# Vampire Uprising Chronicle I

## *Part I of II*

By

Blk Qween Master of Black
Vampire & Lycan Fiction

## Copyright © 2018 by Blk Qween

### All Rights Reserved.

No part of this book may be reproduced in any form or by any electronic or mechanical means, including information storage and retrieval systems, without written permission from the author, except for the brief one-line quotations in a book review for the entire review. Resemblance to actual persons, things, locations, or is coincidental.

### Library Of Congress Control Number: 2021923860

# Dedication

We can soar high through sun drenched skies, we can speed run, we can ride on backs of dragons by day and hunt like vampires at night. We can shape shift into lions, tigers, and dinosaurs. We're aliens with no names, and we own and repair spaceships and space stations. We space travel through time, and we levitate. We're witches who heal and destroy. We're masters of the sea above the ocean and below it.

We're Alphas running fearlessly with packs of wolves, and we're magical Fairy Queens. We marry princes of a royal priesthood, and we love the underdog who has the blood of kings coursing in her veins. We're pirates as we look down into blue waters at our mermaid kin swimming below us in mystic filled seas.

We're black people the proud descendants of slaves we are what and whom we say we are. This Afro-fantasy epic series is dedicated to you precious reader you deserve it your wait is over. You asked for an African American diverse character and a detailed world woven society drenched book featuring us. It is in your hands at this moment.

Welcome to the imaginative mind of Blk Qween……

-You've just been bitten-

# Table of Contents

Chapter 1: Damn This Heat! ................................................ 1

Chapter 2: I'm in Love ........................................................ 7

Chapter 3: The Turn .......................................................... 14

Chapter 4: If I Can't Have You ......................................... 19

Chapter 5: Bloody Tracks ................................................. 33

Chapter 6: Awake .............................................................. 37

Chapter 7: Forget Me Not ................................................. 43

Chapter 8: Welcome Home Pharaoh ............................... 52

Chapter 9: Birth of a Queen ............................................. 63

Chapter 10: The Engagement Party ................................ 75

Chapter 11: Troubled Waters .......................................... 86

Chapter 12: Savage ......................................................... 104

Chapter 13: When Rivers Run Red ................................ 118

Chapter 14: Kill Him! ...................................................... 130

Chapter 15: Father .......................................................... 147

Chapter 16: Joan & Zion ................................................. 160

Chapter 17: Meet Your Maker ....................................... 168

Chapter 18: Cody ..................................................................... 185

Chapter 19: Let the Games Begin! ............................ 197

Chapter 20: Let's Get It ............................................. 209

Chapter 21: Keep Your Head Up ............................... 230

Chapter 22: Pharoah Origins ..................................... 251

Chapter 23: Blood Ties .............................................. 272

Chapter 24: Prodigal Sons ......................................... 296

Chapter 25: Forbidden Fruit ...................................... 321

Chapter 26: Bathe in Blood ....................................... 350

Chapter 27: One More Chance .................................. 381

Chapter 28: Love Is a Serious Business .................... 409

Chapter 29: Twin Oaks the Return ............................ 438

Chapter 30: Hook Line & Sinker ............................... 464

Chapter 31: Strike It Rich .......................................... 482

Chapter 32: Control Your Savage .............................. 511

Chapter 33: The Devil Is in the Details ..................... 531

Chapter 34: Shit Just Got Real .................................. 555

Chapter 35: Liza Hollings .......................................... 579

# Author's Note

Welcome to the best Afro-Fantasy Epic Series you will ever read and encounter, you've made an excellent reading choice. The first chapters in this work of art consist of time travel. When the slaves speak it is improper, therefore the grammar is spelled incorrectly which is conducive to this time era of American history. If you stick with this saga series, you will see our characters growth as you escort them through time and situations.

This masterpiece has been crafted to perfection since 2018 and has been condensed because of its length which is delightful, possessing a high page count. Your dream book is packed with Afro-fantasy, Romantacy, Horror, Drama, Betrayal, Disloyalty, and old earth magic.

Please note the art and beauty I've invested in this masterpiece for you dear precious reader, to represent us among authors in the literary world authoring a book of this magnitude. Book one's paperback and hard copy has been divided into two parts. This is because Amazon allows a maximum of 823 pages per book.

Therefore, this literary binge reader ride book consists of Book 1 part 1 and Book 1 part II. Vampire Uprising Chronicle I part II, Vampire Uprising Lycan Wars book 2, Christmas Cookies a warm hearted BWBM romance, and Male Order Bride and arranged marriage space opera sci-fi romance is available for pre-order. Please Know this is a vampire novel, holding mature content and reader discretion is advised.

I look forward to your thoughts. Feel free to reach out on Facebook, Instagram or Tik Tok to Author Blk Qween. I want to take this time to thank you for choosing to read one of the best books and series you will lay your eyes upon.

-Blk Qween-

*My Personal Notes, Likes & Annotations*

*Vampire Uprising Chronicle I*

# MAP

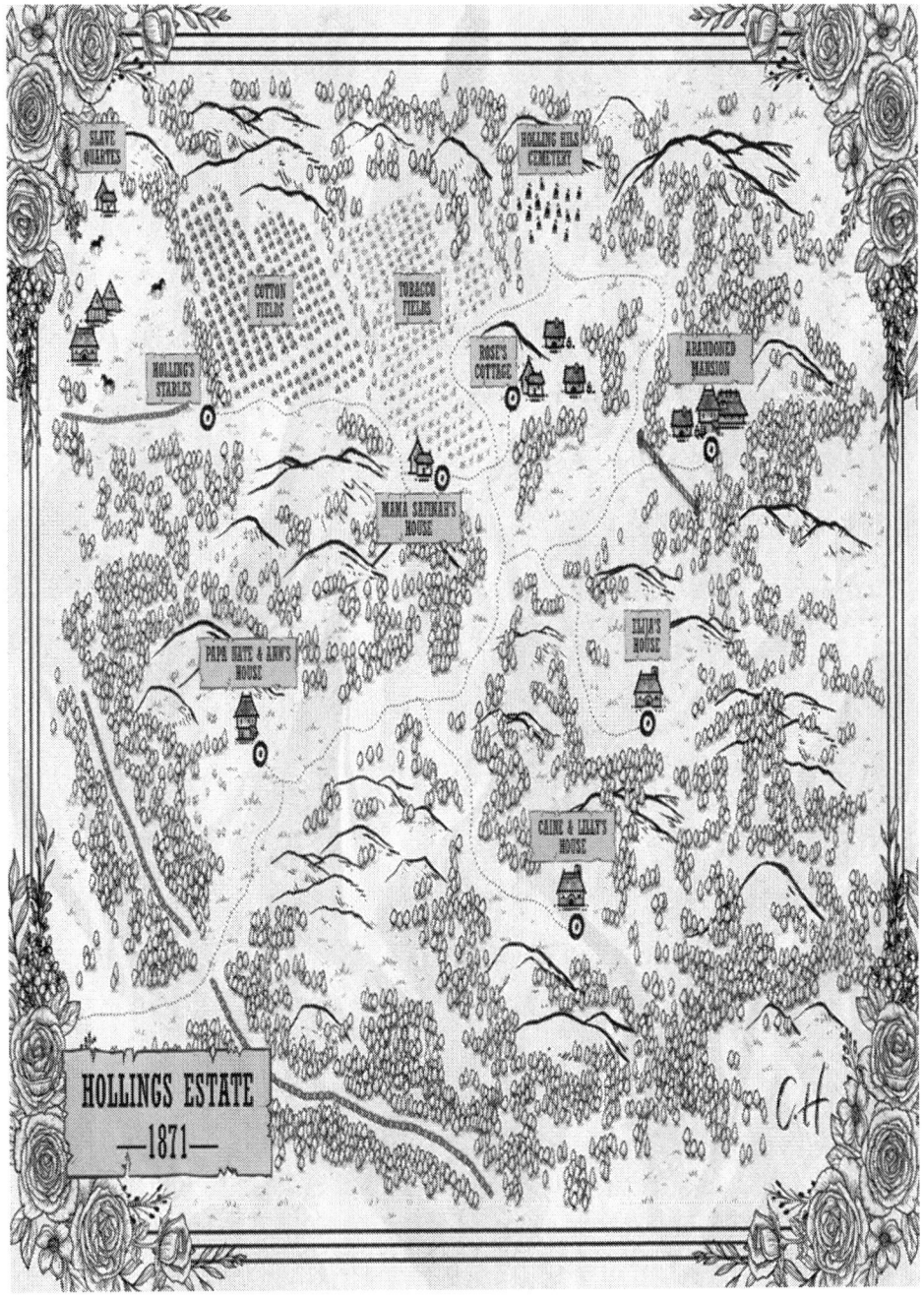

# Chapter 1
# Damn This Heat!

1858....

It was hot, too hot to cart Massa, his wife, and daughter into town. It was four thirty a.m. I feels dew on my neck.

Ise a white slave; my mammy lay wit him willingly, or so she say. Ha' flesh be dark. She ain't get choice iffin she wanna lay a not. Iffin he say it so, then it so. She make haself think cause Massa give worn dresses, spare her pickin cottin, or tendin tobacca fields she think she loved; she not. Dark slaves not kitchen help. Dem tasks fo slaves like me wit white flesh. We's trust by Massa cause our skin white, dey thinks we ain't steal or rise against 'em. We mo civil, respectful dey say…dey wrong.

I put on my pant an ruffle shirt saving da wool coat an' white gloves fo last. I leaves da barn brings da carriage round front da huge house. I cuts cross da tobacca fields to da kitchen. Da smell a wet growin tobacca spun on crisp mornin southern air. Tobacca damp from stormin night befo. Ise hope road be dry so da trip ta town be easy not gettin stuck on a muddy road. I has ta be careful.

Da other slaves goin ta work fields. We nods fast walkin ta chores. Da field slaves walks quick, not ta anger dat ole overseer wit wicked eyes. I walks up the back steps, kitchen Mammy bids me mornin. "How ya sleep Clarence?"

"Da heat keep me up Isabel; it be hot, no matterin how I turn it do me no better den da way I be." "Ya try sleepin up top da barn under da winda good breeze come from yonda mostly Clarence?" "No ma'am" "Ise think after all dis time, ya be good use to dis chere heat seein you growed up chere." "I neva get use to dis heat Isabel" takin a handkerchief from my coat wipin my brow.

"Come sit chere boy, ain't nuttin much dis mornin but a few dinna scraps, eggs, a butta milk, come fo it cold." "Thank ya, ma'am, whatever it is I loves ya fo it." kissing her flour dipped hand.

"Stop dat charm gets ta eatin boy!" clapping her hands for me ta hurry. "You knowed it be Massa first Satday he goes ta harts Clarence." "He ain't playing no harts, Isabel." "Boy. Mine yo bidnes! What I teach ya from picaninny?"

"You ain't know nuttin--"

"I ain't see nuttin, Isabel."

"Good," she whispered, "youse takin em ta town fo haberdashery an da like. Make sho you eats! I ain't need cha faintin in dis heat. All dey finna do is leave ya in a ditch. Finds ya way back iffin ya knowin' what come Clarence." Isabel, gimme me a large jug a cold water.

"Wrap dat up, lest it stay cold in da heat chile." "Yes'm" Avril our house butler come in da kitchen he born on da plantation same as Massa Alex. He take charge a us house slaves. Iffin one a us stole or outta turn Avril ta blame. He an' Massa growed togetha. Massa Alex say Avril raise ta knowed what be xpected, da fault of mis trainin fall on em. Us slaves listen ta keep da lash off em. "You done Clarence. Go round front, dey's comin' open da door." "Yes'sir." I grabs dis tight coat, it gets tight cause dey toss hay in da barn any ol way fa me ta fix.

shakin handin it over." "What wrong you never seent a man nakedness fo?" "Not da likes a ya. Ya ain't got whips, not a one. How a slave yo age ain't got whip scars? Can't be because ya gots white skin I seent white slaves with whip scars fo." "I does as told keep da lash off. Dis da second Massa in a life, ain't had many, dat help too." "Dis be my fifth Massa Clarence." "Any of em treat cha fair gal?" "Dis one ain't to bad I be chere since Ise eight how old ya be when ya come Clarence?"

"Five gal." "I think overseer da devil I seen worse." "It be Massa Alex reign him in. It be days Massa away he gets fixed wit demons when he drink spirits. Steer clear when you know Massa finnin ta go" Her breasts was big, hips round. Look like she has a chile fo I ain't ask. "Who starin now Clarence?" She laugh. "What ya name gal?" "Clover, as in fo leaf." "What?"

"First Massa name me be Irish. Real mammy call me Safinah" Clover gave a welcoming smile. "I does medicine wit god earth plants we knows dat fix ailments an' ill." "Good ta know Iffin Ise ill Clover" grinning, she walked off. "Ise here Clarence." "How ya knowed my name?" "Ya da coachman dat how." Fo da first time I smile inside and out. It be da first time I thinks about lovin a wench, touchin her. *A pretty wench.* he thought, readying himself for the card game.

Clarence dried off combing his hair in a ponytail, placing a bow on it he adorned his trousers closing the barn doors shirtless. Clover saw Clarence pushing them heavy doors closed, watching him from across the fields at the slave shacks she stopped to stare Mmm Mmmh. "What ya starin' at?" Her best friend Ann inquired. "Lookin at the coachman."

"Forget dat white slave you ain't never gettin near da likes a him. Massa Alex treat em like a gold coin Clover." "We see Annie." Smiling Safinah knew she met her husband.

I hears goin back ta Twin Oaks plantation. Iffin I can stop slavery, I does it. I tries not think on it hate creeps in like weeds in a pretty garden. When a man begin ta hate, bad happen. I see Twin Oaks trees at da plantation. Ise grateful ta be out da heat. I stops in front da big house. Avril come out an' afternoon Massa family.

"Welcome home Massa, Miss Minnie Missy Clara. What niceties ya gots?" Avril takes da packages inside. Missy Clara pay no mind to em callin Mammy. I ain't stay, I pass rest a packages ta Avril. Ise not let upstairs or ta come in da front door. I grab da horses' bridle when Massa stop me. "Clarence?" "Yes'sir?"

"Pull around at 7:30 this evening after Isabel serves. "Yes'sir, Massa." I cool da horse's ready em fo evenin I walks round back. I peels off my wet coat an top den rest in da pantry wit curls stuck ta my neck. Isabel come wit tin a water two breads wit jam an tough beef. "Scraps from Massa dinner plates. It be all Ise muster ta save for ya. They ate in town no mid-day meat ta hold." "Much obliged Isabel" "Look chere son, I promise ya Mammy when dey brings ya I looks afta ya as iffin ya my chile. Why dey brings ya?"

"Mamma stop da lash Isabel dey sell me off." "What dey doin dese massa?" She brought her voice to a whisper. "Sendin a picaninny from his Mammy young like dey does? Long as Ise I breathe an God blow breath, Ise take care ya. Go on eat, keep ya strenf up" She give a warm smile. "Lordy deys finnin ta put cha in da field iffin da sun black ya. Stays out da sun Clarence." "How Ise aimin dat Isabel? I carts em to an fo in da sun." She was upset not answerin. I sips an sigh close my eyes a minute, steps outside it cool off some.

"A wind brush me it be five evenin. I goes to da barn cool da horses till dey stops drinkin. I gives em a good brushin on count dey my friends. When Massa goes ta brothel, he wanna show his wealth he say. I readies four nags. I tooks water toss it on my naked body an hair. I opens my eyes and sees da same wench starin wit dark skin clean of whippins wit eyes shape like almonds. She hold somethin wrap in burlap. Hair tie down in a floral scrap.

"What cha want gal?" I snatch da cotton top I wore under the ruffled shirt to dry my private and cover in front her. "Kitchen Mammy say bring fresh cornbread. She say eat it hot starin hand voice a whispa as taught. I pulls in da town stable sat wit slave coachmen who gossips bout who sleep wit who how white misses call slaves fo sex deep night."

"One say he love bein call he love satin sheets. Another say a slave hang when caught she cry rape, course whites say she true. Dey hung em which gentle hearin ways slaves be kill fo dat sorta thing." I sits sippin' warm water listens to em "What bout cha?" A old slave ask. I does wat Ise told. I knows slave's gossip ta share wit Massa's, I never say names or nothin bout our plantation. One taunt me, "You gots a name boy?"

"Clarence be his name; I hear his misses call," other slave say. Dey look fo truth in me ain't find none. Hour pass fast, I wear dat heavy jacket, head where dey eats. "See ya next time," I say on my way out "No boy, we see ya tonight," da coachman smile. I shows to da haberdasheries fo packages. Missy Clara snatch da bag from Ms. Minnie. "Clarence do you like blue?" It be ugly, but I say as Ise taught "Yes'm, Missy Clara, bring out ya eyes."

"Clarence there is no need to lie to her risking your soul getting into heaven over a dress color, if you do not like it, you do not!" "Oh mother, he fancies it I'll ask Isabel to make my dress for the ball next month." Massa left da billiard room when I pass he speak ta his friend bout clubs, hearts, cigars, and bourbon sharin dey secret.

Massa's goes to da plantation a young massa own. He gots no wench, no picaninny he run harts game an dey gets slave wenches an picaninny's all shape, colors, and size. No one look ova thirty year. Willin or no dey must sometime a picaninny be killed. Dem Massa has ta pay fo a dead slave. Slave kin to the dead, be made ta bury em in da fields. Dead slave still make Massa coin. Dere be savagery where a wench ain't walk. Some women liked it causin dey got hand-me-downs money and jewelry, but dey has ta give it to dey Massa's.

I hear gal picnininies scream in pain iffin it be da first time. When dey leave I hands out apples from da orchard on da plantation. Dey grateful. I ain't eat outta shame thinkin bout what

Here he come walkin slow down da wide white marble windin stairs dress crisp, "Mornin Massa." "Good morning, Clarence," He come close, whisperin. "We have a long day and night Clarence. Tonight, will be follies. I for one cannot wait." Massa pat me iffin Ise a slave owner. I smiles as taught. I ain't glad fo him I ain't wanna take part in his lie. Ain't nuttin good bout havin a mistress roun' a wench back ya love. Here she come strollin round dem windin marble steps, parasol in hand swearin she beautiful as mornin sun. "Missy Clara, ya looks beautiful today." Thank you, Clarence, mother is behind me."

"Ms. Minnie mornin ya look a ray a light." "Oh, hush Clarence. Avril used to say those charming words when I was fifteen and married Alexander. Did he teach you that old line?" Ms. Minnie face filla scarlet iffin I means it. "Yes, ma'am he did, but it be true."

I opens the double oak front doors fo em. I rush down da entry stairs to da carriage door fo both misses holding dey decorated glove hands in my glove hand so flesh ain't touch. I once seent a Massa give twenty lashes cause his wife fall off da carriage cause da slave slip her hand. Once Massa enter da coach, I hurry up top to da coach man bench. I clicks my tongue an' away we goes leavin Twin Oaks plantation. When we passes da tobacco fields ya hears slaves callin out. "Ms. Minnie, Missy Clara, Massa Alex has a right good day!" Dey stop chores wavin wit tobacca-stain hands. I looks on one wench starin. She keep a eye on me, she wave.

I knowed she ain't wavin at Massa. I dare not waves back I keeps my eye on da road. Hot water rollin ta my knickers make stick ta my flesh. I hates dis long ponytail hair so fine mind me of em. I wanna shear it but Massa wife say no. A slave needin a yes'sir ta shear his hair. Damn sun addin worse on me turnin it yellow folks asks iffin Ise a slave. I slow da horses so dey ain't tire a thirst, no wind ta cool me. I beg God for somethin' he ain't oblige. We gets in town Ms. Minnie goes ta shop. I jumps grabbin da door takin her hand same wit Missy Clara Massa step last. "I shall return in one hour Clarence." "Yes'sir, Massa" I makes sho I ain't eyeball em, keepin my

# Chapter 2
# I'm in Love

The year 2020

Clarence splashed his face with chilly water, rubbing it through short hair which the Vampire knew would grow. Every two days it grew long, and every two he'd cut it. He was damned with it for eternity. Clarence exited the bathroom "Hey Sugar," wrapping his arms around her.

He loved her full, plump figure. She reminded him of his first wife, Safinah, who loved to eat. He'd buy her food; watching her enjoy herself. He missed food, but wrapping his arms around this full-figured woman from behind made him full and warm. Gabriel faced him, locked in his loving embrace. "Your hair grows fast! I wish my hair grew quick Clarence. You look handsome, not like this bird nest I have," Gabriel sighed, touching her head. "There's nothing wrong with your hair Sugar." "This kinky old thing, I hate it."

Gabriel tugged at her head wrap as Clarence kissed her neck. Her warm veins rolled under his lips. He could hear her heartbeat; it raced at his touch. "May I see Sugar? It is pretty."

He tried to remove her scarf. "No, don't!" Gabriel shouted holding her head in shame. "Besides, how do you know it's pretty? You've never seen it." "I don't care. I love you the way you are." Gabriel had tears in her eyes. "What did I do to deserve a good man like you? Are you sure you love all of me Daddy?" She wondered, looking down at her full body. "I love you," he assured her, kissing her bare shoulder, hugging her tighter.

Gabriel adored his passion, and sweet words. There's something different about him, something regal. Pulling him close, she wanted him because he was the first man who didn't body shame her. Fat, full-figured, curvy, thick, plus, plump, fluffy, BBW, or whatever it's called, he loved it all on her.

Cancer took a lot of her hair; Clarence didn't know it ate away at her little by little. Gabriel had a double mastectomy scheduled in two weeks; she wasn't going to inform him. For the first time in years a man looked with loving eyes, not pity. She embraced these treasurable moments basking in them without regret. Gabriel opened her dress, welcoming Clarence to her, he kissed her lovingly, closing it. Gabriel playfully ran from Clarence in her small, dangerously sun-drenched house. Embarrassed at her failed sexual attempt with the man she loved. Clarence read her thoughts, a habit he needed to break because of privacy invasion.

Clarence heard her thinking, "*I love him so much. I want him in my arms forever. He's wonderful. I wonder why he doesn't want me? I'm too fat.*" "I want you!" Clarence blurted out, holding her dainty hands, kissing her inner wrists. "I don't want to rush Gabriel. I always rush, but not with you; I love you."

Gabriel jumped in his arms "I love you more, Daddy." If he could cry, he would. His crying abilities were touch and go. "I've gotta run baby; my shift starts in an hour. If I arrive when the sun is up, I'll get written up."

"I'm sorry Clarence," she teased, stealing another kiss. The sun was rising faster than he could race. He could smell it; Clarence hated leaving.

He wanted her to know who and what he was, and for the first time in his life he feared rejection. Clarence engaged in a kissing session with Gabriel for ten precious minutes; time did not allot a vampire racing against the sun. Clarence smelled and heard the sun. A clean crisp smell accompanied by the dragging sound of it rising. "Baby, I'm going to be late Gabriel." breaking free of her strong love. Gabriel entered, as Clarence raced home, watching the sun's light reveal itself slowly beyond the horizon.

"Hurry!" He heard his coven members call anxiously. They panicked, waiting at the mansion door with a blanket to snuff sun-fire. The Dr. stood by with a blood transfusion drip, and three quarts of human blood for Clarence; using emergency protocols they hadn't used since he helped slaves escape with Harriet Tubman. Clarence arrived four minutes after sunrise. He pulled up directly to the door; driving a beat up 1999 red Toyota. Clarence breathed labored. The sun scorched his forearm, back and lungs. The guardians removed his burned tank and handed him a goblet of blood. He grabbed it, gulping it down as the burn wounds healed immediately. "Where were you?" A vampress boldly inquired, smelling human female stench.

"Are you questioning me Cody?" not looking in her direction. "No, Pharaoh," keeping her head and eyes lowered, remembering her place. Clarence looked at the guardians, they were afraid they'd lost him. "I'm fine family. Can someone please bring my jacket and phone? It's in the car." "Yes, Pharaoh," the teen guardian volunteered, before retrieving it. "Hey," Clarence grabbed his arm. "Why aren't you in school Isaiah?" "It's closed Great One. It's teacher prep day."

When Clarence arrived in his bedroom his cell rang. "Hello sweet Sugar." "Hi honey, did you get to work on time?" "Yes, ma'am, talking with the guys at the job." The guardians smiled; Clarence loved human smiles. Generations of human guardians protected him. One generation was taught to replace the next. They protected him, and other vampires during sun rise. They're the descendants of humans Clarence saved from lynching's, slave trades, human trafficking, rapes, murder, drownings, and baby killings.

"You made it man!" The 19-year-old treated Clarence like a father. "She's mad at you Clarence. You're in trouble. I see you're holding on to your Georgia accent Pharaoh." Isaiah closed the blinds shutting out sunlight as taught. "Why were you late Pharaoh, you ok?" "I'm good Isaiah." "Yeahhhh?" Isaiah teased. "You got a shorty Pharaoh how she look?" He whispered, or so he thought. "Isaiah, humans can't whisper around vampires, our hearing is extremely good, so why do it?" "I'm unsure" he whispered eerily. "Have you thought about it boss?" "What have I said about calling me boss Zay?" "We aren't on a plantation" Clarence laughed. "You can leave my bedroom when you're ready Isaiah."

"I love it here this coven it has history. Do you remember sharing bedtime stories about meeting Malcolm X? I thought you were pulling my leg until the scroll writers shared pictures of you with him and Ms. Betty. What an honor was he smart as they say?" Isaiah inquired. "Smarter, you should go to college, and graduate from a conservatory. You play the piano excellent, and white people love you. They'd come to see you perform. Have you applied to Julliard Isaiah?"

"Who cares about white people or what they like? When are you going to make me a member of this coven?" "You're too young, we've been over this; I'm tired." Isaiah laughed "You ain't tired! You're tired of me." Isaiah exited Clarence's bedroom sensing Cody. "What do you want Cody?" "Damn, how'd you know? You're not vampire." Cody giggled. "Your hair lingers, smells like candy," he responded, as she locked arms with him. Isaiah loved Cody; however she wanted Clarence, who only used her for sexual pleasure.

Cody, a beautiful half black and native American Indian. Her hair pitch black, and shiny as a moon lit path. Blessed with a thick frame, small stomach, big ass and hips, and a sexy D rack to match. Her kissable lips pink-rose blush. She adorned original tribal markings on her belly, back, and right thigh before tats were in style. Vampires at coven dinners wondered where she was inked, her reply was always, "An old Indian shaman my grandfather." When Clarence saved her from the massacre of her three hundred slaughtered people. She alone escaped death as walked on a field of dead Indians, hiding under the body of her chieftain father, barely alive carrying her dead baby.

Clarence heard her shallow breathing and a faint heartbeat; Cody took a bullet for her baby and was rapidly losing blood which she would've bled to death without Clarence. "Where was he Zay?" "He didn't say. Why didn't you listen at the door Cody?" "He reads thoughts, hearing anything from miles away. He'd sense me at the door trust me."

Isaiah walked the long corridor away from her to his room. "Why're you upset Cody?" "I want to be his vampire Queen. I've been here since the beginning when he formed Covens, bet you didn't know I knew Queen Safinah Zay." "No, I didn't Cody, was she nice?"

"All you've heard and more. Hard shoes to fill, denying vampirism made her immortal. She's been gone for decades, but Clarence never forgets her. Her painting hangs in his bedroom." "He painted that, Cody?" "Yes, Clarence is quite the artist, he knew Basquiat. The painting in his office was a gift from him before he was discovered. Nice man he loved Safinah's portrait. Clarence hasn't touched a brush since her passing Zay." "Cody, Clarence never said you couldn't see other people" she scoffed. "I'm not of this time. Our spirits are one because he saved me, you don't understand Isaiah."

"I understand love. I know when someone doesn't want me." Isaiah walked off. Cody hissed at him, revealing her fangs. "Put those away Cody," Isaiah playfully whispered. Clarence didn't know how much Isaiah loved Cody. The melodies, and love ballads he'd written were for her. At eight, he confessed his love, she smiled tucking him in. "I'm an old Indian. Why do you want an old vampire when you can have a young one?" Cody would kiss him goodnight, he'd dream she'd be his wife one day.

"Hello Gabriel, I'm on break." Gabriel was half asleep because Clarence kept her up all night talking. "Hey, you know what?" I must come up with a nick name for you, Clarence. Your accent is sexy baby!" "You like it, Sugar?" "Yes, I love it when you call me Sugar. Did you call your wife that?" "No honey, I called her Cotton or Brownie." "That's cute Clarence. Did she like brownies?"

"Yes, and would burn them, so I called her Brownie, and it stuck. She had the most beautiful complexion." Clarence gazed at her portrait reminiscing. "So sweet you remember her, I hear love in your voice. Did she ever get the brownies right Clarence?" Clarence laughed remembering how they'd stick to the pan breaking up. *She was no Isabel God rest her,* he thought.

"No Sugar, she didn't, however she never stopped trying." If he could shed a tear he would, but for the first time in a half century, he found himself sharing her memory without sadness, with a new woman who respected sharing his memories of his first wife; loving to hear about her. "You think she'd approved of me?" "What an odd question Sugar, yes, she wanted me happy. She begged me to remarry, and I said yes to ease her mind. She knew I was lying but I'm not anymore." Gabriel smiled "Oh?" It took everything in her not to blurt, yes! "Don't you need to return Clarence?"

"Yes, I should." "Ok, call when you're off are you coming tonight?" "I have a meeting, Gabriel; I don't want to call on you too late." "Call on me.... vintage talk, I like it." Clarence blushed. Years passed since he courted seriously, he didn't know dating lingo. "I'm going back to sleep Clarence sorry." "Get some rest Sugar." "Mwahhhh." Clarence was surprised. "Did you kiss me, Sugar?" "Yep, I'm kissing you whenever we hang up." Clarence smiled. "Do it again." "Mwahhhhhh." "Music to my ears. I'll call later Gabriel." "Ok bye baby."

Clarence showered, changing into his grey lounge pants, and broken in tee. He spoke low calling Zion the Dr. Clarence heard him but received no response. Closing his eyes, he called telepathically. Most vampires rested during the day, as guardians ran the house. Yes *Pharaoh?* Zion responded telepathically.

*Tonight, set a meeting for coven Elders please. Yes, Great Pharaoh, as you wish.*

# Chapter 3
# The Turn

The year of our lord 1859

"Youse chere Clarence?" Avril called. "Yes'sir" "Come get dinner scraps." "Yes'sir! You be out 'till mornin and den gots ta get up ta liffin hay wit dat fool overseer. I swears I hate dat fool." He whispered. He ain't no better sep his skin white dey say he a slave he stole at da general stow. He workin off what he thief Clarence."

"Listen chere, you ain't goin round talkin like he same as us, cause he ain't Avril." Avril looked down. "What ya lookin down fa ole man? Cause he ain't same as us? He ain't he never gonna be. We ain't stole nuttin Avril." Avril smiled, "Dat be da white man in you talkin Clarence he chuckled."

They walked back to the big house. "How ya cummin wit ya letters?" He whispered. "I'se gettin dere. I learn hearin Missy Clara take lesson. Massa has me dust shelves while she takin lessons." "Sometime somebody drop a newspaper, or Massa leave it in da carriage. I sneaks a peak as I cleans da carriage. I ask Massa fo it ta line slave quarters fo extra picaninny beddin, Avril. Truth be, I looks at dat paper good."

Avril stopped walkin he came close speakin low. "I hear Massa sayin it gonna be a war cause dey gots a man name Lincoln, he ain't like peoples havin slaves he finnin ta put a stop to it iffin he gets ta warrin' wit dese white folk Clarence."

"When ya lookin at dem letters see iffin it say somethin' bout dat." "I'll Avril" "Get ya dry goods on u finnin ta go Clarence." They entered the kitchen to Isabel. "Stop fiddlin Clarence, I swears youse worser den when youse fifteen." "It fittin close Isabel."

"I knows Ise havin ta let 'em out tamorrow. I speaks ta Massa, 'ain't no house slave posa be liffin no hay!' It make ya dark an big to fittin dry goods Massa Alex pay fo. Ya ain't servin at da table all dark like did ise sayin you ain't pickin cottin. I lets it out it be all I does Clarence." Isabel exited frustrated mumbling to herself "How ya gonna have a house slave workin fields? It ain't good Clarence!" "Thank ya, Mammy." "I tell ya I ain't ya real Mammy, I ain't takin her name nosir she a fine Misses. Call me Isabel like ya been, in front Massa ya say Mammy chere boy?"

"Yes, Mammy" Isabel tugging at Clarence's pant waistline playfully giggling. "It be 7:20." Avril yawned. Clarence left the kitchen with a jug of water walking to the front where he walked them earlier. "Massa, youse lookin mighty fine. Is dem new dry goods from taday haberdasheries, Massa?" "Why yes, Clarence, it is." Clarence held his gold lion's head walking stick while boarding the carriage. Once Alex sat Clarence handed him his walking stick. Cool air, and the wind rustling leaves were music to Clarence's ears, air blew on Clarence dropping his temperature to bearable. The stars shone bright; the full moon lit the road perfectly. Clarence and Massa Alex arrived at 8 p.m. Clarence steadied the horses jumping down to open the carriage door. "Return by 3 a.m. Clarence." "Yes'sir, Massa."

"Clarence, I spoke with the owner of this plantation. You May take apples off the ground as long as they're bruised. As many as you wish." "Thanks, him kindly fo me, Massa, please. "I shall what do you do with the apples Clarence?" "Give em to the picaninnies an' wenches Massa." I use dey words so he ain't pick up on me learnin letters. "I reckon that's fine Clarence." "Thank you, Massa Alex." "Three a.m. do not be tardy." Alex reminded.

"I be's dere Massa." Clarence drove the carriage to the back of the house, breaking on a ridge on the outskirts of the plantation where apple orchards grew. From there he saw a clock on the wall inside the house. Clarence checked the carriage for a newspaper, glad there was one there he secretly read what he could make out. Clarence ripped paper into squares, wrapping apples, when a blood curdling scream echoed across plantation acres. He thought this normal at first, but each scream warned him something was deadly wrong. Clarence looked in the mansion windows, drapes were drawn. Slaves and Massa's alike fled the big house, no Massa's made it past the white gravel walkways.

Clarence stared in disbelief slave men and women openly slaughtering plantation Massa's. He had heard stories of these happenings on neighboring plantations. Frantic and afraid his thoughts raced. "Iffin I goes witout Massa Alex they kills me, iffin I comes back wit a dead Massa, dey kills me." Clarence thought aloud pacing rapidly a habit he had when nervous.

*Ise fraid I aint know what ta do. Someone grabs my hair from da back chokes me while a knife stick in my side. Long claw fingernails rips open my throat with a swift swipe! I looks down seein my blue coat red. As I lay on crushed apples, I smells blood mix with sugar sweet ripe red apples. Ise dying I ain't hot no mo it be's cold. I rubs my fingers together dat oil? Dat oil bees my blood I ain't fraid no mo. Deep down I knowed I die young at slavery hand.* "Lookey chere! A white carriage man." A tall nigga slave pushes his boot in my chest makin ma' breathin hard. A wench say "Dis aint no white one baby! You gotts ta save em fo me!" "Why?" "Dis da slave boy of da wench dat save me from rape an' whip."

"She takes ten lash den dey sells her boy off ta anotha plantation. Dat be ha' punishment on count she help me. She ain't never got over dat, broke her heart loosin her boy. I tolds ya bout her when we meet member baby?" "You sayin dis boy Mammy a negro slave who save ya from lashin and a Massa rape dis be true wife?" "It be true husband, he a slave like I is." She gazed in her husband's eyes with affection to save the child of the woman who once saved her. The man removed his boot from Clarence's chest speaking at him.

"Black Lilac say yo Mammy good people, den I thinks you good. However, iffin you ain't, I finish what I starts white man." waving his large hunter knife, drippin slick wit my blood over my face. "Go on," the tall man told da wench she smiled "Da way I shows ya woman." Black Lilac sat on my chest leanin over me. "Welcome to life eternal." *She turns my neck bitin hard. Blood ran down her mouth. Is she drinkin blood? Da man chantin somethin I ain't knowed. He bends writin a sign on my naked chest usin his blood. Black Lilac opens my mouth drippin' blood in mine from her mouth. Lilac holds ha' hand over my mouth she holds my nose an' force blood down.*

*Movin' ha' wrist Lilac pour mo ha' blood where he slices me open. Was da screams fadin' or is I dyin? Ripe apples, blood, fresh jasmine be heavy in my nostrils. I be here twenty times ain't never smell jasmine. Lilac spat mo' blood in my mouth. I seent a map come in my head where Ise need ta wait fo ha.'* "Up boy" *she gets me on my feets.*

*How does I breathe or stand? I takes off my coachman coat tearing away my shirt leavin it a top of hundreds of bloody broke apples.* "Start movin up in dese woods." *Black Lilac hold me up givin da was ta go. She teachin a baby ta walk dat baby be me. After a few steps Ise steady nough ta stand alone.* "Run! We gots a few hours, ya gots ta make it fo sunup or ya' be dead." *Confused I runs an' follows da map she show in my head, her footsteps lead da way.*

*Ise running in da woods with a wench leadin me ta a place ha' footsteps light in da ground as I runs. Iffin she turns left, I does, iffin she climb rock I follows. When ha' feets stop, I stops. Lookin, round I sees nothin but shrub an' dead trees.* "Stop!" *Lilac yells in my head. Her eyes stops wit mine. I sees it deep in da brush under fallen trees. I hears water rushin in da rivva but ain't sees it. I smells da sun. How ya smells sun? I follows da rivva sound, steppin in ta rinse dry blood an' dirt.*

*All my wounds be shut I ain't knowed how. I clears brush ta get in da shack. I pushes da door open. I sees Lilac pull leaves, I does da same. She puts em back in front ta hide da shack from slavers, I does da same. I hears her voice say 'close dem shutters fo sun seep in.' Ise tired I ain't look round fo nuttin ta eats. I sees a bed I drags ta da middle flo where da room darkest blocking the door as I slumbers, I thinks bout Clover how I never get ta ask her ta marry me. Ise thinkin how beautiful she look in dat head wrap. I tries not ta love a wench bein a slave it be bad ta do. I sees lotta dreadful things happen when one slave love another.*

*I tries ta shut off wantin da love of a wench, but I sees her bright smile, her dark skin she woke da man in me da one I thinks I kill. I has ta have ha.' I finds a way ta get back. Ise tired I ain't thinkin straight.* Clarence fell into a deep slumber while turning vampire, afraid and alone.

# Chapter 4
# If I Can't Have You

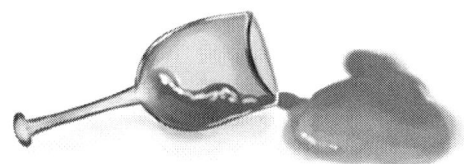

The Year 2020

Zion called the heads of each coven, instructing them to arrive at 7 p.m. New York time. Designer cars pulled up to the mansion. Clarence set many of them free from slavery or a dangerous situation.

The house was a mansion in Brooklyn, New York, off Jackie Robinson Parkway. A fifteen bedroom with ten additional bedrooms built in the basement, six in the attic, and a built-in sub-basement under the house with holding cells. Clarence inherited the house in 1960 from an old, black woman he befriended after the death of her husband. They were friends with benefits, until her natural passing.

Vampires entered, honored to be present. Vampires and Vampress,' which Clarence hadn't turned but gave permission attended. He fed from them, to read thoughts if needed and call on them if he were distressed. Clarence sat in the ballroom on a platform stage as coven Elders entered. Zion sat to his left, the chair on his right remained empty. It was the chair for his deceased Queen.

Guardians offered glass flutes filled with human blood as Elders obliged. Clarence knew people in blood banks, hospitals, and clinics. He owned blood donation clinics around the city. If the blood extracted from a human but proved useless due to medical negatives, he would have that blood sent to the covens.

Clarence recalled being human. He valued human life, although it'd been stolen from him. Zion was a smart vampire but foolishly fell in love with a white woman in the 1950's. He was a negro Dr. working in a segregated hospital as a janitor. Clarence's mind wondered to the day they'd met. Zion's parents struggled putting him through negro medical school only for him to sweep the hospital, not run it. Currently he works for cancer cures, and often uses human blood in his trials. Clarence built Zion a medical lab on the property in the 60's to perfect his lifelong work.

April 1st, 1950
Georgia Dekalb County
Dr. Zion Donovan Origins....

One night Clarence went running in the woods as he often did when he saw a campfire. There he saw six white men beating Zion. Clarence thought he was dead, hearing his raspy struggled breathing. One of his captors was beating and screaming "keep ya nigger hands off our women boy!" A white man took a noose placing it around Zion's neck while the rest laughed. Clarence stepped out from behind the trees in the deep Georgia wood saying calmly, "drop him." They looked, laughing mockingly. "Is he a white man?" One spewed, "no, he's a nigger passing, boy go about your business before you get strung up with him."

"Drop him!" Clarence growled. They tightened the noose tauntingly. Clarence grabbed the leader by his neck raising him ten feet off the ground, holding him with one arm. Eyes raging and blazing with blood lust. He pierced his jugular feasting on warm spouting blood. Clarence decapitated his dinner when he was done. The severed head dropped to dry cracked earth quenching its thirst with sacrificed blood of a good old boy. Clarence tossed his dead carcass one hundred feet west. Using sharp claws, he sliced the strangling noose.

Before the sinister bigots could shoot, Clarence grabbed Zion off blood-soaked ground, disappearing in the dark night. He took Zion to his cabin in record time, covering his tracks with leaves and pepper to throw off blood hounds. As Zion lay lifeless Clarence informed, "You're dying, shake your head if you understand." Zion shook his head, yes. "You don't need to die if you're not ready. I shall bless you with immortal life. This means you need blood to survive, and you'll never see the sun again. If you want to live shake your head yes." Zion thought, *am I dreaming?* No, you're not dreaming. *Yes.* Zion agreed telepathically to immortality. *I want to live sir.*

Clarence held Zion's neck tight biting his bruised, jugular vein right above the rope burn, which stayed with him as he healed. A warm salty blood cocktail saturated Clarence's mouth. He didn't like the taste of his blood; it tasted of death. Clarence moved his mouth, roaring as Zion's heartbeat faded. He tore his wrist open resting it on his neck, the sting subsiding closing wounds.

"Old vampire blood has healing properties Dr. The older the vampire, the faster the wounds heal." Zion screamed as Clarence drained blood into his mouth, pinching his nose making sure he swallowed. He also shared his blood drooling in his mouth. As an old vampire, Zion didn't need much blood.

The change is different for everyone. Some either screamed in agony or laughed for hours, uncontrolled. Some slept for days on and off 'till they slept no more. Some fell into a coma or cried, with extreme human emotions coming out when the human was dying. Zion was a screamer due to the pain he endured. Clarence prayed it wouldn't be for days. Within twenty minutes he stopped falling into a deep slumber. *Thank God, I hate screamers,* Clarence thought.

*Vampire Uprising Chronicle I*

Present Day Hollings Estate
New York Vampire Elders Gathering....

"We're here because our Pharaoh wishes to discuss business please sit." Vampires knew something was amidst. The scroll writer's presence meant documenting something historically important. "Thank you for coming, sorry about this morning. You may've sensed my mishap" he chuckled, holding up his right forearm, proving he was burn free. Elders nodded yes, smiling, daring not ask what happened.

"I'm in love family." The entire room sighed, elated. Cody gloated inside. "Let us hope she says yes, and we gain a new Queen!" Vampire Elders clapped overjoyed they were gaining a Queen. They knew Safinah added softness to their King, bringing forth his gentle side, especially with court cases. Old vampires were inflicted with Clarence's grief when Safinah died; his mourning period three long years. Vampires that were connected to their maker learned to handle the grief he shared.

Zion ran the covens during this time, of course with direction from Clarence. The jails were full of vampires awaiting hearings for months when usually it took days. Safinah handled small infractions, while some were coven matters. Vampire Elders didn't see him during mourning, but knew he lived. The original vampires who were slaves and freed, communicated telepathically and Clarence always responded. Baby vampires named by Clarence because they were turned between the ages of seventeen and thirty felt confused feeling a burden on their spirits. Clarence slept with Safinah's dresses on his bed and didn't cut his hair. He was depressed, but now he allowed its grow in over a century. Vampires aren't allowed to be made or allowed to marry during vampire mourning; it was truly a trying time.

"I'm having an engagement party to introduce my fiancé to covens, Zion will manage the invitations. Thank you for coming out, I need to leave for a date." "Wait!" The Elder of coven four called out, "What is her name?" "Gabriel." Clarence looked at Cody on the library mezzanine overlooking the ballroom floor. She wasn't allowed to attend Elder meetings because she wasn't an Elder. He heard her tears drop. Rushing to his love, Gabriel, Clarence hugged and shook hands with the vampire family he'd created and loved. "Zion, I may not come home this morning." "Is her place sun proof Clarence?" Fear flowed into his voice. "It's ok Zion." "You were scorched this morning." "I was Zion, and guess what?" "What?" "It felt good having the sun on me, even if it did burn a little." Zion laughed.

"Tell Isaiah to get the car please." Clarence called Gabriel "Sugar I'm coming." She squealed excited "I gotta get pretty." "How you gonna do what God already did?" "Aww, baby" "You gonna sprinkle that Jasmine perfume I like Sugar?" "Sure, are we ordering in?" "Yes, get what you want, I ate at the meeting" he smiled sipping his third glass of B positive.

Zion ran to the side of the house with a cooler bag containing four additional bags of B positive. "Just in case, I'll leave it in in the car." "Yes mom." condescendingly as he took the bag, hugged him, and left. "Hey boss, where to?" Zay taunted Clarence purposely using boss. Clarence cringed but didn't correct him for the 100th time "Queens 107th street and Jamaica avenue." They arrived quickly. "Damn, boy you need to slow down" Isaiah chuckled. Clarence called Gabriel, "Baby, open the garage please." There she stood, a shapely woman of 5'8 and beautiful. Her smile was gorgeous, and Isaiah saw love in her eyes for Clarence. *Human* he thought but was pleasantly surprised.

"Gabriel this is Isaiah, my nephew." Isaiah was caught off guard. "How are you ma'am?" asking respectfully, of Clarence's future Queen. "Please, come in guys. I ordered Chinese takeout I hope you're hungry. Get comfortable Isaiah." "Yes ma'am, I'm starved." Isaiah and Clarence entered. The house was as he pictured small, cozy, decorated contemporary, clean, and neat. They ate off fine China.

"These are pretty plates ma'am." "Please call me Gabriel Isaiah." "Like the angel?" "Yes, I see where you get your charm." Clarence drank ice water, the other liquid afforded vampires. Clarence admired her China pattern. It'd been years since he saw a modern woman with an authentic China set.

"They're old. My great-great aunt purchased them after slavery ended from a nice woman in town. It's odd, she remembered the woman's name, said the woman had a pretty smile and wanted auntie to have them because she saw love in her eyes for the bone China dishes."

"Wow, what's the woman's name who sold them Gabriel?" "Clover, Isaiah." Clarence put his glass down, he knew Safinah found items in abandoned houses, or trinkets she acquired in trade, even though there wasn't a financial need. She loved meeting people. Clarence picked up a dish smiling. "The world is small" he shared, speaking his thoughts. "Huh, baby?" she clutched Clarence's hand. "Nothing Sugar." Clarence ran fingers around the gold trim of the plate. "Food was delicious." Clarence smiled at Isaiah over complimenting Gabriel, as if she cooked it.

"Guess I'll go, I don't wanna overstay my welcome." "You won't Isaiah!" Gabriel insisted. "It's 12:30 at night. You can sleep on the couch." Isaiah looked at Clarence for approval who conversed telepathically with him. *I'll need you since I'll be here when the sun is up.* Isaiah nodded lightly. "Yes ma'am, thank you." She went into the closet handing him a blanket and the remote control. "Me casa es su casa, Isaiah." "Gracias's senorita"

Gabriel took Clarence's hand leading him to her boudoir. He was going to reveal he's a vampire and was nervous. "Baby, draw the blinds please." She drew the room darkening shades over double windows. He patted the bed, "come let me to hold you." He removed his jeans and shirt leaving only boxers and a tee. She removed her lounge pants and tee, replacing it with a black robe and nothing underneath. "Sexy," Clarence restrained himself. "I must explain something Sugar." "Oh God you're married" "No, baby!" as she sighed relieved. "We've been dating for two years, we love each other Sugar, yes?" "Yes Clarence," laying on his chest smiling. "Your head is on the left side of my chest; do you hear a heartbeat, Sugar?"

She listened, moving her head around, resting her fingers on his wrist searching for a pulse. Gabriel slipped out of his loving embrace. She was speechless, as confusion swept her loving eyes. "There is a reason my Sugar." "What Clarence? No heartbeat means you're dead."

"In body, yes, but not in here." Tapping his temple. "And not here." Resting her palm over his beatless heart. "I'm vampire, my love." He heard her breathing become rapid. Gabriel's heart pounded; her thoughts raced. *'Ok he's mentally ill.'* "I'm not mentally ill Sugar." she jumped up. *"How?"* staring amazed.

"I read human and vampire thoughts. I communicate telepathically. I don't usually because it's an invasion of privacy, however, don't fear. I'm the man you love." Gabriel sat; her thoughts sporadic as rap music videos echoed from downstairs. "Do you love me, Gabriel? holding his head down.

She lay back down comfortably in his arms "Why're you holding your head down Clarence?" *That's what's special about him. He loves me that's why he wanted to wait for sex, he didn't want to deceive me about being a vampire.* "Are you afraid Sugar?" "No Clarence." "Why not?" "Don't laugh." "I won't" "My aunt who purchased the china, said the lady who sold them said former slave-guardians would help black folks when we needed. Guaranteeing they couldn't be harmed, but their weakness is the sun. If we needed them, they'd help." "Clover, Gabriel?" "Yes, that's the lady." "That was my wife, Sugar." Gabriel smiled. "Clarence, that was after Lincoln freed the slaves in 1863, you're 188 years old?" "Yes, give or take can't be sure they didn't keep birth records of slaves Sugar. To be clear, Lincoln didn't free slaves, Gabriel." "He didn't?" "No, we freed ourselves baby." "You were a slave, Clarence?" "Yes, for the first years of my life I was born into it." "What year were you born?"

"I'm not sure Sugar, but according to Zion, my Dr. and best friend states I was around thirty-three when turned vampire before the proclamation." "You don't look older than thirty.

You're an old man!" "I prefer sugar daddy Sugar." They laughed, breaking the tension in the room.

Gabriel gazed into his eyes kissing him, swirling her tongue with his. He rubbed his hand up her fleshy back. He loved warm flesh on a woman, mixed with fluff. She kissed his neck and ears, his sinful weakness. Fire rose in him one that lay dormant. Clarence fought to hide the vampire inside. It was one of the things he failed to master when he was horny, hiding his fangs.

Gabriel whispered, "yes baby," giving him access to her wanting body. He opened her robe as round heavy beautiful breasts that spilled into his large capable hands. Her nipples stiffened, welcoming his touch. Clarence rubbed them gently making Gabriel moan as he forced himself from thought invasion.

He opened her legs before placing his mouth on her bald, wet pussy sliding his tongue deep inside, savoring her taste, swallowing thick sweet cream. He was enjoying her sexual scent as his tongue teased her. Her trembling being proof his pussy pleasure was fire. Gabriel moaned his name as Clarence placed her legs on his big broad shoulders slipping one finger inside her tight, wet pussy wiggling his finger on swelling walls as she squirmed to get away from his sexual tease as her rising giggles turned him on.

CRACK! Gabriel's bedroom door flew across the room. Clarence raised his forearm shielding Gabriel from its reckless blow. Gabriel pulled the sheet covering her nakedness confused. "Leave Now Cody!" "NO Clarence!" Cody hyper-sped snatching Gabriel from his loving arms. Clarence was livid, never having a vampire do this. He called Zion telepathically, *COME!* Zion dropped his glass hyper-speeding to Gabriel's house.

"Cody, what're you doing?" "I'm your Queen Clarence, not her." Gabriel thought, *Queen?* Clarence spoke with Gabriel mentally, *it's ok Sugar, don't move. I trust and love you, Clarence. If I die, you're the best man I've ever known. Don't talk that way, Sugar we're gonna be fine.* "You're talking to her Clarence, aren't you?! Say your goodbyes bitch."

Cody swiped her French manicured razor-sharp nails across Gabriel's throat, half decapitating her piercing her jugular vein intentionally. Blood spatter decorated her bedroom walls, coating her hardwood floors. Cody violently tossed her broken, naked body to the floor. She fled, stepping over Gabriel's listless body exiting out the bedroom window, shattering it upon her angry exit leaving a dangerous gaping hole one hour before sunrise. Before Gabriel hit the floor, Clarence caught his broken doll.

*NO, NO, NO, NO, NO! His thoughts raced; he panicked. She's not conscious. She can't decide to be immortal.* Clarence decided for Gabriel. Using his fangs to open his veins, he created six gaping gashes. Zion entered Gabriel's house greeted by the bloody scene. "Clarence, Isaiah is barely alive." "Save him turn him vampire Zion." Zion never turned a man but performed the ceremony with ease. Clarence's blood poured into Gabriel's exposed wounds. Her heartbeat was faint, she was leaving him. "Come on baby, come on." He never lost a human during a turn but heard it happens. Opening his other wrist, he held both over the bottom half of her neck.

Clarence prayed. He didn't think God heard his kind, but Isabel said when something bad happens, pray. So, he did, and her neck closed. Clarence laid her on the bed. Gabriel coughed crying. Clarence thought a neighbor would call the police; he smashed her dresser in one blow, covering her windows with splintered wood. Hysterical laughter echoed up the steps. Zion saved Isaiah. Clarence exhaled a sigh of relief that both of Cody's victims lived.

Gabriel slept. He didn't want her waking up to a blood bath. He ran a warm bath placing her in the tub gently. He removed the bloody sheets, the bed, and cleaned the floor before flipping the mattress. Clarence washed her floor and walls within ten minutes before returning to the bathroom to check on her. She was burning up; Clarence ran chilly water in the tub to bring her fever down. "How are you doing down there

Zion?" "I'm ok, Pharaoh. How is Gabriel?" "Burning up Dr." "Isaiah won't stop laughing, is it normal Pharaoh?" "Yes, it's a human emotion dying. He may act them all out before the turn is complete. Stay with him Zion." "Yes, Pharaoh." "When he slumbers come, please." "Ok." Gabriel cried out for Clarence mentally since her voice cords were severed. *I'm cold!* She was shivering in the tub. "You've a fever, Sugar. I'm trying to break it." *Take me out of the water Clarence it's too cold.* Her whispers tugging at his heart strings.

Clarence picked up his bbw Queen as if she were a feather. He hoped she was fine with her size because it was permanent. He placed Gabriel in bed, dressing her lightly. She turned her back to him, crying in pain and shivering. He covered her with blankets before he left to check on Isaiah, who was still chuckling hysterically. "How long Zion?" "Two hours nonstop laughter Pharaoh. What the fuck was Cody doing?" "I'm unsure Zion; however, she'll regret it. Let's move this coffee table." Zion never saw him this angry. Clarence lay on his back meditating. He connected telepathically to ten thousand vampires excluding Cody.

*Family we have a rouge member of our coven. Tonight, I announced to coven leaders that I'll marry. Cody, enraged, followed me to the home of my new Queen. In a fit of jealousy, Cody partially decapitated her, and a day guardian who I raised. She is to be caught, not killed. The vampire who returns her unharmed will be rewarded with one million dollars.*

Zion watched as Clarence communicated with vampires, hearing the message echo in his head. Clarence levitated four feet off the floor, floating effortlessly sealing Cody's inevitable fate. *Cody, there is no use running. I can see wherever you are, and you will die. Why did you choose her Clarence? Love selects for us Cody. If you chose to love instead of greed, you'd understand.* "Zion, she's in Times Square. Zion called the house informing them, "Times Square."

Clarence kissed Gabriel's hand before he adorned her in a lace night gown, praying the fever didn't return. He tucked her in with a blanket. After cleaning the bathroom, he called Elijah. "I'm enroute Clarence." "Clarence" "Yes, love?" "I need Tylenol." Clarence held his laughter as he fed them to her with water. oddly, she didn't throw up. "Thank you, Clarence," holding his waist tight. He brushed her hair and platted it. The braids touched her mid back. *Why didn't she like her hair?* He thought as she slept. Zion tapped the door. "He's asleep thank God the fool wouldn't stop laughing. Cody tore his throat out drinking his blood. Clarence Cody can communicate and track Isaiah now. We need to abandon him." "No Zion." "Pharaoh the boy is in love with Cody. He has been since childhood, it's risky having him near your new bride. He may betray you." "We don't turn humans vampire, then abandon them, Dr."

Clarence whispered to not wake Gabriel. "It's no better than the oppressors releasing us after freedom without 40 acres and a mule. You'll manage Zion, you made him. You will be able to call him when you need help, he must come. I'll read his thoughts daily making sure she's not contacting him bring me a cup of his blood." Clarence closed the door heading downstairs. "We must get this cleaned up Zion."

Zion carried Isaiah upstairs to the main bathroom showering Isaiah off. Clarence took the couch to the garage and placed an older one in its place. He swept, mopped the floors, and cleaned blood spattered walls. It'd been a long time since Clarence cleaned a house. He loved it but remembered why he was cleaning, making his rage grow. Zion dried off his vampire patient, who continued to periodically laugh aloud and cry. He lay him on the dry fresh sofa that Clarence made up with a fresh sheet and pillows. Zion covered him with a crochet blanket he found in the hall closet. "Hey, they're going to be fine. I'm taking blood samples" Zion reassured. Clarence went upstairs lying next to Gabriel. "I'm here Sugar." The doorbell rang "Who's it?" Zion inquired. "NYPD is Clarence here? ... We got his request to come."

"Who's asking?" The officers revealed fangs. Zion allowed them in. "Wait here please." Zion went upstairs two of us at the door Clarence." He covered Gabriel again;

however, she kept kicking the blankets off. Clarence greeted Elijah. When Elijah saw his king, he kneeled with his second in command. "Pharaoh, we're sorry to meet under such horrible circumstances."

"Vampire, if you don't rise, New York's finest is in the house. Zion, this is Elder Elijah. We were slaves together. He's a first-class detective now." "Pleasure meeting you in person Elder." "Same here brother who's this, Elijah?" "My second, he attended the meeting earlier Clarence." "It's an honor Great One." "Same." Clarence shook his hand.

"What's this I hear; you're taking another Queen? Congrats old vampire." "Clarence scoffed "Old? In human years you're older than I." "Don't remind me brother. Sorry I missed the meeting. I was assigned to a robbery-homicide last minute. What happened Clarence?" "I announced my engagement. Cody thought I'd choose her. She tracked us here, attempting to kill Isaiah, and my future bride. She fled, to Times Square." Clarence closed his eyes locating her in seconds. "We put an APB on Cody Clarence in all five boroughs and Jersey. I put out an Amber alert for a missing sixteen-year-old."

"Clarence" Gabriel weakly called to Clarence from upstairs. Elijah, and Clarence looked toward the voice calling. "Is that her brother? Allow me a glimpse Clarence." "No, she ain't presentable Elijah." "Oh, excuse me!" Elijah threw his hands up surrendering jokingly. Clarence went to her, and Gabriel placed her arms around his waist. "I'm hungry." Clarence brushed her cheek lightly, her fever lingered. Gabriel was turning faster than he thought. "Ok Sugar." "Clarence, I need a hospital." "Sugar, a hospital can't help you." "What happened to me Clarence?" "I'll explain when you're better Sugar." "Explain now Clarence. I'm going to throw up." He raced for a bucket. Clarence examined it; her dinner, and a lot of dead blood was purged.

"Elijah," Clarence called telepathically. "Come up." Clarence Covered her, Gabriel's vision was blurred. "Clarence my eyes, I can't see." "It'll return Sugar." She gripped his waist trembling secretly afraid. Elijah knocked gingerly.

"Enter." Gabriel fell asleep and Elijah stood next to the bed on Clarence's side. "Oh, she's a beauty brother. You love thick women," he recalled smiling.

"Your cross cause you can't handle all this sexy woman Elijah." "Not true. You remember when we were free via the proclamation?" "Haha, she was crazy for you Elijah. You revealed you were vampire to scare her thinking she'd go away, making her want you more." "You know we remained lovers until she passed Clarence?" "I recall, how is your wife Mya?" "Good man, nursing at the hospital." "Did you think of converting her to vampress?" "I'm thinking about it. Every year she grows older."

"Patience Elijah, besides, what's this your third wife?" "Yes, all humans. I've buried two, loved them differently but this one's different Clarence." "It's your call Elijah if you want to turn her or not. Does she want to be vampire?" "Yes Clarence." "But?" "If I wanted vampire wife, I would've married one." "Follow the rules is all I ask" "No reminder needed; we've followed rules for centuries. Rules you helped write Elder to govern these covens. You are an original law maker; how can you want to break laws you helped create? Bring her to vampire parties allow her to see we're not bad. I'll hand write an invitation, have it hand delivered with a box of roses. I'm sure she'll say yes to an engagement party Elijah."

"Yes, she will Clarence. Thank you, brother. Man, you got a beauty doll on your hands." Clarence touched her face. "Thank you, she's turning fast, look Elijah," holding her mouth open. "Fangs already? It's usually on day three Clarence." Elijah looked at Clarence laughing. "What's funny?" "You're scared Clarence." "I'm not." "You are," Elijah whispered not to wake her. "I don't want her to die Elijah." "She ain't dying, she's turning Clarence." Elijah went downstairs. "Oh, is that Isaiah laughing Zion?" "On and off, it's annoying Elder." "Your first turn Zion?" "Yes." "Zion, the boy is family. I dated his great grandmother, she was a sexy woman, whew. Lock up behind me Dr." Zion laughed at Elijah as they exited, there were times he forgot Clarence's age, but comments like these reminded him. "Isaiah, rest," Zion laid him back on the couch he stopped laughing. He refrigerated blood samples, resting knowing the days ahead were going to be long and dangerous. His mind raced with unanswered questions.

*What was Cody thinking rising against an old vampire who possessed abilities he didn't share? What was she doing?*

# Chapter 5

# Bloody Tracks

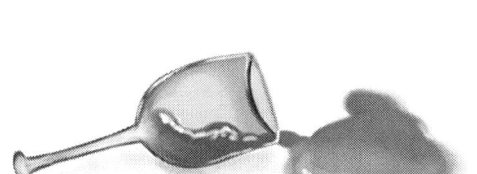

The year of our lord 1859

"WAKE! WAKE! All niggers front and center!" It be early mornin dark when we's rousted outta cabins an outta da big house da overseer be half dressed.

"I bring unwelcome news our beloved Master Alexender died this morning. There was a savage uprising at the Diamond Plantation where he plays hearts! We are going to clean the diamond plantation like good neighbors. Get rags, basins, brushes, and brooms. The wagon leaves in five minutes. Dress and return quick, anyone not here is promised three lashes--picaninnies too!" Mammy gone upstairs ta see both misses. Isabel sends fo Avril.

Dey's hoopin' an' hollerin' dey, brings Massa Alex body home, he axe in da back choke too. Isabel left the bedroom to the kitchen to make mornin' tea. She went to her bedroom off the pantry, closing the door. "Clarence," she called, whining his name in soul wrenching pain falling to her knees holding her belly. Avril entered their bedroom. "Dat boy smart den all us baby.

He walkin slow on count da heat. You knowed dat boy hate some sun, Isabel." Clover entered through the porch door, "Is he here da coachman, Avril?" "He ain't back gal." "Youse goin ta da Diamond Plantation, gal?" "Yes'm, Mammy." "Looks fo em, hears Clover?" "What dry goods he wears Mammy?" "Massa Alex ole suit. Blue coat, white britches gal." "Yes'm." "Here, gal." Mammy gimme cold water an' bread. Hides it under dem skirts. When ya comes back, finds me. We sleeps back da kitchen, me an Avril." "Yes'm."

Clover sensed tension in the air. Her thoughts rested on Clarence how handsome he is. She wanted to know him the moment she saw him. He was tall with big strong arms and shoulders, most slaves had that, but not house slaves. Clover climbed on the wagon, sitting in back with picaninnies on her lap. They arrived at the plantation It was a bloody mess. The sun shone on the road leading to the big house on the plantation. Clover pondered on what she saw, *dem white pretty rocks on da main road got blood on em. Blond hair and white skin scrape on da road. I be a water gal and cook slave fo slave catchers fo dey sold me ta Massa numba two. I learn ta track peoples and what I sees it be ten peoples here dey went up yonder west in dem woods leaving an' dey walks not runs.*

"DOWN, OFF HURRY NIGGERS we ain't gots all day! Who here knows how to run a team of horses attached to a carriage?" "I does!" Clover yelled. "Gather as many horses as you can, separate them by plantation mark gal. Here." Ovaseea throws dirty gloves on da ground. "Ise lookin fo horses, I picks up a strong twig. I ain't like beatin em, but some be stubborn. Ise reckon some come easy being hot wantin water. "The rest of ya get inside, start scrubbin make it spit shine. Any jewels, money, guns, hand it to me"

I hears da overseea voice get low I walks round startin on da hill by dem apple trees. Ise walk up yonder spots foots tracks I follows 'em findin' Massa Alex carriage, one horse, three gone. I runs fast on my foots. I opens da door, Nothing. Cold creep in my blood tho it be heat out. *Bad happen I looks around like dem slave catcher teach me ta find Clarence, so I look to da dirt. Apples were bloody crush. I steps down an' my boot get mud mix wit blood on 'em. It smell a dead rotten, flies. I looks down worms feedin' on blood soaked apples.*

*Three feets prints. Tracks has two peoples one wit lady, and man feets up yonder threw dem trees. Branches...broke twigs a snap in da earth bloody leaves. Folla dem foots, Safinah.* Clover followed footsteps deep in the woods risking getting raped by slave catchers, though she knew most of them. *My feets keep up wit wench, feet prints Ise far from da plantation.* Clover looked farther seeing a ridge. *What is dat? Dat be Clarence coat? Woman feets go down his keeps on.* Clover fought back tears, *He got away he got away! Thank God! He live he live!* Clover hid the coat under her skirt tucking it tight. Wiping stinging tears *he free. He be free.* "Hey gal!" "Yes'sir?" "What you doing so far off the plantation you ain't tryin to run are ya Clover?"

"Nosir, ise callin' Massa Alex horse I see one I call em from yonda sir" *God bless my lie. Soon as I say it, da horse show.* "Take em round back an' water them. No sign of Clarence, Clover Ms. Minnie is worried about him?" "Nosir sept bloody apples. Look likes animals drag em off fo meat." "Damn I liked that boy. He done what I said, no questions. He was one of you better niggers. Go on gal, get them horses watered."

"Sir, ya want me ta steer Massa Alex carriage to da big house? Ain't no one else. Avril too old ta steer a team sir." "I reckon gal it be fine until the misses finds another coachman." "Yes'sir," I walks fast ta get out dat man eye. I use dem apples ta draw nags, an' fifteen comes. We ain't sho how many loss, but Massa Alex goods be all dat thievin overseer care bout. I sees him keepin' ammo, coin, a man ring. He say check pocket a da dead. Dis one slave I hates name John, da overseer friend, he do what ovaseea say. He drink wit him, laugh, steal pussy too. One night, he come my way. I say drink first, we does, an' he go ta sleep wit sleep powder. I takes off his dry goods, he wakes late, the overseer get so mad.

He say how bad I is in bed, "I ain't want her she ugly." Dey laughs, but I ain't want no pink dick. I laughs cause Clarence pink, too. "I gots nags watered an bloods off em, sir. Dey's line up, an' ready, sir. Dem others over yonda ain't Massa Alex horses." "You done a good job gal." "Thanks, ya sir." "Take old Violet up there ta sit right next to ya up front Clover. She deserves a good ride back that be my favorite gal. She found me a diamond and gold ring. She can sit where she wants!" "Yes'sir" Clover moved over.

"Clarence....ya seent sumthin gal?" Violet asked, hushed. "I thinks he dead Violet. I sees blood drag up yonder like da wolf takes em fo meat." "Clarence look out fo us field slaves Clover. He give us goods he finds, food when we gots none, most be scrap, he make sho we gets it. Missy Clara old clothes or old drapes, apples fruit from trees off da sides a' roads he ain't have ta. He better off wit da wolf den da slave catcha I tells ya dat gal." Violet sobbed for her loss. "Violet, why you crying that gal ain't being mean to ya is she?" the overseer called out. "Nosir Ise cryin fo my Massa he gone yonda" she looked at Clover winking. "Violet?" "Yes'sir?" "Master Alex is with God out this heat and we're still stuck here." "Yes'sir."

By time we back I rides to da stable waterin da nags afta Ise right tired. I goes to da kitchen ta see Mammy. I taps da screen door. "Gal, why is you knockin? comes in. Avril Clover back." Isabel woke him, turning to Clover. "Is Clarence dead, chile?" "He live mammy he gets gone Mammy." Isabel dropped to her knees thanking God, he was spared. "How dat be gal?"

Clover pulled the blood-stained jacket from her skirts. Mammy gasped in fear; "I track his feets Avril. He heavy on em first, he run deep into da forest up yonda. I covers his tracks. Overseer thinkin' animals drag 'em off. Dese white folk sick wit worry, they ain't got time ta think a no slave iffin' he escapes. I finds his coat spot where he drops it, feets marks come after. Clarence comes back, Mammy, I knows it!

# Chapter 6
# Awake

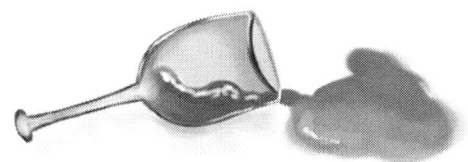

The Year 2020

If he could sleep it would be on this contraption Zion set up called a recliner. *What a wonderful invention. I love recliners* he thought, pushing it. It became a bed for him; he meant to purchase one but didn't. *Clarence, how are you?*

*I'm good Zion, watching Gabriel. How will I explain I turned her?* Telepathically speaking, *explain with love, Pharaoh. Can you get away Zion? Yes.* After checking on Isaiah, he crept not to wake the joker upstairs. "It's open Zion. Look in the bucket, is it normal?" "It's coagulated blood. The blood she's throwing up is dead. Do you mind if I look in her medicine cabinet Clarence?" "Go ahead." Zion returned holding chemo-therapy pills. "Gabriel has cancer. It's what she's purging." tossing the pills to Clarence.

"Did she reveal her illness?" "No, but it's no matter now, Zion." "Are you going to sleep Pharaoh?" "I've been off soil a couple days; I can't sleep Zion." "I haven't slept in five years, Clarence." "Yes, you conveyed that. It'll pass, Dr. I hadn't slept in years. One night I rested, waking the next morning.

They heard giggling again. "Lordy! Let me check this boy." Clarence laughed, "He'll stop eventually, look Dr." Clarence held Gabriel's mouth open. "Thoughts?"

"God already? She's evolving overnight. Fangs usually come in week two Pharaoh." He grabbed his stethoscope from his neck checking her heart. "It beats low. It'll be over soon; then she'll rise to her new life. Does she know she's our vampire Queen Clarence? Does she want to marry you?" "I haven't asked for her hand yet nosy." "How do you know Gabriel will say yes Clarence?" Zion looked waiting for his reply. "Speak truth and free yourself vampire king." "I read her thoughts entering a dream once if you must know Zion."

"Shame on you." Zion shook his finger of judgement playfully. "How do I say you're my vampire Queen?" "You say...you're a vampire Queen Clarence." "You always keep things simple Zion. You're employed at a renowned hospital; you sit on the board of directors. Your parents would've been proud. A thoracic specialist in a white hospital. This is the life you should have." "I have it thanks to you brother, thank you."

"Water," Gabriel whined dryly. Clarence held her head, "here baby." He steadily held the ice-cold water to her plump sexy lips. "Thank you honey," reaching for his hand dozing off again. "She loves you, Clarence you'll be fine." Clarence overslept the next morning. Gabriel was awake singing and bathing. He tapped the bathroom door, "honey, are you ok?"

"Yes, bae I'll be out in a minute." She loosened her plats. *It looks like a rat nest.* Gabriel slipped into warm shower water shampooing her hair, trying to recall what happened a few nights prior. *I had sex I think... warm kisses. Strong hands. A woman kicked the bedroom door, a wife or girlfriend? Clarence explained something, you inquired about a wife. He isn't married. Oh God, he's a fucking vampire. Am I dreaming? Nah Must be trippin, girl you trippin. Those pain pills have hallucinating effects wait. No, you're not Gabriel.*

*You heard his thoughts when he slept. Trust yourself girl you all you got.* Gabriel grabbed her comb, untangling hair knots. *This can't be.my hair has it grown?* Chemotherapy snatched clumps of it. *Gabriel glanced at her long nails, wow this can't be. I feel great with not one ounce of pain.*

Gabriel felt for the lump in her breast. The Dr. said he couldn't get to it in her left breast because it metastasized. *It's gone!* She sat on the side of the tub, placing her arm behind her head self-breast examining again. Not there. *What the fuck is going on?*

"Sugar you alright in there?" "Yes babe." Gabriel stepped on the scale *243. hahah shit ain't change.* Gabriel grabbed her comfy robe before exiting and gazing in the mirror. *Jesus my eyes are prettier, and light brown. What's that brown ring? They look like Clarence's.*

Gabriel smiled. Her teeth had gone back to their normal shade before medication damaged them. She sat on the bed, her eyes blazing fires like Clarence's. She couldn't hear her heart; it beat extremely low. "I'm vampire, aren't I?" Clarence stared in shock, hearing it for the first time aloud made her nervous, hell it even made him nervous. "How'd you know?" "I heard your thoughts you were sleeping" Clarence was speechless.

"Why're our eyes this color Clarence?" "This is how we identify one another. We inherit identical eye pigment. "Gabriel smiled; he couldn't see her fangs. "What is it?" "Fangs Sugar?" "They went in during my Shower." "On their own?" "Yes." "You didn't retract them?" "How do I do that? And why are the windows boarded?" "Sugar, the sun is our enemy." He delivered the news with disappointment; "It can kill us." Gabriel approached the bathroom window. "Gabriel no!" She stuck her hand in the sun. "Zion get up here." He obliged "Show him Sugar." "Good morning, who're you?" "I'm your new Dr., Zion Donovan." She put her hand in the sun. "Can't be," examining her hand. "Gabriel's heart stopped the started Zion" "Anyone hungry?" The old vampires were confused. "Sugar, may we speak privately before you cook, please?"

"Sure babe." Zion exited doing his best to ignore the conversation, but the medical vampire inside thirsted for knowledge. He grabbed his Dr.'s bag drawing blood from Isaiah while he slept and dropped a sample in a petri dish before holding it in the sun. The blood bubbled then burst. *How could she walk in the sun? All species evolve. Is this the evolution for vampires.* "Sugar please allow me to explain." "Go ahead honey," gazing with inquisitive eyes holding his hand "Sugar I'm a vampire."

"I know I read your--"

"Thoughts, I recall, no one can read them Gabriel that's the thing." "I woke thirsty and went for water. I thought you were talking to me, so I answered. When I looked down you were asleep. First your thoughts were unclear then I meditated, and they cleared Clarence." "What did you hear?" "You're worried I'd be upset you turned me vampire without consent, afraid you enslaved me. The icing on the cupcake is, you're in love with me," placing her hand on his cheek. "You didn't want me to die, and you couldn't see your life without me Clarence. Why're you looking that way honey?" Gabriel looked sad.

"No Sugar it's not you." He smiled bringing comfort back into the conversation. Clarence touched a piece of her hair she left out of the wrap, however she held it down to hide it. He moved her hand kissing her fingers.

"It's beautiful like you." He kissed her plump lips. She wrapped her hand around his huge arms, nestling her nose in his neck, smelling him as her fingers crept through his silk hair. "Gabriel, we stay with the same looks as the day we're turned." "Clarence my hair grew. It was falling out. I no longer have bald patches." "May I see." He reached for the wrap. "No Clarence," gently holding his hand in hers. "Not another one." He sighed aloud chuckling.

"What?" "Safinah hated her hair and didn't like me seeing it when we met. There is so much to explain Gabriel." "I'm in love with these vampire eyes Clarence. I can see wayyyy down there. Can I keep 'em?" "Haha." "We see distances as you age, you'll see further." "What was wrong medically Gabriel?" "I'll explain when we're alone."

"Aren't we alone?" Vampires have excellent hearing. Our bedroom in the mansion is soundproof to some. I added led to the walls years ago." "That's not what I meant." "What Sugar?" "I have breast cancer and leukemia third stage." "It's not returning Gabriel" "How do you know babe?" "Zion is an Oncologist when you were turning, you purged cancer out your body last night. You are cursed with me for eternity my love. We don't eat and some don't sleep. We drink blood and water, living normal lives with the humans guarding us in diverse ways. We enjoy wonderful lives Gabriel." "May I go to the kitchen? I'd like a cup of coffee please." "Did you hear we don't drink coffee?" "Yes," I'm going to the kitchen to boil water. Clarence joined her at her 1950's vintage table. In fact, the entire kitchen was 1950 vintage, the items all original. "You like the kitchen huh, Clarence?" "Don't do that woman" she grinned. "What?"

"You read my thoughts Gabriel" "I didn't. You were looking around like you enjoy seeing these items. Do you remember them?" "I do Sugar." "Which one do you like the best?" "The fridge sweetheart." "What do you do for a living Clarence?" "Yes," Zion instigated. "What do you do for a living Clarence?" "I own blood banks and various businesses throughout the city Sugar and I'm the Vampire King." Gabriel poured hot water on top of coffee powder, adding sugar and cream. "Zion, grab that pot please."

"Most vampires were turned by me and in turn they created their own Covens. All Covens pay dues for protection and other favors, but the money goes to our protection and things we need as vampires I provide Gabriel." She grinned. "Vampire King?" "Yes ma'am." "How many Covens do you have?" "Ten" "How many vampires in all Clarence?" "Over 40,000." "Do you have security?" "Yes Sugar." "Where are they?" "Home Sugar" If we were there the attack wouldn't have happened." "Do you've a Queen?" "She died Safinah, she was human and had no desire to be vampire. She died many years ago."

"A person has a choice, Clarence?" "Yes, they can decline under vampire law. No human may be turned against their will. Its punishable by death." "Vampires have laws?" "Yes Sugar." Gabriel slowly sipped coffee as Zion stood behind her with the pot. Clarence glared at Zion. "Do you mind if I take a blood sample Gabriel?" "Sure, no problem, Zion." "Can you share your prescriptions in the last year?" "They're in the bathroom medicine cabinet Dr." Both vampires were shocked she hadn't purged the coffee. Zion removed his phone recording Clarence on bended knee.

"Gabriel, I loved you the first day I saw you. Instantly I was drawn to your beauty and intelligence. Being with you makes me feel alive again. Will you be my bride… are you in love with me?" "Yes, I'm, yes!" Shaking her head excited. "You heard?" Clarence nudged Zion. "Yes, I heard Great One." Gabriel kissed him fervently, wrapping her arms around his neck. "Wait, where's the ring baby?" "I'm going to get you one Sugar." "If you can't afford one its ok honey, we can use my grandmothers." Zion stopped himself from laughing. Did she know his money is as long as a train smoke?" Get it Sugar." She returned fast. "Here it is Clarence."

"Goodness, it's beautiful. Are you sure you want to wear grandma's ring?" "Yes baby." He took the ring out of the blue-velvet box, a one carat, round ruby with one carat of diamonds surrounding the set, in white gold. Clarence removed the ring as he bent on one knee again placing it on her left hand. Zion recorded the entire proposal for the scroll writers.

"It's beautiful on you sweetheart but if you want another ring, I'll buy it baby. Honey, please pack items for a month's stay. It'll be sundown soon. I want us to leave before it sets, ok?" "Yes," Gabriel exited the kitchen to pack. Zion lifted the coffee cup. He held it upside down, looking into the empty pot in awe. "I'm unsure, you're the Dr., figure it out." "Yes, Great One."

"Call the mansion, have them send six motorcycle escorts Zion." "Yes Pharaoh." "Prepare a chamber for my Queen. Have all house staff present to greet her please, especially the guardians and Joan. Tell the baby vamps to take showers." Zion called ahead, handing him a mug of blood. Clarence sipped, ecstatically. He knew before he celebrated his engagement, he had a snake to kill.

# Chapter 7
# Forget Me Not

The Year of our Lord 1860....

It be a year since da uprising. Constables never catch who done it, dey blame us slaves. Fo a year, dey talk durin' carriage rides, dinners, tea, lunch, and whatever else---dey gossip 'bout slaves.

Dere be change, me bein a house slave, den workin fields. Ms. Minnie made me da coachman. Avril an' Isabel put a bug in Ms. Minnie ear, so she say Ise da new one. Ms. Minnie gives me all Missy Clara old dresses.

Twin oak trees, I sees em from yonder. We home thanks Jesus. Fall leaves make da road look colorful. Gots ta be mindful of ditches hidin' under leaves--ain't want no broken spokes. BANG!! Missy Clara hit da carriage wall. "Yes'm, Missy Clara?" "Clover, can we move faster? Mr. Thomas is calling on me this evening, I need to be ready." "Yes'm, Missy Clara." I make da horse trot. "Missy Clara?" "Yes Clover?" "I sees holes in da dirt road, theys cover wit leaves." "Clover slow down."

"Yes'm Ms. Minnie." I hear em fussin. Ms. Minnie say she gots plenty time. Missy Clara been trouble since Massa Alex die, making kitchen calls late an early morning.'She has da slave Massa Alex buy her following her like a puppy, she ole as thirteen. One thang good come, Missy Clara say no man touch her, no overseer, or they gets sixty whips.

I see dat gal alone I say "why Missy Clara say no man touch ya?" "She say she don't want me with no child, cause iffin I is, she ain't teachin no new dressin housekeeper. Ise hard nuff ta teach, Clover." "You keeps bein hard ta teach. When ya gets easy, she gets a new hard one ta teach." "How ya knowed Clover?" "I knows gal. Do as I say, ya hear?" "Yes'm," she skip to get Missy Clara petticoats off da line.

Mr. Thomas ain't no good, callin' on her money not her. Da other coachman in town say he broke hear bout Massa Alex dowry on her and dat all he after. Dat devil too good lookin' ta want her he can have any wench he want. Ain't no way he picks her she ugly inside and out short wit a nose push up like a swine. Hair always look dirty no matterin how much she wash it. She wicked dey right fo each otha. "Gal gets in chere helps me light da oven. You ain't no coachman, taday youse kitchen help Clover." "Yes'm Mammy."

"We gots ta get this table dress. Ise gots ta ready Ms. Minnie. Table settin fo five people: Ms. Minnie, Missy Clara, Mr. Thomas, his Mammy, Ms. Emma. Gets dat fine china out. Avril checks da silver. Make sho folk see dey face in it. Clover, gets ya servin' goods on." "Why me, Isabel?" "Cause I says all hands a helpin." Clover finished setting the table, checking it over, *salad fork, dinner fork, dessert spoon, soup spoon, salad fork, butter knife, meat knife. Dem eatin' tools Ise never eats off 'em. Iffin I does, which ones I eats wit first?* "Table set Avril."

"Good, get ya servin dry goods on Clover ain't no mood ta hear fussin." "Yes'sir." I walks ta where Mammy an' Avril stay, dey makes me a small room wit em off da kitchen. I stays late evenin so Mammy ain't worry. Ms. Minnie say dat be fine betta I be in da big house case dey call on me.

I went ta ready I thinks of Clarence passin as white livin good I wishes he buys me outta slavery Ms. Minne never see me go I knows dat. I watches him a seasons fo he run. Clarence dat boy never smile or talks ta us field slave's cep ole slaves he knowed. damn he pretty. I loves em first time I sees em walkin a nag ta stables. Older slaves say "You betts get ya eyes off dat one he a house nigga we ain't loud ta mix wit em."

"Is ya ready gal?" Clover exited slow and shy. "Aww look ya gots a waistline under dem hundred skirts, ya look mighty fine, Ms. Clover." Avril smiled, handing her white serving gloves fussing over her apron bow. "I hates it Avril. Clarence say Ise right not ta let no one sees my pretty. Dis show em Avril." "You be fine, chile jus fine"

The guests arrived 7 p.m. sharp Avril opened the door escorting them to the foyer. Ms. Minne come down windin steps. "Welcome to our home." Once she reaches bottom, Missy Clara come in a ugly dark dress wit embroidery showing ruffle petticoats. Mammy draw dem corsets right tight round her fat belly. Us slave's lines up in dry goods lookin same, black dress, white buttons, white ruffle apron, white gloves, black boot, black stockin, left hand behind our back. "Stand tall...back straight. Ms. Minnie was lookin ta make sho we takes heed. Ms. Minnie wink at me, brushing my apron lightly she rightly proud a me."

Mammy and us slaves walk behind Ms. Minnie an' her dinner folk. Three a us line up other three goes to da kitchen. I stands close to da door since I be da oldest slave Avril come up wit dat. I stands left cause all service from da left. Mr. Thomas say ta Ms. Minnie he sorry bout Massa Alex when he hear wat savages done, he upset. He ask if dey finds who done it. Ms. Minnie say not yet. He say he hears same happen on nother plantation not long afta. Missy Clara say, "could we speak conversation less upsettin please?" I pass out butter bread, I sees Mr. Thomas eye my tit an hide. I sure I sees it. I helps wit salad. I passes it out I gets ta him he rub my skirt hem under da table. I pretend I ain't see what he done, Ise scared. Last time it done to me Ise tea. I thinks. He drunk da slave tracker who own me kill him after.

He say Ise dere ta track, cook, work an' heal slave gun wounds, he yell mad wit his gun smokin. I ain't knowed what he mean till Ise older. A slave say "ya no good ta him wit baby in ya belly" I knowed what dat mean when Missy Clara say it ta ha' dressin gal. Dat Massa let mens see him kill dat raper fo what he done, after no one look my way. Ole Massa be nice when no one round. I stay by da servin door, I looks up I sees Mr. Thomas eye on me. We serves meat, again I takes da side he on otha gal takes cross from me. Mr. Thomas slip somethin in my apron. I pretends I ain't see nuttin. Ise scared.

"Emma, I have not seen you since we were children. It is good to see you again." "Yes, it is Minnie." "Have you settled in Georgia Emma?" "Yes, we have. We are staying at the hotel until we can purchase a home. Thomas and I have prospects we're visiting this week."

Missy Clara smiles at Mr. Thomas he smiles back ta be nice. "Shall we retire to the parlor room for dessert and coffee Emma?" "Yes, we May Minnie." "What is for dessert?" Mr. Thomas ask looks my way lickin his lips.

"Chocolate cake, coffee or tea sir?" "I love chocolate. I'll take coffee with cake, Clover." "Yes'sir." I looks down not ta meet eyes. As they went to da parlor, we clears da table wrappin scraps fo us. Dere be a lot cause Missy Clara ain't eats. Ise hungry an' wanna eat. Mammy slice cake thin fo ladies thick fo Mr. Thomas.

Missy Clara sat near Mr. Thomas; she make sho she far ova on da settee away from him. Ise sho she wanna touch him fresh. I holds da silver coffee pot servin while Avril puts cane or cream. Missy Clara say no sweet cane she knowed she take two. Ise back by da parlor door. Mr. Thomas, say he need a outhouse. Ms. Minnie say, "Clover show Mr. Thomas the chamber pot in da guest room."

"Yes'm." Ise showin da way once we gets dere he say, "wait here gal." He come close sayin, "you are a sight." He push on me I stay lookin down he licks my cheek sayin, "when I marry that ugly woman, I'll have you every night. You will be mine to do what I please. You are beautiful." His hand went up my skirt "I gave you a gift that Missy Clara gave to me, look at it when you are alone. You will it need it once I become Master of this house."

I stay quiet. Ise angry but mo so scared. I knowed he mean all he say an' worse. Iffin I can spit on em, I would. I walks behind em down those cursed windin' steps. I feels dirty, iffin' I done bad. Dey finish dessert you hears Mr. Thomas ask Ms. Minnie if he could call on Missy Clara again, she say yes, he kiss her hand lookin up, I looks away. When ise alone I sits cryin ova chocolate cake. We gives scraps an' meat bone to da head field slave to share makes soup ta stretch. I gives Ann cake an scraps.

Mammy ask, "Why you cry chile?" Clarence bees back. I tells her an' Avril da bad. Avril leaves ta makes night trays in da kitchen. Mammy lower her voice a whisper. "Iffin he come Massa of dis house ain't much fendin' we does, lessin ya tells Ms. Minnie what he done."

Avril hear an cut in, "No, you ain't! Dey says ya done somethin' make em want ya she be sold next auction cause Clara make it so outta spite. We think on somethin. Let's enjoy dis cake" Avril opened brown paper "Cake scraps for ma' ladies." "You ain't give dese scraps away Avril?" "No mammy I ain't," he grinned. "Clover eat all dat cake. Iffin ya fat sat fool ain't gonna want cha." They laughed enjoying chocolate cake off fine china with real silver forks making them feel free. Clover didn't know why, but this chocolate thing was the best she ever tasted.

Mammy collect our servin' dry goods da next mornin' when da key falls out my apron. "Clover?" She whispers callin me in da kitchen. "Dis falls out ya apron what ya doin' wit dis gal?"

She repeated what Thomas said the evening prior. Clover looked down ashamed. Mammy toss da key on da pantry shelf. "Leave it be. I takes care Missy Clara handin' a key ta ha' bed chamber. I tells her I finds it in the guest commode. She ought be shame fast tail!"

"Mornin Avril." Mornin Clover dis mornin ya takes Ms. Minnie ta ha' bridge game round five at da lady club." "Yes'sir. Avril is Missy Clara comin'?" "No, she stay on count chocolate keeps her on da chamber pot." We laughs. I water horses brush 'em out walk 'em since dey ain't out day fo. I calls da new horse Clarence on count his coat white an pretty. Mind me da time I sees Clarence wit no dry goods on. I saw somethin' way in back da nag stall I goes behind da nag, a white shirt I picks it up, It stain wit old blood. I fast looks round, I ain't see a soul. I hides it under my skirts and goes ta see Mammy. "Mammy," I whisper through da pantry window "What ya want gal? Ise busy with Clara shittin."

I looks round holdin' da shirt. "Dat be my baby shirt Clover." Mammy holds her hand out fo it. "Ya sho Mammy?" "Course I is gal dis chere be my stitchin. Where ya gots it Clover?"

"Back da nag stall ain't dere fo Ise sho of it." "Boy bets not come chere why he does somethin' fool?" "Tole ya mammy he live ya give up hope I say we betts not." "We gots ta burn it, Clover." "No Mammy. I wanna smell em." "Smell it gal den I burns it cut ya a small part." I puts it close ta my face smellin' da neck Clarence put it fo me cause he watch me so I knowed he live. He thinks on me too. I hangs da shirt where it was.

Most gals hitch at sixteen. I hear otha coachman's say no suitors want Clara on count she ugly. Girls on otha plantations mo handsome. She gots da heaviest dowry of all plantation gals cause Massa Alex gots heavy coin. Clara 18 not hitch. I make sho Ms. Minne shot gun inside da carriage. Small gun under da bench. Massa Alex huntin' knife hidin' too. I ask why we need all dat. She say, 'Three women's travel da road alone, we cannot be too careful Clover.' Ms. Minnie say her daddy and brothers teach her ta use dem guns an she knowed what ta do. She teaches me an' Clara how ta use em.

I gets up front where Ms. Minnie be lone. I say, "Ms. Minnie, dat color dress make ya look Missy Clara age!" She laugh an say, "Avril stop teaching Clover how to lie, I'm too old for it." "Ain't no lie, Ms. Minnie." Ms. Minnie a fair

Misses. She listens ta us slave side a story an' 'fo punishment, she talks. Ms. Minnie take ya meal or give 'mo work. Iffin ya keeps doin' wrong she give whips, den it be one. I hold her hand and help her in "Clover are the guns ready?" "Yes'm, ready 'em fo da ride, ma'am."

"Good, keep the small one close. We're traveling after sundown, and we can never be too careful, Clover."

"Yes'm, Ms. Minnie."

We gets to da the lady club on time. I rush ta get da door and grabs Ms. Minnie hand "Thank you, Clover."

I held my head down till she enter da house. I hear ladies say "Minnie you look wonderful! Come sit near me." Dere a lotta gossip and laughin.' I pulls da carriage round back. I ain't go sit wit othea coachmen. I practice letters first. Missy Clara teach her ready gal ta read letters I makes her say what she know." "A.B.C.D." "E."

Clover ran behind the horse, pulling a knife "Who dat be?" she whispered, hiding in the shadows. Someone stepped out, she could barely see who it was, the person came closer. "Come closer" Clover called out blade behind her back. He stepped closer, the light shining on him a bit. "Clarence." Clover dropped the knife, hugging his neck as tears fell. "Ise dreamin." She let go. "Lemme look at cha, Clarence I aint knows iffin I shud be cross, or happy ya live." keeping her voice to a whisper.

Clarences eyes glimmered. "I miss ya, Safinah. Ya got my job, I, see?" "Yes, I did ta look fo ya when I be on da road." "How is Mammy, and Avril?" "Mighty fine. I finds ya coat when dey make us clear da plantation. I tells Mammy you ain't dead, we rejoice at dat news."

Clarence kissed her neck hearing her blood running through her veins, the smell of the sun on her smooth pretty skin. Her breasts pressed against his hard chest made his manhood rise. It took everything in him to keep his fangs retracted. He wanted to bite her, but not turn her into a vampire without consent, enslaving her to this life she never requested. "May I kiss you, Clover?" "Yes'sir." Clarence kissed her.

"Ouch, Ya bit me boy." "Baby, Ise sorry. May I see?" Clover held her lip "It ain't nothin'." she grinned.

"May I try again my love?" "Yas, Clarence" He opened his arms she flew into them he wrapped his arms around her full waist resting his hands on her hind parts leaning looking in her brown eyes kissing her. He opened her mouth swirling his tongue on hers making sure to swallow her blood. He let her sweet warm blood mix with his saliva. Clarence broke the kiss, swallowed, leaning in for more.

Safinah felt his manhood hard on her thigh. She wanted to touch it, but her hands were busy combing his long silky hair. Her nipples hard, Clarence gently massaged them, she moaned at his touch. Clarence broke up the rendezvous to hear what was happening in the house. She explained the changes since he was gone, and about Thomas marrying Clara. She left out what he'd done, she was ashamed. "Ise be watching over you, woman."

"Go away boy," she held both his hands, "get outta Georgia if ya loves me like ya say ya does. Leave me be…free yaself. Iffin ya stay, youse be made slave I ain't seein dat so shoo neva looks back coachman wipin her tears." "I ain't leavin witout ya, Clover neva." Clover smiled, "I thinks ya forgets me." "How I forget ya? I gots a sweet secret ta say. Ise watchin ya a year fo we speaks in da stable Clover I love ya." "I loves ya back. Clarence call me Safinah."

"Safinah, love of my life." He pulled her in, hugging her closely. Safinah was never hugged by a man she wanted his loving embrace it warmed her soul. "How we finnin ta be tagetha Clarence? We gots ta run" "We is I gots it thought out Safinah." "You comin' fo me love?"

"I is you can't tell a soul not Mammy or Avril fo dey own good Safinah." "I stay secret Clarence." She grabbed his cold hands. "I love ya, Safinah." "I loves ya back Clarence." She looked away another coachman was coming, "Who ya out chere talkin' wit gal?" She looked back Clarence was gone. "No one I shoo away a deer." "Come in gal ain't safe slave catcher out."

Clover smelled him on her dress, her lip stopped bleeding but stung. She sat as they gossiped drinking spirits thinking on the day, he would take her away making her free. She knew he was not lying, and for the first time in her life she felt safe. *When? How?* She kept asking herself over and over all she knew was she was ready to spend her life with the man who risked his freedom to see her. Clover wanted to be with him, love him, if she to run, he was worth the risk, or die trying.

# Chapter 8
# Welcome Home Pharaoh

"**S**ugar is this all?" Clarence teased. "You said pack for a while, correct?" "Yes, Sugar." Clarence looked at eight suitcases and three duffle bags. He wondered what was in them but recalled she's a woman. Zion carried the luggage to the trunk with his medical bag and cooler holding the blood samples. Zion tossed Isaiah over his shoulder like a five-year-old.

"Is he heavy Zion?" "No ma'am, vampires have excellent strength." Gabriel looked at a fifty-pound barbell sitting on the floor of her garage collecting rust. "It's been here for years. I never lifted it." "Try it, Sugar." "Ok I may pull a muscle." "One hand Sugar." Gabriel lifted it amazed. "Too heavy?" "Lord no Clarence."

"Don't drop it, you'll put a hole in the floor." Zion drove them home. "I'm nervous Clarence." "Why Sugar?" "I'm unsure." "We're your new family." "What if Cody hurts me again Clarence?" "I have security and NYPD looking for her, they'll find her Sugar and I'll protect you." "How do I look?" "Beautiful Gabriel. I love the light blue dress, it's pretty." Gabriel smoothed it out, a habit she had when nervous. "We're home." Zion announced.

Gabriel cracked the dark tinted window, looking outside. The driveway leading to the house was lit with real fire torches on each side. Tiny white stones glistened in the moonlight. The car pulled around a fountain made of cherubs blowing water from trumpets in front of the house. Clarence opened the door, "Welcome home love." Clarence carried Gabriel over the threshold as they locked eyes gazing lovingly.

Zion entered as two vampires departed to carry Isaiah to his bedroom. "Baby, help me get my bags." "Sugar the maids will bring them." "I want you to carry them." "Yes Sugar." Housekeepers were shocked at his response. Gabriel grabbed her purse holding his hand standing in the large foyer. They were welcomed by fifty vampires, on bended knees.

"Welcome home Pharaoh, and to Gabriel, our new Queen, welcome to your estate." "All you see is yours Sugar," Clarence whispered in her ear. Gabriel wanted staff to stand. It was a lot to process. It'd been three days since her attack Clarence scanned her thoughts. "Please rise." They rose obeying their king.

As Clarence walked, Gabriel held his right arm. Vampires hugged him, relieved he was unharmed. Gabriel smelled human blood and heard hearts pounding in the guardians. Her stomach craved what she smelled. "I'd like to lie down Clarence. May I please have a cup of tea?"

Vampires were flabbergasted, *tea?* They thought but dare not say. Clarence shared a telepathic message *"She isn't like us; she's the next evolution of the vampire. We're trying to figure it out. Your Queen can eat and walk in the light.* The baby vamps stared and gasped. *"Stop staring,* Clarence darted a warning look.

Zion looked for Joan, the lead housekeeper, and one of Clarence's closest friends. She sat in her grandson Isaiah's bedroom, covering him. Isaiah is a direct descendant of coven three. The lead vampire of coven three is Papa Nathan. Joan, his fifth-generation human bloodline granddaughter, and Isaiah is his sixth-generation grandson.

It's forbidden for anyone in Papa Nathans bloodline to be turned unless an emergency arises. There's a treaty with Elders to maintain his bloodline, leaving trustworthy humans to record vampire lines and have children continuing his lineage.

Papa Nathan was the only vampire Elder to have fifteen children before being turned. With Clarence and Safinah's help, they were able to buy back or kidnap fourteen of his children from slavery. His daughter Iris was never found, and Papa never stopped looking for children that may've been born of her bloodline.

"What happened Zion?" "They were ambushed by Cody Joan." "Old Indian?" Joan shook her head. "I told Clarence she was trouble when he began courting Gabriel." "You knew Joan?" "Yes, I knew. I warned him Cody's jealous and look what it got us? Who turned Isaiah Zion?" "I did by the Pharaoh's order.

The boy is a son to him, Joan. Cody tore his neck open, left a bloody gaping hole. We need assurance Cody won't use Isaiah to kill Gabriel. He's in love with Cody, sweetie." "My boy will never betray Clarence." "Joan, I was shaken, and I don't scare easily. It was either turn Isaiah or let him die. Clarence couldn't see you heartbroken; I turned him while he saved Gabriel. Cody half decapitated her." "Jesus."

"It was a bloody mess." "You're telling papa Nathan, not me Zion." "Clarence will speak with Papa Nate. Where is he Joan?" "Egypt, he returns in three days. Thank you for saving my baby, Dr." "You're welcome, Joan." "When will he wake?" "We aren't sure Joan however he will. We need to move his bedroom to the second floor, he's one of us so he should sleep with us. He can take Cody's room. I have soil from Gabriel's house. I'll prepare his bedroom and run the house while you nurse him. I'll handle your duties until he wakes." Joan grabbed his hand, "thank you." Zion reached down hugging her. Then he went to check on Clarence and Gabriel. "Zion Gabriel won't drink blood."

"You must make her drink blood, if she doesn't, she'll die Clarence." "I'm aware Zion, thank you." Clarence entered the bedroom leaving a worried Zion in the hall. "I can't believe I'm a vampire Queen. This room is huge scanning her surroundings. "Where's the T.V Clarence?" Gabriel looked out the window seeing a beautiful flower garden but couldn't make out the types. Her vision was still misfocused.

*I love flowers* she thought. Gabriel smelled jasmine, roses, and orchids. Man! I love that smell! She approached the bathroom and the tub was HUGE! A hot tub with candles, the shower is separated into eight square shower heads, complete with a bamboo shower bench gazing through double glass sliding doors. When she approached the sink there were old female products and perfumes in vintage pretty bottles. She heard someone coming, cutting the light she hid behind the bathroom door.

"Sugar?" Clarence tapped the door, "may I enter?" "Yes Clarence." He was nervous, it was an unwanted feeling. "Honey why are you hiding?" Exiting the bathroom her tears surfaced. "You're with me Sugar, you needn't hide your home." Clarence wiped her eyes sitting on the bed.

"Come Sugar," patting his lap. Gabriel straddled Clarence's lap cautioning her weight, his dick was hard under her. She wanted him badly. He kissed her lips rubbing his large hand up her back. Clarence grabbed her waist, while she twirled on his lap. His tongue was cotton candy sweet. Moans escaped her lips while her body called his. Clarence unbuttoned her pretty, blue dress, pushing it past her thighs, licking her shoulder blowing on her collar bone as goose bumps rose at his touch. Gabriel buried her face in his neck, his blood raced under her lips, the smell was tempting.

"Drink love please bite." "No," she moaned, embarrassed she wanted to feed. He ripped his shirt off tiny buttons landing at her feet he exposed his broad shoulders and neck rubbing herd sweet spots pushing her panties to the side. He stroked her throbbing clit with his forefinger his other fingers glided in and out of moist pussy. "Mmmm," she moaned, eyes rolling in her head. "Fuck, Daddy."

He pulled his sticky fingers, licking them. She grabbed his hand joining him as their tongues met at his thumb. Clarence touched her white sharps seeing them for the first time. She was radiant. He pushed his finger on one of her fangs, his blood dripped on her tongue. Gabriel sucked his finger. Shaking his head, yes, Clarence bit his bottom lip. Gabriel sucked it, feeding her growing hunger. He placed her head on his neck.

"Feed, you cannot hurt me, Sugar." Opening her mouth wide, Gabriel inhaled, biting Clarence arousing him. The smell of her wet pussy mixed with his blood swirling in the air drove him into sexual madness. His throbbing dick ached to meet her sweet sticky gripping walls. He unzipped his jeans holding his hard on straight while she rose slightly for Ms. Kitty to meet his acquaintance. His twelve-inch man glid into her throbbing, slippery, creamy pussy. Tethering her on his saddle he pumped hard and strong holding the bed with one hand and her waist with his strong arm. His moans intoxicated her. She fed... he fucked, moaning her name. "Gabriel, shit woman." The tightness vice gripped him. Clarence inhaled, trying not to bust too soon during his first spin.

Gabriel's pussy sucked him deeper, giving him no break with her relentless grip. He opened her ass cheeks, sinking the entire twelve inches balls deep. Her legs wrapped around him as he took the lead satisfying his new Queen. Baby vamps heard them vaguely downstairs; the boys laughed. "Pharaoh up in it" making jokes. Forty-five minutes, they were still at it. Gabriel held his arms down. "Can you move?"

"No Sugar," he lied seeing excitement rise in her eyes. "You're strong Sugar, how can I?" She held his wrists tight pumping her ass up and down, riding his hard dick. "Damn you're fucking hard." Clarence removed her head tie wrapping his fingers in her thick, kinky, long, tangled hair as it fell to her shoulders. It was beautiful, he loved every strand. He leaned in sucking her nipples. She was about on the edge of greatness.

He could tell by double pump bump of her pussy walls his job was almost done to her relentless sexual satisfaction. Rolling her over, she was his spellbound captive. Clarence tossed her sugar-sweet thighs on his broad shoulders. She was spread eagle across the bed, he sunk in there was nothing between his dick, and her fat, wet, pink, shaven, pussy. "Give me all that dick, take this fucking pussy." Clarence slipped slowly in and out doing pussy pushups inside of her grabbing the headboard.

"Damn!" she looked above her head, his arms straight, pushing off the foot board getting it all in her legs on one shoulder while candlelight danced off his chiseled body. "Sugar, I can't hold it." He gasped, sucking her left nipple before switching right. "Sugar?" "Yes, Daddy?" "Cum with me!"

Gabriel beat him to it, biting his neck trying to catch the fountain of free-flowing blood in her mouth. She tried not to make a mess, squirting cream cum on his hard chest. It trickled down his thigh, shooting on his hard abs and his face. Clarence and Gabriel locked eyes. "Get it, Sugar," shaking his head yes, he licked her cum from knees to inner thigh. "You ready for me?"

"Yes, Daddy!" She purred he pumped, shooting a steaming sweet nut consummating his vampire marriage with his new bride. "AHHH FUCK!" he roared, pouring his love inside her. Baby vampires jumped, grabbing weapons. "Sit, he's fine," Zion commanded. Clarence lay on top of Gabriel as she fed. She felt greedy so she stopped.

"Why did you stop Sugar?" He kissed her hand, rolling off breathing labored. "I ate enough." "No, you didn't. What you're not going to do is start lying. I've been vampire for many years. I understand what new vampires need." She nestled in his arms laying her head on his chest. They were a blood cum mess. "Your bed is messy." "This ain't my bed Sugar," he chuckled. "Oh, whose bed, is it?" "Yours woman this is Safinah's old bedroom." "You guys slept apart Clarence?" "She liked privacy. She took this room cause its sun drenched and faces the garden." "Where's your room, Clarence?"

"Our room Gabriel?" Clarence grabbed a towel wrapping himself. "Allow me to share a marital secret no one knew except Safinah, since we're wed, you can never show anyone it's a security breech Sugar." Clarence moved a chair off the wall, triple tapping it the wall slid open. "Come my love" holding out his hand. She followed him naked and bloody to the next room. It was the same size as hers, the same layout but more masculine. "A TV!" She exclaimed. "You like TV I take it?" "Yes, don't you Clarence?" "I like CMN world news and reports." She lay on the bed on her stomach, hair wild, flipping stations. Clarence entered the bathroom, ran the hot tub lighting candles before sprinkling rose petals on bubbles. Gabriel followed him into the bathroom.

"Man, I thought Safinah's bathroom was big. Why do you've two tubs Clarence?" "That's a pool babe." "WOW! What happened to the water?" "I don't use it, but you can if you wish. Safinah designed both bedrooms You can redesign them as you wish." "No, they're perfect. She great taste." "I added upgrades to the plumbing, as time went by, but the layout is her design, Sugar. Come." Clarence dropped the towel, Gabriel stared at his beautiful body. "Alexis, lights and play 90's R&B slow jams" "You like 90's music Clarence?"

"Yes." Gabriel approached the tub looking at herself in the mirror. She was covered in blood, feeling disgusted. She rubbed dry blood off her collar bone. "Sugar, come." He didn't want her seeing herself. She looked away entering the huge pool style tub.

"Alexis, jets." The pool roared. The warm water on her skin relaxed her mind Clarence massaging her was a bonus. "Your neck. I saw my bite marks Clarence." She looked down ashamed. "Turn around Gabriel look."

Gabriel turned reluctantly. His wounds healed. "What?" She rubbed his neck amazed. "I'm an old vampire our wounds heal instantly. The younger ones like you can heal in an hour.

For now, don't drink from anyone. You drink directly from my veins. It's for your protection. I'll instruct the house not to serve you outside blood Sugar." "Ok." "You must say when you're hungry Gabriel." "Yes, I will. Can I have hot tea?" "Yes Sugar, I'll have someone bring it after our bath." "Food and liquids are, ok Clarence?" "Yes, because Joan prepares the food, I trust Joan."

Clarence kissed her back right below her neck wrapping his arms around her full-figured body. He was thankful they met. Clarence was overjoyed he fell in love again, praying to whatever God would listen to his kind that no harm would come to her. Terror was going to rain on Cody and anyone who assisted her simply to make a statement of his wrath. *These new vampires have not seen the real me. They heard the stories, read the scrolls, heard the readings at certain ceremonies but never witnessed it firsthand but its time. His thoughts spiraled into darkness.*

They took off from the pool cuddling in bed. Clarence used a remote control to draw the blinds. The motor roared loud, and Gabriel covered her ears. "It'll get better Sugar," he reassured, kissing her head. "My senses are off today. My eyes get blurry then fine, my ears crescendo super loud then low, It's annoying. My body is betraying me, Clarence." "Sugar? The human side of you is dying, the vampire is taking full possession. The venom is working its way through you. It's been three days. It takes about two weeks for the process to complete. As a young vampire, I stayed in a cabin for a couple of weeks. I thought I was daft, until my maker who turned me explained things. When vampire laws were created, I implemented during a turn vampire are not to be left alone."

"'Clarence?" Gabriel looked; he was fast asleep. "I don't sleep much, yeah ok." she giggled.

She covered him and wrapped her hair because it was wet and wild. She tossed on his tee before leaving to get a drink. When she walked past the living room baby vampires were on laptops, playing pool and listening to music on a typical Saturday night. They looked young, no older than 25, but

Gabriel knew they were older. When she walked by, they stopped what they were doing, kneeling. "We're sorry Great One, we didn't know we were disturbing you." "You're not."

"Hello, I'm Khrista and this is Kevin in the blue, Rashawn with the pool cue, and Mikala on the corner laptop. They call us baby vamps because we were turned before we reached 35." "Pleasure meeting you all." Giving the room a wave Gabriel reached her hand out to shake but Khrista kissed it. "You don't need to do that Khrista." Gabriel was embarrassed. "Yes, I do." They smiled politely. "Can you please show me the kitchen Khrista?" "Sure." Khrista escorted her. Gabriel went into the fridge, pulling out apple juice.

"Oh, we can't drink human food Great One. It's for the guardians. You may get ill." "Please call me Gabriel."

Gabriel poured a glass drinking it. Khrista waited for her to retch. She grabbed the garbage pail waiting however she never did. Khrista looked like she saw a ghost.

"What?" Her new Queen inquired. "Nothing." Khrista didn't want trouble with the Pharaoh since they were always in his crosshairs for recklessness. Thus, the coven's name them baby vamps. "I loved apple juice as a child, did you Khrista?"

"Yes, my mom made sure I'd have it at lunch." "What a sweet memory Khrista. How old are you may I ask?" "You may ask anything Great One." "Gabriel please." "I'm twenty-three- and 40-years old February 27$^{th}$ Gabriel, I was 29 when married." "How is marriage, Khrista?"

"You have difficulties, however if in love, the downs fade. Trust him even when it's difficult. I'll show you around the house tomorrow if you wish. There's a solarium and greenhouses. Queen Safinah grew variations of plants, roses, flowers, and herbs. When she died, I took over." "How many years ago did she die?" Eighty Gabriel. It was overgrown and dying when we moved in. The Pharaoh forbade anyone to touch it after her passing.

Then one day unexpectedly he allowed me to restore the greenhouses to their original beauty. Joan tends them by day,

I keep them by night." "Do you work Khrista?" "Yes. I'm a real estate broker. I handle all real estate transactions for the covens domestic and international." "How do you show homes by day?" "Oh, I work with a human who helps we're partners." "Awesome. I'm going to bed Khrista. Thank you for the chat." "Anytime. Goodnight Gabriel." "Goodnight."

Gabriel left; Khrista was intoxicated by Clarence's sex scent wafting in the air. She tried hiding it, but he was sexy to her. He saw her as a married child, so she never revealed her feelings. Other vampires are polyamorous. She wondered why he had one bride. "She's different.

Gabriel slipped into bed thinking about her life, how she lacked friends and was abandoned by her mom because of the crack wars. She resided with her grandmother and aunt who raised her. After her grandmother died, she was diagnosed with stage two lymphoma.

>
> They Meet
> Java Jacks
> Queens New York....

Gabriel recalled the day she met Clarence. Nothing good happened for her until a handsome man entered her favorite coffee shop days after her third dismal diagnosis asking her on a date. He approached the barista purchasing madeleine cookies. Those were her favorite things to have with coffee but how'd he know? "Do you mind if we sit and chat?" "Sure," she responded, shocked he talked to her. There had to be a catch. Six feet three in height, fair skinned, with silky long hair. His smile was contagious and spread to her when she saw it. He sat and his cologne swirled about, locking her in a secret trance. *Man, he smells good. It'd been a long time since she smelled fine.* Hell, it'd been three years since her last relationship the last time she had sex.

"Clarence." He held out his hand for hers. "Gabriel, pleased to meet you." He took her hand, kissing it, never breaking eye contact. The barista dropped her bar towel.

Gabriel giggled delightfully. "I purchased a trinket." He handed her madeleine cookies. "Thank you. These are my favorite, although I don't need them" patting her stomach. "What's wrong Gabriel? I adore a curvy, sexy woman like you if you don't mind my saying." Gabriel blushed; Clarence heard her heartbeat speed.

"Thank you." "You're welcome gorgeous. May I leave with your phone number please?" "Sure." Gabriel handed him her phone. "Oh no darling here." handing her a Montblanc pen. *Is this gold?* She dared not ask aloud. She knew it was genuine. He wrote his number on a coffee shop napkin as did she. "Here you go, old school. What time is good for you Gabriel?" "Anytime Clarence, I don't sleep much. I'm up late most nights."

"Great." "Thank you for the cookies" "You're welcome honey." He left but his smell lingered long after he was gone. "That's a whole man," her barista friend teased from across the room.

"Yes, he is girl." Gabriel joked, schoolgirl giggling aloud with her only friend. Best decision she ever made. Gabriel kissed his head snuggling behind him. Staring at her engagement ring, she dozed off grateful she loved again and wasn't alone in this troubled world anymore even if he was a vampire.

# Chapter 9
# Birth of a Queen

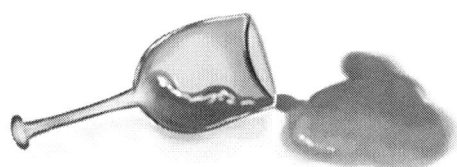

The year of our Lord 1859......

Clarence left Safinah overjoyed, the happiest he'd been since he turned. He would visit the plantation watching her laugh with Isabel and Avril. Clarence memorized her laugh the dimples under her eyes appeared when she laughed hardest. He watched her bathe in the barn, the water glistened off her naked full hips, her beautiful dark silky-smooth sunbaked skin, and breasts. He many chances to leave Georgia but didn't, not without his Safinah.

This was the first step he could take to track her because he consumed her blood knowing if she was in danger. Clarence purchased clothes of a white man, owned a horse and carriage passing as white he reinvented himself; he hated it. Listening to them chit chat about nothing made him sick.

He became wealthy overnight buying and selling properties triple its worth to white people. While gifting houses and land to free slave's property thought to be undesirable to whites because of location.

Clarence made sure it was not too deep in the woods to avoid slave catchers but close enough to the town where people knew they were there. He purchased thirty acres of land, built thirty cabins for families and freed slaves to live. He purchased an old plantation he made home. The former slaves knew what he was a runaway slave passing and most of all that he was vampire.

To the outside world he was a slave owner with a plantation and slaves that worked the land and they, his slaves. It would appear to be his sugar plantation, but it was not. Free slaves grew sugar cane and various other trade items such as tobacco, pig farming, cattle, stone carving, chickens, and engineering. The fields belonged to the free slaves as did all profits. Clarence was the front man sending his "slaves" to town to transact business like whites often did. Selling and trading on his behalf to get top dollar. The oppressors never knew they traded with the actual owner of the business. In turn the free slaves would give Clarence 50% of earnings to purchase more slaves and their families if up for auction. This money also went toward the purchase of the house and land they were on. Clarence often purchased children who were alone or a mother child combination. If a family managed to stay together, he purchased them as well. Pregnant women and young black headstrong men were also on his radar or anyone having the look of freedom or death he purchased often using his last. With all this he could not buy Safinah he could not show his face to his former owners. How he pondered scenarios of escape. My how he worried.

Twin Oaks Plantation........

The buzz around Twin Oaks was huge Missy Claras engagement party came as promised. Isabel and Avril were speaking to the slaves about the party before it began. Ms. Minnie made the mansion look special. A December engagement party would be good so she planned her only daughter's party sparing no money as her father Alexander Dupree would have had he been alive. The coachman and the slaves were gifted new dry goods from the sewing slaves on neighboring plantations.

Safinah recalled what Ms. Minnie said "No one adorns anything tattered or worn. I do not want our guests to see my slaves looking tattered." "Isabel how does I look?" Mighty fine Chile pass me dem plates. Mammy to busy ta be lookin. Missy Clara gimme her goes ta town dresses from three years time. Tara Missy Clara dressing housekeeper as she call her wears a dress from when Clara be 12 herself. She treat Tara like a doll baby. She ain't want no one mess wit dat gal. Ms. Minnie say 'leave Tara alone her daddy gifted Tara to Missy Clara when she was three years of age' Tara still listens to us slaves. She spy on her an' Ms. Minnie den tell us wat dey say.

Tara keep teachin me letters. Now I knowed some letters and words. I puts on a special coat. Ms. Minnie gets me ta ride da carriage in, I goes to fetch Mr. Thomas and Ms. Emma for da wedding party. He finnin ta ask her to marry him in from all dey peoples. I hates dat devil da way he look at me. I knowed he gonna take it from me. I knowed and was nuttin I does ta stop I shakes my head wit worry. It happen ta me once ise a youngin two a time. *You betts not cry Finah youse strong now.* I gets ta da inn evenin Ms. Emma. I opens da coach door takes her hand ta helps her in. Mr. Thomas say, "now Clover are you gonna hold my hand?" Ms. Emma say "Thomas stop fooling around with Clover. Do not mind my son he likes to make follies Clover, says it keeps me young." Devil pinch my thigh fo' he gots in da carriage.

We finally gots ta Twin Oaks. I help Ms. Emma out grabbin her hand cause she old. "Thank you, Clover." Yes'm. Devil jumps down an' looks into me wit dem evil green eyes, "thank you Clover." He kiss at me. I feels sick an' turn away. I put da nags up an' goes ta kitchen.

"Ya stay in chere washin pots an' china ya hear gal? Clover fill dem basins one with cold water an' one wit water I done boiled." "Ise hear Avril."

Clover tossed the drying rag on her shoulder. She heard people laughing, singing, and drinking spirits. She felt eyes on her. It was Clarence, he stood next to the porch. Clover sprinted to the side of the house hugging him tightly. "You look mighty pretty tanight Safinah." "I does?" "You does woman." Safinah kissed him, deep his tongue meeting hers. "I loves ya, lets me come wit cha now Clarence just as we is please" "Light come soon slave catcher be out Safinah seen em when I come." "When ya fetch me, Clarence?"

"Safinah, what be troublin ya?" "Nuttin troublin Ise fixin' ta be wit cha be all." He knew Safinah was hiding something. He heard her thoughts like the woman who turned him, but they were unclear and jumbled. Holding up her chin to eye level, "dat be true Safinah?" "Ise wanna be wit ya Clarence." "Ise comin baby, I swear it," holding her tight.

"Clover!" Startled she looked at the back door "Where dem plates be gal?" Avril asked "Ise comin Avril" "I gots ta go Clarence." When she turned back, he was gone. The party carried on into the morning. Clover washed dishes all night, Mr. Thomas and his mother stayed over. I hears Ms. Minnie make Missy Clara sleep in her bed, she knowed she fresh. Hours later we up early fixin' food, table set. I went to da barn ready the horses ta carry people's home. I strip my dry goods an' use soap Ms. Minnie gimme. I rinse wit water in a empty nag stall. I goes fo my rag ta dry, but it gone. Eyes open, Mr. Thomas hold it out. "Come get it gal."

Across county lines....

Clarence was asleep waking alarmed he felt Safinah's fear worrying her.

Twin Oaks Plantation...

Clover tried not to show fear by gently accepting her drying rag. "Thanks, ya, sir" looking down as taught. "Allow me." Thomas took the other end rubbing it down her back, making sure to rub it up the crack of her hide. Thomas turned her to face him, running his nasty fingers over her nipples gliding them down the middle of her breast to her pussy, shoving his fingers in pulling her close. Clover pushed him off. Thomas grabbed her throat, knocking her on the stall floor. He punched Clover in the face six times, blacking her eyes and busting her lips. Clover tried to remain conscious, scratching his face and neck as he forced himself on her, as he was turned on by the nigger savage in her being his first negro woman.

Clover screamed for help, but he shoved hay and big chunks of horse shit into her mouth, choking her. Safinah prayed, begging God to keep her from seed hold., *not his baby* as she faded away mentally and spiritually removing herself. She saw Clarence's old top hanging on the back stall wall she stared at it crying as she blacked out angry her dreams of being Clarence's wife were dashed dying with her.

Clarence knew Safinah was in danger, he could not leave, it was 8 am, the sun was high in the sky. He paced and screamed in the house. The former slaves now family asking him what was wrong. He paced breaking his glass items and furniture. Finally stopping, he lay down on his marble floor crying in angst, pounding it breaking the marble with striking blows Elijah entered the foyer, "Brother, what is wrong? Say." "Safinah…something is wrong I can feel her feelings she's in grave danger. I cannot go to her I curse the sun!" "Who Safinah, Clarence?" "A slave woman on the plantation where I was a slave, Elijah." "Where's it?" "Two towns over, half a day ride." "I betts head out." "NO! Elijah It's too dangerous." "Clarence, I cannot protect you by day" "Listen, me and my brother Caine is goin, write us a travel note to da plantation we will load up wit coffee, sugar, and tobacca, say it be a gift fo that party ya told tale bout.' Who da Massa dere?" "Alexander, Elijah." "Yas, Alex. You hear bout' da passing when ya return from Europe. Ya sendin fo ya sorrow or fo dat gal wedlock." Clarence wrote the note, they hitched the wagon to four horses to arrive faster. "We return wit news hold on brother." It was 8:30 am when they left.

Twin Oaks Plantation....

Thomas sprinted to the house with ripped tattered clothing dirty and skin scratched off bloody screaming for help. "I chased them off get a shot gun! Hurry." Slaves rushed to get Massa Alex's shot gun. Thomas sat out of breath, "Someone get Clover I think she's gone." He demanded. Ms. Minnie say, "Gone as in run away? Clover would never run away or try that's preposterous."

"I looked outback to fetch her as you requested, when I saw a white man beating and forcing himself upon her. Certainly, I attempted to grab the scoundrel, I forced horrible thought from my mind. What if the ruffian were to return for my Clara or Ms. Minnie. I defended the honor the women of this house as Alexander would have wanted, God rest his soul. I engaged in a scuffle with the charlatan, as I was getting the best of him, he fled!"

"AVRIL! AVRIL!! COME!" "Yes'm Ms. Minnie?" "Run to the stables assure Clover is well." Ms. Minnie paced back and forth she loved Clover as her child ill in her 20's nothing cured her illness. She heard from a slave catcher of a young picaninny who mastered healing herbs. He rented her to the young misses for three months. She cured Minnie then she conceived. Minnie owed Clover her life, and the life of her only child. When the slave catcher returned for his property, Alexander handed him $100.

"Sir, since you took a liking to my picaninny and you need her for healing abilities, while I need her for tracking abilities and preparation skills. I trained her since she was five years of age, be as it May I think your $100 is a mighty fine offer sir." Clara clutched Ms. Minnie's hand "It will be fine mother." Clara heard many times how she lived due to Clover's medicine skill. Avril and other slaves took Clover to the slave quarters across the cotton fields, her blood staining white unpicked cotton.

Avril and Mammy entered the big house crying. Ms. Minnie wailed in pain at the news. "Is she dead Avril?" "No

Ms. Minnie." "Thank God, I must see my Clover." "Ms. Minnie she in no way ta be seen we cleanin her up for ya. When we done, I fetch ya. I goes fetch da constable Ms. Minnie." "Yes Avril, I'll write a pass and a letter for the constable." "Yes'm." The slaves looked in the dirt there were no footprints disappearing into the woods, they knew Thomas raped Clover.

Clover lay in bed breathing shallowly. The medicine woman she trained, Ann was also a slave, they created herbal medicine for all situations including rape. She was not the first and would not be the last victim. Ann arrived on the plantation half dead, raped, beaten, used for pleasure sold for $10 at auction incredibly low for a young woman who could bear more slaves. Alex purchased Ann dropping her to Clover. "Help her please," he left bearing the shame of what his people did. Raped back and front, mouth too. Clover had a job in front of her to heal Ann.

Clover thought *'what iffin dey sells me or somethin happen ta me who fix me up when I fix everybody chere?'* She gifted Ann with her medical knowledge. Ann cried seeing Clover she swallowed her upset knowing she was all Clover had. "You ain't dyin on me gal" clearing her mouth. *Horse shit wat dis nigga done?* Ann wiped her eyes, patting her back to get the rest out. Clover coughed weak the rest hit the floor. One of the female slaves fetched six hot water pans staying to help Ann. "Fetch me da black bottle," Ann pointed out mixing it with boiled water to clean her mouth. "Red bottle." Ann poured the elixir in a tin cup blended with hot water.

"Get behind her, hold her head back her mouth open chile hurry! Pinch her nose." Ann poured the pennyroyal black cohosh tea down her throat. "Clover, you ain't making no baby wit dat bastard. Green bottle gal," she took the third pan of water poured in a green leafy liquid washing her snatch to clean infection same with her hide. "Yellow bottle, fourth bucket chile." Ann poured a black slick oil in the bucket, kept the green tincture close, she swabbed oily water over her whole body, using remaining green water to repeat. "Fifth pan of water white bottle gal."

Ann poured homemade witch hazel into the basin, "hold her arms down chile dis gonna sting." Ann opened her legs drenching her snatch pouring the rest over her body. The two women cried as Clover screamed. "Pick six leaves off dat vine hanging upside down in da corner chile." Ann rubbed the black oil on her eyes and lay large green leaves on her eyes wrapping her head securing the leaves to her eyes. "Come gal hold dis basin." Ann held Clover's head on her lap washing blood & dirt from her hair. She finger picked and twisted it flat to her head. "We almost done Clover." Ann took a clear bottle of oily salve rubbing it on her face and below to dead pain. They wiped dirt and blood from the floor. They placed a clean sheet on her keeping bugs off her.

"You done good Ann," Clover slurred. "Good thanks," Ann kneeled at her bedside, "who done dis Clover?" "Thomas Annie." "I knowed it!" "Shhhhh," Clover shook her head. "Iffin I say dey kill or sell me Ann." Ann cried her friend recalling what she went through when she arrived this wench saved her life. "Stop dem tears, Ise leavin dis plantation Clarence, he comin"

"Rest Clover…Clarence dead, she think she dyin she see da dead chile. You see Clarence, Clover?" "Yes Ann." "Don't go over Clover, you hears? You tell dat fine beau a' yours not chet." Clover slept. Elijah and Caine arrived at Twin Oaks by 1 pm. Five hours they made good time. They pulled behind the house where clarence said Clover was most of the time. Mammy came to the door. "Yas who you?" "Yes'm Ms. Minnie here?" "What you wantin' wit Ms. Minne?" "I gots gifts an' a message from a friend her late husband."

"Come." They stepped into the kitchen. Mammy led them to the drawing room where Ms. Minnie wrote a list of medications for Clover crying. "Ise rightly sorry Misses, dis fo you." They handed the note to Mammy she passed it to Ms. Minnie. "Mr. Clarence Hollings?" Mammy looked at Elijah shocked she been in this house forty odd year and never heard tell of a man.

*'Be my baby!'* Isabel thought. "Doesn't ring a bell however Alexander had business partners I knew nothing of." "Yes'm, will ya accept his gifts fo his sorry ma'am?" "Yes, Mammy will see to it." "Thank you fo your time ma'am." they reached the kitchen, "He ain't dead?" "Who Mammy?" "Clarence Hollings?"

Elijah looked around whispering "no, he ain't." Mammy sat from falling crying tears of joy at news Clarence lived but sorrow about her Clover. "He rapes Clover dis mornin." "Who dat be Mammy?"

"Mr. Thomas, Missy Clara intended." The brothers looked at each other. "She alive Mammy?" "Yes, in da slave shacks otha side da cotton field you pass on ya way out. Here takes dis ta da last shack left side." She gave me chicken foot soup. They gave her two burlaps with ground cane, "For ya Mammy." "Thanks, ya kindly Ise wait till Clover come we eats sweet cakes togetha."

"Yes'm." "You tell dat boy Mammy say we needs him, lijah." "Yes'm." Elijah and Cain stopped at the cabin knocking on the floor seein a sheet covering the door. "Yas?" Ann left the cabin. "Mammy say carry ya dis." "Thanks ya kindly." "Might we see Miss Clover please?" "One only not both ya." "I knows a little docterin' Mammy say what he done." Caine entered wincing at her condition. "She in a bad way, her wounds clean and salved." Ann sat bedside fanning flies. Clover opened her eyes, Caine whispered in her ear, "He comin."

Clover smiled squeezing his hand with all her strength, "Ise ready." Caine exited telling Elijah the condition of Clarence's wife. Enroute home the sun would be down by the time they reached. Elijah whispered to Caine, "there's gonna be hell." "Yas, indeed, brother."

They arrived Clarence was dressed, waiting, his horse saddled in front of the estate. "Least da sunup we gots time ta say wat dat devil done." Clarence paced anxiously, "Brothers what is it Caine. Is she dead?" "No, thank God. A man forced hisself on ya misses Clarence. Mammy sends us ta da slave quarters. She dere wit a medicine woman her name Ann, you knows her, Clarence?" "Yes" Clarence looked out the window as fading sunlight peaked through the glass.

"Where you goin Clarence?" "Ta get Safinah, Elijah." "Oh, dey say dis gal name Clover." "Slave name, her name is Safinah." "Clover can't walk or move. How ya gonna gets her chere Clarence?"

"Run Cain Get me two bed sheets cover em in dirt." The brothers sprinted doing as asked. He took the sheets, tying them around his body, so they would not drag the ground. "Please fix my bed chamber and have someone light candles. Please ask someone ta help when I returns Cain." "I ask my wife she say yas Clarence."

"Fetch clean water please for her bed chamber. Elijah opens the door." The sun sank into the horizon giving way to a full moon, Clarence bolted at super speed to Twin Oaks leaving his horse behind. What normally took a half day took fifteen minutes.

Elder Ainsworth (Ann) Freeman
Origins......

Clarence knocked on the cabin floor. Ann pushed the sheet aside fainting. Clarence stepped over her kneeling at the bed of his beloved as rage embodied within. Ann came to, "Is I dead? Vampire!" "How ya know what I be Annie?"

"I see ya kind in da bayou. Ya kind help free slaves in New Orleans, we calls y'all shadow kings, chain breakers, freer of men, walking Gods. I seent one fo I fell in da slaver trap. He negro. He touch me an' say Ise too beautiful ta be a white man's slave. Me not listenin cuts through swamps. He warns not to walk dat way Ise keep goin slavers trap me. Da glow of dem eyes, like dancing wildfires give ya away." Ann backed up.

"Have no fear Annie, no harm will come ta you." "Granny told us bedtime stories a ya people. I thought dey were tall tales." Ann rolled her tiny fingers over his cold skin amazed. "Cold flesh on such a warm night Clarence."

"I give ya her roots and tonics ta keep her sleep durin healin." Clarence unwrapped the sheets. "Help me Annie," he sat on Clover's bed. "Strap her on my back." Ann knew he was stealing a slave but didn't ask or care, she was happy for her. She feared him more than her Massa. She gently laid Clover's head on his right shoulder. Ann placed her arms around Clarence's torso. He took sheets from the floor, criss crossing them tethering Safinah to his back. Standing, she was light. "Here." Ann tucked four bottles of medicine under the sheets. "Give her three spoons of the black one three times a day till she sees her blood." Ann held her head down her way of telling him what that demon did to her friend.

"I'll return," Clarence punched Ann fracturing her cheek bone. He wished he could carry her too it was going to be hard covering his steps with Safinah on his back. Ann fell unconscious, Clarence ripped her dress open exposing her breasts and vagina as if the "scoundrel" returned. He scratched her inner thighs cutting his palm smearing blood on her. He tossed items about to create the look of struggle.

He took the gas from her kerosene lamp pouring it in a empty bottle. Clarence ran to the woods pouring kerosene on his tracks running in ten circles to throw off blood hounds. Once home, he sent Caine with three burlap bags of black pepper to sprinkle it around the plantation and on his footsteps in the woods in a one-mile circle.

Clarence approached his bedroom of this once abandoned plantation. He untied Safinah, laying her gingerly on their bed. She was asleep. *How happy she'll be to see my face when she wakes*, he thought. A faint knock interrupted his thought. "Enter please." Caine's wife stood bedside, "She's a doll." "Doll?"

"Beautiful. The mens at da saloon say it when a woman handsome. When I hear dat, I know he be a gentle one. She was a light skinned woman with long light brown hair like a white woman, however it shriveled in heat showing her negro blood. She loved her mother, the name she bestowed on her, Lily. A man offered her mother freedom in exchange for her daughter. They agreed she should take it. She left her 13-year-old girl with a saloon owner."

"Allow me ta wipe her off. I don't want fever rest on her. I took me nurse from dis Dr. at da saloon he talk I listen and yes'sir. I learns a lot fixin a gunshot hole. Man get shot fo cheatin' spades dey comes bustin' in my room callin' on doc fo help he goes runnin' I follows. He share how ta pull a buck shot an' fix da hole. No need worry wit me Clarence." She put a cold rag on her head. "Dem her elixirs?" "Yes'm." "You ain't gotta ma'am me. Ise Lily." "I recalls." Clarence sat in the corner dirty. He didn't want Safinah to wake up afraid. He approached her bedside dropping to his knees. Lily stood back, watching.

"Love, Ise here. Ise sorry I made you wait, for fear of our slavers. Tonight, Ann say where she from I'm considered a God. You must wake so we can go to New Orleans, the Bayou so we can learn about me. I loves ya, Safinah, I need ya. Will you be my wife?" He kissed her lips; he tasted dry blood making him angry.

"Clarence? Go clean yaself no needin' she wakes seein ya dirty. Ya cannot hole her dirty da wounds get ill." He rose, "Youse right Lily I'll return." Thinking he should hurry. He knew what would happen to Thomas. He wants to be a savage? I'll introduce him to one.

Caine cooked strong coffee and tea in case Safinah woke. Caine and Lily sat bedside while Clarence changed his dry goods. Clarence needed to go back for Ann. She knew of his kind and Safinah needed her medicine woman and friend. He would return but not civil.

# Chapter 10
# The Engagement Party

Present Day......

Gabriel woke to a dark bedroom covered in blankets, but Clarence was gone. "Clarence?" She called he didn't come; she grabbed her cell. As the phone rang, he entered. Gabriel raised her arms he rushed to her as if she were gone forever. "Hey, what's the matter Sugar?" He approached the hall, ushering in a bouquet of mixed roses. "Joan cut these this morning." "What time is it?" She looked down at her cell. "It's Friday 7 p.m. Sugar" "I've been asleep since Tuesday?"

"Yes love, three days we waited to see if your turn is complete." "Zion took blood. I gave him permission because you were running a high fever but after I gave you a cool bath it broke." Examining her arm and clothes she noticed she was in her robe with her hair untied again. She looked at her ring, a present with a matching diamond tennis bracelet.

"You did this?" "Yes, do you like it, Sugar?" I love it. It matches the ring beautifully Clarence." "I didn't buy the ring. The least I could do is buy a mate." "Thank you, honey. I need the bathroom." He looked confused. "We don't use the bathroom." She rushed to the toilet, peed, and did a bowel movement.

"What is it, Sugar?" "What Clarence hehe?" "Number one or two?" Gabriel thought it was cute. *Is he for real?* "Yes, I'm for real" "Don't Clarence, it's creepy I'm jumping in the shower."

"Baby?" "Yes? I want hot tea please. "Hot tea? Mouthing to himself. "Yes, hot tea." "You heard Sugar?" "Yes." Zion can you provide hot tea please? *Humm.... Ok,* Zion answered telepathically.

When Gabriel finished her shower, Zion turned his back. "Good morning, Great One" "Stop that" He turned around. "I hear you used the bathroom?" "Ok next time, I'll leave a few tubes in the bathroom for samples please." "No problem, Zion."

Zion handed her tea. "Ummm thank you." She sat on the bed turning on tv. "Say Zion, has Isaiah awakened?" "Last night, he's elated with his new looks Gabriel." "I'm glad he's alright."

Zion checked her vitals with his eyes looking at her pupils and counting her pulse while looking at the clock on the mantel, listening to her breathing. "Nothing, perfectly healthy. She's fine" he spoke with Clarence softly. "Gabriel, guess what? "I must ask you to marry me again" "Why?" "Because it must be in front of the covens. We're an old race of vampire; we follow old fashioned ideals."

"Are you going to Inform her Clarence?" Zion inquired. "Say what Clarence?" "Must offer you a dowry." "A dowry is real old school daddy." "Yes, it is Sugar." Gabriel threw back her head giggling. "What're you going to offer? Oh, wait how does this work Clarence?" "We plan an engagement party the covens come. You'll meet our vampire family."

"There's a lot with it I don't want to spoil it for you." "Get to the dowry" Gabriel grinned. "I'd offer it to your living relatives however I must offer it to you since they've crossed home. You need someone to accept it on your behalf." She looked at Zion.

"No, I'm not in this what if you don't like what I accept Gabriel?" "I'll give you the eye like this" opening her eyes real wide they belly laughed.

"However, if I close them like this" slanting her eyes. That's a yes Zion." "Zion can request anything Sugar. A dowry can be paid in jewels, land, cattle, or any combination." Gabriel looked around. "What if I want this house, Clarence?" "I'd give it if it meant I'm able to marry you, but remember Zion must ask, not you." "How do I know you can afford it Clarence?" Grinning like a cat that swallowed a canary. Clarence bellowed a hefty laugh. "I mean this could all be on credit baby." "Zion will discuss my assets. Zion, grant her access to all assets allow her to choose what she desires. I'll present the dowry at the party. Will you accept Gabriel?" "I'm unsure, Clarence!" she teased, grinning before kissing his nose. "We cannot marry without a dowry; it secures the bride in her marriage the Elder vampires won't allow it trust me, Sugar." "When's the party?" "Next Saturday."

"Mr. Hollings you work fast!" "Mr. Hollings." Clarence tipped his imaginary hat. "Baby, have you found Cody?" "No love, she's what we call blocking. Some vampires are good at it. It is rare but because of her Native American heritage she's good at it." Clarence remembered the night in 1968 she taught him to block another vampire from sensing his presence.

Nineteen Sixty-Eight......

Cody sat legs crossed, hands on her knees. "Clear and free your mind. Remove all thoughts" s as the sage encompassed them. "Can you sense me here with you Clarence?" "No Cody."

"I hear your thoughts." Cody smiled with her eyes closed. "Clarence when you open your eyes don't be afraid." When Clarence opened his eyes, he levitated above the bed touching the ceiling. "You're levitating Clarence." "I see Cody." They heard a woman in the hallway scream when they looked, he fell. "Damn!" They were amazed.

Present Day Hollings Estate.......

Clarence recalled as if it were yesterday. Cody blocked him sporadically throughout the day. She was good, but not that good. Cody would slip up and Clarence would catch her. "I need a dress, Clarence."

"Yes, and a new hairdo." handing her his black card. "Wow!" "Worried if I can afford you Gabriel? I'll leave you with Zion." Clarence left. "I'll return shortly Gabriel." Zion returned with six leather ledgers; two he placed on the bed next to her. "Open it, Gabriel." She opened the first book. It contained fifty pages of oil paintings

"This is Andy Warhol, Basquiat, Henri Matisse, Klimt, the kiss. I love this one, Keith Haring." Gabriel turned the pages amazed. She looked at Zion, "choose Great One." "As in a part of the dowry?" "Yes." She opened the next book. "Is this BB Kings, Lucille? Is this Michael's silver glove? Ray Charles' glasses, and his signed first album? James Browns' Cape! Aretha Franklin's signed piano? What's this Zion?" showing him two pages. "Mya's scrap notebook and Langston Hughes' first book draft and rejection letter"

"No way! Madam CJ Walker's prototype hot comb?" She stared at the photos in disbelief. "Yes. Look closely, it has her initials in gold. She traded it to Safinah for a silver candelabra Gabriel" "Wow, the executive manor blueprints."

"You call it the white house; Benjamin Banneker gave them to Clarence as a gift for purchasing his freedom, Gabriel." "Where did he get the rest, auctions?" "No, they were either gifts or he purchased them directly when they fell on hard times." "Jesus! He met these people and helped them, Zion?" "Yes." "Jim Hendrix's head scarf!" "His guitar is there as well, Gabriel."

"What's in this book?" Zion handed her the one on his lap. "Real estate deeds. Paris, Rome, Africa, Egypt, and Spain." "Clarence owns islands?" "Yes, ma'am and this is the financial ledger." "I don't want to see. Thank you, Zion." "What shall we request, Gabriel?"

"Nothing." "Nothing? Great One, we must, it is vampire law. Allow me," handing her the last book of assets. "Tobacco fields, sugar fields in Cuba, cotton fields…Di…diamond mines?" "Four of them in Africa, Great One." "Oil wells in Texas?" "Apple stock, Oogle, Delta. Where's this Zion?" "Gullah Island. It's quaint."

When Gabriel looked at it, she imagined her and Clarence owning it as a getaway spot. Right on the banks of the Gullah islands, eh? She became enamored by this one Zion. "I'll choose for you Great One, yes?" "Yes, but nothing big. I don't want him thinking I want him for what he has, Zion. I love Clarence, not what he owns."

"It's settled then Gabriel." Zion collected the books from her. "Did you look at the black card, Great One?" Gabriel grinned seeing her name. Zion left her to shop. Clarence entered the bedroom, "What're you doing Sugar?" "Dress shopping online."

"We have our own seamstress and tailor, honey. Elizabeth Keckley's great granddaughter is coming tomorrow. She's bringing her grandmother's style book, and Ann Lowe's great grandson will come Sunday to tailor my tux." "Who Clarence?" "Oogle it."

Gabriel oogled the people he mentioned, did you meet them?" "Through Safinah yes. They'd buy fabrics from her. We'd choose bulks during our travels have them sent home." "They know we're vampires, Clarence?" "Yes Sugar, the Black Elite knows of our existence. Let's go for a stroll." She threw on jeans, a pink tee, and white flip flops. "I'm hungry honey." "Come Sugar," Gabriel moved to sit on Clarence's lap. Immediately bit his neck. He held her closer, trying to hide his excitement.

When he first saw her, she always sat quietly reading or laughed with her friend at the coffee bar. There were days he heard Gabriel crying outside her bedroom window. He knew about her cancer hearing her make appointments with specialists.

He didn't dare embarrass her by speaking with her about it. Humans took illness as a private affair, so he waited patiently for her to reveal her past in her time. They left the house for the garden. As they strolled, Gabriel whispered, "Shh." Clarence whispered hearing Isaiah speaking. He was on the phone with Cody, on the other side of the mansion. "Hi honey bear. How are you?"

"I'm vampire because you almost killed me, Cody." "Is that what they explained? Clarence wasn't going to turn you, Zay. You're Nathan's blood, yes? I know how much you wanted to be a vampire. I knew they would save your life, and it worked." "Zion turned me, Cody." "How is his new Queen working out? So, what Zay, Zion is still an old vampire count your blessings?"

"I woke up a day ago. I'm unsure Cody." "Is she in the house with you?" "I'm not sure I want to see you, Cody." "How come, Zay?" "Don't you miss me, Cody?" "Yes." "Halloween, I want to spend it with you." "I'll call next week with a meeting place Isaiah, yes?" "Yes." "Sweet baby, I love you. Good night, my smart baby." "Good night, old Indian." When they finished their stroll on the property, Clarence sent Gabriel upstairs. "I'll be up shortly, Sugar. Do you want tea? "Yes please." Clarence watched Gabriel Walk upstairs.

"Zion, bring Isaiah here please." He spoke in a low tone. Zion went to Isaiah's room and tapped on the door. "Pharaoh wants to see you." Isaiah was nervous, it was his first time greeting him as vampire. The baby vampires embraced him as one of their own. They knew he wanted to be vampire, however they were aware of Papa Nathan's treaty agreement, so no one wanted to face the vampire Elders for turning him. Isaiah entered the large study. Clarence moved to hug him, and Isaiah knelt as he'd been taught by the baby vamps. No direct eye contact they warned, keep your head low respectfully unless he's speaking. Isaiah tried to remember the rules as Clarence embraced him.

Clarence looked into his eyes and raised his lip checking for fangs. "Not yet, Great One," Isaiah responded, nervously. "No worries soon they'll come. Have you played the piano since turning, Isaiah?" "No Pharaoh." "Try the piece you're having trouble with. I have something for you, Isaiah." "Beethoven's fifth?" "Careful. It's old, original ink. He left it on my piano and never collected it. Play for me Isaiah." Clarence and Zion listened as he played, they were impressed enjoying his flawless playing. When done, he stared at his hands.

"It's the vampire in you." Clarence shared. "Our hearing and dexterity are impeccable. This is why you must never compete in schools against humans for scholarships. I'll pay for your education." "Yes, Pharaoh." "Has Zion explained what took place the night you were turned, the savagery displayed by Cody?"

"Yes, Great One." "She attacked Gabriel out of jealousy, not love. She broke the treaty the coven made with Papa Nathan by harming you. Cody refused orders to return and be judged by our Elders for her treachery. I say this informing you that Cody is a vampire fugitive and any vampire consorting with her is a co-conspirator against the crown who will stand at her side during trial before vampire Elders."

Clarence approached Isaiah, "Has Cody contacted you, Isaiah?" "No, Pharaoh. May I say hello to Gabriel, Great One?" "Yes." "Thank you." Isaiah exited in a hurry. Clarence spoke with Zion telepathically. *Isaiah spoke with her tonight on the phone. Pull out the phone record when Papa Nathan arrives for the party and show him Zion. As you wish, Great One.*

Zion warned Isaiah not to side with Cody. He was too young to stand vampire trial. He witnessed several over the years. Punishments were severe sometimes, death by sunrise was the worst. Cody was entitled to representation, but no vampire attorney wanted to represent her. If so, they'd advise her to surrender.

Zion emailed one hundred attorneys versed in vampire law on Cody's behalf. Clarence had an attorney whom he paid handsomely for sole representation. He called when he heard of his engagement to ask if he needed to draw up a vampire prenuptial agreement. When Clarence declined, he decided to bring a draft to the party. After all, Safinah married Clarence for love. What did he know about this Gabriel woman? He didn't want Clarence to be cross with him, but he didn't care, it was his job to protect his maker and king. Clarence entered the kitchen, Joan sat at the kitchen table. "Why're you awake Joanie?" "Waiting for you to explain if turning my grandson has merit."

Clarence looked Joan in her eyes slipping her hand between his, "No one values human life more than I. This is why drinking from humans without their permission without written consent isn't allowed. I'd never violate Papa Nathan's agreement with the covens nor with me."

"Thank you for saving Isaiah's life Clarence." "It wasn't me, Zion saved him. But we have a problem, Joan." "What?" She grabbed the tea bags and sugar. "Zay lied tonight." "He what Clarence?!" "Shhh…I don't want him to know I heard him speaking with her. I need him to lead me to Cody." "That's treason against the crown. He can be killed." "I promise I won't. He's a young vampire petulant. That's why the baby vampires stay here for five years after to be supervised no worries, Joanie." He hugged Joan and in exchange she handed him Gabriel's hot cup of tea. "I was to make this Joan." Do you know where we keep the tea and sugar Clarence? There" pointing out the duo locations. "Thank you." Clarence kissed her hand.

"The dressmakers and tailor are coming tomorrow, Joan." "Yay! May I sit with Gabriel? I love those old books especially the dresses her grandma made for Jackie Kennedy," Joan clapped. "It's time for you and Zion to tie the knot, Joan."

"Please Clarence, that young man doesn't want me. He needs a young woman." "Joan, Zion isn't that old." He pushed the restaurant style kitchen door, leaving her in thought.

*Zion's sixty?* She thought. "Seventy-five!" Clarence called back. "Stop!" She shouted aloud giggling. When Clarence arrived with her tea, Isaiah and Gabriel were laughing. "Isaiah says his fangs aren't in yet. I have mine but I'm unsure how to control them." Gabriel closed her eyes; her legs were crossed yoga style. She thought of Clarence's hands on her nipples making them hard. Thinking of it made her smile, her fangs exposed themselves. "Look Clarence!" Isaiah pointed. "I see 'em pretty and white Sugar" Isaiah bid them goodnight leaving the room.

Clarence lay on the bed. "How many wives can you have?" "What makes you ask Sugar?" "You're a King all Kings have concubines in history." "Elders can have as many wives as they can afford." Do you want another wife, Clarence?" "No Sugar, I'm a one-woman man."

"Were you seeing anyone after Safinah died?" "Yes Love." "Who?" Clarence knew this conversation was coming. He didn't think it would come so soon. "Cody. I cared for her, but I was never in love with her." He took a deep breath continuing. "One day, I took a walk. I heard a woman crying so I looked in the window. That's when I saw this thick, beautiful black Queen with a head full of thick dark cotton billows. She was the prettiest woman I laid eyes on since Safinah. Her skin was like smooth yards of flawless melanin. I became enchanted by her. She received a call from her Dr., who explained she'd begin chemo on Monday."

Gabriel held his hand tighter as her tears fell on his lap. Clarence continued, "I watched over her closed her windows when she forgot warding off pneumonia. I placed packages on her porch so no one would steal them off the sidewalk, along with her newspapers. I watered her shrubs because she was ill. I removed her garbage and rolled the pails back in. I paid the mail carrier to hold her mail while she was in the hospital and sent groceries three times per week. She thought a hospital stipend paid her house tax for the year." "The flowers at the hospital Clarence?" "Yes, Sugar that was me as well." His southern drawl was sexy to her.

"When you saw me in the coffee shop, it wasn't by happenstance Clarence?" "I knew you were going to arrive, Sugar." "Thank you." Clarence rubbed her hand, and, in that moment, his love grew as did hers. Gabriel realized he didn't have to give her anything else, she found a man who genuinely loved and wanted her. He could have any woman, many wives but he chose her. "The day I saw you is the day I stopped sleeping with Cody because I met my wife."

Gabriel reached down grabbing his hardon. She excitedly served herself its thickness. The entire dick tapped the back of her throat. She didn't want sex, she wanted to pleasure him. Her warm tongue circled the tip as she cupped his balls in her soft palm, sliding them past her wet lips, licking and gliding them around her wet under tongue. Gabriel tip-glid his hard dick applying cream cum lip gloss with the tip. Clarence trembled, gifting her with short bursts of sweet pre-cum, begging her to sample suck his sticky treat.

"Is this for me?" Gabriel's sexy look upward from her knees burned his eyes. Hers brimmed with lust swabbing his precum clean. Parting his thighs, Gabriel licked his balls shaft to tip. "You love me daddy?" "Yes Sugar," his fangs were exposed, his breathing labored.

"Cum in my mouth. I wanna taste your load. Please cum, let me taste your sweet nut." Clarence lost his soul, grabbing the bed, ripping the mattress tangling with a certified soul-snatcher. "Damn!" He shook uncontrollably as hot sweetness filled her mouth, filling her cheeks, Gabriel looked in his eyes and swallowed. She held out her tongue showing him she drank her daily dose of protein. Gabriel poured him a glass of ice water and he gulped it down. "Sugar, where'd you learn?" "Grandma Clarence." "Thank you, Grandma haha" "Gabriel what is a BBW?" "A big, beautiful woman, Clarence." "You mean plump? "Yes, hehe thick... has weight." "What dress size are you?" "18 or 20."

"Safinah was a 20, sometimes a 22. It didn't matter. The bigger she got, the more I wanted her. You're not changing, you are forever size 20. I looked this way when I turned. I was a coachman, the overseer had me doing field work. I used to lift hay, that's how I became muscular. Are you ready for our engagement party?" "Yes."

"The covens will show up. It's gonna be a long night. Vampires stay, not to catch light. We get lots of gifts and we must open every single one Sugar. "Jesus." She chuckled. "Can I decline gifts?" "You can however, it's an offense pretend you like it. I'll discard it later." "Mean." "Haha hungry, Sugar?" "No." Clarence got a bottle of blood from his bedroom fridge. "Why can't I drink a bottle of blood?" "Sugar, I don't want you drinking unknown blood. Dead blood will kill you within an hour. "We have vegan covens where they drink synthetic blood. Zion helped create it." "Can't wait to see you in your tux Clarence."

"Joan is going to help you dress. I'll see you the day of the party." "Why?" "Vampire law gives you a chance to ponder if you want to marry me. An Elder will ask if you want to be my wife record your answer in scrolls." "Is there a female Elder?"

"Yes Sugar, her name is Ann."

# Chapter 11

# Troubled Waters

Ann was awakened by the overseer. He stood over her shouting. "Who did this?! He after Ms. Minne and Missy Clara?" Ann was on the floor, her cheek killing her. She grabbed at her skirt covering her exposed vagina.

"Look like he took goodies." The overseer laughed, "RETURN TO WORK NO HARM HERE!" demanding onlooking slaves. It was clear Ann was beaten, raped, and assaulted. "Get yourself together Ann. Cotton need pickin youse my chief picker. Constable on his way. He gonna want to speak with you 'bout the man dat took Clover." "Clover gone?" "Yes, he took her come to finish the job I'm guessin'." Ann was jubilant pretending to cry at the news inside. She secretly celebrated her freedom.

"Ms. Minnie want to see you up at the big house." Ann pulled herself together. She didn't take any tonics because she knew she was not raped. She entered the back door, where Avril comforted a crying Mammy. She entered to the bright dining room, "Yes ma'am." "Ann, lord Jesus, I prayed you were fine." "Yas Ms. Minnie Ise fine." "What happened Ann?"

"A man enter grab me take my womanhood punch me hard. I woke dis mornin. He says he want Clover, an' he be returning fo da woman folk in da big house. I tells him ain't no women folk when he punches me here," pointing to her cheek. "Last I members, Ms. Minnie, Ise scared on count he come hurt ya an' Missy Clara; Ise glad it be me." Ann fake cried instantly; a trick taught to her by her aunt in the bayou.

'Men succumb to women tears use it as part of ya lying truth she'd say.' Mr. Thomas knew Ann lied but how could he out the lie without betraying his truth? "What did the scoundrel look like?" Thomas asked.

"He a white man, stocky, strong he tosses me to da dirt fast, blue eyes and hair sun color." The constable entered gave his greetings hearing her story. "Thank God he got to a nigger, not any of you fine women Ms. Millie. I cannot arrest him on count of taking advantage of a slave, however he stole a slave which is same as stealing a horse: a punishable crime. Ma'am because he has stolen your property. Do you have the bill of sale on the slave?"

"Yes Constable. Avril, get the livestock book, the green one." "Yes'm." Ms. Minnie found clovers bill of sale passing it to the constable. "You are sure this gal ain't run off Ms. Minnie?" "No constable she'd never flee, she has been with me since she was a child. Please find her. I have illnesses only she can cure and keep at bay. "Yes, ma'am. I'll do my best at returning your property."

Inside Ann laughed loudly. She controlled herself from smiling. Her mentor, friend, and sister was free. She felt jubilant as if she were free, not upset, or hateful like some slaves when one gets free. She crossed into the kitchen when she was dismissed. Mamm wrung her apron worried, but Ann could not let her worry. She bent down hugging Mammy, "Clarence took her." Mammy's eyes filled with tears, "What cha say, chile?" Ann whispered, "Clarence he come take her. He hit me so they ain't whip me thinks Ise a part."

Mammy fell on her knees, "Thank God." "Shhhh. Mammy rise, please." "How he look Annie?" "He look good, like he passin fo' white." "Long as he live be all I care bout Annie."

"He be back. I say what dat demon done he looks me straight in da eye an' say I be back anger boilin inside Mammy." She hugged Mammy, satisfied something bad was going to happen to Thomas.

The Hollings Plantation....

"Ann! Annie!" Safinah woke three days later stiff and thirsty. "Ann?!" Her eyes swollen shut everything around her blurred. *Is I lost sight? my head...he hit ya head you alright gal ya lives* she thought. "Hello, who dere?" "Name be Lily." "Lily like da flower?" "Yes'm." "Say Lily, is I at Twin Oaks plantation?" "No ma'am you isn't." "Where I be?" "No need for ya ta be fraid." "I ain't see." "Ya eyes swoll shut. I gots ta tonics. Ya friend Ann gives us em" "Ann here?" "No ma'am not yet she ain't." "Is I'm with Mr. Thomas?" Clover trembled" "No ma'am you ain't." "Where I be, chile?"

"Here." Lily put a glass of water in her hand, "water from glass not a jar or tin cup?" Safinah was afraid. She smelled and drank the water it was to clean for a slave to drink. Lily took the glass resting it next to her tonics. Safinah saw a peek of the colored bottles and recognized them as her own work. The door opened, and footsteps walked briskly toward her. The click of boot heels on the wood bedroom floor alarmed her. *'A white man no slave gots heel boots.'* The person kneeled in front her and took her hands to his face. Hesitant afraid and trembling in for her life she touched his face, his eyes nose and hair instantly crying. Safinah rested her nose to the crown of his head.

"Thank you, God. Thank you, Lord, I prays you hears me thank ya." Safinah leaned her face to his kissing his lips, as tears of joy fell over and over.

"I knowed ya come I knowed it I knowed it." Safinah inhaled the exhaled relived she was free of her slavers. "Ise sorry love; can ya find it in ya heart ta forgive me, please Safinah." Clarence was on his knees begging her. "Please," His tears wet her lap. Lily cried seeing the love they shared. This powerful reinvented white secretly a runaway slave on his knees begging forgiveness from his love, a free slave.

"Forgive what Clarence?" He hugged her gingerly. "You hungry my love?" "I takes broth iffin ya has it." "Yes, I has it love" "I gots ta apply her tonics, Clarence." Lily rested her hand on his shoulder.

"Please stay, Clarence!" "I bees in a chair not five steps from ya love." She held on to him as he walked across the room. Lily poured the tea for a pregnancy not to hold. Safinah smelled it knowing what it was.

"How many days ya gimme dis?" "Three misses." "I take it?" "Yes'm. I hold your nose close, ya gimme a fit, but ya takes it down good." "Ann tell Clarence make sho ya drinks dis teacup full. She say twice a day fo five days, like I say dis here be ya third day. It pass sundown you gots one mo time fo bed."

"Youse in good hands honey." Safinah turned her head to the sound of Clarence's voice. Safinah drank her tea and Elijah brought a large bowl of chicken broth up. "Imma rest this here ma'am, on da bedside table." "Thanks, ya kindly," "Elijah." introduced himself. "Pleasure ta meet ya." Safinah pushed out her hand Elijah shook it softly. Safinah touched her hair.

"Lily, can ya please fetch me a cotton rag? I can ties down dis bird's nest." Lily looked at Clarence for permission to leave, he shook his head yes. "Yes'm. and Lily?" "Yes'm?" "Name be Safinah." "Safinah. what a pretty name."

"Thanks, ya kindly." She felt good inside hearing her say the name her Mammy blessed her aloud for the first time in nineteen years, since she was sold away from her. Clarence rushed over, lying next to her. She lay on his chest crying uncontrollably. Clarence became angry.

"Shhh What happened Safinah?" Safinah explained her interactions with Thomas up to her assault. "When I see ya at da party, I wanna say somethin but Ise fraid dey makes ya slave. Ise fraid dey do worse fo ya runnin, I ain't want dat. I keep quiet hopes he go away but he fix on me."

She trembled in the safety of his embrace. Clarence held her close, he wanted to explain about himself, but this was not about him, it was about her. "Honey? Ise get em make em pay fo layin one finger on ya." "No, baby no, no, no." Safinah sat up frantically. "Yas, Safinah no need discussin furtha now." "Slavers gonna snatch ya Clarence. We ain't togetha long dey takes ya back please stays wit me."

"Honey it be right fine." Patting her back. He blotted her face with his sleeve not to wipe off the salves resting her back in the bed. He sent Elijah with a list to buy medications sold to white people. He kissed her head until she slept. Covering her up he turned the lamp down. He went to chop wood. Caine walked up smoking a cigar. "We gots us enough wood ta burn fo three winters Clarence"

"Sell em in town by tree kind oak fetch mo coin. Dese fallen trees I finds runnin evenin' time drags em fo trade or coin. Uncut in da back barn fo building Caine" "What's fueling yo anger boss?" "I ain't no boss dis ain't no slave plantation Caine we all same chere. All youse work fo yaself, way it pose ta be y'all rents land till it pay itself off Caine." "You our family Clarence. Ya gives us a chance ta hold our head high, give us freedom papers, get our women's an' picaninnies back an' a place fo em ta growed up away from ds evil. Youse full a rage Clarence, rage dangerous lessin you drain it" "Ise finnin ta kill em, he wanna be a savage? He gonna meet a damn savage. Caine get a burlap bag, no marks." "Yes'sir!" Caine rushed to get the bag and Elijah.

Present Day New York Mansion......

Joan helped Gabriel into her waist trainer. "Girl, I don't understand why you're wearing this thing. Your waist ain't going to train." "Joan it's good for tonight to get in this dress. I want Clarence to see my curves."

"Man done seen you all of you before you seen him, Gabriel." "You knew of me Joan?" "Yes, I did. We'd chat and he'd share how pretty and smart you are, and how you're a teacher and love kids and that you've a beautiful flower garden at your house." "I can imagine what weeds are growing there now Joan." "None. Clarence has a landscaper go to the yard three times a week. Don't Inform him I told it's supposed to be a surprise."

"I'll act surprised when I see." "Look at you Gabriel. Beautiful!" "This hair ain't gonna hold long, Joan thank you sis" "Oh, girl it'll last for a day. Your hair is long. Your makeup and eyelashes make you look like a Hollywood rising star, Gabriel." "Like Dorothy Dandridge or Billy Holiday?" "Gurlllll! Clarence went on a few dates with her."

"Who Joan? Billy! Wow!" "What happened?" "Billy traveled a lot. You know, hard to connect." "How was she as a person?" "A sweetheart, this was before the drugs, you know?" "This gown looks gorgeous, Joan." A knock interrupted them. "Enter." Security was outside her door, no one was allowed on the floor except Elders. Ann entered and Joan rushed to her grandma, Ann. She gave Joan a hug. "Look at my little girl all grown up." Ann loved Joan as she was Papa Nathan's first wife's twin. God sent her back when Joan was born. "Gabriel, this is Ann. I call her grandma. She's the female Elder over coven three."

"Hello, look at you! The rumors are true, you are beautiful. Is it true you can walk in the light, Gabriel?" "Yes, it is Ann." "What I wouldn't give to sit in the sun once more. Do you know I have special windows in the house? Vampires love them. Sun rays cannot penetrate the glass. You can sit in a stream of light, and it'll not burn Gabriel." "Yes, I have seen the glass company on TV."

"Gabriel a young inventor asked that I invest in it about thirty years ago. Best thing I ever did, I tell you. I'm trying to convince Clarence to get them, he says the glass is a tease." As they sat in Safinah's old bedroom on her vintage settee, Joan smoothed out Gabriel's gown before sitting. "I know this must be a lot for you Gabriel." "Are you from New Orleans, Ann?" "Yes, how'd you know?" "I hear it in your accent. I love New Orleans."

"When you arrive in the city, you must stay with me, Gabriel I live in the Quarter." "Thank you for the invitation, Elder." "You're welcome, Great One." "How do you feel about Clarence?" "He's everything… my best friend. I'm enamored by him. He's wonderful! I'd die before hurting him or seeing someone hurt him." "I know you do. Get one of the scroll writers please, Joan." Joan picked up the walkie, "Please, send up a scroll writer per Elder Ann."

There was a tap on the door a young woman with a notebook entered, falling to her knees. "Great One, it is a pleasure meeting you." "Thank you, please rise." Ann instructed her to sit and bear witness." Ann turned to Gabriel. "This is a formality, Gabriel. Do you understand you're accepting a marriage proposal from our Vampire King?" "Yes, Ann. I do."

"Do you want to marry him, Gabriel? If not, you can say no." "Yes, I do." "Yes, what Gabriel? You must say the words." "Yes, I love Clarence, I want to be his wife Ann, willingly." "Has it been explained that under vampire law, he can have as many wives and concubines as he can afford?" "Yes, it has." "Knowing this Gabriel, do you wish to move forward with your marriage?" "Yes, I do Ann." "Do you need a minute to think it over?" "No, thank you." Ann nodded at the scroll writer, "You may go." "Yes, Elder Ann." "Joan, can you allow us to speak alone please?" "Sure, Grandma I'll be outside."

Ann looked at Gabriel sensing she loved Clarence. "You're getting a good vampire, Gabriel. Clarence is a brother to me. If he has chosen you as his bride, you must be special." Ann opened her purse pulling an item from it.

Gabriel opened the box, a diamond and sapphire necklace glistened in the light. The sapphires and diamonds were imbedded in a platinum sweetheart setting. The clasp was diamond-encrusted with 22 stones; 11 sapphires and 11 diamonds, accompanied with a matching tennis bracelet and two carat diamond tear-drop earrings. The velvet box was marked Hollings Diamond Collection.

Gabriel's breath seized as the diamonds enchanted her. "Jesus." Ann smiled. She couldn't help but remember her best friend, her sister Safinah. She wasn't impressed with jewelry. In her case, Clarence would've done better buying her new fabric, an odd tree, or a plant for the gardens below. Riding to the house, Ann grinned at the trees Safinah planted through the years; including ten magnolias she purchased for her from New Orleans. They were huge and beautiful reflective of Safinah's personality. She remembered the day she and Clarence got married under the magnolias in Georgia. "You look beautiful Great One. Is it heavy?" Ann inquired locking the clasp. "Yes Ann." Gabriel giggled.

"You'll get used to it, Gabriel." "May I call Clarence Ann?" "You're not supposed to. However, we'll arrange something before you come down, yes?" Nervously, Gabriel agreed. Ann left Gabriel staring in the mirror. She was getting hungry, so she drank a glass of water. "Joan?" Joan entered. "May I have a cup of tea, please?" "Sure. Gabriel." "Please, ensure you make it yourself. There are many people in the house." "Yes ma'am." "Don't ma'am me Joan." Smiling, she put on her black long lace glove with her new bracelet glistening on top. There was a tap on the door. "Enter." "Sugar?" Gabriel ran to the door, but Clarence held the doorknob. "Sugar, I'll see you in a few minutes, ok?"

"Yes," holding her hand to the door. "What's wrong? Are you hungry?" "A little, I drank the cup you sent earlier." They were quiet for a second. "Baby?" "Yes Sugar?" "I'm afraid Clarence." "Why Gabriel?" "I don't want to be married and in ten years, you feel I'm not enough and you want another wife." "Haha."

"It's not funny, Babe." "Sugar, I'm not laughing at you. I'm laughing at the thought of losing the woman I adore over someone I'd never love as much as you." "Open the door, Clarence." "No," he chuckled. "Open it please Daddy!" She grinned wickedly. "Oh, that's dirty, woman." "Hehe" as he fled seductive temptation. Joan knocked as Gabriel snatched the door open. "I thought you were Clarence, sorry." "Are you ready Gabriel?" Joan smoothed her dress in the front. "Yes." Zion knocked. "Enter." He stopped short as he saw her, catching his breath.

"You're stunning, Great One." He couldn't keep his eyes off her. Joan cleared her throat and Zion collected himself. He pushed out his arm, "We have a party to attend Gabriel." Gabriel nervously held his arm, allowing him to lead her to the party. They stopped at the top of the winding marble staircase. A man with a deep voice read aloud the room was pin drop quiet.

"We the Elders of ten covens understand on this day, August 15th, 2020, the 14th hour of the day, acknowledge our Pharaoh has chosen his vampire bride. She has been vetted by Ann Freeman, an Elder of our high vampire council. On this night, she, per vampire law, asked Ms. Gabriel Johnson of Queens, New York, if she accepted a marriage proposal from our king, Clarence Hollings; she willingly accepted. On this night, we publicly ask our king, has he chosen this vampress as his vampire wife and your future Queen. Great King have you, Clarence Hollings, a free slave from humble beginnings from the commonwealth of Georgia, proposed this vampress become your bride?" "Yes, I have."

"Please, allow me to introduce the future Queen of Covens vampires in the United States of America and Eastern European regions, Ms. Gabriel Gail Johnson."

"That's our cue." Gabriel held Zion's arm "Don't leave." She whispered through her smile, not realizing every vampire heard her. They stared in awe of her natural beauty. Clarence sat on his throne as love swept through him. He stood making his way to her. Zion escorted her to meet him in the middle of the ball room then placed her hand in his. It'd been years since the Elders had seen him happy.

Clarence took her hand, ushering her to sit on the podium next to him in Safinah's throne chair. Gabriel looked over the crowd and they clapped as her contagious smile lit the room. Zion stood on her left as Clarence stood before the throne; the room fell silent. He fell on bended knee as Zion handed him a ring box. Telepathically, to *Gabriel, I know you'll wear your grandmother's ring. However, I must present you with a ring of my choosing. It's a formality. I hope you love it. I understand. Thank you for the necklace and earring set, it's beautiful Clarence. It pales to your beauty, darling.*

She leaned in to kiss him. "Wait! He hasn't asked," Zion announced, everyone burst into laughter. Clarence fell on one knee as the camera flashed blinding light. "I'm a vampire who was a slave. I hail from humble beginnings, a coachman for a cotton plantation in Georgia. I came from dirt and mud. You'll be marrying a free slave, a vampire who has a lot but is nothing without your love Gabriel. I ask on this day in front of all who witness, will you have me as your loving vampire husband?"

Clarence opened the box, a 5-carat round cut diamond ring with an additional carat of small diamonds surrounding it, sparkled in her eyes. Gabriel held her heart inhaling. "Yes." Clarence slipped the ring on her finger still on one knee, she bent down kissing him. Both humans and vampires recorded the event. Scroll writers documented this blessed day. Clarence took his seat on the throne seating Gabriel next to him. "It's time to present the dowry." Zion announced.

This is what everyone was dying to hear. Single vampire women sat on the edge of their seats. Many dated Clarence in the past but found him complex or unable to read. They waited to hear what they may've gotten. Zion presented the scroll of dowry requests to Caleb who stood in the middle of the ballroom floor breaking the seal of coven on the dowry scroll to be read.

"Per vampire marriage law, all vampires seeking the hand of a vampire in matrimony must present the intended bride's family with a dowry. In this case, Queen Gabriel Gail Johnson has no living family as such, the dowry must be presented to her. To represent her, she has chosen Dr. Zion Donovan, chief advisor to our Pharaoh, the lead physician, chief of surgery and lead scientist to all vampires.

*On this day Dr. Donovan requests on behalf of Queen Gabriel Johnson, two items:*

*1. The Pharaoh may never marry another woman, human or vampire, lay with or take a concubine as long as he's wed locked with her.*

*2. The five-bedroom cottage on the Gullah Islands which sits on fifteen acres of land and all that's on it including livestock will belong to her."* Everyone was silent. *"This is the end of this dowry request. What say ye, Great Pharaoh?"* Clarence was speechless, "Gabriel, I'm flattered. Is this all my Queen has requested Zion?"

Clarence was perplexed. "Yes, Pharaoh this is all we request for her hand. Do you accept the terms of this dowry request?"

The room was quiet, everyone was surprised. She could have anything - diamond mines, houses, land, and all she wanted was him? Romantic or stupid? Elder Ann knew this woman who inherited the love of her friend's life was worthy of his love. "Yes, I accept the dowry request Dr. Donovan." "Pharaoh!" One of his junior advisors exclaimed, which was fine according to vampire law.

"I must advise you to consider what you are accepting. You must never seek the love of another in illness or disagreements. You cannot break this covenant under any circumstances, you will be bound by your word and by your blood in this contract for all eternity as you're marrying a vampress and not a human. A vampress has no expected date of expiration as a human does. Are you sure you want to concede to this agreement, my King?"

The scroll writers tapped away on their laptops enjoying every moment. No videos were allowed at this time. "I appreciate your advice young vampire, and it's dully noted." Clarence spoke extracting his fangs exerting his dominance. "However, I consent to the dowry I'm love swept by this vampress I'm afraid your words of warning fall upon deaf ears. Please, hand me the deed for the property on the Gullah Island and the vampire marriage contract to sign in blood."

*Why this property Sugar?* he inquired, mentally *This is where I resided when I turned. I love it, it's beautiful Clarence, do the island inhabitants know what we are? Can we go there for our honeymoon? If you like, Gabriel."* He signed the deed transferring the property in her name, pricking his finger pressing down on the scroll; a blood signature, that bound him to the contract until death. Gabriel pricked her finger on a rose thorn pressing her index fingerprint next to his. They rolled the scroll handing it to Zion on her behalf.

"Thank you, Clarence." Vampires clapped, celebrating their love. When Clarence placed Gabriel's finger in his mouth sucking her finger, vampresses were insanely jealous. The catering staff handed out glasses of wine for humans and blood for vampires in flutes. When they came to her, she spoke gently, "Wine please." The crowd gasped as she selected wine over blood. They heard she was a hybrid, but many thought it a lie. "A toast!" Zion held up his glass. "May they love for all eternity."

Vampires gasped; others were amazed as if it were a magic trick. Vampire Queen Gabriel was drinking wine! The DJ turned on the music as guests flooded the dance floor. Clarence stood and grabbed Gabriel's hand. He quickly led her to his study, pulling her in, locking the door behind him. He pushed her against the door kissing her wildly. "What were you saying behind the door upstairs?" "Daddy please open the door." Gabriel spoke seductively, licking her lips as she saw his eyes blaze with lust. "Woman, don't start what you can't finish."

She tossed his tux jacket removing his shirt for her to feed. They sat on his new tufted leather couch, drinking. Clarence held out his wrist Gabriel bit without hesitation. "I know you're hungry." as she drank slowly so as not to spill blood on her dress. "I'm good, Clarence." She stopped sipping." "Ok Sugar." He stared at her in awe. "Why're you looking like you've never seen me?" She kissed him. "You got me wrapped around your finger, Gabriel." Zion tapped the door. Clarence opened it, hugging Zion who was surprised.

"You're not upset, Clarence?" "No, all I have is her Zion, we must return." "I need the ladies' room, Clarence. I'm going upstairs." "Security will escort you, Gabriel." She nodded. Gabriel was escorted by one guard. He checked the room before allowing her in. When she was done, she washed her hands and reapplied lipstick. Gabriel smelled something different in the air, she looked in the corner seeing Cody. "Great One, don't you look beautiful?" Cody flashed a scalpel glistening in the light. "Why do you want to kill me? I could call Clarence, and you'd be captured. However, I haven't. Turn yourself in I'll help you." "YOU STOLE HIM BITCH!"

"How can I steal a man from another sis? Your mind is clouded, you aren't thinking properly." *Clarence Cody is here* Gabriel instantly sent a telepathic message.

Clarence hurried up the steps with ten guards. Fifteen guards were outside the windows. Clarence burst into her private bathroom. Cody grabbed Gabriel from behind holding the scalpel to her throat. Vampire guards burst into the bathroom through the window.

"You're trapped Cody. There's no way out." The guard reminded her. Cody jumped over his head, breaking the bathroom light, cutting the guard's face jumping out the broken window. "Catch her! Don't let her off this property!" Clarence shouted. Cody bolted through the woods, cloaking her presence.

The party was abruptly placed on hold. The house was locked down, windows and doors blocked by steel gates;

infrared beams filled the house in various locations detecting movement. The Elders were led to Clarence's den. Clarence entered the den. "Cody is on the property, Ann." Ann closed her eyes, a mist filled the room. She went through a crack in the wall, her clothes dropping to the floor. The others – Elijah, Clarence, Papa Nathan, Caine, and Lily removed their clothes too. "She's gonna pay for this." Lily seethed, aggravated. "It's ok, love." Caine assured her.

Elijah pressed a square on the wall, they walked through a tunnel naked. The Elders reached a secret door leading outside. Five Elders shifted into dingos. They ferociously ran loose on the property moving as one pack with Clarence leading as Alpha. Zion took the clothes to the barn, stretching them out individually with five basins of clean water soap and towels. The dogs disappeared into the darkness. Vampire securities were taught in school never to shoot or harm dingos as it meant death because you'd be killing a vampire Elder and coven leader. Few people knew it. It was a rumor the council of Elders never confirmed.

Gabriel stayed locked in Clarence's bedroom with one of the guards Caleb an Elder and Joan. She sat on the bed, crying. "I'm appointed by the Pharaoh to be your personal security for the night. I'm the Elder of coven five, the house of seers my name is Caleb Great One." "You are an old vampire?"

"I am." Caleb sat in front of the door with six guns on his person; three for humans and three for vampires." He sat with his eyes closed. Caleb sensed Cody on the property, he quickly shared visual locations to the dingo Elders to track and trap her. Cody couldn't cloak her fear as a high vampire seer, he tracked vampires based on emotions they experienced. The greater the emotion, the easier it was for Caleb to find you.

She's *near... magnolia trees... hurt. A guard shot her with vampire vice grip (vvg). It's slowing her down... making her tired.* Clarence rushed to the magnolias; she wasn't there. Elijah searched the trees while Ann hovered in a shroud of midst over the property. *She's heading to the highway.* Ann sent a telepathic message. Caleb smelled her fear. *Someone's helping her* Caleb advised. Ann didn't see anyone.

*I don't smell any tracks,* Papa Nathan added. *I see her!* Lily rushed to the highway. *Lily don't run on the highway!* Caine warned. Lily bolted onto the Jackie Robinson expressway after Cody and was hit by the car aiding Cody's escape, Z71-985 NYC plates. Caleb concentrated on the face of the driver while Lily shared the plate number with Caleb. *I'll stop them.* Ann headed for the parkway. *No Ann! It can cause an accident on the parkway with the mist! You'll kill humans return to the mansion please.* Clarence gave the order the dingo pack returned to the barn. "Lily!" Caine embraced her worried about her being hit. "I'm fine family. I'll be better after we get the bitch that destroyed Clarence's engagement party." Lily hated turning into a wild dog. Instead of self-shifting, she'd wait prolonged periods of time before changing. Caine would enter the house and have a dingo wife for five days straight. He'd keep repeating, "All you must do is shift at will, so it won't force itself on you Lil." "Leave me be Caine." "Yes, baby Caine chuckled. "Sorry family." Clarence shook his head, aggravated. "Brother, you never owe us apologies." Elijah and Papa Nathan held his shoulder as they finished bathing and dressing. "Thank you, Elijah." They returned to the engagement party, the gates lifted, the emergency security protocols raised.

Clarence made an announcement, "Family, I apologize for the temporary interruption. Please, enjoy the music and food. There will be an exotic blood tasting. Please, enjoy." Vampires rose to dance. The Elders returned to the party. Clarence instructed the caterer, "Please, hand out strong, intoxicated blood." "As you wish, Great One." Clarence returned to his bedroom, Caleb jumped, pulling guns on him. When he saw Clarence, he lowered them.

"What did you see, Caleb?" Caleb glanced at Gabriel unsure if he should speak candidly in her presence. "It's fine Caleb speak freely." "The person who picked Cody up on the parkway is Isaiah Clarence." Clarence approached Gabriel, hugging her tight. "Why would he get himself mixed with her? Get Papa Nathan here, Caleb."

Papa Nathan, a tall handsome older vampire with a distinguished salt and pepper beard, was good-looking with his dark chocolate complexion. His suit was sexy, and Gabriel never saw one like it. She wondered if it was vintage or an old style he remade. "It's a pleasure to make your acquaintance." He greeted her as he fell on one knee, kissing her hand. "I've heard many good things about you. Allow me to introduce myself. They call me Papa Nathan around these parts." "Please rise." He rose, Gabriel greeted him with a hug. He felt her trembling and like a father, he reassuringly embraced her.

"It's ok, my dear." Papa Nate patted Gabriel's back, "You are in the gulf of loved ones. We're your new family, we'll never allow anyone to hurt you, Gabriel." His words were comforting. Gabriel understood why they called him Papa. His words were like the father she never had. "Thank you." She whispered. Clarence requested Caleb to escort her to the party. "I'll stay by her side personally, Clarence." "Thank you, Caleb."

"Do you have a coven, Caleb?" Gabriel asked rejoining guests. "Yes, Great One" As Caleb escorted her down, he said "Wear a big smile, Queen." He held her hand, reading her, envisioning her life smiling. "You love children my Queen?"

"Yes, I'm a kindergarten teacher." "Don't fret. You will have your chance again, Great Queen." "Are you a seer, Caleb?" "That's what vampires call me since I turned. I'm empathic, I see glimpses of people's futures and past." "Say seer, will I be happy?" Caleb took her hands. "Yes, Great One. Your days of unhappiness are behind you." Gabriel smiled, "For some reason, I believe you Caleb." "Let this serve as one of your gifts from me. Clarence won't seek the arms of another man to replace you. There will always be women who want him because of his title and what he owns, he shall never turn his eyes from you. He'd rather walk into sunlight before breaking your heart. Were you aware the other night he stayed over he met the light and was severely burned because his heart longed for you?"

"No Caleb. Your accent is charming. Where are you from?" "The Gullah Islands Gabriel. I grew up there." "I just got a cottage there," she joked. "I heard." "See? A good smile Great Queen. Let's go down and party while it graces your pretty face." Papa Nathan and Clarence sat discussing what happened as they sipped B-positive tox blood.

"This person is young, Clarence. "Yes, she is Papa," Young people's blood is sweet, sometimes too sweet." Clarence held the flute glass down. "What happened Clarence? Clarence explained to papa Nate what happened the night Zion turned Isaiah. "I couldn't let him die Papa. He's like my son." "I understand you love him as much as I. It's been a half a century since my offspring was turned. I recall you were outvoted Clarence, and man, were you upset! How long before we spoke?" "One year Papa."

"The Polio vaccine hadn't been created." "Did you hear it was the genes of a black woman who cured polio, Papa?" "Yes, I heard. Who would've known?" "Where's your granddaughter, Joan papa?" "Upset." "Why?" "Because you are not marrying her, Clarence."

"She knows better. She's like a baby cousin how was I to know papa I thought she has feelings for Zion?" "She swore you read her thoughts." "No, I didn't." "You're going to upset lots of vampress. It happens. That's why I got two wives. They cried when I took the second. They're downstairs; one human, one vampire."

"Who do you love more, Papa?" "Truly?" Mouthing his answer, Clarence read his lips. "Why?" "She reminds me of our human selves. I smell the sun on her hours after she enters the house. I'm in awe of Gabriel's dowry request, I must say I'm shocked Clarence Gabriel asking for fidelity over diamonds haha bold move can't say she aint got moxie." "I'm baffled as well, Papa Nate. I opened the books to her" "All of them, Clarence?" "Yes sir." "Wow! I would've taken a diamond mine off your hands." They smiled.

"Bad news, Papa Caleb saw Isaiah help Cody escape. She drank his blood the night she bit him on purpose directly violating your treaty. I heard her inform him via phone we would've never turned him because of the treaty. Cody didn't bite him when she broke in, she left him to die drinking his blood to use him as her inside man, Papa."

"Isaiah must be punished for consorting with Cody, Papa Nate. I warned him yesterday." "I understand. Clarence." "It's his first vampire infraction, it won't be harsh. You must help me find him before it gets worse. Papa." "Agreed Clarence." Papa Nate worried Isaiah was digging a ditch he had no way of escaping.

# Chapter 12
## Savage

The year of our lord March 1861

Two years before the Emancipation Proclamation.......

Clarence waited patiently for Thomas to marry Clara and become the plantation-Master. All assets transferred to him, because the estate belonged to Master Alex who left Clara everything thing upon his death as his only living heir.

Once married she no longer possessed all that was willed to her, now transferring to Thomas upon marriage. Clarence followed Thomas to slave brothels, where he could be rough sexually, and no one cared. Thomas frequented saloons nightly, playing spades, hearts, losing estate money rapidly. Clarence understood why he and his mother were broke and needed the marriage to survive.

There was a negro playing cards. Clarence sat, playing a few hands, talking to the locals, while they watched him win every hand. Whites would get angry. It was not unusual for the negro player to draw his pistol regularly as he was the main player draining Thomas of his money daily.

A young negro male no older than twenty-five years of age, six feet even in height, about 185 pounds. Clarence laughed inside. Negro saloon ladies swooned over him while white women pretended, they didn't want him. He was a slave, the saloon owner had him play customers for money and all winnings were handed over to his owner.

Trying to show how ignorant negros are, Thomas challenged the gambler to a hand of poker. The stakes were if the negro won freedom would be his. If he lost, he would never be free. Thomas put up a hefty bet of $1000. Having faith in his skills, the gambler and his owner accepted the challenge. It was a day like no other. Negros in town heard of his foolish bet they gathered rendering prayer and strength. The saloon was packed with children looking in the windows. Decent women who wouldn't be caught dead in a saloon stood on the walls to witness this unbelievable event. This day whites bore witnesses to a negro beating a white man at cards winning his freedom and the owner one thousand dollars.

Negros were euphoric as if they were being freed holding hands when the gambler signed the documents attaching it to his bill of sale. Tears of joy fell from every negro in the saloon including men when the slave owner pressed his signet seal at the bottom of those freedom papers. The saloon owner offered him to stay and continue to play for an equal share of the winnings. He accepted not having to leave Georgia within thirty days never returning or risk being enslaved again. However, as an employee he could stay, work and not be subject to recapture under their unjust laws. The day was a good one for slaves for once his freedom gave a sense of hope, something they desperately needed as a race of people.

One night when he left, Clarence followed him, he pulled a pistol on Clarence. "Why ya followin me?" "I want to employ you, Gambler." "Employ me doin what?" "I want you to bankrupt the man you play Thomas." "Why?" "I don't fancy him, Gambler." "That be your issue mister. Don't get me in white folk business." "I'll pay $100 a day ask him into private games and take all he has. I'll front your gambling money."

"You gonna pay $100 a day to do what I does any how and gimme da money ta gamble wit?" "Yes, here is $700 cash to start Gambler."

"Thomas don't come every day." "Think of it as pre-paid wages. Certainly, our arrangement is private, Gambler?" "Yas." Clarence put his hand out to shake on it removing his glove. The Gambler was shocked but shook back to seal their agreement. "What's your name?" Clarence called out to him. "They call me Chance, 'cause I take chances." "Mr. Savage." "You French?" Chance looked away when he looked back Clarence was gone.

The Engagement Party
Brooklyn Mansion New York
The year 2020....

Everyone danced to the electric slide. When Clarence rejoined the party, he stopped in the middle of the dance floor. Gabriel cut through the sea of guests joining him. "I will exhibit to new vampires how to properly waltz." "You guys will love it. This is how you make a vampress fall in love with you." Zion handed Clarence a wax candle and paper base. "Thank you, Elder Ann, and Dr. Donovan. If the candle extinguishes, you failed to waltz properly."

Papa Nathan yelled, "I couldn't get this in 100 years literally." The room echoed with laughter. The DJ played the classic waltz, Clarence took Gabriel's hand, "I'm unsure how Clarence." "I'll lead, you'll be fine close your eyes, feel the music." Gabriel allowed the music to encompass her, as Clarence held the candle between them, twirling clockwise, swaying counterclockwise, sweeping her around the ballroom floor as she closed her eyes entranced by his slow movement. As the waltz echoed, Gabriel was spellbound. Clarence held Gabriel close removing all memories of Cody attacking her, turning back the hands of time in the eye of her mind. Clarence danced as Gabriel forgot.

When the waltz ceased, he held up the lit candle. Gabriel smiled, feeling lighthearted once again; the crowd cheered. Clarence kissed Gabriel's forehead, leading her to her throne chair for gift presentations starting with coven one. Joan and Zion approached the throne holding hands with a gift wrapped in brown paper. The room was quiet.

"Great Queen, we the humans and vampires of coven one, your home coven, the coven of our beloved Pharaoh, present you with this beautiful gift." They carried it to Gabriel, who peeled back wrapping as a gasp swept the room. "It's beautiful." Gabriel looked at Clarence with a glow in her eyes. She held the stained-glass window under ballroom lights. It was a red rose wrapped in beautiful green vines, with stained glass of different hues. Zion handed her the card. Gabriel read it with tears in her eyes sharing it aloud.

"Hello, Great Queen,

If you are reading this, it means Joan has kept her promise, and is giving a wedding gift to you, and your new husband. I created this for you in the event Clarence found love again. Red is the color of blood which sustains him. Green he'll always remember his life as a human, he'll never be fully dead. A rose, a symbol of the love that will grow between you. Yellow, to remind him of the sunlight he loathed in life but loves in death. I pray you love this gift, please cherish Clarence, he's a good vampire. If you're reading this, I know you're a good woman.

With love,

Queen Safinah Hollings

First Queen of vampires."

There wasn't a dry eye in the house. Clarence was surprised she did something noble. Ann reminisced about the day they made the gift, with Safinah needing Ann's help to finish it.

*"Come help an' old slave," she'd say to Ann. "I hate when you use slave, Fi. We been free, an' it ain't funny."* Ann chastised her, making her laugh. *"You sound like Clarence y'all are too serious."* Ann remembered how they laughed and talked of people long gone from the Dupree plantation laughing like schoolchildren for hours. Ann recalled sleeping in her bed, while Clarence would be cross with Safinah for not sleeping with him. She'd be upset with people thinking she was his wife then his mother graduating to his grandmother even if he'd always say she was his wife.

Safinah cried regretting her decision not to turn as she neared death; however, she never shared her regrets with Clarence. *"Ann, I made my bed. I'm mo lay in it. I waited these years to see mother, to have the life with her in heaven that I didn't on earth. I recall the day they snatched me from her loving arms, she screamed so loud. I know the sound of a broken heart, Ann. If I were vampire, I'd never be able to mend her broken heart."*

The tears flowed down Safinah's cheeks; Ann had no idea they were making the window for his future bride. *"It's ok, medicine woman,"* Ann hugged and reassured Safinah. *"You're going to get to heaven and you gon' see your mammy again. It's been long, hasn't it?"*

*"Yes, it has. I never forget her face, Annie."* Ann hugged her. She ate her brownies knowing they'd make her ill. It didn't matter, she wanted her best friend to see her try. Ann looked at the upper righthand corners of the gift, and saw Safinah's fingerprints there, it's how she signed her work. Zion handed her an additional letter, "This is for you to read privately, Queen Gabriel." "Thank you, Zion." Elijah, leader of the next coven, stepped forward with his wife Mya. "You may approach brother." Clarence granted permission as the guards stepped aside.

Elijah's wife handed Gabriel a box, she opened it gasping. Clarence leaned over, looking at the pink, sweet-smelling salts inside. She opened the card, reading it aloud, "May your marriage be filled with flavor." She held up the bath salts pulling paper from the bottom. 'It's a title she turned to Clarence, we own a Himalayan salt mine, thank you Elijah and Mya!" Gabriel hugged Elijah and Mya. "I saw bath salts in your bathroom in Queens, I thought you'd love to have your own mine, my Queen." "Yes, Elijah, thank you again." Caine and Lily presented their gift next representing coven three.

"Great One, we're honored to present you with our gift, we hope you love it." They rolled out an old ornate trunk, "Brother, please do the honors."

Clarence stepped down, opening the trunk, bursting into laughter. He called to Elijah, the three vampires and Lily chuckled. Clarence announced the gift was a trunk full of gold confederate coins passing a handful to Gabriel. The gold was stolen from a stagecoach robbery they'd done in 1895 to cover the cost of slaves they'd stolen, helping blacks being held hostage.

"Caine, I said to get rid of it!" Vampires chuckled. "I couldn't Pharaoh." "I'm glad to have the space back this thing was taking up!" Vampire women tapped glasses in agreement with Lily. "Is it real Daddy?" "Look at the stamp on it Sugar" "Confederate gold 1894 wow" he grinned at her childlike expression."

Papa Nathan and his two wives approached from coven four. "Papa!" The crowd called with glee, waving their hands. Vampires loved Papa Nathan; they trusted Papa with money and goods because he was honest. Clarence loved his congeniality and truth. Papa Nate was the father he and a lot of the male slaves never had. Being older papa was sixty when he accepted the bite, he was in excellent health, not looking his age. All his human adult children and grandchildren were present. Papa cared for his bloodline, living wealthy. His children attended the finest schools, adorned the best clothes and jewels, drove expensive cars who were blessed with trust funds by the age of thirty. They were doctors, lawyers, and teachers running their own practices and schools. Papa raised a senator, a professional NFL player, contractors, a gem specialist to run their diamond mines and a grandson who aspired to be a classical concert pianist, Isaiah.

Clarence envied him because Papa was blessed with a bloodline. He wanted kids with Safinah. He exchanged giving life for life eternal. He recalled buying papa's children out of slavery. Of the thirteen kids he fathered with his wife, they purchased twelve. His vampire wife requested to approach the thrones; Gabriel nodded permission. She handed Gabriel a paper bag from Louis Vuitton, which she opened, "A speedy 25 satchel" The women cheered. "Open it my Queen," his human wife called to her excitedly. Gabriel unzipped the bag, a shiny derringer sparkled in the light. She lifted it, smiling. "A girl needs protection look at the handle. HT." The initials were carved into the handle. "H.T? NO!" "It belonged to Harriet Tubman, she'd a thing for Papa," Clarence shared, and laughter filled the ballroom. "I had a thing for her too!"

Under it a check for two million dollars before she could reject the thoughtful gift *You must accept it, Sugar. It's an embarrassment to the coven if a gift is rejected.* Clarence reminded mentally. "Thank you all." Gabriel blew hand kisses. They announced coven five, and the house of seers stepped forward. Gabriel held Clarence's hand. She liked Caleb, he didn't need to give her another gift. He gifted her the gift of his sight which was enough for her.

Caleb called for a red square box with a yellow ribbon. "May I approach Pharaoh?" "You may Elder Caleb." "This is for Queen Gabriel." He sat the box on her lap gently. When she opened it, a puppy popped out. She picked him up, hugging and kissing his nose. Clarence darted Caleb a look inquiring telepathically, *you know dogs hate us,* keeping a smile and hiding his disdain. "This is a dingo Great Queen." "He's adorable, and his fur is so soft."

*She has a dingo… Caleb staring in his eyes, continuing their quiet conversation. Not like him, you don't Clarence.*

"Take him to our bedroom please." Caleb gave her another box full of gifts for the dingo. His last gift was a white gold necklace, thirty inches long with a white gold skeleton key encrusted with diamonds. "It's beautiful Caleb, thank you." "Always wear it my Queen." He winked. "I will thank you."

"Coven six, step forward." Chance stepped forward with seven vampresses. He was handsome. His wives were diverse types, some vampires some humans. *How many Clarence? Gabriel asked mentally. Five vampires, three humans I think haha Gabriel. All his wives? Some wives, some concubines.*

*Which is the first wife, Clarence? The wife will present the gift. Is she in charge of the others? Yes Gabriel. Are you ok with my dowry request baby. One thousand percent sure love. I'm a one-vampress vampire, always have been Sugar.* "Great One," he called to Gabriel wearing a Stetson cowboy hat and snakeskin expensive boots removing his hat, his burning deep-set eyes drowned against his flawless chocolate skin. His first wife was a beautiful vampress.

"Queen Gabriel," bowing her head, "Pharaoh, please allow Senior Elder vampire Chance Hollings to present both gifts, may we approach?" Clarence allowed Gabriel to answer.

"Yes, you may." Chance's first wife Mary approached with a gold envelope bearing the coven wax signet seal. Gabriel cracked the seal reading its contents, pleasingly surprised before handing Clarence the envelope. He read the contents staring at Chance. "Approach alone Chance please." The scroll writers tapped away on stenographer machines. Chance approached, he and Clarence continued their telepathic conversation. *Are you sure? This is your second big win after Twin Oaks son. Pop, I owe you, my life. I have plenty of stocks, bonds and holdings in Arizona, Vegas, and Atlantic City casinos. I own private saloons, cat houses, and clubs for vampires and humans. I attend high-stake gambling games, yes, I'm sure.*

Chance stepped back, as Clarence held up the envelope "My son has given the deed and title for the Las Vegas Palm

Casino Hotel and Spa." Vampires inhaled aloud. His wives were shocked. *Do you see?* Clarence laughed, speaking with Gabriel mentally. *They're upset. Now he must answer eight wives instead of one.*

Music played and humans were served dinner while vampires attended blood tasting. Glass flutes were marked by blood type. There was intoxicated, newborn, eight-year-old, fat women, skinny men, vegan, pregnant woman, and candy lover's blood offered. Vampires tasted in shot glasses and were given half-flutes if they enjoyed it. Clarence grabbed his bride dancing the night away. Taken by her laugh and exultated he found a spectacular vampress to wed.

"What do you think so far, Gabriel?" "It's beautiful honey. Vampires are nice. It's one big family." "Guess what? You've four gifts to go beautiful." "Oh, wow, honey, ok," Joan approached Caleb informing him humans were finished with dinner. For dessert they served Safinah's brownie recipe with vanilla ice cream. "Are those brownies? I want one Clarence." "It's Safinah's recipe." "Smells wonderful. I'll have Joan bring it with your tea tonight." She buried her head in his neck, licking him. *You're making me hard woman. I know Clarence,* gently brushing her fingers over his hard on. "You gonna get it!" They were seated.

"Coven six, step forth." A tall sexy vampire stepped up. He stood 6' 7" in height and 350 pounds with not an ounce of fat and a head full of large sexy natural curls. "Where's your wife vampire?" "She died some time ago, my Queen." "You've my deepest sympathies." Vampires present from his coven stood at their seats, one of his members rolled two clothing racks on the dance floor, "May I approach Great Ones?" His voice was deep, grabbing every woman's attention in the room. "You may," Clarence nodded. The vampire held out his hand Gabriel placed her laced gloved hand in his hand which swallowed hers.

He escorted her to the racks, "My wife was a size twenty. I was told you're eighteen Queen Gabriel?" "Yes, sir I fit both," she looked puzzled. Clarence read his thoughts; he was enamored by Gabriel's beauty. Niarchos thought her strikingly beautiful and charming, wishing he'd found her first.

"For you." He escorted her to the first rack, which held beautiful, 1920s hand-beaded gowns with matching headwear. "They're 1930's, through the 70's Queen. They belonged to my wife. I'd be honored if you adorned them."

"They're gorgeous Elder." She held a beaded gown in her hand gasping. "Sorry, I didn't get your name, gazing in his eyes." "Niarchos Clarence Hollings, Great One." "Niarchos, such an unusual, nice name." "Thank you, my Queen." "If you do not wish to part with them, I totally understand Niarchos."

"Please, Great One," keeping his gaze down shyly. "Please accept them. I'm sure they'll pale to your beauty; however, wearing them helps me honor her memory. I almost forgot." One of his coven members handed their vampire Elder five velvet covered boxes. Niarchos opened,

Box 1: Which held a diamond and ruby princess-cut sweetheart necklace. Box 2: A diamond and emerald cascading necklace. Box 3: A thirty-inch-long diamond and pearl necklace with matching chandelier earrings. Box 4: Diamond pear-shaped earrings, one carat each. Box 5: A diamond triple row choker holding five carats with a triple row matching diamond clip bangle. "Are these from 40's Niarchos?"

"Yes, my Queen, may I?" He opened the bracelet clasp gingerly with his large fingers. "Let's see if I've lost my touch." He placed the bracelet on her empty arm over her glove with the lightest touch. She held up her arm, everyone clapped. "I love them all Niarchos, thank you." "Wear them in good health my Queen." "One final gift as we depart Great Queen."

Niarchos owed Zion big time. He explained her love for vintage items. Lastly, he held up a garment bag. Gabriel unzipped it, revealing a black sable stole. "Rhinestone buttons, I love those Niarchos." "No, Great One, these aren't rhinestone buttons these are diamonds."

She gasped. He grabbed her arm she was about to faint, making him chuckle. Niarchos took her hand, leading her to her throne. "Pharaoh, I hope I didn't offend."

"Never son." Niarchos smiled. Single vampresses looked on melting and, drooling over him. Although he was quiet, he was Clarence's head of security. Vampresses adored Niarchos. He was a one-woman vampire waiting for the special one. Vampresses recalled his wife's elegant attire. She was a beautiful woman. Vampresses loved when Elders married humas knowing she'd die, and he'd be single giving them a shot. "Coven eight, step forth."

Ann stepped forward, with her second in command, "With such beautiful gifts how can I compete?" Everyone clapped. Her second handed her a leather-bound book along with several letters bound in red ribbon.

"Queen Gabriel, we the members of coven eight welcome you to vampire life. You're sitting in the seat of our first Queen Safinah Hollings. She wasn't only our Queen but a phenomenal woman, and my best friend. Before she transcended, she wrote diaries, one specifically for the future bride of her husband, accompanied by several letters. It has her unbroken signet. I've held these items in trust for the Pharoah's future bride. I have two gifts for you which Queen Safinah willed me upon her death bed, may I approach?"

"You may." The room was full of quiet vampress' holding back tears. Ann handed Gabriel the books and letters, "Please read these in private." Ann handed her a box wrapped with a blue bow. Gabriel opened it, inhaling sharply. "A crown." Clarence smiled. "Not any crown my Queen the first crown forged for Queen Safinah made from the very first diamonds harvested from the Hollings mines," Ann exclaimed. "May I?" She placed a small tiara on Gabriel's head.

"Wear it in good health Great One." The last package was brought forward. "Pharaoh you may want to have a seat for this one" Clarence sat laughing. Guests were swept with excitement. An excited Gabriel opened a blue blood-stained torn jacket, then old Ann passed her a note that Gabriel shared aloud.

*"Dearest Beloved;*

*This is the coat my husband wore the night he turned vampire. As a young slave it stood as the only proof he lived. I'd fall asleep with it as comfort so I could smell him. Please let this coat serve as a reminder he turned vampire not of his will but by force. He sacrificed his human life in exchange for our freedom physically, mentally, and spiritually. Please love him as he loves you.*

*- Queen Safinah Hollings-"*

Clarence adorned the jacket for the first time in a century. Gabriel rose wiping his face. Zion came to take the gifts away. "Pharaoh? May we take photos of the jacket for the history vault?" "Yes please" Zion handed the coat to the scroll writers. Gabriel hugged Ann. "Thank you." "You're welcome." "Coven nine, come forward."

A young vampire stepped forward. "He's young Clarence." "No, he's not. I turned him when at twenty-three years old. It's against vampire law to turn a child." "Where's his wife?" "You mean his husband honey?" "Ok." Gabriel smiled. His vampire husband walked behind him. "Pharaoh, Great One, we vampires of coven nine salute you." Vampires of his coven stood mostly transgender male to female. All vampresses presented a gift wrapped in gold paper. "May we approach?" "Yes, please your name?"

"Vaughn" Gabriel opened an oil painted, at the bottom signed DaVinci titled "The Madonna." "He painted it then threw it away creating the Mona Lisa my Queen." "It's beautiful I love it. I'll cherish it." Gabriel stared at her black Madonna eyes aglow. "Thank you, Elder Vaughn," "You're welcome my Queen." "I'll have it hung in my boudoir." "Last but never least, coven ten."

The vampire stepped forward, with him stood young vampires dressed stylishly like they stepped off magazine covers. They were no older than thirty-five. He himself looked young" "Queen, may I approach?"

"Yes please." "Is that vintage Willie Wear you adorn Elder?" "Yes, it is." He was impressed she knew her fashion. "My name is Elder Blaise." He gave her a white box with a black bow. "For you" He held his head down kneeling. She pulled the string, car keys. Zion pulled the curtains to the ballroom windows; everyone rushed looking outside at a 1950s Rolls Royce vintage white convertible sparkling in the moonlight. "It's registered, see the plates?" "Qween... I love it Blaise.

"It sat in my garage I have no use for a convertible." "Certainly, you can have a sexy moonlit drive up the shore with a special vampress Blaise?" "I have no one special, my Queen," "There's plenty of single vampresses here." "Do you always see the silver lining Gabriel?" "Don't you Blaise?" He understood why Clarence chose her. She was good spirited, innocent to a default and regal minded. "Thank you, Gabriel." "For?"

"Making me feel human…for a fleeting moment." Gabriel hugged him. He took her to Clarence. "Pleasure Pharaoh." "Thanks Blaise." Gabriel yelled, "DJ, the electric slide!" Young vampires rose the older ones. Clarence danced with her. "You, electric slide Mr. Waltz?" Gabriel teased. "I do, the running man and moonwalk." They danced until her feet swelled and curls fell. The celebration continued until 4 a.m. Guests left to beat the sun. Intoxicated visitors were escorted to guest bedrooms.

"What gift is your favorite Gabriel I think I know the Rolls sugar?" "Nope you Daddy," snickering leaning on him, she was drunk. Clarence drank eight glasses of intoxicated blood. He was drunk which in turn intoxicated her when she fed after tea. Totally naked, she became his pillow princess cumming in his mouth as an additional gift from him. Gabriel wore the long strand of diamond and pearl necklace Niarchos gifted her. Gabriel passed out in Clarence's arms. He kissed her good morning, brushing cotton curls out her face, closing his eyes worried he called Isaiah.

*'Yes Pharaoh? Boy, what' are you doing helping a fugitive? She tried to murder Gabriel, you, and me.' 'No one is helping her Pharaoh.' 'Return home at sundown, Isaiah.' 'No.' 'I gave au an order Papa Nathan wants to see you.' 'Not without Cody, I love her Pharaoh. Would you leave without Gabriel or Mama Safinah?" "GET HERE!"*

*"No."* Clarence connected Papa Nate telepathically, in the conversation. *'Isaiah. It's Papa, aren't you going to allow me to see you as a vampire? There aren't many of my children walking time with me. You're special because I lost your mother, please come see papa, no harm will come to you.' 'Ok, Papa.'* Clarence ended communication with Isaiah continuing with Papa Nate. *Powerful gift, telepathy.* Papa said to Clarence. *You think he's gonna show Clarence? If he doesn't, Papa we gonna hunt him down.* They heard a light bark. The dingo was fast asleep on the bed with Gabriel. *He ought to be shot!* Papa spewed, as the dingo snuggled next to his new mom. Clarence laughed *who the dog or Caleb papa? Gabriel needed him, he said. You know Caleb has the gift of sight Clarence. In a few weeks I'll turn dingo and run with him, so he knows his alpha Papa. You got a fine Christian woman with a good spirit Clarence did she know you were wealthy?*

*No Papa never purchased an expensive gift either, yet she loves me. You done well boy Ise proud of ya.* Clarence doted on Gabriel, loved, and cherished her. *You got it bad boy. Yes Papa. I do.*

# Chapter 13

# When Rivers Run Red

The year of our lord 1858....

The burlap blood hood was hot, he was glad to remove it, eyes a blaze, teeth sharp. The savage was out to play…there was no putting him away. A young vampire's blood thirst needed quenching only human blood would do for such a joyous occasion.

Tied to a chair, Clarence snatched off the burlap hood of his prize. Fear gripped him as terror ran rampart in his eyes, arousing the devil in Clarence over his first human kill. Chance, Elijah, and Caine dared not make sudden moves; they were paralyzed with fright.

"Get Safinah!" Clarence growled pacing back and forth rabidly with wily ravenous eyes. Caine hurried to the house. His meal pissed himself. Clarence laughed raucously embarrassing him intentionally, bending down eye level Clarence asked, "You knowed her?" "Who is she sir?" growling scratching the kidnapped man's forehead with double long claws, blood streams masked his pale skin stinging his eyes.

"She was a nigger girl slave!" the captured yelled. "What ya done?" Clarence carved a hole tracing the back of his ear peeling flayed flesh excruciatingly slow licking his fingers, and detached ear. His blood curdling screams echoed across cotton fields, "Please I'll give you my plantation and all I own!" Chance approached withdrawing a billfold opening it "Ya means dis Thomas? I won yo plantation two nights ago, an' all dat be on it" Chance smirked, blowing cigar smoke in his face. "Who's going to believe a nigger owns a plantation?" Thomas laughed nervously, spitting blood on Chance's boots. Chance grabbed the back of his head wiping his boots with his face. Chance handed the deed for Twin Oaks to Clarence. "Pleasure doing business with you Mr. Savage."

His spurs rang as he walked away guarding the barn door. Cain walked Safinah to the barn holding her hand. She was dressed in frilly fineries, a long robe trimmed with powder pink satin ribbons, with satin house slippers. Cain escorted her to the stall past Chance and Elijah. Clarence turned to her; Safinah gasped resting her right hand over her heart at the ghastly sight of what Clarence had become as Safinah was introduced to his inner savage for the first time.

Caine held her up from behind in case she fainted. Clarence felt shame holding his head down, seeing fear sweep her eyes for the first time pertaining to him. Safinah approached him touching his silk hair as she'd always done, lightly brushing her dainty finger on his cold cheek. Clarence leaned into her loving touch as the beauty calmed her beast. Safinah hugged him kissing his blood-stained lips.

"Ya thinks dis stops me from lovin ya Clarence?" Safinah looked to the back of the stall, seeing someone she couldn't make out in the shadows. She held up the lantern sharply inhaling. Anger seized her reasoning, losing her composure, Safinah rushed to her rapist violently punching him repeatedly, her white gown covered in blood spatter. Safinah pounded his head, ripping patches of blonde hair out the roots, scratching, spitting, and gouging continued. She picked up horse manure, shoving it in his mouth, squeezing his nose, pushing, forcing his mouth closed. He choked on the triple pile of horse shit.

Thomas spat the manure out, Safinah cried hysterically digging her nails in his face and neck. Clarence hugged her, passing her over to Caine. Caine and Elijah watched the savage grab what remained Clarence pushed his head forward chin to chest holding him still effortlessly despite Thomas' futile struggle.

Thomas screamed begging for forgiveness and his life, Clarence opened his mouth wide, sharp fangs extended, showing Thomas what he was so his adrenaline would race, making the blood extra warm. He descended on Thomas biting into the back of his neck, feasting on his warm salty sweet sacrifice. Fifty-five minutes on and off he fattened himself on racing blood. Thomas convulsed, went in and out of consciousness, whined, cried, and begged.

Clarence knew where to bite thanks to a book he purchased on human anatomy. He released every ounce of deserved pain, drinking until content, then loud slurping to torture Thomas who was seconds from death's door. Safinah left with Caine, returning with a metal milk canister draining him for her husband's morning breakfast from existing wounds. Safinah held his hanging head up releasing a wicked diabolical shrill-mocking laugh. One the men never forgot.

A brick was lifted off her chest, it was the laugh of freedom from his unspeakable act that tried to break what hope remained in her getting her through slavery mentally. Now Clarence was her slavery chain breaker mentally and physically. Thomas died Safinah spat on him. Clarence stopped drinking seven minutes later. "Why ya stop Clarence?" "We aint pose ta drink dead blood. We gets ill, Safinah. I stops when his heart stops." Clarence kicked him black and blue. He wrapped Thomas in a manure-stained burlap. He adorned himself in his burlap hood with no holes cut out "Where ya goin, Clarence?" "Home to his Clara."

Safinah smiled deviously. "Wait, Chance, ya gots a blade?" He handed Safinah a huge hunting knife. She untied Thomas' trousers grabbing his dick, hacking it off with the serrated bear knife, stuffing it in his mouth. Safinah made sure to shove it way down in his throat with the tip facing the opening so there was no mistaking what it was.

With her satin ballerina slippers she kicked his chin shutting his flesh stuffed mouth. "Damn! Hahaha!" Chance belly bellowed. Clarence kissed her head, joining Chance in the laughter. Clarence tossed Thomas over his shoulder I'll return in 45 minutes or less, love." "I love you." "Not more than I love you, cotton." "Cotton? Hehe, I gots me a pet name, Chance, ya hears dat?" "Yes'm, I reckon I does." Clarence handed Chance the deed for Twin Oaks. "It's yours you won it fair. I'll handle the details." "Thanks, ya kindly Mr. Savage." Clarence left. Chance, Caine, and Elijah escorted Safinah to the house.

"I ain't never met a white man dat love us niggers much." "We ain't niggers, neither is ya, Mr. Chance." "What is we, ma'am?" "We's God's chosen dat why dey mad." "I reckon, where you hear dat missus?" "My mammy, says dat fo she die." "Smart lady, God rest her soul." "Clarence ain't none of em neither," Elijah hushed Safinah.

"No, Lijah Mr. Chance one a us it be fine I gots me a good feelin' bout Mr. Chance," Safinah was holding his arm he knowed we good folk." Chance looked at her confused. "Clarence like us God's chosen." Chance stopped walking, Caine raised his shot gun cocking it, Chance ignored his warning sound. "God's chosen, is you sure Misses?" "Course I is, hehe you knowed dere be white slaves, ain't cha seen any Mr. Chance?" "No ma'am."

"Now ya is, it be our secret ain't dat right Mr. Chance?" She kissed his cheek, sealing the secret. "Yes, ma'am dats right." For the first time since Chance was a child, he felt safe. "Ya stays wit us now ya hear? Youse family, youse home." "Yes ma'am."

Twin Oaks Plantation
Sunrise......


"AHHHH THOMAS!" Clara let out a blood curdling scream fainting on the cold marble floor. She looked for her husband who often stayed late nights and was frequently seen sneaking back from slave quarters in the wee hours of most mornings. Clara was determined to catch him sneaking back from the slave quarters. She walked gingerly past her mother's bedroom, which was once hers, making her way down the cold marble steps barefoot not to make noise with slippers. At 4:30 am before sunrise she opened the large oak double doors the body of her new husband battered and bloody lay listless.

Thomas' mouth popped open exposing his mouth shoved bloody penis. Thomas' pants rested around his ankles exposing a hole where his manhood once was. Clara's eyes filled with horror and stinging tears as truths cold hands clutched her into the reality of the man she married. No expense was spared breaking her heart by the demon who butchered, bit, and bled dry her love. Ms. Minnie rushed to her daughter, seeing the blood pool around her daughter's knees. Clara held Thomas' limp battered body in her arms. Slaves hurried to the big house gasping at the sight of savagery shown to him; shock turned to happiness.

"Who could do such a heinous act mother?" Clara fainted. Ms. Minnie turned away instructing the slaves to wrap him up and to fetch the sheriff. She gave them linen wrapping him gently, carrying him to the barn. When two younger slaves arrived, they dropped him on the ground carelessly, opening the bloody sheet having a kicking party.

They knew what he'd done to several slave women, children, their wives. They broke his arm, listening for the crack, gut punching him till their fists were bruised and raw then called the female slaves to have fun. They shitted and pissed in his mouth. The slaves wrapped him back up, wiped blood off their shoes and faces, exiting saddened. Word spread like fire of his death, and the condition of the corpse.

The sheriff came to Twin Oaks, questioning the family. "Were you aware Thomas had a terrible gambling habit Mrs. Dupree?" "No, sir we were not." "In fact, he lost a large amount of your holdings and real estate in hart and spades. I hear he lost this plantation to a nigger." The slaves were shocked, as were Minnie and Clara. "A nigger slave Sherrif?" "No ma'am, a free nigger he must have done this, and we're looking for him ma'am." "I'd like for you to get the papers to this plantation back from him immediately Sheriff." "Yes, ma'am. Ms. Minnie, May I view the body?" Clara cried as Mammy consoled her. "Surely, Sheriff.

"Avril, escort them to the barn please." "Yes'm" Avril walked the sheriff to the barn making sure to look at his face as he drew back the sheet, he lived for his reaction to laugh with Isabel. The sheriff threw up, Avril covered Thomas swiftly. They walked back to the big house. Avril fetched him a glass of water, spitting in it, a practice he'd been doing since a child. The Sheriff drank the water straight down. "Mo sir?" "No boy." Avril took the glass, tossing it in the rubble.

"They say this nigger plays the saloons most nights. I shall arrive tonight to get the deed from him. Free or not he gonna give up the title to this plantation. I do not care how he got it. No worries, ma'am," patting her hand reassuringly. The Sheriff approached his horse while thinking he'd retrieve the plantation deed and marry Clara or her mother, whichever he could persuade. They needed his protection. He informed every white, red, chink, and nigger he was looking for a gambling nigger called Chance.

Present Day......

Gabriel woke someone was playing Tchaikovsky's Swan Lake. Pano notes glided on the warm breeze into the bedroom window intertwined with the sweet smell of jasmine flowers. It was dark. She slept through the day again. The music continued to play; after using the bathroom filling the sample cup, she followed the alluring sound. The notes were perfect, calling her out of sleep. When she arrived downstairs, Gabriel was surprised to find her fiancé playing perfectly. "It's one of your favorites, yes Sugar?" She stood in awe gazing. "You don't need sheet music?"

"No, I memorized it." When he finished, Gabriel clapped as did the baby vampires in the next room. They loved hearing him play, although he didn't often, except Gabriel infused his heart with the love of music again, enticing him to return to his abandoned lover, his piano. "Where did you learn Clarence?"

"A young deaf man who was once an African slave lost his hearing to the slap of an overseer as a three-year-old boy. I met him inquiring he teach me. He did and later became famous Clarence began to play moonlight sonata. You know him as Beethoven the name white men created for him. He played symphonies for them in their grand halls not allowed in because of his dark skin. I own one of his spinets and Chevalier as well. Beethoven gave it to his prized student as a gift after mastering the piano. "In turn I taught him how to"--

"What Clarence?"

"Waltz. It's not easy teaching a deaf person to dance to music they cannot hear." "Did he learn?" "He did Sugar. It's me you're talking about haha." "What shall we do tonight? It's Friday Chance invited us to the clubs." "Which vampire or human love?"

"Vampire." Clarence whispered the baby vamps entered kneeling, "Pharaoh, Queen," the eldest vampire spoke. "We're going to Club Ambrosia if you guys are free tonight, come, blood on me." They bolted up the steps excitedly. Khrista returned inside the den Gabriel followed her. "Khrista, are you and your husband coming?" "He's working Great One. I'm waiting for him to arrive."

"But--"

Clarence who entered behind Gabriel tapped Gabriel's knee, she quieted. Once alone he explained. "It is against vampire law to interfere with marital affairs between two vampires unless there is violence or breaking of vampire law.

A vampire attorney's presence is needed before judgement is passed." "We have vampire attorneys Clarence?" "Yes, they're lawyers in the human world representing vampires and humans. Once they get a law degree in human law, they must attend two years of vampire law school, take the exam, and pass."

"Oh, that's why the lawyer asked you not to sign the dowry." "He's my junior law advisor. Under vampire laws legally, he has the right to inform me in front of witnesses he didn't agree with my decision. Come Sugar let's ready ourselves"

Gabriel adorned a sequin black tank with matching black jeans and leather open-toe heels. She struggled with her straight iron *Why couldn't he change me when I straightened it,* she thought *damn that Cody bitch.* Clarence knocked on the bathroom door handing her a tall glass of his blood. "How'd you get it neat in a glass?" "The wrist." She drank fast. "You look wonderful sugar." He slyly grinned. Bikes were lined up.

"NO!"

Passing her a helmet with her name on it, "You're a bike virgin Gabriel?" "No" "Yes, you are." he gave her a boyish grin hop on Sugar. Twenty bikers are outside with women on the back." Zion stood next to Clarence's Indian. "Indian I'm impressed Clarence. Zion are you coming?" "No, Gabriel. Joan and I have a date." Gabriel clapped lightly "yayyy." Clarence helped Gabriel on the bike by hopping in front of her. "Lean into turns Sugar, hold on we'll arrive in twenty minutes. "Is Chance there, Clarence?" "Yes, Papa and Ann too. Ann's staying at Papa's house, Gabriel." "Papa playing with fire hehe." Zion looked away. "What?" "They were married but that's a pillow talk story Gabriel." Clarence put Gabriel's tortoise shell helmet on her, he put his on to avoid the law. The ride was fast. The view across the Brooklyn Bridge was breath taking. Gabriel squeezed him tight; he loved it. Clarence got off his bike, and one of the baby vampires parked it. He and Gabriel entered the club. The music stopped, as vampires dropped to their knees. Clarence and Gabriel crossed the dance floor with vampires clearing a path. Gabriel squeezed Clarence's arm.

"This way Pop" Gabriel gave Chance a hug Once they sat as Clarence gave permission, "rise children." The music blasted, vampires continued dancing and enjoying themselves. Drinks sent to the table were vast, blood Jell-O shots, and his favorite blood types. Clarence gave them to the baby vampires ordering his drinks of choice for him and Gabriel "Do you want to dance Gabriel?" "You can dance like this?" "It's a two-step wanna see Sugar?" "Sure" Clarence led her to the dance floor. She turned her back, grinding and bounced in his crotch. Vampires tried not to watch but couldn't help themselves. She turned to him, Clarence pulled her closer with her legs around his thigh he kissed her neck nicking her not, spilling not a drop he bit her in several spots feeding from her sweet blood she never knew she was bitten. When Gabriel opened her eyes, vampires were below her in awe, the women were wet with excitement.

She gasped, "Baby!" "Yes Sugar?" "Put me down please." "As you wish." He dropped his screaming Queen. Clarence reached the dance floor before she hit the glass tiles swinging her facing him smiling. "You want to continue?"

"Entranced by his charm yes baby." She licked his neck right behind his ear lobe. He knew she was going to feed he loved it. He wanted gossip to get out in the covens their Pharaoh levitated. Chance stared amazed. They were back on the dance floor when Clarence spotted her. *Come to the back of the club, ALONE!*

Clarence walked Gabriel to VIP seating asking Chance to sit with her. "Where are you going baby?" "I'll return shortly Sugar. Chance, stay with Gabriel." "Niarchos is here Pop." "Where Chance?" "Upstairs in a private card game winning." *Niarchos. Yes Pop? Come stand by the back door inside the club, she's here.* Niarchos adorned his guns loaded with vvg bullets dipped in dead blood, enough to make a vampire sick but not kill one

*Old Indian? How does she know you here Pop? She can sense me she consumed my sperm and blood Niarchos. Not enough to overpower me but enough to sense my whereabouts. It wears off as women stop drinking. Now you say Pop? I told you back in 73' a vampress can track you by drinking sperm you forgot Niarchos? I did pop.*

Clarence stepped outside the club. The alley was dark; being nocturnal, he saw no one. She stepped out from behind the dumpster falling to her knees.

"My maker, I beg for forgiveness of my transgressions please allow me reentry into your coven." Faced down, she was dirty and disheveled. "You've been V-basing Cody. Show me your eyes now." The wildfire in her eyes snuffed out by the drug hiding the vampire color which makes your eyes look human. The problem is the drug causes a vampire to bounce back and forth between human emotions and vampire emotions, that's where the high is.

It cuts vampire reasoning to mere human reasoning, then boosts it in a rush to vampire reasoning. This happens on and off for 24 hours until you land back on vampire emotions where you started. Sometimes vampires die, because when they drop to human emotion levels, the brain makes them think they're human again. They believe it walking in the light.

"Isaiah jumped out from behind the dumpster popping a shot Clarence levitated Niarchos kicked the back door open BANG! Isaiah was hit in his leg. He dropped to the ground withering in pain. Cody looked back and hopped over a car in double lane traffic making her escape. Clarence looked down at Isaiah, "Clarence grabbed Isaiah by his collar punching his jaw knocking him out cold.

"Take him Niarchos lock him up, he's standing trial." Niarchos was shock-shook. "Papa Nate?" "He tried to take my life Niarchos. Get some gloves son." Clarence pulled the bullet from Isaiah's leg. "Bag the gun as evidence. It's in the hands of Elders now."

Niarchos obeyed, lifting Isaiah one handed tossing him in the back of his dark tinted SUV with glass from Ann's factory handcuffing him with pharaoh's steel. He checked Clarence's bike for a bomb, it was clean.

"Pop I'mma need you to leave the bike is good." Clarence entered the club sitting with Gabriel, raising his wrist. *You're hungry. I can wait baby. We're leaving Sugar. What happened? Chance cut into his mental conversation, Clarence was now speaking with Gabriel and Chance. 'Cody had Isaiah tried to assassinate me, Chance and Gabriel darted a look of shock.' 'What the fuck pop?' 'Isaiah tried to shoot me. The bullets were acrylic, translucent plastic with a metal needle tip filled with dead blood.' 'I'm going away for a few days. I left Niarchos in charge of security. He's moving into the house. Tell Zion to give him Gabriel's bedroom.' 'Ok, Pop, I didn't know you could fly.' 'Not fly, levitate, Chance. I gotta find this bitch or she's never going to stop.' He only allowed Chance to hear him.*

*'I'll return soon we will never be happy if this keeps happening Chance. Leave Isaiah in jail until I return. He has a right to be processed within thirty-six hours unless I request an indefinite hold.' 'You never used your legal seniority, Pop.' 'I am now Chance, get the boy a vampire attorney. He's going to need it.'*

"Come Sugar." Gabriel rose, the music stopped, and everyone was kneeling. Clarence held Gabriel's hand and waist. "I give you your future Queen Gabriel Hollings." She waved vampires clapped. The royal couple crossed the dance floor, exiting through the front, while Niarchos waited on his bike. "Why is Niarchos on your bike honey?"

"Protocol." Gabriel knew he lied, sparing her of her own fears. She didn't want to do it; however, she listened in on his thoughts. They got on the bike. He put the helmet on her, she laid her head on his right then wrapped her arms around his rib cage, creeping into his thoughts undetected. How could she without an old vampire noticing? She rubbed his stomach holding him lovingly, she was in.

*How could she? She couldn't have thought we'd wed. Tricking Isaiah how can he avoid death? He tried to kill me; the Elders will seek death by sun light. I love the boy. What did she do to convince him to end my life? I'm way too old to be killed from dead blood. Gabriel, are you listening to my thoughts? No...yes how'd you know? I was quiet bae. I didn't until we hit a pothole, I heard your fear, Sugar. You can hear fear Clarence? Yes, it's part of our hunt when we feed off humans, which is a story for another time Sugar.*

*Where are we going? Away for a week, Gabriel. Baby, I don't have clothes. I'll buy them, no worries. Ok.* It turned him on her calling him daddy he never knew why he'd been waiting for Gabriel to call him daddy during sex. If she calls me that during sex, I'm busting hard in her. Clarence shifted his thoughts back to the alley moments before.

"*Gabe?*" She was out of his thoughts. Clarence had a telepathic conversation with Cody in the alley of the club. *I'm going to kill your Queen; this time I won't miss then your next! How do you intend on doing that, little girl?* She fled, and Isaiah fired the shots. Clarence sped up on the FDR drive in New York. The view was breathtakingly stunning.

Gabriel didn't understand what was happening. All she knew was Clarence reassured her it would be fine, to her his words were golden.

# Chapter 14
# Kill Him!

The year of our lord 1861

Ten oppressors dragged, kicked, stomped, and strapped him to the back of a wagon, they dragged him to the river over a gravel road then tried to drown him. He would not die he was owned by them his whole life minus nine days of his freedom. He would leave this world on his terms not theirs.

"WHERE'S IT BOY!" The sheriff yelled one hundred times over in between slaps, burns, punches, and beatings. Chance spit in the sheriff's face laughing maniacally. He and Clarence were partners in ownership he remained silent. "A nigger owned plantation?!" They were livid. "We ain't gonna get nothing from this nigger, kill him," the sheriff instructed his blood thirsty henchmen. "Hell, he's already dead sheriff." "Let the wolves finish him off," the deputy spat on Chance.

Hollings Estate Georgia....

Clarence stepped on his porch, the rancid smell of dying human blood mixed with gardenias floated a warning on warm night air. "Cotton please, hush." Safinah stopped her wedding prattle. "Chance is in trouble cotton. Get a room ready with medical supplies please. Call Lily, you will need her baby." Clarence left following the aroma of metallic blood.

When Clarence arrived at the moonlit riverbank, wolves lingered waiting to rip flesh from bone. Clarence fell on all fours popping his fangs, growling at the wolf Alpha threateningly. The wolves rushed off fearing the glint of death in his dingo-colored eyes. "Chance? Oh, God no." "Clarence, dat be you boss?" His voice was raspy blood pooled in his throat. "Wees goin home, Chance." "I ain't tell em shit boss," he slurred Chance grinned showing teeth blood stained, "fuck em boss." Clarence picked him up tears stinging his eyes feeling guilt for involving him in his revenge plot. laying him over his shoulder "Ahhh!" Chance screamed in pain. "I gots ya Chance.

Clarence arrived at the house. Safinah checked Chance thoroughly telling Clarence what his injuries were. "His ribs broke both sides. arms broke three places from wat I feels, left leg too, blood come from da ears mean he bleedin inside. A bone poke somethin' important. Lily says Ise right Peety. Dis do dad ya gots me say his heart movin real slow from da sound it pound. an' dem medical book say, dey broke he aint hearin good no mo."

"Clarence Safinah whispered, cause' he bleeds inside he ain't finnin ta see mornin Ise sorry Peety." "Clear da room please." Everyone left except Safinah. "You, too, woman go on." "No Clarence." "Sho' ya wanna see dis Cotton?" "Be wantin' ta knowed who Ise wed wit." "Don't open the door…draw da drapes, call Lijah and Chance he gots ta be hold down."

Safinah fetched Elijah. "Brother, he gots ta be turned." "Turned Clarence?" "Vampire Lijah, iffin not, he die. Lessin, I calls don't come near dis bed Cotton." "Chance!" "Mmmm boss." He moaned. "Brother, ya seen what I is, knowed what I is, ya has choice!" Safinah handed Clarence smelling salts. "Thank, ya kindly Cotton, stay back please." "Ise sorry Peety" He waved salts under Chance's nose. "Humm?!" "Brother squeeze my hand iffin ya understand!" "Chance squeezed his hand, "brother youse dyin, youse bleedin inside, we ain't stop it. Iffin ya wanna live you sees da sun no mo an' drink human blood ta tarry. Ya wanna be vampire or die?! Tarry squeeze once die twice!" Clarence yelled cause his ear drums were broken.

A minute passed Chance squeezed once strong as possible. Clarence, enticed by his blood, wanted to drink but controlled himself. Ripping Chance's shirt, pushing his neck left, he held it steady. "Elijah hold his feet." "Yes'sir." Clarence opened his mouth wide candlelight flickered off his white fangs. His eyes widen a fire blazing bronze brighter than the roaring fireplace. Duo Canine teeth slipped from his gums razor sharp. Elijah was impressed. Clarence bit Chance, his screams violently ripped through the plantation windowpanes rattled Safinah grabbed hugged herself nervously.

*How do I care for a vampire?* She thought. Clarence sunk his teeth deep in his jugular vein rushing blood pounded against his teeth as vampire venom virally spread in his blood stream. Clarence dug deeper his fangs met with blood-soaked flesh trapped between them. AHHH! AHHH! Chance screamed as Clarence bore down trying to push him off Clarence rested his body on his chest.

Clarence gulped as much blood as possible to track him, so no one would hurt him again. Stopping his feed Clarence bit his wrist dropping sharing his blood Joining them to time walk sealing his immortality.

"We is one. We help one anotha." Chance was his first vampire turn his son. "Safinah?" retracting his fangs "Please you an' Lil clean up" Safinah puckered her lips for a kiss "Likes dis cotton?" "I loves all a ya Peety." Clarence obliged her. "Hehe." Clarence rubbed his bloody face all over Safinah's. "Stop Peety hehe." Clarence exited the room Elijah chased him. "Clarence I wanna be vampire." "Why?" "Ta be like ya."

"If ya want this, for 21 days ya can't go out sunup?" "How Imma do chores an' tend da bees?" "Dat be fo ya ta figure. After dem days we talks." "Yes sir."

"Good can I cleans up Lijah?" "Go head." "Hahaha." "Will Chance live Clarence?" "Long time Elijah." As Clarence bathed, he heard her voice in his head.

*'Ya make a man tanight?' What need lookin fo? 'Madness iffin it happen takes his head den burn him in da light. I seen vampires turn an' kill a whole vampire nest. Firstly, dey talks crazy an' act wild likes a trap rat fo days. No second guessin Clarence. Mind me now. Dey mind too weak fo us venom it make em sick be no fixin dat. Has no pity put em down like a rabid dog. Youse a pappy now Clarence, he be yo first pickaninny, an' youse mine.' You abandoned ya pickaninny leaves me be in dis world ta rot.*

*He kill ya dead outta jealousy you knows dat. I save ya by stayin far, but I sees ya by my blood dats in ya Clarence lookin handsome livin like one a dem devils foolin em real good ya is. Ise mighty proud a' ya. Youse gettin hitched? Yes'm. She white? No, slave like us she gots dark flesh pretty likes you. Good Ise right happy fo ya. I try an' make da weddin. Thank ya kindly, ma'am. Fo Clarence? Savin me Black Lilac. Ise goin handsome, we talks soon. I reckon we will Lilac.*

Clarence was alone in thought. *What did Safinah think about what she seen? Will Chance be fine?* Clarence cleaned up returning to the guest bedroom. He sat by candlelight and fireplace next to Chance's bed all night with Safinah, Elijah, and Lily who all worried. Chance was twenty-three years old, his first vampire turn and a part of their secret circle blessed to be added to their blended free slave family as they worried, he may die.

His breathing was shallow, a bad sign, his bones cracked miraculously fusing under bruised dark skin before their eyes screaming in agony. Clarence and Elijah held him down as he withered in excruciating pain. Safinah prayed hoping God would listen to her keeping this new negro vampire alive holding his hand as he died to be reborn.

Present Day 2020

Clarence raced to Teterboro airport for thirty minutes. They boarded his private plane beating the sun by minutes. Gabriel lowered the window shutters. "Pharaoh and Queen Gabriel welcome aboard. We'll arrive in Georgia in two hours. Your limousine will meet you on the runway." "Thank you, Gil." The pilot kneeled he left for the cockpit. Clarence placed his arms around her; she leaned back on his strong chest; he raised his wrist. Gabriel enjoyed breakfast, dozing off.

Clarence was tired but didn't sleep until he arrived at the Gullah Islands. He loved it there, understanding why his maker kept a place to herself. Certainly, he remodeled the tiny shack through the decades adding on to the original structure. Safinah hated the Gullah Islands because it reminded her of slavery down to the Geechee language, when he'd go, it was alone.

Safinah loathed Georgia begging him to move north where she was free to express her love and dote on Clarence openly. She was his wife, not his slave or housekeeper like she pretended in Georgia. She hated the south for forcing her to hide her love many years after the emancipation, leaving the south to move to New York. Zion called "What happened Clarence? Joan is in tears and Niarchos is here."

"Isaiah tried to kill me. Niarchos witnessed it, Zion. I took a blood sample from Isaiah. Check it. Cody was high." "High...Cody?" "Yes Zion" "Oh, God what the hell is going on Pharaoh?" "Call Papa Nate inform him before he leaves town. Ask him to sit by the boy until he recovers. Please give Papa the room across from mine."

"Yes, Pharaoh." "Zion? How was your date with Joan?" "Interrupted. Niarchos entered as we were headed upstairs." "Haha you're responsible for Isaiah. He's your turn and son now." "This is exactly why I never turned anyone. I don't want the responsibility, Clarence. Where are you headed?" "It's best you don't know Zion." "Travel Safe."

The plane landed on the walkway leading directly to the limo with not an ounce of light filtering in. Gabriel stopped. "You smell the sun, Sugar?" She grinned. They entered the limo. "We sure ride in style, don't we old man?" "Is there another way?" "I'm sticky." "Welcome to Georgia, Sugar, my home state."

He fell back on the seat; she pounced on him; he welcomed her affections. "Why are we here early Clarence I thought we're honeymooning here." "We can return; I need to keep you safe while I think things through." They were driven to a marina, waiting as they set up a tunnel to the yacht. They walked down the boat steps when sun tapped his forearm. "Shit" Clarence grabbed his scorched arm. In French, a deck hand yelled, *"tu l'as brûlé idiot."* Clarence yelled back *"sa fin ne vous inquiétez pas frère.* Gabriel said, *"Il sera bien." "C'est bon vous parlez et comprenez bébé français, Gabriel?"* "Oui."

"Wow where did you learn French Sugar?" "In college." Gabriel held up her wrist to her fiancé. "No, thanks." "Close your eyes." She closed them. He nicked her feeding. "Why are we on a boat?" "Didn't you read what you signed Sugar? The house is on an Island."

It was a four-hour boat ride. By the time they arrived, the sun had set. It was humid walking the dock to the house, Caleb greeted them. "Cherie." Gabriel hugged him while his coven members kneeled. "Please forgive my attire family." "I took the liberty of choosing some clothing my Queen. Here we are, wala" Caleb opened the cabin door. "Oh, Clarence, it's all I thought it would be and more." "We didn't have much time to prepare but we hope you love your dowry choice. We're honored you chose our little island as your gift."

The log cabin had a facelift. There was a massive wood burning fireplace encased in red brick, and a seat made from slate stone was in front of the fireplace. The ceilings were high, and windows were around the top of the cabin which were tiffany-stained glass. While Clarence slept, she opened the skylight windows with an old fashion iron turner. "They're on remote control room darkening shutters, but you can open them by day Gabriel." "Are you gay, Caleb?"

"What is gay …happy?" "You know what I mean." "When you've walked through time long as I have what is gay? I believe in reincarnation strongly. Let's say you die, and Clarence died, assuming you both were humans, in this life he's male you're female right Gabriel?"

"Yes." "Now you both return your love will gravitate toward each other like invisible strings. You both are reincarnated except you both are women. You don't understand your love, it's meant for the two of you to love no matter what. If you were to you return as a woman you should ignore what you feel naturally Gabriel?" "No, Caleb" "Makes sense Queen?" "Yes."

"Secret?" "Yes please" "You and Clarence were here before you knew one another. I knew it the day he saw you in the coffee shop. He's Pharaoh, he and I are connected through his blood. I see a lot regarding him, most times I see clear occasionally not." "Alexis, play 'oh, happy day." Caleb yelled smiling. "I love this song, Caleb!" "Me too." Gabriel grabbed Caleb's hand twirling with him while Clarence showered, upset the humidity was unbearable.

"Alexis air on." Clarence liked breathing thinner air. He loved Colorado for this reason. He exited the bedroom to the balcony seeing them dancing on the patio outside the living room. "Sugar, may I speak with Caleb please?" "Yes boss." "Ohhh, hee-hee." "What's funny Caleb?" "Gal, don't you know that's a bad word in the covens?" "What boss?" "Yes, ma'am that's how we addressed our oppressors." "I'm sorry guys I didn't mean to trigger."

"It's fine Sugar, we know you didn't." Gabriel walked up to ready for bed Clarence met her halfway on the stairs blessing her with a peck goodnight, "Caleb tomorrow?" "Yes, Queen tomorrow sweet dreams." Caleb went for fresh cold human blood passing Clarence a mug. "What happened why you here?" "Isaiah tried to kill me. The boy was on drugs."

"Someone hypnotized the boy, Clarence another vampire not her, one who stands behind her." "An Elder?" "Hell, no, Clarence." "Can you see his face, Caleb?" "No, he cloaks himself however he has a tattoo on his left forearm. You gotta smoke him out. The wedding Clarence?"

"No Caleb, I gotta think on it." "I told Zion take the boy's blood, don't look way Caleb. He deserves a fair defense, and Zion is a new vampire. He needs all the help he can get." Someone was at the door "Come In" Caleb called. A woman entered. "This here is Cheri Bell Clarence." She kneeled as though Clarence was her king; she wanted to be vampire badly. "Please rise." She stood smiling.

"I've heard much about you." "Thank you. Is the Queen asleep?" "She's Cheri." "Were you born on Gullah Island?" "No, I was born in Dekalb County, Georgia." "You're one of us Georgia born and raised." "Yes, ma'am I sure am." "You've your accent after all this time charming." "Do I now madam?" She flirtingly giggled. "Southern charm I love it. I see where Caleb inherited it." "Honey, can you wait in the car please?" "Yes, dear it was a pleasure meeting you, Pharaoh." "Same." Cheri was excited; she met vampire royalty. "Sorry Clarence." "Ah don't be, she's crazy about you, Caleb." "Yet, she'll never be my wife." "Ahhh, the gift is sometimes a curse. Have you seen your wife?"

"Yes, she's six." "Wow haha." "I saw your wife when she was eight." "Thank you for not telling me." "You're welcome. Niarchos is fond of Gabriel." "I know, I read his thoughts. He's enamored by her beauty, and personality Caleb." "He's harmless. Gabriel is beyond in love with you Clarence. She'll never look at another man the way she looks at you. She thinks you're the handsomest man she's ever seen." "Do you have the carriage ready Caleb?" "Yes, I know you love your carriage while visiting the island. No cars for you."

"Poukisa ou monte alantou nan ansyen cha lagè a?" (Why do you like riding in Massa's old carriage Clarence?) "Se sa ki te transpò amoure a te fè pou de Clarence? Mwen te panse li te bon. Espesyalman jodi a li te ansyen ak tout. Fi renmen yon woulib cha. detann! chwal nwa tanpri." ("The carriage is made for two. I thought it charming; women love a carriage rides black horse please Caleb.")

"Ok, goodnight, the remote control is there to block the light. I'll have fresh blood delivered in the morning Caleb." "Human?" "Yes, when you gonna let Gabriel drink other blood?" Caleb peered over his sunglasses in judgement.

"When we catch Cody and who she's running with Caleb." "Makes sense the help laid your fresh soil. See you tomorrow night brother, call if you need me." Clarence locked the doors and windows. It'd been decades since he locked his doors. Clarence rinsed the glasses checking his healed arm. Entering the bedroom, the smell of fresh apples lingered.

"Sugar?" Clarence shook her to see if she was in deep slumber. "Ummm?" "Nothing, Sugar, sorry." He covered her with a blanket, she loved blankets. Staring, fear brewed in him, which he hadn't felt since Safinah's incarceration. Clarence brushed stray hair from her face, seeing her clearer he spooned behind her praying he never lost her. His large muscular body and ripped stomach cradled her thinking of ways to end Cody's reign of terror. The next morning Gabriel woke refreshed.

"Wake up old vampire," "Ummm?" "It's beautiful here the housekeeper is knocking." Gabriel chipperly opened the door. "Hi Great One, I'm your housekeeper Lulu." Gabriel pushed her hand out. Lulu shook her hand.

"How old are you?" "Nineteen ma'am. I'll prepare your tea." "I'll take it in the rose garden thanks." "But ma'am, the sun?" "Yes Lulu?" "Nothing, remembering her place. She took the tea with fresh lemon and fresh honey to the patio surrounded by red roses. Gabriel stepped into the light. Lulu was shocked saying nothing. *She's human.* Gabriel read the morning paper, the Georgia Sun Times. "Lulu?"

"Yes ma'am?" "Are there boutiques to shop?" "Yes, in town and oh, a carnival coming. Vendors will be out all night." "When Lulu?" "All week, Great One." "Sounds good." The landline rang. Lulu brought it to her.

"Hello?" "Sugar, why are you outside in the light?" "I wanted to take tea on the patio babe, why?" "Sugar, I can't protect you in the light please come inside." "After I take tea, Clarence." "Gabriel, please." She left her teacup and newspaper storming inside straight to the showers. Clarence tried to join her; she exited.

"Sugar?" "What?! I'm not marrying you to control me, that's not love." He grabbed her lotion massaging it on her back. "I'm sorry Sugar" butterfly kissing the nape her neck moving her hand to his massive throbbing twelve-inch-thick dick. "I don't want to Clarence. I want to finish tea please. Thank you." "Outside?" "Yes."

"Ok." Gabriel dressed, exiting to the patio with a fresh cup of tea. Clarence sat at the kitchen island peering through patio doors being extra careful not to allow the light to touch the tips of his toes. "You're going to sit there and watch me huh?" "Yep! I'm not bothering you. I'm enjoying your new house." She grinned at how silly he acted. Clarence smelled the sun and roses swirling in the heated air. "Why did the room smell like fresh apples last night? Did someone bake a pie before we arrived Clarence?" "Come inside, and I'll explain. You wanna see something Sugar?" "Yeah"

"Come." She turned around peering at him. "This better not be a stunt mister." "It's not." He went to the fireplace pulling down he and Safinah's wedding photo. "You ready Sugar?" "Yes."

"Close your eyes." Sighing, she obliged him. "Open." "Wow look at you her dress is beautiful." "She and Ann made it. I think her seamstress days are behind her." "The detail in the gown is incredible. Look at you all suited up what color was your suit, Clarence?" "Navy blue." She kissed him. "I see the happiness in your eyes."

"When black men wanted to marry and thought it a blessing instead of a curse. It was against the law for slaves to marry, however we found our own ways. Broom jumping or secret ceremonies. I never wanted a wife before becoming vampire made me free. I couldn't see myself sending my wife to the big house as a comfort girl. I've seen men kill themselves over that or kill the woman.

Clarence explained what happened the night he turned and why the room smelled of crisp red apples. "Why're you crying Sugar?" "Because you had to go through it alone. I couldn't imagine being left during all that." "I came here to turn Gabriel." "Wow!"

"The cabin belonged to my maker she's dead now. She was killed in a witch hunt in the early 1900's. I have a surprise for you Gabriel." She stepped outside the door. "Jesus its muggy Clarence." "Imagine having to sit up top driving a coach in a wool coat they gave you in this heat?" "Oh, honeyyyy its wonderful, a buggy ride for two so romantic Clarence." Gabriel let go of his hand running to the carriage peeking inside as he stayed on the shaded porch. "This is yours Clarence?"

"It's yours Sugar the estate and everything on it remember?" "Oh no, honey, I couldn't." "Too late we signed in blood," teasing playfully. "The horse too?" "You mean horses?" "How many Clarence?"

"Four, do you know negros were not allowed to sit on a horse and look down at a white man in the south? No horses for slaves." "That's crazy!" "Who's driving? You could have forgotten it's been a while Clarence" "No, it's like riding a bike but we can go at sunset Sugar." She hopped in the seat. There was a carving on the stool, it read S + C with a heart around it. "Did you carve this Clarence?" "No Gabriel, Safinah did." "Aww cute."

Clarence knew Caleb took the carriage out to make money riding tourists on romantic tours at night, marriage proposals or services needing a horse and buggy combo. Caleb asked Clarence if he could borrow both the two-seater and the six-seater. He agreed if he took care of them.

Later that evening Clarence and Gabriel went to the fair in the buggy of course. They arrived in town, the streets were strung with fairy lights, children were excited and jovial. The smell of fresh roasted popcorn filled the air mixed with sweet cotton candy. Children ran to amusement rides including a Ferris Wheel. There were games for prizes and vendors as well as fortune tellers and past life readers. "Baby, let's get a past life reading."

"Ok honey." Clarence kissed Gabriel's hand. They entered a small living room with red velvet curtains, a dim kerosene lamp, and a basic coffee table. They sat on the love settee, on top of a genuine Turkish rug. There were salt lamps plugged in the walls, which were a pale green color. "Are you nervous Sugar?" "About?" He chuckled. A woman appeared she was about eighty with a multi-colored silk scarf on with prescription glasses. She sat across from the settee. Her eyes were drawn to Clarence. She looked at him giving him a huge smile.

"Hello Mammy T." She stood hugging him. Clarence picked her up off the floor. "Que fais-tu ici?" (What're you doing here?) "Avant un voyage de noces, voulais voir comment ma future reine obtiendrait sa dot." (On a pre- honeymoon trip I wanted to show my future Queen her dowry). "I'm Gabriel we call Mammy T." "Hello, it is a pleasure to meet you. I hear your getting married." "Yes," the couple replied in sync. Gabriel held his hand, which she did when she was nervous, afraid, or unsettled. "What can I do you for you honey? "We'd like a past life reading please." Mammy T bellowed out a light laugh. "Clarence's life before this one?" "Yes, ma'am."

"I must go way back. He cheated death this one." "It's what you say to all vampires, we cheated death Mammy T" "It's no true vampire?" He shook his head no. "No man cheats the angel of death. We pay for it, everyday drinking blood as a reminder Mammy T." "Sulking over your turn again, I see vampire."

"You can't escape destiny. I explained this when I was sixteen, remember Clarence?" "I do and I remember your graduation dance." "Ahh the eyes when I entered with you vampire, yes?" "Yes, Gabriel Mammy T didn't have a prom date. The boys were afraid of her because of her gift."

"Clarence being a gentleman he took me Gabriel. You should've seen him Cheri he showed in a 1930s white tux in a Rolls Royce. He sho can dance gal." "Back on you two!" Mammy T pulled out a black satin bag asking them to touch it. She dropped the bag of old cat bones sorting through them.

The room was pin-drop quiet except for the jovial sounds on the streets. "You were a man two lives ago…you've an assertive side, you try to control but you being Queen, there will be many times in your husband's absence you must use this skill. You were a dominant man and often you didn't like to be told what to do, you like to create your own pathways and walk them right or wrong at least you did it your way. However, you must submit to your husband in this life. One life ago you were a woman Gabriel and successful. You find love but your dominance causes you to lose it in some way."

"What happened this morning Gabriel you challenged your husbands' dominance, what was it?" She looked at Clarence, he shook his head in approval for her to answer. "I stepped into the light to have a cup of tea, when Clarence asked, I come inside, I did but was cross with him, and went out again against his request"

"Une journée de Marche? (A Day Walker Clarence ?!)" "Oui. (Yes)" "Comment est-ce ? (How is this possible ?)" "Nous examinons main'tenant. (We're looking into it)" "Mademoiselle…do you know this vampire would walk in the light sacrificing his life for you if you were in danger?" Gabriel looked in his eyes. "I'm sorry."

"He'd die for you then see harm come. You must understand, he is an old one, an Elder, these vampires don't think of love like the men you know today. Love is a serious thing to them. Old fashioned values and a wife is his responsibility. It's how he was raised. Things will never change, not even with time passed. You must understand this. There will be times to exercise dominance but not in love because it never works in your favor, yes?" "Yes." "Good. Your turn." She shifted the bones. "You were a woman before this life. A black woman you wanted to return a man, so here you are. She died early you drowned in a boat accident that's why you hate boats." "You do Clarence?" "Yes Gabriel."

"You hate being on the water. You were married they killed your husband; it's why you love hard you're afraid of dying and loss vampire. It's why you were depressed when Safinah passed you were lonely. How does a king, a father of thousands feel lonely?"

"Without love or no one to love me why live Mammy T?" "See? He loves hard Gabriel." Mammy T laughed again shifting the brittle bones. "Did you make her think you were a common man when she met you Clarence?" "Yes ma'am"

"This love is what you had with Safinah did it work?" Clarence gazed at Gabriel. "Yes" kissing her forehead. "The two of you in other lives and this one lost love. Love is important to you both. Yet you found one another." Mammy T shook her head in approval pushing the bones around. "Long life I see. Mammy T will be a distant memory you two will be here in love. I'm glad to know you both. Clarence, may I speak alone for a minute?" "It's ok Sugar." Gabriel went outside to wait. Clarence closed the stained-glass door.

"Yes ma'am." "Don't you ma'am me. You're older than me. Trust her, don't crowd her she not born of your time. don't smother her love. She's a day walker and she's naturally going to gravitate to the sun. Inform her why you are this way make she understand better... yes?" "Yes Mammy T."

"Be careful I see a red eye surrounding her. A jealous eye...bring she harm." She whisked her hand at him kissing her teeth. "Give her space vampire! Yes?" "Yes Mammy T." "Good Clarence. Do she know how jealous you be?" "Not yet," he smiled. "Sagittarius men jealous souls." "How do you know my month of birth?" "The cards years ago telltale. You born December's time crazy vampire" "Thank you beautiful." "You're welcome." She opened the door sitting on the bench outside. Clarence hugged and kissed Mammy T again, slipping a gold confederate coin in her apron.

Clarence gave Gabriel two gold Confederate coins. "How much are these worth Clarence?" "A small fortune but it's blood money in my eyes, slaves were purchased with it. That's why I give it away to our people... profit for the generations of free slaves. What next Sugar?"

"Ferris wheel." They rode six times. "This is my favorite ride of all carnival rides makes me like a bird Sugar. Do you regret meeting me?" "No honey...why do you ask?" Clarence held his head down, "I'm unsure." Gabriel pushed his chin up. "Baby? I love you for you not for your looks or your money or the hustle in you. You're the father of many. I've loved you since you blessed me with those Madeline's and smiled. Oh, that was a contagious sexy southern smile. Right there you chased the darkness away. I'm in love with you honey I am, if you leave, I know I'd die inside." She leaned into him kissing his lips with both arms around his neck, she pulled him close snuggling her nose into his neck smelling his aura.

Gabriel did something to him. She softened him. something Safinah never mastered. Safinah showed love and affection but could not express it with words, only action. Gabriel did both. He'd sneak into Safinah's thoughts, hearing how much she loved him, and yet, find the words were rare. "I want a teddy bear Clarence."

"Yes, Sugar." strolling to the game section they ran into Caleb. "Hey!" Caleb hugged Gabriel. "Clarence gonna win me a teddy bear." "I gotta see this." Caleb grabbed his phone recording.

"Pick a game any game!" The game attendant sing-songed aloud. Gabriel chose shooting. There were bull's eyes set up on an enclosed field 25 to 400 yards. The farther the range, the greater the reward. She knew his sight was excellent but was he good with a pistol?

"Shot gun or pistol, sir?" Clarence looked at Caleb. shrugging his shoulders. "Which one, coachman?" "Gimme the shot gun sir." Caleb, and Clarence's fiancé, stepped aside, "which range Sugar?" "400."

"Woah. We got a bold one here folks gather round!" People crowded around, especially menfolk. Clarence handed his jacket to Caleb. The women gazed and looked at his sexy physique. He turned to the side holding the rifle as men side betted with the game owner. Gabriel put up $100 for the win. The gun cocked he fell to one knee holding the rifle steady. He moved the rifle over by two inches. "What're you doing Clarence that's off target?" "Quiet Caleb." Gabriel giggled. He took a deep breath holding it.

THE SECRET IS YOU NEVER PULL FAMILY YOU S-Q-U-E-E-Z-E. Bang! "You've three shots sir." "I don't need the other two, thank you." The game master mounted his horse riding down returning with bull's eye in hand. "Give the lady what she wants!" Holding up the bull's eye, men cussed upset. The ladies were joyous. Gabriel collected $200 and a large pot belly panda. "Bye, old friend," the game master handing it to her.

"How? The shot was off Clarence? I know our eyesight ranges far I but didn't know you were such a good shot." "I was a coachman. I to protect the master, right? I learned to shoot long ranges Caleb. Shooting from the carriage to the hills I had to be dead on or we would've died." "Who taught you Daddy?" "Avril he was like a dad to me. He helped raise me. He's buried at house here in Georgia, he, and Isabel. She was like a mom after I was sold away from my real one." "Those were your parents then Clarence." "Yes Sugar, they were."

"How old were you when you turned? Slaves were considered property like a cow or horse. I have no written record of my original birth. According to Zion, my bone structure, body size, and teeth indicate I was about thirty-three guys." "Sugar I'm ready." "For?" "What you wanted earlier." "Taxi!" Gabriel giggled jokingly.

Caleb opened his palm. "Are you donating that gambling money we won to the church Caleb?" "No." "Sure, you are. I partly cheated give 50% to the church Caleb. It would please me." "Yes Pharaoh." "Let me steer the horses, Clarence pleasssse."

"No Sugar well wind up in a ditch. I'll teach you tomorrow." "Promise?" "Yes." Gabriel laid her head on his shoulder as the cool night southern air combined with the gentle rocking of the carriage slowly lulled her asleep. The night was quiet as the half-moon lit the road perfectly before him. Someone was in his head.

*Father? I'm Father now Isaiah? Where's Cody hiding? I'm unsure Great One. You lie for her even though you're clapped in irons. Where's Papa Nate, your grandfather? Here Great One. Papa taught me to reach you telepathically even though I've never tasted your blood."*

*'What did you learn Isaiah?' 'Cross telepathic communication through drinking blood of someone who has had yours Pharaoh.' 'Humm. all you can do is say where Cody is holed up.' 'I can't.'*

Clarence blocked Isaiah in the middle of his lies. He scanned his memories. Cody egged him on to assassinate him. She got Isaiah high, made false promises of loving him, being there, wanting him she bewitched him explaining she'd be hunted no more if he killed him. She lied.

"Sugar we're home. Vampire games; I think I'm going to start them, Sugar." "What is that, Clarence?" "Games of strength like gladiator games, not to the death Gabriel." "I'm unsure, honey, what would be the reason?" "We can discuss it later sweetheart." "Yes, sure Clarence."

Clarence escorted Gabriel inside thinking as they readied to shower. *He was deep in thought. I need to see the skill level each vampire is on and record it. Start keeping records as a security measure because vampires lie. They can't lie if under the pressures of survival. I'll need to show my skills, so they know who they're fucking with.*

# Chapter 15
# Father

The Night of Gabriel's Turn....

"I've been at his side since Safinah died now, he announces he's marrying a human? What does she have that I don't?" Cody paced the floor so hard the baby vampires heard her pounding. She heard Isaiah passing her room, so she quickly snatched the door open and pulled him inside. "Where are you going Zay?" "I'm driving the Pharaoh to Queens." "When you arrive, text the address. I want to send flowers to our new Queen Zay." "You're not upset?" Isaiah asked warily. "Why would I be sweetie?"

"I'm unsure…maybe because you wanted to be Queen? Anyway, I'll text when I arrive." Cody grabbed her jacket skulking outside impatiently waiting for the address to be texted. As soon as it arrived, she hyper-sped to Queens New York from Brooklyn in ten minutes. *I want to see if she's beautiful as I.*

Cody peeped through the window seeing them eat and laugh. When the Pharaoh's bride to be wasn't looking, Clarence gazed upon her, melting as he doted on his bright star. Cody was disgusted.

He never looked at her with such adoration. "If you won't love me, you won't love her." Rage with a dash of anger, a lethal mix. A vampire enraged was a violent recipe for a blood disaster. She circled the house slowly as the savage in her grew impatient. The predator was present and lurking, it wasn't going away. Cody smelled the blood of her prey through the glass window. She stalked, tracing her vein lines with her eyes, pre-selecting her attack spot. She had it planned, she'd kill her for stealing the vampire she loved, robbing her of the dreams she'd for 30 years being his stand in wife. Someone was going to pay for her broken dreams and fractured heart!

Her eyes a blaze the savage knocking wickedly at her soul, clawing to be released. It'd been a decade since it was released free to wreak havoc. Aways able to control it, subdue it, but tonight, the savage demanded blood for the disrespect shown to its master. Cody waited for the house to quiet, tapping the door with her clawed forefinger Isaiah opened the door. She snatched his hair gouging his neck wide open biting deep, ripping his young flesh from his bones leaving a leaking bloody messy hole.

She wanted to kill the boy Clarence raised as his son. If she was going to be destroyed so was her maker. Laying Isaiah's body quietly on the blood drenched floor she crept slowly and silent as taught by her chieftain father how to sneak up on your enemy without being heard. She embraces her native American honing skills to kill the woman he loves.

Moans and giggles escaping the bedroom were shrill upon her ears. Anger gave into rage as she kicked the bedroom door in lunging for Gabriel's throat. She wasn't worthy of her bite popping razor-sharp nails Cody ripped Gabriel's neck across the front, as a jagged cut exposed her insides to the outside world. Blood spattered everywhere on her and Clarence's faces.

She segued out the window leading to the garden below. She heard Clarence whispering words of love through blood-stained tears of undying affirmations speaking to Gabriel. she segued through the window. She heard her Pharaoh yell out in agony, begging his love not to die from the lawn below.

"What had she done?" It was too late for regrets. What was done couldn't be undone. She slammed her cell to the ground, destroying it. She hyper-sped to the nearest bank, withdrawing $1000 then destroying her card.

"Where can I hide?" He had eyes on every corner and beyond there was no place to go. She needed help but who?" "Miss can I borrow your phone please?" "Sure, sweetie," thinking she was helping a 16-year-old girl. "Chance? It's Cody. I'm in trouble, Daddy. Please, help me."

The Hollings Estate....

Papa Nathan and Elder Ann arrived at Clarence's mansion the next night. Niarchos sat outside of Isaiah's cell. Papa came down on the elevator to the jail, four floors below the mansion. He and Elder Ann walked down the corridor to the gate where Niarchos stood. "Open the gate Niarchos." "No Pharaoh's orders" Papa called Clarence who texted Niarchos he opened the cell. Isaiah lay on a cot inside. Papa sat, hugging his grandson.

"What happened, boy?" Niarchos gave Ann his seat and walked down the hall near the elevator to allow them privacy. "Papa?" Isaiah hugged his grandfather crying. "They treat ya, ok?"

"Of course, papa. Niarchos is getting me a radio." "Talk to me boy," "Cody needed help papa Nate. I love her, always have. I didn't know she was going to hurt Gabriel or me papa." "What do you mean?" Ann looked down the hall giving Papa the eye. "Don't speak to anyone except Zion, until we get a vampire attorney Zay." "Why only Zion papa?" "He sired you, it's his job to assist in keeping you alive. What has he done so far?"

"He took blood samples from me as soon as I got here. He also took my clothes to check for residue, and samples from my gun hand.

"Did he ask questions son?" "No papa, he said wait for Elders." "Good Once Elders arrive all you say is between you. No other witness can say what they heard if you were speaking with your lawyer Zay." "Will Clarence, I mean Pharaoh, seek death?"

"He has the right. You tried to kill our king, there are vampires that'll snap your neck for that. Clarence's turns will end your life because he was there when they needed him. He hasn't turned one vampire who didn't ask for it. He rescued me from slavery and whips risking his life to save the lives of children from slavery. He could've left Georgia, but he didn't. He bought our children's freedom." The tears fell from Papa's eyes like huge rain drops, he removed his cotton dress shirt turning his back to his grandson.

Whip marks and gaping wounds adorned the back of his neck and buttocks covering him like an unforgettable shroud. Papa held out his wrists showing Isaiah the cuff marks from irons he'd been forced to wear during sale transfers. He removed his socks and shoes to show him shackle marks cut into his ankles and feet. He held up his forearm to show he was branded. "You see this? Proof I was owned by Massa. Clarence is the vampire who saved me from this!"

Ann cried holding Papa's shoulder. "As I walk through time, the memory of what happened never goes away. These scars are constant reminders. How could you allow a woman to convince you to kill the vampire who set me and ya grandma free?"

Isaiah burst into tears. "I'm sorry, Papa and Grandma."

"He could've passed as a white man and got away with it not helping us not one bit he didn't! He returned for every one of us. He loves us like we're family. We all we got boy!"

Niarchos held his head down, recalling the cruelties of slavery as a child shaking his head at the nasty memories of sexual rapes he endured. He was forced to lay with white women because his manhood was large. He remembered the night the overseer was stopping him from leaving, Clarence stopped it. Niarchos grinned thinking of it. Clarence would always be his hero and father. He'd kill anyone who tried to harm him. Niarchos knew Isaiah would've died had Clarence not pushed his gun.

"I blame myself for not educating my children," Papa began. "I wanted to forget the past so much I forgot to show you how I got here, and the man who made it happen." Isaiah wiped Papa's face with his sleeves and hugged him. "We'll return in two days with a vampire attorney. Think on your action's boy, understand?" "Yes Papa." "Niarchos?" He opened the cell and locked it when they exited. Ann hugged Niarchos, she loved him, he was fair in her eyes. Papa hugged Isaiah goodbye. "You fucked up Zay." "Royally Elder."

Joan & Zion......

Zion lay in bed when he heard a faint knock on his door. It was Joan. She entered, "Can I cuddle with you?" Zion was shocked, "You wanna cuddle an old man when you can have a young one?"

"Have you forgotten we're only a few years apart?" Joan approached the other side of the bed and got under his comforter, drawing close to him, wrapping her arm around his waist, resting her head on his chest. "Is this your first-time cuddling with a vampire?" "Yes." "You afraid Joan?" "Boy, bye."

Zion bellowed out a room filling laugh, "You been hanging with the baby vamps." She smiled, "I look like I'm sleeping with my son." "Don't start that mess again Joan. You know darn well I ain't nowhere near no son's age." He tapped the back of her hand, "Don't worry about Isaiah, alright? I'll do my best for him. You know that, right?" "Yes. What got into him Zion?" "I'm still running tests on his blood. Clarence said the boy was high Joan." "High?!"

"Yes, Clarence called to tell you that Zion? "Yes. He's still helping him. But the council votes on his fate at trial. You know Papa Nate and Grandma Ann are gonna say no. We have eight other coven Elders to worry about. Niarchos is on the fence that leaves seven. All we need is 6 votes for Joan." "You have two Elders; you need four. Lily and Caine you gotta get past Caine Zion." "You know Clarence, Caine, Elijah, and Chance are close Joan they usually vote the same on death trial matters." "Vaughn?" "You may get Vaughn Zion he deals with a lot of young vampire issues he's more understanding."

"Chance adores you Joan speak with him." "You sound jealous." "I'm not." "You are," she teased. "Can we move on Joan?" "Ok. Hehe" "I'm seeking a lawyer, but no one wants to take the case for fear."

"What about Lee? She's quite the attorney. When I was a kid, I heard she retired, living in Cairo. She's not afraid of Clarence, especially since he turned her, they were once lovers Zion. He it bad for her, however she chose her career. He said he wasn't in love, however, I never believed him Zion."

"It doesn't matter sweetie. He's marrying Gabriel. He's enamored with her." "She's a good person Zion, I like her. Every time I bring tea, she says 'you didn't have to or thank you so much.' I tell you; she means it. She's a sweetheart and will make an excellent Queen. She adds zest to Clarence that fills a void in him Zion."

"I'm looking for a psychiatrist to document everything. I never knew Cody would stoop this low. Why involve my grandson in your scheme Zion She's out to hurt everything Clarence loves because she's hurt. Did you know Gabriel isn't allowed to drink any blood but his Zion?" "Yes. It's to protect her. He knows no one will tamper with his blood. He's smart. I'll say that sweetie." "Have you read the scrolls on Clarence, Zion?"

"No, I've heard them at parties when they're read by the scroll writers. The writers read what they select, not what you want to read."

"You're considered a mid-level vampire, and hand to Pharaoh, the scroll library is at your disposal Zion." "Clarence was a hot mess back in the day, smart as hell but with a nasty, violent streak. Few of us today have seen when he was ravenous decades past." "What is he today, Zion?" Zion shook his head. "I'm unsure we don't want to find out Joan d we?" "Read the scrolls it's worth it. Ask for scroll 39 Zion."

"I read it when I was 12. I was in the vault with Papa when they were documenting his story and the scroll was on the table, Let's say Clarence knew I read it. He stated he'd clear my mind if I asked. He assured me he'd never harm me. I chose to keep the memory Zion, read the scroll."

The Gullah Islands......

The mood was set entering the candle-lit cabin rose petal covered floor. "First a traditional carriage ride and now this you make me feel special daddy thank you."

Gabriel approached the bedroom and Clarence followed. She needed the lady's room when she looked down, she had her period. "Man!" "What's wrong Sugar?"

"Nothing," using tissue to make a pad. "I have to go to the store, is there one open Clarence?" "Should be what's wrong, Sugar?" "Can you pass me the phone, please baby?" Clarence restrained himself from scanning her thoughts and tried not to listen to the call. "Hello?" "Hi, may I speak with Zion? It's me Gabriel, Joan?"

"Hold on, Zion It's Gabriel." "Great One is everything ok?" "Yes and no I got my period… hello Zion?" "Yes, Great One I'm here sorry." "Please call me Gabriel." "Gabriel, is it a heavy or light flow?" "Normal, not heavy or light." "Any clotting?" "None so far." "Does the blood look fresh or old?" "I'll take a picture and send it Zion hold on." She took a picture of her pink, red stained panties.

"Sugar you, ok?" "Yes Clarence. I'll be out in a minute!" "Who are you talking to?" She didn't respond "Did you get it,

Dr.?" she whispered. "Yes, it looks normal Gabriel how are you feeling?" "Tired, no more than usual when I have my period." "I'll document it. How are your bowel movements?" "Less now Zion." "It's to be expected. How many per week?" "About 4." "Any headaches, nausea, or weakness?" "No just tired you know?" "Let's count the days if it starts clotting, call. No need to worry its dead blood which is to be expected but no clots larger than your fist ok?" "Yes Zion." "Oh, no tampons. How do I get past Clarence for pads without telling him?" "You don't he's your husband. Goodnight my Queen."

"Goodnight, Dr." Gabriel looked at the panties exhaling soaking them in cold water. She exited the bathroom, dressed.

"We need to go to the pharmacy I need something." "This?" Clarence removed a bag of sanitary napkins.

"Where'd you get them?" She smiled relieved. "Caleb placed them on the carriage seat, it wasn't until now I opened it." "Creepy." "You'll get used to it, trust me. Go run the tub." "Ok," she wrapped herself in a towel, ran the hot tub and turned on the jets. Clarence entered naked, she stared at him in the candlelight. He was well-endowed with 12 inches flaccid. *His dick caused the period*s to herself. Clarence slipped inside the tub. "Come."

"I have my period, and you want to bathe with me?" Gabriel floated over sitting on his lap wrapping her legs around him resting her head on his shoulder. "Its blood doesn't matter where it comes from, I'm nasty. What's the matter, Sugar? Start at the top. "Why do I have a period aren't I dead?" "Honestly, Sugar we don't know. You're the first vampire to be partially alive. Zion is running tests he's an excellent Dr. He'll learn what's going on, patience young vampress." "Ok."

"Next question." "You can't put Isaiah to death daddy." "It's out of my hands Sugar. Evidence will be presented like in human court. He's safer in jail than on the streets. It's against vampire law to mistreat another vampire in custody unless directed to do so by the Pharaoh."

"Do you have say in the vote Clarence?" "Yes." He was hard under her his thoughts trailed off. His penis floated in the water between her legs. She grinded lightly on it rubbing her clit losing her concentration, the warm water combined with clit rubbing and him rimming her hard nipples with his tongue aroused her quickly0.

She couldn't think, her breathing was rapid. "Sugar, you were saying?" he moaned licking her nipples like ice cubes on a warm summer day. "I'm on my period." Gabriel whispered her secret. "So, I've heard." The jets roared tapping her clit and his tip making them extra sensitive.

"Oh god the water is hitting my clit along with the head of your dick." She moaned aloud. "Unn, get it Sugar you love me?" "Yes Daddy. I love you" "Then fuck this dick like you want it." She kept her stride letting the water do the work. "It's fucking huge, and my clit is swollen tight." "Touch me Gabriel." "No." sucking his lip teasing. "Why?" "Cause you're about to cum daddy." Clarence gasped as her legs tightened around him.

"God!" She whined out as he continued to take turns, teasing her nipples, sucking soft then licking hard. "Fuck!" She gazed at him, her eyes a burst of blazing colors. Her fangs extracted, she pushed his head to the left, feeding and creaming. He slid down, entering her pussy. She was always tight because it was that way when she turned. The savage was out of her he knew it as he'd seen it in vampire women prior, but they were never allowed to drink from him. It felt good having a vampress drink from him. He held her down on top of him afraid the water would sweep her away.

"But--"

"But what?"

"You're mine." nibbling her ears. "Say it." as he thrust inside her holding her waist. "Say it," grabbing a fistful of her hair, holding her head back her eyes rolled up in her head. "I'm listening," he growled, fucking her harder. "I'm yours. I belong to you, body, and soul vampire."

He opened his mouth, fangs waiting biting her neck deep into her jugular. "Ahh!" She closed her legs tight as the reality of being engaged to a vampire set in.

"Shh..." He sucked and licked absorbing her pain. He knew it hurt, but he had to do it in case something bad happened to him, and he needed her blood. It was the first time he bit her with four fangs. Safinah fed him and she was human, so he spared her no expense being hybrid. He held her back pounding. "Daddy, I feel like I'm going to faint." Her eyes rolled in the back of her head; she went limp . "Gabriel!"

Hollings Estate New York....

Zion's phone rang early morning hours. "Hello. Wait... slow down, what happened Clarence? She won't wake... how long has it been? About 10 minutes." "She blacked out during sex Zion. I bit her." "With how many fangs Clarence?" "Four. Zion, help me brother. She's convulsing!" *Caleb! OH GOD CALEB HELP ME GABRIEL IS DYING! Caleb was at the bar. He heard him clear across the island,* hyper-speeding he was there in three minutes. Clarence covered her.

"The bite, was too much." Clarence was crying calling her name. "Caleb?" "Yeah Zion? Do you have anything for the worst snake on the island, what type is it, Caleb?" "A black mamba Zion." "Get the antidote Caleb and a syringe, hurry! Clarence call on facetime now!" Clarence called shaking. "What's happening Zion?"

"Gabriel is dying open her eyes let me see her iris.' closer" "Ok her pupils are dilated. Start sucking as hard as possible where you bit her and spit it out. Where's Caleb?" "He went to get the snake medicine." "Keep sucking Clarence." "Gabriel, wake up Sweetie please don't leave me." Caleb rushed in, "I got it!" "Wipe her arm with alcohol." Zion ordered. Caleb rushed to the bathroom while Clarence kept sucking and spitting on the floor.

"Ok pull 100ml about 3.38 oz Caleb." Caleb held the needle to the light, plucking air bubbles out the syringe. "Ok, got it!" "Let me see the needle. Looks good now stick it directly in her heart, inject the antidote." "Zion we're not snakes." "HURRY Clarence!" Clarence took the syringe stabbing Gabriel directly in her heart. "Push it all the way in draw out the needle and perform resuscitation Clarence. Hurry."

"She's spitting out water and blood," Clarence announced, kissing her forehead while holding her limp body. "Caleb, I need you to take a blood sample and refrigerate it in a glass jar please." Caleb did as Zion instructed. He used to work in a negro hospital during the civil war as a trained nurse. Later in life when negro nursing schools came about, he got licensed. "Keep her up for 30 minutes, Caleb." "Her temperature at 104.1 Zion." "Not bad for vampire, guys I've seen worse." In fifteen minutes, Zion called for a temperature check. "Thank God it's dropping 102.2 Zion." Caleb put the sample in the fridge.

"Caleb, swab the blood and saliva Clarence spat on the floor and place it in the fridge please. We'll arrive tomorrow night. Please, arrange a boat at the docks for pick-up, brother. The pilot said we'd leave at 4am. See you soon." Clarence placed a cold rag on Gabriel's forehead.

"Baby, I'm sleepy again." "Caleb, turn on the air conditioner. Make the house cold." "No Clarence." Her voice was weak as a child's. "The cold will keep you awake reversing the disease, Sugar." She looked at Caleb when he returned.

"That's some sex huh?" "Hehe best I ever had." He chuckled at her witty reply. "You're gonna be good, Great One you're with Clarence.

"Clarence, has an hour passed?" "Not yet, Sugar." Her eyes were heavy, they were like iron. "Water, Baby." Caleb sat her up giving her small sips of water. "Thank you." After an hour passed, Clarence and Caleb left her for a minute to get blood and talk. "What the fuck happened, Pharaoh?" "We were having sex. I bit her." "With all four Clarence?" "Yes." "That's a lot of venom. You're the master vampire, the one who has four fangs that's turning venom injected in her times four instead of two. Blood leaving her body to too fast, possibly?"

"I'm unsure." Caleb cleaned while Clarence sat with Gabriel. *She isn't going to die. She's special. I'll consult the cards while she sleeps.* He pulled his tarot deck. He preferred doing readings when people were asleep bedside, their souls were open, they weren't awake to block pathways, truths, or future sights. He would do one on Clarence if he could catch him asleep. Clarence lay next to her worried. "What did I do?" "She's fine. Don't beat yourself up Clarence it was an accident."

Telepathically, Clarence sensed a visitor in his mind.

*"Where the hell have you been?" You miss me, Love? "I do." I felt distress pulling heavy is your new wife, ok? "She will be." I hear she's a good person. Zion sent me an e-mail about Isaiah's charges. "Lee, I can't discuss it with you if you're to be the boy's attorney." That Serious? "Yes. Where are you?" Egypt you know that. "Zion is on his way. He arrives tomorrow. I'll Inform him to call. You were absent from our engagement party?" I wasn't ready to see you in the arms of another. "I understand. I love you always, you know that."*

She exited his thoughts. Clarence never wanted two wives but if he were forced to choose a second one, it would've been her. He was in love with Gabriel, whatever was between them is no more. Lee never allowed him to fall in love with her. He was close to it when she left him. *It would be interesting seeing her again. Damn. Why choose her to defend him? Why pull her out of retirement? She teaches vampire law classes in Egypt five times a year - 5 weeks of classes on the old laws and 5 on the new ones. She hasn't defended anyone since her retirement.*

Joan called while Zion slept. "Clarence? We should arrive in 45 minutes." "The limo and boat are waiting Joan." "How is she?" "Sleeping." "Did she wake up Clarence?" "Twice." "Coherent?" "Yes Joan." "If she wakes again, ask today's date, her name and who's president. I want to give Zion news when he wakes."

"Yes ma'am." "Don't ma'am me, old vampire." Clarence loved banter with Joan, she was quick-witted. "Clarence." Gabriel whispered his name; he hurried up the steps to her. "Thirsty." "Water, tea or blood?" "Coffee."

"Lulu, can you bring up a cup of coffee, light and sweet please?" "Yes sir. In five minutes, there was a faint knock. "Enter." Lulu entered with a coffee tray. Clarence took the cup Gabriel whispered, "Thank you." "You're welcome, ma'am."

She sipped. "Mmm java is life…" She held her mouth. "What Sugar?" "What is this it wonderful?" "Coffee roasted in human blood ma'am." "What?" Clarence smelled the coffee. He smelled the blood hidden in the roast. "How does it taste Great One?" "Like heaven." Clarence tasted it. "No, I'm throwing it out." "No, you won't Clarence." Gabriel clutched the mug close.

"Where did this come from Lulu? How dare you give the Queen this coffee without permission when you know she's already ill." "Honey? Don't yell at her, please." "Don't drink it, Gabriel. I'm unsure whose blood is roasted in the beans." Gabriel put down the mug remembering Mammy T's advice. It's someone else's blood Sugar. Lulu left, thinking she was trying to help. As she left, Clarence sat on the side of the bed with his head in his hands thinking about the weight of protecting a wife again. "Do you regret being with me Clarence?"

"Never Gabriel. Sugar, you worry much. Lay with me," patting his chest. She obliged picking up his wrist to feed. He drew her as close as possible with his free arm as he sang, her to sleep.

Let me to call you sweetheart I'm in love with you let me hear you whisper. You love me too. Keep the love light glowing in your eyes true. Let me call you sweetheart I'm in love with you.... Clarence kissed her forehead, cutting out the light.

# Chapter 16
# Joan & Zion

Hollings Estate

Georgia 1965....

Joan wanted to travel with them as vampires, but her mother forbade it. "You'll never be vampire so its best you don't fall in love with them or date them."

Joan listened to her mother until the day Clarence came home with a young black Dr. from Georgia. He was there on business and saved a young man from the kkk. It wasn't odd for Clarence to bring people home he'd saved from violence. During this time in her life, Joan's mother was dying, she assumed her mother's position as lead maid. She'd been groomed for this moment lifelong. When she married, Clarence gifted her the cottage outback for privacy, which she adored.

When her husband returned home from Vietnam in a flag covered box there was nothing left to do but raise their daughter and keep the house under the tutelage of her dying mother who was 88. All the family members came to see her mom.

When the Dr. diagnosed her mom with three months remaining, Papa placed a bed in her room, sleeping there until her passing. This gave comfort to the children in his bloodline, Papa being there for every birth and death.

Joan was 30 when introduced to the young Dr. who tended to her mother before her demise. As soon as she saw him, she was smitten. He was handsome with a baseball player's build. A dark-skinned vampire with curls that sat on his head like large round bubbles. It was the 60's, his face was clean, shaven, with a short haircut.

He wore a white fedora hat with a navy-blue suit. The fedora was a navy one, and when he tilted his hat locking eyes with Joan, his eyes were a gorgeous vampire blaze.

"Joanie," as Clarence called her, "this is Zion." He stretched his hand to shake hers, she stared speechless, looking foolish. "Joan?" "I'm sorry, Zion, it's a pleasure to meet you." "Pleasure, ma'am," smiling with perfect teeth. "I'll show him to his quarters Joan." The vampires walked away chatting. Joan entered the kitchen grabbing a glass of ice water. No vampires, she reminded herself. "Mommy who are you talking to?" Her eight-year-old daughter, Anya inquired. "Is a newly made vampire here?"

"Not sure if he's new, you stay clear, at least while he controls the thirst." "Yes, Mommy." Joan grabbed a large mason jar filling it with ice water carrying it to the vampire floor where he slept. Before she could knock, "Enter." Joan opened the door. "How'd you know I was here?" "I heard your footsteps." "I'm sorry if I alarmed you. I brought water."

"All for me?" "Yes, it's cold. It's warm out I didn't want you getting thirsty, not knowing your way to the kitchen. Thought this would hold you till morning." "Thank you, kindly ma'am."

"You're welcome Mr.--"

"Dr. Zion Donovan."

"Irish?" "My grandfather was a black Irishman, born in Ireland through indentured servitude. He came to America after he served his time. A mistake he begged our forgiveness for until his death." "Goodnight, Sir." "Please call me Zion."

2020 Present Day

"Baby," She shook his arm, "We're here." Zion slept the entire trip. He grabbed the bags before he knocked. When the door opened, Clarence hugged him so tight he thought he'd break a rib. Clarence led them to Gabriel. She and Caleb were watching TV.

Gabriel hugged Joan. "Happy you're here Joan" She liked Joan as most people did, especially the women of Clarence's past. Its Joan who didn't like the array of women coming and going after Safinah's passing.

Gabriel was sweet, reminding her of Safinah. "I got your bag." "Thank you!" "Clear the room please, I need time with my patient." Clarence, Joan, and Caleb exited while Clarence remained in her head telepathically listening. Gabriel tapped her head and Zion nodded then whispered, "Brother, it's ok. You can let go." Gabriel shook her head yes, letting Zion know he released her thoughts. Zion checked her vitals and reflexes. He conducted a breast exam inquiring about pain there. He pricked her finger checking sugar levels. All was normal as expected for someone like her – a vampire hybrid.

Her eyes healthily were vampire-colored, a good sign. He checked inside her hair for knots, bumps, or bruises. Zion removed a list of 50 questions inquiring about her medical past then, had her sign a medical records release request from the human hospital. As her new physician he wanted to know how medically fit she was when she was human as well as any pregnancies, abortions, or miscarriages. Zion administered activated charcoal and prescribed a vitamin B shot. "For the loss of blood," handing her the tablets. "You must ask Clarence if I can take those, Zion." "You're my patient I won't ask permission to treat you Gabriel." "He's overprotective. Please, do it for--"

Zion tapped her knee, using an inside voice. "Brother, come." Clarence entered. "Gabriel needs activated charcoal to cease the stray venom, and a vitamin B shot for loss of blood."

"Give it to her. Why are you asking?" Zion looked at Gabriel, who looked away. "Sugar Zion is my brother; I trust him with my life and yours. You can take anything he gives. He'll never harm you, alright?"

"Yes Clarence." "I'm sorry, Sugar. I'm making you as paranoid as I." "Yes, you are." Zion chimed in breaking the tension. "I'm doing a before and after blood testing. I'll return in an hour to get another sample after the medication. Can you stand Gabriel?" "Yes." "I'd like you to exercise around the house today. Do nothing strenuous. Would you like to sit on the patio with Joan for tea?" "Yes, please." They exited the bedroom to speak as Gabriel dressed.

"What do you think it is Zion?" She's half human. That's why she has food cravings. I'm not 100% sure but when you bit her that's enough venom to turn a human. From what I'm guessing, two fangs are feeding fangs and two are used for turns. I've never asked this of you but I'm going to need a venom sample." "How?"

"I'll have you bite into something. I may be able to save turns from dying and counteract the venom if it's too strong." "I'm unsure if I want people to know about me. It's a breach of security Zion." "I understand. What if I document it and give you the findings to keep in a location only known to you know?" "You'd have it in your head, Dr. as long as you're alive, it's a breach of security. There are people who'll hurt you for your knowledge. It can fall in the wrong hands, creating a war between vampires and humans."

"I won't let it happen Pharaoh." "I made a promise to your mother no harm would befall you. It hurt her when she discovered white folks strung up her son. I intend on keeping my promise." "I'm not a child Great One. I can defend myself."

"You're my vampire child my son or have you forgotten your vampire blood oath to me Zion? I'll make a deal with you. When you become one of our dingo pack, I'll consider it." "Why?" "If you're captured, the way to free yourself is to shift handcuffs. Zip ties don't fit dog paws. No one expects a dog to walk out of holding. This is why we keep the change secret. If you change, we can revisit this agreed Dr.?" "Yes." "Niarchos hasn't changed Clarence." "Niarchos is huge doesn't mean it won't happen Zion." "What about Caleb?" "Seers don't change. What's wrong with my bride?" "I'll know after results are in."

Gabriel felt good wearing her comfortable clothes. She walked downstairs barefoot to avoid falling. She met Joan on the patio to enjoy the sunset. "Hey girl" Joan handed her iced tea.

"I'm unsure if I can drink this," Gabriel teased looking over her shoulders. "Mmm girl don't upset me." Joan giggled. "I remember when he and Safinah weren't speaking for weeks. Girl, I watched the king of vampires lose himself. She'd go out by day and stay out. He swore she was with a man one day. Safinah woke and Clarence locked the doors instructing us not to let her out. But my mother said, "Don't unlock this door.""

"I witnessed a 68-year-old woman climb out the bathroom window *'Nobody stops this ole slave from being free.'* She waved at Clarence from the yard taunting the vampire as she ran to the bus. He stood in the window watching her in the sun. The second, I mean the instant, the sun disappeared, he left on foot following her scent to town. Clarence arrived catching chatting up a man in front of a vintage 1950 beautiful mint condition white Cadillac"

"She traded things she owned of value for this car remember I said she took the bus? Here he comes… big, bad, your new husband was about to take the man's head off. *'This is who you've been running around on me with?'* The salesman asked, *'Who's your son? No, my husband. Oh, you like 'em young, eh?*

"Safinah and the salesperson laughed of course, Clarence thought it was at his expense you don't laugh at an angry vampire, he grabbed the man off his feet. He controlled himself from revealing he's vampire. The sales associate removed Cadi keys shaking them screaming. *'She purchased you a car! She's making drapes for my wife in exchange for the Cadillac.'* The man peed his pants. Safinah kept begging Clarence to put the man down. "Hahaha, that's too funny. Girl, he worries too much." "I know Gabriel but there's nothing he won't do for you he loves you."

"Enough of me. What's up with you and Zion? you were in his bedroom when he called. Love connection girl?" "I hope Gabriel." "You love him, Joan?" "For years. I could've been turned when I was younger however it's forbidden 'cause I'm papa's blood. It's not fair, it shouldn't be up to a treaty. It should be our choice. I went before five Elders, they refused, afraid the flood gates would open, and the other family would want to be turned. I don't look my age, do I Gabriel?" "No, but black don't crack Joan hehe"

"Zion wanted to marry me when I was 31, but he was clear he wanted a vampire wife. He didn't want to fall in love and bury me. Papa wouldn't bend we ceased speaking eight years. Zion and I have been apart since then. We're taking it slow and I'm ok with that Gabriel." "He's a good vampire Joan I'm sure you'll be together." "Are you having a wedding shower Gabriel?"

"Things have been advancing fast. I don't have family or many friends." "You have family, or didn't you see your engagement party girl?" "Will you host one Joan please?" "I'd be honored."

Zion scanned the spare bedroom. He removed his petri dishes, microscopes, and other items setting up a temporary lab. He reused the sample from Gabriel's turn the other sample was taken weekly for him to compare. He dropped the tray on the table pacing, frustrated with Clarence for not relinquishing the venom sample. He needed it to connect what was happening to Gabriel. "Joan!" Zion called. "Yes?" Joan entered. He grabbed her, hugging her tight.

"What's wrong Zion?" "I'm sorry I didn't marry you when we were younger and that I didn't turn you and deal with it later." "You could've been put to death Zion, it's ok." "No, it's not my love." "Were you listening to Gabriel and I on the patio?" "No, I was working. I put your bags in my room." dropping little kisses all over her face and neck. "You're sure about this Zion going public?" "Never been surer love." Joan tiptoed for a kiss when she turned to use the bathroom, he slapped her butt.

Zion wanted to make it special for Joan as it was their first time. He activated the six head showers and invited her in. Then, he rubbed her with soap, watching as the water slid down hugging her melanin skin. He kissed her back and neck rubbing the soap on her vagina, stroking her clit. Moans and sighs escaped her unwillingly, so she sat on the bamboo bench because her legs betrayed her.

She wanted his touch. He kneeled under misty rain shower head warm water cascading on them resting in all the right places. Zion placed her legs on his shoulders licking up and down her pussy like a frosted cupcake topping it off with a suck of her cherry-colored clit. He repeated it, demanding his prize - his cream cum coated tongue.

He loved the large amount of cream shot down his throat. It made her night, she wanted to see him look at her as he fucked her, she watched the fire in his eyes to see if they'd switch colors when he cums She exited the shower grabbing a towel, making her way to their bedroom warmed by the Georgia heat seeping through the open windows.

Joan lay on the bed, showing off her freshly waxed pussy legs wide open inviting him in Zion placed her feet firmly on his shoulders. He spread her legs at arm's length pushing inside her he inhaled, smelling her sexiness, feeling her wet excitement over him. He kept stroking Joan till he heard her wheezing. *Asthma?* He knew the sound. "Babe?" "Keep going Zion."

He kept up deep steady strokes, pushing 10 throbbing inches dick deep. Joan clutched his back, sinking her nails into damp skin. Her smell and expressions excited him. She was so wet, he lost control pushing her to the wall pussy pounding. Clarence and Gabriel heard the banging. It was her night he showed her how much she meant to him. Gabriel's jaw dropped like a little kid making Clarence laugh. Joan sucked Zion's neck as he came, leaving a temporary hickie before dropping on the bed uncovered, gasping for air. Zion went for her asthma pump. She slept before he could get to her. Zion cuddled her as he slept for the second time in five years.

The visceral scream of a woman rang out in wee morning hours. Clarence rushed to Zion's room. Joan stood in a corner, shocked and pointing. Clarence looked to the other side of the room, as a young dingo approached him. Clarence picked him up sensing it was going to happen due to his heightened agitation, smell and long sleep when traveling.

"I've been waiting for you Zion."

Joan fainted.

# Chapter 17
# Meet Your Maker

Clarence picked Joan up calling Caleb telepathically. He arrived in ten minutes. "He's tiny. I never saw you all when you first shifted. Were you this small?" "I'm unsure." Caleb took a picture for Zion. "What's her issue?" Caleb asked, staring at Joan. "She fainted. They thought it was a rumor about us being dingos. I'll make her think Zion went to town for a few days." "I gotta see this." Clarence held Joan in his arms gently. When she opened her eyes, she was afraid.

"Shhh...," stroking her face keeping her in a state of twilight. "You made love to Zion; you'll recall I sent him to town a few days to get medicine for Gabriel. He'll see you in a week, is this understood Joanie?" "Yeessss." "You'll wake rested. Goodnight Joan." "Goodnight Clarence." she slurred. Clarence put her in bed carrying a sleeping Zion in his arms

"What's up with the housekeeper? I heard you petrified the gal by yelling at her." "She served Gabriel blood roasted coffee Caleb." "Did you allow her to explain Clarence? She tried to pitch a business venture. What's his name back in the day? Garret--

Garrett Morgan.

Yes, he tried to sell you shares on that heart do dad thingy you said no. 'When it's time for humans to die, they should' were your words, now look now…The heart pacemaker Pharaoh." "I messed up Caleb." "Sure did." You're doing it again, give Lulu a chance besides when did you stop investing in the solid dreams of black folk? You're our Pharaoh, our dream weaver, you make dreams reality. If not you who Clarence?"

"I gotta go downstairs and get my phone, Clarence closed his eyes. When he opened them, he was on the kitchen floor. He grabbed the phone thinking, *"What happened?"*

"What the hell was that, Clarence?" "A new gift I'm guessing Caleb." "Superhuman strength, speed, agility, reflexes, breathing under water, endurance, stamina, senses, healing, adaptation, and our durability are superior to humans. If they had the gifts as humans, it's amplified once vampire. They can taste blood and see truths or lie I know of one vampire who has that gift." Caleb stared at Clarence.

Set up a coffee tasting with this girl of yours. Invite vampires on the island for a meet and greet." Zion barked Clarence wrapped him in a blanket. "Vampire games is what I'll call it. What do you think of skill matches Caleb, top vampire battles?" "Vampire Elders can't enter Clarence. I won't fight my brothers and sisters." "Agreed Caleb." "We're having it here on the Gullah. We'll keep the money here for our people. Must find an arena. This is going to be better than the gladiator games of Rome Clarence…" "Without death Caleb, I don't want anyone slain. We can't have games before we find Cody Caleb, why can't you get a handle on her? When she sleeps, her guard is down. I need you to find her."

"I got it Clarence hear this idea. This competition may smoke her ass out. We'll invite vampire exiles; who must fight for coven reinstatement and pardons Clarence." "There's gotta be rules put in place governing their return. Put them under Niarchos Caleb. You know he'll kill any vampire if they get out of hand."

"Will you tell stories at the coffee tasting? I'm going to tell my coven for the first time how I was made, they always ask and you?" I'll let them choose Caleb."

Zion hadn't turned back, and Joan kept calling his cell the next morning. Gabriel went to the shops with Joan to get her mind off Zion. Clarence went to shower and when he reentered, Zion lay on the bed, confused. Clarence locked the bedroom door. "Welcome back, brother." "What happened Clarence. Why am I in your bed naked?" Clarence removed his phone sharing of himself holding Zion as a dingo. Zion held the phone in shock. "When we're dingos, we can eat food and walk in the sun. I gave you a hamburger Zion." "Did I love it, Pharaoh?" "Look," he showed a video of him eating a burger he cooked.

The coffee tasting event....

Gabriel dressed casually in a pair of jeans, a fancy black sequin tank top adorning the pearls Niarchos gifted her. Her nails were painted. Her hair was silk pressed by a local vampress. "You look beautiful, Sugar."

"We match hehe," Clarence wore black jeans and a tank accenting his large biceps, long wild hair and a gold link chain dripping with Hollings diamonds, a matching bracelet and a vintage 1978 Rolex. The medallion was a glass gold globe in the center two carats of loose mini diamonds.

Gabriel held the globe shaking it, looked her fiancé in the eyes asking, "Is this real?" Clarence laughed incessantly. Caleb insisted on knowing what made the vampire laugh, who rarely does. Gabriel held the chain looking seriously at Caleb. "Do you think this is real?" Including Caleb in the joke. Gabriel pulled Clarence aside privately handing him a remote control. "What's it for Sugar?" "Read my thoughts." Clarence opened his mouth, shocked.

"It's inside you? Yes, when you hit the button, it vibrates on my clit. You can make me cum all night." You sure about this Sugar?" looking devious. "Are you drinking intoxicated blood tonight, Gabriel?" We're trying new blood blends and coffee. It's a tasting I wanted to surprise you to see if you like a specific blood blends." She kissed him happy she was allowed to try new blood, "Thank you, Baby."

The living room was filled with fairy lights and paper flowers hanging from the 19ft wooden ceiling. There were old photos of Clarence in the room through the years. Gabriel looked at them with him as they walked around. "You were a confederate soldier?" "One of my costumes to help free slaves to the border." "You looked handsome. What about this one?"

"I was on my way to the slave auction. Safinah snapped it before I segued, she made the garments herself." "Who's the little girl in this one Clarence?"

"She was our daughter. Rose. Safinah and I raised her." "Is she alive?" "No, she could've had her coven been a vampire Elder. May I discuss what happened another time, Sugar?" "Sure." Gabriel saw the hurt in him. There was a lot she needed to learn about him. The live band arrived. They looked like an old school 1940's swing band. "Where's Caleb Clarence "Right here darling." He entered with his coven. Gabriel and Clarence sat in front of the fireplace holding hands.

"Allow me to introduce you to my coven. Arise, children." They rose from bended knee, smiling at the man on a personal level they'd only heard of. "Please enjoy yourself. Drink, mingle and allow the humans in." Everyone was jolly as Caleb read from the list, "We're going to hear from a bright young lady who put us on the map with science contests. She has received several scholarships offers from Ivy League schools. Without further ado, I present Ms. Lulu Cartwright." The crowd whooped as she approached the front. "Thank you." She stood next to the royal couple reading notes as samples were served.

"Great Ones, it's a pleasure to stand in your presence. A few years ago, I worked in a coffee shop discovering how much money the coffee business generates annually after conducting basic research. I went to the lab and created an arabica hybrid bean grown from soil, watered with a synthetic blood and sugar blend. The blood is lab-generated safe from my own ingredients, and it's taken ten years to perfect. The sugar cane has been doused and grown in an identical solution."

Someone handed Gabriel a mug. Caleb handed one to Clarence. *Did you pour this Caleb? asking* telepathically. *Yes, stop worrying.* "Vampires are not allowed to drink anything except blood and water Lulu continued, or they get ill as Elder Caleb has pointed out. Thank you, Elder. I give you Pharaoh's Coffee, a blood blend-roast SALUTE" Mugs were raised but no vampire dare sip until Clarence and Gabriel had.

Clarence sipped as vampires watched his reaction. "Mmm… this is good," he wasn't lying. "I'm waiting to get ill." vampires laughed with him. "Pharaoh, I'm sorry about before," Lulu apologized. "Water under the bridge, child." Zion drank the whole cup. It'd been decades since he had coffee he was elated. Clarence thought the same, "I haven't had a cup since the 1800's." he shared aloud.

Caleb carried the coffee pot, serving Gabriel seconds. "Pharaoh, if I may?" Caleb handed him a black bag with a gold foil face of King Tut on the front the words read, 'Pharaoh's blood roast.' "I'm proposing we go global distribution with vampire coffee in every vampire clubs, restaurants, spas, hotels, gaming houses and casinos. We'll market it as grown directly from the Gullah Islands in Georgia, home, and birthplace of our Pharaoh!" Clarence smiled, nodding at the idea. The room of vampires hooted and barked happily. Clarence rose, the room grew silent.

"Lulu, have you written a proposal for the Queen?" "Yes, sir." "She'll read and return it to Elder Caleb will that work?" "Yes, sir." She was overjoyed hugging Gabriel. The crowd sighed shocked until Gabriel returned her affections. After a while of talking, mingling, and enjoying coffee with various blood blends Caleb invented, he stood tapping his whiskey glass with a fork getting everyone's attention.

"Take your seats. Hope everyone is eating, drinking, and enjoying I'm unsure if you're aware Pharaoh however, my coven has never heard how I became vampire." The lighting dimmed as candlelight set the mood.

Elder Caleb Origins....

"I was a slave on a plantation 75 miles west from here. I was owned by an oppressor. I oversaw his books and paperwork. I had no other duties, and I was forbidden to do any work but prepare him for trips. I'd travel with him but never abroad as slavery didn't exist in other countries. Many slaves gained freedom abroad with no help from the law to retrieve lost property. He wasn't going to allow the same fate to befall him since he'd trained me from childhood."

"He owned a four-floor library with a mezzanine carefully without teaching me to read, he taught me to file the books and scrolls properly. Every afternoon, he'd give his daughter's reading and writing lessons. Unbeknownst to him, I learned with them. When they were taught to play the violin, harp and how to read music, I also learned. It was my job to put the music sheets, books and scrolls back. As I filed them, I read them. By the time I was 15, I secretly drafted a book using paper and pencils the daughters would desugared. When attempting to write music or love letters. Using hair ribbon and a leather warped leather ledger, I kept my writings hidden within the floorboards of the library. This continued until I was 23. At 17, I'd met another slave I fell in love with. She dressed the master's daughters. Together she and I asked permission to marry. He agreed if it didn't interfere with our chores. I made sure it didn't. At 24, with a two-year old daughter..." The crowd gasped.

"Yes, I had a wife and child." The room became pin-drop quiet. "Some years passed, and my wife met a woman who came onto the plantation when she was drawing water from the well. The woman spoke of freedom, a subject we visited secretly. She explained we would walk north to get it. She'd gone that way many times. She visited plantations, asking slaves brave enough to flee. She allowed my wife ten minutes to get me and our daughter, which wasn't hard because it was day's end, and we were retiring to the slave shacks. My wife came to the big house, whispering to grab my book and follow her I did."

"Once we arrived beyond the fence the woman waited. My wife grabbed fruits, food, and scraps from the kitchen garbage plus whatever she could salvage for our daughter. The woman said to bring scraps of cloth, salves, pepper, bullets, and weapons, if possible. I tied my daughter securely to my wife's back with rags. I wrapped the book tight with more rags as we began the journey to freedom. The woman explained it would be a long journey but there'd be rest and sometimes, we needed to keep our daughter from crying. If we couldn't, she'd give her a root to help her sleep."

"When we heard blood hounds we quieted. When they distanced from us, we crossed a river. One of the blood hounds spotted us alerting the slave catchers. We crossed a rushing river, my book dropped in the raging river. I chased it down stream. The woman grabbed my wife and child pulling her from following me forcing her to go forward, then she came for me."

"The book floated away, the slave catchers were so close, we could hear their voices. The woman drew a dueling pistol from her skirts and said, 'Let's go leave without the book or Ise leave ya behind.' I declined then; she shot me in my chest." He picked up his tee shirt, showing the bullet wound to the room. Vampires were in tears. "It missed my heart by inches. I was sure to die, my arteries were knicked and blood floated into the water. She walked over my body to shoot me in the head when a man stepped in front of me demanding she stop." *'Move, white man. This be no business of yours,'* she held her pistol to his head, but this man covered me with his body, taking a bullet for me in his back. The woman was shocked when the bullet pushed out of his flesh onto the muddy riverbank."

'I ain't not white Ise a slave like ya. Dis man is good as dead, leave or dey catch ya.' 'I knowed where ya is iffin Ise caught, Ise comin fo' ya, white slave. Harriet Tubman be's da last name ya hear fo I takes ya life. I ain't knowed what ya is, but I sho finds a way ta kill ya.' "With that she fled."

When the slave catchers arrived, the man who saved me held his gun on me. This is your nigger, sir? Yes, He tried to escape but I caught him. You sure you be fine sir? I'm fine loading me on his wagon.

"I came to bleeding out, the white man sat next to me on this very floor. *Do you wanna die? Blink once for yes, twice for no.* I think I blinked twice 'cause I'm standing here. *'I'm gonna gift ya life eternal, but you'll be damned ta never walk in sunlight. You must feed on the blood of men or animals to survive. Do you want this gift?*

"I blinked twice; he placed his hand on top of my chest. With four fangs, he bit into my flesh. It hurt way worse than the bullet I'd taken. He poured blood in my mouth, and I blacked out. When I awoke, I was vampire. My mouth tasted like metallic, teeth stained with blood."

"I had a bad knee; I didn't anymore. The asthma I suffered gone. I woke 3 weeks later with a stronger gift - the gift of sight. It was crisp, clear, and concise. I slept through my entire turn, the first thing I remember is waking, crying. I was heartbroken thinking how foolish I'd been returning for a damned book! Instead of seeing my wife and child to safety, watching my baby girl grow into a woman a...cursed book...damn that book!" One day our king returned from a business trip in the north. He sat with me fireside delivering good and sad news.

'Your wife and child made it up north Caleb. How do you know Pharoah? I saw the woman who shot you one time since your turn, caught up to her up north. She stated they lived with a white family, a good one, not mean like these are down here. She was working as a housekeeper for fair wages. Some people helped with our cause of freeing slaves. Your wife and daughter were told you drowned.

"Why?" I asked upset. Harriet shot you Caleb with that shot, you be dead. How is it you live? We cannot risk anyone finding out what we're, I'm sorry.

"I cried for a year mourning the loss of my wife, child, and book. The life I could've had as a married free man and father. Thankfully, I'm alive due to this vampire, my brother, friend, maker, and father." He pointed in Clarence's direction.

Vampires wiped tears, smiling, laughing, and clapping Caleb hugged Clarence. "I didn't know you play the harp Caleb, can you?" Gabriel requested His coven shouted "Yes!" Jovial laughter filled the room.

Telepathically Clarence requested a performance *Caleb, will you play for me? Of course, Pharaoh.* Caleb sent members of his coven for his harp. The caterers passed out dessert - more coffee blood and wines. Joan brought Gabriel a large hot cup of tea with lemon. The room once again watched in awe to see her drink without illness.

"Without further ado, our king, our Pharaoh let's give a warm welcome. Clarence stood, "I'll do it differently tonight. What would you like to know about me?" No one called out. "Don't speak all at once." Laughter filled the room. One male vampire raised his hand, "Pharaoh, may I?" "Yes, you may. I'd like to hear of a time you were truly afraid and how you overcame this fear." No one dared leave, no one wanted to miss this. Some vampires sat on pillows arranged on the floor, while couples were snuggled up.

He thought of telling them about the night he turned. He never heard the story read it in the scrolls. He was looking forward to this moment as much as Gabriel. "I was a young married vampire. Back then marriage was a privilege. My wife was human, we were slaves together on the same plantation. We didn't marry until after I was bitten.

The first Queen loved people much like the present Queen. She used to acquire vintage items, trading them for new goods to sell or keep buying me gifts although we were beyond wealthy. She wanted to buy it with her 'own' money vampires you know how vampresses can be." The vampires nodded, agreeing jokingly.

"There was a wealthy white woman who sold a complete set of her mother's bone china from France. Safinah paid purchasing the china in a signature keepsake box. It was 7 a.m. when she went to the trader's market. A white man walked up examining the china. He lay it down and left, then returned with the constable demanding he arrest Safinah for stolen goods which was a hanging crime. It was custom-made for his mother her name was on the back of each plate. Without explanation, they arrested Safinah. A white woman, spoke on her behalf explaining it was a mistake. They insisted on making a public spectacle of her by dragging her out of the market clapped in irons. My Queen in irons! Back then, I had no telepathic abilities. Yes, I'm telepathic." he chuckled.

"Therefore, I had no way to communicate with her. One of the black women from town who knew where Safinah lived, sent her 9-year-old who went running to fetch Safinah's Massa, not husband although Massa and husband were identical. Elder Lily, who was the steward of the household at the time, was not vampire yet. She opened the door hearing the dreadful news. I heard the child upstairs. As soon as the sun set, I went into town with Elders Elijah, Chance and Caine who were human. Elder Chance, who's my first turn, returned to the plantation standing guard in our absence."

When we arrived at the jail, I was dressed as a proper slave owner with the paperwork showing that I sent my slave to town to trade and make purchases on my behalf, and I gave her the money to purchase these items of value as well. I brought out the book showing the day I gave Safinah the money, proof I owned her as a slave though I never did. People were kinder with the law if I were to take responsibility for her actions as a slave. As a free woman, she'd have to hang."

"I showed the bill of sale signed by the man's daughter for $3 for a full set of china. The sheriff had gone for the day, he was not to return until the next morning. Anything could happen to her overnight - rape, or a murder which they'd claim was by accident, of course. I explained nothing better happen to my property, and I meant nothing or I'd have an attorney there to sue who ever touches or harms her, demanding they be jailed for the amount she cost me plus interest of loss as the girl had been a slave since I was a child and was a gift from her deceased parents. They better see that not a hair on her head is harmed. Back then, my tear ducts were dry so I couldn't cry. I couldn't leave when the sun was coming up, I couldn't leave!"

Clarence's voice was filled with passion and anger. Everyone's souls quaked at his emotion as it rattled the room. Vampires cried. Clarence walked outside the circle clockwise they formed on the large living room floor.

"Children and family, there are no friends here. What I need you to understand is this woman, this person held the heart and soul of this vampire in the palm her hand. If her life were to end, mine would end with hers. I already murdered her rapist he was my first human kill. I hadn't anything to lose. I was the prominent white owner of a plantation. I owned 60% of the sugar cane fields and 40% of the tobacco and cotton fields by age 40."

"Money! I thought returning to the sheriff's office. *I don't have time for this! How much? I have business in three counties in the morning. Sorry sir, we must wait on the sheriff before accepting a donation,* though I knew he wanted to take it if a new employee hadn't been present. Elijah and Caine and I slept in the carriage. Caine woke walking around the jail to find Safinah's window open at 4am. The sun was due to rise at 5am. I could smell the sun."

*Cotton,* I called her. She stood on her bed holding the bars. I wrapped my milky white hands around her chocolate ones. 'Did they harm you, love? *No Clarence.* 'One been real nice tellin me make sho I tell ya bout it when ya comes mornin. Go home, coachman. That's what she called me. It was the job I was enslaved to do."

"Today, I'd be called a chauffeur." I approached the coach wrapping myself in 5 blankets. I bent to my knees, properly dressed, and dug with these two hands a hole 5-feet deep. I then lay in the ground with a top over my face. Elijah and Caine covered me with earth outside her window in a dark alleyway, yes children I ordered them to bury me alive. I heard Safinah speaking telling me what was happening although I couldn't reply. *The sheriff is in court late. 'It be 3 o'clock, coachmen. He's not here, he's at a public hanging.*

"Elijah left after inquiring on my behalf, 'I'm fine.' I responded. I heard her while I was in the ground asking, 'Transferred where? Is it in this jail or another? This jail, where?" I heard they were moving her within the jail till I heard her no more, the feelings I was experiencing were cataclysmic. The sun was bearing down through fresh earth, warming but not touching me. Fear crept through me. Where was she transferred to for this fictitious crime? What if they kill her? What if?"

"After what felt liked forever, Elder Caine and Elijah unearthed me as the sheriff entered 15 minutes prior. Elder Elijah briefed me as to what had happened as I changed into fresh clothing. *The sheriff has letters from the mayor and county clerk's office to aid you in any way you need. I explained what had occurred. I wrote a note in your hand on formal stationery adding your signature and signet. I said you sent it.* I hugged him thanking whatever god listened for me to teach him to read and write. This is why it's important not to keep each other down as black people but as brother Malcolm X, taught Each one, teach one."

*"The sheriff offered a coffee. I took it pretending to sip, spitting back in the cup. The bailiff brought her up unharmed. I showed no affection. 'What did you do?' I asked. 'Nothing Massa but sell dem good you gimme to.' 'Is this true?' I inquired of the sheriff. I presented him with the signed receipt. 'May I hold this to show her brother his sister sold the china?' 'Of course, as long as I get it back.' 'Of course,' the sheriff said. 'May I collect my wench and go? It has been a long day.' 'Of course, sir.' They removed her irons. 'Elijah?' 'Yes Massa.' 'Take her to the wagon.' I rose to leave. 'Sir? the*

*Sherriff called as I wiped the wretched Georgia heat from my brow. 'Yes? I replied. 'The night guard mentioned a donation...' He looked afraid to speak. 'Oh yes, for you.*

"I removed $500 from my billfold. *I'll assume this shall cover this incident and any others. Going forward, you will see this once per year provided, we do any business, there shall be no need to see my face or my wench in irons, agreed?* Of course they agreed. Once privately down a dark road, Elijah stopped the carriage and Safinah exited the front coach entering the carriage with me. We drew the curtains, kissed, and petted the rest of the way home. Let us say those proper clothing items I wore were almost off."

"It would be 100 years later I met a beautiful woman who offered me tea. She served me with a teacup and saucer from the exact set my first wife was jailed for attempting to sell a century earlier." Gabriel inhaled shocked *"Is it true?* telepathically messaging. *Yes Sugar, it is. It's an extremely small world.*

The crowd clapped and snapped with love, some even shed tears. The coven was jovial to hear something personal about their king.

"Game time," Caleb said, standing up. "Since you're telepathic and can read minds, let's play 'what're they thinking'." "Ok," Clarence smiled, showing his top fangs. Clarence walked around the room touching a male vampire. "No, I never whipped a slave as I was a free one. "I won't answer what you're thinking," Clarence blushed as he touched a girl. "I don't have a favorite color. I'm unsure what sign I'm because I don't have a birth certificate."

He touched a human. "I play piano, I learned from Beethoven himself." He removed his hand and put it back. "Yes, he was black." He touched vampire male, "What's the worst thing you witnessed during slavery?" He heard his thought and said it aloud. The room was silent once more. "Using babies for sport and I won't go into details with vampresses present. However, I'm sure you can imagine the horror."

Someone was blocking him from getting in, a skill not possessed by a new vampire but why the block? He wondered. He walked till he got closer to the block, touching the girl next to the blocker.

"Yes, they used to make us have sex with each other to make more slaves they'd blindfold us. We didn't know who we were impregnating as slaves. We could be having sex with our own mother and not know it. I was precious to the people who owned me I'm unsure why" She lowered her block. Clarence walked off; *I wonder if he knows she's with Chance.* Clarence grabbed the young man by his arm gently requesting, "Zion, take this young man upstairs."

Caleb was shocked but he continued the game, and everyone clapped in awe at the parlor trick. "Last, but not least, which one of you ladies ever wondered what it's like to waltz?"

Vampresses swooned while clearing the floor of pillows. "Who'll be brave enough to accompany me?" Gabriel handed him the candle. "May I try Pharaoh?" A young woman inquired.

"Step up, young vampress. What's your name?" "Valerie, Great One." "Valerie, you don't need to know how to waltz. Follow my lead, ok?" "Yes pharaoh." "We will know we've waltzed correctly if the candle is still lit in the end." The band played the waltz. Clarence twirled her around the room. '*Great One, can you hear me?*' Clarence didn't reply. She squeezed his hands. He looked into her eyes scanning her mind. '*Great One, can you hear me?*'

*I can. You're extremely handsome Great One. Thank you dear. You must be careful Pharoah. While in Vegas two weeks ago I was working, one of my vampire clients became intoxicated blurting how he was in a gaming house where Cody served drinks. She plotted mentally on killing you. She was asking him chemical questions because he's a chemist. She was asking something like if a pen touches something, can a person die instantly or if it's in the shampoo? Chance shut her up instructing her to leave immediately. The vampire client said he was irritated and angry she was speaking this way of you.*

*When the waltz was over, he kissed her, biting her lip and drank her. It was light she barely felt it. He handed her a handkerchief and said, "Thank you. I'll make sure you've my personal cell number. I've tasted your blood; this makes our bond stronger Valerie. You're safe.* "Did you enjoy our dance?" "Loved it, Pharaoh. You're all vampires say and more." "Thank you, child."

"Mastro music!" Vampires danced as Clarence made his way upstairs while Gabriel watched. Zion sat next to her as protection in the absence of the Pharaoh. Newly turned vampires walked up to her making introductions. "Why does the Pharaoh have you separated, boy?" Caleb asked. He declined answering, looking down. Clarence entered the room "Get me a chair Caleb this won't take long." Sitting on the chair directly across from the vampire Clarence asked, "what's your name?" "James."

"Look at your Pharaoh when he speaks," Caleb ordered. "It's James Great One." "How old are you?" "Nineteen Great One" "A young vampire... who taught you thought blocking?" "Cody in case I need it Great One."

"Don't look away. If you do, you will feel as if you're drowning." The boy looked away he began choking. "Look and live vampire." James looked in Clarence's eyes, his mental life jacket heaving for oxygen. "What is Cody doing with Elder Chance?"

"They're lovers. They have been on and off many years Pharoah." "How do you know?" "I'm an online gambler. I've been invited to play in person by Elder Chance more than once, I have seen her in his private suite on his arm many times. "Did Elder Chance know about her attempt to assassinate me?"

"One of the girls who runs the vampire lounge in Vegas said he didn't know. She arrived a few nights ago half dead from dipping with vampire street drugs Pharaoh. "Who's telling you all this?" "A bartender vampress named Venus Great One."

Clarence closed his eyes using her body to spy on Venus herself. When he did, Venus dropped a glass inhaling at the feeling of the master vampires' eyes on her. *Yes, Great Pharaoh? She whispered respectfully, trembling at the feeling of his presence.* "I'll call when I'm off I'm constantly being watched is this ok, Great One? Yes. Thank you, Pharoah."

"She's going to call in an hour's time. You're going to forget all of this. When you hear from Venus, you'll go to Elder Caleb and Inform him all she shared with you. Hold up your finger." James held up his pointer. Clarence knicked it with his fang, drinking of him.

"You will awake in the hallway walk down and report the Queen Gabriel. You were sent to see if there's bathroom toilet paper for the humans." Caleb laughed. Caleb walked him to the hall while returning, Clarence broke his connection to him.

"Chance would never betray you, Clarence." "Vampires change, brother." "Not Chance Clarence, anyone but him." Clarence and Caleb rejoined the party. Caleb stood in the middle of the dance floor holding up his hands. "I understand our Queen has a beautiful voice."

Gabriel smiled and shook her head, "No…no." "Come on," the crowd shouted, urging her to sing She approached the front, whispering to the band, "Before I start this song, these words are from my heart. I mean every word. Daddy, this one is for you I love you." She blew him kiss.

The vampresses were glued to her while vampires doted on how humble and beautiful she was. She sang one in a million you. As she sang, she felt the buzzer zapping in her clit. She tried to hold her composure while singing.

Clarence saw her struggling as it turned him on, but he stopped to allow her to get through her serenade. When she smiled, her fangs popped pretty and white. The men melted at her sexiness; her new teeth looked petite.

*You devil. I should've never given you that remote. You almost made me cum! You hid it well. You're lucky I didn't enter your thoughts planting memories of our sex sessions.* He kissed her by knicking his wrist, draining his blood into a whiskey glass with ice for her. *Sexy shit*, the vampress women thought.

Clarence laughed inside hearing their thoughts. Vampresses admired her engagement ring, the rock was huge. When they were leaving, one asked Gabriel if she could try the ring on. The other vampire nudged her and apologized, "I'm sorry Queen Gabriel, she's new." They held their heads down when they looked up, Gabriel handed it to them to try. "It's not as heavy as it looks go on try it on." she urged. "Queen Gabriel thank you."

They were shocked at how sweet she was. Gabriel looked and saw copious amounts of money on the patio with men shouting, "Roll the dice." at Clarence who loathed dice games. Caleb looked through the patio doors winking, "He's happy again Gabriel." "Is he Caleb?"

"You make him this way by being yourself," Caleb hugged her waist. "You're a good vampress Gabriel. Come on, meet the other vampresses. Clarence wants you to hire a lady-in-waiting." "A what Caleb?" "An assistant." "I don't need…" She took a deep breath, "It's a lot to accept Caleb."

"You'll get used to regal life love. Trust me on that one."

# Chapter 18
# Cody

The year of our Lord 1916.........

"The American's signed the treaty Father." "What does the white man know about keeping his word? Look at the Lakota, the Cherokee. They promised a treaty but what is it now but ash and lies Anahu?" "Papa, it's for change, for your life, mine, and your first grandson." "You speak as though the stars lay at your feet son." "This treaty will help." They passed around a peace pipe amongst the village Chieftains. Ahanu, the name given before his warrior's name, picked up his things exiting to his tent with his princess wife, Hausis.

She was a spirited Indian, the chieftain believed she'd been in this world before. Wise for her age of twenty-three, and blessed, inheriting her mother's looks. One day her mother wondered half dead into the camp escaping slavers. It was her father, a black foot Indian prince of tribes who, mentally nursed her to health while falling in love with her. Their spirits intertwined; it was meant for them to join. The great ancestral spirits sent her to him so she may live, bringing forth the offspring of a strong Chieftain.

He fell in love with her sweet nature and beauty, she fell in love with his warrior spirit and soft hand. They had a black foot traditional marital ceremony under the night sky thanking the star gods for leading her to him.

It was better than she could wish. For the first time in her life, she felt love. It didn't matter if they weren't negro, they were her family now the only one she knew.

She was accepting of this of him, running her fingers through his raven-colored long hair. He adored her curly coils. He taught her the language and ways of the Indian in turn she taught him English. It was best for a future chieftain to know both. In a year they bore a girl blessing her as Hausis, meaning "old woman." When born she didn't cry, her eyes were wide open taking in her surroundings, never smiling, only looking. When her grandfather blessed, her he declared his wife reborn in Hausis. She died the winter prior to her spring birth with the blessing of the tribe and the love of his people upon her shoulders Hausis grew engulfed in love. At the age of sixteen, it was time for suitors to fight if they wanted the hand of a Blackfoot Princess. They had to prove worthy to lead as chieftain since the current Chieftan bore no sons.

Hausis' mother Nutah, the name her husband gifted her meant heart had a young Indian boy in mind who was brave and gentle. Her father invited him because he came from a line of warriors trained for this moment all his life. Hausis had her eyes on someone else no one suspected. A quiet warrior, six feet tall, huge strong arms, and long black shiny hair. She loved braiding the designs of her mother's people dressing it with traditional items of her father's tribe.

The secret couple spoke of what they wanted in life. With the weave of each hair strand and dream they fell deeper in love. Village children learned English from her mother, the former mistress to her master who secretly taught her to read and write during private pillow talks. The village appointed her teacher to learn the white man's customs, body language, and mannerism's when transacting business.

Hausis worried she'd lose the man she loved; Spotted Horse was a threat to her future happiness.

They discussed the competition, together they strategized. She knew Anahu loved her and if another man won her hand, he would die inside watching her live the life he should've with his adversary. She had wanted Anahu since childhood, they were inseparable, but this had nothing to do with who'd be Chieftain of the tribe. Three days before the competition, Hausis' friend suggested a root be crushed and placed in Spotted Horse's water.

"He won't taste it Hausis, it won't hurt him make him slow to give Eagle...Anahu, a chance." "It's dishonorable Nika, and not becoming of a Queen." "You're right Hausis I'm sorry to think this." The day the competition arrived; her friend was the water girl for all warriors. After ten rounds of hand-to-hand combat Spotted Horse and Spotted Eagle were left standing.

Spotted Horse never looked at Hausis loved her, he wanted a title not a wife. He spent romantic time with her friend who was in love with him and upset he entered to compete for Hausis' hand. Both men were battered, bruised cut and tired. The current Chieftan called for a water break. Hausis' friend handed out water as she did the previous 10 rounds. The men drank with one minute to return to combat.

"Spotted horse I love you please withdraw." "As Chieftain can I have you and Hausis as wives you both are like sisters anyway. It'll mean nothing to have you both."

"I won't leave you my little flower Nika." Hearing what he had planned Nika couldn't leave fate to decide the outcome of the battle. Nika took the sleepy root powder sprinkling it in Spotted Horses water swirling it making sure it dissolved without detection. The men threw punches. Spotted Horse became dizzy not understanding why. Three more punches and Spotted Horse fell to the ground.

The chieftain announced Spotted Eagle the victor and future chieftain of the tribe. The wedding was scheduled in seven days. Hausis was overjoyed with love and excitement, ready to be his bride and in his arms forever. Later that night she woke sneaking out the tepee to see Eagle. "Eagle?" his mother came to the teepee exit. "Hausis your mother is going to kill you. You're going to be my mother in seven days would you tell on your only daughter for loving your son? How is my husband doing?" "He's asleep Hausis." "I'm not mother." Hausis knelt at his side kissing his lips in the dim lantern lit tepee. His mother saw the love flowing in their eyes. "How are you, my love?"

"Terrible but you are worth it ache and pain Hausis." touching her full lips. "I'm going to be yours in seven days Eagle." "I heard." smiling "Return Hausis you know how your mother becomes; she'll kill us because you're here without chaperone a few more moments than you go child." Eagle smiled sharing plans with his future bride. "Tomorrow, I'll choose a spot for our tepee. I hunt for buffalo with your father to cover it and feed our village. Go now, I have an early day. I love you Hausis."

Present Day Las Vegas Nevada 2020....

"What the fuck did you do Jesus!" She held her hand to his face high and faded. "What the hell are you on you a junkie now Cody?" "No Chancie" "Go to the bedroom, sleep it the fuck off, and don't leave the bedroom. No one can see you here, dismiss the housekeepers, they're vampires. No vampire staff or humans can know you are with me Cody."

"Why honey?" slurring her words. Chance grabbed her arm, "You tried to kill the Pharaoh, have you lost your mind? If Clarence wanted, you dead: you'd be dead. You're lucky he hasn't imposed a bounty on you Cody." "Can't you speak with him Chance?"

"Admit you're here, and commit treason by harboring the person who tried to kill his Queen?" "She's not his Queen Chance." "She is, they signed a dowry contract in blood. Gabriel belongs to him." "She doesn't know it Chance" her words trailing off as she dozed from her high. "Gabriel thinks a Christian wedding makes it official." Chance dragged her into a cold shower, dropping her in. "Ahhh! Eeee!" "Get yourself together woman!"

Chance left her in the bathroom calling the front desk "No housekeeper or blood service until further notice. Keep everyone out of my penthouse." "Yes, Elder Chance. The Pharaoh called." "When John?" "An hour ago, Elder." "Is he in Brooklyn John?" "No one knows where he is since the attempt on his life. Elder Chance?" "Yeah man?" "Don't get involved, we don't want problems with the Pharaoh. I dated a scroll girl once and I read a scroll, the Pharaoh is extremely violent."

"I witnessed most of what happened in the scrolls John, I know what he's capable of." Goodnight John. Goodnight Elder. Chance called the scroll writers. "Good night, this is Elder Chance Hollings." "Goodnight Elder Chance, how may we help?" "Can you please pull scroll 13?" "Yes Elder, call on facetime, to confirm its you." Chance hung up shaking. Few things made him nervous but there was something about this that made him uneasy, like a game he knew he'd lose after placing a sizable bet, feeling lady luck leave the room. She was not with him at that moment nor at this one. He called on facetime.

"Elder Chance, as handsome as ever, please check your email and docu-sign you're requesting I read this scroll." "Have you ever read scroll 13 dear?" Chance wondered as she unwrapped silk binds.

"No. I'm nervous I've heard about it from a retired scroll personnel, but none of us have read it Elder."

*Scroll 13*

*May 18, 1897*

*Clarence was on his nightly run in the woods of Georgia, he heard visceral screams When he saw what was happening, he became enraged. Four* white men were taking turns demining, raping, defecating, urinating, biting, beating, slapping, cutting, and burning two colored young women. Clarence's savage instantly emerged hearing the intoxicating sound of blood coursing in their human veins, the smell of adrenaline oozing from their pores, excited him to a hard-on before the kill.

The two women were defenseless tied to a tree, Clarence hyper-sped to the first white woman beater, with one blow of his left his hand a decapitated head fell to the earth rolling in his own blood dirt mix. Clarence grabbed the second rapist biting into his skull cracking it open with four fangs, sucking brain blood from his skull through the holes. Clarence slurped blood through an eye socket after he removed the eye squeezing blood from it like a grape. Holding the skull, tipping the small hole to his mouth hitting the back of the animal's head draining it dry.

After dropping the carcass to the ground, he wasn't satisfied the savage yearned for more. Clarence levitated into thin air raising his third victim off his feet with him who weighed 200 lbs., biting him 42 times on his neck, shoulders, arms, and back. When he dropped him from 15 feet above the earth, a skeleton weighing 60 pounds thumped the earth below.

The condition of the corpse? Flesh hung from bone with extraordinarily little blood left in his body. The fourth man grabbed one the victims who was barely alive threatening to finish her off if the savage didn't allow him to live. The savage tilted his head vertically sizing his prey, plotting with a sinister blood thirsty grin tattooed on his face revealing four fangs arguing with himself internally about how he should be killed. "Drop her, I'll let you go" he growled. Being too trusting the fourth rapist dropped her fleeing into the woods. Clarence counted singing his voice echoing through the open airy woods.

"Beautiful dreamer, Wake unto me; Starlight and dew drops are waiting for thee; sounds of the rude world heard in the day Lull'd by the moonlight have all passed away....." The rapist hearing the song shitted himself. 'What type of killer sings?' He thought as his heart raced.

Clarence counted loudly to 5 in an eerie song. I'll give you a head start killer! The man sprinted as humanly fast as possible. Struggling to make it to a public place. When he arrived at the tree line Clarence greeted him there. Using his sharp nails, he flayed then peeled skin from his chest licking the bloody side, exposing his heart keeping him alive to feed. Clarence cracked each rib in the cage one by one snapping them, sucking and licking the bones clean, making sure the heart kept beating he stayed awake through it all.

Clarence carefully sliced out his liver and kidneys, squeezing the blood in his mouth his head tilted way back. Then helped himself to his left wrist biting the vein leading to the heart, gulping mouthfuls of warm sweet blood, leaving the heart for last exposed and pumping fast plump, and ripe, he placed his head in his chest cavity sucking the blood from it until it beat no more. His blood clinging to his flesh like a dark shroud.

Going back to the victims one remained alive he carried her to her parents' house with a note which *read, "take solace in knowing the white men who did this to your child are dead." The survivor? He offered immortality and she accepted. To protect her privacy, he refused to name her.*

*End scroll.*

"Hello, Pop." Chance sipped a much-needed whiskey tox calming his nerves after what he heard. "Are you having a party?" "Where are you? You don't say. Have I seen Cody? No pop If I do, I'll call. Say hello to Gabriel for me. Goodnight, Pop."

Chance flew Cody to Vegas. She'd stay for weeks, gambling, drinking, and living the Vegas high life. They were jet setters traveling globally on weekends enjoying trysts and staycations. He fell for her hard. She was thick, sexy, and beautiful with long flowing hair down her back accented with deep set dimples.

A true beauty, a vampress desired, smart, beautiful, gentle, and understanding but Clarence never fell in love with her. When it came to looks, Gabriel bested Cody in his eyes. What did Gabriel have that Cody didn't? Clarence was head over heels in love with her and Cody lost him. *What possessed her to get into this mess?* He thought. *She's lucky Niarchos didn't get her, or she'd be dead. I need to convince Cody to surrender once her mind is clear of drugs.*

Las Vegas
Chance & Cody....

"Chance please, can I have a glass of ice water" "Yes Ma." He made her shower covering her up, to sweat out the drugs. He wrapped his arms around her whispering, "You're going to be fine Cody."

Gabriel & Clarence
Gullah Islands......

Gabriel woke, running to the bathroom, locking the door in tears. Clarence was downstairs making tea when he heard her screaming. He ran up the steps to a locked door. Clarence restrained himself from breaking the door, respecting her privacy. "Sugar?" He tapped on the door. "Are you alright?" "Go away" "Honey, please open the door." Gabriel opened the door and when Clarence entered, she sat on the floor knee to chest like a child, holding a cloth to her face and trembling.

Clarance sat on the floor with her, careful not to sit in the sun because she opened the window for fresh air.

"Sugar, please come close." He held out his hand. "No." "Sugar, don't make me enter the light." She slipped further into the light. "Sugar?" Caleb and Zion heard what was going on but dare not interfere. "I had a nightmare when I was ten years younger. Those were the happiest days of my life before the deaths of my aunt and grandmother before cancer snatched them away. I was crying and walking in a place I'd never been. It was sunny and I was heartly happy. I used to wear these yellow sunglasses. There was a man I approached as he held my waist loving me. He pushed me against the wall, kissed me and whispered how beautiful I was, how he needed me. The whole time I heard a voice telling me to remove my glasses. Each time I tried; he distracted me with kissing."

"Finally, I removed my glasses. I looked and saw the face of a demon. When I put them back on, the man's face was normal again. He held me tight and said, *"You know what I'm. Do you love me?"* "The demon was you, Clarence." Gabriel glared through bright sunbeams as gripping terror swept her eyes. She glared at him infused with fear, it upset Clarence deeply, but he didn't know what to do.

*Caleb, help me.* He called mentally sensing he was close. "Clarence don't step in the light please. Get Gabriel to come willingly. If you grab her, you'll scare her more." "Gabriel Sugar, I made your favorite tea. I'll go and get it." "I'll wait for you in our bedroom. I'm not leaving you baby, I love you, Sugar. I'd never do anything to hurt you. Follow your heart. I'll be waiting sweetheart."

Checking his watch, 10 am quickly turned to 1:30 p m. *Yes Zion?* feeling him in his thoughts. *The venom is causing her to have nightmares, it's dying down in her system. It's a side effect. I'm testing the samples, but the venom tripled because sex boosted the adrenaline spiking its potency. I remember Safinah saying you were stronger during sex. You need to concentrate on weakening your strength during relations Clarence.* Gabriel opened the door. He sat on the bed not moving. "I'm sorry Clarence."

"Sugar, its fine you don't need to apologize." She sat on his lap hugging him tight. He wiped her face. "It felt real, Clarence." "Sugar, it's my fault. Zion explained my venom is potent when I'm in a state of arousal. When I bit you, I released a double dose."

"That's why the night Cody attacked; you healed fast. When I bit you, I injected you with the side effects which include nightmares and hallucinations." He held his head down ashamed. "You know? You're the first vampire human hybrid? I'm learning I'm sorry Sugar."

She pushed his chin up. "Kings don't bow their heads." "This one does before the feet of his Queen." He got down on his knees. "I love you. I'd never ever harm you. I'd walk in the light before I inflict harm on you or allow it to happen." He laid his head in her lap, he could smell her period through her clothes which turned him on, but he didn't mention it. Tea Sugar? Gabriel laughed because it was cold.

Clarence went to the kitchen to make Gabriel dinner. "Vladimir called Clarence." Clarence took a deep breath. "He called to remind you of the yearly meet next month in Budapest." "Who's Vladimir?" Joan asked.

Vladimir Gobetrov Origins....

"The vampire who heads covens outside the United States. He runs Europe the surrounding areas including Egypt." Zion responded. "A lot of black vampires left his rule migrating to the United States joining our covens." "Who's older?" Joan inquired.

"I am." "Why don't you rule Europe too Clarence?" "Technically he does Joan. He's the vampire king when he's in Europe. They have their own vampire council. Clarence is head of the council, he left Vlad in charge in his absence." "Did you turn him; Clarence? Thank you, Zion, for replying?" "Yes Joan." "A white boy?" "It's a long story." "We got time Clarence."

"I was in Budapest, trying to see what I could learn about our kind studies that led me there. He was a young librarian, full of knowledge of our kind. In fact, it was his lifelong work. He was the laughingstock of his profession and was thought to be losing his mind to believe in mythical vampires. Despite ancient beliefs, a book on our existence is in the Vatican under heavy security. Vladimir was going to be allowed to view this so-called book the Roman Catholic Church had.

I met this fool in Budapest. I have no idea how he figured out what I'm, but he did. In one week, he was scheduled to fly to Rome. I was to accompany him to hear what he'd learned. I arrived at his flat opening the door he slit his wrist twelve inches up his arm. I was forced to save him. How else was I going to get information about us?" I bit him to save him, which was what he wanted! I was damned angry." "Did he ever see the book?"

"No Zion, the Vatican is consecrated ground. It's forbidden for the dead to walk inside the Vatican or even on the blocks it is built on. The second he put his foot on the church steps, he got ill as a dog and could go no further. They knew what he was and tried to kill him but failed. Vlad moved swiftly and got away. I've offered large sums of money for anyone to take pictures of the pages, video the pages or something. No luck."

"Clarence never forgave him for that, deep down," Caleb "Why make him ruler over Europe if he's unscrupulous Clarence?" "Who else Joan? He has two covens of 800 vampires there haven't been problems We meet in person once a year to discuss issues he may have. I hold court via Zoom call for his high offenders." "He has an engagement present for you as he couldn't make the party which was insulting. He needs reprimand Clarence."

"He's not comfortable Caleb the Elders knew he tricked me into a turn. He's white. Would you come to a party where you're loathed? He's a good kid. The main thing is he obeys me." "They drink from the vein, it's old-fashioned Clarence." "It's safer Zion, makes you a stronger vampire." "Why did vampires cease vein drinking practices Clarence?" "I forbade it Joan unless the host gives permission. Humans were being attacked; it was out of control. Everyone sipped and chatted as Clarence cooked.

Gabriel looked at engagement party photos to choose from when her cell rang, "Hello, Gabriel. It's Cody."

# Chapter 19

# Let the Games Begin!

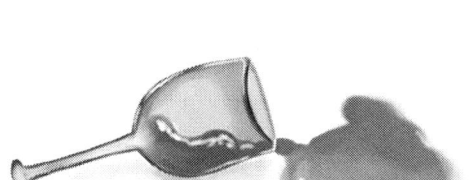

Hollings Estate New York....

"Welcome home, Pharaoh." "Thank you, Khrista. How are things?" "They're fine." "Are Papa Nate and Ann here?" "Yes, Pharaoh. They've been awaiting your return." "Joan, can you catch up with Khrista please? The trip made me tired." Gabriel grabbed her overnight Louis Vuitton bag that Joan packed. "Sugar, we don't carry our bags," Clarence smiled. "Then, carry it for me," she snapped. "I'm drained and I need it, Clarence." touching his wrist gently. "Of course, Sugar"

The baby vamps looked on not saying a word. Guardians knew not to get involved. She was a good wife, the humans thought, smiling, he finally met his match. Joan and the other vampresses purchased Gabriel a large teacup the island gifted, to surprise her. It read 'Bride' and was decorated with hearts and ribbons with a matching saucer and lid. "Was it relaxing Joan?"

One of the guardians Joan worked with for over twenty years asked. "What?" "You and Zion?" she whispered. "Yes." Joan whispered back. Her friend hooped and hollered.

"Girl, how was it, not him per say but the whole vampire experience?" "Keep your voice down girl." "It doesn't matter if we whisper, they'll hear us, Joan." "I'll explain today when we get groceries. Are we low?" "No Joan." "ARE WE LOW Lena?" "Oh yes, we're low." "We leave in a few. Stop messing with Niarchos." "Who me?" "Yes, you Lena" "Have you looked at Niarchos Joan? He's a whole vampire boo." "What you gonna do with all that sexy vampire Lena?" "I'm unsure Joan but, I'm willing to find out. Shoot." They snickered low. "Go give Gabriel her tea. I gotta take Niarchos, and your grandson some blood. You going to see him?" "Yes." "Ok. cause Zay's been asking for you. Papa wants to see you." "I only got back damn Lena." "I know girl."

"Alexis, turn on the air conditioner." Clarence removed his shirt. Gabriel loved seeing him undressed. He was a beautifully made man with natural cuts in the right places. His hair was beautiful and as soft as his smile. He possessed a humble spirit and was a man who was so in love with her she wanted nothing. What had she done in this life to deserve such love? She treated him horribly that day in the bathroom. He was forgiving and unmoved by her actions. "You hungry?" "No, thanks." "Must leave for a few hours to sign paperwork. The lawyers are coming. Papa and Elder Ann want to see me." "You're going to visit Isaiah?" "No, it's against vampire law. Any contact may be seen as tampering." "Use telepathy. No one can prove it." "I'll consider it because you asked Sugar." Clarence sat next to her.

"Can I ask something Clarence? Why did you choose me?" "I saw you and was smitten. You got me at hello." "Hehe, you're full of it!" Clarence left to attend his meetings. Someone knocked on her bedroom door. "Come in." Niarchos entered kneeling. "Please, rise." He rose walking towards her towering over her. "You're wearing the pearls." "Yes. I love these thank you Niarchos."

Niarchos thought she was gorgeous with plump lips and matching sexy hips, silky skin like yards of perfect brown fabric, her hair thick and wild with a beautiful smile that did something to him no woman had in years. She was sweet, kind, and good inside. In a fleeting time, he knew why his father loved her. It was also why he loved her. The time he saw her at the party, his heart melted. He wasn't smart enough to block his thoughts. He didn't think of it when he was there.

"Are you going to bed Niarchos?" "No ma'am, I sleep by day. I have a surprise for you. When you get it, call. Do you have my number?" "Yes." "Do you mind if I sweep your bedroom Queen? I did it two days ago, but you can never be too careful." "Sure."

Niarchos checked leaving a descrambler on the dresser. "This will destroy cameras or bugs my Queen. Please, tell the Pharaoh what it is when he arrives?" "I sure will. Are you going to the basement?" "Yes, my Queen." "Tell Isaiah I'm working on it Niarchos." I'm sure he'll be glad to hear good news." She went to her Louis Vuitton bag to remove some things.

"Here Niarchos." She handed him magazines on music, art, Ebony, and Jett magazine with articles about Black issues and "Up from Slavery" by Booker T. Washington. "Powerful book Queen." "Inform him he must read this. It's important for him to learn about black people. It'll help him understand the mentality of the Pharaoh." "Yes, Great One. Thank you, on his behalf. Do you need anything before I go?"

"No, thank you Niarchos." "I'm downstairs. If you need anything, don't hesitate to ask Queen." "I won't." Niarchos bowed his head exiting the bedroom. *She smells so good.* He swooned internally. He was intoxicated by her.

"Joan?" "Hey girl, I'm on the way up. Can you ask one of the maids to make Niarchos a cup of blood roast and one for the Pharaoh please? Ask them to put a coffee brewer in the family and security rooms please." "Yes Gabriel." Her landline rang. "Hello" "Coffee?" "Yes, Niarchos."

He loved her saying his name. "I appreciate the gesture, but I'll get dog ill." "Niarchos?" "Yes, Great One?" "Do you trust me?" "Yes, my Queen." "Sip."

He took a small sip. "It's delicious. I'm not ill. How?" "It's a blood roast." "A what?" "Blood roast. We're starting a vampire coffee line everywhere. All vampire businesses will carry our roast." "You're going to make money Great One." "Do you want to partner with us Niarchos?" "Silent partner?" "Sure."

"I ain't business minded like you and the Pharaoh. However, I have money for investment if you need it. I know you don't need it, Great One apology." "Stop. You don't need to watch your words with me Niarchos." "Will the Pharaoh mind if invest?" "It's a shared business venture. I'll run it how I want. I already purchased land on the Gullah Islands to grow the beans and a warehouse. We're going to grow, package and manufacture the coffee then, ship it from the main warehouse."

Joan dropped off the tea and left for her Walmart run. "Zion," she called as she was going to the car. "We're going to Walmart. Do you need anything?" "Bubble bath. A birdie stated someone likes bubble baths." "Who honey?" "Your mom." She burst out laughing. "Do you know before she passed, I asked her for your hand?" Joan was shocked. "Even though it's forbidden?" "Yes. I said if I could convince Papa one day I want to know I had her blessing Joan."

"What did she say?" "I'll explain if I get Papa to give me his blessing." "Not fair Zion." "Bye." Zion approached the sample fridge holding up a blood sample he diluted.

The Gullah Islands......

Upon going to the garage on the island, an old carriage sat in the corner. He recalled the conversation he and Clarence had about its history in his life. *That's the carriage I sat in the night I was turned. Why did you keep it, Clarence? I'm unsure... Chance needed the space. I had him send it here for Caleb.*

Zion walked around the carriage noticing small red faded stains embedded in the leather hood. He took a plastic baggie from his pocket and with his Swiss knife, scraping old, dried blood. *Pharaoh's human blood? Can't be. What're you doing Zion? Nothing Great One.* He didn't want to get his hopes up. The blood could be too dilapidated to test for DNA, but he had to try.

*If I can get a sample of the synthetic blood from Lulu, I may be able to replace the missing DNA in the sequencing to complete the pattern creating synthetic blood for feeding and vaccines. Zions Medical mind was at work.*

The Hollings Estate New York City....

The digital phone chime interrupted Gabriel's thoughts. "Gosh hello." "You alone?" "No." "Why are you lying? It's Friday he's downstairs, signing paperwork. It's the first Friday of the month the lawyer will arrive in 15 minutes Gabriel." "What do you want?" "I want to come home." "You know that's not going to happen. Ask for something reasonable like 'I want to turn myself in.'

"Hee-hee that was good Gabriel. Can you talk to him for me?" "What can I say to sway him from a decision of your own doing? It's not up to him anyway, the Elders are involved. You tried to kill us and now, you want to be pardoned? Is this a joke Cody?" "No, Great One."

"What can I do for you? I'm not a Queen yet. Even if I were, why would I listen? You tried to kill their king!" "Our king." "No, their king. My husband." "Should I beg Queen?" "No." "I'm in love with him. I need him." "You can't have him, Cody." "Why not?"

"He doesn't love you like that. You can't make a man love you as old as you are you don't know this? You can have babies with him, cook, and clean shit sparkling clean if he doesn't love you, he's not staying. That's something my grandmother taught me." "I'm scared Gabriel." "I'd be scared too." "Help me Great One, please." "I could get in trouble for talking to you. I'm not good yet myself Cody."

"Yes, you are if you only knew how good. You signed a blood oath at the engagement party which you made before a traditional wedding. He laid claim to you puy you on paper, no vampire can touch you and all you do is considered a royal act. Why do you think he gave you access to his books? I'm begging, that's all. If there's any human left in you, please help me Great One." "Do you know Isaiah is facing death by sunlight? Hello."

"I'm here." "Your stupidity over a man has a young vampire facing the gallows. I'll speak to him. One ripple in an ocean... see what you've caused? I'll see what I do Cody, no promises. Any more death attempts, all deals are off." "Thank you, Great One." "Don't thank me yet, I gotta go." Gabriel hung up hurriedly.

"Who was that on the phone Sugar? Wrong number. What're you doing back so soon?" "How long do you think it takes to sign papers? Coffee is a hit. Who was it?" "No one Clarence." Clarence popped his top fangs attempting to scare her into truth. "Who?" His eyes blazed as Alexis turned up the air conditioner.

The wind blowing made her nipples hard through her tee. He stood in front of her with his eyes glowing brown, green and hazel color blends. He pinched 1 nipple while caressing the other. Grabbing his button on the fly of his Levi jeans, she attempted to unbutton the top button when he grabbed her hand. "Who was that on the phone?"

She stopped but his bulge was calling her so she grabbed a handful of what she could, she bit the bulge spot, sucking through the jeans while using her left hand to rub his chest and nipples. His moaning was driving her insane. He was growing impatient and horny, a lethal combination for vampire. He grabbed her throat hoping it would scare her.

"Who called?" He pressed his hand on her neck, squeezing tighter, smiling. She finished loosening his jeans. His 12-inch hard as fuck dick popped out of the boxer briefs. He grabbed her hair, pulling her head backward exposing her neck. Gabriel snatched away tethering herself to her throbbing treat. Her mouth was wet dripping with spit, sliding down her sexy lips. "Do you want to get bitten woman? Who called?" She stared uncooperatively, closing his eyes, he licked her cheek picking her up by her throat off her feet, 1 inch off the floor before tossing her to the dresser. Her perfume bottles broke on the hardwood floor.

He knocked the wind out of her. He heard her grasping for air. She was holding her stomach killing her thoughts. "Stop locking me out," he growled low. He raised up her robe from the back holding her down with his forearm across her shoulder blades. She tried to wiggle free, but she was trapped under his sexual restraints.

"Who was on the phone Gabriel?" He growled, spreading her feet apart pushing his fingers in her asshole. She gasped because she never had anal sex. The pinch of first-time penetration drove her wild.

"Who?" Now with two fingers, he spit on her asshole, gliding them in and out teasingly. "You know what's next?" She moaned about to cum on the edge her wet pussy dripping, shaking her head unable to speak. Her bare ass was up and naked for his pleasure.

He kept her legs spread as white cum rolled down her thick thighs rubbing her ass softly as possible blowing on the wetness reveling her excitement as goosebumps rose at his touch. "I asked 10 times, who was it? "And 10 times, you've refused to answer Gabriel."

1. pop.2. pop 3. pop. 4. pop 5.pop. He gave her five slaps on her bare-naked ass. "I'm in pain," she whispered. "It can stop if you want Sugar. Who called?" He reached down pushed fingers from his other hand, pinning her down as she squirmed in ecstasy. Silky cum lined her walls. She begged as his fingers went in and out of her pussy slowly, then fast then, twirled them around rubbing swollen walls ending it with clit pinching. He put his wet, slippery fingers to her mouth. "Suck them clean," he demanded. "Who called?"

She shook her head no defiantly while tasting herself. He licked her back, his teeth scraping her shoulder. Blood oozed, resting on top of the forearm holding her down, blood pooled between her shoulder blades on top of his fore-arm, as he slurped trickling blood off her back the vibration rolling down her spine while holding her clit as his hostage. He let go shaking uncontrollably. "Did you ask to you could cum? Stop."

Gabriel inhaled ending her orgasm. 6. smack 7. smack 8. smack 9. smack 10. smack 11. Smack. Wincing with every pop, she whined in heat poking her ass out, begging to be fucked. Grabbing a handful of her hair, he picked her up, turned her around pushing her on the wall dropping her, she suffered a hard fall landing at his feet. Slowly tilting her head backwards, he slipped on top of her ramming 12-inches in her mouth. Gagging, her eyes teared he pinched her nose in five intervals. "Who?" Pinch. "Who?"

She gagged on his dick, almost throwing up her tea several times. He pulled his sloppy toppy, wet, hard, dripping dick from her mouth. She fell to the floor on all fours gasping for air. As she crawled to the bed, she was heaved for air pulling herself up bent over. He pushed his jeans off, kneeling behind her holding her waist. He slammed his dick into her fucking her hard from the back. He had to remember she was a hybrid. "Blocking thoughts? Naughty," he moaned as he grinded, deep, and slow. "I love you, say it." He whispered. Digging balls deep, her legs trembled as she tried to scoot away.

"You running from this dick?" He held her in place while inside her shifting positions, he sat on the edge of the bed dick up. Gabriel bounced on his hardness. "Your shit is hard as fuck shit, Daddy." He slapped her ass holding her throat. "Don't talk unless it's who the fuck was on the phone woman. Keep bouncing." He laid back she bounced hard "I'm gonna burst all up in this wet tight sweet pussy."

Her pussy would tighten then loosen while he was still inside. "Don't fucking move." "Heheh yes Pharaoh," her legs quivered rubbing her arms and breasts with her eyes closed licking her lips. "Ahhh Sugar mmmm." By her count he pumped thirteen times in her the throbbing of his dick bounced on her sensitive walls breaking the levy on her triple orgasm.

His nut tangled with her cream slid down his legs and hers. He licked the blood off her back. "Stay right there," he fastened her to his saddle wrapping her with his huge arms wrapped around her. He sucked her neck sure not to bite though it was hard as her nipples. They gasped for air breathing heavily like animals he flipped her on the bed eskimo kissing her causing her to giggle. He went to the fridge to get ice water.

"Here Sugar." "Thank you." He rested next to her and tapped his chest. She snuggled close laying her head on his chest. "What did Cody want?" "Hehe you knew the wholetime you rascal!" "I'm an old vampire, my hearing is supreme. I heard you crying in your house in Queens 3 blocks away." "You knew what we discussed? Eaves dropper!" "I wanted you to say Sugar." "I would've Clarence once I figured a way to help."

"Yes, love. If you can convince the vampire Elders not to put her to death especially after trying to kill their maker and king, your good. To vampires, I'm a god thus the name Pharaoh. I didn't self-give the name, Sugar. I have saved many from slavery, the whip, rape, murder, cancer…" "Yes," rubbing his chest inviting her to lay on it.

He kissed her hand. "These vampires will kill her for that. I'm a fair king. We all make money. We're comfortable financially. No one suffers in any house. This stops jealousy and rage from rising. If you want more money, there are job listings within the businesses we own salaries are above what humans pay. Take Khrista whom you are fond of, she handles real estate for vampires all over the world. She has several licenses allowing her to conduct business in 40 states and 15 countries." "Why do they live here?"

"Her husband wants a spot on the security team they would to move to Georgia where training takes place on the plantation Gabriel." "Plantation?"

"It's what we vampires call the first house I owned it was originally a plantation. Niarchos grows sugar cane and tobacco on it. Safinah gave it to him some time back." "You let her?" "It was hers Sugar, it reminded me of slavery." She comforted him holding his hand. "Those years hurt the pain never ceases. Some Elders like Papa and Niarchos have whip marks." "Why don't you have them, Clarence? I mean, thank God but, why?"

"Safinah asked that very question when we first met. Let's finish with Chase first. He wants to join our security so; he must live in Georgia with Niarchos joining his coven. She loves it here, she doesn't wanna switch covens. They're coming up on five years. They must decide. "She's fond of you Clarence, makes her decision harder. Can they stay?" "Yes Sugar, until another vampire is made. We need the bedroom for them."

"I don't have lash scars because I'm a white free slave. They considered whipping us unkind since we looked like them. Who wants to see a white man tied to a whipping post? We weren't savages like the darker skinned slaves so no lash. Thier words used to divide us as a people. Isabel and Avril taught me how to avoid the lash." "Smart woman, my mammy Isabel." "You think you can help Cody Clarence?" After her dragging Isaiah, the Elders sweetheart into this mess? Let's wager Sugar. "Ok, what type?" "A suitcase with one million dollars in cash. All 100-dollar bills Clarence." "Fine." "What would you want?" "Something no woman has ever given me anal sex." "You want to fuck me in the ass Clarence? ok you're on!"

Niarchos was checking the perimeter of the estate when he heard them having sex. He couldn't help himself from listening to her moan in ecstasy hearing her cum. She was so sexy that after his shower, he lay in bed grabbing his 15-inch dick, yanking, rubbing, and pulling a palm full, of thick sexy hardness dying to be fucked. Echoes of whining in heat and hearing the squirt slip down her curvaceous legs started a fire within he thought extinguished with the death of his wife. Niarchos vividly imagined himself inside her, exploding on himself. He wanted a vampress he couldn't have, it's not to say he couldn't dream.

The Gullah Islands....

Caleb found an old warehouse near to Gabriel's coffee warehouse. He purchased it for a little less than one million dollars. This would be their arena for vampires in the United States and abroad to compete for money, forgiveness, and pardon. Many types of competitions and categories would be on public display. A show to end all shows. Excitement ignited Caleb as he theatrically yelled it to his coven members.

"The Queen needs a security detail one vampire to stay by her side and guard her in the Pharaoh's absence. It pays two million dollars per year you must show worthy to protect a Queen. Twelve matches will be held in her honor. In the end a fight with Niarchos. "I thought no Elders were allowed to compete Elder Caleb?" "We shall see my children." He ran around the arena happily yelling to the construction crew that they had work to do!

The year of our lord 1863

Hollings Plantation

Dekalb Country Georgia....

"Ya makes it back from da whoopin dey puts on ya." Safinah wiped Chance's head with a cold rag. "You gots a fever cause a da' healing going on inside ya. Ain't no elixir I gives ya, all I does is make rightly sho youse above ground." Chance opened one unswollen eye "Look, he gots eyes like ya Peety real Pretty wit dat fire in em" Clarence looked, "I see Finah lookin good." "He looks like one of ya now a vampire," she smiled at Chance. "He one now Safinah." "Chance real slow now." Safinah reminded him to help him sit up. "Thank ya kindly." she gave him a sip of water "Wait 'fore you stand Chance."

Safinah collected dishes from around the room five nights passed waiting for him to wake "HE WOKE!" her shouts echoed through the house as their blended family cheered and clapped. Chance was chipper at the amount of people glad he survived his attack. "Looking glass ma'am?" he asked with a raspy voice.

Clarence fetched one from Safinah's vanity. "Sometimes ya cast no reflection, sometimes ya does Chance" "Shucks, hardly looks like nothin happen ta me Clarence." "It did almost die. Youse like me, vampire no sunlight, it kills us. We're connected by blood you, my kin. Ise in danger, you feel ta help me, it's a naggin pull ya gets Chance."

Chance stood, "I see far hear across da fields." "Tanight, we feeds." handing him a glass of cow blood; he drank it fast. "Ya gets used to it you my first turn. Obeys me always, follow da rules of our house, be my right hand, young vampire."

He kneeled Clarence touched the crown of his head "Tagetha, we gonna free other mens, women's, an' picaninnies trapped in slavery. We gonna walk time together as father and son." "Yes, papa you saved me, I owe ya, my life. Ise never betray ya." Chance stood. Clarence hugged him, "welcome ta ya family vampire."

# Chapter 20
# Let's Get It

TO ALL COVENS VAMPIRES DOCUMENTED OUTCAST ACCUSED AND EXCOMMUNICATED

FUGITIVES RUNNING FROM VAMPIRE JUSTICE

You're cordially invited to the 1st annual vampire games. ALL VAMPIRES are welcome to attend for a chance at rejoining or joining a coven. If you lose and you are a vampire fugitive, you'll be placed in custody pending a vampire trial. If you're an excommunicated vampire, you'll have a chance to regain entry to a coven. Competitions will be held as follows:

    1. Any form of Martial arts.

    2. Boxing: For this division there shall be no weight or height requirements bare knuckle only.

    3. Fencing: Must have knowledge of the sport; no protective gear is to be worn during this competition. No neck, heart, or head wounds immediate disqualification if inflicted.

4. Archery: targets will be 20 city blocks, then 40-city blocks and the last 100 city blocks.

5. Runners: Destination to be determined.

6. Axe/hatchet throwing: All contestants must come with vampire subjects. Vampires will toss chosen weapons around your subject, hitting the subject will result in loss. Protective neck and head gear will be supplied.

7. Find it in the dark: Contestants will be transported to a dark location whereby you've 3 minutes to find 20 specified objects. The vampire who collects the most items wins.

8. Sharp Shooting: Shooting targets will be set at various distances, vampires must hit all marks to advance, advancement continues as objects become more distant the vampire who doesn't miss wins one target wins.

9. The Crowns Hacker: Vampires will be seated at computer terminals in the arena they have 2 minutes to hack into the Pharaoh's encrypted diamond mine accounts. The vampire who succeeds hacks his encrypted bank account within the vampire bank and trusts you will have two minutes. The vampire who wins becomes the top IT person for the vampire crown with a salary of one million dollars per year to start.

10. Security: A threat will be placed on the grounds of the arena. The vampire who finds and eliminates the threat advances to the final round in a ring. They'll have to pass our head of security Elder Niarchos Hollings for a spot as second in command on the Pharaoh's new Madjai Elite. You Must get past Elder Niarchos to grab a flag. This will be the sole competition an Elder shall compete.

11. Knife fight: You'll be tied with another vampire and the first vampire to draw blood wins.

*The winner fights the next vampire. This consists of 10 rounds advances victor.*

*12. Last and final round, instruments voice, and art: Vampires will choose an instrument to play, a piece will be given to this vampire to perform you'll hear the song one time before re-play if one note is off, you're disqualified. Same rules apply for voice. Voice and Instrument may pair up, however one mistake from either, both face elimination.*

*Art: you'll be given a photo to either paint, sketch or create your own masterpiece. You'll have 1 hour to complete and or re-create it. Please bring your own materials for this competition.*

*Vampires are allowed to have other vampires represent them in a competition for reinstatement however if your vampire champion loses you won't be allowed coven re-entry. Ending the games will be a masquerade ball & award banquet ceremony with a chance to have drinks with the Pharaoh, Queen, Elders, and their companions.*

Hollings Estate New York City
Pharaohs holding Cells....

Waking up, Isaiah looked at the person standing outside of his jail cell kneeling. Clarence handed him an envelope leaving.

He nervously opened it sure it had his trial date; but it didn't. "Niarchos, it was a way-out man!" "It's great kid, you've a second chance." Isaiah was elated. "I'm getting out here." he gloated "Boy? "Yes, Elder Niarchos?" "What're you playing you can't practice cause you're here." "I never thought of that. Can you ask the Pharaoh for a keyboard Elder?"

"Can't ask the Pharaoh, I'll ask his Queen. Pharaoh can get in trouble by coming here to give you that, he risked you going free by contact." "She's a nice vampress Niarchos." "You tried to make her a widow boy." "Don't remind me Niarchos.

Las Vegas Nevada......

"Wake Up." "What is it, Chance?" Your lifeline." Cody cracked the black envelope adorned with gold letters and Calligraphy. Reading it. "Why Chance?" "To find snakes you beat grass. You're not thinking of doing it are you woman?" "I gotta try daddy."

"If you lose, you'll be taken into custody. I'll be forced to judge you Cody." She lay her head on his shoulder, "Clarence won't put me to death." Chance's laughter rang out, "He'll. Pop will give his life to protect that vampress, when he falls in love he falls hard. You weren't there in the beginning with Safinah. If someone looked wrongly at her, he'd lose it if they spoke harsh or rude Niarchos and I had our orders.

If he did with Safinah, do you think he calmed over the years concerning Gabriel? Pop was an intelligent human slave. Don't underestimate him as an old vampire. What will you do to gain freedom Cody?"

"Karate."

"Haha you?"

"Allow me to show you something." Cody opened her email, pulling up pictures. Chance looked at them, "I'll be damned." "There's a lot to more to Cody than looks boo." "You were taught by Bruce Zee?" "Yes, I was his side girlfriend before he met his wife for five years, he was a street boy." "Does Pop know?" "No one knows, except you Chance." "When was the last time you practiced?" "It's been a while."

"You've forty-five days to get it right. I'll get you a trainer. What belt are you, Cody?" "Black. I need a sensei with a degree and higher to teach me."

*'John its Chance, ask the concierge for the highest degree karate master in Vegas.' 'Yes Elder. Call as soon as you find someone, please.'* Chance ended the telepathic conversation.

Hollings Estate New York....

"Someone is at the door Clarence." It was 4:30 a.m., the sun was down. Clarence opened the door. "Sorry to interrupt Pharaoh, we got a ping on Cody's emails, she accessed pictures we've taken the liberty of securing her location from the pictures she accessed passing him a manilla envelope." "Good job Shawn, are you competing for the hacker's division at the games?" "Thank you, Pharaoh, I'll consider it." Clarence closed the door dropping it on the nightstand climbing in bed. "What is it?" "News on Cody Sugar." "Lemme see," Clarence passed her the envelope pulling the blanket over himself. Gabriel laughed.

"What?" She handed him pics of Cody and Bruce Lee as lovers. "I knew, I read her thoughts one night when the story of his life premiered on TV. They loved one another, but when fame found him, she didn't want to let go. Cody was in every London tabloid I sent Chance to Inform her to end her relationship it was to public for a vampire." "Bruce knew she's vampire Clarence?" "Yes, the Chinese know of us. We have a name; we're considered ancient creatures. I know something you don't know Sugar." "I'll give a task; call the scroll writers ask to draw scroll 34." "I'm not your Queen, will they obey?" "Gabriel, I have something to confess, you're my Queen under vampire law."

"I don't understand were married when?" "Under vampire law, yes, the night we signed dowry paperwork. You were my wife when I saw you in the coffee shop Sugar" "I love you because you love me, you're special. I knew it when you asked if you could call on me daddy." He grinned, revealing a shy side he didn't let anyone see except his wives. "Cody's in Vegas at Chance's hotel. I think it's time we took him up on the passes he gave at the engagement party. What do you think Clarence?"

"I like Idea. We get up like we're going for a stroll instead we fly to Vegas. I'd like to see him scramble. I'm going to bite him to see the truth." "What do you mean Clarence?" "When I sip blood, I see a truth they may be hiding or lying about Sugar." "What did you see the night you drank my blood?" "You were touched by an uncle as a child inappropriately, he didn't have intercourse with you because your grandmother caught him. You were six." He held his head down," sorry honey."

"I'm glad you saw it. Now you can fix what's broken and love me better Clarence." He kissed her lips chuckling. "What?" "I saw your first kiss, a boy you cut with your braces. You cried for days." She covered her eyes. "It was horrible Clarence that reminds me, do I need to sleep with retainer?" They laughed while laying down.

Ann & Papa Nates Room......

Ann woke Papa "Clarence was downstairs with Isaiah Nate. I heard the day guardians talking in the garden." "What you mean he wasn't supposed to be. Ann?" "Yes, Nate it's a legal breech?" "He's the Pharaoh, this is his house he can do what he pleases in his house Ann." "There are vampire laws we created for a reason."

"Yes, that Clarence can override us as Elders any time he wants but doesn't. You know he abides by the laws like the rest of us. He loves the boy like his own." Papa turned over Ann held him from behind.

"Wives ain't gonna like me and you messin around Annie." "What they know about this love Nate? Where they slaves with us? Or there when we guarded the plantation by day while Clarence and Chance slept? How about when we found you? Or when I nursed them whip wounds on your back ta closing?

I sutured them wounds closed best I could ta keep infection off ya. No one tells me when I can cuddle with my nasty Nate."

He sighed aloud. "Ann you're to jealous, we ain't good no more you know this." "Nate?" "Umm?" "You love me?" "I wasn't the one ask the Pharaoh fo no divorce you done that Ainsworth, now you regretting ya decision some thirty odd years later?" Ann was quiet. "I loves you Nate, I ain't sharing shouldn't have ta. Aint no changing my feelings."

"I love ya muffin," holding her. No one understood him like Ann. She helped find his kids during slavery. They knew her as mother and grandma. The great grands, nieces and nephews call her grandma, Mema, or any form of grandmother; she adorned all titles with pride.

Papa Nate Origins
Dekalb County Georgia
Hollings Plantation
1862....

Nate held Ann's hand thinking of the night he and Clarence met. He was at deaths door the night Clarence found him tied to a bloody whipping post. It was the fifth time the oppressors caught him running, but no one knew why. This time they issued thirty lashes leaving him in the wintry night tied up, wounds exposed with frozen blood on his back he was stark naked. The slaves stayed up knowing not to touch him they snuck him water quoting the bible for encouragement. Clarence smelled the blood knowing someone was hurt.

He walked up the middle of the slave quarter straight to papa looking him in the eye. Papa Nate asked, *Is ya Gabriel, da angel come ta carry me ta Jordan? Why ya ask? Ya eyes bright like fire made from heaven's coal stoves. Ya hair long like the trumpet blowers of heaven you sho you ain't here ta carry souls? I is, but not ta Jordan.* Clarence popped his binds tossing him over his shoulder exiting as slowly and easy as he entered.

"Ya sees nothing," he called out to slave on lookers disappearing into the dark wood. Thats exactly what the following morning, nothing. Clarence carried him to the medical room Ann and Safinah set up for people Clarence would try and save. Papa Nate was going to make it. He'd lost a lot of blood. Clarence poured his blood in a glass, they gave it to Papa and soaked rags with it, laying it on the worst of his wounds. It helped his bleeding cease, healing his wounds faster however they needed to be stitched. Ann was better at stitches than Safinah. She didn't get nervous when they'd scream. Ann would keep stitching.

Safinah and Ann worked all night to stitch Papa Nathans back or fold the skin over and tape it a technique Lily taught them where flesh was too thin to stitch. Safinah gave him herbs to keep him sleeping for a few days not to disturb the wounds. Clarence didn't like anyone drinking his blood, but his maker said it had healing properties, and to use it sparingly. Messengers and slave catchers carried bulletins looking for a runoff slave. Clarence invited the messenger in for brandy as they sat fireside talking.

"What're they saying this nigger did? lighting his pipe casually making sure to use English as proper as he could. "He runoff five times sir looking for his family, other niggers they probably dead." "Shame he would try and run he should know better." "Yes, he should sir." "He hasn't come past here. My slaves would say a nigger's been hiding on my land." They finished brandies by the fireplace Clarence saw him out. Clarence drank blood and water mixed, but it looked like brandy to the human eye.

Tossing his glass in the fireplace Safinah entered, "what he say?" "Looking for a runaway slave, hope dis Lincoln hurries an' sign dis proclamation. Its rumored he gots negro blood." "Who do Clarence?"

"Dis Lincoln fellow be president up north, they fights ta make him president over da unions south too. It be talk no one seen evidence of his black blood Cotton." "Dey aint Peety." "I'll be here when they expose him, you can too Cotton." She nestled her head in his neck shaking her head, no. "Why not?" Sucking her full bottom lip, holding her on his lap whispering fresh talk. "Ya fraid?" "Yes'sir" "Of?" "I ain't see my Mammy gain."

"Oh, ya wanna see my mother-in-law humm?" cupping her ass. "Yes'sir, Ise say I marries a white man." "Hahah." "When we's broom jumpin? It be two plantin season past. We's livin in sin Clarence." "Who gonna marry a negro an' a white man?" "A negro and a negro Clarence. Ya ain't foget dat" "In dey eyes ise one of em. I knowed wat is woman ain't no need mindin."

"You ain't Dem Peety." "Thank God for dat youse my wife here." touching his heart and head. "Youse mine no paper say what ya is ta me. Iffin broom jumpin ain't in a man heart he aint hitched." Safinah raised her dress untying her petticoat resting on his huge manhood. He slid down in her Queen Ann chair welcoming her sexual advance.

She rode slowly, staring in his eyes as fireplace flames danced off her flesh rippling thighs enhancing the glow of love flowing between them. Safinah grinded gripping her pussy, twirling her waist wildly. Opening her blouse, she gave him something to suck taking control. He sucked a sweet nipple hearing soft moans. *I love you Safinah.* She increased her stride unwrapping her hair wild kinky cotton billows falling in his face the smell intoxicating him. Clarence shifted trying to hold his nut she rode hard the chair moving by inches with each land of her bounce. "Cotton Imma release." She kept going, he held her close listening to her heart Dam! *"Ya knowed what dis do I aint control it yet Fi.' 'Don't worry you've years to practice.'* "Hehe!"

A gripping scream came from the medical room Clarence ran to the commotion *draw the blinds Ann* Safinah yelled. Clarence Chance and Caine entered the room. Papa pinned Ann against the wall with a broken bottle at her throat. '*Where I is?!*' "Put da bottle down, please, yose safe here. How ya hear me thinkin you a demon?" '*Ya save me why a white man wanna save me?*' "Aint white no demon." Papa dropped the bottle jaw dropped shocked. "Look!" Ann yelled. "Ya break ya sutures. Please rest!" Papa was too weak he did as Clarence asked. "We gotts ta tape it close Fi."

They explained what was going on but not what he and Chance were. *'I can't stay I gots ta find my picanninies an' wife.'* *"Ise help ya iffin ya stays put till it safe."* Clarence read the bill post to him. *'Ya reads?'*

*Ise self-taught as a slave.* "Y'all reads?" Papa Nate asked Caine, Chance, and Ann. "Clarence taught us we teaches each other." Caine replied. Papa was amazed. 'Ise stayin' "Ya ain't go out it be a while I has ya word?" "Ya gots my word long as you helps wit my chillen." "Clear da room please." Clarence requested and Chance stood outside the door. "Dat why ya run?" "Yes'sir Ise free once but I return fo my family. I caught dey steals my freedom."

"When Ise free I become a vicar has a secret church here in Georgia.:" "Youse a preacher?" "Yes'sir I ain't got papers causin they tooks em when ise caught. Ise ordained dat what word dey say when dey gimme dat paper." Clarence fell to his knees before him holding his hand crying. "Keep secret youse a preacher. I gots a favor ta ask." "Ask it boy." "Will ya hitch me and my misses iffin I get da paperwork ta sign? I teaches ya ta make ya x mark." "Anything, ya save me." "What ya name be?" "Nathan, they call me Papa Nate." "Clarence." The vampire and the preacher shook hands.

Ann nursed papa back to health. He was helpful around the house with anything that needed to be done. Clarence sat with him asking questions about his children and wife he'd go to auctions looking for his family. When Harriet Tubman made him an underground conductor, he'd let papa hand out food and supplies to see if the runaways were his family. They told Harriet the last plantation his family was on in case she went there to lead slaves to freedom, getting information if possible.

The severely wounded stayed with Clarence, others went with Harriet continuing the arduous journey up north. The slaves who stayed with Clarence gave their stories as he documented facts and anything they could recall. He took a thumb print in blood as a code of silence and a x mark in ink.

Clarence documented Harriet's story one night whenever she rested there which was often. He read the names to Papa Nate to see any story was familiar which discouraged Papa Nate who confided in Ann. There was a large night auction three counties over five hundred slaves for sale, the largest combining the counties. Slave catchers were present with bounties in case any slaves fit descriptions of runaway slaves. Clarence notified his growing blended family to ready themselves and the wagons.

They attended with six covered wagons and ten thousand dollars in cash between them. Papa Nate, now shaven with fifty pounds, changed his appearance. Clarence sat inside by the window to hear papa say if one of the children were his he was grateful the auctioneer changed the time to evening at the bribery of Clarence of course. He wrote personal notes about slaves, their former owners and branding burns. He sketched portraits of the slave, birth marks and scars to discuss with Harriet in case she freed slaves seeking their kin. Clarence always purchased children out of slavery they kept his secret, he raised them as his making them productive members of society.

Adorned properly in white plantation owner attire he adorned gloves a ruffled shirt jacket, knickers, cufflinks a top hat and a slave on call on a plantation owners top accessory he looked perfect for the part complete with a silver topped walking stick.

His slaves dressed clean which was unusual, but it was the way Clarence saw Alex treat his slaves, so he mimicked him so as not to raise suspicion. Except for Caine who loved tattered clothing. Lily hated it when he wore them, however it kept eyes of suspicion off them. Clarence gave a bag of gold coins to tip the auctioneer for bids to sway in his favor for whatever slaves he wanted. The auction continued, none of the children thus far belonged to Papa.

"Next, we have this lot of old trustworthy niggers the previous owner stated they never tried to run. They cook and the butler will oversee your plantation and house slave property. This mammy is baron, but this trained Mammy makes dresses, drapes mends, cooks, repairs, she's a lady's maid, and rears children with forty-five years of experience and southern hospitality to boot per her previous owner.

Clarence looked up from his pipe careful not to show excitement. These two can be bought together or separated let the bidding begin together at $25. Clarence bid. "Do I hear $30." "$30!" "$40 Clarence bid. "$40 going once twice sold to the young plantation owner for $40 in the creme colored dry goods."

"Next these fifteen picaninnies must be purchased as a lot starting bid opens at $200." The room buzzed owners combined finances for purchase because of the high opening bid was high. "Clarence, shake your head if ya hears me." Clarence gently shook his head yes. "Four of em be my picaninnies." Clarence blew smoke out the window, a sign they knew he heard them and would bid. The bid rose quickly along with papa Nates anxiety. "Going once going twice at $800--"

"One Thousand!"

Clarence spit tobacco on the dirt floor. The room filled with whispers, smoke, and stares towards Clarence. "The higher bid was received by the young man on the front row anyone? Going once...going twice..." BANG! "Sold to the young master for $1000."

The auction continued, "buy her" Clarence heard Elijah whispering "She's a pretty flower. Ise pay when we get home." Here is one for you gentlemen to have comfort on nights your wife's unwilling." Gruff laughter filled the air looking at her naked curves. Her hair was dirty and matted. Her skin was filled with dry spit blood and cum stains as she tried to hide her breasts the auctioneer kept removing them. "Seventy-five dollars is the opening bid for this comfort gal still in childbearing years. She can make mo slaves with the right stud." Clarence let the bid rise. "Two fifty is the current bid do I hear $300?" The room grew silent "$300" Clarence added with a southern drawl letting them know he was one of them.

"Going once going twice sold for $300 to the Hollings plantation." Men hooped and clapped. A white slave owner leaned forward; you can make plenty more slaves with her," patting his shoulder. Clarence smiled but inside was disgusted. The auction ended Clarence paid collecting the bills of sales for each purchase without them he could never give legitimate freedom papers or claim them as property if they were stolen and reselling was attempted. He made sure the bills of sale were detailed mentioning birthmarks or scars to each slave he'd purchased with full descriptions and features. Elijah and Caine rustled eighty souls into the wagons. Ann Safinah and Lily gave out food and water inside covered wagons. Clarence whispered to Caine. Do not lets Safinah see da old folks put em in wit papa an' his picaninnies.

Yes Massa! Caine said loudly making it look good scurrying away fast to get the job done. The auction owner gave Clarence the list of where they'd be the next five months. "You own plantations Mr. Hollings?" "I have five hundred acres out of Dekalb County. I grow sugar, tobacco, and cotton. I own an orange grove and apple orchard this is why I need these niggers to work my land."

The auction owner shook his hand. "Thank you, Mr. Hollings." Take these two slaves free they in bad condition but ya slaves look like you take care of em. I'm sure you can patch these two right up. Clarence approached his six-passenger velvet lined gold trim expensive carriage imported from France. Elijah helped him drive home.

Safinah sat inside the coach with Clarence curtains drawn cuddling him. 'Anyone need medical Safinah?" "Minor Clarence, I say dat right?" "Yes Cotton." The ride was long they beat sunrise. "Bring the old ones to the kitchen please introduce little flower to Elijah," they chuckled. Caine walked them through the back they sat at the kitchen table. "Cotton come to the kitchen please." "Clarence suns comin." "I knowed it baby." "Ise tired Peety Ise bring ya a blood fo bed come on lessin we go ta bed." "Woman comes to da kitchen."

Safinah entered the kitchen instantly crying, falling to her knees at Isabel's feet putting her head in her lap. Avril grabbed "Clarence boy I knowed youse alive. I gets ta holds my boy looks at cha...a plantation Massa. Ise gettin tears an' dirt on ya good dry goods." Clarence cried hugging Avril "I ain't care bout dese white folk dry goods." Avril laughed through tears of joy.

"Stop dat Avril we's da same slaves ya knowed." Safinah hugged Avril "Ann!" Safinah called! Ann here too? "Yes Isabel." "Dey say she dead Clover" Ann entered the kitchen "God in heaven!" Ann hugged Avril and Isabel in tears. "Where yo tea pots Clover?" "Mammy you ain't no maid housekeeper chere." "Gal dis my kitchen you ain't gots no mo kitchen."

Clarence shrugged his shoulders at Safinah. "Let me show y'alls sleepin quarters" "We stays together Clarence." "I knowed Isabel" Clarence held her hand reassuringly walking up winding steps "Where's we's goin boy?" Avril whispered. Clarence opened the door to the huge master suite. Avril refused to cross the threshold staring at the huge room. "Dis can't be fo us. Ise gonna rest a spell, wit Isabel Clarence." "Go on Avril I knowed yalls tiresome" The fought back tears. Safinah showed them where everything in the house was to help themselves. Isabel sat on the huge bed she was only allowed to fix for her misses.

She cried thanking God Clarence spared them from their unknown fate. Ann remained awake in case they needed anything, assisting papa with the children. When they were in the wagon his oldest Nathan Jr. crawled to him in tears. The next oldest girl remembered the day the masters traded her papa for bags of sugar and cotton.

"Papa?" She hugged her father crying tears of happiness. The younger kids didn't remember him, they were babies when he was sold. "Dis is our pappy." Nate junior informed the twins who were now six. Papa held out his arms and they greeted him trusting their brother. "What a ya mammy?" Holding their heads down "she gone on a year we think papa." "How Junior?" "Massa put a baby in her, midwife say it in her wrong. She losses blood doc say he can't fix it."

Papa cried, "how y'all get sold?" "Massa lost money selling off sickly livestock. Folk come fo dey coin constable say he gots ta pay what he owe. Kids makes da most at auction. Ise able to keep us together dis da first one we's at papa." "God be praised da older ones?" Far as I know they at da plantation papa." "All nine junior?" "Far as when we tooken yes'sir. Massa make Daisy his comfort gal she say he not rough wit her." "She gots picaninnies Junior?" "When we tooken no papa." When they arrived, everyone headed to the big house.

Papa Nate and the children followed Elijah to a newly built 5-bedroom cabin. "Aint finished yet papa we put a pot belly in chere. Da out houses out back two of em. Dis fo ya from Clarence an' us fo when we find ya picanninnies. He speaks wit ya bout terms. We ain't lowed to cut no bushes on da fence line keeps eyes out an' folks from trespassin."

"Since youse, da first house on da land youse da eyes now." Elijah handed him three shot guns, "for ya an' ya olda boys. "Clarence say shoots first asks questions later." Papa was in tears, grateful. "Can ya ask Ms. Ann ta come Elijah?" He hugged Elijah, "I asks her, she sleep in da big house. Welcome home brother."

Ann came with clothes for the children, fruit, honey, meats, dishes, and other gifts neighboring families donated as welcoming items. "Ann, you has your own house?" "I sleeps in the big house Nathan I ain't married." "Ya wanna help with my chilens?" "Thank ya kindly Nathan but I ain't wanna get good den we finds ya wife." "Wife dead picaninnies say she die berthin." "Ise sorry Mr. Nathan" He kissed her hand. "I helps ya however I stays in da big house till we knowed one another Mr. Nathan." "Yes'm as you say."

## Vampire Uprising Chronicle I

Current Day the year 2020....

Caleb's coven was planning the games. The building was close to being completed. It was designed like a roman arena. Three Thousand seats and a holdover house with 100 televisions from the basement to the 6th floor eighty-inch screens installed in the main arena with several types of lighting.

The battle ground easily switched from sand to dirt to mud or grass depending on the sport. Caleb was excited. He created a champagne room for the Pharaoh and his Queen to entertain vampire dignitaries.

Gabriel dialed the scroll writers "this is Gabriel." "Great One what do we owe the pleasure?" "The Pharaoh asked I call, and request scroll 34 please." "Great One I'm sending a document for you to e-sign." Gabriel obliged her returning it." She untied the leather strings gently unrolling the old parchment. My name is Sharon Great One I'll read your scroll today.

*Scroll 34*

*January 21st, 1910*

*Zhou Xie*

*(pronunciation: Zow-She)*

*He began entering over 200 death matches he knew 22 styles of karate. Experts weren't able to assign a degree to his skill set because he surpassed them all. In 1925 Zhou entered a competition for five million American dollars for 10 rounds of excruciating combat. Zhou completed the rounds in one hour emerging as the sole victor. He was invited to enter an illegal competition that promised to double his winnings. When Zhou* arrived, men placed large bets, Clarence was one. The fight began, Zhou was winning.

Round one ended with the promoters bringing water to the fighters, in it, white oleander root undetectable to taste or smell in humans. Clarence smelled it and by the time the scent made it to him Zhou drank the poison. Clarence knew the round was going to end badly for Zhou. Despite the poison coursing rapidly in his veins, he broke his opponents' ribs nose and arms sadly he was severely beaten once the poison set in. Elijah and Caine grabbed him before the men could finish the warrior off. They took him to his hotel Clarence sat bedside. "You're dying from poison and inside wounds. You'll be dead inside of an hour. You can become immortal Xīxuèguǐ a vampire, but you can never walk in the sun. You must drink blood to survive. This is the price for life eternal nod your head if you understand Zhou."

"Shì de, wǒ zhīdào wǒ jiāng chéngwéi xīxuèguǐ" ("Yes, I understand I'll be vampire.") "Wǒ jiāng chéngwéi shén, yǒngshēng" ("I'll be a God living life eternal") Clarence nodded to Caine and Elijah who held Zhou down. Clarence turned him vampire sharing his blood to heal his wounds.

The year 1955……

Zhou Xie has a wife, as she walked home, she was robbed and murdered. The duo responsible were caught and tried under human law and assigned a prison term of ten years each. Zhou hated this because he like the negro was not wanted in America. These men served eighteen months of a *ten-year term. Zhou consumed with rage begged the vampire Elders to seek revenge for the loss of his wife. The vote was 6against. Zhou wasn't allowed to avenge his wife. The Elders felt it would draw attention to Zhou placing him under arrest and being exposed as vampire.*

*Zhou defied the Elders; his warrior spirit wouldn't allow him rest. In one blow the first man was decapitated. His head rolling into traffic was crushed by a bus. He did this in a busy shopping district. He went to the home of the second man he sat at dinner with his wife and children terrorizing them. Zhou put his fist through the killer's chest, holding his beating heart in his hand. He placed the heart on his wife's plate wiping his bloody hands on his daughter's blond hair.*

*Zhou was judged by the vampire Elders on June 6th, 1957. He was found sane, however, because of the violent nature of what Zhou did. He was the first vampire to be excommunicated for Elder defiance. The Pharaoh was said to shed tears publicly followed by months of depression as Zhou is one of his turned sons.*

*End scroll.*

Clarence entered the bedroom with tea, "Gabriel what's wrong?" "They read scroll 34, sorry for your loss." She dried her eyes. "We speak of this to no one. I sent Zhou an invite to the games." "Does Chance know about Zhou?" "Yes Sugar, however, I think he's forgotten him."

Clarence's text chimed. He read it, handing it to Gabriel. Zhou:我会在那里带铃铛的兄弟。

"What does it translate to Clarence?" "I'll arrive with bells on brother." She shook her head sighing "Cody is in trouble Clarence." "You prepared to make good on your bet Sugar?" "Hehe"

Las Vegas Nevada....

The private plane landed in Vegas by 7pm when the Pharaoh and his Queen approached the desk, the vampire clerks were shocked immediately kneeling.

"Please rise." "We have your suite ready Great Ones." "It's beautiful Clarence." Gabriel was in awe of the original chandeliers above her. "Tell no one I'm in the hotel John." "But Pharaoh." the male vampire nudged her.

"I'm sorry sire, forgive her ignorance." "Speak freely.

"Elder Chance said if you arrive to alert him ASAP. "Tell no one." "Yes Pharaoh." "Let's go to Chance's room Gabriel." Clarence knocked gingerly smelling Cody's strong scent. Chance opened the door shocked. "Pop what're you guys doing here?" "Kneel."

It been many years since he knelt, Clarence held Gabriel's hand walking past his kneeling son. He nodded at Gabriel, "please rise Chance." When he rose, she hugged him, but Clarence didn't. Clarence struggled to control his rage, Cody entered, Gabriel walked behind Clarence afraid, before Cody could speak, he teleported across the suite grabbing her throat pushing her on her knees. "Guard the Queen. Don't leave her side Chance." "Yes Pharaoh." "If you try anything, I'll kill this bitch and then you." Chance was afraid Clarence sensed it. Chance stood in front of Gabriel, "Pop please...." Chance begged his father for Cody's life. Clarence growled slow and low. "You hid the vampire who tried to kill my Queen! And now you ask to spare her life when you should have concern for your own?!"

Security burst through the doors, once they saw it was Clarence they dropped their weapons kneeling faced down.

Gabriel trembled. "Don't fear Sugar, these vampires won't harm you." "Clarence pointed to one of the guards, "blow his head off" pointing to Chance who begged for his life. The vampire cocked his gun. "STOP!" Clarence laughed maniacally giving the cease order. "Pop please allow an explanation." Clarence dropped Cody, "don't move or I'll kill you bitch."

Security turned their guns on Cody. He clutched Chance's throat careful not to snap his neck. Clarence sunk his fangs into his jugular, blood spilled hitting vampires like rain. He struggled to free himself Clarence tightened his grip. He dropped Chance diverting his attention back to Cody. Vampires opened the circle allowing him through. Cody was scared she'd heard of his temper but was fortunate avoiding the receiving end until now.

He held her hair in his fist, her neck straight, feet dangling he stared listening to her beg for her life watching her squirm with a diabolical vertical stare. "Please Clarence forgiveness." He pushed his face into hers, peering deep into her eyes gripping her in fear. A fly caught in a web Clarence bit her cheek with four fangs Her screams were shrill echoing through the casino over slot machines, rolling dice, and jovial winners as he pulled a chunk of flesh from her spitting it out at Chances feet across the room exposing her teeth and gums. Clarence tilted her head, blood from her open cheek drained into his mouth filling him. "I'm dying Pharaoh, you're draining me." Cody cried out. Gabriel squeezed Chance's hand afraid. "How rude do you want some, Sugar?" "No thanks daddy." She didn't want anything from the woman who tried to end her life.

Gabriel trembled like a leaf, and Clarence and Chance smelled her fear. He drained Cody inches from death. Clarence used her hair to wipe his mouth and hands. He tossed her across the floor she landed at Gabriel and Chance's feet. "Lock them in separate cells." "He's a vampire Elder he can't be arrested!" Clarence hyper-sped to the mouthy vampire security bloody and stained Clarence drained him as an example. They picked up Cody and Chance, who were unconscious tossing them over their shoulders, showing Chance extra care as their maker. Clarence and Gabriel went to their suite. "Place four security vampires outside this door at all times." "Yes Pharaoh."

"Send John up with tea for my wife please. The vampire left swiftly tripping over his shoes, afraid. Gabriel's phone rang. It was Niarchos. "Hi."

He was chipper to hear her voice, it made his day. "You, ok?" "No." "Is the Pharaoh there Great One?" "Yes, hold on." She handed Clarence her phone. "I tried to call pop." "I was busy, do you need me Niarchos?" "I arrive by morning pop." "Ok see you soon son"

Niarchos hung up texting Gabriel.

Niarchos: It'll be ok Gabriel. I'm coming. "What did you learn Clarence?" "Chance didn't know she attempted to kill any of us. He wasn't a part of her plot Sugar. He was going to say but didn't know how."

"Chance loves her Clarence." "I know I saw it in his eyes. Sugar come" he patted the sofa. "No, you're dirty." "I'm a savage you saw my true nature exposed. I understand if you call off our engagement although I'd be heartbroken. You saw what I am Sugar" "Engagement huh? You said I'm your wife."

"You are Gabriel." "If I call it off, am I still your wife Clarence?" "Technically yes, however I'll sign a blood separation oath." "I don't want one." Clarence rushed kneeling before her." "You're a mess daddy" she took off her top wiping blood off his face. "Do you mean it Sugar?" "I do, what part of I'm in love with you Clarence didn't you understand?"

He went to kiss her, "NO!" She ran around the suite giggling as he playfully gave chase.

# Chapter 21
# Keep Your Head Up

Las Vegas Nevada....

"Pharaoh what a surprise. "Please rise John." "I'm pleasingly surprised to hear of your arrival. We didn't get to prepare Great One." "How long has Cody been here John?"

"I'm unsure Pharaoh. When I asked, the desk said two weeks." "You're in command when Chance absent?" "Yes Pharaoh." "I'm implementing a cease and desist on making and indoctrinating new vampires for this coven. The coven master of this house betrayed me. He must stand before the Elders for his treachery." "May I order you a drink perhaps a vintage whiskey tox Pharaoh?" "Tox blood whiskey strong John thank you." "Pharaoh permission to speak?" "Speak freely."

"I run the hotel and coven; I live in the suite of the attic has--"

"Three hundred rooms John." "How'd you know Pharaoh?" "I drew the blueprints." "You're an architect Great One?"

"I learned from Benjamin Banneker; I haven't received formal paperwork. I have the original blueprints for the executive manor. You know it as the White House. He completed it after the architect abandoned the job, I assisted some nights he rewarded me with the blueprints John." A young vampress holding the drinks on a tray and her head down shyly arrived to serve the drinks. "What's your name child?" "Mara, Great One."

"You'll make drinks for my bride and I during our stay. No one fixes, nor brings them except you Mara." "It'll be an honor to serve you, Pharaoh."

Mara thought *gosh he's fine looking at his smile. His fangs are gorgeous. I'm too fat to be beautiful.* "How dare you say you're too fat to be beautiful! Have you met my Queen?" "No Pharaoh, I haven't," she was confused, wondering how he knew her thoughts.

"Were you aware in my time vampresses and women were considered destitute if they had no weight? People pointed and laughed at how poor your house was. It was embarrassing to be seen with a slim woman Mara. This is John, Chance's second Gabriel and this is Mara." Hello Great One, your beauty and charm precede you," "Thank you John please rise." "Mara thinks she's ugly because she's robust. Mara, this is Queen Gabriel. My Queen," Mara nodded.

"Girl, we're winning," Clarence used his strong arms to grab her hips turning her toward him before grabbing her thick thighs slipping his tongue through Gabriel's pretty teeth. Mara smiled, feeling better about herself. "When I wake John, I'll visit Chance. Have a chair in front of his cell. I'll need privacy please. Turn off recording devices he may choose a witness to be present John." "As you request Pharoah." "Hello Niarchos bring coffee and soil please." "Yes Pop."

Clarence let Gabriel sleep the next morning. He went to Chance's suite to search. Security swept every inch of the penthouse. It looked like a jail toss when they were done. "Leave it this way." "Yes Pharaoh" security obeyed. He entered the jail. Vampire security escorted him to the chair he requested. They were joined by a scroll writer who was vacationing in Vegas. "I'm glad you're here Steven. I'll float back lost vacation time for servicing the crown today. Thank you, Pharaoh. "Steven, you're standing witness today. Create two scrolls when you're done bring them for my blood signature. Please call with the scroll numbers."

"Steven removed his stenographer as Clarence glared at Chance. I thought of the night I turned you, how afraid I was for you to die. I had no other vampire to protect me. You let your love cloud your judgement. No longer are we equals. We ran from slavers. My wife saved your life when you were on your dying bed and my new bride held your hand last night as you were chastised fearing for your life." "The love we have for you runs all through these covens and you risk losing it for a vampress who doesn't love you, Chance." "You've found love twice Pharaoh but what of me?" Clarence paced calming himself.

"Yes Chance, from a woman who deserves you. I fed from you, taught you business. I know you've nothing to do with Cody's treachery. You'll go before Elders for aiding and embedding the vampire responsible for an attempt on three lives. It'll be fast, so you don't need to remain incarcerated. Do you want council?"

"Yes pop" "Who?" "Jackie Robinson." "Bring the phone please Steven, please call vampire attorney Jackie Robinson for the senior Elder." Clarence handed Chance the phone. "Take me to Cody," She kept her back turned he sat with tension boiling over. "Why did you pick her over me?" We don't choose love, it chooses us. Why did you love spotted Eagle Cody?" She turned around, her face was healing but swollen her eyes were black, as his bite marks were present. She stood head up before his judgmental eyes with bloodstained matted hair and clothes. She needed blood to close her wounds, she was in searing pain.

"He was my love my spirit chose him, although fate didn't see it that way. My husband was a warrior who've lost to a stronger one--"

"Not if you had anything to do with it," "I knew nothing of her plot, Clarence." "When you discovered her plan, you were obligated to alert the Elders in the village, but you didn't Cody. The lie would've died with you and your village until I saved you." Cody darted a hateful look through black eyes. "You made my son deceive me as you deceived your father moons ago. Deceit is imbedded in your character. Lying to Chance about the nature of our relationship? We never agreed to being open, you decided that for us."

"I smelled him on you Cody and you wondered why I never ate your pussy, but you love me, Cody? Deceit! You swore you'd stopped dating Bruce a month prior, yet your photos pop up in London tabloids." "Why did I choose Gabriel Cody? You're a creature of spiritual background reach back. I've studied under great Indian Chieftains and Shamans your spirit and intent are in the wrong place.

"You set out on a path of deceit from an early age. Your deceit graduated into treachery, your treachery shifted into drug use, your drug use morphed into attempted murder climaxing into treason. Those small lies have cursed you for generations and led you to your reckoning at this moment in time! It's time to pay the piper. Pray, meditate, call on ancestral spirits for guidance and understanding because you'll need them vampire."

"Get them showers get Elder Chance anything he wants. He can conduct business as usual. Blood as many times a day as needed, A positive no tox. He's not to leave his cell. Only visits from Elders or his attorney. Call me when Jackie Robinson arrives," "Yes Great One. What of Cody?"

"Blood five times a day, A positive. Shower by armed guard. Make sure the vampire is male security on staff and gay wanting men only," "Yes sire." "Place him to guard her so she won't tempt him sexually. No one is to converse with her.

She's awaiting transport for trial. Set up a hotel room for Chance's trial, "Yes sire." "Steven?" "Yes Pharaoh?"

"Make sure you're there to document scrolls, call Margaret and have her explain how legal scrolls are written. How long have you been with the scroll writer's division?" "Five years Pharaoh," "This is a special assignment for you?" "Yes Pharaoh." "This is your shot don't blow it Steven." "What's your name officer?"

"I'm vampire security Nathan Great One at your service." Clarence looked at him thoroughly. He favored Papa Nate before he turned thick and stocky with a beard. "Who named you vampire?" "My mother sire" "Say of your lineage what do you know officer?"

"My great-great grandfather was a slave. He had thirteen kids, I think. They were separated during the slave trade he tried to find them. He was killed by the slave catcher's for running. Mom said my great-great grandmother was his daughter sire." "She survived as he whispered a lone tear running down his face, Clarence smiled holding his head in his hands. Forgive me sire I don't understand." "Your great-great grandma what do you know of her Nathan?" "I met her a few times when I was a baby. I remember her saying I looked like her dad and her brothers. She has a diary, mom has it Pharaoh." "Your mom is alive?" "Yes sir." "Do you've siblings Nathan?" "One he's incarcerated." "Do they know your vampire?" "Yes, how could I explain the eyes to my mother when I wasn't born with them Great One? She'd heard stories about black vampires who helped slaves escape. Her mother was senile when she told those stories, we ignored her thinking she was getting senile prattling on Pharoah." "Can you get the diary please Nathan?" "Yes of course Pharaoh," "Assure your mother it'll be returned. I'll compensate her for allowing me to borrow the book. I'll need you here when the Elders arrive. Please be our personal security until Elder Niarchos arrives." "I've always wanted to meet him. Is he strong and fast as they say Pharaoh?" "I have a challenging time keeping up when we race Nathan. Will you compete to join Madji Elite?" "Yes Pharaoh" "Good to hear Nathan."

Clarence entered his penthouse falling into bed. He didn't undress, he was exhausted. Gabriel raised the blanket. "Alexis turn the air to 65." Clarence spooned with her falling asleep. Niarchos arrived late, with four bags of coffee, soil, and a surprise for Gabriel. When he got off the elevator security blocked his path. "I'm Elder Niarchos, step aside." They didn't move.

*Pharaoh* Niarchos mentally called his father. Clarence came to the door reminding them "Let all Elder's in officers." Niarchos opened a bag removing her dingo. "He missed you Gabriel" Niarchos smiled at Gabriel's reaction. Clarence shot him a look of disapproval. "What pop," he mouthed silently. Niarchos made coffee, "Our new addiction." He and Gabriel sipped and chatted. "It is Niarchos. What's this, the coffee clutch club guys?" "Yep!" Clarence laughed at their joined response.

"What's up Pharaoh?" Clarence updated Niarchos. "Old Indian was always trouble, but this shit here takes the cake. The phone rang, Gabriel answered. "Ok thank you. Jackie Robinson is here." "Shit just got real. Haha" "Niarchos! A lady is present." "Apologies Great Queen." Jackie knocked. "Come" Niarchos spoke low. Jackie was short, 5 ft 7 inches, stocky built, extremely good looking, well dressed in a pin stripe tailored suit. He knelt before Clarence and his Queen. "Please rise." Clarence loved when Gabriel requested the rise instead of him. "This is my Queen Jackie. Great One? It's a pleasure. I'm sorry we meet under such unfortunate circumstances." "Thank you, Jackie." "Niarchos, let's watch 90-day fiancé and let them talk" They entered the bedroom sipping coffee with Jupiter, the dingo following.

"Have you spoken with Chance Jackie?" "I have Pharaoh. Please be lenient. If you are the other Elders will too, but if you're hard they'll follow. Please before they arrive will you share your thoughts?" Clarence paced. It was something he did when worried.

"Loss of privileges and I implemented a cease and desist on this coven. I'm thinking 10 years. He must be made an example of. Lying by omission can't go unpunished Jackie. Will he testify at his trial?" "I didn't advise it Pharaoh." "I think he should. Elders will want to hear what happened from his perspective and will be lenient with judgement. If he doesn't speak in his defense, what will they think?"

"What of Cody Pharaoh?" "If you wish to represent her after Chance you may. It's a hard case, are you brushed up on vampire laws?" "Yes Great One." "It's your call Jackie. Who's paying you for her defense? Don't say." "Trust me Pharoah I'm charging Elder Chance for that love because her case is attempted murder on two Royals." "You'll go down in the scrolls for these trials are you ready counselor?" "I am." "Who's your lawyer Pharaoh?" "Hunter Jackson he's sitting quietly taking notes for Cody's case and to advise on maximum punishments per vampire law."

"Thank you Great One. I'm going to freshen up hit the books if that's ok." "Go Jackie, I'll see you tomorrow call anytime. Whatever you need call John." Clarence saw Jackie out. "Honey, can we see Vegas tonight?" "I can't leave sugar, I'm in the middle of somethings." Clarence handed Gabriel $10,000 from the safe. "You wanna go with Niarchos Sugar?" "Sure daddy." "You like him, don't you?" "Yes Clarence." "Why?" "He's funny he makes me feel welcomed. He was glad she'd made friends. "Y'all have fun bring back something sexy Sugar." She adorned pink lipstick grabbing her jacket. Niarchos grabbed his biker jacket. "You ride?" "My bike is in the garage." "Make sure you don't go fast with her Niarchos." "I won't dad." he joked.

"A Harley huh?" "Yes, ma'am hop on." Gabriel held him tight he smelled her pussy when she opened her legs. He wanted to eat her out. He had to control his thoughts he was getting hard. They rode to boutiques, she shopped till she dropped while he stood by her side with a watchful eye, guarding her with his life.

They went for a ride and wound up in the park square. There was music, humans dancing, laughing, smoking weed, drinking nutcrackers, and making out on the lawn. "This reminds me of Washington Square Park during the 90's in New York. My mom used to take me there selling bracelets we made. She'd make a killing dressing me in a set of earrings, necklace and bracelet having five like it for sale. I remember customers asking her; you have that one? pointing to my neck. She was smart, my mom." "How'd you become vampire Niarchos? You can say." Gabriel resting her hand on his. Niarchos removed his sunglasses.

Elder Niarchos Hollings Origins....

"I was a young boy on the plantation the white owners raped us making us wear our pants under our ass to show everyone they'd anal sex with us. It was to break our spirit. They called it breaking the buck. This happened frequently but the man who raped me, the master of the plantation, he was killed thank God. One night I was in the barn when his son demanded I bend over. I told him his father already did it. He claimed to be the new master, and it was his turn. This was the night of the emancipation I was free to go, he didn't want to free me." Gabriel cried.

"I'll stop Great One. I didn't mean to upset you," wiping her tears. "No Niarchos go on." "I was infuriated I pushed him away knocking him to the ground. He pulled a pistol shooting me. I reckon he was scared a huge negro coming at his ass? Guess he didn't know what to do. I remember being picked up by someone struggling to carry me."

"Three weeks later I was a vampire in a house with other vampires and your husband was the leader. He asked my name, I said I ain't like my name. Pop said I could choose another, but I didn't know what to call myself. Safinah, my mother, had a name chosen course I asked her what it was, mama smiled... *"Niarchos."*

"I asked *'what'*?" Gabriel laughed. "She repeated *'knee-r-koze.'* I asked where she got the name. It was her baby brothers name, he died in childbirth. I was honored to carry it. Upon legal adoption, I became their son Gabriel." He wiped her face with his handkerchief. "They treated us badly Niarchos." "It's ok we have psych's if you need one Great One." hugging her.

"Good to know Niarchos thank you." He knew she cared for him, it felt good. A human woman walked past. "You married daddy, cuz damn you fine as fuck!" "Go away." Niarchos demanded. "Damn you ain't gotta be like that." Gabriel burst out laughing. "That's funny Gabriel. haha?" "These human's get on my damn nerves, especially the women only wanting to fuck sick of it." "The vampresses want you." "It's because I'm an Elder with a coven most are fortune hunters Gabriel."

"How'd you meet your wife?" "Her family owned a haberdashery we did business with. Elijah would help shop for our estate. Her mother held inventory asking I pick it up." He smiled, which was rare. She saw the sharps of his fangs; but they weren't out. "I'd get the items, and my late wife would stare at me. In my time this was the way a woman showed interest in a man. Her mom invited me to dinner, but I declined. I asked pop how to handle it because I knew I'd be invited again. I wanted her from the first time I saw her. She was beautiful like you with pretty hair and smile she was shy and smart Gabriel." "How'd you get past dinner?"

"It was Christmas and Pop hosted the annual Hollings party which was huge for many reasons including arranged marriage proposals and business connections amongst black people county wide. The black elite and common man attended. If you intend to make money hand over fist you better be at the Hollings Christmas party." "Dang like that?" "Yes, the Hollings name holds a lot of weight in Georgia and New York."

"Some were leery thinking pop was white. We explained Pop's mother was black and he identifies as such. The business owners and neighbors arrived, it worked out, making us stronger than the whites in business. This was after the proclamation we secretly did business with one another, causing whites to lose money. The food was buffet service, I sat with her and her parents. I said I'd eaten earlier. I had cookies in hand though. Pop taught me to give the illusion I was eating. I'd crush the cookies allowing the crumbs run down my sleeve." Gabriel laughed. She picked up his hands, they were huge, she rubbed them.

"When we were alone, I explained I was vampire. I showed her what I was. She didn't scream, she touched my teeth and said, aww you are a huge teddy bear sent as a gift from the heavens." "I kissed her for the first time and asked her to marry me that night." "How many days did you know her Niarchos?" "About twenty."

"No way!" "A man knows if he wants to marry a woman in less than ninety days Gabriel." "I say it takes longer." "If we love each other then I'll marry right away. "Men of your time were different Niarchos they knew what they wanted and wasn't afraid to get it."

A man interrupted "Do y'all swing?" Niarchos took off his shades growling the man sprinted off. "I killed a man over Pop. It shocked him so he taught me to control my temper but that's a story for another time."

"It's almost twelve, we gotta go Gabriel." Niarchos enjoyed every minute he spent with her. He took her home and told her, "Good night Great One." "Tomorrow, coffee!" "Yes ma'am." She entered the bedroom as Clarence sat on the bed. "Do you see the time, Gabriel? "It's twelve." She undressed for a bath. "Why're you going to the tub so fast?" "Are you serious?" He walked up on her and bent down smelling her pussy. He fingered her, looking into her eyes before licking his finger clean. "How does it taste? "Faithful." Gabriel stormed off sleeping on the couch, making sure she opened the blinds before dozing off.

Morning arrived as Clarence stood in the bedroom doorway of their sundrenched penthouse. "Draw the blinds,

Gabriel." "No!" "Draw the blinds please." "No." "Security." A guard entered making sure not to step in the sun. "Close the blinds officer." "Pharaoh?" "I need to get to my wife. She's been given a gift from God himself to remain half human she's abusing this gift. If you don't close the blinds I, your Pharaoh will die. What's your job vampire?"

"To secure the Pharaoh at any cost." "He stepped a foot into the light screaming. "Stop!" Gabriel screamed upset. She closed them and went for a glass of blood. "Better?" "Yes, Great One. I'm sorry." "It's ok officer." She dashed into the bedroom crying. "You may leave. Take the rest of the week off I'll add a bonus to your pay vampire" "Thank you Pharoah." Clarence was on his knees in front of her in the bedroom. Gabriel, she slapped him. He grabbed her hand kissing her inner palm.

"Forgive a fool. You have a jealous husband, Sugar." "You told me to go Clarence." I'm trying not to imprison you as I did Safinah. I was selfish with her love because I never knew love Gabriel. What excuse do I have when she died loving me? She sacrificed having friends so jealousy wouldn't take hold Sugar."

"Love isn't selfish you made me feel dirty Clarence." "You must be hungry Sugar." "I don't want your blood you're a bad person. You'd let a vampire die to get to me?" "I'd let thousands of vampires die to get to you with no remorse woman." Jupiter jumped on her lap growling at him. "I'll never do it again Sugar." She hugged him, biting his neck, she fed as he held her close.

"Niarchos is a friend. He would never do anything against you daddy." There was chatting in the living room of the penthouse. Elders were mingling happy to see one another. Tables were set, the stenographer was there for Steven to create scrolls. The coven was praying for their maker's fate. They waited for him in the halls to encourage him as he approached his private trial. Chance was escorted by vampire security with guns on him knowing cuffs were worthless. "Open the cell." Niarchos hugged his brother.

"It's not gonna be bad." he whispered, "We love you." Cody yelled down the hall, "I love you daddy! You gonna beat this!" Niarchos shook his head. Chance arrived at the penthouse surrounded by guards who were instructed to shoot at will. Gabriel was on the witness list. She wasn't allowed to judge but being Queen of covens, her words weighed heavily if asked her thoughts. Chance sat at a table with Jackie. Clarence and Gabriel sat next to Steven. Clarence instructed her never to rise or kneel when he entered a room to show equality. The energy in the room was nervous. This is the first time an Elder was judged. Steven read the charges.

*As per our Pharaoh Clarence Hollings was born a slave from humble beginnings, made vampire first of his kind freer of slaves, the breaker of chains. The following charges have been placed against Senior Elder vampire Chance Hollings.*

*1. Aiding and embedding a wanted fugitive.*

*2. Treason.*

*3. Lying to the Crown.*

*4. Guilt by omission.*

*End scroll.*

"Permission to speak Pharaoh?" "Permission granted Jackie." "I stand before you today with a humble heart. We have no defense. Instead, we open the floor for questions and allow Senior Elder Chance Hollings to answer his brothers and sisters' questions. Elder Chance hasn't anything to hide." "He may not skip questions and will answer all questions inquired." Clarence demanded.

"I must advise against this." Hunter interrupted. "Why Hunter?" "Pharoah, I advise Elder Chance's answers may directly affect Cody's trial. Therefore, some of his answers should be stricken from the scrolls until her trial is complete. "Jackie, do you agree?" Hunter gave Jackie the eye. "I do Pharaoh." Niarchos asked the first question. "Did you know Cody planned to kill the Pharaoh or his Queen Chance?" "No, I didn't Niarchos." "I'd like to submit evidence; proof Elder Chance received no calls from Cody within 110 days until the night of the murder attempt.

As for the second attempt on Queens Gabriel's life, Elder Chance attended the engagement party is this correct Elder Nate?" "Yes, Niarchos it is." "Papa Nathan your question?" "Do you know how Cody entered the engagement party Chance?" "I don't Vaughn." Clarence heard his thoughts so far, he wasn't lying. "Elder Ann you have the floor." Hunter advised. "Why did you lie when the Pharaoh inquired if you'd heard from Cody Chance?"

"I was trying to protect the woman I love from death Ann." "Do you want the Pharaoh dead Chance?" "No papa Nate." a lone tear rolled down his cheek. "Elder Elijah the floor is open. "Thank you, Jackie, what happened the day you were turned by the Pharaoh?" Chance explained how he and Clarence met. There wasn't a dry eye in the house. "The best part is he promised I was no longer alone. *I have a son; you are my son together we will walk time. You'll protect me and I you.*" Chance shared the message to Clarence telepathically along with the memory. "He could've let you die Chance?" "Yes, Elijah." He risked going back into slavery to save you knowing the Sheriffs were after you? "What happened to the property you won?"

"Pharaoh gifted the plantation his childhood home to me Elijah." "All 16,000 Acres of it?" "Yes Ann." "Did you have a family before you met Clarence Chance?" "No Elijah." "When Clarence came for you after the lynching, was close to sunrise Chance?" "I wasn't conscious, so I don't recall Elijah." "Elder Lily? What time would you say it was when Clarence left?"

"About 40 minutes till sunrise Elder Elijah." "He risked himself to save Chance's life Elders?" "Yes." Lily replied. "Thank you, Elder Elijah...Elder Caine you have the floor." "You sorry bro?"

"I'm sorry I didn't Inform my father Cody was here. I'm not sorry for helping her Caine." "Your coven lost their way Chance. One bad apple spoils the lot and improper thinking breeds contempt and disorder. I'm not happy with you nor anything I've seen regarding this coven thus far. They are unruly and have not been taught the way of the vampire" Clarence informed the Elders angrily.

"I'd like to ask Queen Gabriel a few questions as a witness if I'm allowed Hunter?" "Permission granted by the Pharaoh Jackie." "Thank you. Queen Gabriel, please step forward." Clarence stood behind her while she spoke. "Queen Gabriel What happened when the Pharaoh found Cody and Elder Chance together?" She explained what she saw. "When the Pharaoh commanded Chance stand by your side while he held Cody by her hair draining her blood for treason, what did Elder Chance do?" Gabriel explained all she witnessed.

"Elder Chance knew she could be killed, yet he protected you over Cody at the Pharoah's command. He didn't attack the Pharoah, watching the woman he loves face a violent deserved chastisement?" "No counselor, he didn't Jackie." "When Pharaoh chastised Elder Chance, did he resist?" "No."

"As an older vampire he could've gotten free yet didn't try Queen Gabriel?" "He couldn't get free Jackie." "How'd you know Great One?" "Clarence is older, swifter, stronger, he was vampire years before Chance was turned there was no way he could free himself from the Alpha vampire." The room was shocked, she was aware. "How'd you come across this information Queen Gabriel?"

"I can't say Jackie." "Queen Gabriel, we implore you to speak truth a vampires life hangs in the balance."

"I heard it within my husband's thoughts Jackie." "You mean he explained telepathically?" "No. I heard him thinking of when he turned Chance. He was melancholy I looked at him and heard." "Thank you Great One." "I have a question, Queen Gabriel? Did Cody mention during the second attempt on your life anything about Elder Chance?"

Gabriel was confused, "second attempt Hunter?" "May I interject?" "Yes Pharaoh, please." "My wife knows nothing because as we waltzed, I wiped her memory of the disheartening ordeal." Elders gasped. Ann smiled. "You can clean a person's memory Clarence."

"I can hypnotize, clean or add thoughts not memories Ann." Papa smiled tapping his arm "You've grown powerful since we were slaves in Georgia huh Clarence?" "Wow." Niarchos added. "She has no recollection. I'm sorry Sugar. Cody ruined my formal proposal, and you were elated at the engagement soiree. I didn't want bad memories interfering with us Sugar forgive me." "It's fine honey." The room was filled with understanding for the love they shared. "I'd like to call witnesses to testify on behalf of the crown if I may. I call Elder Chance's first three wives, Mary, Christina, and Azalea."

Clarence knew Mary she was the only child to former slaves like them. His questions would be directed at her. They were given seats next to Chance. "Mary, I called you to this hearing to ask questions." "Yes Pharaoh." Jackie was nervous. "Mary did you know of the relationship your husband had with Cody?" "Yes, Great One." "How long did it go on?" "I'm not sure Pharoah" "Christina do you know?" "It's been years on and off Great One." "Mary were you happy with this?" "No Pharaoh." "Why not?"

"I heard she was one of your concubines. The Pharaoh's concubines weren't to be shared." "Did you speak with your husband on the matter Mary?" "Yes Pharaoh." "What did he say?" "You didn't claim her, and as per vampire law all concubines must be claimed on paper and coven Elders notified of the agreement Pharaoh." "To your knowledge did Chance check with the marriage commission to see if I had this agreement?"

Jackie interrupted. "Forgive me Pharaoh, was there an agreement on parchment claiming her as your concubine?" "Steven please hand the scroll to Jackie. Please say what you are holding Counselor Robinson?"

"A concubine agreement between Cody and yourself Pharoah." "What date is on the scroll Counselor?" "May first, 1953, Great One." Is that my signature and was seal binding the agreement on the scroll? "It is Great One." Niarchos shook his head. "Steven, is there a dissolved agreement signed in blood ending this contract?" "No Pharoah." "Ladies do any of you want your husband to take Cody as a wife or concubine?"

"No Great One." the ladies answered. "Have you all expressed this to your husband?" "Yes, Pharoah they answered together. May I speak free Pharoah?" "Please Christina." "My husband is a good vampire, but when it comes to this vampress, it's like she placed a curse on him. I've seen this in my country. Something is done to the vampire then, he isn't right. Its Santa Ria Pharoah voodoo." tears rolled down her face. She scuttled to Clarence and Niarchos cocked his gun blocking her path. She fell on her face grabbing at Clarences feet. "I beg you Great One, forgive please." she cried hysterically.

Clarence and Mary looked on with sympathetic eyes. "Pharoah, I tried everything. Chance stated he'd separate from me over a vampress who tried to kill the vampire who saved our lives." she cried. "Azalea...will you stay if Chance marries Cody?" "No Pharoah." "Mary?" "No Pharoah." "Christina?" "Yes Pharoah, I won't separate from the vampire who saved me from human trafficking." "Thank you, vampresses." Do the Elders have additional questions?" "Yes Hunter." "Elder Blaise you've the floor." "Does any wife think the Pharoah is in danger by Elder Chance?" "No." The wives responded in agreement. "Chance, do you have anything to add prior to break?"

"Yes, Vaughn I was foolish not to alert you Pharaoh that Cody was here. For the first time I request leniency and forgiveness from my Elder vampire family." Chance held his head down. "VAMPIRE! Hold your head up brother!" Chance held up his head smiling at Blaise. Ann pushed her chin up staring in his eyes.

"Slaves hold their heads down Chance, by the Pharaoh's bite we're free." Clarence smiled shaking his head yes with his fangs showing. Steven documented their unity; in the middle of disagreement, they still stayed together, he was impressed. Gabriel's phone buzzed. It was a message from Niarchos.

Him: You, ok? I heard he went off last night. What's wrong? Her: Stayed out too long. Him: I heard you were crying. Did he hit you? It's against our laws for vampire to hit his wife. Her: He didn't Nicky. Him: Coffee during deliberation? Her: Of course!

Jackie, Chance, and security left. Nathan from security pulled Clarence to the side. "Were you able to read the diary Pharoah?" "Yes, can you arrive to my suite tonight at seven?" "Sure, should I bring my mom and wife Pharaoh?" Nathan asked. "Please Nathan, especially bring your mom. I have a surprise to present." Clarence approached Papa Nate who was sipping tox gin. "It's early for that."

"No, it ain't Clarence. I need a drink behind this." "I'll need to see you tonight at 8 bring Ann. I have a surprise for you." "Better be good, to get me away from the tables. Chance gave us $10k each." They sat with drinks. "This a whole mess. You're not in danger Clarence." "Caleb, do you sense danger?" "No Vaughn he's remorseful. You won't see any trouble from Chance." "I wonder if Chance gets out, and she's freed, can he control Cody Caleb?" "Lily, what man can control a woman? I been trying to control you since saloon Sunday's shidddd." "Caine, you play too much!" "Who's playing papa Nate?"

"I've implemented a cease and desist. I request a turn lock for 10 years." Elijah cut in. "Are we letting him out of jail?" Clarence let them speak. They agreed to release Chance. "All in favor of vampire turn lock?" "How many vampires do they have Clarence?" "Seven fifty."

"Fine all agreed 20 years of no turns?" "Yes," the Elders agreed. "Loss of coven Clarence asked?" "This loss is too massive a hotel, casino, and spa, who's gonna run it, Clarence?" "His second Ann." "He'll lose coven leader profits Pop." "Niarchos, all profits will go to an escrow account in case of coven emergency." "How will he live, Clarence?" "Let him gamble, Blaise." "Clarence are you serious?" "Let him keep the coven. How much does Chance pay for vampire tax Clarence?" "Same as you all 2% of profits Vaughn. It's an old contract that needs to be renegotiated." They grumbled.

"Tax ain't been raised in over 50 years. Who was President when 2% was implemented?" "Raise it in ten years Clarence." They were careful because it could be them. "Thirty percent for ten years. No new wives' concubines?"

"I disagree Clarence. We aren't slave masters. We cannot direct his life. I hated they wouldn't allow me to marry Lily, it killed me." "Same with Safinah Caine."

"We can't repeat mistakes of those who had us in chains. Hell, if it were me and I loved a woman, I'd drop all this shit. Don't underestimate Chance's gambling skills. I seen the vampire take one hundred dollars turning it into one million over night. Who wouldn't drop everything for love?" "Pop, would you keep all you've or drop it if you couldn't have Gabriel?" Clarence gazed across the room at her. "I'd be poor again Niarchos and Caine."

"I can't" "Papa Nate made the silent room laugh. "Fuck that, sorry ladies." "Shoot see Clarence was a house nigger. People like Niarchos, Ann and I were in the field. He doesn't know hard ass work."

"Papa Nate we've been over this you think the masters were easy on me because I was a white coachman?" "Yes!" they chuckled. "Ann?" "What?" She looked the other way. "Don't involve me, Clarence." "Caine?" "They treated us fucked up, him too. It was the white man's way to divide us mentally and its working. Listen to y'all, we're all still in chains."

"Stop spoiling Clarence Caine." Clarence laughed. "Ya'll think it was easy? Safinah was a chocolate woman it was hard work." "She was a good woman God rest her" "Thank you, Ann." Clarence got back to business. "Chance and his wives need permission to enter New York." They agreed. "Can the Pharaoh randomly check financial records?" Ann asked. "Yes, they agreed. Steven, please read the agreement."

"As per Pharaoh Clarence Hollings King of Covens the Elders present pass judgement accordingly for the crimes and charges presented, documented & written in the sacred vampire scrolls the following shall occur for the fore-mentioned charges.

1. No vampires are to be turned for 20 years or added by other covens.

2. Your coven and vampire tax will be raised from 2% to 30% quarterly for the next ten years.

3. You Must alert Elder Niarchos Hollings in formal writing for permission to visit New York City.

4. All 750 coven members are to give the Pharaoh blood before his departure. Including wives and documented concubines.

5. Financial records and books are to be sent to the Pharaoh's accountants monthly. The Pharaoh has access to the coven and financial records pertaining to the coven its subsidiaries, sister, shell, and parent companies and any business established within the ten-year tax. Upon request financial records from spouses as well.

6. All security shall fall under Elder Niarchos Hollings.

*7. A formal apology will be given to the Pharaoh and Queen Gabriel at the discretion of Elder Vampire Chance Hollings.*

*End scroll*

"I'll bring the scroll for ink and blood signatures Pharaoh. "I'll see you all tonight at 7." Clarence and Gabriel approached the elevator.

Clarence held Gabriel's hand pushing her onto the elevator wall, tonguing her down. He put his hand up her skirt, twiddling her clit. Security remained faced front smiling, pretending not to smell her sexiness. The elevator stopped and Clarence tossed her over his shoulder, whisking her to the bedroom." I love you, Clarence. Was your wife raped?" "Yes." "Did you get the man who did it?" "He was the first human I killed; he wasn't a man he was a savage Sugar." "Did you enjoy it?" "I always love a human kill." Puckering her lips for a kiss.

"What other memories have you taken from me?" "None Sugar." "Promise you won't do it again Clarence." "I didn't want you thinking vampires are animals based on our encounters with Cody Sugar." "Replace, the memory. "I can't Sugar, it's gone my love." "What other skills do you hone Clarence?" "How about I explain as a wedding gift Gabriel?" "Yes," she clapped. "By the way Niarchos is falling in love with you." "How do you know?"

"He let his guard down." "Why do you sneak into people's heads Clarence? It's not polite I don't like it." "I wanted to hear how the Elders felt about Chance's charges. When I got to Caleb, he said '*get the fuck out of my head.*' "Good for you!" "Sugar, let's fuck." "Niarchos' thoughts don't bother you, Clarence?" "No, I want my head of security to love my wife." "He's shaping up to be my best friend. We're coffee clutch buddies." rubbing his dick.

He spread her legs, pushing his face between them, slipping her panties to the side spreading her pussy lips tongue in first, exposing her clit, sucking on her cherry lollipop. She never had a man suck her clit.

Gabriel grabbed a fist full of her hair. Clarence I can't breathe oh god." she moaned as he thrust his untamed tongue deep in her pussy. He licked both lips, graduating to the pink of her pussy rising to clit, starting the ride again from start. She wiggled; he grabbed her, tethering her to his face. "Cum in my mouth." "What?" "I know you heard me, Sugar." "BABY! MOVE!" "Squirt my treat." "Ahhh oh god Clarence!" She tried to back up, but he kept working that fat ass clit.

*Cum, so I can taste you. This is what happens when you don't gimme pussy. I'm a southern boy, we're nasty.* She heard him in her head, trying badly to hold it. "I gotta pee, let me go!" *Pee Gabriel let it go.* His persistent perfect pressure licking and digging his tongue as deep as he could, drove her to sexual madness. Cream cum covered his lips he kissed her first pair of lips as she trembled beneath him

"Ahhh ahhh shiiiiitttt Daddy." "Umm." Clarence moaned as the reward of her double orgasmic rivers flowed into his mouth. Looking up as she slept, he smiled, covering her after licking his fingers clean.

# Chapter 22
# Pharoah Origins

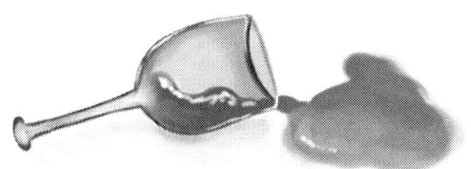

Guard Nathan arrived his mother, and grandmother. The Elders with their spouses joined Clarence for dinner in his suite. "I'd like to read something if I may." Opening the diary guard Nathan loaned Clarence as Steven created a scroll.

"*April 4, 1875....*

*I have learned how to write and read from a man who employs me. After President Lincoln freed slaves, we met in town. His wife passed; he was left rearing twin picaninnies I help with. Thank God he's a Christian like Papa and was a quarter master for us slaves.*

*He's from London. There slavery doesn't exist, he wants to return abroad and asked if I'd accompany him for a better life.*

*Twenty sixth day of April 1875....*

*Some soldiers passed on the road wearing civil war uniforms, and we gave water and bread.*

*I questioned soldiers asking of my brothers hoping they didn't change their names. No one heard of Nathan or Matthew from Harrison plantation, that doesn't stop my asking.*

*June 11, 1875....*

*I miss my mother, there are days I swear, she's here. I ask God to forgive my ill thoughts of that animal filling her with child. That baby was the devil that killed my mother. She birthed thirteen of us with my Papa Nathan, no one died. I'm alone. I can't find my father, sisters, or brothers. Master laid with me I prayed a child don't hold. A few weeks later the proclamation came about Ise free to live with no slave master baby inside. I ran like Papa done as soon as I heard the news. I'm glad I did. He killed half the slaves before they could run.*

Clarence looked at Papa and Ann who were crying. He handed Papa Nate a photo of Iris. Papa Nate held the photo staring in disbelief. "There's more papa, I sent it to our vampire genealogist. It's authentic." Baby Nathan's grandmother stepped to Papa Nate. "You look like my mother." touching his face as he kissed her hand. "Your mother was Iris?"

"Her name was Iris on account --"

"It was her mother's favorite flower."

Papa recalled the night he and his late wife named her. Papa Nathan put it together. "Am I your grandson Elder Nathan?" "You're the offspring of my first-born child Iris Freeman Baby Nathan." Baby Nathan's mother spoke with Papa Nate. "I knew she was talking sense. She'd share stories mentioning you and her siblings." "I'm your great-great great grandfather, they call me Papa Nathan. Chance is missing this Clarence. Let him meet Iris's." Clarence consented. Niarchos left to get Chance. Papa explained everything, introducing Chance to his family. "Do you know how many years we've searched for Iris's children?" Papa Nathan asked clutching Iris's diary.

"Nana...Mama this is my coven leader, the vampire who saved my life, Senior Elder vampire Chance Hollings." "You saved my Nathan from dying?" Baby Nathan's mother asked Chance.

"Yes ma'am. Twelve bullets center mass he wouldn't see morning." "I never wanted him to be a sheriff in the deep south Chance." "He's my head of casino security ma'am." "You may lose him if he joins my coven, Chance." Papa teased. "Shall we go to my suite to talk family?"

Papa Nate tapped papa Clarence on the back "This is the best gift you've given me." "Better than the diamond mine or immortality Papa?" "Yes, Clarence thank you." "A century ago, I promised we'd find your children if you performed my marriage to Safinah. Tonight, that promise has been fulfilled. It's not Iris but it is her bloodline papa." Papa Nate hugged Clarence. "You are debt free my vampire maker."

Chance was escorted back to jail by Niarchos. "I see the way you gaze at Gabriel, out of all the vampresses in the world you chose pops wife?" "It's a crush Chance, it'll pass." "It won't and you know it, Nick." "She's pretty, smart, funny, cool and--"

"The Pharaoh's Queen Nick. She loves Pop. She'll never leave him. I know women, she looks at him like Mary once looked at me." "You must fix shit with Mary nigga. She has been with us since the beginning Cody's going to ruin you. If the Pharaoh ain't want her, she's trouble." Niarchos locked his jail cell. "Later Chance."

The Gullah Island
Vampire games preparation....

The bed and breakfasts, hotels, basements, and attic apartments, were booked on Gullah Island with no vacancies. Caleb set up cots in the basement under the arena and the coffee warehouse. Vampires slept on floors, campers and tents set up in the surrounding woods. There were vampires who hadn't seen one another in years. Vampire fugitives were held in prison waiting to compete. Gabriel and Clarence arrived on the island from Vegas that morning lodging at her inherited cabin.

"Someone is knocking Daddy." He was irritated with the biziness of the house. "Enter!" Zhou Xie entered kneeling with his face to the floor. "Rise." He embraced Clarence. "I've missed you brother Clarence."

"This is my wife, Gabriel, I've missed you Zhou." He was a tiny man, standing 5 ft 5 inches and 140 lbs. "It's a pleasure Great Queen." "Are you ready for the games Zhou?" "Yes Pharaoh." Clarence threw a punch at Zhou; he jumped up and didn't come down. Looking up, he was on a beam above them. "Still slow Pharaoh when do the games begin?" "Tomorrow night take any room available Zhou welcome home brother." "Thank you, Clarence."

"He's so tiny babe." "Sugar, that's a case of dynamite, trust me." Caleb had carriages waiting outside. He'd restored the one Clarence drove the night of his turn, it held five vampires. His private carriage was a two-seater. Clarence pranced down memory lane circling the vintage carriages. The coachman on top, of the second coach looked down at him smiling. "Honey you, ok?" "Yes sugar, let's go." helping Gabriel into the carriage hopping in next to her.

"Who's our driver, Clarence?" He adorned leather gloves seizing the reins. "You sure you know what you're doing? You may've gotten rusty over the years." grabbing his arm nervously. Clarence ignored her smiling, clicking his tongue as the horses obeyed his signal slow walking down the dirt road. The passenger coach following held Joan, Zion, Elijah, Mya, and Zhou.

It was a 30-minute scenic stroll across the seasonally warm island to the club. Gabriel heard an announcement over a loudspeaker. "The Pharaoh and Queen have arrived." It became quiet and Niarchos stood in front of Gabriel and Clarence as they walked the red carpet. Vampires kneeled before them. They were escorted to the VIP booth suspended over the dance floor in a glass mezzanine box. There was a vintage disco ball that bounced colors around the room.

Vampresses stared at Clarence lustfully, as did vampires at Gabriel. The Elder vampires were never short of attention. "My feet are killing me, Joan." "I said not to wear those heels, Gabriel. Comfort over cute, you'll learn." Mya agreed. "They're sexy Gabriel, I love the gold vine climbing your leg." "Thank you, Mya." Joan scoffed jokingly.

Music played the house lights dimmed. The dance club setting transformed into a lounge scene. Mara came for orders, Niarchos allowed her to pass after frisking her, which made her wet. She handed menus to the Elders. "Mara hi." Gabriel gave her a hug. "Hot tea?" "Coffee please Mara, and a glass with one cube of ice and a water please."

"Pharaoh?" "Four Henny-Tox shots extra strength Mara." Gabriel spoke with him telepathically," *you're gonna be fucked up daddy. Then I'll fuck you good Sugar. Yass.* They kissed for fifteen minutes. Vampires smiled pointing at their King's behavior. Clarence and Gabriel didn't care who watched. Elijah cut into Clarence's thoughts. *Vampires are watching you. Let them, Elijah. This is how old vampires love publicly, or have you forgotten?*

Joan was busy with the menu; Zion checked the scenery as was Niarchos for exits. Joan and Mya ordered steak dinners. "Elder Zion were you ready to order?" "I'm not an Elder dear." "Dr. Donovan." Joan corrected her nicely. "I apologize. "It's fine Mara. I'll have two blood-tox shots, mild, and a cup a coffee." "Yes Dr."

"Elder Elijah?" "Same as the Pharaoh Mara." Mya darted a warning look. "We're on vacation." "Vampire Zhou?"

"Three B-positives, please Mara thank you." "Elder Niarchos?" "Water." 'Thats it?" "I'm working Mara."

She ordered A positive for him-weak blood without alcohol. Mara was crushing on Niarchos. He didn't want her, but that wasn't going to stop her from trying. Caleb took center stage on the first night. "Thank you for attending the first annual vampire games. Tonight, we have a treat!" Vampires read poetry and some sang. The comedian joked about being turned and human reactions when they have sex with old vampires.

"Some vampires are 300 years old, and can't fuck, ain't that right vampresses? He made everyone laugh, even Niarchos. He made jokes of human and vampire paternity testing. "I pay child support, so humans won't request my dead DNA, fuck it I'm they daddy now, right? I got 14 human kids and counting haha."

"I see our Pharaoh is here tonight." Claps filled the air. "Can you imagine him a slave once? I'm unsure how the Elders did it cause my ass would've been locked up in a hot box every day. Hell, I would've been dead cause, I don't listen." "I heard Elder Niarchos took a man's head off for looking at him wrong shiddd I know he did. I see why the Pharaoh turned him, he's a massive negro ain't he haha. Ladies tell the truth, y'all think y'all can handle him sexually? Elder Niarchos will hurt ya, have you walking home like this." He held his private area walking funny. "Easy girl, I should've known better!" Giggles filled the air.

"I think every 20 years or so another Elder gets popular with the vampress population. Who was it last time?" the comedian asked. "Elder Chance!" One heckled "Elder Blaise!" confirmed another. "Elder Chance," he inhaled then exhaled. "I sat at a gambling table and lost my life savings in ten minutes. Haha true story Elder Chance saw me down at the gas station begging for change. I was tow up from da flo up! Elder chance wired my $10 life savings back and I was good, haha."

"Vampresses want Elder Blaise. Vampires you don't want your vampress hanging with him. Nossir. He got that black unity, join the black vampire revolution shit going on haha."

"Elder Elijah, ladies don't know his wife will drag yo ass into the light haha." "Don't play!" Mya tapped Joan laughing.

"Elder Vaughn, Owwww." the comedian meowed snapping his fingers, with his lips poked out. "Chile you ain't ready." he stared, his eyes growing large, playfully mocking a feminine gay male. Gay vampires meowed like cat's Clarence and Vaughn laughed. "Y'all ever hear Elder Vaughn speak? He doesn't speak, his husband speaks for him. He's on some sexy shit. When you see Elder Vaughn, he whispers to his man then his husband says tox please! You be like I'm a damn vampire, how couldn't I hear you? Elder Vaughn on another level up in this mother fucker haha!"

"Elder Nate, the original Mack. Women called him Papa, before the term Daddy was sexy. Papa Nate smooth as hell, baldheaded, bearded, a modern-day Shaft up in this bitch." The chuckles were endless.

"When you meet him, he'll say darling call me Papa. Shit I'm a man I be like yes Papa. For real though, he's like all our grandfather's ain't he? Papa will correct ya ass real quick, like your grandparent's did you in public. 'Hey boy, sit up straight when you're out with me.' 'Yes sir!' Make yo ass feel like you 8 again. A true Mack too. Three wives you know they friends. You know he a Mack when they look out for one another, not stealing each other's weave glue and shit like human poly women do hahah. Let me to sit my ass down. Elder Caleb tapping his vintage rollie backstage."

"Oh shit, I almost forgot lordy my Coven leader, the vampire who saved my life, Elder Caleb have any of you met him? Some yes, some not... ok"

"He's a seer. I'm getting dressed and Elder Caleb walks up on me. Don't wear that shirt tonight, you are supposed to wear it on Friday. 'Why?' 'You'll see.' What happens will I die in this shirt Elder Caleb? 'Not yet!' hell, kinda answer is not yet from a seer?! How you live with them vague answers Pharoah? One hundred years of cryptic shit haha." Clarence and Gabriel laughed. Caleb leaned in from behind, "He's funny right guys?" "Heck yeah." They agreed when Gabriel's phone chimed.

*Caleb:* Babe, can you sing for us? I want people to see another side of the Pharaoh's Queen.

*Gabriel:* Sure.

*Caleb:* I want to surprise him. Inform him you're using the restroom and get Niarchos to escort you on stage please.

*Gabriel:* Ok.

"Clarence, I need use the ladies room." "Take Niarchos with you Sugar." Caleb took to the stage grabbing everyone's attention. "Vampires and guests, the Pharaoh is to marry his Queen. She's much like his first. She's a beautiful vampress inside and out. I'm sure you've heard rumors she can sing. Did you hear a vampress inquired to try her five-carat engagement ring on, she removed it from her hand, obliging her?" Caleb smiled bragging about his Queen. "Allow me to introduce our Queen of covens in the United States and abroad, Queen Gabriel Hollings."

"I didn't know Elder Caleb was going to ask I sing but I want to share something with you since we're vampire family. When I was human, I was lonely. My last two family members died within two years of one another. Taken by cancer, only for me to learn I was next. I didn't have many friends. My boyfriend broke up with me when I was diagnosed. I cried like a baby. I went to get coffee one day and a man chatted me up. He was fine as fuck, and I couldn't stop staring."

"He was strong with broad shoulders, brown hair with blonde mixed in. His arms were like two guns bulging through his tee. Tall, adorning the most gorgeous smile I'd ever seen. He gave me Madeline cookies, which were my favorite at the time, then wrote his phone number on a napkin. I'm unsure what I did in my life but someone in heaven blessed me. This song is for you Daddy. Thank you for saving me."

"Natalie Coles, Morning Star melodically floated on the air of the arena. The crowd sang along. Vampresses stared at the infamous diamond ring, glistening in the light. Clarence joined her on stage, dipping and kissing her before levitating her twelve inches off the stage. He twirled her in a circle of radiant light the crowd went wild. They waved to the crowd before floating off stage. Niarchos texted Gabriel. *Niarchos:* Your voice is pretty. *Gabriel:* Thank you, honey.

He didn't mind being friend zoned. He loved her. He had nothing but time and patience. Clarence carried Gabriel on his back to their seats with security in tow. Some vampires were surprised at how giddy in love he was. Clarence didn't care how he looked or what vampires thought, not to mention he was drunk.

"Mara, three whiskey tox-shots please." Clarence requested. Zion picked one up replacing it with B positive. "Zion put it back." "Clarence, do you think you've had enough?" Clarence ignored him reaching his hand under Gabriel's blouse, rubbing her nipples. "What do you say we blow this juke joint Sugar?" "Ok." "Niarchos?" "Yes boss?" "Don't call me boss Niarchos we ain't--

"On no plantation!" The Elders cut him off playfully. "Pop, get in the truck. I'll bring the carriage home later." "I'm reading you both of your thoughts. Why're you scared Sugar?" "I don't want an accident, Clarence." "Niarchos, get the carriage." Niarchos did as requested but followed the carriage on his Harley. "Go Niarchos." "Pop, it's my job to protect you. I can't leave." "Sugar, if I were poor, would you want me?" "When we met what was your profession, Clarence?" "Construction." "You lied to me daddy." nervous about him swerving on the road.

"I did, to make sure you wanted me, for me Sugar." "What did your secret teach you?" "WHOAH." The horses stopped. "You love me, Gabriel." "Oh lord, let me find out you're a crying vampire drunk." hugging him giggling. "What's wrong?" Niarchos appeared, with guns drawn. "Nothing son."

They arrived home safe. Gabriel showered when she came out Clarence was sleep. Someone knocked.

"Enter. Hey Zion." He brought water to Clarence. "Brother, drink," trying to sit him up but he wouldn't budge. "Let him sleep it off I'll leave the water in case he's thirsty Gabriel." "How are you Gabriel?" "I'm fine, thanks Zion." They bid one another good night. There was another knock on the door. "Come in." "I'm leaving." He sat a hot cup of tea next to Clarence's water. "Why aren't you staying Niarchos?" "Pharaoh's order. He doesn't want too many Elders under one roof. I'm closer to the holding cells in case vampires try something." "Thanks for the tea Niarchos." Niarchos undressed him. "I tried but he's too heavy for me...Thanks." He exited.

Niarchos' phone rang. "Who dis?" "Mara the server from tonight." "What's up?' "Are the Pharaoh and Queen, ok?" "Yes ma'am." His deep voice made her melt. He was so fine, towering over her she loved that. "Can I ask something Mara?" "Sure." "How'd you get my number? "Elder Elijah. Do you want to hang out. I know you're busy." "I'll let you know when I'm free." "Ok, goodnight, Elder" Niarchos ended the call shaking his head he texts Elijah.

Niarchos: Why'd you give Mara my number? Elijah: Stop crushing on Gabriel. Niarchos: I'm not. Elijah: Nothing can come of it Nick. Mara is a sweet vampress she reminds me of Liza, God bless her. Niarchos: You're a matchmaker now? We got hella criminals here to compete including Cody. I have better shit to do then to think about pussy Elijah. I'm unsure why pop gave Cody a chance. She'll lose Elijah. Elijah: Who says? Niarchos: Zhou Shi's here Elijah: It's over for her. Niarchos: Haha

The town was busy. Gabriel, Joan, and Mya woke early to shop. Niarchos had a human guard accompany them. They purchased lingerie. "What about this?" Joan and Mya looked at the sexy number. "You sure he's gonna give you time to slip it on Gabriel?"

"We can hear y'all and we're human Gabriel" "Thats Clarence" "Thats you hehe enjoy your man." Mya whispered wear him in good health." Gabriel tapped her arm giggling. They arrived home. "Is he up?" Zion stared saying nothing. "That bad? Gabriel entered their bedroom "Honey, you, ok?" "My eyes are sensitive Sugar." He was adorned in black sunglasses.

"Allow me to see." pulling them down. His eyes weren't fire colored. "Did you speak with Zion?" "He wants me to drink water." She poured a glass he pushed it away. "Please Daddy." "Let's take a bath, Gabriel." She helped him in the tub and sat on the side washing his hair. "Feels good, Sugar.' "It's long again."

She finished washing him then she washed herself. Standing she put one leg on the tub washing her pussy and ass. He stared up through dark lenses, as she rubbed her soapy double d tits. Large bubbles strolled down her body, refusing to pop as his eyes lustfully followed their slow descent as they rolled over every curve.

"Turn around." Her ass was fat, shiny, and dripping wet. She sat on his lap with her legs open. He slipped in, rocking gently. "They can hear us." He smiled, fangs out. "Is this why you're being gentle Sugar?" She bumped quietly as she fed.

His moans echoed as she covered his mouth. His laughter muffled under her hand. The more she rocked, the harder cumming at the same time.

"I feel like a teen." "You had to hide having sex as a teen Clarence?" "I was fucking the master's wife." "How old were you?" "Thirteen Gabriel." "He knew?"

"He would've killed me, but it's what they did, endanger us for their own gratifications. I was pulling out. "Avril was a dad to me. Can you imagine older slaves teaching younger slaves' sexual survival?" "Sorry baby" She kissed his shoulder blade. He fell asleep in her arms.

*Vampire Uprising Chronicle I*

The Vampire Arena
Game Day....

They were driven to the arena that night and escorted to the balcony, where Elders waited on them. Clarence and Gabriel were amazed. It looked like a replica of ancient Roman coliseums. Flags of the Covens adorned the walls, vampires and humans waved smaller flags, representing their covens. Rap music played as vampires traveled from around the globe to their temporary Mecca.

"I want a flag, Mara." "Yes Pharaoh." She returned giving each Elder the flag for their coven. "Let me see Clarence." He looked at his coven flag smiling. It had a rose with a drop of blood dripping from it, behind the drop of blood was a bowl of red apples. "What's with the apples honey?" "Remind me to explain Sugar."

The word's read: All men should be free Clarence recalled that night he recited it to Caleb. All flags Caleb created had a quote the Elders shared with him. Elijah's had sugar cane and honeybees is what made him rich. The cane fields and bees still operating today with the quote humble beginnings make a man great. Clarence laughed, "It should say, hard work never killed nobody." the Elders laughed. Blaise was handed his. It was a black power fist on an African flag with the quote #staywoke.

"I love this, Clarence." "Me too, Blaise." He wanted to see Niarchos' flag, but he was working. "Mara?" "Yes Pharaoh?" "Please make sure I have two of each flag. I'd like to put them in my greenhouse. I'd like to have large ones made with flag poles before I leave the island. Inform Elder Caleb to have them embroidered please Mara." "Yes Pharaoh."

The crowd roared as 10 horses trotted in carrying larger versions of the flags. Vampires representing each coven rode with pride. "Look, it's Khrista Clarence carrying your flag." The flag bearers exited the arena waving goodbye. The arena darkened shifting the mood as bullet proof glass rose in front of the vampire Elders.

Sharpshooter competition....

The first two opponents hit a target two hundred yards away before the first vampire shot the second. Khrista rode out, returning the targets for scoring. Caleb put them on a projector, which showed on TVs around the arena, bars, and lounges. The winner was shooter two, so he advanced. The targets were moved farther out. "This ends the sharp shooter's competition. They'll continue tomorrow. The winner's excommunication will be lifted." Caleb exited the announcer circle.

Dancers were on stage, gyrating to Sean Paul's Gimme a light. Vampresses danced out their seats, grinding on males as fireworks lit the sky of the open ceiling arena. Mara took orders before she left, running into Niarchos in the hall. "May I call tonight? It May be late." "Sure, I don't sleep Niarchos." "It'll pass I went four years with no sleep." "Man, I hope it's not that long." "Won't be Mara."

Niarchos looked her up and down. She was in attractive shape a big girl, his liking. She wasn't a beauty, Queen like Gabriel; he loved beautiful women.

Competition Two Knife Toss......

"As per the Pharaoh, protective neck gear must be worn, or participants cannot compete."

The house lights dimmed; a female vampire was tethered on a board with infrared dots surrounding her frame. The target is 250 yards away. A vampire was given nine knives. Clarence was nervous, sitting on the edge of his seat. He didn't want his vampire children to die. He tossed the first blade above her head and the crowd gasped as anxiety grew. The next blade at her crotch, "AHHH!" Vampires screamed. Last aiming next to her ankle. He missed. Cameras zoomed in on her ankle. He nicked her, blood pooling from her foot.

"They almost made it." Caleb said, "this doesn't mean they're disqualified. We'll see how the others compete before a winner is announced."

The games went on, each level higher. The larger matches were saved for the weekend, Clarence was scheduled to speak at a venue called the making of our Pharaoh. Clarence had no idea Caleb arranged it. All proceeds went to Blaise to fund the Afterschool daycares and Inmate Reform Programs in black human impoverished neighborhoods. A lot of vampires, including Gabriel wanted to hear the story of his turn. There was no time to go to the cabin and freshen up when he was scheduled to speak at 12 p.m., and it was now nine. He went to the limo with Gabriel locking the doors they fed, he slept. "Wake me up at 11 Sugar." "Yes baby."

Niarchos called, "where y'all at Gabriel?"

"In the limo. Niarchos" "I'm panicking because we can't find pop." "He's sleeping off the tox off headache." "Cool, as long as y'all ok." "I'm excited. I've never heard his vampire birth story Niarchos." "That makes two of us. Pop doesn't like talking about it. See you later Ms. Queen." Gabriel closed the phone smiling.

"Who was it Sugar?" "Niarchos." "Is it 11?" "No, you're still sleepy Clarence." "I know, I'll sleep tomorrow, Sugar so I'll be good for the night games." "Do you like being King?" "I think you're the first to ask. I'll say yes and no." "Do you like being a Queen?"

"No. I like being your Queen, but not everyone's. It takes getting used to daddy. A few months ago, I was a nobody, dying from cancer. Today I'm a Queen over nine covens." "Ten covens Sugar. We have eastern Europe however they're independent." "You asked if I loved you in the carriage. I fell in love with you the first time I saw you Clarence." "I know sugar, I read your thought's when I entered the coffee shop, they were inviting." He chuckled. Her mouth opened in shock before she smiled. "Cat got your tongue?"

Rolling her eyes, she turned her back, laying down falling asleep. Gabriel popped up "Baby, wake up, it's 11:15," tugging his arm. "I overslept," She shook Clarence awake. "We'll be fashionably late. Sugar," he yawned. She opened the door. The cool air of night rushed in. Clarence undressed, she handed him his fresh clothes, a toothbrush, and water. She took his comb replacing it with his brush and rubber bands.

Once dressed, he assisted her. The driver dropped them in front of the arena camera's flashed as they walked the red-carpet wearing matching crowns. Clarence and Gabriel were seated in the skybox with the Elders. "How many of you know this story?" Elijah raised his hand. Clarence exited to go on stage.

As Niarchos escorted Clarence to the stage he asked, "Do you like Gabriel?" Niarchos looked down surprised. "Yes, are you vexed with me pop?" "No, because you haven't shown anything but love and respect our relationship if it remains this way we have no issue son. A vampire can't control his heart, but he can control his impulses. Now let's get this done so I can sleep big baby." Niarchos smiled at his father. Caleb took to the stage.

"Without further ado, the vampire of the hour, the chain breaker, freer of slaves, Father of us all, our Pharaoh and Eldest Vampire of all covens, king Clarence Hollings." The room went into a thunderous uproar as he walked center stage, wearing the blue blood-stained jacket. There was a stool, a bottle of water and a spotlight following him. Three scroll writers documented the origin telling. The best written story would make it into permanent scroll vaults.

"Good evening children. I'm no good at this, however Elder Caleb insisted I share this horrible story. So my vampire children would know from whom they were made," The room was silent. He sat on the stool with all eyes on him. "It was a hot night in Georgia, I was the family coachman. For those of you who aren't familiar with this job, today I'd be called a chauffeur. I did plantation work when needed, but because I was a lighter-skinned slave, I wasn't allowed to participate in field work."

"The white masters didn't dark skin slaves walking the big house. This day started like any other. The oppressor who owned me asked I drive he and his family to town to shop. Once per month he'd visit another slave plantation. That night I was in the barn bathing when I'd spoken to my first wife, Queen Safinah for the first time. The house Mammy, Isabel sent a message to hurry it was getting late and I must leave soon. She'd raised me as her own since I was taken from my real mother at the age of six, as punishment for something mother did."

"When she entered the barn, I was wet and naked. She stopped dead in her tracks, staring. She relayed the message and inquired why I was absent of whip marks on my back. I was irritated with the heat, responding sharply, 'why are you staring? Ain't you seen a naked man?' Later I'd discover she hadn't which is why she stared," women cat called men chuckled.

"I dressed, wearing this jacket," turning around in the spotlight holding his arms out. "Queen Safinah found it, dirty bloody tattered and torn. Do you see this hole? Remember it. My master attended card games once per month. These weren't ordinary games. The owner endorsed prostitution, women, men, and children for coin. I have seen men who weren't gay made to engage in gay sex. Women being raped and beaten forced into rough sex. Our people forced into deviant unscrupulous sex acts."

"There was nothing I could do. Women were carried out unconscious or killed. Masters were part of it "by participation or bringing slaves to participate. When I'd go, I parked the carriage on a hill in the apple orchards. I chose this location because I could see into the house. There was a large clock on the wall. I was told by my master when I see the hands in a certain position, come to the front to get him. He was careful not to teach me to tell time. Here I was looking down the hill, inside the house when horrible screams shrilled into the dark night. It was horrible like nails on a chalkboard. I jumped down looking through the 20-foot windows and saw negro men and women inside slaying every white person in sight."

"I thought, oh God an uprising! I tried to run when a man appeared out of nowhere, slicing my throat with his bare hands jabbing a knife into my ribs." He pointed to the hole in the jacket. "I fell to the warm ground amiss crushed red sweet macintosh apples, life was slowly leaving. I remember smelling blood but didn't think it was my own. I looked at his hands, they were drenched in blood. The tall black man standing over me was holding my oppressors walking stick, asking if I was on my way to fuck slaves."

"This young woman yelled at my assaulter, *'Stop, no, he a slave like us! You killed a slave! I know his Mammy; we be on a plantation together. She save me from da lash!* "I remember the man asking," *'What cha wanna to do turn em?' 'Yes, baby please he finnin ta cross.' 'Ya says his Mammy save ya from da white man whip?' 'I says!'* The vampire lit a cigarette dropping ashes on me. *'Go head like I show ya.'*

"She sat on top of me with her legs open bending down whispering," *'Ise gonna make ya a God, walking through time among men.'* "She smiled then shifted into a fanged monster. I thought I was in hell. I saw this pretty woman's eyes, brown and glowing. She opened her mouth two teeth sharp as thorns appeared. She comforted me saying, *'<u>don't be afraid you a walking god now.</u>'*"

"I closed my eyes and thought *'I can't die, not like this, with no children, or wife.'* I hadn't purchased myself out of slavery before I could finish my panicking thoughts, she pierced the left side of my neck, feeding off me."

"She bit her wrist exposing her veins, her blood dripped on me like an open faucet. She opened my mouth filling it with warm blood I swallowed still choking from a slit throat. She covered my open wound in a ripped rag soaked in her blood from her dress. She gave me the location of a cabin she acquired from an old dead woman. She helped me on my feet, ushering me into the forest, helping me get my bearings. She sent a message using telepathy saying, *'I'll come see ya when able.'*"

"*'Do not walk in the sun, drink live animal blood nothin' dead.'* "I dropped this jacket on the crushed bloody apples running as fast as possible. I ran until I got to a river crossing and swam. When I emerged, I was clean of blood and all wounds were closed. I heard far and saw in the dark afraid, alone, and shaking I should've died but didn't. I arrived at the cabin cold, dirty, afraid, and alone. There was a looking glass, I looked in it and saw that I wasn't casting a reflection. I broke the glass in a fit of rage. I covered the cabin with shrubs and leaves, closing the windows, blocking all sunlight. I lit a fire and pulled the bed in front of it. I slept for one week straight."

"Thank God, I awakened one night and upon entering the forest I saw a deer eating elderberries. I held him down feeding, careful to listen to his heartbeat, making sure it didn't stop as I fed. It was the most terrifying time during my walk-in time, I saw my maker three months later. Her maker was a jealous vampire and didn't want her to have anything to do with me. I was her first turn. Later she was burned at the stake in the Salem witch hunts. The minute they dragged her in the sun, I felt her pain. She talked to me, commanding I do not save her." He wiped his eyes as his voice cracked mentioning her.

"There was nothing I could do. The vampire who sliced me orchestrated the vampire uprisings with a young man by the name of Nat Turner. He was caught and charged with committing murders by uprising. A public hanging was to take place, but he never made it to the noose. I'm unsure when I was born. Dr. Donovan puts me at approximately thirty years of age, give or take when I was turned. I don't celebrate birthdays because I'm unsure when it is. I've kept my first name because I know my birth mother bestowed it on me. I own the plantation I was turned on the apple orchards remain on the land today. My wife asked why our bedroom smells like fresh red crisp apples. Now she knows the soil I sleep on is from the place I was turned, an apple orchard."

"I don't regret being vampire I see the good it's done, the children I've saved and sired. I do miss being human at times, because I was a slave and as Elder Caleb pointed out, we went directly from slave to vampire. We were never free men. I'm unsure what steak tastes like, Brandy, Hennessy, French fries, or seafood. I won't know what it is to have biological children watch them grow and marry and become and grandfather. I was never fond of the heat of the sun; however, I miss the warmth mixed with breeze on my skin, on a spring morning as I sip coffee waiting for my day to begin."

"If I weren't vampire, I wouldn't have saved my first Queen from slavery or the second from cancer. I would've never met the Elder's who've enriched my life and become my family walking through time with me. The people we purchased out of slavery nor the black civil war soldier's, we gave Christian burials would've never had one they would've been buried as compost." Clarence passed the jacket around vampires held it as if it was the holy grail.

"This jacket informed my first Queen I was alive, when she cleaned the bloody mess of the vampire uprising the next day. She feared she'd find my dead body; however, she found this jacket in its place. Queen Safinah discovered my bloody footsteps, which she covered with her bare hands, sweat and tears so my master's wife wouldn't send slave catchers or dogs after me. This was her glimmer of hope I'd return for her. If I hadn't she was fine with it because one of us escaped." Ann and the Elders were in tears. "I have over two hundred human bloodlines from children I purchased off slave auction blocks and adopted. Some died off over time and some are alive today."

"No one knew he was turned and left alone. That's why he's adamant about vampires not being alone for the turn." Ann whispered to Lily. "Thank you for listening but your Pharaoh is tired...too many tox-shots last night." He raised his hand goodnight, exiting stage left receiving a standing ovation. He took Gabriel's hand, escorting her to the limo. She sat next to him, laying her head on his shoulder.

Looking down at her she cried. "Sugar, what's wrong?" "You were all alone." She hugged him. "Sugar its' fine." "You're so strong Clarence. You've been through so much. Everyone was in awe of your rich history; we sat on the edges of our seats." They petted in the limo like teens. She lay on the seat; he was on top of her. They were parked, kissing under moonlight for ten minutes before arriving home.

"Sugar, we're home." "Are we Mr. Hollings?" "We can finish this inside honey." They undressed one another slowly before lying in bed staring using body language. The love between them was real. Gabriel cuddled Clarence telling him how much she was in love. They made love she gave herself to him as it were her last night on earth. She wanted him to be human, if not she'd make him feel as if he were. Hearing his story touched her in places emotionally she never felt before. She kissed his forehead, lips, neck, and eyes, caressing his back and arms. He entered her slowly.

She kept him in missionary position. She wanted him to see the love in her eyes. "I love you." "I love you, Sugar." Holding his head with her tiny hands, she forced him to lock gaze with her opening her legs wider, as he slipped into a deeper connection. "I need you Clarence, promise you won't leave." "I promise Sugar. I won't let anyone take you from me." He stroked upward staring deep in her eyes, forcing himself not to read her swirling thoughts of love.

"Gabriel, I can't hold it." "If you love me, cum inside me. If we were human, we would be making a baby tonight. Let's make love like we're trying to create the children you wished you had daddy." He sucked her bottom lip, grabbed her waist pulling them together so there was no space between them. He came deep and hard inside her. "I love you Sugar."

Elijah looked at his wife. "Get it." "Shut up, you need to get it." "Haha." Zion looked at Joan shaking his head. "What Zion?" "She's a vampire-human hybrid. I warned him to be careful. We don't know what we're dealing with."

"He's in love guys." Elijah reminded them. "I ain't never seen him like this, not even with Safinah. He loved her, don't get me wrong, but he's different with Gabriel." "She put it down on him, you're talking different sex styles Elijah." "He's had other women since Safinah passed Mya." They heard her moan his name looking at the bedroom door.

"I don't like it." Zion stated. "It's the medicine man in you talking Zion. I loved his story tonight" "Thank you Joanie Goodnight see y'all in the morning family!" Clarence called for the master bedroom making Gabriel giggle.

Clarence for the first time since Safinah died felt real love; if his heart could beat it would.

# Chapter 23
# Blood Ties

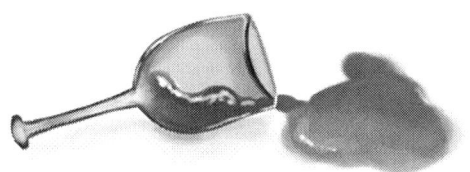

Las Vegas Three Days Prior......

Chance and his wives sat to hear his fate. They gasped at the 30% tax hike. They knew their husband was an excellent gambler, who created income to fill a deficit.

Mary was a ghost dress designer, behind one of the black couture labels of Paris. When they read about all the subsidiaries and businesses associated with Chance Hollings, it upset her. Clarence tied in all her personal income leaving out his private game winnings.

"Is there anything you or your attorney would amend Elder Chance?" "Yes Hunter, not being able to be in New York at identical times as the Pharaoh."

Clarence stared at Chance not breaking his angry gaze. His fangs out, asserting dominance. "Elder Hollings, what would you like amended?" "What if I have business in the city Hunter?" "You must send someone to tend it Elder." "How long will the band be Counselor?"

"There's no date of expiration listed Elder. The Pharaoh reserves the right to lift the restriction or enforce it hence forth at his discretion. He's your maker you must obey you've no choice Elder the decision is final. Chance held his head down. "UP!" Blaise yelled across the room as Chance lifted his head with pride. "Elder, additional questions?" "No Counselor."

*"By power as Pharaoh of 10 covens here and abroad this order is passed. I sign my name in blood, an oath written on two scrolls sealed along with my brothers and sisters. Do we agree?" "We do." The Elders answered.*

*"I hear by order the release of Elder vampire Chance Hollings to walk on his recognizance by power, blood and word I end this scroll."*

The scroll writer provided the stick pin to each Elder they stuck their thumbs pressing it on the parchment next to their names. Niarchos looked before he pressed, he stared at Chance. "I love you big brother." Chance gave Jackie a hug, leaving the room. Mary approached Clarence, Niarchos blocked her path.

"Move before I push you." Niarchos smiled stepping aside. Mary gave Clarence a hug. "Thank you I'm sorry Clarence" "It's fine Mary." Lily and Caine requested an audience. "I'd like to ask the Pharaoh's permission to start our own business. I would like to start an exclusive vampire dating app." "I give permission to set it up on the vampire network. You can promote it when we get to the vampire games Lily. Does your husband agree?"

"Yes Clarence" Caine replied. "I'm excited Lily!" "Shut up Caleb, you don't need no one." "You don't know what I need Blaise." "Haha." "Ya'll behave like bickering brothers. Anyone else?"

"Me pop, I'm bottling honey. Caleb is helping me get exposure and expansion. We're in the southern states. We have small grocery stores and haberdasheries, but we haven't gone global. Thats what Caleb wants to help with if that's ok." "It's fine Niarchos." "The bees are doing well Nick?" "Yes Elijah." "How many hives?" "Seventy Come see them. I have your hives separated the others, Elijah." Niarchos reached into a box gifting everyone a large pickle jar of honey.

"I know you have humans in your homes this is for them." He wrapped them in gingham ribbon with gift tags. He did a special one for Gabriel. "Pharaoh May I?" "Yes son." Niarchos handed her a jar with her name on it. "I figured you could use the empty jar for make-up brushes."

"Thank you." Niarchos excused himself. He forgot Lily so he went to get one. Gabriel entered the bathroom. "He's crushing on her Clarence." "I know, Caleb. Its harmless, make sure you add him to the dating site Lily." She giggled.

Vampire Games Day Three....

"Caleb No." "It's all in fun Clarence, what if Gabriel says ok? All funds are going to the vampire college fund." "I thought the story the other night was for that Caleb." "Those monies are going to Blaise Clarence." "A lot of vampresses will pay top dollar to go out with our Pharaoh, please." "Please what?" Gabriel cut in fixing a cup of coffee. "They want me to enter a date auction to help the vampire college fund."

"Why don't you? I trust you, if I didn't know you, I'd like a chance too." "Thank you, wise Queen." Caleb agreed. "As long as Gabriel is fine with it." "Gabriel you too?" "No Caleb absolutely not!"

"It's ok Daddy." Gabriel sat on his lap; he held her tight. "Hell no." he whispered. "Daddy, I have an idea, you bid." "Sugar, you're right." "Cheaters." "Why not Caleb, who can out bid a billionaire?"

"We're auctioning personal items What's up with the jacket you were turned in?" "No, it meant something to Safinah the scroll writers want it for the historical archives." "Fine, then what?" Clarence exited returning to hand him a rag. "Let me see." Gabriel rose to look, it was a tennis bracelet with four rows of diamonds, eight carats set in white gold. "I had it made for Safinah." Caleb bellowed a laugh.

"You knew damn well FI wasn't wearing this." "Fi Caleb?" "It's what I called her, like I call you Gabby." "It's old made from the diamonds honed from the first African diamond mine I own. Take it unless Gabriel wants it, Caleb."

"Why wouldn't Safinah wear it, Caleb?" "Safinah didn't do flashy, said it reminded her the slave masters wives trying to outdo everyone, flaunting money." "What type of gifts did she enjoy Caleb?"

"See them sycamore trees and roses in the yard at the New York house? Those were gifts to her from her Peety." Caleb teased, pinching Clarence's cheek. "The magnolias are the prettiest Caleb." "Yes, they're gifts from Ann Sugar, however they pale to your beauty." "I'm sick" Caleb chuckled.

"Elijah donated a savings bond from 1899. It was authenticated on the treasury web, they offered $80k. I'm creating a book of items for the auction tonight guys." "What did Niarchos donate Caleb?"

"His motorcycle Harley Davidson 1929 Clarence he didn't like the feel of it." "What're you doing for my vampire children with low funds?"

"Beauty basket's, 100 of them with coffee, salt, blood and hone donated by Our Queen and Elder Niarchos Clarence."

"Go to town and buy the most expensive Rolex watch they have Caleb. One for a vampire and vampress and one hundred diamond tennis bracelets. Start the bid at $1 compliments of the King and Queen of covens."

Vampire Date Night Auction
Vampire Arena.......

The night before the games vampires arrived for the auction. Caleb opened the event. "We have Vampire Elder, Ann Freeman. Ms. Freeman is a vampress entrepreneur who's sexy and was turned at the tender age of 29. You can learn a lot from this beautiful Elder vampress. Let the bid begin at $100. Do I hear 100?" Caleb bellowed excitedly.

"One hundred." said a sexy, young male vampire. from vampire legal. "Two hundred." another shouted. "Do I hear $300?" Caleb asked. "Three hundred!" "One Thousand!" the young lawyer bid.

"Do I hear 1,100?" Caleb inquired. "Eleven hundred." a bidder yelled. "Eleven hundred, going once, going

twice--

"Two thousand!" "Thirty-five hundred!" "Sold for $3500 going once...going twice sold to the second chair, legal team vampire counselor Jackie Robinson. Thank you!" The crowd clapped.

"Next up, Our Vampire Queen, Gabriel Hollings." Murmurs of shock filled the air. "Do I hear $100?" Caleb asked. No one bid out of respect for the Pharaoh. "One hundred? Anyone?" Clarence bid "$100!" "Two hundred!" Niarchos called out. "Three hundred." "One Thousand!" Clarence bid. "Two thousand!" "Ten Thousand dollars!" Clarence shouted, taking the lead. "Twenty Thousand." Niarchos bid. The crowd buzzed.

"$25,000?" Caleb asked. "$50,000!" Niarchos called out. "$100,000!" Clarence chased his offer off the table from the balcony, puffing his Cuban cigar. "Isn't this nice?" Caleb was nervous for Niarchos. He was worried he was upsetting Clarence even though the proceeds were for the vampire fund. "$150,000." Niarchos shouted as gasps filled the arena.

"Going once, going twice… Sold to our vampire Elder Niarchos Hollings for $150k! Please see Khrista for payments, thank you." Caleb requested smiling before moving on. "Elder Blaise!" Caleb welcomed him to the stage. Hearts were in the eyes of vampress'. *'This is going to be a cat fight,'* Caleb thought to himself, starting the bidding. It ended in $70,000 from a vampress. She was an artist who studied under Basquiat before his passing.

Gabriel auctioned Caleb. Men and women bid on him; a vampire won at $80,000. He owned a Texas oil ranch they dated once upon a time. Caleb continued the auction. "For the final auction we start at $10, as per the King of covens." Clarence came out with his muscles oiled, wearing his crown with no shirt. His Jean's showed his hard print, and his hair was wet and curly. Gabriel dressed him well.

"Oh?" Caleb teased, "ok now." Whistles and cat calls echoed. "He's wearing his royal crown and his jewels ladies." Caleb fanned himself. Vampire ladies were meowing, loving what they were seeing excited, the bid jumped to $20,000 in minutes.

"One Million!" a vampress bid, everyone looked back as whispers floated to Clarence's ears. It was a vampress who owned spa chain franchises. "Going once, going twice.... sold to vampress Daisy Kelly!" Caleb ended the bid.

Her vampress crew cheered her on. "I won't go if you don't want Sugar. I'll do whatever you say my Queen." Clarence entered the sky box kneeling before Gabriel laying his head on her lap. Gabriel kissed the top of his head. The Elders were shocked she wrapped him around her finger. He was never submissive with Safinah.

"Go with Niarchos when I'm with her Sugar. That way I know you're safe." Clarence phoned Daisy. "It's him." Daisy hushed her girls. "Good evening, Great One." "Good evening vampress I owe you a date tonight. Where are you lodging?" "Hinton Regency Pharaoh."

"I know the place. Dress down, it's a surprise I'm sure you'll enjoy Daisy." "I'll be ready Pharaoh see you then." Clarence called Caleb. "Hey, I need the carriage ready with four horses, bottled blood and daisies, fresh cut." "Yes Pharaoh." "I don't want to go."

"I know you don't Clarence, but you must interact with your children. You can't be so engulfed with your Queen, you forget everyone. These vampires have your venom coursing through them. They owe you a debt they'll never repay."

Later That Evening....

Niarchos waited for Gabriel to come down as Clarence paced in the bedroom. "Why are you pacing?" Gabriel stopped applying make-up looking in the mirror which cast no reflection.

"You're jealous and possessive. It's only Niarchos, dang." "You gotta put lipstick on Sugar?" staring at her full lips. She wiped it off. "Better?" Elijah looked at Niarchos. "I hope you're happy Nick." "He'll be ok Elijah." Niarchos ignored him playing candy crush.

"I know you hear that, Nick." "Did you want her to go with a stranger? He'd never allow it. You know no one bid because they were scared or broke Elijah." "I wish I could arrest you, Nick" "Only to let me go?"

"Is this top to your liking vampire king sheesh?" She and Clarence bickered as they came downstairs. Clarence was pouting like a child. "Is my date ready?" "Yes Ma'am."

"Tonight, no ma'am, Queen or Great One. It's Gabriel Niarchos." Clarence talked to him telepathically. *Keep your hands to yourself and be back before light. Of course, pop.* Niarchos gave Gabriel a helmet. "Why not take the car Niarchos?" "Clarence, let Niarchos take her out his way." Elijah asked.

Gabriel stuck her tongue out at him before blowing him a kiss. "I love you." Clarence started to walk out behind them, Elijah grabbed his arm, "Let her go, if you smother her, she'll hate you. You smothered Safinah" "No, I didn't Elijah."

"She'd call, saying you're driving her crazy." Don't you have a date?" "Yes, with an air head vampress." "She's smart enough to run a beauty spa and pay our tax be charming it's one of your entrancing qualities Clarence."

Georgia Peach Regency Hotel.......

Clarence arrived at the highest-class hotel on the island. He strolled down the ornate halls with the original moldings and chandeliers from the art deco period. Clarence knocked on her door hearing women giggle before one opened it. "Pharaoh welcome." a vampress greeted him with her head lowered. When he entered eight women kneeled. "Please rise. Is Daisy here?"

"Yes, Great One, she'll be out soon, would you like a drink?" "Water, please." Clarence sat waiting. "How old are you Great One?" "Kira!" "It's fine ladies, over 200 years old Kira." "Were the women different compared to today?" "They weren't outspoken Kira." "We're men worse then or now?" "There weren't laws for black people then, women were considered property. Unfortunately, many men treated them as such."

"Name something about a woman you detest Great One. My name is Lisa?" "I despise deceit." "Can you read minds?" "Yes Kira." "What am I thinking Great One?" "You want parlor tricks ladies? You like my cologne, Kira." "Yes!" They giggled like schoolgirls.

"I have a friend who was at your engagement party. She shared you waltz eloquently, a demonstration please." Kira clapped excitedly. "Do you have a candle? We need waltz music ladies."

A vampress found it online as the other returned from the desk with a candle. Clarence locked onto her mind. *Can you hear me, Kira? She smiled happily. Yes Pharaoh. Good, allow me to lead, keep looking in my eyes, you'll be fine.* The waltz echoed as they danced with the lit candle in his hand, he twirled and wooed her. They moved in sweeping circles as one. She couldn't believe he levitated 36 inches off the floor, and she never felt it. Clarence turned her mid-air counterclockwise gently descending counterclockwise. He held out her hand bowing and blowing out the candle as she curtsied. The vampresses clapped amazed at his skill.

"I have a question, Pharaoh; how does one get a coven?" "Old vampires earn covens. Vampires who display excellent leadership qualities and are 100 years of vampire age may apply Lisa." "May we see your fangs?"

Clarence opened his mouth; his fangs slid out sexy slow. "They're beautiful." "Thank you, Kira and Lisa." Daisy joined them. Clarence handed her flowers. "Thank you Great One." "You're welcome." "I hope my friends haven't upset you with questions Pharaoh." "On the contrary, we've had a ball, haven't we vampress'?" "Yes, Great One."

"Shall we depart Daisy?" offering his arm. Daisy took it. Arriving outside, the carriage waited with four horses. "Have you ridden in a carriage Daisy?" "No Great One." He helped her in as a human drove them.

"It's a beautiful night it's smaller inside than I imagined are the lanterns outside gas or electric Pharoah?" "This coach seats six, their gas, and yes its mine, Daisy." "Yours as in, you purchased it back in the day Pharoah?" "Yes, in the early 1900's." The ride across the island was scenic and fragrant as the sweet smell of mixed wildflowers scented the vintage carriage floating in on the evening breeze.

Clarence opened a picnic basket. "Water Daisy?" "Please. taking the glass bottle, sipping slowly soaking in her surroundings. "Are you nervous?" "Yes Pharaoh." "Why? Speak freely." "You're our maker the way you were turned I can't imagine. What if the slave catchers caught you?" Shaking her head with teary eyes.

"It was horrible the atrocities we suffered wasn't it Great One?" "Yes Daisy, I've seen horrible things I choose not to discuss." "Sorry you went through that Pharoah," touching his hand. "Thank you." resting his other hand on top of hers. *I made the Pharaoh smile, she thought.*

"We've arrived." before hopping out of the carriage. He grabbed the door and basket helping her down. The full moon lit their path on the empty beach. He spread the blanket removing the ice bucket, adding ice before placing bottled blood and water in it.

"Have a seat," helping her on the sand. The stars danced like diamonds as waves gently crashed. "I wasn't sure what type you drink so I purchased one of each and two tox-bloods for you."

"I'm good on the tox Pharoah. I'm an alcoholic. I don't partake thank you for thinking of me." "May I ask how you were turned, if it's not upsetting and what coven are you from?" "Elder Chance, Pharaoh, I hope I didn't upset you." "I love him, he's the first vampire I turned." "He brags about it. Especially when one of us is in trouble." Daisy mocked Chance *'don't you know it's a gift to be undead...a gift to walk through time? I'm my maker's first reborn.'* Her voice was baritone.

Clarence laughed. "That sounds like him." "I'm a lead vampire in the coven." "Concubine Daisy?" "No sir. My grandma was a strict Christian. She'd turn in her grave if I didn't make an honest woman of self." "I haven't heard that term in decades." "She'd say, 'Daisy you ain't finnin to be whoring around. You is a honest woman and gonna make a man a good wife one day.' Daisy gazed at the stars.

"I miss her when she died, I drank and gambled the money she left. I inherited two addictions. I left Chance's casino one night. I was $80k deep in debt. The bookies worked me over God awful. They wanted me to prostitute to work off the debt. When I got home, they waited. When they were done my ribs, arms, legs, and face were broken. They intentionally left me alive to suffer before death."

"When Chance entered, I was shocked to see him. He followed me. He heard from a friend that the bookies were after me. When he saw what they'd done to a woman, he removed his hat crying. I never saw a man cry over me Pharaoh. Do you know what he said as I was begging God to allow me in heaven?"

"Look what they did to a beautiful Black Queen. If God sent me here to give you a second chance, would you leave the booze and cards to make your grandma proud?" "I must've said, yes." Daisy was trying not to cry. "If you want to be vampress walking time with me blink once. I blinked. He stated I'd never walk in the light again. Then we recited together as Clarence said it with her--"

"*'You'll drink blood of men and animals for the rest of your days, your reward, immortality to time walk with me. I'll care for you, and you will care for me.'*"

"How'd you know we recited that, Pharaoh?" "I said it to him." Clarence looked down, remembering the night he saved his life. "I woke 3 days after the bite to a dark room in the middle of day and I was completely healed with these sexy eyes." "Haha sexy I never thought of that Daisy."

"Chance paid for college. I got a bachelor's in business, he partnered with the spas. I never looked back. I never saw those men again; however, I did see an article they were found dead with their necks snapped and blood drained," rolling her eyes.

They discussed spa expansion. "Do you've a spa in Brooklyn Daisy?" "No sir." "If you open one, I'll finance the build out. There's one condition." "Yes, anything." "It must be in Bedford Stuyvesant, Brooklyn."

"Why, may I ask?" "Do your research and e-mail the answer Daisy." "I will." Clarence texted the driver who arrived on the beach with two saddled horses. "Do you ride?"

"Yes." He helped her on her horse, getting on his, giving her a tutorial on rein control. The horses strolled slowly on white sand. "I hope we don't run into anyone Pharoah." "We won't dear I own this beach. The houses you see up there, no one's allowed in them tonight." They rode to the end of the beach, turning the horses around "Let's race to the other end Daisy."

"Oh god!" "Come on live a little on your mark, get set, go!" "Whoooo wow that was wonderful!" fixing her wind tossed hair. "Again Daisy?" "Yes Pharoah!" They raced twice before retiring to listen to the radio, scanning through different genres of music. "Do you have artists you prefer Great One?" "Yes, John legend, Elton John, Billy Joel, Jill Scott, Jamie Foxx to name a few."

"What's your favorite Elton John song?" "Candle in the wind Daisy." "What about Billy Joel?" "All of them." "You can't say all of them hehe." He grabbed a CD putting it in. Sarah Smile began to play, they sang together. The night began to shift to morning giving way to sunrise. "The sun is going to rise soon Daisy." "How do you know Pharoah?" "I smell it." "How does it smell?"

"Everyone asks that. Close your eyes." Closing her eyes, he stood behind her. "Can you feel the coolness of the air?" "Yes." "It's leaving." touching her skin with his fingertips. "If you concentrate, there are warm hints in the breeze breathe deep. The sun has a certain scent and sound, it's different for everyone. It's not like anything you've smelled." "I smell it heating the saltwater Great One."

"The sun is warming the sea, Pharoah." Daisy turned to him. "Pharoah, may I ask a huge favor?" "Ask." he whispered as the sea air brushed their cold skin. She looked down. "Head up vampress." "Can you bless me with your bite?" "Why Daisy?" "You will know if I'm in danger and Its sexy." "Where Daisy? You donated for this date, it's your call." "My neck please." "Front or back?" "Back please." "Left, or right?" "Left please Pharoah."

He hyper-turned her holding her tiny waist. She was afraid and excited at the same time. "Child always remember, your original maker loved feeding from the vein, it brought out the savage in him."

He floated her off the beach in his arms, biting and licking her sexual spot unbeknownst to him. She orgasmed in his arms he held her close. She came repeatedly. The adrenaline rushed her blood into his mouth, A woman cumming as he fed, gave him a rush. When she was done, she fainted with excitement. He carried her to the carriage arriving at the hotel, he put her to bed.

"Please get two A positive blood bottles." Clarence ordered. A vampire worker who delivered the blood Daisy sipped slowly. "You were a wonderful date, Pharoah."

"Thank you for your company child. I must go."

"The sun?" "Yes, she's close sleep well" He kissed her forehead. When he exited, he heard vampress laughter and a battery ram of questions. His job was done. Now home to his Sugar.

Niarchos & Gabriel
Beehive Caves......

Niarchos sped with Gabriel on his bike. She loved it. He took her to the other side of the island where beekeepers waited in bee suits. She dressed and met him at the hives, he taught her how to extract honey the way Elijah showed him. She poured it into a jar, he held her hands, helping. Niarchos loved being close to Gabriel. He loved how she squeezed him tightly on the bike. His vampire nose smelled her natural vaginal scent mixed with her cherry blossom scented hair. He did his darndest not to get hard. Thankfully, his jacket hid it.

She smiled withdrawing the honey excited. "Look Nicky. I didn't have friends when I was human. I stayed to myself, withdrawn. What I'm saying is, besides Clarence, you're the closest I've had to a friend."

"I'm not friendly Gabriel it's nice having someone to vent with." Her smile under her bee mask lit his heart. She put the honey in her backpack. "I'm taking you around the island to show you some night sights Gabriel." She hopped on fastening her helmet. He sped off Gabriel signaled Niarchos squeezing his waist. "We're being followed Nicky."

"Hold on." picking up speed. Gabriel was afraid. She looked at his odometer, he sped at 100 miles per hour. "It's ok Great One I'll protect you." He shifted down, turning the s-bend dangerous mountain, almost touching the ground sure they'd lose them in the shadow of the moon.

Rapid gunfire rang out, they were the targets. Gabriel was in the back and sure to get hit first. Niarchos sharply turned the bike in the opposite direction of their assassins. Niarchos shot the back passenger who fell off the bike. He was hit. Niarchos felt ill realizing he was shot with a vice grip filled bullet. Vice grip raced through him as fast as he sped on his motorcycle, as vines of poison seized the warrior vampire.

"I'm ill Gabriel." He knew he would never make it back before sunrise he had to stop, or he'd black out killing them. Blood flowed from him, drenching her blouse as she tightened her arms around him applying pressure to the wound while he struggled to keep them alive.

He shifted fast up a hill he knew of. "Hold on ma." He was coming to a cliff with the shooter on his tail.

Niarchos picked up speed to 245 miles per hour jumping a river wide gap landing on the other side. Gabriel's screams echoed through the valley as she closed her eyes flying across the gap and over the moon. It was a jump he always wanted to try but was too afraid, today the fear left him he had a life to save there was no room for doubt.

When they landed, she looked back the masked shooter turned back. Niarchos rode in a cave dropping the bike, falling to the earth beneath him.

"Nicky! Nicky!" The sun was up. She could go outside and walk back, but what if they were human and looking for them? Gabriel tried her phone but had no service. She took a few branches looking around before she went out to cover the bike tracks. She remembered Clarence's story of how Safinah covered his bloody footprints. She cried and panicked. "He's gonna die." whispering to herself.

Niarchos breathed labored, he was hot and shaking. Vampires are always cold to the touch. She opened his eyes, the colors looked dense.

"Jesus, please help me. If you're listening" Niarchos' phone was no good. They must've been too deep in the valley. *Think Gabriel! Sex yes!* Her fangs popped, she nervously bit deep into her forearm opening his mouth, tilting his head back her arm to his mouth. He woke up choking on her blood.

"Nicky thank God" she whispered so she couldn't be heard if scouts were around. He sipped slowly.

"I have the Pharaoh's blood in me. It must heal you." She laid on top of him to keep him warm as his temperature shifted drastically. She didn't care if she blacked out from blood loss. She didn't want her best friend to die. "Nicky?" He didn't answer, drinking until he finally stopped, the wound closed. She looked at her phone it was 1 p.m. She wrapped her arms around him her head on his shoulder.

'*Baby help, help.*' she blocked her fears out, opening her mind. '*Clarence, help. Gabriel?*' "I got her!" He yelled to the Elders.

*Baby we're in trouble. Sugar, where are you? I'm unsure. We left the bees when men started shooting at us. Don't cry Sugar, your emotions block me, I'm unsure why. She calmed down. They shot Nicky with a liquid, he's sick bad baby. I'm unsure what they hit him with. It looks like black vines under his skin. Don't touch it Sugar it's contagious it's vampire vice grip. Is he going to die Clarence?*

*No Sugar, he's an old vampire. Niarchos is huge. One bullet can only make him ill. Then what happened Gabriel? He rode us into the woods. He jumped over a huge water gap. Caleb said he knows the spot, Sugar. We went over the cliff, then into a cave, he passed out. I'm coming at sunset Sugar. Ok.*

She cried again. He lost communication with her. Clarence was livid. He slammed his fist on the marble kitchen counter, breaking it. "If we shift dingo, we'll find them faster Clarence." "Good Idea Cain" "What time is sunset Caleb?" "6 p.m. Clarence." "Get the pickup truck and bikes we ride to the cliff at five." Clarence ordered.

"It's not safe for all of us to shift into Dingos. We need Chance, Clarence he's the next strongest vampire." Caleb suggested. Clarence grabbed Zion's wrist.

"Set up the medical room for Niarchos. Have Chance fly in." Papa Nate sat him down. "He's already here Clarence." "He's not supposed to be here as long I'm here Papa Nate." They looked away.

"How do we know he isn't behind this to free his woman before her competition?" "Never Clarence. Chance is your son and our brother." "My son deceived me, Papa Nate." "Clarence, calm down." Papa Nathan was the only Elder who calmed his temper.

"It was my idea. If you want to blame a vampire, blame me. He arrived last night at 11 o'clock. He was with Ann and I, we discussed getting you to squash this. The Elders despise division, you know this Clarence, this isn't who we are. He's here to assist your Queen Clarence. He wouldn't hurt Gabriel. You scanned his thoughts, let him help. We don't know what we're up against and Niarchos might be dying in a cave while your bride is struggling to keep him alive. Chance is an old vampire we need his strength. Don't push him away not when Niarchos is in danger."

"Since it was you who defied me, it's you who'll stand trial as his co-conspirator if he's behind these attempts Papa Nate." "I don't take issue with that Clarence." "Fuck!" Clarence shouted, lying on the floor meditating. Caleb got on his knees next to him. "Caleb, do you see something? Connect to me. Say you got something seer." "Not yet quiet." Clarence levitated 30 inches off the floor, the Elders were in awe. No one made a sound. "Gabriel's watching the light. She has four of Niarchos' guns, ready to shoot in the dark. I can see through your eyes Clarence. Caleb smiled the connection worked. "I'm coming my vampire bride."

Clarence changed into grey sweatpants with no underwear and a hoodie. Ann looked down as he walked by. She knew he was hung from the few times they were naked when shifting. "Ann, I'll need you to go ahead of us when we arrive hover where you hear them please. When we see you, we'll meet you there." He shared Gabriel's shirt they, sniffed it getting her scent.

When evening approached, Caleb drove to the jumping cliff. They navigated around rocky terrain to get to the other side which was roadless as they waited in the jeep for sunset. A car pulled up behind them and they drew pistols. "It's Chance."

Papa explained he wasn't shifting. He and his grandson would keep guard while they were in dingo form. Baby Nate was excited he'd heard of vampire shifters but thought it was myth. Papa Nate informed him, "You can't discuss our change with anyone. When you marry your wife can't know. When we're dingos we're vulnerable humans or vampires can easily kill us. This is why we don't share it, understood?" "Yes Papa Nate." "I need you to kill anyone headed at us don't hesitate. It could mean one of us dies." "Yes papa."

He hugged his grandson and Chance. "I feel good you're here Chance." They stripped, leaving their clothes with Caleb. Ann left after kissing Papa.

"See you later free slave," misting far away. Nate beheld her one minute, the next she evaporated into tiny particles blending with the night. Ann went into a twirl, wisping into the air, moving into the woods one with the fog and sweeping winds. The Elders split up when Baby Nate heard barking.

"Watch the cliff, when you get to it, run and jump. Chance, you'll know it when you hear water." "Ok papa Nate." Caleb sat in the jeep, with security guarding him. He concentrated on seeing their location through his third eye. "Shoot anyone approaching, understood." "Yes, Elder Caleb." His security obeyed. Caleb closed his eyes. He saw Gabriel in the dark, with her phone light on. He connected telepathically with Clarence. "Look for a phone light in the dark." Clarence heard him but was unable to answer as a dingo. They ran as one arriving to the cliff. Clarence found it and jumped from rock to rock until he was valley low leveled with rushing river water. Rocks connected leading across the wild river. His pack stood behind him looking for another way. Clarence looked at Ann hovering over the rocks, telepathically informing them this was the only passage across. Clarence, being the Alpa dingo, led the way as the Elders jumped on the rocks behind him. Upon arrival, there were more rocks and a steep uphill, but it was better then being washed away.

Clarence trusted Ann again, who now hovered over a flat terrain. *Nicky?* Clarence heard her thoughts she was weak she opened her wrist feeding Niarchos more blood. This time he held her wrist hostage to his mouth, savagely sipping. "Nicky, easy." she begged. He was draining her unconsciously.

"Nicky easy." She called weakly trying to escape the grip of a 100 plus year-old vampire tethering her wrist to his mouth vice grip tight fracturing her wrist. "Ahhhh!" Her screams echoed off mountain walls alerting Elders to her exact location. The Elders followed her blood smell. It was heavier her screams clearer. Ann went straight to the cave, shifting to vampire from Dingo. "Gabriel honey?" "Ann?" "Yes honey, please don't shoot, put the gun down."

"No offense Ann, but how'd you know I was here?" "Gabriel Honey please, we're all here. Clarence will be here in less than five minutes. Can I come in?"

"No!" "Ok honey. I understand you're scared; but I must stop Niarchos, or he's going to drain and kill you. I hear your heart slowing, sweetie please." "NO Ann!" Gabriel clutched Niarchos' gun. "Anyone entering the cave is gonna get shot Ann these vice grip bullets too." Chance arrived. "Gabriel, its Chance. May Ann and I enter?" She popped a shot, they jumped back.

"She's dying, I hear Niarchos draining her. Where the hell is pop, Ann?" "Right here Chance." The Elders shifted vampire, peering in the darkness of the cave. Lily sat in a tree to see if anyone was coming. "Sugar, it's Clarence. Lower the gun baby or you'll hurt me." She didn't reply. Clarence ran in with Ann and Chance. Gabriel passed out on top of Niarchos. He had her wrist in his mouth. His fangs were in her. He was unconscious and full of black veins. "Clarence, she needs blood now." Clarence opened his wrist holding it over her mouth.

"She's not drinking Ann." Chance and Cain were giving Niarchos blood. Lily howled. Elijah and Blaise headed to the cave. "Come on boy," Ann demanded slapping Niarchos' face.

"Sugar, don't you die on me." Her arm wasn't healing. Stinging tears welled in his eyes. "Don't do it boy." Clarence looked at Elijah afraid. "Save her, ain't no time for tears she be fine make her drink." Clarence held her in his arms he poured his blood in his mouth. He opened her mouth pouring it in pinching her nose. Gabriel woke up weak coughing blood. She grabbed his arm hungrily feeding.

They heard Glocks cock outside as dingos looked to the sound of gunfire stirring the quiet mountain terrain. "Is she awake?" Elijah made Clarence focus on Gabriel. Clarence picked up Niarchos' handing one to Elijah. fast gunfire continued for five minutes then ceased. Niarchos crossed five languages feverishly warning Clarence the grey coats were shooting at them in French.

Clarence went outside with two vampires in custody. Cain, Chance, and Elijah held them at gunpoint. "Put them in the UV holding cell Cain." Chance grabbed Niarchos' bike to make the jump.

"I'll carry Niarchos Elijah. We can cross the river letting the water carry his weight. We can't cross rock barefoot, not with his weight on us."

"Where's Chance?" "Here pop" "You're taking Gabriel on the bike. I'll need to help Cain, Elijah, and Blaise get Niarchos across the water gap." Lily entered the cave. "I found this. It was an old makeshift wooden raft made from logs. We can get Niarchos across on it. I tightened it with braided vines. It should work guys." "Ann, guide us across. Help find shallow waters please. Good eye Lily" Ann misted out.

Clarence grabbed vines from a tree. He and Lily braided several together to tie Gabriel onto the bike and reinforce Niarchos' raft further. Clarence tied Gabriel to Chance. He wrapped and secured her legs around his waist. "If she dies, you die." he growled. Chance held his head down. "Yes Pharaoh."

"Get her to Caleb. Inform him to take her to Zion and return with blankets for Niarchos. Take the pick-up truck leave our clothes on the side the road Chance." Chance went to the cliff staring at the gap *this negro is crazy as hell,* shaking his head. "Hold on honey." Chance secured Gabriel tight to him.

He u-turned around revving the engine, making sure her helmet was strapped on saying a prayer to whatever God was listening. Chance revved his engine rolling with excessive speed over fallen leaves and dry branches. Chance clutched the handles hyper-forwarding his body bike bumped advancing forward flying across the water gap at 325 mph. Their silhouette looked like wings shadowed within the full moon. As gravel from the cliff dropped below. The bike dropped to the earth across the gap. The motorcycle slid as Chance used his foot controlling the bike's speed. He smiled looking back at the jump he made overjoyed they were alive.

Gabriel awoke, biting Chance then feeding. "No honey." He tried moving her head, but she needed his blood. *Damn she's sexy.* He wiped her mouth before meeting Caleb. If he told Clarence, he would be more cross and jealous, so he hid it. He met Caleb, guards rushed to Gabriels's aid getting her in the truck with Caleb who sat in the back with Gabriel staring at Chance. "You're in trouble negro." "Quiet Caleb don't say a word. It was an accident. Don't discuss it he hates me." Chance paced upset. "Pop said return with the pick-up for Niarchos and bring blankets after dropping Gabriel Caleb."

When they arrived to the cabin Zion had a blood transfusion IV blood drip ready the second Caleb carried her in "Whose blood is this on her shirt?" "Chance, Niarchos, and Clarence."

"Is Chance, ok Caleb?" "Yes Zion, Gabriel bit him by accident, thinking he was Clarence." "Jesus, as if we need more problems Caleb" They handed Caleb guns through the door. "I'll return with Niarchos Zion." "Take her to the bedroom in back the kitchen Joan. We'll prep Niarchos' room Caleb." Zion carried her to the bedroom and Joan cut off her clothes, covering her with a sheet.

"You're ok honey. Unfortunate thing, she has an open wound Zion." holding up her arm it was bleeding from Niarchos' punctures from his bite. Zion injected Clarence's blood into the wounds they closed painfully slow. "Joan, tea please?" Zion shook his head, no. "The Dr.'s trying to transfuse blood in you Gabriel." "My arm hurts Joan. Nicky...Nicky?" Gabriel called incoherently. "Who's Nicky Zion?" "Niarchos Joan." Zion administered a sedative. "Why sedation Zion?" "She needs rest, and WE stay out of issues that aren't medical woman." "Hehe yes honey." Clarence and Elijah carried Niarchos to the pick-up. Papa met them at the riverbank with baby Nate. "Gentle watch his head!" Clarence yelled. Clarence sat in the truck bed with Niarchos. "Don't touch him, Clarence." "This is my child my son I will touch him, Caleb."

Ann touched down behind Papa dressing. The prisoners were apprehended by Papa and Baby Nate. They returned to finish their botched assassination attempt failing. They arrived at the cabin with Niarchos. "All of you shower! Decontaminate!" Zion instructed as soon as they arrived at the cabin. Zion filtered six bags of blood for Niarchos because he was huge.

The Vampire Holding Cells....

Elijah and Caine dropped the assassins at the jail, questioning them for three days with no sleep.

Caine saw they were native American Blackfoot Indian. Cain, learned the language from Cody speaking the language, asking who sent them. They were out of it from the gunshot wounds Niarchos put on them.

"Lock them in the UV cells." Security grabbed them. "N.B.O, no blood order." "Yes, Elder Caine."

The Cabin......

Clarence rushed to Zion after his brief shower "Gabriel?" "I sedated her. She's getting your blood by morning she'll be good as new. I set her arm stitched a few punctures Niarchos' bite is deep to the bone. She saved Niarchos' life Gabriel, kept him alive Clarence. Niarchos almost drained and killed her. Gabriel exchanged her life for his as any good Queen would."

"Allow me to see her Zion." Zion left Clarence and he locked the door. He lay next to Gabriel on the bed, holding her waist crying because he loved her. All these things happening, he feared she'd abandon him and his love for her. "Don't leave Sugar." She picked up her hand resting it in his hair, moving her finger's. "Shhh...I'm here," she whispered over his tears.

It was a rough night. The games were suspended, gossip floated amongst the covens of the attempt. No vampire knew who they were after or why.

They heard Niarchos killed one the shooter's and made an impossible jump over the river gap causing vampires to visit the iconic spot taking pictures, selfies, and videos. Scroll writers visited the jump spot taking pictures to document a scroll. The jump made Chance and Niarchos vampire motorcycle gods.

Chance and Mary guarded Niarchos room while Elijah remained bedside. He was a little brother to them; they were afraid for the first time one was going to die. No Elder was supposed to die, they were immortal made to walk time as one. Clarence wouldn't open the door. "You know I can knock it down Zion." Joan joked. "Have you both lost your minds, Zion and Joan?" Caleb inquired. Clarence gives Niarchos blood he had flown in from his blood banks. As soon as it arrived, Niarchos used ten bags per day to chase the poison out. "How's Nick doing Zion?"

"We must clean his blood, Chance. "Has he wakened Zion?" "No Chance." "Call as soon he wakes, keep a blanket on him please." Chance was scared for the first time since his lynching. Clarence handed Joan three bags of his blood for Niarchos through the door locking it behind him.

She brought the blood to Zion; everyone cleared the room. "I'm not leaving him alone. He hates being alone," Chance said pulling his baby brothers blanket up." Clarence left Gabriel attempting to wake Niarchos via telepathic chain link, with no luck. "I'm here big baby." Clarence whispered the nick name he and Safinah called their son.

Zion tapped the door, Clarence didn't answer. Joan knocked he opened it. Zion was on Joans back "Check her vitals and wounds. Inform me if they've healed, please Joan." "I will honey." "Did Gabriel wake Clarence?" "A little."

"Caleb said she and Niarchos will be fine, he saw it." "I've been linked to Niarchos telepathically, he's not speaking. He always speaks Joan." "He's sedated heavily. I'm worried about you Clarence my mother said your sensitive and one day I'd see. I guess today is that day. What's wrong."

"What if she breaks it off Joanie? Three attempts on her life in three months." "We don't know what happened Clarence. We must wait till they wake. We can't make assumptions. She's stronger than you think, and you know what? This woman loves her some you! She's crazy for you Clarence. I'm unsure who's worse, her or Safinah."

"Me." They heard Gabriel confess dryly. Joan grabbed water, putting the straw in her mouth. Her heart pumped on, and off as Zion monitored the machines attached to her on his phone's medical apps. "Get her some tea, please Joan." "Zion must clear it Clarence, I'll get him." "How are you feeling Sugar?" "Tired, are vampires supposed to feel tired daddy?"

"When they've lost as much blood as you, yes Sugar." "Nicky Clarence?" "Resting he'll be fine, he's strong. He saved your life, and you saved his. Giving your blood kept his body at vampire temperature, not allowing the vice grip to kill him, Sugar." "Help me up Clarence." "No Sugar."

"Help me or I'll walk down alone." Zion gave the nod of ok; Clarence carried her. Elder vampires kneeled before her for the first time out of respect instead of obligation because she risked her life for their brother.

"Y'all excuse my hair." She used her hand brushing it off her face. Clarence sat her on the chair in Niarchos' room. "No response Elijah?" "Not yet my Queen." Gabriel held his hand which swallowed hers as the house fell silent. Vampires looked in or listened.

"Nicky? Wake up please gimme something Sweetie." His eyes opened, weakly turning his head, he smiled for her. Moaning. "It burns Gabriel." Clarence cried for his son's pain. "It's the charcoal arresting the vice grip Niarchos. Get some sleep. I need you, my gladiator," touching the crown of his head. He squeezed her hand. "Let my patients rest please." Zion pushed a wheelchair in for Gabriel.

"Pop, I got one of the bastards. They thought I was you." "How son?" "The helmet has your name on it. My chin strap was broken. I borrowed yours. They weren't after Gabriel they were after you." Clarence told the Elders what Niarchos revealed as someone knocked at the door. Everyone drew weapons. The security gates of the Cabin were down. They rolled Gabriel back into the room with Niarchos. Ann and Vaughn guarded them heavily armed all vampires popped their fangs.

"Who's it?" Elijah yelled with baby Nate standing on the sides of the door, gun in hand. No one responded. Elijah opened the door slowly, his rifle locked and loaded.

"I'm an old friend of Clarence Hollings." "State ya name?" "Spotted Eagle."

# Chapter 24
# Prodigal Sons

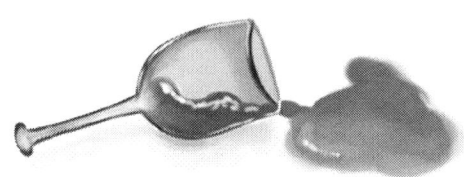

The year 1901

August 1....

Clarence was coming from town with cigars and brandy with former slave owners. He did this monthly to keep up appearances and get information regarding negros in the county. He wanted to make sure whites weren't plotting anything wicked when they did, he was made privy to it before the plot was carried out.

There were issues with Indian's, however he wasn't clear on what. On his way home, smoke filled the air. He rode toward the smoke, arriving at a blood bath. There were dead Indian's everywhere. Some sacrificed themselves as human shields and some were scalped. There were no children only men and older women past childbearing years. The younger women were gone. Selling Indian women as wives to white men wasn't uncommon.

He popped his fangs in case someone was still around. He tried not to step on the dead as he crossed the bodies checking the mud houses and teepees for signs of life when he heard faint crying.

He pulled the rug in the teepee reveling a hole with a young woman holding a dead baby. "Stay away!" she screamed clutching her baby drenched in blood.

"I'm not going to hurt you. I'm not a white man, I'm a free negro. English?" "I understand, go away!"

"Young Ms. you can't stay. The savages who did this will return. Give me your hand.... please. The sun is coming up, gimme your hand!" She gave him her right hand, clutching the baby in her left arm close to her bosom as Clarence pulled her out of the ditch.

She walked behind him through the bloody carnage, afraid. "Eagle?" "Who are you calling Ms.?" "Husband." She gingerly gave Clarence her baby before dropping to her knees after discovering her father's body on top of her mother's. Clarence grabbed her arm, watchful of the time. She fled; he held the baby who had a bullet hole in his chest. *Poor baby*, Clarence thought.

"It's my husband. Can you help him?" Clarence looked down, his breath was faint and raspy. "Is he a good man?" "What?" "Is he a good man Ms.?" "Yes!" Clarence bit his wrist because there was too much blood on his neck. If the blood was dead, he didn't want to risk illness. Clarence bit him, he didn't have a choice of asking him because his pulse was fading, and sunrise was upon him. Clarence shook him, looking in his eyes, which remained human colored.

In fear of sunlight, he left him in the ground. If he were vampire he'd turn during the day. There he'd be safe from the sun. Clarence escorted his Indian wife to his plantation. She met his family and wife Safinah who pronounced her son dead. Hausis laid in bed for six months and didn't come out of the room. She didn't speak, only sat near the window staring out chanting Indian songs. It didn't stop Safinah or the other women from caring for her and incorporating her in daily chores.

Niarchos buried the baby in the Hollings cemetery. She couldn't bring herself to cremation which would free his spirit from this world. The next night. Clarence went to the tepee, moved the rug to find her dead husband the way he left him, unturned. He dragged him out of the ground, opened his eyes to see if the venom took hold. It didn't. He saw no sign of vampire or human life.

He placed him on a sailboat on a nearby lake, shot a flaming arrow at it to set it on fire as his wife requested, setting his soul free. She didn't want him to be placed in the ground. The body needed to burn so the spirit could rise with its ancestors. Feeling empathy, Clarence granted her wish. When Clarence returned with the news, she sat on the floor chanting and wailing in her native tongue, heart heavy and tears falling like hail. Clarence left her to the women.

Present Day......

Elijah let Spotted Eagle in carefully. They kept 15 guns pointed at him. He had long black shiny hair wearing black. Elijah placed handcuffs on him with a UV tablet in the center of the cuffs. If the vampire attempted freedom, the tablet would break over the wrists and once the UV entered the blood it would kill in one minute.

"This is a precautionary measure." Elijah warned Eagle didn't object. Clarence glared at him, unable to read his thoughts. "How?" The Elders were shocked he knew him.

"I woke on fire, once that was out, I traveled to our sister village with warning. I was shocked when the sun hit my hand, burning it. Our shaman stated I was a holy half dead, a God among men in turn for this gift, I couldn't see the sun. I was to survive on blood of the living. The village fed me blood in exchange for protection. I never knew how I ended up this way. I knew from legend something bit me, but the question was what, who and why? I'd get my answer years later when I saw this." Tossing a London vintage gossip rag on the table dated the 60's. Its headline was 'Bruce and a mystery woman who is she?' He paused enough to give Clarence a glance, still unable to read his thoughts.

"I tracked her, which led me to you my maker who stole my wife leaving me for dead." "Is this what you think happened Eagle?" "You're holding Hausis in captivity. Her only road to freedom is to fight in a competition Clarence." "A competition she chose rather than face trial for her treacherous ways Eagle."

"Treachery is siring a vampire and setting him to flames. You will release Hausis immediately, return her to her tribe seeing her no more. Chance connected to Clarence telepathically. *Pop please don't.*

"Was it you who made the attempt on the life of my wife and son last night Spotted Eagle? If so, you committed treason because you are aware that I'm your maker, no matter the circumstances, you've attempted to kill members of this coven."

"I didn't have knowledge, they acted on their own they're in your custody, do as you see fit Clarence" "Of course, not before questioning to see if you had any involvement. It was and is my intent to speak as leaders of a tribes, to speak as two chieftains should." Clarence spoke to Eagle in Siksika Blackfoot. Spotted Eagle concealed shock he spoke his native tongue.

"You have no coven. Your tribe is mine, vampires within it are all my children. I'm your father, you're a lost child, my prodigal son. One lost who has no idea of his heritage. You've gone many moons and many sun sets now you've returned this is a joyous day for me. This is a misunderstanding which must be cleared up. What we are and what you are. Do you see all these vampires? They were made by me and never have I left one. Some are your age on the date of their turn, some older. Yet they sit before me as you do. Your home, you've no enemies here Spotted Eagle."

"Do you care to hear what happened the night you became undead? Why you woke alone?" Clarence looked in his eyes, his hard exterior fracturing. It was strange seeing vampire-colored eyes on Spotted Eagle. His black hair made the eyes stand out.

Spotted Eagle was confused, this isn't what he imagined. He thought they'd have discord or a fight over the woman's freedom. He wasn't expecting peace or a warm welcome from his maker.

Clarence continued, "you're a part of me and us. I'll love you and your people as I have loved the ones before you. We can discuss Hausis and her fate. I'm not promising you, her freedom. I'll grant you permission to speak with her. I'm sure she'll be as shocked as I. Please be sure to speak using your native tongue as I'm keeping the conversation confidential."

"The meeting must be here on this compound and heavily guarded because as fore stated she'll be in shackles because she's a strong old vampire like you and me. Please know the woman you once loved has been lost many years ago. If you can restore her mentally, I welcome this attempt to save her from the path of self-destruction." Spotted Eagle held back tears. Years of anger, rage and hate melted away. "How'd you learn the tongue, Clarence?" "Hausis Eagle." "She taught you to speak Eloquently. You speak great ancient Blackfoot. Some words I speak with Elders of my tribe have been long forgotten. I remind them as we converse.

"Thank you, Spotted Eagle." The vampire Elders were nervous. They couldn't understand and didn't know what to expect. (Still peaking siksika) "Does Hausis know you live Eagle?" "No Clarence." "Why do you look at me with sadness Clarence?" "All these years she sought love like you and she shared, what took you so long my son?" "Foolish pride."

"You're back finding your way home. Please, when you're ready to hear what happened that night the stars aligned and made you a vampire God I'm here. Leave the address to where you're lodging with your new vampire brothers, they'll come in two moons to meet with Hausis. Unshackle him." Cain did as commanded but was hesitant. Their guns still pointed as the UV cuffs were removed.

"Lower the guns." "Pharaoh?" Clarence gave a look, and Cain complied. "This is your brother Spotted Eagle my prodigal son. Treat him as such." Spotted Eagle went to the door. "Goodnight Pharaoh." Bowing his head he stepped backwards, disappearing into the foggy night.

The Next Morning....

"Steven, hi, it's Gabriel. Are you here for the games?" "Yes, my Queen. Goodmorning."

"Great, can you come to the cabin? When you arrive tell the guard at the gate, I sent for you please." Since the attempt on his life, Clarence had gates installed around the acres. She sat in Niarchos' room a week after the attack. The games resumed however they weren't in attendance. Gabriel loved martial arts, so Caleb moved it to the end accommodating her. Niarchos was awake but weak. They were sipping coffee as usual. Gabriel fully recovered.

"Look Nicky surprise!" Taking out a honey bear shaped glass jar with a gingham bow tie. He smiled at the honey packaging.

"Do you have a name for your honey?" "I do, Nicky's Honey." Gabriel met Niarchos' unbreakable gaze. Elijah entered the room. "Guess who's here, negro? "Who Lijah?" "He landed to compete in the gun range competition Saturday night. GRIP BOY!"

Niarchos teared up Elijah hugged him. "Yep, he wasn't gonna come but I called and told him what happened. Clarence sent for him he came ASAP. I begged him to compete to get his excommunication lifted. His wife Ginger helped me convince him Nick."

"She good Lijah?" "Yep but said she can't watch haha." "She needs to bring her ole ass down here too. She plays too much Lijah." Niarchos sat up wincing in pain "Grip don't fuckin play! These vampires don't know how to handle a vampire nigga like Grip. Sorry for cussin Gabriel haha."

"What did I say about using that dirty word around me Niarchos?" Clarence entered the room to check on him. "Sorry, Pop I didn't see you there." "May I have coffee please daddy. You want one Nicky?" "No thanks Queen." "I'll bring it, Sugar." "Thank you, Clarence." "Why didn't you ask Nicky?" "Pop can hear like five blocks away woman; whispering won't work." "Hehe." "Cause he's king he's not to serve me nosey."

"He's your father. Don't parents take care of ill children Niarchos?" Clarence returned with a serving tray with two coffees, Niarchos smiled. Clarence whispered, "I'm never above serving those I love." "Hehe told you Nicky. Who's this Grip? Call the scroll keepers you're an Elder let them read for us" "I've never done that Gabriel. "Why?"

"I was there for most of it. Some of its sad I don't wanna relive it." "Pleasssssse Niarchos." "Ok ma. Alexis dial the scroll writer's division."

"Hello, how may I help" "This is Elder Vampire Niarchos Hollings." "What do I owe the pleasure of this call Elder?" "I'd like to hear the scroll written on Tavarus Grip Griffith-Hollings. "Of course, Elder. How are you feeling?" "I'm recovering." "Glad to hear it Elder. Steven will write your scroll on what took place at the epic cliff jump as soon as you're well. Elder, please check your e-mail."

"What do I need to do?" "Sign Elder." Gabriel signed his name. "Elder Niarchos, the signature doesn't match." "My dexterity is off due to the poison." "I apologize. Elder, I'll phone on facetime. You're looking well Elder Niarchos." "Today I'm privileged to be your reader my name is Tiyee Thomas." "Love the name, Tiyee was the wife of Ramses the third. She was involved in a harem plot to assassinate her husband for the throne ascension. The plot was discovered, the Queen was tried in court. Nothing is known of her fate. I'm assuming he killed her." "Elder, I'm impressed." "Why Tiyee?" "No one, I mean no one knows that!"

"I study the Kings and Queens of Egypt to learn how to lead people. I read and watch history channels. No matter what city they bring Egyptian artifacts I always see what's on display." "Elder, you look young." "Tiyee?" "Yes Elder?" "The scroll?" "Oh yes, Elder please excuse me." He mouthed to Gabriel, "This is why I don't call." "Hehe."

*Scroll 36*

*Tavarus "Grip" Hollings*

*Origin Scroll*

*August 8th, 1951......*

*Tavarus "Grip" Griffith, a 1951 bad boy was compared to a black James Dean. To support his mother and eight minor siblings after the death of his father Grip raced cars against white rich people's children. Grip would win the race selling the cars to keep food on the table and land tax paying for land his ancestors received after slavery, forty acres. He was 26 years old.*

*Grip stole cars occasionally when times were rough. One night, he found his way to the Pharaohs property in Georgia, where he saw a barn full of vintage cars and motorcycles. In his mind he stepped into heaven. With so many choices to steal from, he chose a 1940 Rolls Royce, which happened to be the favorite car of the Pharaoh. Grip stole the car not realizing who he was stealing from. He rolled the car to the gate, started the car driving away. Grip did this in broad daylight. When vampires in the house heard the car being stolen there was nothing they could do.*

Clarence forbade his wife Queen Safinah to go outside in daylight with her shot gun, a 1940 Winchester Rifle purchased for her as a gift from Elder Chance for her birthday, to stop the car thief. Pharaoh watched from his window, standing out the sun getting a good look at his face as his body smell wafted through the open window. Grip looked up at the window in the shade of the magnolia trees waving goodbye to the pharaoh smiling before exiting the property. As soon as the sun set the Pharaoh searched for the thief brazen enough to break into his home to steal his car in plain sight. He arrived at a back dirt road where Grip finished racing against a rolls Royce owner, winning the person's car. Crossing the finish line, the white car owner refused to relinquish the key to Grip which angered him. Grip threw a punch, and brawl ensued. Grips gang against a gang of white boys. The white boy was upset because this'd be his third loss, fearing someone would inform his father of his losses he shot Grip in his stomach.

When the gun shot rang out, his friends and girlfriend abandoned him to die alone. Clarence stood over Grip, who struggled to stand to his feet.

"What're you doing here.... how'd ya find me mister?" "I have my ways you're going to die boy." "Don't call me boy peckerwood! I know I'm dying you think I'm stupid?! If imma die I ain't letting no white mother fucker call me boy as I leave this world and I ain't dying on my knees." Grip looked at Clarence with fire in his eyes. "I can't die." "Why?"

"My mama got eight of us by her lonesome she need me. My daddy dead, I'm the oldest. I got seven *little ones myself." "You're young to have seven children you married?" "No, it's a long story white man everyone ain't had a rich life handed to em' like you!" "Get off my car you're bleeding on it." Clarence pushed him off. What if you didn't die, if you could live forever, would you?" Grip clutched his stomach dropping to the ground.*

*"I wanna see my little ones and siblings grow," wincing in pain. Clarence draped him up, dropping him in the Rolls Royce, driving onto a back road.*

*"You'll die; however, I'll bring you back, stay out the sun, and drink the blood of humans and animals to live...yes, or no?" "White nigga, will you help me or fuckin not shit this fuckin shit hurts?!"*

*Clarence grabbed Grip, tossing him on the hood of the car biting into his salty neck. Grip screamed as Clarence bit down without care or mercy. Clarence opened his vein dripping blood into Grips mouth making a mess but not into his wound to close it faster making his turn painful, long, and drawn out.*

*Grip was in agony. Clarence dragged him by the ankle into the house, dropping his leg on the floor like a stray dog. Safinah dashed to Grip. "Peety what's wrong with him?" "He's turning Finah." "Why's he screamin so badly?"*

*"The vampire venom burning him, Cotton. It's killing the human inside Cotton and it's annoying. Have Niarchos drag him to the west barn woman that screaming has me on edge." "I won't! He's negro like us, he deserves his turn to be better than a common animal." Clarence locked himself in his study. Niarchos carried Grip to his room to a spare bed where Grip resided for 10 years.*

*The year 1962....*

*Tavarus Grip Hollings now the adopted son of Clarence Hollings met a woman named Ginger, a former escort in New York. He began a new life with her moving out of Clarence's house. Grip, a thrill seeker began robbing banks across the south, working his way up the east coast.*

*June of 1961 Grip & Ginger robbed the Dime savings bank of Williamsburg Brooklyn. 'A modern-day Bonnie & Clyde,' as they were dubbed in the negro papers also revered them as heroes of their time. When they were caught, Clarence alone went to bail Grip out, but not his wife Ginger as he was married unsanctioned by the vampire crown. "You've heat on you we cannot afford for you to bring attention to us Grip. Stop this foolishness, I command it."*

*Grip looked at his maker defiantly, "No." Grip was the first of the Pharoh's sons to defy his order. "You will stop or face death by sunlight Tavarus." "You never liked or forgave me for stealing your car pop."*

*Clarence growled at Grip, banging his fist on a table, frustrated with his actions and stubborn ways. Grip kneeled at Clarence's feet, face down remembering whose presence he was in.*

*"STOP BOY!" When Grip looked up, Clarence was gone. Grip bailed Ginger out, they got lawyers, and both were given 15 years in prison. Ginger convinced a judge, by giving him a blow job, to allow her home with a date to turn herself in. The*

same day of her release, she got her guns shooting her way in and out with Grip on her arm who was taken into custody on the spot. Ginger took a bullet in her back which lodged in her spine breaking him out of jail.

Grip turned Ginger vampress in a dingy pissy alley without the Pharaohs permission behind the jail if not she would've perished in his arms. Grip & Ginger disappeared off the grid for six consecutive years. No calls, postcards, or letters. The Pharaoh was unable to reach Grip telepathically, but knew he was alive from his blood chain connection.

Spring 1968....

Grip called the Pharaoh, who informed him the Elders and council excommunicated him from his coven and childhood home. He's not to call, nor contact the Pharaoh, or any member of his coven again. Any vampire caught helping Grip would face judgement by the Pharaohs hand. This decision was due to the rash of bank robberies the last one leading to the death of four bank security and two federal agents. This led the F.B.I to Clarence's door with a warrant where they trashed his home looking for stolen treasury bonds.

"Do you have anything to say Grip?" Before hanging up Grip simply said through broken tears and realizations, "Papa, I love you."

End scroll.

Gabriel sniffled wiping her eyes "Is there anything else Elder Niarchos?" "How many scrolls are written about Queen Gabriel to date Tiyee?"

"Four Elder." "Thank you Tiyee." "Get better, Elder." "Thank you Tiyee." "Look at us being nosey Nicky hehe." "We can't be nosey we're royalty Gabriel, best you accept it." "It's a lot. I was human six months back, with no love life. Today I'm vampire Queen," putting her hand on his. "Your hands are massive Nicky." "Your hands are tiny my Queen."

Someone knocked, "Enter." They never broke their gaze, forgetting where he was, and who he was gazing at. "Look who purchased you flowers Niarchos?" Lily entered with Mara, who was shy and nervous. "Great One I didn't know you were here." She fell to her knees. "Please rise." Mara's eyes were closed, Niarchos grabbed Gabriel's wrist she snatched away, giggling inside closing the door behind her. "Can I get you anything Elder?" "Sure, water Mara."

Gabriel approached the master bedroom. Clarence was stretched out with one foot on the floor head resting on his pillow remote in hand, flipping channels. "You look at TV Clarence?" "Yes, since my wife spends so much time away from me." She sat with her legs across his lap, he looked around her at the TV. "You're jealous." "What if I am Gabriel? "Why would the Pharaoh be jealous?" She leaned in seductively kissing him. "Hug me." He dropped the remote, hugging her.

He rose off the bed she found herself under him, drifting down like a petal in the wind. She screamed playfully and Elijah kicked the door off the hinge to find them suspended in midair.

"WOW!" Elijah looked up smiling as Clarence held her in suspension.

"How high can you go Clarence?" "Pretty high Elijah." "Caleb requested a ride up the other day like a big kid." "Me too Clarence!" "You can't be serious?" "Hell yeah, I'm serious." "Why didn't you use it to glide across the gap the other night?" "I haven't mastered it. For example, it's hard for me to talk and concentrate on staying in this position without us dropping to the bed Elijah." "I'm helping you?" "Yes, as always." "Can we come down daddy?" Elijah and Gabriel laughed, as Clarence floated down. "I'm glad you two find it funny. Fix the door Elijah." "You promised shopping today, Clarence." "You know it's not safe Sugar." "It's driving me nutty being cooped up in here." "A little more time." "Are we going to the games this weekend?" "Yes Sugar, someone's at the door." "I heard no bell; the gate keeper didn't call Clarence." He smiled. 'Ding dong.' "Stop that Clarence!" "Haha"

Elijah went to the door. "Who is it?" "WHO DAT IS BOY?" Elijah snatched the door open, picking Grip up crying. "Damn you a welcome sight boy. Wait till Clarence sees you" "Papa here Elijah?" "We all here boy!" "WHO DAT IS?!" Niarchos yelled from the back room.

"My nigga back there?" "Your father's here, you know he despises that word Grip." "Sorry, Lijah my bad" "Pay your respects to the Pharoah before you see Niarchos." "Elijah, you know pop hates me."

"Why do you say that? It's not true Grip. He was hard on you because you don't listen you put us at risk of being exposed as a vampire coven because you chose to live reckless. You're the son of the Pharoah who does what he wants instead of what Clarence says. I hope you're different or coming home to coven ain't gonna work if you're not going to obey your father."

"I'mma listen." "I miss you negro I'll lead you to speak to Clarence Grip give a proper greeting." "What happen to the door Elijah?" "I kicked it off the hinge, like I'm do your ass if you fuck up again negro." Elijah knocked on the wall.

"Enter." Elijah entered kneeling head lowered formally because Grip was there. Grip knelt next to him with his head low and arms crossed in an X with two black power fists. "Great Pharoah, I appreciate you allowing me home." "Grip?"

"Yes, Pharaoh?" "How'd you get past the gate security undetected?"

He looked at Elijah. "I jumped the fence, so no one saw Great One." "Why?" "Permission to stand." "Granted." Grip stood with his eyes closed becoming invisible for twenty seconds, then returned. "Jesus!" Gabriel gasped, clutching her husband's arm. Clarence and Elijah were shocked. "How long have you had the gift Grip?"

"About six months Great One. It doesn't last long." holding his eyes to the floor. "Wow! You can disappear like the invisible man and return?" "Yes, ma'am." "That's incredible Clarence" Elijah tapped his arm, "that's Queen Gabriel, your father's new vampress bride."

"Apologies, Great Queen. I've heard nothing but praises. Please forgive me for speaking out of turn." "It's fine, you don't need to be formal with me Grip. Welcome home, son of the Pharoah." Gabriel smiled showing excitement for her husband she intentionally masked.

Grip was shocked that his father's new Queen was warm and welcoming. Clarence was mean in his eyes, but he was blessed with loving women. "Allow me to say Pharaoh, that Ginger and I were saddened by the passing of mama Safinah. My heart was heavy when I received the news. Please allow me to extend my deepest condolences for your loss Great One and please forgive my absence." "Thank you Grip, for the flowers they were her favorite yellow African daises." Grip was surprised, Clarence knew he sent them. Clarence hugged Grip "I've missed you my son." A lone tear streamed down his cheek.

Grip was in awe. His father never hugged or joked with him. Grip never understood why Clarence was hard on him and easier on Niarchos and Chance. This was part of the reason he returned; to learn why his maker hated him. Grip held tears back.

"May I see Niarchos, Pharaoh?" "Yes, you may son." Grip left without turning his back. "It was a pleasure meeting you,

Great Queen." Minutes later Elijah appeared with a goblet of warm blood, a blood offering from Grip Clarence. He sat in on the nightstand. "Why did he give you, his blood? Daddy." "Grip is A/B negative. He has a rare form of blood six percent of humans have it." Gabriel put the goblet in the fridge. "How can you like cold blood Gabriel and that's for me so we can blood lock?" "I'm unsure, tastes better cold Clarence. You're sharing I wanna taste it since it's rare." She plopped next to him he tickled her. "Hehe."

Downstairs....

"Who dat?" Grip grabbed Niarchos and hugged him for five minutes "They tried it, didn't they big bro?" "They almost had me, Grip." "Almost ain't good enough, nigga! If they was smart, they would've got us 'cause that's what it's gonna take for us not to head hunt them fuckers."

"Show him Grip." "Ok Elijah. You looking Nick?" "Yeah Grip." Grip closed his eyes, fading out. "What the fuck?" Niarchos smiled, his fangs showing. "Look at this shit here." "It's hot gift right Niarchos?"

"Hell yes! Elijah, damn!" "When I run it stays a little longer. It's how I got past the gate men. I ran, jumped, faded returning on foot." "Zion's gonna want a blood sample Grip," Elijah and Niarchos said simultaneously. "Haha no worries, Elijah" "Where's Ginger...how she?" "Man, she sent me to break the ice. She'll come out once me and pop finish fighting."

"Gimme some water Grip." He handed Niarchos a water bottle. "Remember that Indian bike you stole for me Grip? I still got her." The trio continued to catch up on old times.

Upstairs....

Lulu knocked on the wall outside Clarence and Gabriels bedroom "Come" Lulu moved the sheet aside.

"Great Pharaoh, Steven is at the door for Queen Gabriel." "Let him in. Sugar Steven is here." Gabriel whizzed past him down the stairs. "Shall we sit on the patio and take in the night?" "Lulu tea please, Steven?"

"Blood mix A and B positive If you have thank you. How may I service you Great One?" "I'd like a scroll written please." Steven removed the laptop. Lulu brought the drinks. "Please close the patio door Lulu thank you." "You're welcome Great One," as she exited the patio.

"I want to write a scroll as to why I love my husband even though there have been a few attempts on my life. I wonder if he knows why I love him? No man should wonder so I'd like this scroll to serve as a memory for him in case something happens Steven."

"Of course, when you're ready Great One."

*Scroll 300*

*Origin Scroll*

*The first scroll of Queen Gabriel Hollings*

*August 2020....*

*I was lonely. I had a few male suitors and a couple of serious relationships, however they never ended in marriage. I lost my mother by the age of 7 to the crack wars and had to live with my aunt and grandmother who raised me. By the time I was 28, my grandmother passed of old age and cancer and by 32 my aunt died of cancer.*

*By 33 I discovered my fiancé was sleeping with my cousin who he met at my aunt's funeral and by 35 I was diagnosed with rare lyophobic cancer. It had metastasized to my bones. I was in stage four,*

Dr.'s informed me to get my affairs in order I had six months to live.

The day I got the news I cried. I didn't cry because I was going to die, I cried for the loss of myself, I never lived. I never did anything I'd regret. Never made love on the beach, swam naked in the moonlight in the Caribbean, or sunbathed nude on a secluded beach. I never drove down Mulholland drive at night in a vintage Rolls Royce or parasailed over Egyptian waters. I'd yet to genuinely enjoy the zest of life.

There was so much I wanted to do marry have children and yet my time was up. I was never loved. I had the love of a mother, grandmother, and aunt but what of the love of a man? I mean what was it like to have a man adore and love you so badly he was willing to do anything to have you? To revere you as a gift, to want only you? Where would I find such a man? I cried for the woman and the dreams scheduled to die with me.

One day on my way home from my first chemo appointment, I stopped to get coffee. A man entered the shop he was handsome; correction, he was beyond handsome. His radiant eyes were the most beautiful eyes I'd ever seen on a human. On top of it he had gorgeous hair. It looked as though God took silk straight from heaven's looms placing it on his head strand by strand. His body was perfect, not a blemish or a mark on it. He was radiant.

He purchased Madeline cookies gifting them and reassuring me, "I'm going to make everything ok." in that second in time, I trusted him wholeheartedly. I fell in love with Clarence fast and hard. I didn't know his name; however, I knew this man was going to love me, behind his eyes revealed his truth.

For the first time in my live he was mine, something that belonged to me. I lived the year; it was his love I lived for. When Cody sliced my throat, I said to myself, 'not like this. I don't want to die.' I heard him say 'I love you Gabriel, on this night, you shall live and leapfrog through time with me.' Do you love me, Sugar?' 'With every fiber of my being Clarence.' That night the human perished; and the vampress emerged. No pain, sickness or worry with an instant no exportation date added to my dismal six-month diagnosis. A part of me is happy Cody attacked saving me from death. She guaranteed I spend eternity with a man that's mine immortalizing me in his eyes. For this reason, I forgive her transgressions.

He's my secret, the diary of my heart, the love of my life and my best friend. I'm enamored and hopelessly in love with him. The regret is I can't bear his children see him in them. Other than this, I have none. This life is the one I was meant to live happy and free. Clarence is my life and strength. I'd give my life gladly in exchange for his. He saved me mentally, spiritually, and physically. I owe him a debt I'll never be able to repay. I'll love him until the end of time.

End scroll.

Steven cried; they laughed through tears. "Were you afraid once you knew what he was?" "No Steven. I was afraid once I saw what he could do in anger." "Did you want to leave him Great One?" "Yes, to get my bearings Steven it's how I process things. I need alone time to sort my thoughts." "Will you and Elder Niarchos give us a scroll on what happened with the assassins Great One?" "Yes, when all this dies down. Do you love your job, Steven?" "I do, I'm a historian over our vampire histories. I was appointed by the Pharoah personally as I was a negro librarian in the human library which was rare back in 43 that's how we met. The Pharoah was the largest donator for school textbooks. Steven smiled he found out what books the white schools were using, purchasing our children the same books and all the supplies they needed from kindergarten to high school. Then he paid one year for the entire graduating $12^{th}$ grade class to go to college.

Steven sighed. "I'm gay and I had a hard time not falling in love with him Gabriel." "Hehe yes he is very easy to love is he not Steven?" "Yes, my Queen he is. These scrolls are particularly important. Did you hear about Pharoah's auction date Great One? She bragged he's a wonderful vampire." He explained the details of their date. I heard she requested he drink from the vein to be blood locked he obliged her my Queen." Gabriel's eyes squinted.

Mara & Niarchos……

"Goodnight Elder." Mara left Niarchos' room seeing Gabriel. "Ummm, you were in there a while." "We talked and looked at television." "You're returning tomorrow, Mara?" "If Elder Caleb gives me the night off, which I doubt. Good night Great One." "Goodnight Mara."

Gabriel went to Niarchos' room. He sat in a chair trying to stand prematurely. "Close the door, Gabriel." Niarchos took a pad handing her a note.

**I love you, Gabriel.** Gabriel read it smiling. She wrote back *you can't love me Niarchos I belong to the Pharoah, but I'm flattered. Why me?* You're a smart and beautiful vampress. she read it replying, *If I never met the Pharoah, I'd date* *you. You're a good vampire fine too. You know we can't Niarchos.*

I understand, however, it won't stop me from being in love. I'll always love you Gabriel. She hugged him, kissing his neck. Why are you crying?

*I never thought anyone would love me after my diagnosis Nicky.* He hugged her, still writing, "You're everything a vampire could want. Why would you think this way? Stupid I guess, she wrote before running her fingers over his 360 waves locking eyes with him. Shh, he wrote Pharaoh will want to know why you're crying, he reads thoughts. I know, she scribbled. He wiped her tears.

**I'll always be here for you, no matter what. You saved my life. I'll always be in your debt, Great One**, he wrote kneeling. She kissed the crown of his head writing *you owe me a date Nicky ;)*. I do he smiled; she touched his fangs before he kissed the palm of her hand.

He burned the notes. She smiled, wiping her face, blowing him a kiss leaving. She purposely stopped thinking about him declaring his love before seeing Clarence who was playing chess with Zion. "Check Mate Zion." "Where?" "In three moves look there Zion." Zion knocked down his king.

"I never knew you spoke Blackfoot siksika. How many languages do you speak Clarence?" "Ten. I picked some up and others I've mastered through private lessons." "You always improve yourself Pharoah. Which languages?"

"Siksika which is Blackfoot, French I learned from you Caleb, Haitian creole, Chinese I learned from Zhou, Russian from Vlad, Mandarin Cantonese, Swahili learned vampires that protect the diamond mines in Africa, Italian Arabic and Spanish." "Impressive goodnight, Pharoah." "Goodnight Dr." "Is the bedroom door repaired Elijah?"

"I'm starting to think you lost your touch. When we were slaves, this door would've been repaired in ten minutes." "The door is repaired Clarence haha you wish I lost my touch Goodnight vampire." "Goodnight, friend."

Gabriel went to her private bathroom, closing the door. She drew a bath tossing bubbles in when Clarence entered sitting on the toilet staring at her. "What's on your mind Gabriel?" "Nothing." "We lie to each other Sugar?" "How was your date with Daisy." She was mad when her fangs popped by accident. "Hungry?" "No, I had tox whiskey blood." "No, you didn't Gabriel, I'd smell it." "Leave it alone." she turned her back on him in the oval shaped tub. He undressed, joining her.

"Gabriel wash my hair please." "No." he handed her the shampoo. She threw it in the water low growling. "Gabriel what's wrong?" She started in on him. "This is about the date. Is it because I drank from her? Did you know I can drink from any vampire on command, they can't deny me?"

"Gabriel, I'm thirsty, feed me your blood." her arm rose against her will. She tried to stop herself and couldn't, "How?" Her wrist was at his lips. She fought hard to lower her arm but couldn't. He kissed it releasing his magnetic hold.

"It's not the same. Daisy asked and you obliged Clarence." "True, I love drinking fresh blood from the vein." "Drink mine you don't need nobody else." She held her wrist up as an offering. "I can't it's dangerous." "I fed Niarchos Clarence." "Yes, almost dying in the process Sugar. You're not strong enough." She mashed her palms to her face crying. Niarchos was sleeping, his eyes popped open when he heard her sobbing. He hated that sound. He stared at his door trying to stand to check on her, but he was weak.

She held up her wrist. "No Sugar." denying her again enraged her she slapped him before exiting the tub. He grabbed her ankle, breaking her fall, catching her in a cascade of brimming bubbles, cradling her body, she was gorgeous in his huge arms. No words were exchanged, Gabriel held up her wrist.

"Zion's going to kill me." Upon biting, her blood rolled down her wrist to her forearm turning iridescent bubbles crimson red. His fingers twirled her clit clockwise and counterclockwise under the water. He rubbed fast matching the speed he drank as warm water filled the tub raising the temperature of her blood flowing into his mouth. *I accept your offering vampire bride.*

Gabriel was sexy to him he took small sips from one hole allowing the other to close pretending to suck while he fingered her deep applying the right amount of pressure on her g spot.

"Baby, I'm coming for you," she moaned, squeezing his large biceps. Licking her, belly to chin she squirted creamy cum between his fingers as he sucked her nipples through red stained water.

"I don't like you drinking from vampresses. They can get the wrong idea Clarence." "I won't say I'll stop; however, I'll try Sugar." "Then I'll drink from a male vampire and try too." "Gabriel? Don't get that vampire killed." "If it's nothing, and I'm a Queen, why can't I drink from the vein also?"

"Gabriel there are things that come with drinking straight from the vein. You as a baby vampire don't know as I haven't discussed with you." "It's why we discourage vampires under 10 years turning to drink from the vein." "Like what?"

"Another time." "I'll ask Niarchos." Clarence closed his eyes. Niarchos?

*Yes, Pop. How are you feeling? Better still weak can't stand up long pop. It will pass I promise, don't force your healing. Ok pop. If Gabriel asks why young vampires can't drink from vein to mouth, don't reply, refer her to me. Yes, Pop.*

*Thank you for saving her life son. You're welcome, it's hard telling her no pop. It's hard for me too Niarchos but we must understand this young vampire-hybrid. Something we've never encountered. We don't understand her anatomy. Niarchos were you aware you bit with four teeth, she almost died? Zion is continuing the examination of her blood so what may apply to a normal vampress doesn't apply to her son. Gabriel is a feminist pop you despise their thoughts. How'd you end up with one? Little did I know I had two son. Your mother was a feminist, but she never knew it haha. In this situation, she has no options. If she decides to try things on her own, it can have horrible effects Niarchos.*

*She's going to try food pop. It's fine, let her get ill a few times, she'll stop Niarchos. A reminder from God, we're not human. She cares for you a great deal. If anything were to happen to me, I'm trusting you to love and care for her as I' would've. Yes, Papa. I'd be an honor. Goodnight Niarchos. Goodnight pop.*

"Caleb?" "Yes Clarence." Caleb opened the bedroom door. "We're coming Thursday through Sunday to the games. I assigned a guard from my personal detail. Isaiah arrived with Papa Nate; they flew in from New York to compete. You're scheduled to play piano before the competition begins Friday you open Clarence." "See you then Caleb."

"Blaise?" Clarence called him on the phone. "What's up brother?" "Any news for me?"

"From what my sources say the Indians acted alone with no permission from Spotted eagle. rouge vampires Clarence no coven connections." "Thank you, Blaise see, you at the games" "Right on." Clarence called Vaughn. "Vaughn, has the fresh blood from the banks been delivered to my hotel suite?" "Yes, Pharaoh. I'll bring it as soon as the sun sets. I'm waiting on the ice coolers." "No one handles the blood but you Vaughn. Not even your husband." "Yes, Great One I agree." "Lock the coolers don't let anyone know you're coming. Mental message me and I'll send the car for your safe transport."

"The fall collection is out Clarence." "You buy my clothes Vaughn you've access to my account buy what you like." "I'm excited." "I need a wedding suit Vaughn I'm getting married haha." Cody got one of the guards to give her a phone she called Chance who stepped outside to talk. "Hello." "Hi daddy."

"You hanging in there Indian?" "Yes, Chance They moved the competitions what happened?" "Niarchos was in an accident Cody." "Is he ok Chance?" "Yes, he'll live." "Tell him old Indian said get better." "I will. Cody, do you love me?" "Chance that's such a silly question. Of course I love you." "Will you marry me Cody?"

The line was pin drop quiet. "I don't want to be one of your wives Chance we've discussed this." "What if I divorce them?" "Even Mary Chance?" "Yes Cody, even Mary." "Yes, Chance I'll be your wife. Cody squealed with glee making Chance smile.

# Chapter 25
# Forbidden Fruit

"Up!" Cody was laying on the side of her cot sitting up slowly staring at the guard who interrupted her much needed sleep. "Stick out your hands Indian." They made sure an old vampire like her was heavily guarded. She pushed her hands through the bars, above her a UV lamp a reminder to behave.

"Open 17." The bars were made from remnants of torn down churches that were blessed on holy ground. The materials weaken vampires by touch. They never understood why they'd get ill after wrapping their hands on the bars but after a while it dawned on them not to touch.

"Where am I going? competition is in two days I want to practice this morning." They put Cody in a limo. "Look up." Caleb's guard commanded with his thick Jamaican accent. She obliged. "I'll cook ya, if ya try the doors or windows. The back is rigged with UV ray panels embedded in the doors, walls, door handles, seats, and the windows which activate if you try to open or break them. You like my design Indian hahah? Lock up for prisoner transport."

## Vampire Uprising Chronicle I

Vampire security arrived at the cabin six military hummer jeeps deep following the security caravan. Clarence wasn't underestimating her. He was the vampire she'd been with he knew Cody was a cunning, sneaky, manipulative liar. She wasn't wife material, but he waited for her to realize it. "Indian you know where you are?"

She pushed her hair back, trying to look decent. She was clean of drugs looking healthy.

Vampire guards deactivated the car, opening the door as six guards held guns on her. "All this for little ole me?" Cody winked at the Jamaican guard which oversaw her risky transport. "I like you Indian, you're a firecracker, eh?" He walked behind her with a vice grip loaded nine glock pointed at her skull. That pistol was taped to his hand, with a hair line trigger. She entered the living room.

"Sit." "What's your name security?" "Jamaica and you?" "Cody." He secured her to the self-designed chair with handles made from identical material as the cells Pharoah's steel is the street name it was given, cuffing her to the chair she heard a faint beep. "What's that Jamaica?"

"UV needles stab ya in da ass, pop out the seat if ya stand without permission, its boobie trapped." Cody smiled defiantly "In another life, we could've been good together Jamaica." "Haha if you say Indian."

Cody looked around Clarence joined her speaking siksika. "I have a surprise for you Cody." "Why're you speaking siksika Clarence?" "Have you forgotten your tongue princess?" "No never." "You know what they say." a voice echoed from the back, "If you don't use it, you lose it." Cody froze. She knew that the ancient Blackfoot dialect was taught by royal chieftains to their sons and daughters. Tears rolled down her cheeks. He knelt before her, kissing her shackled hand, she rolled his jet black long hair between her fingers. He kissed her, wiping her face.

"Is this a trick of a shaman to punish me for my wrong...have they given me something to make me hallucinate?" "No love. I have been told the story by my maker."

Clarence sat silent on the couch, where four guns were buried. Chance was in the open kitchen watching with five Elders. "Great Pharaoh permission to be unchained to hug him?"

"Don't stand Indian." Jamaica un-cuffed her from the chair. She cried, holding handfuls of Spotted Eagle's hair smelling it. Clarence explained the charges Cody committed to her husband; Cody sat with her head down ashamed of herself hearing what she'd done aloud. "Hausis, is this true?" "Yes, my love." "Why baby?" "Because I loved and lost Clarence, he's like you, kind, gentle, loving, and patient. It was as if I found you again Eagle."

"Princess Hausis, or Cody as we call you, I'll grant a pardon if you leave with Spotted Eagle to Colorado today. He's proven he can care for you financially. He's a furrier and a chieftain of vampires for the Blackfoot reservation nation. Here are photographs of his home," handing her the pictures. "He'll join our covens and be placed in the scrolls as a vampire of age and my son since I'm the one who turned him. In time he'll get a coven and become an Elder since his age dictates, he can become one. If you say yes, you may leave on a plane with a signed pardon but if you stay you fight Zhou Xie, I have no doubt you will lose and walk away pardon less."

She sat teary eyed staring at Chance. "Hausis, do you love me?" "Always my spotted Eagle." brushing her hand over his cheek. "Let us have the life the stars aligned for us. Where does our son rest."

"He's buried in the Hollings cemetery next to mama Fi. He was a beautiful child Eagle."

*Cody. Clarence mentally messaged her. Stop looking at Chance it's not his choice Cody, I love you as my child, lover, and friend. I always have this is your way out a gift from my hand. This is the way I justify to the Elders why I let you leave without judgement a clean slate to start your life again. Take it woman...please. If you fight Zhou, you'll lose, I'll have to place you on trial. if you leave, Isaiah's case becomes weak, and I'll have to release him with low consequence. I'll deal with Chance; vampire law states you belong to me it's legal and binding for me to turn you over to your lawful husband. Look at your husband kneeling before you.*

Hausis looked in Eagle's eyes, although vampire colored, they were still kind, loving, understanding and most of all non-judgmental. The memories of the love they shared flooded her soul. "Yes, I'll go with you warrior spirit." Cody hugged a crying Spotted Eagle.

"Steven Please bring the scrolls you created, including the pardon." He brought what was requested Clarence signed the scrolls freeing Cody from her crimes. Steven passed Clarence his signet ring, he dipped it in red wax pushing it down while it was hot on her pardon. A quiet curl crept on Cody's lips as the emotional anchor dropped at her feet with the flick of Clarences wrist.

Steven hand wrote the scroll making sure he added Spotted Eagle responsibility for her actions moving forward. Any attempts on any vampire's life meant Cody's death via sunlight. Cody and Eagle signed the scrolls.

"Jamaica, Cody is no longer our enemy. She's the wife of our Coven Chieftain Spotted Eagle who was lost to me and has now returned. Please escort them to the airport, they're leaving for Colorado Springs." "May I have a moment to say goodbye to Chance please Clarence?" "Yes Cody." granting her request.

She stepped into a blind spot on the patio, away from prying eyes. Chance was crying, she'd never seen him cry. "I love you, don't let anyone make you think different Gambler now and always." They kissed fervently and she used her hair to wipe his tears. He held her hand as she left her old life, starting her new one. Chance didn't want to let go but did. Cody never looked back at him. Chance and Clarence were her great loves in her life, but Spotted Eagle was her soul mate. When she lost him, she lost herself knowing their love would never compare. Cody knew if she remained, she'd wonder about her life with Eagle. Eagle called his second in command she hugged him hard it was her baby brother.

"How?" "I was fishing the day of the massacre. I went for help when I returned with help everyone was dead." "Clarence, Chance this is Khaede, my baby brother." Niarchos come to say goodbye to Old Indian "You out Cody?" "Yeah, big baby, take care of yourself losing herself in his body swallowing hug." "Always" Clarence was relieved, but Chance was angry.

"How could you let her leave Pop? You know nothing about him!" Chance cried Grip Elijah and Niarchos were there for him. Niarchos went to the fridge and got eight extra strong tox-bloods. Clarence ignored his son going to see his wife.

They got drunk talking about each other's women. Papa showed to the cabin once he heard what happened, joining the drinking fun. The women were in Gabriel's room gossiping about Cody and how Chance considered leaving Mary.

The men were getting on each other. "Who remembers when Papa Nate had a thing for Harriet Tubman?" laughing loudly. "She was a fine lady, however she hated Clarence. No matter what he did to help the cause, she hated him, all on count he was a light skin slave. Harriett couldn't stand him passing as white no matter what the reason!" Laughter and cigar smoke filled the air.

"Who remembers when Billy Holiday was crushing on Clarence?" The Elders gruffly chuckled.

"A toast to Harriet and Billy." "What y'all fool's up to?" Caleb entered crashing the party. "Seriously? Y'all too old for this." "Caleb they're toasting to ya girl Harriet." "I'm unsure why Clarence, she don't need no toasting!" Papa Nate snickered, "She killed me!" "I heard you can fly Pop." "I levitate Niarchos birds fly." "Lift me up Maker!" "He may drop you, Elijah." Caleb, who was the only sober one, cut in. Clarence stumbled from his chair and Caleb stood behind him. "Don't fall Clarence stop this mess you're too drunk to levitate." "Haha I'm fine Caleb!" He stumbled as Caleb kept his arms open behind him.

Zion entered. "Why did you let him drink tox Caleb?" "He was this way when I arrived Zion." "I'm fine Zion." pushing Zion away, causing him to fall by accident. Belly laughs filled the air. Clarence picked him up but fell as he bent to help him up in Zion's lap. Zion guarded his head in the fall. "He stood stand here Lijah!" "Don't go high Clarence." Clarence held Elijah under his arms lifting him halfway up to a 15-foot ceiling. "Ok Clarence, bring Elijah down please."

Clarence brought him down, stumbling to his chair happy Caleb? "What else can you do Clarence?" They asked. Clarence disappeared and the Elders jumped in shock. "Where'd he go?" Niarchos drew his gun drunk as hell running around the cabin stumbling. They heard a knock at the front door Caleb went gun drawn, snatching the door open. "Don't shoot!" "Haha."

Clarence was at the door. "I can't control it, Caleb. Show em Grip." Grip closed his eyes, becoming invisible returning in 30 seconds. "Told you" Niarchos yelled clapping.

"Jesus!" Have you turned to a dingo?" Grip looked confused. "He's not old enough Niarchos" "That's enough tox." Caleb warned collecting glasses on a tray.

"Guess what? I'm giving Pop a bachelor party. Grip and I are getting vampire bitches to strip. We can drink from the vein Sodom and Gomorrah in this peace."

"Hell, no Niarchos! Gabriel will kill me." "You're whipped Pop." "No, I'm not Niarchos." "Yes, the fuck you are." They agreed with Elijah. "You never cut Safinah slack pop." "Different times, Chance we had to be protective. A black woman couldn't go to the store without being raped or killed." "Sorry brother, but your woman puts it on you." "All your women got you, so shut up Chance." Niarchos aided Clarence "Chance, you've 7 wives?" "Yes, baby Nate.

Why do you want one Pop?" "Women want to feel special Chance. How can she feel special if she's one of seven? I won't share, why should I make her share?" They planned a wild vampire bachelor party. Grip was glad he was back; he missed his vampire family.

Meeting in the lady's room....

Gabriel, Joan, Mary, Mya, Ginger, Lily, and Ann were in Gabriel's room. "You been through some shit sis huh?" Ginger was outspoken and gorgeous. "I sure have Ginger." "The nerve of that hussy doing what she did Gabriel." Ginger hugged Gabriel showing sisterly support. "Did you ladies know Chance was going to leave his wives for Cody even me?" Ann looked at Mary shocked.

"I explained this back in 1903 to you Mary--"

"Here we go again Ann." "I told you then I'm not with no concubines or other wives Mary look at Papa Nate when he came with that mess--

"He presented it to you Ann that's my point."

"And what did I do Mary?" "You left Papa Nate, to return Ann." they giggled as Ann sipped her red wine blood tox staring over her glass at Mary "Nathan is mine and always will be, I ain't worried about them other wives cause they're leaving him one by one wait and see Mary."

"What I should've done is what Gabriel did for her dowry, but my father negotiated with Chance some horses and land." Gabriel inhaled shocked. "Don't listen to her Gabriel I was there for her dowry and the land she speaks of she owns today. Her haberdashery sits on it and the twenty-five blocks surrounding it in prime downtown Georgia so please." Mary snickered at Ann and Gabriel's reaction under her glass tapping her lap playfully.

"Oh God, I was shocked." Lily said, making Gabriel laugh. "Why Gabriel? Girl you could've requested anything, and you asked for him couldn't be me. Clarence is the richest vampire in DeKalb County Georgia" "Don't you get it Lily?" Ann cut in, "Gabriel's gonna get anything her heart desires because all she wants is Clarence. Clarence is a die-hard romantic, he needed a woman to want him, not his money."

"Ginger! We missed you." Joan shouted! "I got y'alls Christmas cards, thank you." Ginger said, opening her arms as Ann, Lily, and Mary hugged her.

"Joan when are you marrying that fine ass Dr.?" "I'm waiting. You think he's gonna ask guys?" "We do!" they giggled her reply.

"Grandma Ann, can you please ask about me being turned vampire?" Zion wants a vampire wife please grandma. The room went silent. "I'm old enough. I don't look my age grandma please while I still look young."

"I requested for you Joan. Clarence shut me down, something about a treaty?"

"Yes Gabriel, the vampire Elders signed a stupid agreement with Papa Nate saying none of his kin can be turned unless it's an emergency, like what happen to Isaiah when he was with you and Clarence."

"You could have an emergency, Joan." The women stared shocked at Gabriel. "Don't talk way Gabriel." Ann corrected her. "Why Ann?" "It's considered plotting against an Elder or intentionally breaking vampire law. You can be brought up on charges its treason against the crown Gabriel."

"If I want something bad enough, I'm going to get it even if I have to plot to get it that's me." Gabriel said shrugging her shoulders. "See the difference in the era of time with the way we were raised as women in this room?" Ann said scoffing. "Gabriel is a modern-day woman. We're old school and hush." Ginger broke the silence "Hehe." "We know Clarence ain't charging you with a crime." Mya giggled sipping tox smiling under her glass.

"What Mya?" "We can hear you girl. You gotta give us some sex tips." "Like what guys?" "We don't know, give us something." Mya coaxed her. "Ok use pop rocks." Mya laughed. "Ann Lil and Mary can't use that, it's food Gabriel." "You can and Joan can use it."

What's pop rocks? "It's candy that pops when you put it in your mouth Mary." "What you do with it Gabriel?" Gabriel looked at Mary shyly as Ginger died laughing. "You put the candy on your tongue as it pops you suck his dick Mary the candy pops off the head and shaft as you slurp him." "Oh." Giggles filled the air as she thought of her swift tutorial.

"Girl what's up with Niarchos and Mara?" "He doesn't want that girl, Ginger. Elijah hooked them up." "She's sweet Gabriel. She may be good for him." "Maybe Mya but he's gaga over Gabriel. Niarchos wants you girl." "He's a sweetheart Mya, however I'm getting married." I can't blow it with Clarence, I love him. I couldn't see myself with anyone else." "Let us see that rock, Gabriel." She passed the ring around the room. "Y'all think it's real?" 'Heheh."

"Give us something sexual Gabriel. Something not involving food." "Ok Ann, I'll say dirty talk." Ginger smiled. She was an escort before Grip. She knew sexual secrets, and this was a huge one. "Oh, and acting defenseless during sex, like a kitten." "Show us Gabriel." "No y'all, I'll sound silly." "Come on they urged."

"So, you're having sex right? You say something like daddy please help me, you love me, don't you? Help me cum mmmm Daddy, I'm there a little more please fuck me real good right there you know my spot. Cum in me if you love me nut in this pussy." The room was quiet. Ginger smiled. "I should've had you working for me before I married Grip got damn!" Lily smiled, she used to work in the saloons. "You would've made an excellent saloon girl. They would've never freed you." Lily shared with Gabriel.

The room rang with bubbly giggles. "Ok one more Gabriel." "I feel silly and embarrassed guys." "You don't need to, Gabriel we're your sister's." "Make him watch you masturbate he can't touch you do it until you cum, then let him in. I haven't done it yet to Clarence. Oh, they can't touch themselves either, tie them up. If the try to get lose slap him hard open handed then stare."

"Tie up vampire and slap him?" "Yes Ann." "How Gabriel?" "In here Ann." tapping her temple. "Shit Clarence is gonna get a run for his money." "heheh" they giggled while getting drunk. "What's up with a bridal party Gabriel?"

"I don't have friends, and my family passed Ann. I'm the last of my line." "What're we Gabriel...chopped liver?" Hugging her she felt good inside. "Clarence is your family now and all who're tied to him. "Thank you Ann I'm sorry. I'm getting used to all this. I'm overly blessed."

The house cleared Gabriel turned off the lights in the bedroom. She knew Clarence could see in the dark, so she hid behind a curtain. They walked him to the door, knocked and opened it. They were drunk and singing loudly.

Zion, Joan, Elijah, Mya Grip and Ginger spent the night because sunrise was close. Niarchos went to his hotel room to check on the jailed prisoners. The house was in a love making mood. Gabriel had on a night shirt with no panties.

"Sugar?" He slurred. "I smell your snatch sexy. I know you're in here beautiful." He whispered following the smell of perfume stumbling in the dark. When he got to the curtain, she pushed him, Clarence fell to the floor on his back. In a haze of confusion, Gabriel hopped on top of him to fuck. POOF! He was gone! "AHHHH!" Gabriel drunk herself searched under the bed patting the floor as if she'd lost a contact lense.

Elijah pushed the door open gun drawn Gabriel sat on her knees "I pushed him on the floor and like that." snapping her fingers, "he was gone Elijah!" "Oh God!" Vampires exited the building calling his name. "FOUND HIM!." Grip found him in their tub asleep. He tossed him up over his shoulders, laying him in bed. "He has a new skill. I'm thinking because he's in his home state where he was turned it unlocks abilities. Look at Caleb, his empathic abilities are amazing because he never left Georgia Grip." They exited the bedroom.

When everyone exited, Gabriel grabbed her robe and slept in Niarchos' room. Jupiter followed her gnawing quietly on his bone. She smelled Niarchos on the sheets damn he smelled good. His blood smelled like cotton candy to her. She could smell his head on her pillow. He made her feel safe, more than Clarence, that was bad. She'd no idea why she felt this way.

She pulled up the covers dozing off thinking too much as her grandma would say. *He knew what he could do and didn't say, what else was he hiding?* Her text notification chimed:

Nicky: You sleep? Honey: Nicky: Wyd? Honey: In ur bed. Nicky: What're you doing downstairs? Honey: I tried to be with your father intimately, but he disappeared right out from under me. Nicky: Haha. Honey: It's not funny Nicky. Nicky: Its ok. Honey: No, it's not. He knew he could disappear and didn't share it. He may be the Vampire King, but he's also my husband first. Secrets in any relationship are never good.

Nicky: You're right. Wait till pop is sober. We were drinking too damn much. He doesn't know he did it, trust me. I'm fucked up but I'm in a bigger body, so I absorb liquor handle it easier. Honey: Blame it on the Alcohol Nicky? Nicky: Yeah, shit why the hell not? Honey: Fuck it Nicky: Listen bae, don't take life too seriously. Take it from someone who's been around a little minute. Honey: Bae? You gonna get both of us in trouble. Nicky: Apologies Great One. Honey: None needed. Delete these messages, so will I. Stop with the Great One mess. You're the only one who makes me feel human. Everyone else walks on eggshells, but you don't. Don't change please Nicky. Nicky: I won't. Be nice when he wakes, you know he can't deal with it when you're upset. You're his world.

Honey: Thank you.

Nicky: Call later today. Honey: Ok. goodnight

Everyone was asleep when Gabriel showered, dressed, and left. The warm rising sun felt good on her skin, she needed to clear her head.

She went to the garage to get a car. There were 14 of them. WOW, she grinned. Of course, she went for the Rolls identical to the one Grip stole years earlier.

The key was already in the ignition. "No wonder Grip took it," she whispered. "It's a beautiful car." She wore her straw Chanel hat, tied a bow under neck adorned in her Jackie-O sunglasses before driving out the gate. "Good morning." "Good morning, Great One." They were shocked she was in daylight and alone. "Open the gate please."

"We've been instructed not to allow you off the estate Ma'am." "Who is it?" "Yes, ma'am vampire security team Elder Niarchos gave the order." "When?" "Last night Great One." "Who's higher in rank Jonathan...Elder Niarchos or the Queen of covens?" "You are Great One." She removed her glasses eyes glowing, proving she was vampire. "Maybe we should call the Pharaoh."

"The Pharaoh is asleep and won't be pleased when I explain you refused to open the gate. Do you want to be vampires one day?" "Yes ma'am." "I'll be sure to put in a word with the Pharaoh and Elder Niarchos, I promise," smiling seductively. When they saw those sexy white fangs, accompanied by her sexy rack, they opened the gate immediately. "Thank you, vampires!"

Gabriel drove enjoying the quiet of the countryside morning she stopped picking wildflowers off the side of the road. No vampires, only the clean crisp morning country air and private thoughts feeling free and alive.

*Free from? Being cooped up,* she thought. She arrived in town pretending to be normal people around her did the same. Everyone knew who she was but thought it was a rumor she could walk in the sun until they saw it first-hand. Gabriel ordered a blood roast sipping slowly, looking out on the street as the town woke, pretending not to hear the whispers. No one said anything bad. One woman said, "look at that rock on her hand glistening."

"How many carats do you think it is?" She grinned behind her cup when a text interrupted her solitude. Clarence: Sugar where are you. I'll send someone to get you. Sugar: I don't want to come home. **Clarence: Sugar Where are you? Sugar: Am I incarcerated Clarence? Clarence: No sugar, you aren't. Sugar: Do you know your wife? Clarence: Yes, I think I do. Sugar: Where am I?**

There was a pause. She hadn't let him tap into her mind, closing her eyes, blocking him out. **Sugar: Stop using your vampire skills, use your heart and what you know of me. Clarence: Caleb's coffee shop. Sugar: Yes Clarence: Do they have Madeline's? Sugar: I'm unsure, didn't ask. Clarence: I'm coming. Sugar: No, you can't walk in sunlight. I'll be home shortly. I'm going to shop. Clarence: I'll have shopkeepers come here. Sugar: are you placing me in a pretty prison? Clarence: No Sugar: Sugar: You are Clarence. Clarence: Gabriel?**

She ignored him, enjoying her coffee. All she had were gold coins. The server came over. "I'm sorry all I have are these." Removing gold coins from her purse. "Elder Caleb said don't take money from you Great One." "How'd he know I'm here?" "He's seer ma'am." "Oh yes, that's right. Take it as a tip, I'm sure Caleb saw that too." "Hehe" the server smiled wiping her table.

*What's next, I got it!* She drove to Niarchos' hotel enjoying the scenic drive across the island. There was pool. She purchased a swimsuit in the hotel's boutique and went swimming. There were families and kids there. Everyone was having fun. No one was afraid of her. *Do they know what I am?* She played Marco Polo with the children. She taught kindergarten for 6 years prior to her illness and she loved kids. Gabriel was promoted to head the kindergarten division before her life shifted gears. She sat pool side holding a baby for a lady snuggling the bundle of joy. A man walked up snatching his child, "I don't want you getting hungry."

Gabriel was appalled at his ignorance she went to shower and change. When she exited the pool, she went to the desk. "What suite is Elder Niarchos in?" "Room 404 Great One. Should I alert him?"

"No, thank you." She knocked on his door. He opened it, grabbing her inside. "What're you doing here Gabriel? They're going nutty looking for you." "He'll be alright." She sat and he handed her water. "No thanks" "Blood, B positive." "You can't drink that the Pharaoh will know and put me in jail Gabriel" "Was he like this with his first wife Nicky?"

"He was worse, but times were different. We were slaves, hunted you've no idea what the hell we were in our women couldn't get water on our own property without being raped. When we lived with pop, he gated off our land. Thank God you'll never know what we endured or the shit we saw." "What happened...sorry if it's too personal Nicky." "Nothing is when it comes to you, beautiful." "I was a slave, born on a plantation with ignorant owners. Some owners, like pops, treated slaves non-violently, only issuing punishment when the slaves disobeyed severely.

Niarchos Hollings Origins
Emancipation Night
First of January 1863......

Some were sadists, mine was one. At 13 he forced me to penetrate him because--"

"What?" "I'm well endowed." "Oh." she giggled "Fast forward I'm 25 years old I think, the plantation is a buzz because the emancipation went down. He was frantic once we got news, we were free. Black people migrated in the middle the night ignoring the dangers of it. Some stayed thinking it was a lie, until a constable came reading us Freedom law.

The constables said *'y'all niggers can go and not be shot. Go on, get out here.'* I went to the barn collecting what pennies I found over the years on the roads and whatever I was given for work from neighboring slave owners. I had broken silver spoons and forks, trash I found that I could get coin for.

I think it was worth $10 which was a lot back then for a slave. I grabbed a horse I found abandoned in the woods stuck in mud half dead. I nursed him to health and restored a broken saddle I found on the roadside. When I was leaving the master pointed a gun saying I wasn't going. I was his property and no nigga loving President was gonna change that. The devil bucked in his eyes. He yelled, 'take off your pants!' He unbuckled his pants while he held a shot gun on me. Then get this Gabriel, this fuckin idiot says, *"I love you."*

"What the fuck?!" "It Infuriated me. I replied, *"I fuckin' hate ya die, MOVE!"* The base and hate in my voice startled him as I pushed past him going for the door, he shot me twice." Niarchos opened his shirt. "Here." pointing to his arm and right lung. Before I hit the ground, Pop caught me. I thought I died because a white man was holding me, keeping me from hitting dirt. Gabriel cried her tears were broken by laughter when Niarchos continued.

"Blood was everywhere. He laid me down gently. I saw him snap the man's head slurping from his eye sockets. I said, *'I'm a dead man'* mentally. Pop bent down stating; *I'm going to make you a God among men big man. Do you want to live?* I heard myself say, *"no."* "Why? Cause' a' what dis demon done?"

"Yessir." *"Live let me walk ya into da life youse born ta have. We will paint dis plantation red with the blood of his offspring."* I smiled shaking my head, yes. There was something in pops eyes something truthful, trusting. He bit me... I blacked out. I woke two weeks later, a new man; no pain or nothing but scars from lashings and these bullet holes."

"Let me see?" "No Gabriel" "Why not Nicky?" "It shames me." "I'm your friend, no need to ever be ashamed with me." He turned around. He was a huge, strong vampire with massive shoulders and strong arms. "Another time Gabriel." She stood hugging him holding back tears popping her fangs. She bit his chest right above his nipple as her lips and tongue rolled over it as she sucked causing him to rock up. Instead of pushing her off, he held her closer, trying not to moan. "Gabriel, please don't do this." His dick throbbing his voice low and wanting.

He gently pushed her back, closing his shirt shyly. "He'll kill me ma." "I drink if I want, he does." "No, you can't Gabriel you aren't pop you're vampress." "You taste so sweet Nicky." licking her full lips with her eyes closed. "You belong to him woman." He grabbed a cold towel, wiping her mouth.

"Here drink this, Gabriel." "O positive blood its Nasty Nicky." "Drink, it'll hide my blood smell." He checked her shirt for blood spatter. "Soon as the sun drops, I'm taking you home." "You don't have to take me home, I'm leaving." She grabbed her Chanel purse, heading for the door, Niarchos blocked it.

"Move...Move, Nicky. I command you step out of my way please." He stepped aside. "I love you too Gabriel." She slammed the door. Niarchos called Clarence. "Pop, she was in the pool came to say hi."

"You let her leave Niarchos?" "Yes Pop. I blocked the door, but the Queen commanded I step aside, twice." Clarence hung up abruptly calling Gabriel again.

Niarchos needed to rest for the competitions. His dick was rock hard fourteen inches of sexy hardness. A knock interrupted his sexual fantasies. Answering the door, it was Mara. Niarchos' shirt was open, she fixed her gaze on his large chest. "Elder, did I interrupt?" Niarchos grabbed her inside, slamming the door tearing off her blouse. Her D size, plump breasts popped from her bra. Shocked, she crossed her arms over her chest. "I'm sorry, I'm sorry." Mara jumped and Niarchos caught her in his massive arms pressing her against the wall pinning her with his weight as his loosened his pants releasing his throbbing manhood.

Lowering her to the floor, he tore off her skirt, followed by her panties and the remains of her bra. Mara trembled with excitement. Niarchos cupped the d-twins together, pulling her hard nipples he rolled them between his sexy lips sweeping the tip of his tongue over trapped sweet nipples. He switched back and forth between sweet hard nipples.

Pushing her legs open he worked the fire out of her fat, throbbing clit blessing her with his mouth game. He sucked pushing his tongue in, fingering her placing his head game on repeat until her drip warned him her sexual dam was about to break. Mara pushed his head away, "Stop."

Niarchos stopped staring up from between her legs "Cum in my mouth. You want this dick, ma yes, or no? Cause a nigga can stop." "Yes, please dick me down." Moaning her response while releasing herself to his capable sexual prowess. "Then cum for me ma, stop playing. I can taste you its right there let go."

He started in on her clit again, finger fucking her using sensual circles. Mara grabbed the rug, holding handfuls of it before grabbing his head, burying his head deeper in her snatch.

He raised her legs resting them on his shoulders, she was spread eagle holding his body in push up position. "Count me off ma." "Mmmm...1." He pushed deeper and slow "2." Deep fast and hard "3." Now halfway in teasing her pumping walls. "4," As deep pop combinations rang out. "5." "What?" Mara was barely able to think. "I can't hear you, ma," he whispered sucking her ear lobes "5." His sex was as wicked as his mouth game.

Niarchos deep dragged the dick in and out painstakingly slow forcing her to edge with him several times only to revoke the gift of intense release. "6 .... Oh my God...seven."

Banging all his dick up in her relentlessly BANG BANG BANG "8." Dick half in, teasing. "Why are you teasing me stand up in it Niarchos please. 9." Her breath was short he pulled out super slow balls to tip. Niarchos smiled at his cream covered dick, proof his stroke game was on fire. "You ready ma?" "Yes daddy, 10," Mara whispered in his ear.

She held on to his huge arms for his rough ride finale. Wet pussy popped her cum splashing in his face banging her orgasm forward. "Ahh..Fuck...Yes!" The housekeeper leaned on the door hearing the finest Elder ever bang sexual frustration out of somebody's daughter.

Niarchos flipped her over, raising her on all fours locking her into back shot position. He opened her pussy lips bending down licking her ice cream crack. No sucking, only licking white cream from clit to split.

"Jesus." "Call on him you gonna need him when I'm done with you, ma." He tongue stroked twenty pressure perfect licks back-to-back releasing his untamed savage on her inner pussy lips; sticking his slippery tip tongue in her ass, rimming her back door. Niarchos sat on his knees, popping her up and down off his hard shaft reverse cowgirl as she locked her legs behind her around his waist securing herself to his saddle.

Pushing her back down on all fours before him, his throbbing dick owned her hot, wet pussy. Niarchos polished her off doggy style. He looked down at a moaning Mara, but Gabriel looked back at him. He thought of Gabriel sucking his chest minutes earlier, the smell of her hair ripe on his skin, the feel of her full lips rolling across his hard nipple drove him to a deep fuck drive. Grabbing a fist of Mara's hair, he banged balls deep, trying to bang away his feelings for his father's wife. Mara made sure the neighbors knew his name.

"You ready for me, ma?" "Yes love!" "Say you ready." "I'm ready big daddy." "Did I stoke your pussy good ma?" "Yes Daddy, you fucked me so good." Grinding as far as he could get it inside of her, he opened her pussy spitting on the glistening split jack rabbiting her hot, swollen slippery pussy. Niarchos stood tethering her in his saddle, busting a hot fucking load in her. They lay on the floor, desperately grabbing for air. He rose getting ice water he returned she was fast asleep on the floor. A devilish grin crept on his face. *Happens every time haha.* He lay her in his bed cum comatose. Niarchos showered, called the boutique ordering her a new set of clothes and flowers.

Mara;

I saw you and was turned on I hope I wasn't too much. I purchased a new outfit for you. I put you at a size 20? It's in the garment bag on the bedroom door. I hope you like it. I called Elder Caleb explaining you weren't coming in tonight. No worries he'll make sure they're served by good people. I'll pay your salary for the night and return before sunrise. If you want to wait for me, you can. Text me or call when you wake. The lilies are for you order anything you want from room service.

-Niarchos-

Mara was overjoyed. "Hello?" "Hey girl, guess who I got with? Elder Niarchos...No, I ain't lying bitch! "How was it?" "Like a vampire who been fucking for 100 years, that's how! He went to work and said I could wait. No, I'm not leaving." "Girl, leave." "Why the fuck would I do that bitch?"

"He ain't your type that vampire is out of your league trust me, Mara." "Whatever he doesn't think so I'm waiting, Girl he took the pussy hehe, I entered, and he ripped all my shit off!" "Gurl! I'll call you later Elder Chance emailed the new schedule I'm on days again fuck." "Ok girl later."

Niarchos was feeling guilty, fucking Mara. He loved Gabriel and deep down he knew she shared her feelings. He stopped thinking about it because he was getting hard. He fucked the shit out of Mara, chuckling to himself. Is that how badly he wanted Gabriel? It took everything in him not to grab her and make love to her controlling his sexual savage.

"Siree Call Grip" "What's up fool? "Shit where you at Nick?" "On the way to see you compete and blow these fools away. You nervous baby bro?"

"A little Nick." "You got this. Grip? "Yeah man?" "I almost had sex with Gabriel today." "Like clothes off, fuck? Or you wanted to fuck but didn't?" "I wanted to, she did too Grip." "And?" "She fed from me." "Nigga have you lost your fucking mind that's way worse than a fuck. Why the hell are you telling me Nick? Pop hates me. If he finds out I knew, we both hang."

"Cause you're back and you my nigga that's why Grip." "Damn Nick, you love her, don't you?" "Yeah, in the worse way." "Nick, you can't love her. She's pops wife listen to yourself you know she can fuck you and he'll forgive her but pop will never forgive you. You'll face death by sunlight for that shit. Trust me he ain't gonna excommunicate you like he done me over his bitch."

"You done forgot how a nigga act over pussy Nick? I heard she puts it down." "She does." "How you know nigga?" "Hear it." "Man, you got it bad Nick." "Haha." "What's funny Nick?" "I fall in love after 30 years and it's his damn vampress." "Keep ya head up and leave that woman be Nick! Leave her the fuck alone boy. We don't need me in and you out. I can't watch you die ya heard?" "Yeah, I heard Grip. "You fuck that girl Elijah put you on to Mara?" Niarchos gave a sly smile.

"You beat it up?" "Hell, yeah put dat ass to sleep." "Nigga like I taught you, rock a bye baby." "Haha later fool." "Later Nick."

The Cabin......

Gabriel pulled up to the house by 3 p.m. Lulu ran to the door. "Hi Great One." She ran the Rolls Royce to get bags. "Do you want these in the master bedroom?"

"Please Lulu." Gabriel entered the master bedroom removing her sunhat and glasses.

"Out!" Clarence shouted everyone went to their bedrooms. Clarence was piping mad. *Don't smother her pop.* Chance shook his head, remembering how Safinah would escape with him to get away from his jealousy. He mentally messaged his father praying he'd take heed.

She walked past him to the bedroom, closing the door. She sat on the bed waiting for him. "Why woman?"

"Why go out and enjoy a day to myself Clarence? Am I your prisoner?" "No Sugar." "Enslaved?" "No."

Ann listened smiling, remembering the days Safinah cried because he was being too controlling. She was glad he met his match. "Do you envy I'm a sun walker?" "No Sugar." "Then why can't I leave this house, or any other Clarence? Why can't I go for a cup of coffee, or visit a friend and swim? Because that's all I did. Answer me, am I incarcerated?" "No sugar."

"Don't sugar me! Guess what? You tried to keep me locked up like a pretty bird in a pretty cage and 3 time's you've failed." "There isn't anything you can fucking do Clarence." "Watch your mouth woman."

"If someone wants to get me, guess what? They will. Don't make me regret being your wife. I won't be imprisoned by your love." He went to hug her Gabriel pushed him away gently. "Sugar please." Papa Nate chuckled "don't beg her man."

Ann slapped his knee. "You need to beg your wives for forgiveness for not allowing them here. You're in trouble too Nathan." "I'm with my wife Ann." kissing her. "Beg her." Elijah whispered, knowing Clarence heard him. "Mind your business, Elijah." "Yes Mya."

"Baby please." "Do you have something to say?" Clarence looked confused. "Oh? No one explained what happened last night. That's rich." "What Sugar?" "You don't recall Mr. Tox blood?" "Sugar, say what I did." "This is gonna be good Papa and Ann snickered as they dressed." Gabriel explained how he vanished. Grip found you in the tub, asleep." "Sugar, it happened one time. I wasn't sure what it was. Zion took blood and was going to read it when we got to Brooklyn. I wasn't hiding it. I've been trying to master it. I'd never intentionally hide anything from you. Remember we said we'd discuss my abilities when alone. "He circled his finger informing her the walls had ears. "As my wife you will be the only living being to know all abilities."

She tried not to think of Niarchos, drinking from him was addictive. His blood was sweeter, the smell of it made her horny; she didn't understand why. She bit Clarence without warning, straddling him open leg, pinning him down. "We don't have time Gabriel."

"I'm hungry besides that's not what your second head is saying." She drank for 30 minutes piercing his jugular for faster blood flow. *We're gonna be late.* Clarence sent Elijah a telepathic message. *I'll tell Caleb.*

The house was emptied, she fed, sparing him no expense, He held her on his lap, allowing her to eat. "The Alpa-Vampire is built to feed his children at length" he whispered. Clarence opened his pants tearing a hole in the middle of her black lace panties, helping himself to her tight wetness, careful he didn't slip out. She dismissed all thoughts of Niarchos bouncing the horniness out of her.

"Sugar what's gotten into you?" Tearing off her bra. A woman riding always made him nut fast. This was worse. She locked her pussy on him, feeding at the same time attacking his dick claiming it, making it her own.

"Baby." Gabriel ignored him grinding down harder rocking back and forth. He bit into her shoulder licking streams of warm blood off her nipples and collar bone. They connection fed locking themselves into a spiritual blood bond. "God Gabriel." She ran her fingers through his hair turning him up more.

"Ahhhh." he moaned, her nails clawing his back as her cupped hands full of ass cheeks open sinking as deep as possible as her gripping walls bounced on his throbbing vein. "Ummm, cum real good sugar nut," she kept drinking. Her pussy invited him in refusing to release him until he gave her what she came for.

"Fuck…damn!" He released in her burying his face in her neck "fuckkkkkkkkkk mmm mmmm." She grabbed his hair two fists kissing him lovingly long staring into his eyes. "We need to dress, we gotta go Sugar." They showered together. "I'm in love with you Sugar." "I'm in love with you too vampire." "I'm afraid Sugar "Why?" Washing his back. "Safinah was raped."

"No one is gonna rape me." "I had to send Caine and Chance to see her in the sunlight when they were humans.

When I got her, she was torn.... down there. Her eyes beaten and blackened shut. That's why I panic. I'm not controlling Gabriel, I'm afraid. Safinah was raped and I wasn't there. I never forgave myself. It would be a year before we could be intimate 6 months for her to heal and another six before she wasn't jumping at my touch."

"No one knew?" "Certain things you don't discuss outside the marriage Sugar, that's between man and wife."

She rinsed his hair and kissed his back.

"No one is going to hurt me; they fear you too much. If they don't fear you, then we'll remind them why they must. Those two criminals, have you judged them?"

"No Sugar, why? "Bring the Elders together publicly tomorrow night, judge the assassins." "It is death by sunlight Gabriel?" 'No sunlight they battle you in the arena for freedom. Show all your children why no one should cross the Pharaoh. He leaned in sinisterly "I love your wicked streak." "Hehe."

The Vampire Arena...

Vampire King and Queen arrived 10 minutes before showtime. Niarchos led Clarence on stage and Gabriel to her chair. When they were alone in the hall, they hugged. "Sorry, I got upset." "It's ok, not here Gabriel." "He drank from me today, Nicky." Don't let him for a few days. The taste should be out by then."

"You taste sweet Nicky." She gazed at him wanting.

"It's why you don't drink from the vein its addictive Gabriel." "I had sex and had to block my feelings of you."

"They're not your feelings, they're mine. You drank from me sometimes it transfers a person's emotions, sorry."

"No, you're not." "I'm not." 'Hehe" "Let's go we can talk later Great One." "Ok," holding his finger as they walked. He dropped her at the sky box for the musical competition. Caleb was on stage.

"Many of you don't know our Pharaoh learned to play piano many moons ago, from a young African whom he became close. In exchange the man wanted to learn the waltz. Sounds easy enough, right? This gentleman couldn't hear music and if he couldn't hear, how would he waltz?"

"For that matter, how would he play the piano? We learn later he used his mouth and fingers to feel the vibrations of music. Ludwig Van Beethoven was of African descent; the truth of his ethnic origins was covered up through a mixture of white powder worn on his face when in public. He used body doubles for portraits, and "euro-centric" historians, hiding the truth of his genetic heritage."

"One night at a party for blacks, he entered playing the piano. Our Pharaoh knew who he was requesting private lessons. Historians claimed he was completely deaf, we discovered from our Pharaoh he was only partially deaf. Tonight, our Pharaoh will play the piece taught to him by his once good friend Ludwig, before the world would come to know It. This is the favorite sonata of our Queen. Here to play for us tonight, I give you our Pharaoh with Moonlight sonata."

Caleb walked on stage. The light shone on Clarence in a tux Vaughn made for him. He looked handsome to Gabriel. She matched him in a black sequin wrap gown. The notes played as the judge's and Julliard graduates listened closely. The notes floated on the air, hypnotizing all who listened. "He plays beautifully Gabriel." "Thank you, Mya."

Clarence did something new. He connected telepathically to every vampire in the arena hearing him declare his love.

*Gabriel, will you forgive an old fool? I'm nothing without you. I love you. There's nothing in this world I wouldn't do for you. All I'm and all I have is yours. You're my world. I have not seen a sunrise or sunset in 200 years, when you open your eyes in the mornings there is my sunrise, and when you close them at night there is my sunset. It's not easy being the father to many children. Sometimes I forget how to love. It's why I choose you to remind me there is a fraction of a man in me one deeply in love with you. There is no vampire I wouldn't kill if harm befell you. Walk with me love. Gabriel, my angel sent from heaven dance with me on the stars of time as they align at our feet. Allow me to share all life has to offer. You alone are my joy, life, heart, love. I need you forever, I cherish your love. This is what I think of when I play this sonata. Until the end of time walk with me and you'll see the best is yet to be.*

He ended telepathic communication finishing the sonata. Clarence stood vampresses were in tears, the men in awe. No one clapped. The judges stood, tossing roses at the perfection of his performance.

"Bravo!" The crowd followed. When Clarence arrived at the skybox Gabriel cried tears of joy. Mara and Joan inquired why the vampresses were crying. Elijah explained what Clarence did. They were amazed.

"Every vampire Elijah? There must be 2500 in the arena Elijah." "It's 3100 Joan." Zion leaned over to Joan, "he's more powerful than he lets on." "Umm humm."

Gabriel kissed him with the spotlight shone on them. He wiped her face, kissing her tears away. Niarchos looked on smiling inside to himself at what almost happened. Clarence handed her a case. "You purchased the anklet back?" "Of course." "Shame on you." Gabriel passed the box to Ann; she remembered the night Safinah wore it.

*Does it look silly Ann? "Why would it look silly darling? Don't Queens wear diamonds? I'm a slave from humble beginnings Annie. You have a wealthy husband Safinah, Enjoy the damn money we been free."* A tear rushed Ann's eye she missed her friend.

Caleb introduced the players. There were violins, harpsichords, guitars, vampires competing for freedom money or a pardon. "The Pharaoh is giving out 3 pardons in this category however one vampire can win the money, as per the Vampire Elders." Caleb Introduced Isaiah. Immediately the crowd booed knowing what he'd done. Clarence telepathically linked with every vampire.

*Silence! Unless you know all the details of a situation, how can you properly judge?*

"Papa what happened the room went silent?" "Clarence told everyone to shut up in a nice way, Joan."

Caleb continued, "Tonight playing Fir DeLise, a complicated Beethoven piece, vampire Isaiah Freeman."

Papa had a professional sitting with them to make sure he made no mistakes. They recorded the performance in case there were grievances as this was the key to his freedom. Clarence listened sitting on the chair's edge.

*Papa?* Clarence mentally spoke.

*I taught him this as a human. It will get him into Julliard. There is no way he can mess this up. Let's pray.*

The Elders listened close, so far so good. Isaiah played recalling his lifelong lessons taught by Clarence.

*Stop dragging the notes Zay, at 5 a pop on the fingers with a ruler, at 10 don't get cocky you're good but not that good. At 14 why are you holding the last notes stop! Ruler out again. At 16 he won several competitions.*

Clarence erected a trophy case in the main entry for everyone to see, raised as his own son, how could he be blind? Clarence held back tears. his piece was ending. Clarence paced the sky box. Ann and Papa held hands tight with Joan and Zion. *Don't hold it, Isaiah reminded himself, don't hold the notes, its 1 half beat then release.*

"Pop the key," Clarence mumbled. *Pop the key* Isaiah reminded himself hold pop! Done.

The judges were impressed by Isaiah, he didn't make one mistake. They never heard anyone play the piece, not dragging the ending notes. Clarence grabbed Gabriel hugging her when Papa hugged him. "See Ann? you were upset over the ruler! I explained if Ludwig popped me, a grown man, it wouldn't hurt the boy." Ann and Joan cried, this was behind them, at least for now.

"The judges will share the results tomorrow evening. As we know, pardons and rewards will be given on Sunday night. Saturday evening Karate begins promptly at sundown. fifteen rounds. The winner advances to the final round. To recap, archery, knife toss, and running competitions are complete. Next is our singing competition. I have a special treat for you, I pray he doesn't kill me. Elder Vaughn and his husband Ebon designed the tux the Pharaoh is wearing. If you want to order one, please see Elder Vaughn in the lobby at the vendor's circle.

Niarchos escorted Papa on stage. Everyone chanted PAPA! Baby Nate smiled, proud of his great-great Grandfather. "No, he didn't pull me up here. I don't sing in public but Elder Caleb says I have a nice voice. I'll let y'all be the judge. I dedicate this song to the young vampire males and human's when I say young, I mean anyone younger than me in vampire and human years. That includes our Pharaoh, doesn't it? Y'all see he's a hopeless romantic? Bet the ladies love him" They held up phone lights hooting, "GO PAPA!"

Papa Nate pointed at the live band. Caleb already gave the selection. One hundred ways by James Ingram played. Caleb smiled passing Papa a note we need more time. Papa cut his eyes at Caleb who exited waving.

"I dedicate this next song to my second wife. Y'all may not know, Papa was a married man before he was turned. I lost my wife to the slave owner and childbirth, then I met Elder Ann. She helped raise my kids, as bad as they were. When a woman loves you and ya bad ass kids, she's a keeper." Joan held Ann's hand.

"What's he doing Joan?" One of their Grand babies walked on stage, "Annie will you marry me again?" Papa asked. He picked up his grand baby, they flooded the sky box with sparkling soft pink light turning on the mic.

"How many carats is it Nate?" The women laughed clapping. "Seven, woman!" Vampires wowed.

"What do the ladies and vampresses think?"

"Yes!" They chanted. "Yes Nate!" "Once again, Annie? Let's do this" Joan gave her grandma a huge hug. "Gabriel, we're getting married again!" She smiled hugging Ann.

She was elated for Ann. In her eyes, they should've never separated. Papa Nate made his way back to the skybox kissing Ann. "Without further a due, our top five singers in this competition, since no one is seeking a pardon, the crowd chooses the victor." Caleb announced. The singers performed beautifully.

Gabriel loved the vampire who sang Luther but a vampress sang Whitney and Gabriel was a diehard Whitney fan. Gabriel didn't see Mara, she texted her.

Queen: you, ok? Mara: Yes, Great One Queen: Are you here? You're missing a good night.

Mara: I thought Elder Niarchos would've explained, he got me the night off. Queen: Oh, he must've told Pharaoh. Mara: Sorry Great One. I can come If you wish? Queen: No sweetie, you're good.

Gabriel was jealous, not understanding why. It is the blood, she reminded herself. They chose the winner, the vampire who sang Luther.

"People love Luther and Whitney too I was sure Anita Baker had it Gabriel." "Over Luther Elijah? You trippin hehe." During intermission Gabriel requested ice water. The others ordered tox bloods. "Excuse me. I'm going to the lady's room." Niarchos escorted her to the Elders lounge. She entered the bathroom and threw up shaking. "Not again." She breathed heavy sitting on the porcelain floor in front of the toilet.

"What you mean not again Gabriel" "Stop ear hustling and go to Mara ain't she waiting for you?"

"What woman haha?" "Your vampire you heard me negro," purging in-between insults. "You, ok Gabriel?" Niarchos held back her hair "No Nicky and don't tell anyone." "Arghhh...damned, ice water." spitting in the toilet sitting on the floor breathing labored. "Ice water doesn't make vampires ill my Queen. I'll take you home Gabriel."

"No, it'll ruin Clarence's night. She paced kicking off her heels. "Get Zion, Nicky, be discreet please." "Ok" He rushed returning with Zion. Niarchos stood outside the door. When Zion entered, she was rinsing her mouth with warm water. "What's wrong Gabriel?" He raised his hand to her forehead. "I keep throwing up Zion?" "How long?" "A week now." "Bood?" "No, water, coffee, tea and solids Zion." "You're completing your turn, Gabriel. You wanna go home?" "You're not ok you have a fever."

"What competitions do we have left Dr.?" Gun competition Grips competing." "I'll be fine Zion." "We better return." "Gimme a minute Zion. "I'm going so Clarence won't start looking for us Gabriel." "Ok." Niarchos entered, looking down at Gabriel, she gazed upon him lovingly. Their eyes locked with blazing passion; he held her close to him. Her faint heart beating on his chest, entranced by his father's wife as all sense and reasoning escaped him.

Niarchos bent his head reluctantly, kissing Gabriel's warm, plump lips with a peck at first, then fervidly.

# Chapter 26

# Bathe in Blood

*I*nstructions for your pregnancy test: Take a sample, wait 5 minutes. One purple line means you aren't pregnant, two means you are. This is nutty girl you're a freaking vampire what the hell are you doing?

Gabriel exhaled at her silly thoughts as urine tinkled across the stick lightly hitting the water beneath her. It was 6 a.m. Clarence was asleep. Gabriel sat on the toilet reading directions. It was the longest five minutes of her life. A text interrupted her thoughts.

Caleb: CONGRATULATIONS MOM! Gabby: Caleb stop hehehe. Caleb: Do you know how long I've waited? Gabby: How long? Caleb: Since the engagement party. Gabby: Boy or girl? Caleb: I'm unsure sweetie. Gabby: If you did, would you ruin the surprise? Caleb: Yes haha. Caleb called. "Goodmorning Caleb." "May I speak free Great One?" "Always"

"Niarchos will never marry if you don't release his heart. I know you're falling in love with him, but you'll never love any vampire as much as Clarence. I'll see you tonight?" "Yes, Caleb thank you." "Hello, Nicky I'm pregnant." "How haha?"

Niarchos sat up in bed listening to an unsure Gabriel. "Your guess is as good as mine." "You tellin pop?" "I don't want him to marry me because I pregnant." "You're married already Gabriel under vampire law. I'd be upset if you were my wife, pregnant and didn't say. Besides, we were born in the 1800's men didn't run from family obligations."

"Is Grip happy Nicky?" "Hell yeah, he didn't miss one target. He's an impressive a sharpshooter." "That sounds good Nicky." "You get to choose a Queens guard." "I chose you." Niarchos smiled," what Pop say?"

"No Elders hehe." "We'll see Gabriel." They ended the call she left the bathroom. "Clarence, are you awake?"

He lay on his back groggy, tapping his chest; laying her head on him spooning close. "Do you like children?" "I love children Sugar, I raised lots of kids, I have over one hundred human blood lines through legal adoption." "Did you want biological children?"

"I look in your eyes and desire children. It's the price I paid in exchange for immortality, my body is dead." "Are we married Clarence?"

"Sugar if you want, I'll call a human judge to marry us tonight in front of the Elders, but we're one under vampire law. We're going to have a huge wedding, I promise. Is this about the other night the date thing?"

"No honey. You're sure you can't get anyone pregnant?"

"Pretty sure the dead can't create life Sugar. I purchased a baby once." "You better not say that in public daddy hehe how old?" "Eight months, a girl." "What was her name?"

"Rose." "What happened to her?" "Died giving birth happened a lot in the 1900s." "Sorry honey." "I Gave her a huge wedding. She married into a prominent black family. Married a black Dr. who graduated from Tuskegee institute." "Is it in the scrolls Clarence?"

"No, Safinah called the writers burning all scrolls concerning her. It's the time she abused her power."

"No vampire can destroy a scroll unless its authorized by my blood print. I don't speak on Rose's death." "When I arrived with such a pretty baby from the slave auction, Safinah held her asking How much? "Hehe" "Two hundred dollars was a hefty price for a picaninny as they called us Gabriel I had an arrangement with the auctioneer, he called the prominent plantation owners with the healthiest slaves I was number one on his list. "Clarence?" "Yes Sugar?" He yawned.

"I'm pregnant." Clarence smiled, anxiously sitting up. "Zion, come please." He and Joan entered worried about Gabriel's fever the night before.

Gabriel handed Zion the pregnancy double line purple positive pregnancy strip. Joan peered at it hugging Gabriel. "How Clarence?" Zion asked amazed, "You don't know haha." Clarence picked Gabriel up, "Ima be a Daddy, Joanie!" "Hehe" "Zion are you done with the blood samples explaining what you know so far?"

"Here is what we know from the blood drawn at Gabriel's turning Clarence. Vampire cells are dead even though eggs and sperm are still present. Gabriel was on high doses of chemotherapy from I-V to vein. Doctors were trying to eradicate an aggressive cancer in her before it metastasized to her bones. Without it she would've died within six months.

As we know chemotherapy is radiation in humans it kills cancer and other cells, however in vampires it awakens dormant cells. This is why your body functions as human Gabriel. You took chemo treatments every day for month, correct?" "Yes Zion."

"When Clarence bit you and vampire venom entered your blood stream it attached to the chemo. Radiation + chemo kills everything bad in humans allowing only the good to thrive.

Your eggs? Alive. His sperm? Dead, when his sperm passed through the radiation in your blood stream your body did something to it. It needed live sperm for the live female eggs in Gabriel.

The radiation jump started your dead sperm healing them, giving them life thinking her body needed the repaired sperm to fertilize the living eggs! Quite amazing guys. How long the chemo lasts or if it runs out, I'm unsure but I'm thinking if it blended with the vampire venom all of it from the first bite and the large dose Gabriel received the other night when you bit her this is what also helped massive amounts of venom."

"It's why you didn't die when Clarence bit you, or when Niarchos almost drained you, because the radiation acted as a natural super anti-body for the human side of you quickly repairing the damage. It's why you walk in the sun. The human body needs it for healing, for the record this is theoretical so don't quote me." "Haha. Hehe" His excitement made them happier.

"Zion, gather the Elders tomorrow before competition, no scroll writers only family."

The next night....

Elders and their spouses gathered with Eagle on face time. Gabriel sat next to Niarchos nervously holding his arm, while Clarence grabbed everyone's attention.

"We have an announcement, were having a baby!" "When is the adoption?" "Annie, Gabriel is pregnant."

"Can't be," crisply inhaling. "She is Caleb and Zion confirmed." "It is Clarence's child. I saw it the night of the engagement party." Caleb confirmed. "Congratulations! Blaise yelled, breaking the shocking ice. Papa Nate was thrilled. "Zion is going to explain." "You've got super sperm Pop!" "Thank you Grip." laughter filled the air.

"I ask that none of you discuss this, we don't want vampires grabbing humans on Chemo attempting to impregnate them. Anyone speaks of this outside the Elders you'll be jailed for treason against the crown." "I'd like to say something please." The room grew silent.

"I want to thank God for you all. Two years ago, I had no one. Today I live, a King made me a Queen, and now mother. I have a large family; they love me, and I love them thank you." Gabriel cried the women hugged her.

Later That Night....

Caleb rushed Clarence to dress on time, but Gabriel dragged feeling tired. "I'll send Niarchos to get you Sugar. You don't have to go." "I need to see if you can protect me?" "I showed you in Vegas, you almost left me sugar." Clarence kissed her, leaving the house with Caleb.

Niarchos searched the limo and driver with his guns drawn. He wasn't getting comfortable again. "Gabriel, we're going to miss it." Entering the limo, he hugged her. "Nicky, I'm pregnant and married. Move on, get married, be happy." "You don't mean it. I know you don't." kissing her head. "Loving me is going to bring you death Nicky." "Let it come. I fear death no more. I'd rather die knowing I loved twice in my life." Tears rolled down her cheek. "What did I do good in life that God blessed me with all this love Nicky?"

"It's odd I'm this Queen, but with you I'm Gabriel, the Queen stuff melts away. You're my big teddy bear." snuggling her nose in his neck. "Nicky, I beg you, .let...go." "Never Gabriel, I understand what we are. I love you, honey. I have since met you. How about we go to Queens?" "Yeah, since Cody's out the picture, why not? I love you, Nicky. It's not like the love I have for Clarence."

"I'll take it pop's a hard act to follow." leaning in for a kiss. They arrived at the arena, it went black as a spotlight shone on Caleb, center stage.

"On August 20th, 2020, five days ago, an attempt was made on our King's life. Duo rouge vampires acted alone. They failed, thinking they were shooting vampire vice grip at our Pharaoh, they were wrong. They hit Elder Niarchos, rendering him within inches of his life because he adorned the Pharaoh's helmet and rode on his personal motorcycle confusing the killers.

Queen Gabriel Hollings was with Elder Niarchos saving her life by escaping the sniper's, jumping a river gap the size of half a football field, securing her safety minutes before sunrise. Elder Niarchos hid Queen Gabriel in a cave before blacking out. The deadly poison crept through his blood, slowly killing him.

Queen Gabriel telepathically called our Pharaoh who couldn't assist because of his natural aversion to the sun. For hours, Our Elder clung to life while Queen Gabriel knew he was dying. Alone, scared, and unable to hear the Pharaoh's voice, she fed Elder Niarchos from her vein. Elder Niarchos was unable to control the thirst and drained forty percent of her blood, almost killing her. Tonight, the Pharaoh will battle the assassins responsible for these heinous crimes.

These Vampire criminals are charged with the following crimes:

1. Death attempt on the Pharaoh.

2. Attempted Murder of Queen Gabriel Hollings.

3. Attempted murder of Elder Niarchos Hollings.


As per the Pharaoh and vampire law when an attempt is made on our King, he decides their fate, he has decided a death match. The Pharaoh asks all human guests to exit only vampires should remain." The arena filled with fog as Caleb exited the sand.

"You nervous Pop?" "Niarchos cut my hair." "What pop?" "Cut it Niarchos!" "Yes Pop." "Never hesitate when I give an order you know better." "Yes pop." Clarence removed his shirt and shoes. Grip, Niarchos, Elijah, Papa Nate, Caine, and Caleb had their guns cocked. Zhou sat in front in case he needed to hop in the arena.

They'd lost faith in his abilities; thought he'd gotten civilized, blending with society, forgetting the dormant savage within. Gabriel was right, he needed to show his abilities reminding his kingdom why he's Pharaoh.

The light dimmed except for one light shone on the sands of the arena. Vampires were on one end as Clarence entered from the other. Clarence homed in on five senses on his prey, as they breathed rapidly... unsteady. Clarence cracked his neck and back, flexing his muscles bending down rubbing golden sand together between his palms. The vampire duo ran at him steadfast, feet dug in the sand.

Vampires kicked sand in Clarence's face to blind him. Clarence blew the sand back in their faces blinding them instead.

Clarence jumped high landing behind the killer who kicked sand, grabbing his long hair wrapping it fist tight savagely dragging him across the sand isolating him. Clarence pulled him slowly, exposing his throbbing brain, one of the organs still alive in vampire.

His prey fell to his knees barley alive Clarence exposed four fangs biting into his throbbing brain draining blood via frontal lobe. The vampire stared up at Clarence as warm blood blinded him his life force quickly escaped him.

Popping his long sharp nails, he scooped warm brain from his cracked skull. Clarence held it in the palm of his hand, slowly walking across the sand to the second vampire. Clarence raised the pumping brain to his mouth with exposed fangs he drained the membrane before it died licking it clean along with his fingers staring at the remaining vampire. He proudly stood in the middle of the area drenched in bone, blood, and brain matter.

Clarence telepathically locked to every vampire in the arena connecting his five senses to theirs sharing the taste the warm salty blood running down his throat the excitement he felt killing. The second vampire was older and stronger. Clarence tucked the brain away in his pocket as a souvenir.

The last vampire ran toward Clarence hyper speed zig zagging on the bloody sand. Clarence disappeared in thin air! The crowd stood in awe as gasps filled the arena. Vampires stood on their feet, looking in peril through the dark and fog. Materializing behind the assassin blending with the fog, Clarence levitated him in the air pushing his neck left. In siksika he asked, "Any last words?" "I was sent by an Elder."

Clarence tore into his flesh, removing the brain from his pocket and shoving it in his mouth. The body dropped out of the sky before hitting the sand. Clarence hyper-sped glaring up at the vampire, telepathically suspending him mid-air turning him slowly upside down his blood dripped ferociously from a gaping neck wound. Clarence stood directly under him bathing himself in warm crimson blood enjoying his bloodletting. He loved the oil slick sticky feel of fresh blood rolling on his skin, the metallic smell of blood strong in his nostrils. He enjoyed himself reveling in it, as blood rain warmed his cold skin.

Clarence held his head to the heavens, stretching his arms to his side with his mouth open catching the sweet sprinkling shower of fresh blood. He drank, bathed, and enjoyed the blood clinging to his skin until the rouge vampire's breath ceased. The arena was silent. Shock, respect and fear gripped onlookers. Clarence exited the blood-stained sand with his back turned. He looked at the vampire suspended 25-feet above him with blood pooling on white sand. "KNEEL!"

Vampires rushed to obey, including Elders. Gabriel moved to kneel. "Not you, Great One. Please sit." Zion requested. She knelt anyway. The entire arena saw it and was surprised. Gabriel knew what she was doing. He released his telekinetic hold, allowing vampires to feel the pain, excluding his Queen. As he exited the sand a large crack echoed in the air as vampire's neck twisted backward. Clarence released his children from the mental incarceration of shared pain. Niarchos, kneeling, gave him a towel. Niarchos and Grip walked him to the Elders lounge. Gabriel wore a new outfit waiting.

Clarence showered thinking of Gabriel. He had it bad for her because she carried the child, he thought he'd never have. Vampires went wild in the arena when they witnessed his capabilities. Clarence mentally spoke with Niarchos while showering to get Gabriel.

Niarchos went to the sky box walking her to the lounge. "What happened?" "Nothing Gabriel pop wants to see you." She entered, smelled the blood in the air, it caused her to throw up. Niarchos held her hair back placing a bucket in front of her.

Clarence exited the shower wrapped in a towel; he ran to Gabriel holding her hand. Niarchos looked at his father, afraid. "It's ok, Niarchos she's pregnant." "Nicky?" "Yes, my Queen?" "May I please have hot tea with a shot of honey?" "Grip went for it Gabriel. He'll return shortly." "Thank you, Nicky." Clarence handed her a handkerchief. "The blood smell...the baby didn't like it." "Haha. I'm sorry, sweetheart." He mentally connected with her; *One of the Elders is dirty Sugar.*

She was surprised, however she kept sipping her tea slowly thanking Grip. *You can't tell anyone, not even Niarchos. I won't. What happened? The second vampire said that before I could save him. I bit too deep. Who's it Clarence? I'm unsure. However, I'm going to find out. Drink their blood to get the truth. They'll wonder why. It'll cause problems with the innocent. I'll figure it out Sugar.*

Gabriel finger combed his hair "Where's the hair you cut Nicky?" "In his gym bag." Clarence winked at her, causing her to smile and show fangs. "Your teeth are out." Clarence touched one Gabriel covered her mouth, "I can't control them yet daddy. "They look sexy Sugar you're around vampires. Teeth showing reinforces dominance. It's fine, darling." "You and I'll figure it out this Elder thing."

"All three of us?" He hugged her waist, kissing her tummy. "Yes, all three of us Sugar." She kissed the top of his head, full of wet brown and blond curls. "It's not Nicky, Clarence. He'd never hurt you or I." "How do you know Sugar? I can't explain it. I know when I look at him." "You're trembling Sugar," He cut his wrist as she rested on his lap, sipping slowly dozing. "Did I scare you, Gabriel?" "A little."

"I'd never hurt you, Sugar." His eyes were ablaze with seven hues of brown glowing and swirling around his pupils, fading in and out. "What?" "Your eyes," she held up a mirror. "I get to see my reflection today what a treat sugar." "When was the last time you saw yourself?"

"Three years ago. I stopped looking to see if it shows I'm getting older. Is that a wrinkle Gabriel?"

She hugged him, "hehe." Niarchos handed Clarence his bike jacket. Clarence saw Gabriel's lipstick stain on Niarchos' neck. "Did you hug Niarchos?" "Yes, in the limo. Why?" "I smell your perfume oil on him." "Why did you ask if you already knew Clarence?" "To see if you'd be honest Gabriel."

Clarence held her hand as they walked. "He's my best friend that means a lot." They sat in the sky box; the male vampires greeted him with handshakes while the vampress' remained silent. Mary, Ann, and Lily knew the savage inside but Ginger? It was her first time she was so shaky that when Grip returned, he ordered strong tox bloods to calm her. Zion had no idea how swift Clarence had become or how strong his telepathy, teleport and telekinetic powers were.

Steven entered the sky box, "Pharaoh, please forgive our intrusion. We seek your wisdom, please. The scroll writers are arguing over who should document tonight's scroll." Clarence grinned. "I don't want the other writers cross with me. Steven, what did Margaret say?"

"She says I should ask you, and whomever you choose is who'll write it Great One." He looked at Gabriel, "Your eyes are beautiful, honey." She grabbed his hand and rested it on her stomach. "Clarence," Elijah's voice interrupted the kiss. *The scroll writer's division is waiting."* The Elders chuckled it was amusing seeing them together.

Clarence and Gabriel never broke their gaze. "Put everyone's name in a hat bring it let fate decide." "Yes

Pharaoh." Gabriel touched his hair. "Were you turned on seeing me kill Sugar?" "Yes." "I have bad news - no sex for three months." "Says who?" "Zion." "Why?" "Give the baby a chance to take hold Sugar." "Three months…Hmm. We can do other things." "Like sexy?" "I'll show you old man."

Caleb center stage vampire Arena……

"In the competition for the runners, there were several items placed on main roads around the island. The runner to return with the most items wins the competition." There were 6 runners, 22 were seeking pardons - one for the murder of a human, the other for treason against Vaughn and his husband.

Clarence received thousands of texts from vampires, saluting him. Infrared heat images showed vampires on the start lines. Caleb gave a play by play as they bolted around the island. Gabriel's mind wandered to her childhood. She was in her cozy Queens Kitchen as her grandma told her about vampires who helped black people. She walked home from work and foolishly, she cut through Central Park at night which was a no no.

However, she couldn't miss her train to Brooklyn because the next one was arriving an hour later. She was nineteen years old. Two men jumped on the cobble stone pathway one behind her and one in front of her. One ripped her dress off while the other held her down. A man appeared out of the woods, grabbing the first assailant off her, tearing his head from his body.

The other man tried to run but her hero caught him, flying him up in sycamore trees. Her grandmother saw the hero drinking the man's blood pinning him to a high branch. When he was done, he put his coat on her shoulders escorting her to the station. He explained about black vampires, how they'd been around for hundreds of years. Her grandmother had a diary. She needed to get to Queens to see if she could learn more. She remembered clearly what her grandma shared, "If you meet one, don't be afraid, they're gonna help you." At the time, she thought it was a scary bedtime story she imagined. Now, she knew it was true "Sugar." "Yes?" "You, ok? You zoned out on me." "I'm fine Clarence."

The runners returned in under ten minutes. "All winners will be announced Monday night," Caleb announced. Steven arrived with the hat Clarence turned on the mic speaking to Caleb who was still on stage. "Elder Caleb?" "Yes Pharaoh?" The sky box was lit purple. "It's come to my attention the scroll writers disagree over who should write the scroll for tonight's executions. "I've asked all present writers and I emphasize present scroll writers to drop their name in this hat. I'll ask Mrs. Mya Roberson, Elder Elijah's beautiful wife to pull the name of the writer to emboss this blessed vampire scroll. Did you know she's also a midwife and certified doula Elder Caleb?" "I did not Great One." Gabriel was ecstatic to hear that. "Ms. Mya will you please pull a name out of my handsome hat?"

She smiled; joyous Clarence included her in something. "Please read the name before you?" "Wednesday Ahtase." She'd been writing scrolls for a year. The writers were upset that someone with little experience got to document one of the greatest scrolls in history.

"Do an excellent job and as with all scrolls, be truthful and accurate Wednesday." She kneeled below them on the main show floor. The next event started. The sand was clean, as a stage rose beneath it. Hackers were pre-seated in front of twenty laptops.

Clarence turned on his mic. "How do we have more hackers than runners Elder Caleb?" The crowd laughed. "I have no idea Pharoah however, the first one to hack a fake account of the Pharaoh's and send him a text message through this forged account wins THERE CAN BE ONLY ONE! These vampires must get through sixteen encryptions, sixty viruses without shutting down, and 42 fire walls. Please, open the envelope before you."

A baby vamp from Clarence's coven was competing. Gabriel's dingo slept in her lap wearing a diamond collar yawning. "Why is Jupiter here, Sugar?" "I take my dog everywhere. He's, my baby." "Sugar, he's not a dog." "He's adorable, isn't he Clarence? He's a puppy he needs us" She put a shirt on him. "You dressed him?" "Yep. Turn your phone on Clarence they've gotta text you." Clarence handed her his phone. She looked at the texts and saw the vampire he went out with texting him along with his responses.

**Clarence: I'm a married vampire Daisy. Daisy: You're our maker. You can have as many wives as you like. Clarence: It's part of my wife's dowry, I belong to my Queen. Daisy: I was turned on when you killed those vampires. Clarence: Daisy? Daisy: Yes, Great One? Clarence: Have a good night.**

Gabriel leaned in kissing him, leading them into a short make out session. Zion cleared his throat. *"I spoke to you"* he reminded Clarence telepathically. Gabriel rolled her eyes at Zion; he didn't care there'd be many days ahead she'd be cross with him. This is a miraculous child, a key to unlocking a lot of questions. He wasn't going to let their horniness ruin it.

"What happened to the play egg Sugar?" "It's home. You know it makes me want to fuck. You gonna fuck me daddy?" "I'm gonna do whatever you want." "Sugar, what about our baby? "You can do it halfway and gently tonight." "What if I eat it?"

"Before or after you go in?" She loved his huge curls, sexy smile, body, and mind. She loved all of him. He touched her kinky pretty, thick hair. 'Cotton billows' is what he named her hair. He dubbed Gabriel 'Sugar' on account of the packs she'd pour in her coffee when he'd watch her in the coffee shop. "Pharaoh, it's me. Did I chime you first? It's me. Shawn!"

It was his coven member. He broke into the faux account under three minutes nine seconds, impressive. Clarence opened his mic. "We have a winner Elder Caleb." Other vampires were upset, however they kept working on the hack.

"Shawn of coven one," clapping was thunderous as geeks shook hands. "Second, James from Papa Nathan's coven! Third vampress Sandra from Elder Blaise's coven!" Blaise ran on stage picking her up. He was whooping and praising his coven, raising the black power fist. Sandra waved her flag to rep their coven. "Congratulations to all winners. You may not work for the Pharoah but Elders have assured you will get a position within your coven's excellent job vampires."

The stage was cleared, and art easels were set up. Caleb announced, "The Pharaoh has changed the rules the artist must create a painting of the late great Malcolm X, the Pharaoh will personally buy a year's worth of art supplies and purchase the painting for $500,000. He'll ask Vampress Sarah Grandalay of Chelsea One Galleries to feature the painting in her next show!"

They knew who she was and what she was capable of she could jump start an art career!

Gabriel text Niarchos....

Honey: It's Mara Ncky! Mara can paint? Ncky: I guess. Honey: Shame on you. Ncky: Why? Honey: It's called get to know her before you fuck Ncky: I'll explain why I put the horse before the cart over coffee. Honey: No more coffee for now. Ncky: Don't let them make you crazy. Honey: Zion told Clarence we can't have sex.

Ncky: Pop is crazy I'm not letting anyone say when to make love to my wife. Honey: You're crazy! Let me pay attention cause we're buying the painting because I select the winner. Hope Mara wins. Ncky: Whatever Honey: Be nice dang, you're mean

Ncky: Why I gotta hear this?

Honey: Bye negro dang hehe

Gabriel's text chimed...

Mary: It's Mary, did you pick someone to make your wedding dress? Gabriel; No Ma'am Mary: If allowed, I'd be honored. Gabriel; I'd love it, do you specialize in BBW dress cuts? Mary: Girl, thick women ruled in my time.

Gabriel: Did Clarence always like full figured women? Mary: Yes. Gabriel: You're a couture designer, for one of the houses which one? Mary: Victoria Giovanni is my couture label, Gabriel. Can you tell Clarence I have a gift for him? The house where he lived as a slave we're doing renovations. A wall was knocked down; we found old books in the wall. Can you get me an audience? …Meeting sorry.

Gabriel: Yes, what time?

Mary: 2 pm?

Gabriel: I'll Inform him.

The competition was over. Caleb rose. "All paintings are with no names. They'll be taken to the Pharaoh's personal estate to be judged by the Elders. The one they pick collaboratively is the winner. Winners will be announced Monday night. This concludes in two nights. Please, support local vendors. We have many items for sale in the lobby."

"Please return tomorrow at 6:30pm for what we've been waiting for - our boxing and karate competitions." Caleb exited the stage. "I'm going to shop Clarence." He went into his pocket, handing her $1000. "If you need more, text me Sugar." "Thank you." Ann, Joan, Ginger, and Mya joined her. "Niarchos, go please." "Yes pop." Clarence smoked cigars with the Elders sipping brandy tox.

The ladies excitedly buzzed about the secret pregnancy. However, it didn't stop Ann and Mary from buying a baby blanket hand crocheted as a gift before they exited the island for the baby shower. Gabriel and Ginger looked at the jewelry. Gabriel saw a sterling silver set of hand carved orchids. "Look Ginger. It would look pretty on you." Niarchos blocked the door allowing no one in the booth while Gabriel shopped. Ginger liked that kind of attention, Gabriel didn't, it gave her an idea. She phoned Caleb. "Hey, announce as a surprise, I'm hosting a 'Meet your Queen' session."

"Where Gabriel?" "In the Elders Lounge." "Ok. In half an hour Gabriel?" "Ok, cool." "Have Jamaica block the door. Niarchos will stand with me please."

"I'm sure he will" "Shut up its innocent Caleb." "When are we meeting Gabby?" "Tomorrow, 2pm. Clarence has a meeting with Mary." "Alone?" "Yes, why?"

"Chance doesn't want Mary talking to nobody alone. He's possessive of her. Mary can't talk to any vampire; he doesn't care about his other wives. Mary is a diamond to him." "A diamond he treats like glass Caleb?"

"Stop. I know Clarence explained you can't speak on vampire marriages Gabby?"

"Caleb, do you see what you did? If we were human, would you be mentioning this? "No, Great One I'm only trying to protect you because you are new to our laws." "Don't 'Great One' me I'm Gabriel Caleb and thank you. See you don't get it and wonder why I'm around Niarchos. He treats me normal, Caleb." "It's your hormones honey It's ok. Is that why you love Niarchos?" "Yes." "Wipe your eyes. I don't want your husband doing to me what he done to them vampires, oh chileee Gabriel." "Hehe!" "Half hour?" "Yes."

Niarchos eyed a beautiful red Moroccan hanging lamp. "Buy it Nicky." "Too expensive." "You're rich." "I'm a Billionaire to be exact woman."

"How much Nicky?" "$300" "Buy it. Put it in your bedroom corner with a comfy chair and small table with a candle on it." "I'm good Gabriel." He exited the seller's space. "Mary? Can you do me a favor please?"

"Sure." Gabriel gave her money. "Have the shop keeper wrap the red hanging lamp and ship it to Niarchos' house. He's too cheap to buy it." "Yep, that's Niarchos hehe." He escorted her to the lounge. "Is Jamaica at the door?" "Yes, my Queen." Someone knocked. It was Clarence. "Hey baby." "You forgot something Sugar?" placing her crown on her head. "How'd you? --"

"Caleb put it in my gym bag 4 nights ago." "Spooky. How do I look guys?" "It looks pretty on you." "Thank you, Nicky." "I like this one best Clarence." "I'm glad you love it, Sugar knock em dead. You look beautiful my love. I'm going back to the skybox." Clarence entered the hall vampires kneeled as he walked past holding out their hands as Cain guarded him.

Niarchos took couch pillows laying them on the floor in front of Gabriel. "They'll kneel before you as per vampire law Queen." He tapped the wall, "Jamaica, let the first vampress in." Vampress Daisy who won had a date with Clarence showed. She stood there staring glossy eyed. "Kneel." Niarchos demanded blocking Gabriel. "Kneel daughter." Gabriel requested. Daisy refused a direct order from her Queen. "I'm not your daughter." Niarchos drew his gun cocking it. "I'm going to steal your husband out from under you," she slurred. Gabriel cackled aloud disrespectfully.

"Are you daft?" Daisy asked, popping her fangs. "He can't be nourished from you because you're weak. He loved it you know, sinking his fangs into my subtle skin, rubbing my hard nipples with the tips of his fingers he wanted me she smiled oddly. His dick was hard as he pressed against me when we floated above the earth at dawn." Niarchos grabbed her throat squeezing, forcing her to her knees. "Nicky!" Gabriel called let go.

She wickedly laughed through raspy gasps for air angering him. "Cuff her." Niarchos placed her in cuffs at Gabriel's command. "Lock her up until further notice." Daisy giggled maniacally loud as she was being dragged out. "He's mine. We're gonna be sister wives Gabriel!" She yelled diabolically. Her friends entered, begging Gabriel for her release, "Great One please, she had many tox bloods this isn't like her. We don't understand what happened." "Keep your eyes to the floor!" "Yes, Elder Niarchos." "Who's your Coven Elder?" "Elder Vaughn, Great One."

"Call Vaughn Nicky. You vampresses stay here." Niarchos got on his walkie calling Vaughn in the skybox. The vampresses remained kneeling facing the floor in fear. Jamaica returned with Vaughn and his husband. Vaughn and his husband knelt before her. "Please rise Elder. Who's this Vaughn?" "This is my husband Eban Great One." "We've met a few times before, Great One."

"Sorry Eban, I'm bad with names. I know you as Vaughn's husband forgive me. Vaughn, a vampress… won the auction date with Clarence do you know her?" "Yes, Great One. Daisy."

"She's in violation. She defied Elder Niarchos' command as. to kneel she declined. I commanded her identical to Niarchos' request. Daisy defied us, threatening to take Clarence away. Daisy repeated something that bothered me, Vaughn. She stated he's unable to feed from me because I can't sustain the power of his bite. How'd Daisy know this when it's known to Elders? If we speak freely with Elders, how can we trust it'll be kept private Vaughn? How'd one of your members know the Pharaoh is unable to share his bite? Daisy spoke about their private date openly. Why is she discussing what the Pharaoh does with his vampires?"

"I do not know, my Queen. Please, allow me to investigate so I may come with a proper answer?" Gabriel was livid, "I'll wait Elder, I won't allow anger to dictate my decision." "Thank you, Queen."

She turned to Niarchos. "I'd like to go home please get Clarence Nicky. I'll allow Clarence to finish this discussion, Vaughn. Please, come to the house at 4pm tomorrow and bring Daisy with you. "Yes, Great One. Again, my apologies." "How many more vampires, Jamaica?" "Twenty my Queen." She met them, ending the event. "Nicky please take me to the limo I'm tired."

"Yes, my Queen." Niarchos stood outside the limo, waiting for Clarence. "Siree call Lulu?" "Hi, it's me Gabriel. Can you please drive the rolls to the front of the cabin?" "Yes, Great One." "Do you know of any bed and breakfast or room for rent?" "It's not fancy like the cabin, but my aunt has a private converted quaint barn turned into a guest house. The windows have blackout blinds. You are good on the sun. I like it. It's romantic, the set-up Queen Gabriel." "Can you see if I can rent it through Monday night Lulu, please?" "Sure, Great One." "Gabriel." "Sorrrrrry Gabriel." "We're partners, remember?" "Yes ma'am. I text the address." "I have your aunt's money.

Please inform her we'll be arriving tonight. Is 11:30 p.m. ok Lulu?"

"Sure. She's up late nights Gabriel - insomnia." Clarence came to the limo, "What's wrong Sugar?" "Nothing. They discussed the competition upon arriving home. "Why's the rolls out front Sugar?"

"We're going for a ride." He entered the rolls. Gabriel used her GPS to find the rental. Lulu's aunt exited the house leaving the keys on the porch with a note 'Welcome. We can square up when you're ready.' Get the bag, babe. Put the bloods away bae. The tea bags on the table please." "Sugar, why're we here with no guards?" "We don't need guards after what I saw do, we Pharoah?"

"This is nice Sugar," walking up the winding staircase to the loft. This is where they held hay in my day, this where I slept as a slave he smiled"

"I see," she responded, pointing to the fresh hay blocks holding up the pillow top mattress, Decorated pillows and a blanket made it pretty. There were beautiful piggy tail amber Edison lights strung throughout. The blankets were white goose down, and a small fridge with a outdoor shower. The shower was open behind a decorative Chinese screen, with a pull chain. Lulu was right. It was romantic. Clarence lit the square firepit in the loft. It was chilly. He wanted to keep Gabriel warm.

She undressed opening the double loft door as the night air kissed her flawless skin. The moonlight struck the blond hay as moonbeam's caused a sexy glow. She smiled tapping the bed enjoying the summer cool air wrapping her skin. "Take off your clothes Clarence." He was reluctant so she removed them for him, laying on top of him. "I put someone in jail tonight, daddy."

"I heard what happened Sugar?" She explained the ordeal. "What you gonna do Sugar?" "You mean what's the Pharoah doing?" "Haha, has she broken our laws?" "Yes, she has." "Call Jackie in the morning."

"I think he's here Gabriel they may be possible misdemeanors?" "Vaughn is coming to see you with her at 4." "To see us at four?" "Yes, she exhaled."

"That's good. Why did you kneel when asked not to Sugar?" "No one is above the Pharaoh, not even his wife. In your eyes, we're equal. In the eyes of others, we're not. Until the level of respect is reached, I'll do as they do." He was surprised but happy she humbled herself for him. "Gabriel?" "Yes?" "Do you love Niarchos?"

"Yes, he's special. However, I'll never love a vampire more than I love you. Clarence Hollings, I'm in love with you 1000%." She rubbed his arm as he closed them around her. "Gabriel? I informed Niarchos if anything were to happen to me, he's to care for you and the baby. He's to move in the mansion." "Why?" "Because he loves you. He'll be good to you and our baby. If I'm in danger, he'll gun down anyone for you, even an Elder. Niarchos is dangerous. I've taught him to control his anger but it's with limits. I've watched Niarchos crush his man's skull with one hand."

Are you afraid of me Sugar?" "Sometimes." "I'm afraid of you too, Sugar." Scoffing, "Me, why Clarence?" "You're the one who has the power to break my heart and make me cry." Squeezing her close. "I need you, Gabriel. You saved me." "How?"

"My heart was hardening. I was thinking I couldn't love again. The pain of loss, my wife getting old and dying… I saw you and the pain melted away. I know it's a lot a new husband and a baby, all within 6 months? I know you wanted me all to yourself tonight, yes?"

"Yes, we haven't had time to celebrate over our pregnancy or discuss anything like names." "I'm sorry Sugar, I must remember you're a private vampress." His phone buzzed as did hers.

"Sugar, they're worried. They'll start searching. One call Sugar please." "Ok." He called Niarchos. "We're fine Niarchos…on the island. I'm unsure where. Gabriel won't say.

Ok, hold on." handing her the phone. She opened her legs exposing fat ma he covered his eyes boyishly grinning.

"Gabby?" "Yes Nicky?" "I gotta know where y'all are Gabriel please, send the address." "You promise not to share it?" He was quiet. "Ok." "I'm commanding you not to share." "Yes, Great One where?" "Over the moon hehe," she hung up. "Sugar, not nice," "Hehe."

Niarchos called Clarence's phone Gabriel picked up putting him on speaker "Gabriel, if you don't say, I'll find you." "Good luck vampire." "You have no idea you triggered a master tracking monstrous vampire haha." "Thats funny vampire king? Hehe." "Zion and Elijah are calling Sugar." "You can protect us fine. Thank you!" She was agitated and he tried to calm her. "Gabriel, its ok." "No, it's not!"

"Sugar, calm down were pregnant." He took the phone. "Zion, tell Elijah we're fine. I'll return before competitions." "In daylight Clarence?" "Yes, Zion Gabriel will get me home." "Pharaoh, Gabriel who can walk in the light, will get you home, sunup ...alone. Did I get that right?" "Goodnight Zion."

Elijah turned to Zion. "The vampress has his nose open! He's not thinking. When was the last time he was alone in the light? The morning, he burned coming from her house Elijah." Papa cut in. "Gabriel's afraid with all she's been through, have y'all thought of that? Tonight, we saw he's more than capable of protecting himself. Clarence is a grown ass vampire let the negro be. Y'all finnin to push that woman away and where she go he go no matterin where dat be." They were quiet seeing papa Nate upset. Cain shook his head scoffing at their worry.

Niarchos gave Jupiter Gabriel's sweater. Jupiter started the search and Niarchos finished it. "Come on boy. Let's find mommy," following Jupiter who was leading him right to them. "Find mommy, good boy." Niarchos smiled sinisterly because Gabriel taunted the savage in him.

Vaughn & Ebon....

Vaughn was livid. "What the hell were you thinking repeating the shit I explained privately, Ebon? Do you think Gabriel wants to hear Daisy was drinking breaking her sobriety? She's upset because they knew her fucking business."

"I'm sorry, Vaughn." "I'm sorry Vaughn that's all you ever say...Ebon, you talk too fucking much. I know Clarence will pursue it because it upsets Gabriel. We gotta be truthful and ask for mercy. Clarence has telepathic abilities or ain't you seen him tonight in that fucking arena? Lying ain't an option. If he chooses to drink your blood, he's gonna get the truth anyways Ebon." Vaughn got his car key. "Where are you going Vaughn?"

"For a drive." Vaughn loved his husband but wished he wasn't flashy and loud. He hoped he'd grow out of needing to be the center of attraction hell it'd been 30 years already. Vaughn arrived in town knocking on the back door of one of the vintage river row houses, visiting one of the artists from Ann's coven. "Did you finish the painting?" "Sure did." "I love the black and whites with red splashes if you don't win, I'll buy it Brandon how much?" "I don't care about the money, Elder. It's getting hooked into the gallery connect that's all I care about."

"Clarence knew Malcolm X. They were friends in the civil rights cause, Blaise too. He was at the Audubon Theatre during the assassination. He has the shirt with Malcolm's blood on it, they keep asking him to donate it to the African American museum. They authenticated it and Clarence couldn't part with it any more than he could part with Harriet's manifest, a book of every slave she took north. He won't hand it over."

"Why Vaughn?" "Cause Harriet asked he not. He won't give details." "Impressive. Elder, what's up? What brings you by this late?" "To talk. You're easy to talk to."

"What's on your mind?" "Have you ever been in a relationship with someone who's too all over the place?"

"I'm not sure what you mean Elder."

"Brandon, we've been friends for years. Call me Vaughn." "What's wrong Vaughn?" closing his paints to listen. "You know I'm married. I love my husband. I'm want him to understand I'm an Elder vampire. I've been an Elder since the 50's. I've never had an issue with Clarence now, I do. "What did Ebon do?"

"Bran, like any couple, I inform him of things trusting my husband not to repeat what we discuss. Sometimes, spouses are invited to hear private parties, or I share an Elders problem for advice. Ok Brandon? You can't repeat what I'm to share." "I won't Vaughn. You have, my word as a vampire." "The Queen is half human Bran--"

"Which is amazing Vaughn." "It is. Isn't she prone to human illness?" He explained her DNA make up. Clarence has four fangs. Two tops, two bottoms. His venom is extremely strong. There are times we bite humans, and we can't bring them over because they're too close to death?" "Yes Vaughn."

"Well, his venom can seize death and bring them back or in Gabriel's case the opposite which, almost killed her. Zion is always studying our African American DNA infused with vampire venom. This has always been in vampires, but Gabril is the first vampire human hybrid. We can learn so much from her scientifically. We feel she is the next evolution of the vampire. Through his studies, he was able to reverse the strong hold of the venom from killing the human in her, saving her life. I told Ebon this however, Ebon gossiped with the vampire who went on a date with the Pharaoh. She saw the Queen and refused to kneel. When Niarchos demanded she kneel, she disobeyed an Elder and a high vampire royal." Brandon's jaw dropped. "Oh my god, what?"

"The Queen arrested her, demanding to know how she knew about the bite. I know she's going to push the issue." "Maybe the Pharoah won't listen to her." Vaughn burst out in laughter. "What's funny Vaughn?"

"He's entranced by her more than his first Queen. He's crazy over this vampress. He'd move heaven and earth for her Bran." "Wasn't he like that for his first wife?" "It's different. The love is deeper. It happens with us vampires in time, you'll see." "The Pharaoh and his Queen look like good vampires speak truth Vaughn. Do it without Ebon present. Is Clarence your maker?" "Yes"

"He'll know you better than anyone. He can sense if you're lying as your maker. Be like Pharaoh, I got me an out-of-control bitch." "Haha."

"That's the long and short of it, right Vaughn?" "Yes." "How old are you, Elder?" "Twenty-three and 103 on May 19th this year. You?" "Twenty-one and Thirty." Vaughn smiled. "I was 30 once Bran what a wonderful age to be turned forever 21." "Haha how old is Ebon?"

"Twenty-six and seventy." "Next time, pick someone older." "It won't." "Why not?" "Because you're thirty." Brandon blushed. "Elder how were you made?"

Elder Vaughn Origins....

"I was a victim of a gay hate crime. Of course, back then, it wasn't a crime. I lived in New York, born and raised. I was sleeping with the son of my mother's employer. A prominent white politician who shall remain nameless because his family is in power today. We were in love but of course, it was a no no.

He was betrothed since the age of ten - a football quarterback, prom king, you name it. Every chance we got; we were together. This lasted years till after he married, I then graduated from Pace University, a prominent college and went to Brooklyn Law school. He'd call and I'd meet him at a posh hotel in the city. He had a friend, a black woman who he'd send to make the reservations pretending to check in. He'd walk into the hotel as a guest already registered entering the room. One day, I was waiting for his arrival when three men raped and beat me badly. Brandon, I had a cracked skull in two places, broken ribs, leg, arm, nose, and collar bone. They cut the tip of my dick open and a broken femur."

Brandon cried clutching a pillow at the chilling horror. "I was going to die. My mother cleaned these white people's fucking toilets to put one of her nine kids through law school only for her to see her son killed, like this? I was drowning in my own blood; it filled my lungs quickly. Clarenc entered asking....

*'Do you want to live?' 'No, allow me to die.' 'Why do you want to die?' 'I'm ill I love men when I should love women.' 'You are ill because you believe you shouldn't be free to love whom you choose; I ask one last time live or die?' I gurgled the word 'Live.' 'You'll never eat human food or walk in sunlight. You must feed off the blood of humans and animals to survive.' I nodded yes then; he blessed me with the feeding me his blood healing my injuries."*

Vaughn sighed. "He and Queen Safinah took me home with them where for the next five days, I screamed in agony as the venom reconnected and repaired every broken bone in me without pain killer. It burned like fire searing my veins." "Did you ever learn who sent those animals to the hotel was it him?"

"No, it was his wife's brothers." "Wow. Did you see him again?" "No, the Pharaoh forbade it. He was high society. It would draw attention to us, I knew it was also because he didn't want me getting hurt again. Three weeks later her brothers were found drained of blood dead in a lake near the family estate. I looked at Clarence crying tears of joy because he avenged me"

"How is Elder Niarchos as a vampire Vaughn?" He's Clarence's hit vampire. If Clarence says, 'Shoot him' Niarchos won't hesitate or ask questions its done in a blink of an eye. I've seen it happen several times. He's a good vampire why did you ask?"

"I'm asking because he looks so serious Vaughn." "He's the Pharaoh's Cappo. I'd gun anyone down for Clarence, he saved my life, accepted me, loved me when I didn't love myself and forced me to accept who I am loving all of me even the gay me if that makes sense. He's the father I never had Brandon." "That's heavy Vaughn." "You know Ebon never inquired about my turn?" "Why?" "Who knows Brandon?"

"Was she nice" "Who Bran, Mama Fi?" "Yes, she was like a vampire mother to us all." "What about Queen Gabriel?"

"She's a sweetheart too Clarence has excellent taste in choosing women with humble loving spirits. She saved Niarchos' life, almost losing hers and she didn't care. Clarence chose a good vampress." "There's your answer Vaughn." "What Bran?" "She's a good vampress. Talk to her without the Pharaoh. Explain exactly how you did it. Don't vary. How can she not be empathetic? She knows how bitches can be. She's young like my time."

"I'll, thank you Bran." "You're welcome." "Did you graduate law school? You're a vampire attorney?" "Yes, Bran that's how I know how she can be sentenced. It was a misdemeanor when Niarchos told her to kneel. It became a felony when she ignored Gabriel."

Brandon walked Vaughn to the door, Vaughn thanked Brandon for helping him solve his dilemma. Locking eyes as crickets mated outside Vaughn swept Brandon up in his arms. Vaughn pushed Brandon inside, closing the door behind them.

Clarence was asleep when Gabriel woke. She closed the window before sunrise covering Clarence with a sheet. Gabriel heard scratching at the door grabbing a sheet and her husband's gun she opened the door, "Jupe, how'd you get here baby?"

The sheet was open when she looked in the corner seeing Niarchos stuck in the shadows. She closed the sheet however it was too late. He saw her for two minutes and his dick was semi-hard licking his lips. "Nicky, what're you doing here?" "I explained I'd find you. You shouldn't have taunted me and told me what I wanted to know Gabriel."

"Why're you standing in the corner?" "Sun." He was backed in a shaded spot on the porch where there was no sunlight. She took a seat on the porch in the sun, fanning herself. "Whew ,it's warm, isn't it Elder?" Smiling wickedly.

Jupiter sat next to her, drinking from a water puddle on the porch the rain left. She crossed her legs under the sheet Indian style swinging on the porch swing staring at him like a spider with a fly caught in a web. "Looks like you're in a bind Nicky. All this Georgia sun and you're stuck in one tiny corner till sundown. If I don't open the door, you can't run in. You're gonna get burned. When was the last time the sun scorched you, Elder?"

"Many years ago, my Queen." "Say, does it hurt as bad as vampires say?" "Yes, Great One." He was staring at her curves under the sheet. She saw his hard dick, his breathing picking up. He didn't try hiding it, he wanted her to see. She licked her warm lips staring as it grew. "I thought I said not to find us how'd you?"

He looked at Jupiter, "He missed his mommy. He needed a good run anyway."

"Gimme kisses, baby. He's a savage. Like someone else I know," She elevated Jupiter while elevator eyeing his bulging hard on her final resting place. He made it jump, she devilishly grinned. "Come out the corner." "You must open the door; the burn won't be bad. I can hyper-speed in the house. The sun is making me weak Gabriel please, open the door before I fall and die."

Gabriel popped up as fast he could smell her sweet pussy mixed with morning sun. "Hurry Gabriel please," he whispered. She snatched the door open. Before she could turn to close it, he was inside laughing and scorched on the top of his arm. He went to the fridge for A+ blood.

Clarence looked over the loft's edge. "Shame on you Niarchos." "What's funny Clarence?" "Are you going to tell your Queen or shall I Niarchos?" He shook his head no laughing.

"Ok, I'll tell her. Sugar, when we'd get caught in sunlight in the old days, and we needed a human to let us in until sundown. I taught the vampire Elders a trick we don't use much. If a woman answered the door, play on her sympathies like 'Ma'am, I been shot, please allow me in before I faint and bleed on your porch. Please ma'am I mean you no harm.' If they won't open the door, they pretend to weaken. Hold yourself up, look weary, play on human emotions. That's what he did to you Sugar." She hit Niarchos playfully. "Shame on you! Using Jupiter to find us!" "If you don't want to be found, stop wearing Egyptian musk oil. It has a distinct smell. Next time I say where are y'all? Don't hang up." She cut her eyes at him. She walked upstairs lying down, feeling sleepy. Niarchos lay on the couch, falling asleep.

She whipped out his Clarence's dick, sucking sweet. Clarence resisted. Slapping his hand hard, she snatched his hard-on demandingly from him, wrapping her thick sexy lips around his fat shaft sloppily gliding him in and out her mouth. Tip to the ball's saliva slippery spit dripping from the dicks tip.

Gabriel twirled her head wild, riding his shaft relentlessly with her tongue. He grabbed a fist of hair; she reached up slapping his hand a second time. He moved his hands behind his head she had him under sexual arrest.

He grunted standing attempting a futile escape from her sexual prowess. Gabriel pushed him on the loft's wall falling to her knees. Loud gagging and sucking to the underside of his thick dick accompanied by shaft licking from balls to tip of his second head snatched his soul. Gabriel worked her man adding combinations of heavy sexual inhales and soft blowing exhales drying him between sucking sounds echoed off the loft's walls sent goosebumps up his spine.

She tapped her phone "Alexis, play Curtis Mayfield pusher man." The music floated loudly as she burned a beckoning stare through his soul. Clarence was trapped in her web of lust. His massive wide candy spit slick dick choked her, but losing oxygen for a few seconds to mystify and ensnare him didn't matter to her. All she cared about was getting all of him down her tiny throat. Forcing him deep running pre-planned blow job combos on him, working his sensitive tip slurping then spitting pre cum back on him only to lap it up like his good vampire slut while he watched her work her mojo.

"Fuck me daddy." "No Sugar please don't do this." Gabriel swabbed his hot dick with an ice cube, she whined sexually upset as the cube circled the hole. Her naked red tongue up under his second head rimming it round and round with spit drooling from tip to tongue falling out the sides of her mouth as she locked on the sweet cum filled throbbing head, driving him to the peak of desire.

"Daddy please," she started to cry solo licking the shaft of his dick balls to the tip, lapping up her mess his bitch in heat. Niarchos heard her begging, it was music to his ears. He was close to a nut as his dick throbbed through his grey sweats.

*Pop.* he couldn't get a connection. *Clarence!* He yelled in his head. *Yeah?! Don't fuck her, pop. The baby, don't. She'll help herself. She makes me crazy; I can't resist her Niarchos* he popped his teeth, biting into his arm to prevent himself from biting her. I can't control myself when she does this. Niarchos heard him mentally now that they were connected, she was sucking fast & hard longing for pre-cum.

"Oh yeah daddy I'm gonna suck the fire out this dick since you won't fuck me, I'll break your will eventually. You're gonna learn to gimme what I want," she got her wish swallowing the whole 12 inches. Clarence opened his eyes to her tongue on his balls, the tip down her throat and her lips on his stomach.

He trembled, forgetting to unlock Niarchos from his thoughts. Niarchos could now hear and feel everything Clarence felt. He grabbed his chest with all his might dragging to the bathroom falling to his knees on the bathroom floor, doing his darndest not to yell or moan her name, he rolled on his back pillow to his mouth. He opened his pants his hard throbbing dick jumped out hot, long, sexy, and thick. "Fuck!" Niarchos held a towel tight biting it.

Clarence closed his eyes; she slapped him a third time "Open THEM!" Niarchos felt the slap heeding her command,

"Keep your fucking eyes open." Clarence opened his eyes, Niarchos shared his makers sight, her begging for his nut on her knees submissively, urging Clarence to cum jerking his shaft with her soft tiny hands Pop. Niarchos was ignored. Gabriel slowed her stride licking out the hole. Gabriel guided him to a space in her cheek while he thrust fucked her mouth. "You ready for me woman?"

"Yes nasty," Gabriel moaned entranced inviting him to her while Clarence slid down her throat. Gabriel tickled his balls with her tippy fingers locking her mouth airtight engaging him in her wicked suction suck lock down trapping 12 inches of man securely between the roof her mouth, and untamable tongue. He was hers. "Mmm um hum mm fucking sweet, I'm in need daddy... mmm mmm please give it. Do you love me, Clarence?"

"You know I do." "Nut in my throat please daddy, I need it all that salty sweet sliding down my throat"

Clarence grabbed the edge of the wall, putting a hole in it. Gabriel nodded "Yes" looking up at him, innocent, sexy, slutty. He burst an overflow of wet, sticky load in her mouth dropping to the floor, his knees buckling under her fire soul snatching head. Gabriel let his sperm drip from her mouth in a cup, picking up the cup sipping her sweet treat as the hoe in her stared in his eyes unapologetically.

Niarchos' dick vein pounded. He burst a hot, sloppy nut in the towel filling it while breathing hard on the bathroom floor muffling what he could. Clarence slept, unlocking him...finally. He saw her naked body. She lay on his skin, her hair, the softness of her back on his fingertips as Clarence drifted to sleep. He smelled her horniness as he lay on the bathroom floor on his back looking down through Clarence's eyes at Gabriel sleep on his chest. He smiled at a dream future that was not his own. He wondered if the Pharaoh knew he had the ability to allow vampires to see what he could.

"Can you hear me Niarchos?" Gabriel mouthed with truly little sound escaping. "Yes, Great One." As he looked down at her through his father's memory "That's what you get for coming here hehe." Niarchos grinned. She no idea she just sucked his dick.

# Chapter 27
# One More Chance

Zion sent the limo to Gabriel and Clarence. "Niarchos, can you get the carriage when we get home, please?" "Which one pop?" "The one for two please." Gabriel rolled her eyes at Niarchos who scoffed uncaring. "She's cross with you son." "I know pop," he whispered, chuckling. She cracked a slight smile. Arriving at the cabin, Gabriel got out opening the cabin door. Clarence and Niarchos hyper-sped behind her. "You got burned, bae?" "A little." Clarence showed his left hand. She kissed it, licking her blood-stained lips. "What about you Nicky?"

"Same place again." "She got them blood." Niarchos sipped grudgingly, "B positive Gabriel?" "Oh, was it?" She knew he hated B positive blood. He sipped it laughing inside at her digs.

"Clarence, you got Mary at two and Vaughn at four." "You mean I have Mary at two. You've got Vaughn at four Sugar." "By myself?" "Did you speak with Jackie Sugar?" "I did." "What did he say?" "Vaughn is a vampire attorney he explained the vampire law. Felonies of a certain class get jail."

"Yes, they do Sugar eighteen months minimum up to five years maximum.

Did you know Daisy has a lucrative spa business? She pays 2% vampire tax and we're silent partners? She doesn't know you and I are silent partners because Vaughn set it up. If she goes to jail, we lose personal money, and the crown loses tax money. The money I get from her business funds Blaise's afterschool programs and daycares in black neighborhoods. The mothers don't pay for services or summer camp as long as they remain employed or in school.

"You're making me feel guilty Clarence, she was wrong." "Sugar, your royalty now you, must understand vines run deeper than a bruised ego or jealousy. I'm not saying she shouldn't be punished however; incarceration is hurting you and I and innocent children more than her remaining free."

"Nicky?" "Don't look at me Gabriel. I ain't in it. Use your heart. You know what you're doing. I'm going to look at 90-day fiancé come with?" "Yep." Clarence changed into a suit as he did with all business meetings.

"Knock knock family" Mary let herself in. "I'll be down in a second, Mary" Clarence spoke from his bedroom. He walked down, hugged her, offering her a seat. "This settee is cute Clarence." "Gabriel loves vintage furniture." "Twin Oaks have her come and pick whatever she wants there is an attic and barn full."

"I'll Inform her if she goes alone. I'm never stepping foot on Twin Oaks property again they enslaved me there." "Clarence, Chance and I live there."

"No Mary." "Alright," tapping his hand, the pain showing in his eyes. All these years, he hurt from slavery it showed on his face. Mary remembered a little she was five when the emancipation passed. She was exposed to racism, hate and colorism more. She removed four leather bound books from her bag and opened one she marked.

"Read it, please Pharaoh." handing it to him.

Eighteen hundred and thirty

First day of May

The year of our lord.

"Today, Alexander purchased new slaves one is a picaninny who looks white. I inquired if the boy were certain he was not white, accidentally mixed with nigger picaninnies. He explained his mother was a slave. I inquired about his name. He mentioned the name Alexander bestowed on him upon his arrival Clarence.

Our overseer inquired of the original owner the boy's age, as per Alexander he's five years of age to date. I do not want him in the fields. I have charged his care to our kitchen help, Isabel and Avril, our coachman, per Alexander's request.

These past five years, I have been extremely ill, I fear the worst. Alexander has been out late, not coming home. This may be because I'm unable to bear his children. The boy is handsome and can pass for white. He has not mentioned his mother. I inquired of Alexander 'May we raise him as our son.' He declined my request. Such a handsome boy could easily be raised as our own child, why would he deny me the chance of being a mother?

Mrs. Alexander Minerva Dupree

"A gift for the Pharaoh," bowing her head respectfully, raising the books as an offering kneeling. "Thank you, Mary you know I'm a historian of sorts, what's wrong?" "Permission to speak freely?"

"Of course, please rise." "I come before you requesting a legal vampire marital separation from my husband. I no longer wish to be married with him." "Is it the spike in vampire tax Mary?"

"No, Clarence. I don't want to be with a vampire who runs his life using his lower extremities instead of the brain God gave him." Mary stood rubbing her necklace of pearls pacing.

"I've put up with a lot over the years. I've dealt with him wanting me to exchange my sexual desires to satisfy his by seeping with women. When I declined, he married multiple ones. I didn't complain. I loved a human once, I purchased a quaint villa in Paris engulfed in an eclectic mix of sweet-smelling florals, hidden back on the property from the main road. A vintage cracked fountain of cupid greeted you; as birds of various breeds melodically sang into sunset. A slice of paradise and Safinah loved it, Clarence."

"She knew of the human Mary?" "Don't look shocked she was my friend and mentor. I wasn't returning to America, Chance knew it. I woke with the human next to me, drained of blood. Chance sat in the shadows of the corner drenched in blood which stained his shirt face his eyes were blazing from the fresh blood feed. He said *'You killed him, Mary. Did you think I'd let anyone take you from me?'* "He snatched away a man who truly loved me."

"Chance killed a human…why didn't you report it? What if he'd been rabid?" "He showed no signs besides jealousy." "What year was it?"

"Six months ago, Clarence I requested a divorce after the ordeal, he refused. When we loved as slaves what happened, Great One?" "They'd kill the one we loved or both if we ran, they'd kill the loved ones we left behind Mary." "What's different about what he's doing?" "Do you love Chance Mary?"

"No Clarence." "Ann sat where you are conveying the same. Papa Nate signed papers broke his heart. They've found their way back Mary. Is this what you want because Chance won't let go. He'll fight you for money or anything else he doesn't need because he can't say he'll die without you." "I was forced into poly life Clarence I want my own vampire not one I'm forced to share."

"Have you chosen an attorney?" "I don't need one. If you grant the divorce, your word is law." "Bypass my son without speaking with him I cannot do this. You have no idea how bad his temper is with romance Mary. Let's try mediation?"

"Zion Please call Chance to come." "He'll be here 3:30 Pharoah." "Mary I'm sorry." "It's ok, Clarence. Is Gabriel in?" "Yes, in the back with Niarchos."

He opened the door where Gabriel and Niarchos were. He was on the floor in front the bed sipping blood, she sat on the bed with her legs crossed Indian style. "Mary is here to see you sugar." Gabriel exited the room.

Clarence sat, "Niarchos?" "Yes, pop" he muted the television. He didn't look back knowing this conversation was coming. "Do you love Gabriel?" "Yes, she's, our Queen." "Look at me son." He raised his eyes. "Are you in love with my wife?" Niarchos hesitated. It took three minutes for his answer. "Yes pop, you're the father I never knew. Forgive me." Clarence was impressed with his honesty. "You cross with me pop?"

"No if anything happens, get her to safety. I'll map out plans I'll share with you alone. You're to tell no one where you are. When you arrive, destroy cell phones use cash. Respect my relationship do nothing you don't want done Niarchos." "Yes pop. Pop earlier when you mentally connected to me, I saw and felt everything you were doing with Gabriel. Were you aware?" "Did this happen Today?"

"No pop. "When?" He looked ashamed. "No haha!" "I'm sorry papa I tried getting your attention." "I ignored you Niarchos I'll assume blame. This gift I'm learning to control it, our secret son?" "Yes pop." He recalled bringing Niarchos home.

Niarchos Origins II
One week after the emancipation...

"He's huge," Chance complained, carrying him up the stairs in the house.

They gave Niarchos Clarence and Safinah's bed he didn't fit the others. He fell asleep while Safinah washed his wounds. They healed slower than other vampires, she dressed and kept him clean. "Clarence, it be two weeks he ain't woke once." "Safinah ran her hand over his cheek youse sure dis be our new baby? "Yas Ise sho lighting his pipe."

"I sho hope he heal fast I needs my bed woman." Safinah hit him playfully. "I likes da smaller bed; Youse force ta stay close ta me dese slave massa beds to big ta fixin sick of em hehe." Safinah practiced her reading when she heard, "Ma'am, is I dead?" "Nossir, I fetch my husband," returning with Clarence. "Ya husband white?" He sat up afraid. Safinah laughed, "He tells ya."

The men and Chance entered as Clarence explained his story. Niarchos was wide-eyed like a child. Clarence saw he was mentally younger than he looked. He purchased a large milk can with cow's blood commanding him to drink. Without question Niarchos drank all of it

Chance whispered to papa Nate, "he a huge nigga." "What I say bout usin dat cursed word round me, Chance?"

"Sorry Clarence." "Why ya cuss? We aint nuttin what dey say. I looked da word up in a dictionary, do ya knowed what dat say Chance? An ignorant black person, lackin good smarts. Stop usin it Chance." "Yes'sir." Safinah pushed through the men. "Move over," she fussed walking to him fearless, the men had guns hidden in case he was crazy.

"Niarchos was huge 6 ft 7 inches tall and 295 lbs. Solid muscle no fat on him. "Dis be my new baby, he be a big ole baby. Look at him." She rubbed his curly afro and grown out beard hugging him, he hugged her back. "I be Safinah, like ya Mammy."

"I never has a mammy ma'am." "You does," kissing his forehead you ain't knowed her that be all. Youse safe chere ain't no harm come ta ya chile." Clarence shed a tear at her mothering. His decision to bring her a son was good. Isabel corrected her when she was wrong, and Avril got on Clarence when he was. Those were the only parents. They knew his blended family was complete, he had a wife and son.

Current Day....

"I have a question for my wife, how can a dress make you more beautiful Gabriel? You see this, Mary? A snake charmer." "Hehe, I haven't heard that saying in years. "Your four o'clock is here Gabriel. Niarchos will stand with you, Vaughn will keep things civil." Vaughn met Gabriel in the Kichen as Clarence used the living room. Mary and Chance sat together. "You guys want anything?" No, thanks pop."

"Chance, Mary has something to say please hear her out son." "There's no way to say it softly Chance, I want a divorce." "No Mary."

"Chance, Mary isn't happy. She no longer wishes to remain in the marriage." "Pop she's the wife I have under human law." "Vampire law is what matters Chance you know this." "Mary, I can't let you go." "Can't or won't?" "I love you May." "You love me? Hehe...that's rich! We haven't been intimate since 1980." "Each time I try, you jump at my touch May."

"I don't want you anymore Chance! I want my OWN man. Mine! Not one to share with six other women. Cody called stating you were gonna leave your wives for her, and you agreed." She played back the conversation. "I recorded the sneaky bitch. I want what you offered Cody. Chancie, remember when it was only us? The night you made me? I'm your first turn and your first wife and I deserve better. I'll stay if it's us, no more wives."

"I'm not letting you go May that's final." "She's not a slave Chance, she's your wife. You can't do what the master's did, she's free to go if she pleases. If you won't sign the paperwork or give her what she's requesting, I will Chance. Don't force my hand."

Chance grabbed Mary's throat. "Niarchos!" Clarence called. "Drop her Chance!" "Mary, I love you. I won't let you go." "Chance don't!" Niarchos' voice echoed. Clarence closed his eyes taking control of Chance's mind and body, *'Chance put Mary down gently.'*

Niarchos knew what Clarence was doing because of the night before. Chance got on his knees and placed his hands behind his back unwillingly. "Shoot him, Niarchos." He shot Chance in the spine with a tranquilizer.

Clarence disconnected from Chance. "Mary! Zion! Oh god Mary....Mary sweetheart stay with me honey!"

Zion rushed from the basement. "Help me get her downstairs Niarchos."

Niarchos carried her to the medical infirmary. "Her neck, Chance fractured it." Zion whispered seeing the position her head hung.

Vaughn knocked walking in with Eban, looking at Clarence shocked. "We can return, Great One." "Vaughn call Jamaica inform him to come immediately. He'll be transporting a patient/prisoner."

"What's his charge, Pharaoh?" "Are you, his vampire attorney Vaughn?" Vaughn looked to Chance who was unconscious, "Yes Clarence." "When he wakes inquire." Vaughn checked on him while Joan came from the infirmary. "He's sedated Vaughn, he cracked Mary's neck. You're sure you want to represent him?" Clarence looked disappointed at Chance "When did his emotions become erratic Clarence?" "Joan, draw blood from Chance." "I object Pharoah." "On what grounds Vaughn?" "He's not awake and unable to give permission for blood extraction." "Niarchos."

"Yes Pharaoh?" "Vaughn is representing Chance, and he's opposed to a blood draw. Vaughn's stating, he can't consent verbally. Please, mentally record what I'm saying as a witness because you're an Elder."

"I, the Pharaoh, am concerned that Elder Chance Hollings is in the beginning stages of vampire rabidness. He has displayed behaviors indicating thus. For it to be reversed, he'll need immediate treatment. I hereby, as the king of covens exercise the right to protect all vampires from a potentially ill vampire who in sharing his blood, may infect others. I turned Chance. I, his maker, decree under Nas Feratu vampire maker law and blood bond attachment he's to remain quarantined until testing is complete, and he is cleared medically and mentally sound by vampire Dr. Zion Donovan. Do you agree this to be vampire law I quoted, Elder Vaughn?" "Yes, Great One." "Joan, draw the blood please. "Yes Pharaoh, as you wish." "Eban, go to the back room. Wait for Queen Gabriel to arrive please." "Yes, Pharoah."

Jamaica arrived to escort Chance to New York. "A nurse will meet you at the landing strip Jamaica. Keep him under 24-hour guard until his tests return. No exposure to vampires or humans." Clarence knelt holding Chance's head in his arms crying. "I promise papa will fix it I always do. Clarence rested his palm on the crown of his head, eyes closed. Take him Jamaica."

Vaughn joined Eban while Niarchos joined Gabriel in the living room. "Honey, you, ok?" "No, Sugar I'm not." Gabriel hugged Clarence wiping his eyes shh...shhh. Joan and Zion stared watching her calm him. "Let me get rid of this meeting and I'll come up and see you straight away daddy." They kissed and Clarence went to collect himself.

Vaughn & Ebon's meeting....

Vaughn and Ebon knelt before Gabriel. "Please rise, have a seat." "Permission for my husband to leave the room, Great One?" Eban was shocked. "Of course, Elder." Ebon left reluctantly. "Great One?" "Please call me Gabriel." Niarchos stood behind her. "Vaughn, you're aware of what happened."

"Yes Gabriel." "The Pharaoh informed me you are a vampire attorney so you're aware of all charges and the time they hold for each. Vaughn, may I speak honestly with you?" "Of course, Gabriel."

"I was angry, not because she failed to kneel, but because she revealed what took place between, she and the Pharaoh. Part of it was a lie, the Pharaoh never rubbed her nipples. You and I know Clarence would never violate a woman."

"I agree Great One." "I won't have her besmirching his sparkling reputation especially within the vampress community. She revealed something shared with the Elders. How'd she the Pharaoh can't feed from me Vaughn?" "Gabriel I'm a married man as spouses do, they share information with one another, I was not talking badly of you. I explained you fell ill; please believe I wasn't gossiping. Ebon is friends with Daisy he shared personal information of the crown with her, I'm sorry. I accept responsibility for the action of my husband. I ask your forgiveness and leniency in the matter."

"What do you think is fair punishment Elder?" "An apology from both and three months in jail." "No jail time. $40,000 donated to the vampire education fund. If she declines, her vampire tax rises 2% until forty thousand is paid, her choice Vaughn." "That shouldn't be an issue Great One. Daisy will be released, and I'll see her tonight at the games in the presence of the Pharaoh on bended knee for the apology."

"Agreed. I'll speak with your husband." Ebon nodded his head taking a seat. "Ebon?" "Yes, Great One?" "Do you know how important it is to be Vaughn's husband?" "Great One, sorry?" "Do you understand your role as his spouse?"

"I believe I do, please bless me with your infinite wisdom Queen." "Ebon we're in a unique position, we're both married to powerful vampires who hold positions within the crown. It's your job to help him run his coven.

"You'll hear things as the husband of an Elder. Sometimes you'll see things you were not meant to, like today with Elder Chance. Your husband should be able to share anything, and it never leaves you. Every time you betray confidence within your marriage you assist in sealing its fate. Once trust is gone what is left Ebon?" "Please forgive me?" "You were forgiven before arrival. Daisy must pay a $40,000 fine, and you're to help her, pay half not Vaughn, you."

"I understand my Queen." "Tonight, you'll apologize publicly at the games. Once this is done it's behind us." Ebon agreed he and Vaughn left to get ready for the games as Vaughn checked on Chances hospital arrival and care. Clarence entered the back room "I'm proud of you Sugar." Siree play for the love I give by THR Del phonics. Clarence danced with her in the living room as his mind back tracked into memories long past.

July 1868....

"Why pick July Lijah?" "Stop complainin' evenin air be cooler. You fixin ta change ya dry goods again haha. Ya gots so many now?"

"No Elijah." "Lemme me fix ya scarf den." Clarence stood straight. Elijah fixed the silk light blue scarf under his cream-colored shirt and\ jacket. "These damned tights under dese knickers. How I look Lijah?" "Married haha." "Ya got da the rings Lijah?" "Fo da 100th time, yes'sir."

"Is everyone seated...the children?" "Yes, the barn is romantically decorated as Ann, Lily, and my Little Flower say." "I swear this day never come; Papa Nate ready?"

"Yes, wit paperwork Clarence." "What time it be Lijah?" "Seven, the sun been down hour ago."

Clarence and Elijah approached the garden. Lily was on the piano playing the wedding march everyone stood. Avril held Safinah's hand, walking her up the aisle. Isabel, Niarchos, Chance, and Ann sat smiling. This was a great ordeal for them and other free slave families. It was the first formal wedding after the emancipation where their negro neighbors attended.

They didn't discriminate, they did business with every negro. They allowed the outside world to believe this was a mixed marriage to keep appearances, but free slave neighbors knew Clarence was one of them.

The garden was beautifully decorated with trellises adorned with red, yellow, and white roses hanging from a pergola Niarchos saw in a catalog building it as a wedding gift for his mother. Safinah walked under them on a red carpet that stretched from the house and to the altar.

Mason jars with candles were in the ground on the sides of each aisle and hanging from surrounding trees. Ann and Nathan Junior released five hundred Monarch butterflies as Safinah made her way down the aisle.

One of Papa's daughters dropped white rose petals on the red rug in front of Safinah. The fragrant smell of roses caressed the noses of guests in the warm air, notes of the wedding March floated on night breeze, entrancing the guests. A candlelit wedding at night; beautiful. They never saw anything like it amongst their people.

Clarence's smile invited Safinah to join him as she floated on cloud nine to the love of her life, adorned in all lace. Small dainty, embroidered roses, hand stitched by Mary, who took a year to complete the dress, with the matching veil.

Lily begged Safinah to dress her hair. She combed it as straight as she could get it, hearing Safinah scream and cry being tender headed causing Clarence to check on her.

He had no idea her hair was long and thick. "What cha lookin at coachman get out!" She yelled, wiping her eyes taking her pain out on him as he entered. Lily wet, oiled, and twisted it as tight she could in coils wrapped in cotton scraps. Safinah walked slow enough for Avril, glad he didn't miss a step.

The guests enjoyed the ambiance, she never imagined it'd be this beautiful. Her eyes glanced over the white wooden chairs as she held back tears of joy. Never as a slave did, she think she'd marry, more less the man she desired.

*Scroll 3*
*Nineteenth Day of July*
*Eighteen hundred and sixty-eight*
*The marriage of*
*Clarence and Safinah Hollings*

"Who gives this woman to be wed?" "We do, her father an' mama, Avril an' Isabel Hollings." "Please place her hand in her husbands."

"Do you, Clarence Hollings, take Ms. Safinah as your wife, to love, cherish, trust, and honor as long as you live?" "I do."

"Do you, Ms. Safinah, take Clarence Hollings as ya husband, ta love, cherish, trust, honor, and obey long as ya live?" "I do."

"By da power invested in me as an ordained preacher in the great state of Georgia able to unite in holy matrimony, I Nathan Daniel Freeman pronounce you wedlocked husband and wife. You may kiss your bride son."

Papa and Ann released 500 fireflies, as Clarence lifted the veil.

Lily made her a daisy chain, crown four rows adorned with baby breath in her hair. Clarence didn't kiss her, he stared at her hair. It was the first time he saw pretty, long thick hair down her back. He kissed her. She allowed Lily to give her a little lip stain and rouge. Jumping the broom everyone clapped. The newlyweds walked the white carpet under the rose decorated pergola as multi colored *rose petals were tossed, congratulating them on their union.*

*End Scroll*

The wedding was beautifully planned. They drank, danced, and enjoyed the festivities. Juke joint, blues music played all night. They hired local blues singers to come, and boy did they show up.

The music was grand, people were happy, drinks flowed, and glasses remained full as cigarettes were freely given being he owned a tobacco field.

People were drunk as Clarence Niarchos and Chance drank blood. Avril kept identical marked wine bottles for the servants who were their older children to serve vampires of the house for the night.

Mary & Chance Origins....

Chance danced with Safinah's dress maker all night. She was talented and her esteemed family owned one local haberdashery; they ordered goods from them for their plantation. There were several former slaves who owned businesses Clarence worked with and this one, Mary's haberdashery general and dry goods.

They sold them Tobacco from Papa and Ann's fields, cotton from Lily and Caine, honey from Niarchos and Elijah's bees, wool from Avril and Isabel's sheep, dishes, and other item's Safinah would trade in various markets, she also raised goats for milk and cheese, chickens for eggs, cows for milk.

Everyone did well financially. Clarence charged what they agreed upon to purchase their land within the gates of the plantation. Once your acres were paid you owed no more money to him, owning the parcel and everything on it which made for 100% profit.

"I haven't seen you in some time Mr. Chance." "I say identical young miss." "Why is your father staring young miss?" "He knows your sweet on me hehe." "Who say it be so?" "Your elder brother Elijah."

"He may be on to something this time young miss." Mary smiled she was young and beautiful, her dark skin smooth and flawless. Her teeth were white as snow and her hair thick brown billows rolling down her back. She was slim waisted like he liked his women. Her bones were petite, eyes round as silver coins. She was beautiful spoke good English not broken like him; he was enamored by her. "Shall we dance young Miss?" She gave him her hand. They danced, laughed, and sang together. He tried to teach her how to play hearts and win, however she couldn't get it. "You're a gambler?" "Yes ma'am, best in the business." "Is it dangerous? You don't need to do it. It's obvious you and your family are wealthy all negros know the Hollings are well to do, and Mr. Clarence is nice for all he does. Why risk life gambling?"

"It's the thrill of winning and losing, but I always win. Chance looked in her eyes. Mary looked away shyly. "Mary?" "Yes Papa?" "Come inside go find ya mother." "Yes Papa" Mary walked off staring at Chance. "Sir?" "Yes Mr. Hollings? "May we speak please?"

"Yes, you may. "I would like your permission to start courting your daughter sir." "That is fine what day would you like to come to dinner Mr. Hollings?" "Tuesday sir? "That'll be fine. Stop by the store say six?" "Yes, sir see you then." Mary knew what was happening, she was full of glee.

Meet His Maker....

The night continued. A woman dressed in a cotton gown with long gloves arrived, the second she entered the door

Clarence sensed her. He approached the entrance hugging her tightly. "How'd ya know?"

"I sensed your happiness, and talk from vampires we's proud, mostly me."

"Let me introduce ya, Black Lilac this be my new wife Safinah. Cotton this is my maker." Safinah's jaw dropped then she hugged and kissed her; "This is the best wedding gift. You saved our lives Black Lilac." Safinah kissed both her hands with tears in her eyes.

"Nooooo brides ain't lowed ta cry on a weddin day it be bad luck my old Mammy say." "Love please go back in I'll be along." "It was nice meetin' ya will ya come fo a glass a blood?" Sofia was shocked she knew. "Thanks, ya kindly ma'am." They rested on a bale of hay. "How ya been Lilac I be missin ya sorely?" "I be chere an' dere." "What happened to ya husband Lilac?"

"He round, but Nat Turner be dead Clarence." He rode with Nat Turner Lilac I seen dat in da white man paper?" "Nat rode wit my husband he start dem uprisings burning plantations to plantation crops an' all massa an' misses trap on dat land I have ya knowed." She held her head up smiling with pride. "Nat gets credit fo my husband doins. I love em though he brave an' sweet, God fearin Nat was."

"He knowed da good book good. When Ise down I hears him reading scripture he say 'Black Lilac? God don't want you feelin low.' "I say Nat, God ain't knowed me no mo ise damned." "He say God knowed all his creatures big and small, see? Say so right chere.'"

She always made Clarence smile. "Dis be ya wedding gift." "A photograph of other men folk Lilac?" "See dat one far left?" "Yes Lilac." "There be ya kin dats ya brother Clarence." Clarence looked surprised. "You sure Lilac?" "Oh, Ise sure. Hehe" "I knowed you an' him looks like. Ya Mammy makes me swear by God ta tell ya one day. I go back an' see her after I turn ya, tell her wat I done. She ask iffin I does it fo ya kin folk to so y'all be tagetha. I pays fo' dat copy from da photo man. He sell it a quarter fo me but fo white he say 2 bits. He lucky Ise vampire and has coin. I say dis be fo my best turn makes me rightly proud."

"She says fo I vampire 'promise ya find my boys.' I say I does anything fo ya she since she save me from a raping and lashes I finds out weeks later ise pregnant from my husband. "You gots a name Lilac?" "No 'sir. I ask round' in saloons no one say. I offers money no one want nigga coin so I stops askin. Dis I take two towns over dey gots mines up dere. I reckon he come through after he free. One da negro bar men's say he ain't sell himself back in slavery. Iffin he done I'd surely get him out, bring him chere."

"You hungry Lilac?" "I is." He raised his sleeve she fed five minutes. "You always sweet ya taste like dem red apples I turn ya on." They laughed. Clarence escorted her inside introducing her as his business partner. "Chance this be Black Lilac my maker." "What's we got chere?" She smiled beautifully at Chance holding up her hand instantly attracted to him. "Pleasure ma'am." Chance kissed her hand keeping her gaze.

"Don't ma'am me gambler." He looked shocked "I seent ya many a night winnin gold coin. I knowed ya vampire however ya never knowed ya grand vampire sire be starin right at ya now did ya?" "No ma'am I recon not."

They laughed she was charming, funny, and loved male vampires. She enjoyed music, the company of the vampire she turned and his new wife. The night continued as music floated on the wings of butterflies and spirits on the backs of fireflies.

The Wedding Night....

Safinah and Clarence bid the guest's goodnight right before sunrise he put her on his back carrying her up those winding stairs to their bedroom. "Shhh stop screaming" he whispered, "you're going to make Niarchos come out." She was drunk giggling loudly.

"What happened to Lilac?" "Chance took her to her hotel in town Cotton. I'll pay her a visit tomorrow check on her." He removed her veil, playing in her long thick kinky beautiful black hair. "No 'sir it gettin wrapped tomorrow coachman."

"Why cotton? It looks beautiful." "Ya fancy da Georgia heat Mr. Hollings." "I despise dis heat Mrs. Hollings." "How ya ask I leaves it out wit all I gots ta do in dis heat sir?" He kissed her neck.

She jumped up running. He chased her around the room. "Ya know you ain't faster than me cotton." "Tonight, I is," pushing a chair in front of him he jumped over it. "I have you cornered woman"

"Back up!" Safinah raised her skirts showing her thick thighs, his dick rocked up by her sexual taunts and he loved it. "Move hehe" showing deep cleavage. She ran to the bed jumping up and down on it." "Cotton?" "Humm?" "Get down." "Come up!" "I'll break the bed woman." "Buy a new one Mr. plantation owner hehe." "The champagne is talkin." "Get up here big man." Alright he removed his clothes. Her jaw dropped. "You pretty Peety." staring at his hard dick.

He rose on the bed but refused to jump. He pushed his hand under her dress. She locked her legs. He jumped the bed caved he caught her before she fell. "Heheh!" Chance and Elijah entered caught him naked with a hard dick holding her standing in the middle of a broken bed. They closed the door quickly chuckling.

He pulled the mattress off the bed on the floor. Help me get out this thing, he unbuttoned 33 tiny buttons which felt like forever because his hands were massive. He pushed the dress down, helped her out her petti coat and corset.

"Lily got me ladies' nighties like what she wore in the saloon when she worked there Peety." He enjoyed every minute or her being drunk because she was always serious and loving but afraid to let go and be emotionally free. "Do you want me to wait, cotton? If you're tired, I can wait until tomorrow. Guess what? I have a special wedding present for you."

"Where Clarence?" She sat on the mattress clapping her eyes closed completely naked.

He gave her a black velvet box. "Jesus," she held it as it glistened in candlelight. "Clarence. It's beautiful but you knowed I ain't a fancy type. "When I saw it, I knew it be beautiful on ya skin, please cotton, try it."

He wrapped the four-row diamond bracelet on her wrist. "It is beautiful however never as beautiful as my wife Fi, I love ya." She leaned in for a kiss hugging him, turning her head to the side. "What ya doin?"

"Drink my blood Peety."

"Safinah baby no." "Yes, I knowed ya want it. I see da way ya look at me some mornins. Den, ya rush out ta get blood cause da thirst done took hold whiles ya rest. Ise ya wife now we's one drink be from me Peety. It be my weddin gift go on...takes it Peety."

He nodded yes kissing neckline working his way to her bare breasts sucking her nipples softly. He opened her legs gently smelling her growing moistness kissing her sweet pussy. "No Peety." "Why Cotton...who done dis to ya fo'?" She looked away tearing up. Clarence wrapped his arms around her "it be fine shhh kissing her neck. No bad memories on dis chere night no ma'am Mrs. Hollings dis be our good night." Safinah hugged him smiling as he rested his body on top of her.

"Ahhh!" The bite startled her as she surrendered to her creature of the night blood binding her soul, body, and mind to his. Clarence entered her slippery pussy at the same time to ease the pain of her virgin bite long stroking, rubbing her clit sipping her gifted blood. Rich red blood pumped fast; he closed the wound using his blood sexually excited about her blood sacrifice.

He rested her legs on one shoulder, thrusting deep inside rubbing her clit wanting to suck her pink pearl badly, it was large, fat, and juicy surrounded by pink and brown lips. He pushed in her while she invited him deeper.

She sucked his neck he fucked deep, it's the first time she let him push hard he loved it as did she. Safinah came three times by his count he released in her they spooned he held her as close as he could falling asleep to the sound of her beating heart. Safinah slept in his arms wearing nothing but the bracelet on her flawless dark skin as the full light of the silver moon drenched the sparkling diamonds in the amber glow of the room. Dozing, he was finally legally married.

The next morning Clarence walked into the kitchen stopping at the door, Isabel hurriedly closed the shutters.

"What is ya doin in my kitchen? I oughtta let da light fetch cha." Kissing her, "good morning, Isabel." Avril teased him, "what cha done ta dat gal last night boy haha?" "Youse ain't speaking on my picaninny iffin she a saloon whore. She married, a respectable God-fearin young Ms."

"Yes ma'am." Clarence and Avril quieted smiling. "Takes her dis here tray Clarence, tells her I say drinks da jug a water first. I puts two licks of head powder in it on count her havin spirits. Ain't no fussin Mammy say swalla it. Dat be all."

"Yes ma'am." Clarence carried the tray of water, juice, fresh fruit, sausage eggs and biscuit with a large bottle of lamb's blood for him, warmed. He sat the tray on the floor next to her beautiful hair messy on her sexy crown.

"Clarence what is we doin on da flo?" She looked at arm her jaw dropped. "Baby? this here be beautiful." "Ya saw it last night Fi." handing her the powder mix. "I did?" "Yes, Mrs. Hollings." "I thanks ya proper?" "Oh yes ma'am." "Fresh hehe!" "Why da flo?" "Ya jump on the bed askin I join ya." "Sweet baby Jesus hehe." She wiped loose kinky billows from her face. "My dress?" He pointed in two directions. "We has us a good time Mrs. Hollings." She ate laying back down, he lay with her. "Do ya gots farmin Clarence?"

"I do not. I'm spendin a week with my new bride showering her with gifts once a day. Ya have one from last night peek out cha window." He backed up across the room avoiding sunlight. Safinah cracked the shutters to Elijah holding an expensive horse with a carriage made for two. The carriage had a bow on it, in the back the initial their last name a cursive H. Elijah waved at her excited she waved back. "Clarence is he mine honey he so pretty da horse. That the carriage from da catalog from France?"

"Yes love, the horse and carriage, I saw ya eyin it in town and she pretty Cotton." "I love it. When we ridin?" "Tonight, to da lake." The women tapped the door he handed her a robe. "Enter." They looked around snickering.

"I'll return" Clarence exited to read the paper. The bracelet can we see Fi?" She removed it passing it around. "It's flashy I love it Ann but ya knows I'll take a bulk of cloth before this thing." "Hush ya mouth he thought of ya, papa would neva buy me no diamond."

"One day when dem picaninnies gone, he gonna buy you da world wait and see." "I hope Fi." "How he? Did you do what I said Safinah?" Lily inquired. "Ya'll acts like dis our first time." "Married it is Fi married special." "I aint know much after dem spirits. I hear we has a time Lil" They giggled loudly it rang through the house.

Knock Knock. "Come." Caleb entered with a wooden box. "Mornin ma'am I has a gift." "A dog Caleb." "Yes, ma'am seeing how you likes ta ride the fence line and goes to town ta trade, this one here they call a Pitt Bull, he good fa huntin pigs and rats, his jaw locks he crunch bone. What cha name him Fi?"

"Caleb." "Missus how we know if ya callin me or him?" "Ise say big Caleb when I call." "Alright." "I love him, thank ya kindly. Clarence knowed you gots me a dog? Peety hates em say da slave Massa use em ta find us." "We usin him ta find them first if dey be near our land Fi." Safinah smiled.

Safinah couldn't walt for the sun to go down, she loved the horse & carriage more than the bracelet. She went to the barn to hitch it and pull it up front herself she was so excited.

"All hitched and ready to go Cotton?" "I use ta be a coachman, old one died I got the job." "He died Fi?" He chuckled. "Slave died; da rich man come fo me." "Here Fi," she took the picnic basket and blankets.

He placed two rifles under the seat, push ya foot hard Safinah. A shot gun popped out the floor which Clarence caught. There's a pressure spring ya push it back in when done. "See a secret pocket?" "Where Peety?" "Look harder." she stared. "A door." Safinah pressed it, 4 short throwing knives were lodged inside the door.

"One on each side ya practice Fi?" "Yes'sir." "Test tomorrow from dis here carriage." "Ise ready." They enjoyed the ride and each other's conversation.

Clarence set up the blanket and food basket under a tree close to a huge open area with lots of lush green grass the glowing moon shined bright. Clarence struck a match against his boot heel lighting five pickle jars with candles. He then dropped large patches of mint around the blanket corners. "What fo Peety?" "Mosquitoes they hate the smell a mint."

"I love ya smart where ya learn?" "A book on bugs when I enter town. How ya doin wit ya letters Fi? I haven't been on ya bout cha letters, we have this wedding behind us your reading start again wit Lily and papa. I think our picaninnies need schoolin one of ya need to master it Fi.

If I build a schoolhouse on the property, would ya teach?" "Yes, Peety please!" "Learn dem letters woman."

They cuddled enjoying the star lit sky "do you hear dat Fi?" "Hear what honey?" "A woman and man screaming?" "Where?" "Close hurry get on." Safinah climbed on his back. "Wrap your legs, hold me tight don't let go cotton." She closed her eyes when she opened them, they were farther in the woods. "Shhhh it's Chance."

Clarence kept quiet they were fighting over Money Chance won in a card game. Clarence saw seventeen-year-old Mary in the back.

Mary Hollings Origins....

"Get the nigger gal he sweet on." "I'll give your money let the girl go." "No, you gonna give us all we lost and whatever else you gots, like that gold time piece on your waist." Chance removed his watch emptying his pockets dumping everything on the ground.

Safinah mouthed 'help them!' Clarence waited, he knew these types, never happy, you do as they say it's never enough. Clarence quietly removed his boots Safinah was scared and excited at the same time. "Quiet." he mouthed absent sound to his wife.

"Let the girl go!" One licked her face while cupping her breast reaching under her dress, Chance knocked two of the robber's unconscious, Clarence shot out grabbing the third man from behind, but not before the robber threw Mary to the ground, her head hitting a large rock cracking her skull.

Clarence pushed three men off a nearby cliff. Chance knelt "Mary honey?" She opened her eyes blood soaking her canary yellow sweater. "She's going to die if you don't hurry Chance. "Can you turn her Clarence?"

"Do you love her?" "I care for her; I don't want her to die." "You have my permission ta turn her, but ya gotta ask if she wants to be vampire Chance." Chance fell to his knees at her side holding her head bleeding gently in her arms.

"Mary?" The moonlight glistened off the blood-stained rock Safinah tore her dress edges wrapping her head. "Mary you gonna die baby." "Chancie, I love you, don't allow me to die." She slurred losing consciousness swiftly. "You can live but you aint walkin in da sun no mo' and we live on blood. We ain't havin picaninnies in exchange fo' long life." "I can't have our baby Chancie?" "I'm vampire we can't make life May." "May I be your wife?" "If ya have me baby."

Chance pushed her head exposing his fangs in glistening moonlight sinking them into her jugular as he fed unconsciousness consumed her. Chance opened her mouth dropping his blood in. He pinched her nose holding her mouth closed causing her to swallow before coughing violently. "She takes it Chance?" "Yes Safinah."

Chance picked Mary up, Safinah got on Clarence's back follow me. When they got to the carriage Chance was out of breath. He put Mary inside with Safinah. Clarence tied her to the carriage seat. "We're running alongside the carriage while Safinah races to da house Chance."

"Sunrise, I smell it. You ready Cotton?" "Yes Clarence." "Not too fast Safinah." Coachman, I knowed how ta run a team." "Yes, coachwoman." Clarence winked. They were home before sunrise. Isabel, Ann, and Avril waited in the kitchen. Isabel cleared the kitchen table, laying her on it.

"Let us women folk work."Safinah requested. The men exited the kitchen to give Mary privacy. They cleaned her and gave her fresh clothes, she woke... "Chance!" He rushed to her side he picked her up carrying her to his bed the women followed finishing what they started.

Once clean and dressed they left her in his care. "Look Clarence, Mary ain't let go Chance's hand. Gals grip tight while sleeping. She loves him, like I loves ya Peety." As they readied for bed, Caine knocked on the door. Its Mary's kin, Clarence she never show home."

Clarence tossed on long johns and pants, escorting her parents to her bedside. He explained the entire story except the part where he pushed the robbers off a cliff. Safinah explained she shouldn't be moved due to her head injury. Thank God Mary didn't open her eyes, they may've passed out.

Her mother cried; thankful they saved the life of their child. Clarence offered them a room in the house next to their daughter. Her mother decided to stay her dad returned to open the haberdashery. They agreed Chance should explain to her mother about Mary's eyes as Clarence rode shot gun. The sun rose and set three times, when Mary woke at 9 p.m. her eyes were blazing. Safinah wrapped her head for appearances.

Chance was drinking a milk bottle of blood in the kitchen with Isabel & Avril nervous cause he fetched hisself a young bride. "You loves her ain't cha gambler?"

"I do Avril." Avril sipped black coffee staring out the windows as his good memories danced under the stars. Slave Massa try and rob us a' lovin Chance, say we savages we ain't knowed love. I done love dis woman since first seent. She ain't want ole Avril, I keeps trying. Took me fo' years fo' Isabel gimme a lookin haha."

"Ain't no four, be five don't cha come storyin on me ole coot hehe." "Izzy Ise love to death gambler when dey take us from Massa Alex Ise rightly fraid. Old slave like me and my Misses? Ise on plantation since Ise nine I thinks. Dey ought be shame sellin us one by one 'cause Missy Clara husband dead. Some say he owe a heap a gamblin debt Chance."

"Avril right Chance, Ms. Minnie holds us last, make da slaver try his best sell us as one. God shine on me an' Avril when I seent my baby from da auction block. My heartbeat rightly for the first time in long." Isabel grabbed Avril's hand. "I done somethin good when I raise dat boy Chance." "You did ma'am." They didn't know Clarence & Chance owned it, they processed the paperwork in his company name.

Lily ran to the kitchen "She up!" Chance ran up the steps. Mary's eyes a brown glow. Her mother hugged her, what happened to her eyes Safinah?

Yes, Emily Mary hit her head da blood loss change he eye color dat be normal when a head hit hard as hers is." Mary drew her mother's attention away from the bogus explanation. Mama, I have something to explain, please don't be cross, I wed Chance when we went on a date. Emily was an educated woman. Her slave master made projects out of her slaves teaching the savages how to read, write, and conduct themselves properly. She took a fancy to Emily teaching her how to run a general store from the age of six including where and how to order goods. When Mary was raised after the emancipation, she passed on her Masters ways including reading writing and proper diction. At seventeen Mary completed a colored teaching school in Boston and was a certified teacher. This was a huge reason Chance wanted Mary; she'd be an asset to the Hollings family. "What Mary...are you with child?" "No ma'am! We haven't had relations mama." "I'm not gonna tell ya daddy you come home have Chance ask for your hand proper. I'll make sure he says yes. If not you will leave his house without his blessing and we do not want that."

Mary smiled reassuring at her mother. "Mr. Clarence, had a white Dr. Look at me he say for me to stay out the sun until he says its fine mama." "I know you ok, these good folks. Mr. And Mrs. Hollings I hold you personally responsible for my Mary's chastity." "Yes ma'am" Clarence agreed. "Mama, can you get me cold water please." "I shall return shortly baby." Safinah showed her to the kitchen. Mary smiled.

"What cha doin May? It's a secret, ain't it Chance? Quickly blood." Chance cut his finger staining her head dressing. Her mother returned handed her water but Mary dropped it." "I feel dizzy mama."

"Ooh, she's bleeding. She needs to rest a spell I change it whiles you go to da kitchen fo Mammy ta feed ya Emily." Lily escorted her to the kitchen to chat with her about spring colors after Emily thanked Safinah. Chance stared at Mary, "you hungry?"

"You gotta feed her Chance." Chance bit his forearm holding it to Mary's dainty lips. "Thank ya, Fi."

Morning came, there was a knock on the house door, Mammy opened it. "Is the plantation owner here?" "Yes'sir." "Get him." She fetched Clarence, he was asleep. "Wake up! Law mens at the door." Isabel whispered. Safinah helped him dress properly and fast. She wrapped her head like a slave adorning tattered clothes, as did the others when white visitors were in the house.

Safinah led them to the drawing room. She opened the shutters making sure Clarence's chair was situated outside the sunlight that kissed the floor at his feet. "Gentleman," he smiled, smoking his pipe, "how can I help?" "Good day sir. We are going from plantation to plantation looking for three men. They been missing a spell. They removed sketches--this one here, the mayor's grandson and this one, the constables nephew."

Clarence took a long look. "Can't say I've seen them myself, however, I'll ask my niggers if they have." he handed Safinah the papers, "Show this around wench."

"Yes'sir." "I'll do anything to help the Sheriff and the Mayor. I voted for them. I do business with the mayor; I have attended his annual ball." "You and your missus good sir?" "God called her home two winters ago I'm afraid gentlemen, consumption." "Sorry sir, I lost a relative or two myself condolences. I have a sister you may want to take a gander. She's beautiful sir." "Is she? The mayor's ball is in a few weeks will she be in attendance?" "Yes sir." "May I count on you for a proper introduction?" "Yes, you may sir." Safinah returned. "No, Massa, no one knowed dey face."

"My niggers are not allowed to leave, though, they're free by law. Inform them if they leave, they're not to return. As you see you need permission to get on and off the property, they want to be paid they won't leave the plantation."

"Yes, I see." "It is to keep them in keep an eye on my assets prevents theft. Niggers cannot be trusted even though they're paid fair." The men laughed "We understand." Clarence walked them as far to the front door as he could. "If you gentleman need me, please do not hesitate to call on me." Isabel opened the door seeing them out. "Who let em on da plantation Clarence?"

"Papa Nate in charge a' da gate. Honey we must let constables on. White people don't hide from da law?" Safinah trembled taking a seat before her knees buckled from beneath her. "Why ya shaky Cotton? Show her family." Avril, Niarchos Chance, Caine and Elijah came from hidden positions inside the house with loaded rifles.

Papa, had two guns, Ann, and his daughter and sons, are in the windows of his house with rifles, near the gate in case they run. "Papa Nate?" "Ise chere Clarence." "How he hears ya from dat house Peety?" "Years ago, there was a tunnel, we cleared it to lead us to Papa's house from under the floor." He raised a trap door under the carpet. Safinah looked down the escape shaft. "Papa hears everything going on in here he knowed ta shoot fo' dey reach da gate Cotton."

"Meow" Safinah lifted the tablecloth in the dining room knowing they didn't allow cats in the house. Lily was on her belly holding a loaded rifle. "They may get in, but dey ain't gettin out Cotton."

# Chapter 28
# Love Is a Serious Business

Present Day
2020 Gullah Island
Vampire Games...

"What the hell is this, Joan?" "Come look." "What is that swimming in the blood?" "I'm unsure Zion. It's the sample you took from Chance. The blood is magnified by One hundred I pray no one fed from him."

"They look like a parasite Joan." "How does a parasite live on dead blood?" "Call the hospital to inform staff when drawing Chance's blood treat it as contaminated. I'll be in New York Wednesday they are less aggressive in O negative blood. They become aggressive in Tox blood which Chance drinks at card games, look Joan." Zion put a blood sample in a Petre dish injecting Tox blood the parasite moved angrily.

"Zion its drinking the Tox not Chance's blood and releasing something white. Look's gooey, they're moving slow in the goo." "Joan?" "Yeah bae?" "Will you be my wife?" Joan sat shocked. "I know you were looking for a romantic way for me to ask,

I thought of 1000 ways, none made sense I--" "Yes Zion!" "I'm going to ask papa for your hand Joan and offer a dowry. Is there anything you want?" "To be vampire Zion, please ask papa Nate." "Anything for you love."

New York City
Our Lady of Lourdes Hospital
Safinah Hollings Memorial Unit
Infectious Disease Unit....

The hospital phone rang disturbing the peace. "How are you feeling?" "I'm throwing up pop."

"Your sick somethings wrong Chance, medical will find it. Zion is directing our vampire medical staff on handling your medical care." I want to see Mary pop." "She hasn't awakened son." "I'll hate you if you take her from me pop." Chance cried speaking weakly. "Get better Chance, I love you son." Clarence and Chance hung up feeling despair. 'Baby, He's sick it's not Chance speaking." "I know Sugar."

Elder Vaughn & Ebon
Gullah Island....

"You tossed me under the bus Vaughn, you told the Queen I told Daisy." "It's true, I won't lie for you Ebon." "You didn't defend me Vaughn we're married." "I took responsibility for your actions Ebon that's what a husband does. You're embarrassed you were reprimanded publicly." "I love you Ebon but we're vampires, there are laws we must follow. Apologize tonight I command you as your maker, Elder and man. Gabriel didn't deserve that."

Mya & Elder Elijah
Gullah Island Georgia....

"Do you know Gabriel asked I be her mid-wife, Elijah?"

"Clarence is not going to allow it, I'd feel better if Zion handled it, this baby's not a regular, anything could happen I don't want you responsible Mya." "I can work with Zion I think it's important Gabriel has a human female in the room to make her comfortable." "Agreed babe if you're aiding Zion as his nurse, no problem." "Did Clarence dote on Safinah like he does Gabriel Elijah?" "Yes, however he is more into her." Mya wondered why. "I'm worried his love may cloud his judgement one day bae."

Papa Nate & Elder Ann...

"My wives know I asked you to Marry me again Ann." "Do they know you want a divorce Nate?" "Not yet." "Who is upset Penny?" "How did you know Ann?" "Penny never liked me; her glare was venomous." "The one I'm concerned with is my human wife, Shelly, she may harm herself." "Why?" "She was a foster child aged out of care and started being homeless. When we met, she'd started prostitution."

"Shelly came from a good family Ann, mostly Doctor's, her parents died in a car crash when her grandmother took her in but died at 93." "How'd you meet Nathan?" "Shelly offered me jelly roll Ann. With one look I knew she was raised better than that. She was twenty-four, I took her on as a housekeeper. She kept me company when we separated. We'd laugh, play hearts and before I knew it, ten years passed. I fell in love and asked she marry me." "Ten years you never had sex Nate?" "No Ann." "Why?" "She needed to heal, mourn, and get her mentality right." "You don't have to leave Nathan. I understand she comforted you. Do you want to stay married to her?" "Not if it means losing you again Annie." "You won't lose me Nathan ever again, she's human, I'll have you to myself again one day Nate, I love you."

Mara & Elder Niarchos....

"Hi, Mara, sorry I've been busy, can we meet tonight after the games?" "Sure." "Where are you?" "In my room it's not a suite Niarchos." "You think I always had suites?" "Hehe no." "What've you heard about me Mara? "You were a slave, you love motorcycles, fast cars, you were married once, your wife passed, she was human. You're picky over women you date is that true?" "Yes." "Why?" "I fall in love fast. I think it's a lost art, vampires admitting they love. can I call you back Mara?" "Sure."

Niarchos & Gabriel......

There was a knock on his hotel door. "How'd you get here?" "I drove." "Can you drain your blood in a glass Niarchos?" "No Gabriel." "I can't stop thinking about it." "Does the Pharoah know you're here?" "No Nicky." "Where does he think you are?" "Shopping." "Did you shop Gabriel?" "Yes." "She plopped on the couch handing him a high-ball glass." "If you want my blood drink from the vein Gabriel." "Nicky we can't that shit's exotic hehe."

Niarchos removed his shirt using a thin razor cutting his neck, "come." She looked away embarrassed of her lust for his blood, smelling the sweetness and aroma made her stomach growl. The day he was burned she controlled herself from attacking him, his rich red blood oozing thick calling the vampire within.

"It's making a mess Gabriel come before I close it off." The vampress in him cowgirl straddled him licking blood off his shoulder bicep up to the open wound. She sucked, feeding from him moaning rubbing his back and shoulders lost in his smell.

Coming up for air... "am I hurting you Nicky?" "You're funny," exhaling a sexy whisper. Gabriel bit again because the cut closed, he growled turning her on. "Why did you bite me,

Gabriel?" Lying... "I wanted to see if you'd jump Nicky." "From a mosquito bite?" "Hehe."

Niarchos rubbed her back feeling the warm split of her pussy ride his lengthy shaft through his jeans, she sucked his sweet spot, his hard on had her name written on it from shaft to tip. She pressed her weight on it grinding seductively slow knowing it was hers. The more he groaned from her grind ride the more she sucked, as she guided his large hands through her untamed hair. Niarchos restrained himself from unhooking her bra. "You done?"

"Don't you like holding me, Nicky?" "Too much." He looked away answering her so she missed the surrender in his eyes for her. She pushed her 200 plus pounds on his throbbing dick the wet of her pussy now outside her jeans on him. Niarchos tossed his head back biting his bottom lip high of his new drug called Gabriel. "Do you feel weak?" "I'm an old vampire, it takes more than forty minutes of feeding to drain me, Gabriel." "Why does your blood taste like that Nicky?" "Like what?" "Coffee with a lot of sugar." "I'm unsure," he grinned shyly. "The baby craves it, Nicky." "You wanted it before the pregnancy Gabriel."

She washed her face rinsing her mouth shaky because she almost had an orgasm on his lap. "You must feed from pop before the games Gabriel." "I'm full Nicky." "It looks suspect if you don't pop knows you're eating for two you have to feed with him as long as you did with me until your content Gabriel." She looked at his dick. "See what you did?"

"How you gonna remedy it?" licking her lips "You wanna watch Gabriel?" "Oh gosh, I almost forgot, hold this Nicky," handing him a gold medallion with the coven crest, on the back, the day Clarence was turned. "This is nice Gabriel." "Clarence is nosey, hold it so he doesn't find it at the cabin please. oh, and add a chain if you want to spice it up Nicky." He pecked her opening the door reluctantly. A housekeeper saw Gabriel leave, she called Clarence informing him.

The Cabin........

"Calm down Clarence! You always get crazy over your woman." "What was she doing in his room?!" Zion and Elijah tried calming him when Gabriel entered. "Hey all." Lulu ran for her bags scurrying away. "Clarence rushed Gabriel at the door where were you, Gabriel?" "Shopping, you know that." "Where else Sugar?"

"Coffee look," ...holding up a baby romper set. "I got blue for a boy cause' I know you secretly want a son honey." She pecked him ignoring his upset. "Why're you looking at me like that Clarence?" "Leave." Elijah and Zion stayed. "Now!"

They exited staying close. "Vampires are my children when they see something they're taught to report, they're my eyes, where were you woman?" "I told you." "Don't make me scan your thought, Gabriel." "Go ahead." He tried she blocked him. "How'd you learn that?" "Old Indian."

"Don't make me bite you, Gabriel." "Bite and you hurt the baby. Your venom is too strong you'll kill both of us two for one." He hyper-sped grabbing her waist. "AHHHH!" Elijah rushed in; Clarence had Gabriel pinned to the bed. Zion ran in. "Don't bite her Clarence, I'm begging you!" Zion begged.

"Leave!" He ripped her yoga pants and panties off, pushing his tongue into her pussy gently. He tossed his head back swallowing her truth. He didn't need her blood for a truth pull any bodily fluid would due. Cody taught her well before she left with Eagle, because she was a hybrid the whole truth including her session with Niarchos was missing.

Gabriel trembled in fear she almost peed herself. Her head turned so she wouldn't meet the savage. His breath was rapid and dick hard. She punched him in his chest "Don't fuck me! DON'T! I don't want you inside of me ever again! Let go you're hurting me pressing your weight on my tummy!"

She scratched his neck biting his shoulder, attempting to push him off open slapping him wildly. He got off shocked she thought he'd rape her. She grabbed her purse, ran to the bathroom locking the door, crying, and screaming loudly sitting on the floor under the sun calling Niarchos. "Nicky?! I want to leave now!" "What happened Gabriel?" "Come get me Nicky, he's trying to hurt us! "I'm coming Gabriel." "Ok," she cried sniffling.

Niarchos called Elijah. "What the fuck is happening?" "Gabriel was seen leaving your room by a housekeeper in Caleb's coven." "

Caleb told her to bring the medallion they're presenting to him at the games. Caleb said he always finds our gifts, he asked she drop it to me because he's busy and didn't want to risk losing it." "Elijah explained what happened to Niarchos." "Pop pinned her down for fucking what Lijah?!" "Niarchos? Stay where you--"

"Hello Nick? Jesus." "What now Elijah?" "He's on his way. We don't need that huge negro vampire in here fighting Clarence this is a mess he has to control his jealousy Zion." Gabriel exited the bathroom packing her clothes, she wasn't speaking but was still crying. Clarence sat watching her every move, she went for the door. He blocked her. "Move!" "MOVE NOW!" He stepped aside she raced down the stairs running for the patio, but he beat her there, "move now Clarence!"

Grabbing a sterling silver candle stick she tossed it through the patio door breaking it, the sun scorching his back. Clarence hissed in pain fangs popped he moved out of sunlight but before she could get to the door, he swept her up in his arms blood dripping, skin slipping carrying her back to the bedroom locking the door as she beat, scratched, and slapped his third-degree burns. The pain was searing but he refused to drop her. Open the fucking door slapping and

Punching him, he turned his bleeding back to her, blocking the door, his pain at an all-time high. Zion came to the door. "Great One?" "What!" They said simultaneously. "Clarence, please open the door. "She's not leaving Elijah." He breathed raspy his lugs seared badly as he grew weak. "You can't hold her against her will, Pharoah? You're breaking your own law."

"Clarence it's Joanie, Gabriel is still half human you're scaring a human woman she doesn't understand our ways fully please honey open the door all this stress isn't good for the baby the pregnancy is still young." He held his bleeding head to the door wiping his tears sniffing while she punched his bleeding back. "May we see Gabriel? Zion's worried about the baby...please Clarence." He stepped aside. "Gabriel don't leave, tell him why you were with Niarchos" Elijah begged, Niarchos explained it to me.

"If I say, Caleb is going to be upset he worked hard on this he needs to trust me. Did he treat his precious first wife this way?!" Elijah, I'm commanding you and Zion to hand me all your cash. "My Queen?" "Money! Give me all you have please," still sobbing mascara running. *Don't give her a dime* sending a telepathic message to Zion and Elijah. "We can't Gabriel." She opened the door running into the sun Jupiter barked running after her. Clarence watched as she started the Rolls Royce. "Get in Jupe!" "You shouldn't allow a woman to drive angry Clarence, what happens if she has an accident?" Elijah was livid. "What the fuck do you think I was trying to do Elijah!" "Did it dawn on you we're all excited over a blood born vampire birth Clarence? This is more than a blessing or miracle, it's science and bigger than all of us. It's the next evolution of the vampire. I warned you, Safinah was smothered stop before you lose Gabriel Clarence and your child along with her."

Gabriel hopped in driving to the gate, "open it." "Pharoah said not to." "Open the fucking gate or I'll climb it, if I hurt myself who's head will roll?" The human guard opened the gate. She peeled off heading for the main highway out of town. Clarence blew up her phone while they fussed over his inflictions, he locked on her mind sensing hurt outrage and fear. He connected to her mentally begging her forgiveness.

Gabriel heard and ignored him. She looked at her texts it was Caleb.

Caleb: Look in your glove compartment. Opening it there was $30,000. Gabby: I'll pay you back. Caleb: You'll do no such thing that's coffee money to the rich you'll catch on. When you calm down call your husband, Clarence is a good vampire but has a flaw...jealousy. He wasn't going to rape you I promise that he was trying to be sexy his attempt failed sweetie that's all. If I tell you something you swear never to repeat? Gabby: I swear. Caleb called her.

"Hey sweetie Chance was madly in love with Safinah as Niarchos loves you they had an affair. It's in her diaries, that's why Ann told you whatever you read hold it in confidence. Safinah wanted his new wife to have them, there is a reason for it. Niarchos will give his life for yours, he would defy the Pharoah, that's how deep his love is. You must never use the love of these vampires for you as weapons to be used against father and son. Do you think Clarence let any woman beat on him? I saw that and said sock it to him honey!" She giggled through tears.

"It's ok to love two vampires, you can't step over the line. She hung up with Caleb thinking of her aunt's words. *Gabs! You don't run when things get hard, you hang in there you always run, weak women run.* "Yes, auntie, I hear you," she whispered.

"Caleb, can I sing tonight?" "Of course, before the games begin? Yes, I sent clothes to the rental." Gabriel returned to the barn space taking a hot bath in the sun lightning bouncy bubbles. She sipped tea enjoying the peace unwinding. It was evening she heard birds singing. She knew when the sun dipped into the horizon Niarchos would be at her door. He was.

Jupiter growled, warning her someone was there. "It's fine baby." Gabriel went to the window looking down at Niarchos in the bathroom hiding in the shade of the tree line out of the sun. She left the tub smelling like cherries, he could smell her bath water from outside. Gabriel opened the door as he hypersped from the tree line to the barn house. He sat on the couch.

"Burned?" "No worries, Gabriel its minor," as she passed a bottle of blood to him. "What happened?" Patting the empty sofa cushion next to him.

"A housekeeper said I came from your room." "Nosey jealous ass bitches them be the same hoes leaving filthy panties on my pillowcases or under my sheets. I told Elijah it was because of the medallion if it weren't for that you wouldn't have come Gabriel." "Yes, I would've Nicky. You're the only friend I have. Look how fast you helped me. Clarence pinned me to the bed. I was screaming and guess what? Elijah and Zion walked in and saw me, that way he told them to leave, and they did Nicky. He was hard, doing that, turned him on. The worst part is he pressed his weight on my stomach he could've hurt the baby. He was checking to see if we had sex Nicky."

"We can smell another partner days after the deed is done. You women can't smell it, but we can especially when it was left by a human Gabriel. He should know I would never do that I love you, but I won't have sex with his wife it's wrong looking down in shame."

Gabriel moved closer to him. "Don't feel ashamed because we love one another it's not our fault." "What do you mean?" "My grandmother would say love is love if you find it once you're blessed twice fortunate three times downright lucky. I found you and Clarence, I guess that makes me fortunate Nicky. Look, pulling a strand of Pearl's. You gave me these for my engagement, remember?" "I do." "I carry them all the time." "Why Gabriel?" "Cause' you gifted them to me Nicky." She snuggled close with the pearls wrapped around her fist. He wrapped his huge arms around her making her feel safe, something Clarence failed at lately.

"If you were there and he commanded not to assist, would you listen Nicky?" "No, I was prepared to be court marshalled pop broke his own laws. I was getting in the limousine when you called. Elijah begged me not to come, he knew shit would get real." "I broke the patio door exposing him to the sun."

"Haha you're crazy Yoooo haha! Pop loves you real talk." "Was he like that with Safinah?"

"Yes and no, it was a different time, white people were tripping our women couldn't go to town alone for fear of rape or death. I understood it then but now it's different." "Did Clarence have a girl when Safinah died Nicky?" "Yep, her name is Lee, she's a lawyer like a Johnny Cochran for vampires, she only works death cases." "What happened with them?" "I think they grew apart ma. She didn't want to marry, and pop did. He's the marrying type real old school. You feel nice next to me Gabriel." He pulled her closer. "It's gonna be ok; you get to calm down and so does pop."

His phone rang, he showed her the caller's ID. "Yes Pharoah...yes, she was Pharoah. I can't say why she was there Great One, don't you trust me pop? I'm your son I would never betray you." There was a pause, "You'd take the word of a chamber maid bitch over your own wife and child pop listen to yourself? No pop I can't tell you why she was here, you'll learn soon. If you don't learn by night's end, I'll explain before sun rise, agree? No, I haven't heard from Gabriel. Yes pop, see you tonight."

"What'd he say?" "Pop said tell you he's sorry and please come back to him his heart is aching." She rolled her eyes hugging him tighter. Niarchos called out 'Siree play Wyclef Jean 911.' This is bad what we got Gabriel," as the music echoed. "Yes, it is Nicky." Niarchos approached the door "I'll see you in the sky box beautiful." Pecking her, she grabbed his leather biker jacket pulling him into her magnetic energy, kissing him ardently this time with her soul.

He grabbed her waist, picking her up, pressing her to the door then putting her down, opening the door swiftly leaving. Gabriel sighed thinking about Niarchos, how tall and he was she loved strong men, that's one of the reasons she loved Clarence, but Niarchos ignited her fire. He was bad for her a vining weed in her garden. She sat on the edge of the bed with the balls of her feet heels up on the floor. She thought of his hard dick under her as she fed dry humping him, the smell of his flesh as horniness rose in him, the taste of his blood, how his hands molded to conform to the curves in her back. Her heat index rose feeling his hands roam over her massaging as she drank from him. She imagined unzipping his Jean's giving that hard beautiful dick the space is needed to grow, raising her body up only to slip down on top of it giving it the attention it deserved. Her fingers wandered to her throbbing clit, before she started, she set up her phone recording her sensual performance.

Gabriel sat rubbing ready to burst, gliding her fingertips over rising nipples, pulling her clit pushing her fingers in and out of her pussy tasting herself. Consumed with lust for him whining "I want you Nicky," rubbing faster, harder busting, a cum squirt puddle pooling at her stretched toes she popped her fangs, calling his name lost in her private moment. "Come fuck me Nicky please." She was nutting again remembering how sweet he tastes and what the ride on his dick would feel like. She was so horny this baby was making her want to fuck and Clarence was refusing... she needed it. I need you inside of me imagining she was tearing that fat hard long dick up, bouncing on it fucking him good and proper. Popping a nut again arching her back holding her feet up legs open rubbing swift and hard her fingers moving a mile a minute.

"Ahhh see what you make me do?" She sent the video to Niarchos deleting it. Niarchos saw a video from her but didn't open it. He escorted the Elders to the arena for the games. Elijah, Mya, Zion, Joan, and Clarence exited the car

when they arrived, Gabriel was already seated Elijah pointed to her whispering, "trust the process," patting Clarence's back. Gabriel greeted everyone except Clarence. Niarchos escorted her on stage "I sent you something. Nicky" "Am I going to regret opening it? I'll open it when I'm alone." Staring, eyes blazing. "Delete it, I command you." Mouthing the words something they did so no one would hear embarrassed now that she had time to think. He bowed his head in submission she kissed his palm. "Thank you, Nicky."

"Tonight, on our last night of the first annual vampire games, our Queen Gabriel Hollings will perform. Clarence was surprised Gabriel was performing. Niarchos blocked the stage entrance he loved all of her including her voice. The spotlight was on her.

"Thank you, Elder Caleb." Gabriel held the mic, looking down as a silence swept over the crowd. "If you know this song; a million reasons by Lady Gaga please join in. For you.... bowing her head closing her eyes in respect for the Pharoah." Gabriel held up the number 1 while singing, all vampires held their phones high, lighting the dark arena. "Look at that," Elijah whispered to Mya, "vampires adore her."

"She's singing to Clarence." Ann whispered to Papa. Vampires gave a standing ovation not because she was Queen, but because they heard how she handled the situation with Daisy and Niarchos. Gabriel princess waved and smiled exiting stage left. Caleb hugged her "beautiful honey. Thank you." Vampire Elders stared at Clarence. "What?" "You know what Blaise responded." "Ok" "Okay what?" Papa pressed. "I'm sorry." "And?" Elijah chimed in. "It won't happen again." "No, it won't." Caine added.

"We don't enslave, and we don't scare women Clarence especially pregnant ones I don't like what you did not at all," Lily added. "I'm crazy for her." "We understand Clarence but you're scaring her." "Ok Annie." "Caleb entered the skybox "Calm down or you're going to push her and that baby away. Your heart is gonna break if that woman doesn't want you cause your jealous. This ain't 1865 women have choices Clarence." "Gabriel walked in they ceased their chastisement toward him. "You were wonderful honey." The women hugged her. "Thanks ladies."

"Good news I've spoken with Zion, he agreed to me aiding with the birth Gabriel." "Thank you, Mya," hugging her. Joan held out her hand flashing her engagement ring. "A Doctor's wife! Impressive. Now that's a rock Joan" "Thank you girl." Gabriel sat next to Clarence he tried kissing her she moved away. He put his hand out for her to hold, she refused his olive branch.

He left it open refusing to close it. She held it, he took his other hand rubbing the top of hers, staring sorrowfully. Vaughn arrived with Daisy and Eban. Daisy fell to her knees before Gabriel "Great One I'm so sorry please forgive me?" You're forgiven. Ebon kneeled before them I'm sorry Great Ones." "Has Elder Vaughn explained your fines, Daisy?"

"Yes, Great One, may I give you this? Elder Vaughn said you love baths." She handed her a large gift basket packed with expensive bath items." "Wow this is beautiful Daisy thank you." "It's from Ebon and I so sorry." "No need to keep apologizing once is enough whether people accept your apology or not, the point is you tried."

Mara ran into Niarchos in the hall. "Can I see you tonight?" "Sure." She puckered her lips he bent down pecking her." The stage was set for boxing papa's phone was chiming "any of you betting? One million on who you think will win. Clarence bet one million who else. Niarchos?" "Same. The boxers were vampires. Boxing began. Fifteen grueling rounds, no bells, hard hitting, no head gear and no gloves. Grip kept order around the ring with Niarchos.

The boxers arrived at the final round. Hurricane, a member of Elder Blaises' coven, vs. Mark Magna representing Elder Caine's coven stood. Caleb announced from the skybox, "as we have intermission, we'll return in thirty minutes." Blaise checked on Hurricane after taking an ice-cold shower. They fed him blood soaking his hands in ice decreasing the swelling.

Blaise gave his own blood, him being an older vampire sped the healing. Caine did the same. Vendors were open. Gabriel left to shop. Clarence handed her $5000. "Thank you." Niarchos escorted her to the booths. She saw a black braided bracelet in leather, "this one please." The shopkeeper wrapped it in brown paper with a red bow.

He showed her a bracelet it had an opening for spice. "If you get nauseated, you put mint in the tiny jar the smell can help we have the set, Queen." "I'll take it." She walked with Niarchos clear the way! Vampires stepped aside kneeling.

The fight resumed, hitting, pounding, and straight blows. It was brutal, magna fell they began the count, he couldn't steady on his feet. Hurricane won the vampire boxing match. Vampires were mad tearing up betting slips, but a lot were happy screaming.

"Fifteen rounds by TKO HURRICANEE!" The crowd roared wild vampress' lined up to meet both boxers. "I think I found you a guard Sugar." "Who ?" "Magna." "No Clarence, Nicky is my guard. You said I choose my guard." "You can, but he's an Elder he can't run a coven and guard you too." He saw upset in her. "Can we discuss it later, Sugar?" "Yes." kissing her hand. "Thirty million on Zhou Papa Nate!" Clarence yelled over the crowd.

"I'm tired, you can stay." "Are you sure?" "Yes, I'm going to the rental. Niarchos." "Yes pop. I'll ask Jamaica to stand in my place ringside" "Can you take my wife to the bed and breakfast... stay until I return, please son." "Yes pop." "Take the limo it's bullet proof. Gabriel kissed him bidding everyone goodnight." "You sick?" "Cold Nicky." He gave her his jacket and they got in the limo; she fell asleep on his shoulder. They arrived 'Alexis turn the heat to 75'. Niarchos carried her upstairs, He covered her with blankets exiting the loft. Clarence phoned Niarchos. "Is she sleep Niarchos...is she ok?" "Tired pop, tell Zion she complained of being cold." "We don't get cold, only hot son." "I know, I'm worried she fell asleep like in 5 minutes flat. She had a long day." "That she did. I'll have Zion look in on her tomorrow, Niarchos." "Ok." Niarchos fell asleep locking all doors and windows.

Martial Arts Competition......

Zhou fought 30 contenders. He took water and blood from Grip who was his corner man. Clarence instructed no vampire to nourish him except Grip who was assigned by the Pharoah to personally guard him remaining ringside the entire competition. Ten vampires remained. Zhou was undefeated. A master at his craft, he taught himself all forms of martial arts, whatever form of martial arts his opponent used, he matched it making it extremely hard to defeat him.

Round Thirty....

Zhou was tired but ready against his Chinese opponent, Chen Li Pei. His pardon depended on his return. The last few weeks were wonderful. He had an undocumented coven in chine with vampire rouges he helped discipline through mastering the arts and meditation, but it wasn't the same as being with his maker and his vampire American family. They respectfully greeted one another. The vampire warriors fought vigorously under bright arena lights as an authentic Chinese band played warrior music ringside. As the rums beat louder anxieties grew with every shocking blow. Karate, Kuma tae, crouching tiger, praying mantis, the styles kept coming as the crowd roared seeing them hyper speed switch styles like rapid fire.

Zhou triple tapped his neck then his forehead sweeping the bridge of his nose triple tapping his right temple, his opponent froze. The crowd inhaled, as silence and shock gripped the crowd. Clarence stood as the large TV caught the look of amazement on his face as he stared glued to what Zhou had done. Zhou looked around the astonished crowd, circling his prey, triple tapping his spine, shoulder blade, and rib cage. Before he could regain dexterity, Zhou pushed both palms into his chest knocking him out the ring rendering him unconscious. The crowd exhaled standing on their feet at the stellar unforgettable performance. Caleb walked in the ring naming Zhou the victor. "What the fuck was that?!" Papa yelled; they were in awe, whistling at his skills but not Clarence who was proud of his turn clapping knowing what he was capable of.

"Tonight, before we move to pardons and awards, the Elders want to present our Pharoah, with a gold medallion.

On the front, the crest of his house, a red rose with blood drops from a thorn. The back, the date he was made vampire. We recently found out our Pharoah is 190 plus years old. I'll save the plus, it's not polite to tell someone's age, but he old! Haha." Jamaica escorted Clarence on stage. "We had a time keeping this from you Great One." Caleb hugged and shook his hand. "I had Queen Gabriel pick it up at the coffee shop and drop it to Elder Niarchos so you wouldn't find it." "How do you hide surprises from a vampire who reads minds family haha?"

"On behalf of the Elder's, your bride Queen Gabriel, and all your vampire children here and abroad, we love you and present you with this hand pressed beautiful medallion forged on the Gullah islands. We love you Pharaoh, husband, father, brother, freer of men and friend." He accepted the medallion *you should feel bad,* Caleb telepathically speaking.

*I do* waving, smiling, and acting normal, Caleb handed him the mic clapping fake and plastic. "Thank you I want to say to my brothers and sisters who are Elders, thank you, the centuries with you have been colorful and exuberant my we usher in the next 100 with grace and change for our people. Thank you for not being afraid to check and love me when I'm wrong. I especially want to thank Elder Caleb and his coven the house of seers for all they did preparing this major event in such brief time." The claps were endless. "Our Dr. Zion Donovan and his fiancé Ms. Joan Freeman thank you for being on call you have no idea what you both mean to me."

"My security team, Elder Niarchos my son, vampire Jamaica, and his superior staff from Elder Blaise's coven thank you. To my son Prince Grip Hollings, thank you. Last but always first, I thank my wife and Queen, she went home, she was ill. Thank you, Gabriel, for loving a foolish, jealous, stubborn old vampire. I'm sorry sugar, I love you." Exiting the stage. Clapping and whistles echoed in the sir as the first annual vampire games came to a successful close.

Pardons Awards & Accolades......

Grip and Zhou Xie were pardoned for winning the competitions. Isaiah was pardoned for winning his piano performance. Not only did the judges state it was flawless, but they wanted Isaiah to start at Juilliart in the fall. Clarence enrolled him without his permission paying for the entire year tuition in advance. Mara won the painting contest the Elders chose her Malcolm X painting because she captured him wearing a fedora the Pharoah's favorite hat as well. It was a side of the late minister people rarely saw.

Clarence turned to Vaugh questioning him. "Vaughn?" "Yeah, Pharoah what's up?" "What are you doing with that young vampire, and you're married?" "He's a friend Clarence." "Vaughn, I know you be careful, Eban has a violent streak, I know his kind." "What kind is that gay Clarence?" "Don't mess with me Vaughn, you know I don't give a damn about your sexuality, or I would've never sired you I could care less who vampires love you know this. I say 'his kind' meaning, sweet on the outside, a volcano inside, watch yourself Vaughn. I promised your family I'd care for you; I'm keeping that promise. Don't think I am not informed about the domestic violence acts between you Vaughn. Your thoughts cry out to me when you slumber. I have been waiting for you to come to me. If you mess with this new vampire divorce Eban this is my counsel to you as you maker and friend, am I clear?" Vaughn hugged him.

"Yes, my maker. Any words on Chance Clarence? I phoned he's cross with me." "He'll be fine Pharoah." "Thank you, Vaughn." Clarence stayed late signing pardons in blood, so he didn't have to do it in the morning, all he had to do was hand them out. Clarence was anxious to get home to Gabriel, he hyper-sped to her ignoring Jamaica who begged he get in the limousine. Clarence knocked on the door, Niarchos drew his gun. "Who?" "Open it." "What time is it pop?" "Hour before sunrise." "Niarchos, I'm sorry." "It's cool pop, you need to say it to her she fears you. You can't do shit like that." "I know Niarchos." "She thinks you can do anything, and no one will help her pop." "I know you'd help Niarchos." He grabbed his jacket and helmet. "Take my bike son," tossing Niarchos the keys. Niarchos looked to the loft hearing Gabriel light snore exiting the renovated barn.

Clarence lay behind Gabriel spooning, she lay on her back looking behind his eyes feeling let down. "So sorry Sugar," kissing her neck and face. "You forgive me?" "You're scaring me, making me feel unsafe like I'm not your equal but your slave." "Gabriel, Sugar, please," she turned her back crying. "When I requested Zion and Elijah give me money, I commanded them as a Queen you said no Clarence, I heard you." "You heard me telepathically?" "Yes." He was shocked she heard him. "I know vampire law says I belong to you, but I belong to God and myself. I'm his child first, he loaned me to you. He trusts you to care for his child and what you did today, that's not caring for a gift he loaned you is it?" "No sugar it's not." "I don't care about your status or that you're King of vampires."

"I know the man who assisted with my garbage because I couldn't walk, mowed my lawn because I was too sick to stand, the man who'd pretend he was working a construction site and would come straight over after work. You hand spooned me soup you making me eat when I didn't want to. That's who I fell in love with, not all this, not who I saw yesterday! I'm not your prisoner, I'm not incarcerated Clarence. This is 2020 not 1800, I won't get raped because I went to the store."

"Gabriel, I love you. I'm afraid to lose you. I'm jealous I'll work on it." "You don't say?" They smiled. "I'm a vampire who has flaws, that's one, forgive me." "You embarrassed me smelling my pussy, like I was a whore." "It won't happen again," kissing her face. "Alright? I'll call Vaughn and ask him to draw up our new marital law, fix it so it works for wives of vampires, and you." Kissing him, "thank you." "We shall call it Gabriel's Law."

She kept kissing him, opening her legs and robe. She bit into his neck feeding. He got on top slipping in the head only. "If you're sorry gimme all of it sniffing tears scratching his back. He pushed himself in as gently as he could, thrusting short gentle strokes. She rubbed her clit while he pushed watching her on his knees, he saw everything her breasts, thick thighs, fupa and pink pearl pussy as she worked her pearl rubbing with four fingers fast. "You're gonna make me bust watching you." "Don't watch hehe."

He leaned in sucking her nipples. She slapped her clit making it red and swollen. The popping sound was music to his ears. "Spit on her Clarence make her purr for you." He let spit glide down in one long spit stream lubricating that juicy ass pussy making it shine, driving him mad, she pulled her pink lips apart showing him exactly what she was rubbing. Closing his eyes fuck he mumbled tossing his head back fangs on fleek. "Open them daddy." He stared watching her pinch, pull and tug her large clit, he pushed harder, not paying attention, to the Doctor's warning. Her flesh juicy thighs rippled with every push.

Her tummy wiggled sexy he loved the fat stomach, juicy thighs, fat tits and dimpled ass, he worshiped all of her loving every inch. Clarence bit his wrist dropping blood in her welcoming mouth. Gabriel grabbed his wrist sucking sweet rubbing his open vein on her nipples and clit. He pulled out sucking his blood from her clit licking her up the middle of her stomach slurping warm blood from her breasts. The savage emerged, he couldn't take her seductive teasing, rubbing, moaning, the beckoning, mixed with her sexually blended cocktail of self-pleasuring awakened every sensual sense within him. "Move," pushing his head. "If you're not gonna fuck me, I'll cum alone."

Clarence tethered to her clit holding it hostage it was his now to please her. Gabriel squirmed begging him to stop. Her pleas were ignored as Clarence clit locked her pearl to his throbbing tip tongue. Gabriel relinquished herself into his capable hands.

Clarence don't stop daddy please right there. Ahhh Clarence, baby... ah Clarence... ah baby shit!" He hopped on his knees slipping back inside tapping steadily, her legs spread eagle his hands on her ankles. "Pussy is so fucking tight Gabriel mmm."

Clarence held his head down pussy water splashing, wetting his hair, locking his curls as he attempted to loosen her tight snatch licking her off his lips. "Open your eyes no cheating daddy hehe!" She looked in his eyes. His iris colors were insane while he nutted, "FUCK!" He panted heavy, trembling, holding on to the head bored. "You think you can go seven months without this pussy Clarence?" "I don't think so Sugar haha." "Gabriel? I didn't mean to scare you, I'm a foolish jealous idiot." "Who called you Clarence?" "One of the maids." "You trust her over me?" "Yesterday Niarchos admitted he was in love with you Sugar." "Would you rather he lie daddy?" "No. I don't get it why're you drawn to him Gabriel?" "He makes me feel safe." "Over me?" "After today, yes." "I'll work on it Sugar." She dozed off thinking of Niarchos.

As soon as Niarchos dropped his jacket to the chair he played the video. He was aroused so much he licked his phone. Them thighs and sugar hips, fat ass full round plump tits, she aroused his sexual savage. He watched ten time's his dick leaking. *Delete it* he heard her command watching it again glued to her contours, the arch of her feet as she burst into sexual flames. *Delete it*, he heard her warning again. How she bit her lips, pulled her hair, called for him *'Nicky,'* he growled loud and angrily pressing delete.

He paced the floor, hands on his head. Damm! Remembering the smell of her open pussy as she sat on his lap, the lingering scent of her hair, neck, and cleavage, she had it bad for him and him for her. "I want to taste her," he whispered to himself knowing damn well he couldn't stop at that. His breathing rapid, fangs popped, he needed to fuck and now. "Hey, this is Elder Niarchos. What room is Mara in?" He went to her room.

Niarchos pushed her inside the room on the wall sliding her panties to the side. He pounded so hard the wall dented. Niarchos raised her to his mouth, legs on his shoulder's facing him as he indulged Ms. kitty, flicking her clit off his tongue. Tongue tip clit spanked her into sexual madness. "You like what this mouth do?" "Fuck yeah daddy," trembling she was excited and afraid she'd fall. Mara held his shoulder's tight fuck! Cum cream leaked rivers down his throat, beard, and chest. He lay on the floor pulling her on his face sitting session cowgirl ride. She rode his tongue when it wasn't deep inside her. Mara tried hopping up, but he locked her on his mouth massaging her thighs as he made her pussy his second home. Holding on to the bed corner she muffled her screaming, shooting cum down his throat.

Slipping out from under her they stood as he lifted her like a two-hundred-pound rag doll. "Bend over in front of me grab my ankles, Mara." Obeying her sexual master, she bent over ass up clutching his ankles while he doggy dug. He thought of Gabriel cumming on the video, calling for him, opening Mara's pussy releasing a load in her seeing Gabriel's face. Mara's legs were unsteady as his cum leaked down her thighs, he lay her on the bed pillow talking.

He kissed her thinking of Gabriel. "Elder?" "Yes bae?" "Do you like me?" "Yes why?" "I'm unsure." "You want to make sure it not for sex?" "Yes, sort of." "I don't do that have you heard any rumors of me sleeping with vampires? Going to strip parties other than work?" "No Niarchos." "If I didn't see a future with you, I wouldn't speak, do you wanna go for coffee publicly Mara?" "Sure thanks."

Gabriel was awakened to a foot massage. "Goodmorning how do you feel?" "Ok." "I must hand out pardons we leave tomorrow if you're up for travel Sugar. I'll see if Niarchos can sit with you while I'm at the cabin. Zion should be here by 3 o'clock. If I leave now, I'll return by six thirty." "Movie night honey?" "Yes, Sugar anything you want." Clarence dropped Gabriel at the main Cabin for her exam with Zion.

Zion opened his vintage Doctor's bag. "Look what the hospital sent as a gift. We plug it into an iPad, and we can see the baby." "I'd better wait for Clarence." "Don't you want a memory for you mommy? They'll be plenty of sonograms Gabriel." "Ok." "Your iron is low thus the cold you felt. I'll prescribe a low dose iron tablet to see if the vampire within you will allow it." He smiled happy to treat her.

She handed him her iPad he plugged in the sonogram equipment applying the warm gel to her belly. "Ok who do we have here mommy?" Rolling the sonogram ball over her 1-month pregnant tummy looking at her amazed as she positioned the tablet for them to view. Hold on using his stethoscope for clarity as a huge smile crept on his face. "What Zion!" "Shh Gabriel please, I can't hear." Rolling still snapping picture's he wrote in her chart removing the stethoscope holding her hand handing and the iPad. "There are three people in there Gabriel, one he pointed two and there is number three Mommy." "Oh man Boy's girls Zion?" "Can't tell yet sweetie. Triplets"

"After you get to New York nothing strenuous or upsetting please. Sorry about yesterday Joan reamed me out and Mya reamed out Elijah when they heard what transpired. When a woman is in trouble or needs help, we help moving forward no matter his temper Gabriel. Do you accept my apology Great One?" "Do I have a choice?" Tapping her tummy playfully. "They need their uncle Zion." "Yes, they do," hugging her. Niarchos showed as Zion left. "Knock knock," standing in the threshold staring at her sitting on the bed looking at marriage boot camp. He took his phone texting...

Nicky: You can't send videos like that Gabriel: I did what I felt. I thought I asked you to delete it, did you? Nicky: With hesitation yes! I fucking love you Gabriel don't you get it? It's not a normal love like I had for my wife, it's something else, I can't explain. Do you know what I did when I saw it? You better not fucking laugh. Gabriel: What? Nicky: Licked my screen She burst out laughing, making him laugh.

Gabriel: Let's enjoy what we have let it grow organically.

Nicky: You don't know what pop's capable of I do. You'll live he'll kill me. Gabriel: I'll NEVER let you die Nicky! If you die, I'll go with you, I promise. He kissed her hand, licking her fingers. Gabriel inhaled excitedly as his twirling his tongue graced everyone.

Closing her eyes electricity surged down her spine. Niarchos turned her wrist over, looking for her blessing to blood-join with her. Nodding her consent... he slowly slipped his fangs out licking her first softening her flesh, sinking his fangs into the side of her wrist. She jumped from his erotic pinch at the same time her panties moistened. Niarchos fed from her engaging in a private spiritual blood-locking ceremony with Clarence's bride unbeknownst to her by soaking up her memories and feelings which he denied doing during past feedings, becoming one with her soul. Holding out his huge hand wrist turned up, she bit drinking of him, licking when it dripped. Niarchos bit his bottom lip as their wordless blood bond was quietly and secretly attained.

When she stopped his blood soaked her lips. Sucking her bottom lip, she opened her mouth dripping rich red blood into his as it slip slid off the tip of her tongue. He reached his hand under her dress. Gabriel grabbed his wrist shaking her head no. "Please baby," he whispered resting his forehead on hers trembling sexually edging himself privately as the tv played loudly, swirling his tongue on her fingers begging "please...please ma."

Nodding yes, granting him permission to her heaven. He soft fingered her as his fingers rubbed her inner lips up and down gently, she low moaned in his ear which was his green light to push his finger deeper rubbing the sides of her wet walls. Niarchos intentionally breathed open mouthed to digest whatever he could of her moisture that were trapped in particles of dust and air surrounding her snatch. He was lost and intoxicated by the smell of her neck burying his face panting uncontrollably.

Niarchos removed his finger. She pushed it in his mouth joining him in sharing the exclusive taste of Gabriel. He was intoxicated by her, swept up in her sensual seduction mixed with heaps of her swirling aromas. He was spellbound with no escape route. Niarchos held the side of the bed with both hands grabbing a pillow screaming inside of it releasing in front of her. His explosion was sexily massive he was shuddering, and trembling as she scratched his back moaning making it worse. Grabbing her hand Niarchos breathed uncontrolled. You're beautiful she mouthed kissing the tips of his fingers tasting her sweetness losing track of time.

Gabriel pointed to the bathroom. Returning he tossed a half bottle of blood on the floor as if it were spilled by accident. "Why?" "Blood covers the smell; a vampire will always smell before anything else."

She used the bathroom rinsing with Listerine. When she walked in, he mouthed, "No, never try and mask blood it gives you away, drink another blood," handing her a bottle. His phone rang. "Hey Mara, I leave tomorrow Pharoah's private jet. Sure, you can ride with me. I'll send the limo. No problem, I'll call you tonight, bye." Gabriel was upset. "I gotta keep up appearance's bae." "Niarchos it's fine I can't be a married woman and want two vampires." "A Queen or an Elder can have two husbands or wives." She grabbed her purse, handing him a box. "You got me something?" "Well two things, one is waiting for you at home."

"Speaking of the home, when are you coming to see what my mama left me lady?" "Invite me to dinner and I'm there Nicky." "Where do Chance and Mary live?" "Twin Oaks, pop hates it there that's the plantation he grew up on. He hasn't been there in five decades." "That's a long time Nicky." "Bad memories who want to go where they were enslaved Gabriel?" "True."

"Open it!" She clapped excitedly. It was the leather bracelet; his name was engraved. "Turn it over," her name was on the back in gold. "It's beautiful honey." "Let me put it on you, I made them add enough string so it will fit over your hand, perfect as she drew the leather strings." "You don't need vintage furniture Gabriel; between Mary and I you've ten yards full. We've them old oil paintings of the masters." "Why not sell it?" "To auctioneers' honey?" "Yes and donate the proceeds to charity."

'"I'll tell you what, you come, and we'll bring the furniture to the barn and have a county barn yard auction, I gotta clear my attic and I know Mary wants to clear hers." "Look here the man of the hour finished with those pardons pop?" "Sure did." "Grip's so happy he cried call and mess with him about it Niarchos. I said I've never seen a vampire cry happy tears over inheriting vampire tax." "Haha what about Isaiah?" "He was nervous Caleb had my king's chair present remember it Niarchos?" "Dam where'd he find that pop?"

"Who knows? I was on it with the stool for my feet and red pillow for kneeling." He made a show of it removing his diamond crown handing it to Niarchos for safety. "Isaiah trembled I said by the power invested in me by ten covens, ten Elders I issue you this pardon. I welcome you back into the fold you are no longer a vampire without a maker or a rouge vampire without a home. Don't squander this opportunity, use it wisely." He fell to his knees crying. "I touched him with my sword, by the power invested in me as Pharaoh creator of all vampires I decree you are free from exile welcome home. He cried like a baby papa and Ann too."

"We cried when shared we're having a baby. He was happy then I said, 'you didn't drag the notes.' It was a moment I tell ya." "Zhou pop?" Smiling, that fool kept bowing. "Papa and I were bowing till Elijah said 'I ain't bowing no dam more,' we laughed. It was a good day!" "What y'all about to do pop?" "Watch twelve year's a slave." "What?" She laughed.

"Ain't funny I told her there's nothing funny about enslaving a free man pop. They did shit like that, it's a true story. I'll break my dam T.V watching that shit for real pop sorry for cussin Gabriel." "It had a happy ending if you both must know." "Thank you, Sugar." "I promised to drop Mara to Vegas if that's cool pop." Niarchos held up his hand like a phone to Gabriel, she shook her head yes as he left them.

"You ready for this binge watch daddy? Look," shaking a box of popcorn. "You remembered." "Of course I did Sugar!" "Play Equalizer Gabriel." "I love Denzel Washington Clarence." They were laying naked cuddling in the cabin as the Elders packed to leave. "Clarence?" "Humm sugar?" "Zion came by." "Sorry I missed him, how'd it go?" "He did a sonogram." "Is everything fine Sugar?" "Yes, it's fine." He kissed her head sipping tox blood.

"Baby?" "Gabriel, are we watching a movie or talking?" All five of us can watch the movie Clarence sorry I'll be quiet daddy war buck." "Alexis pause the Equalizer. Five?" He sat up smiling holding her tummy. "I'm worried." "Why Sugar?" "Can you afford three babies Clarence? Your money looks light to me." "Haha Sugar you're funny... boys or girls?" "We don't know, can you come down from there Clarence hehe?" He levitated down calling Zion "NO STRESS AND I MEAN NONE! LET HER HAVE HER WAY ALL THE DAMN TIME HEAR ME?" "Yes Doctor." "Good cause I'm the boss for the next eight months." "Yes, Sir." Clarence hung up and Gabriel called Papa Nate.

"Papa?" "Yes ma'am?" "Can you marry us?" "Baby you're already married." "Not by human law." "You mean the white man's law what ya husband say about that?" "He said I can have whatever I want." "Then the answer is yes sweetie. When?" "Tonight please." "May I speak with Clarence please Gabriel?" "Yes Papa Nate." "Yes, Papa Nate I'll tell her okay goodnight." "Papa said he loves you but this ain't no shot gun wedding. Ain't no child of his gonna rush to get married pregnant or not. Papa requests you be proper about. He said too many of us want to see you get married and he ain't trying to upset you, but you can't upset him either. Papa said when Mary gets better imagine her and Ann's disappointment that we eloped." "Ok. Daddy or papa Clarence?" "I'm unsure Sugar let them pick."

"Please be one girl," kissing his hand as they sunk in the bed watching Denzel.

Zion went to the lab to show Zhou what he set up. Zhou had a medical background in holistic medicine, he looked at the sample under the scope, parasite. "What?" "Parasite, we call it burrower." "You've seen this in vampires?" "Yes, they sell it in china to harm vampire. This baby burrower...small." "They grow Zhou?" "Grow abundance they multiply one hundred daily Doctor." "What does it do Zhou?"

"Make crazy, violent, make walk in sun. Parasites need sun to kill only way. Sun kills parasite, vampire no sun.

I help slow down multiply; no stop slows down. No feeding contagious pointing to the dish." "Chance is quarantined." "Good call." "Clarence call," Zion called. "Clarence sorry to bother," Zion repeated what Zhou shared.

"Phone! Phone!" "Hold on Clarence he wants to talk."

法老王，这种寄生虫在中国是一种蠕虫，它在血液中繁殖。每天50到100。最终，身体与它们一起运转过度，以至于它们可能会穿过您的皮肤，因此被称为掘地者。它通过皮肤进入，因为它需要阳光。它会迫使主机在阳光下行走，因为这是唯一杀死它的东西(Pharaoh, the parasite is a worm in China it multiplies in the blood. One hundred per the body is over run with them so bad they come thru your skin, thus the name burrower. It comes through because it wants sun. It forces the host to walk in the sunlight.)

您如何感染寄生虫？(how do you contract the parasite Zhou?)

血液……某人可以将它们滑入您的饮料中，因此它们无法通过静脉转移到嘴中，因为旦空气接触到血液，它就会在嘴中死亡。有人故意将它们放在他的饮料中。**他们必须深入黑市才能得到它们，因为他们没有在美国拥有它们**。(Blood, someone can slip them in your drink they can't be transferred vein to mouth because it will die in the mouth once air hits. Someone purposely placed these in Chance's drink. They dug deep on the black market to get the parasite they don't have them in the U.S) **我可以混合粉末减慢加工速度，但是阳光是我们所知**

(I can mix powders slowing the process, but sun is what eliminates them, sorry old friend). They ended the call Clarence sat up crying angrily pounding a side table breaking it to splinters.

"What's wrong honey?" "My son is going to die Gabriel." "No, he's not Zion, is a medical genius." "One of those bitches fed him a fucking parasite Sugar, before I leave Georgia, I'm going to find out who the fuck poisoned my son." "Calm down baby calm down." "Call Niarchos Sugar."

"Niarchos...as soon as you drop Mara to Vegas return to Georgia tell Grip, Elijah, and Caine to meet us."

"We're going back to Twin Oaks."

# Chapter 29

# Twin Oaks the Return

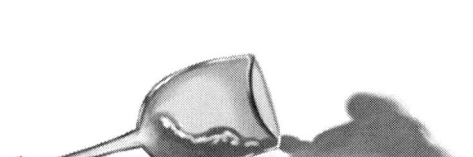

Niarchos and Mara entered Chance's hotel. "Elder Niarchos, it's a pleasure. Will you stay?" "No, I'm flying out this evening John." "Can we get you anything Elder?" "I'm good John thanks." Mara escorted Niarchos to her room, it was cozy. "Vampires are whispering Niarchos. "Let em' whisper ma." "I never asked Mara, who made you?" "Elder Chance." "What an honor."

"I see when vampires hear an Elder made you it's a massive deal, why Niarchos?" "Makes you stronger bae." "How?" "You never fed from an Elder Mara?" "When Chance turned me." Niarchos cut his wrist, Mara accepted his blood offering. Moving his wrist from her mouth, "how do you feel bae?"

"Super energetic, like I can fly jogging in place." "You're crazy haha." "I'm serious Elder." "Ok Mara sit, close your eyes, focus, think on me. What do you see?" "A map leading me to you Niarchos." "I can see an identical map once I drink your blood bae." "Drink from me Elder." Niarchos exposed his fangs.

"Man, they're sharp and long." "They get that way as you grow older it's how we know young vampires from aged ones." "Who made you Niarchos?" "Pharaoh." "Were you scared?" "I was unconscious. How were you turned Mara?" She looked down ashamed.

"You ain't gotta share. Sometimes a vampire's turn is personal babe." "I trust you." "I tried to push up on Chance." "Chance doesn't like big girls." "Yes, he does Niarchos."

"How you know?" "You can't tell." "I won't." "I let him feed when I was a human. It was sexy Elder." "How'd you meet Mara?" "I saw him and said you're the finest man I've ever laid eyes on. I was nineteen, it was true until I saw you Niarchos. I asked he make me vampire, he declined. Chance spent a night, back then we had sex regularly. The African American high rollers of Vegas are well known, especially him because Chance can't be beaten. One night he visited, after an extended six-day poker game. Intoxicated he needed blood to get straight, I offered. I was laying in the bed, Chance spooned and fed nothing unusual. He held me tight; I was getting lightheaded."

"*'Oh god'* I thought. Chance kept drinking. I tried wiggling away. I screamed feeling life leaving me. When I woke, I was in Chance's suite he was next to me. He explained he was drunk, not in control of his senses. I thought about it the next day. He explained he had to turn me, or I was going to die. He gave me this room, a job paying good he never touched me again. One day a scroll writer called asking how I was turned, Chance stated to make something up, I did."

"Wait Chance altered a scroll, Mara? When the writers called Chance said lie?" "I wasn't supposed to Niarchos?" "Hell, no bae, the scrolls are legal documents, a part of who we are. No vampire is allowed to lie on a scroll. You must amend the scroll, Mara." "Chance was adamant not to. He's, my maker. I cannot defy him Niarchos."

"We'll see." "Niarchos baby? You promised." "Mara, he made you lie on a legal vampire document. There is more going on with Chance then you know. You know as an Elder I must report it?"

"Niarchos please." she unzipped her hoodie exposing her breast. "You ain't learn your lesson vampress?" Mara lay down he slipped on top of her, spreading her legs, biting her jugular as she squeezed his arms. "You ok bae?" His deep voice whispered in her ear. She trembled nervously. He drank ten minutes; her blood wasn't rich or sweet like Gabriel's.

"Chance is gonna be livid when he finds out we're dating Mara." "We've been done for years Niarchos." "Chance can be possessive." "You're not Elder?" "No ma'am our passions are worse cause' we're vampires. We own vampresses they're like our property. We'd never say that shit aloud, but it's how it is, once claimed you belong to that vampire, and no one can lay claim to you without that vampire's permission." "Can you claim me Niarchos?" "If no vampire challenges me Mara, you're all mine."

"What if you're challenged?" "He has to prove you're his on paper." She stared at him. "What ma?" "I signed some stuff." "Did Chance explain what you signed in front of a witness?" "No Niarchos." "Did he give you copies?" "I have something." She handed Niarchos a document from a drawer.

"It's a coven agreement. Vampires get this once they're turned so they're clear who they answer to and who's collecting tax on behalf the Pharaoh. Where's the rest Mara?" "Chance didn't give it." "If you signed a concubine agreement Chance has ten days to file, if he missed the file date his hold is void."

"Nice bracelet Niarchos." "Thanks, Queen Gabriel gave it." "Are you, her guard?" "Elders can't be royal guards. Mara this Elder is old, I need a nap ma."

"Yes Elder." kissing his forehead. "Stretch the blanket on the floor." "Niarchos no! You can't sleep on the floor." "Mara stretch it out and lay next to me please." He heard his phone chime and looked at it before texting back.

Nicky: Hi, Gabriel. Honey: Wyd? Nicky: Laying on the floor with Mara. The bed's small.

Honey: Is your bed big? Nicky: H-U-G-E and a custom-made hot tub. Honey: I'll find our REAL soon Nicky. Nicky: What do you mean Gabriel? Niarchos' phone rang.

"Pop is there? Give him his bedroom, he gets anything he asks for Viola, and please bring Queen Gabriel a hot cup of tea with fresh honey three times per day even if she does not ask for it. Only you Viola not the others. "Yes Elder."

Honey: "I love it here Nicky. Nicky: Wait till I show you the bees. Honey: Can't wait, we'll go for a stroll, you can show the property. Nicky: Stroll on eighteen hundred acres Queen? Honey: I'll buy a horse and buggy, or do you have one? Nicky: Yes, ma'am I have my mother's old one. Honey: See you soon Nicky.

"Can we nap Mara?" She lay her head on his chest falling into a deep sleep. Niarchos awoke, noticing his plane was leaving in an hour. Kissing her forehead, he freshened up quietly leaving her room.

Dear Mara,

You were asleep, I didn't want to wake you. My plane leaves in an hour, and I hate goodbyes. Call when you wake. Go to the gift shop. I hope you like it.

-Niarchos-

Mara woke up reading Niarchos' note. She dressed and was reporting to work when her friend ran out of the gift shop approaching her excitedly. "Girl you're the buzz in the coven shop, fucking an Elder. The vampress' are jealous, he's fine!" They arrived at the gift shop, "hi I'm Mara." Introducing herself to the attendant. "Elder Niarchos gifted this Mara enjoy. Please sign here." "Thanks."

"Girl its Tiffany." her friend stated the obvious gazing at the diamond bangle as Mara cracked the light blue box. "It's gorgeous Mara. The Elder's crushing on you."

Niarchos Georgia bound....

If Niarchos could pace on the plane, he would've. He was anxious to see Gabriel. As the plane cleared the runway, he jogged to the Hollings private hanger, strapped his helmet on, hopped on his motorcycle speeding off eating the road. Gabriel heard his bike grinding the gravel, grinning. "Your other husbands home." Clarence teased. Gabriel ignored his jealous statement.

Niarchos knocked on the bedroom door. Gabriel ran to open it. He picked her up, swinging her around.

"Y'all act like it's been years." "He's miserable Nicky."

"Pop what's wrong?" Niarchos inquired, hugging Clarence. "Gabriel, please get me an ice water." "Ok Daddy." Gabriel went to the kitchen. Clarence was on the bed staring as tears rolled. "It's where your mother and I spent our wedding night, in that corner on the floor where we were blood-locked as the moon exasperated our sexual prowess. There is where she confessed her love, there is where her vanity sat with the jewels, I gifted her. There is where she cried the day Isabel died. I'm melancholy is all son."

Niarchos looked at the table, chairs, and marble coffee table. Accented with a red Moroccan lamp set in the corner smiling. "Papa its ok." Clarence approached the fireplace, pulling his mother's Winchester rifle down the chimney.

"Thank you pop, I was going crazy looking for it. What other hiding spots are in the house?" Clarence stomped on the floor by the window, the floorboard popped up. Niarchos reached in the hole. "Pop, thank you. I kept them in case you remarried." "Mama's wedding rings, oh man thank you."

"Those were the second set. I buried the first with her Niarchos." "Will you visit her while you're here pop?" "Of course, she'd kill me if I didn't. We've a long day tomorrow. Get your guns ready. God knows what were gonna run into. Elijah and Grip are sleeping at Chance's house to see what they can learn." "How's Chance pop?"

"Zion gave him the parasite powder three hours ago. We'll see if his blood is less aggressive. Zion's working on a vaccine Niarchos. Go with Gabriel, your anxiety is aggravating. Inform her to bring the ice water first please." "Yes Pop."

Niarchos went to the kitchen sharing Clarence's request. "Gabriel, meet me on the porch when you're done." Gabriel took Clarence water. "Clarence? I have your ice water you, ok?" "Yes Sugar. Do you want to see where I was made?" "Sure." "The apple orchard isn't far; however, it snake infested. I don't want you bitten so we can do a drive by." "Who stays in the house Daddy?" "No one humans tried purchasing it for decades."

"Why not sell?" "I get top dollar for the apples." "Can I, have it?" "No Sugar." "Why?" "It holds bad memories. I was murdered there. I don't want my wife and children where I was killed. "Why're you angry you were turned vampire Clarence? God chose you." "Why'd you say that, Sugar?" "If God allowed it to happen it was for good reason. He gave you what you wanted Clarence. A wife who loves you and three babies on the way a reward for your obedience over the centuries. I'm here I love you."

Clarence fell asleep in minutes. Gabriel pulled a sheet over him exiting to the porch. She sat on the porch swing enjoying the melodic hum of crickets during a warm southern night. Niarchos joined her.

"Nicky, I think Clarence knows about us." she mouthed. "How?" "He said your second husband is here, when he heard your bike." "Pop's tripping I told him he's jealous can I share something with you?" "Sure." Niarchos explained about Mara and Chance. "What you gonna do?"

"Haven't decided. I'll see what Chance filed and ask Vaughn if its valid." "You're serious about Mara Nicky?" "I like her. If she ends up with me or anyone else, Chance shouldn't have a hold on her." Gabriel looked down; enjoying his porch swing. Niarchos texted:

Nicky: What Gabriel? Honey: Nothing. Nicky: I love you, Queen. Honey: Nicky, go be with someone. Nicky: We've been through this. Niarchos texted staring, burning a hole in her head. Honey: Let go, Niarchos.

Nicky: Baby, follow your heart. We love one another. How do you make that go away ma? You'll marry my father. I'll get a girl, but we'll be in love. Honey: You don't want to get married to Nicky?

Nicky: I must be deep in love, and I'm in love with you. I got it bad for you Gabriel. Honey: I love Clarence. Niarchos gave her a look. Honey: Stop Nicky.

Nicky: Do you want me sexually Gabriel? Honey: What kind of question is that? Nicky: An honest one Queen. Honey: I make love to you every day in my head. Nicky: I'm glad I'm not alone.

"Do you like your gift Niarchos?" "I love it, do you like yours?" "I didn't get it yet?" "Follow me," walking her to the end of the porch outside his bedroom window before uncovering her eyes. "Nicky!" She screamed, jumping in his arms. "This is the third Rolls Royce. This one's pretty and girly." "It was my wife's car Gabriel." "Oh no Nicky, I can't accept it." "I want you to have it please." kissing her hands.

"I love it Nicky, thank you. She works?" "Of course, come." "Where are we going Gabriel?" "To the gate and back Nicky." She drove down the dark road getting to the gate making a U-turn. Niarchos innocently kissed her cheek.

"No... hehe." holding her delicate hand to his chest pushing him away playfully. "He can smell you silly." He kissed her again. "Stop Nicky hehe." her gentle voice blending melodically with the rustling leaves of the night.

She attempted to pushed him over, "dang you're heavy Nicky." "Stop the car Gabriel cut the light." They got down, Niarchos drew double guns from the glove compartment. He saw four dingos on the property, they weren't their Elders the scents were different. He glared as they made their way toward the house, letting them pass.

Niarchos got out running, gun shots echoed in the night disturbing the silence waking Clarence who grabbed his rifle jumping out the second story window without shoes half dressed, four vampire guards followed Clarence across the property. Gabriel returned to the house alone head lights out staying in the car doors locked as instructed. She waited 15 minutes to step out of her car when A dingo cornered her growling.

Gabriel froze, Jupiter bolted out the house attacking the dingo, tearing off his ear. Jupiter bit into the stray dingos neck, causing his retreat into the woods. Jupiter chased the dingo attacker. "JUPE NO!"

Niarchos picked Gabriel up, running into the house slamming the door running back into the night. The housekeeper implemented a house lockdown the windows, doors, and chimney were shut off with bullet proof metal, the property flooded with light.

"Open the door, Gabriel?" She unlatched the door, and Jupiter came running in bloody wet, "oh no Jupe baby." "It's not his blood Sugar." "Where are your clothes, Clarence why're you half naked?" "I was sleeping this way when I heard the gunshots, I jumped out the window to find you." "Naked?" "You were in danger Gabriel" kissing her cheek.

"Open Jupiter." He obeyed his mom, opening his mouth. "JESUS!" A Human ear fell to her feet. "Sugar calm down."

"Clarence, I saw Jupiter rip a dog's ear, not a human." "Maybe, he met a human in the woods Sugar."

"There was no human's Clarence." "Sugar, rest. Viola is bringing Chamomile tea. She grew the leaves herself; I'll go downstairs to call Papa, Elijah, and Caine. Stay with Gabriel Niarchos." "The rabid dog was going to jump on me Nicky. Jupiter ripped his ear off in a fight." Gabriel kept repeating what she witnessed, convincing herself of what she saw. "It was a dog ear Nicky not human." "Ok relax my Queen and get under the blanket. You're cold, did you take an iron tablet today?" "No Nicky." She was shaky.

"Why not?" "I Forgot." "You can't forget Gabriel." He went into her purse, seeing the pearls. "You have to take it with blood." Popping his fangs he bit his wrist "Come on." She drank for four minutes. "Guess what ma?" She didn't answer. "I left a blanket on your side of the bed. She gave no response, trembling. Viola tapped the door with a tray. "Thank you, Viola." "You're welcome honey." Niarchos opened his wrist again, she declined. "Gabriel please honey," he mouthed; she turned away.

"Sip this tea ma." She started sipping slowly and confused. Gabriel lay her hand on top of Niarchos', rubbing for comfort. "Is Clarence a dingo Nicky? Don't lie." He burst out laughing, gaslighting her. "Not that I've seen ma." "Why was he naked?" "He went to bed with boxer's and a tank. Where are they Nicky if he removed them before bed?"

"Gabriel baby, please drink your tea." wrapping his arms around her for comfort. In minutes she was fast asleep. He looked in the tea leaves seeing white residue. He called and questioned Viola. "The Pharaoh put it in there Elder." Viola volunteered, before he could ask. "What is it?"

"Sleeping powder Elder, because her nerves were rattled." "Where did pop get it?" "A hiding space in the kitchen that I never knew was there. Pharaoh said Queen Safinah gave it to white people who came being nosey."

"Goodnight Viola." "Goodnight Elder." Niarchos stroked Gabriel's face. "Nicky?" "Yes bae?" "Do you like my gift?" "I love it honey, thank you." "I wish we met first."

"Me too." Niarchos opened the door for Clarence. "Keep the gates drawn until we can figure out what happened Niarchos." "I watched them head here and tracked them to Chance's house pop. Where are your clothes?" "Someplace outside Niarchos."

"Do you've identical item's Pop?" "I think so why?" "Gabriel was looking for them, they're not here. She asked if you're dingo." "She's a smart one Niarchos."

"Open your closet for me Niarchos, please push all your clothes to one side on the clothes bar." Clarence entered the huge closet, dipping his head under the clothes bar. The wall opened, Niarchos followed Clarence. "It's huge in here Pop, what're you looking for?" "Identical underwear son." Clarence looked in the drawers for something close. "All those times you kids looked for your mother and I and couldn't find us? We were right in here, frolicking. I built it to hide Safinah, and you kids in case the oppressors discovered I was passing."

"It's amazing Pop." "Thanks. found some, these must do. Now let us come out the closet." "Man, she's knocked out. What's in that tea Pop?" "Your mother had her herbs. If she were alive, she would've found a cure for Chance Niarchos." "I'll find her medical journals get them to Zion pop. He may be able to find something to help Chance."

Niarchos rested in the chair Gabriel gifted him. "Who do you think it was tonight, Pop?" "I'm unsure Niarchos, but we're going to learn who's ear it is." Clarence closed his eyes scanning her thoughts about the dog ear incident. Clarence removed the memory, but he kept searching. Niarchos was nervous. Clarence saw the memories but couldn't hear them. He saw her drinking tea questioning Niarchos about his missing clothing. Clarence deleted those memories along with

*Blk Qween*

her thinking he was a dingo. Clarence opened his eyes, "it's done."

Morning arrived, Niarchos gave Jupiter a bath. Clarence entered Niarchos' room he got on all fours rubbing his head on Jupiter's head low growling. "We're leaving in twenty minutes Niarchos." Clarence approached the limo under the UV resistant car port leading from the door to the car.

"The car port is nice Papa." "Ann invented it Niarchos." Clarence held up his hands, "see? No burn. The glass windows are better." Clarence Niarchos Elijah, Grip and Papa rode to Twin Oaks. Clarence looked out the Limousine window. "Damn those twin oak trees," as they rode up the mile long drive to the house set back on the property. "Why hasn't Chance removed those slave shack's Elijah? They're an eye sore."

"Those eye sores have made this property declared a historical landmark, the museum conducts tour's here. Chance gets special funding from Clarence. We have one of the largest negro burial grounds with records in Georgia." "I wasn't going to let them burn black soldier's bodies or sell them for compost or cadavers, Elijah. It's our blood stained on the American flag and our backs built this country brick by miserable brick. Black slaves died for our flag; their families deserved a proper Christian burial." "A girl Chance was dealing with had both our lands declared historical landmarks pop." Clarence got everyone's attention.

"We're in Chance's house to place his vampire staff and wives under arrest." "Is the jail in his basement Pop?" "Far as I know Grip, yes." "Don't answer any questions and put Mary in the jail with everyone else." "Mary Pop?" "Everyone goes Niarchos. Chance is clinging to his fucking life someone is folding." "Elijah when we go in the house announce the Pharaoh seize decree, please." "Yes Pharaoh." "Guns up!" Niarchos shouted. Niarchos kicked the front door in with Grip at his back. Vampress' screaming, servant's running the house was chaotic. Elijah read the law as follows:

"Vampire Law Article 32 Sub code 653-741. This coven has been seized and reverted to the king of covens Clarence Hollings. The Pharaoh has the right to seize any vampire coven he declares may be a danger to itself or to other vampires. If the Pharaoh suspects foul play, he may take control of the coven, house, or business attached to it. The Pharaoh has a right to place all vampires under arrest, question, judge and execute all vampires without an Elder council present, hearing, or trial. All vampires will be judged by the Pharaoh, he alone will hand down judgement accordingly or decide if a trail is necessary."

Elijah nailed the decree inside the front door. The rest grabbed vampires placing them under arrest. Clarence grabbed a girl, "how old were you on the date of your turn girl?" The vampress spat in his face. Niarchos slapped her to the floor so hard she broke the marble tile. "Do you know who's face you spat in bitch?" Niarchos grabbed her hair lifting her off the floor, feet dangling. "Line everyone up." "Yes Pharoah" Elijah Cain and Grip wrestled the women doing as commanded.

"Separate Chance's wives Grip. Open the front door Caine." He kicked opened the oak double doors. "Toss her into the sun Niarchos." "Clarence mercy I beg of you." Mary fell to her knees. "Mary, she's an abomination, a child. What is a child doing vampire Mary?" "Pharoah mercy" Mary cried on his shoes, "please Great One." "Look here child, are you sorry for spitting in the face of your Pharaoh?" Clarence inquired, she spat again.

Niarchos tossed her into the burning son. Screams mixed with shrieking tapered off into painful screams. The silence in the house commanded respect speaking volumes because shit got real. "Get me a chair Grip." He returned with a chair for his father. The sound of whimpering fear bounced off the walls of the old mansion. Clarence sat removing his fedora as a curl fell in his eyes while he fanned the heat of the old plantation away.

"No trial, no jury, no stories today is execution day ladies." Clarence wiped his face with his handkerchief. "I'd rather not drain you one by one, but there is an illness running rampart in this coven isn't there vampresses?" Niarchos towered behind all twenty-three vampires. Grip and Elijah were behind the wives. Caine and the guards ransacked the house. "Which vampire can say why I'm here? Don't be shy. Speak up" The front door remained open. The smell of high noon rolled in mixed with charred flesh and ashes.

*The one in the black robe* Clarence telepathically spoke with Niarchos. Niarchos dragged her in front of Clarence. KNEEL! She scrambled face to the floor.

Clarence squatted looking in her eyes, "why is Elder Chance in the hospital?" "I'm unsure Great One." Clarence nodded; Grip shot her in the head with a UV ray bullet. Screams rang out. Remaining vampires backed up in fear. Clarence opened an umbrella to keep his white suit clean as blood and flesh flew everywhere leaving a blood spatter flesh mess. Niarchos licked his fingers growling. Grip wiped Clarence's shoes white again.

"Why is chance in a hospital? Anyone?" *Red shirt.* Niarchos grabbed her neck, dangling her in front of Clarence as she gasped for air. "Do you have something to say vampress?" Niarchos tightened his grip. Clarence nodded. Niarchos pulled her neck to his mouth, draining her blood in one minute. She struggled kicked and gasped for air she never got. The vampress slapped and hit Niarchos for air, CRACK! After snapping her neck like a twig Niarchos dropped her to the floor kicking her twenty-five feet across the floor. The loud thump of her dead body hitting the wall like a dead animal drenched the room with understanding.

"Great One?" Clarence asked again. "Please I beg, may I speak with you privately Pharoah?" "No, you may speak in the presence of the four Elders present." He held up his hand helping Mary off the floor. Papa Nate sent a telepathic message *please meet us in the kitchen.* Papa Nate sat with Clarence and Mary. Papa got her a glass of water. "Clarence what's going on?" "Why is Chance in the hospital Mary?" Clarence scanned her thoughts she was clueless. "She doesn't know Clarence.

You know Mary would never ever hurt Chance, would you darling?" "No papa Nate, I wouldn't"

"These stray's he picks up runs the house, no respect as you saw. It's vampire nest not an elder sanctioned coven Clarence." "Mary, you never said it was this bad." "I'm sorry Clarence." I need you to pretend with the other wives until we find the underlying cause of this mess Mary. Did you know there are four outside dingos on the property? Niarchos tracked them here last night. Mary instantly cried. "Is there anyone who may want Chance dead Mary?" "The last four wives Papa Nate."

"Why Mary?" "Money Clarence. When Indian and him finished, he cut ties with his vampresses. Let's say all his wives aren't financially set guys." "Makes no sense Mary, Chance signed agreements with all his wives were they filed?" "I made sure mine was filed, and never withdrawn. I can't speak for the others Clarence."

"Grip?" "Yes Pharaoh." "Contact the scroll writers have them pull all marital and concubine agreement's concerning Chance's wives." "Yes Pharaoh." "Grip take Mary back to the other wives, be rough with her but not too rough. Make it look good." "Yes Pharaoh." "Hello? Yes, Gabriel, I'm fine. No Sugar I'm not stressed. Yes Sugar, I'll bring you fresh mint tea it grows wild on this plantation. I know exactly where it is."

"Nausea ...have you had blood today? Get a bottle of blood from the fridge, the yellow top is my blood; I'll be home soon. Do you want to call Zion Gabriel? You're not troubling him Sugar, I'm paying him for house calls. Did you take your iron pills? No? Not good Sugar please take one with the blood baby. Gabriel, can I finish, and come home to you? Thank you. Yes, it's, plantation hot Sugar. It's not funny," grinning to himself.

"I love you more Gabriel." "She drives you nutty Clarence huh?" "Yes Papa Nate, Jesus." "You ain't seen nothing yet. It gets worse as she gets bigger." "Thanks for the warning, Papa."

Clarence approached the foyer wearing his white suit, matching fedora, white shoes, and an Egyptian cotton tee. He looked sexy as hell. He slowly sat with a bottle of ice water from the limo.

Agitated he scanned thoughts. There was a lot of mind blocking. Some were good at it, some horrible.

Clarence chose who to question first by who blocked him the hardest. "Niarchos, Caine, and Grip take the wives place them in jail. Strip, and frisk them thoroughly, private areas too." Clarence spoke with Grip telepathically, *shoot anyone who resists. Use a rifle, the shot commands respect.* "Yes Pharoah."

"Niarchos? What should we do with the rest?" "We gotta go home, Gabriel called pop." Papa continued searching the house. "What you got Papa?" "Diaries Clarence?" "How many?" "Twelve." "Give them to Niarchos, he'll have some reading to do tonight." Clarence looked at the young vampires.

"Rainbow hair." Niarchos grabbed her hair dropping her at Clarence's feet. "Do you've news for me? Niarchos close the door please turn up the air. It's the Georgia heat in this mansion Rainbow hair, holds the heat. Did I mention I grew up here?" Vampires were shocked at his admission. "I was six when they sold me to the master of this plantation. In its hay day this place thrived. Rainbow? Do the cotton field's still grow?"

"Yes Pharoah." "Does Elder Chance have it picked?" "No Pharoah." "Must be a mess now Rainbow. What about the Tobacco fields?" "Yes Pharoah, Chance harvest's the tobacco and sugar cane." "I guess he ain't picking no more cotton." Clarence burst out laughing alone. Niarchos failed to smile. "I don't blame him. Darlin how old are you?" "Nineteen and Twenty-three Great One." "A baby. Say what you've heard of me?" Sipping his water. "You're fair Great One."

"I'll be. Say child." popping his fangs. "What do you know of slipping a foul worm placed in someone's blood from china?" She looked back at a male coven member who was Chinese. Clarence gave a look to Grip. Grip dragged him, placing him next to the girl on the floor at Clarence's feet. Niarchos' phone buzzed; he ignored it. Clarence's phone rang, "yes Sugar? Nicky's busy. Not mint tea, raspberry tea Niarchos." He nodded head yes. "I'll call you when I'm on my way Sugar, yes? Good speak soon love you too."

"Rainbow where were we?" "The worm Pharaoh, he may know more." "Thank you, Rainbow hair. Vampire where are you from?

是谁造的(who made you?) The vampire shocked he spoke Chinese. *你扔在阳光下的*。 (The girl you tossed in the light.) You allowed a child to make you? *你让一个孩子让你吗？她饿了，所以她在这里咬我* (she was hungry, she bit me then fed me her blood.)

"The worm, it's from China great one. A parasite lives in blood, multiplying until it forces the host to walk in sunlight." "How'd Elder Chance drink this parasite?" "I'm unsure Great One I swear by the ancestors." "Niarchos, escort and lock everyone downstairs."

There were six cells Clarence cramped twenty-something vampires into with no air conditioning. "Niarchos, stay until Jamaica, until his staff arrives. They'll be here tonight. Water, no blood NBO order. If anyone is caught feeding, shoot them. Question Mary every five hours, when you do, treat her well but return her appeared roughed up, but don't hit her." "Yes Pharaoh."

"No blankets, no air conditioner, no pillows, only truth. Turn the camera's on with audio listen when the guard's leave, and record everything Niarchos." "Yes Pop." Elijah and Niarchos left once Jamaica arrived. Grip and Papa Nate stayed. Niarchos: Hello Gabriel, please turn on the air conditioner in the bedroom. Pop is agitated. Honey: Ok Nicky.

"Driver?" "Yes Pharaoh. "Please, stop at the market and please turn up the air." "Yes sir." They arrived at the market. "Driver, can you please get one flavor of mother earth hot tea bags please? Make sure to get raspberry, mint, lemon, and sleepy nights tea."

"Yes Pharaoh." He exited to fill his request. "Why is Chance allowing children to be vampires? Has he lost mind? His coven isn't in order. You see a bitch spat in my face twice?" Niarchos shook his head. "I was shocked Pop." "I gave her a chance to repent Niarchos. We're having an Elders meeting when I return to New York."

"How long without blood Pop?" "Until they start talking Niarchos. This isn't a game. Someone in that coven committed attempted murder of a vampire Elder. This is serious. What if Chance dies? God help me if a human's involved." "Why do you say that Pop?"

"As I scanned thoughts, I heard Rainbow say the man who gambles paid them. I'm going to press her tomorrow. She's a weak link. You know how Chance is with cards. It won't be the first time a bounty was on his head." The chauffeur returned, handing Clarence the bag of teas. They arrived at Niarchos' house. The limo driver opened the door; Clarence approached the house holding the bag of teas. "Sugar I'm home!" peeling off sweaty clothes. The room was nice and cool.

"Gabriel?" Clarence entered the bathroom. She sat in a cool tub. "Come in honey." Exhaling his stress filled day away he joined her. Gabriel rubbed his back washing hair. "Look at these sexy curls." separating and straightening them one by one, watching them snap back. "You like playing in my hair Gabriel?" "Yes hehe, I hope it's not aggravating baby." "I like it its relaxing honestly."

Sitting behind him Gabriel rubbed his chest and dick under soft scented waters. "Don't." grabbing her hand. "Why not, did you hurt me the other day daddy?"

"No but we were lucky Gabriel. I once had sex with a human who was pregnant. I didn't know until we finished blood was everywhere. She screamed, and I rushed her to the hospital, however she miscarried. Dr. said she should've refrained from sex in the early months if so her baby would've lived."

"What year was it?" "70s Sugar, not long ago." "I know you're horny like I am Clarence. It's a warm sultry night but cool enough to crawl all over one another" Gabriel jerked his manhood under iridescent bubbles rippling on the surface. "I'll eat you real fine Sugar, finger you slow, and make you cum, but I won't penetrate until you're five months."

"You can't be serious Clarence." "Sugar don't be cross. I have a surprise for you." "I don't want it." She went for his dick again running her fingers in his hair. He popped up grabbing a towel, "come see what I got you."

"Clarence ya dick is hard as Chinese math." Gabriel inhaled, grabbing her robe. "Sit sugar," handing her the tea filled gift bag. She looked inside smiling. "I thought of you. Niarchos gave me flavors you like look." He gifted her a bag from Target, with an electric tea kettle. "You don't have to wait on tea anymore, Sugar." "Thank you." kissing his lips stretching his curls.

"You're a beautiful looking man." "Beautiful?" "Your beautiful inside and out Clarence" "No one's ever said that to me Gabriel." "It's true." He looked away shyly. She lifted his chin staring deep in his eyes. "If I saw blood coming because I couldn't wait for relations, I'd never forgive myself. These are our miracle babies Sugar. We must be careful." Clarence's phone rang, "hello Zion how is Chance?"

"Better. We aren't out the woods. I have him sedated, sleeping slows the aggression. I prescribed A-positive, blood drip, combined with Zhou's powder. It slowed down the illness by eighty-five percent."

"I'm sending Safinah's medical journals there may be information we can use." "That'd be great. We may find something to assist." "Have you tried infusing my blood Zion? "No Clarence, I haven't. I'll try it."

"Very well, Zion, Good night." "Good night, Pharaoh." Clarence knocked on Niarchos' bedroom door. "Get your mother's treasure chest from the attic. Bring all four of them please unless it's too heavy Niarchos."

"You're funny Pop." Niarchos passed the master bedroom where Gabriel. He knocked checking on her. "Come in." "I heard you're denying Pop feeding you Gabriel."

"Stop" Niarchos mouthed, "or I'm not sharing my blood." "I'm going home to New York Nicky I won't be a problem." "You're not going home Gabriel; we've got issues at Chance's house. Pop must arrive per Pharaoh's law." "It's that bad?" "Two vampires were executed today, Pharaoh's order ma." "I wonder who carried out those orders?" "I'm the Pharaoh's gun hand always have been. If the Pharaoh gives the order to kill, I'll kill."

"What if he orders for you to kill me Niarchos?" "I'd run with you. If you die, I die," touching his heart. "I'll return, heading to the attic." Niarchos returned quick, "open the door, Gabriel." "What's all this?" "Pop and mama's storage chests" "Which ones are Clarence's?" "These two." Niarchos left, "wait here Gabriel. I have a gift for you." Niarchos entered with a 1940s chaise lounge chair. "Close ya eyes nosey!" "They're closed Nicky." Niarchos walked the pink lounger over to the window. "Open." pulling the white sheet.

"Oh my god, an original chaise lounge are you serious!" running to the chair. "How do I look?" sitting on the chair posing like a black Hollywood starlight. "Sleepy." "No silly, you're supposed to say like Dorothy Dandridge." "Ok, like Dorothy Dandridge. Here Gabriel help me find the medical journal's please." Niarchos carried the first chest to her. Gabriel pulled an old Smith & Wesson. "Get ya hands up BANG!" "That was my first gun." "This can fetch a penny at auction Nicky."

"Ain't for sale hybrid vampress. I killed a slave catcher holding a gun on pop my first human kill with old Betsy. Our private plane leaves in three hours so I can carry the books to Zion at the hospital in New York." Niarchos handed Gabriel a picture of Clarence and Safinah on their wedding day.

"Clarence look daddy" He entered with her snack. "Thank you, Clarence." "The camera caught me that day. It was hot in them dam tights Sugar haha."

"You were handsome with your long Safinah's dress was beautiful. May I have this photo of the wedding Clarence?" "Sure Sugar."

Gabriel shifted through old photos. There was one of Chance, Caine and Elijah dressed in Confederate soldier uniforms sitting on three chests of gold coins. One was presented to her as an engagement gift. "You can't have that Sugar haha It's evidence we stole gold from confederate armies." "Clarence the men in this photo are dead boy stop hehe." Gabriel took a picture with her phone sending it to Elijah, Caine, Papa Nate, Lily, Mya, and Ann. "Papa said 'Clarence you weren't complaining about the heat that day.'" "Tell him we were trying to avoid real heat." There was a photo of Clarence and Chance at Twin Oaks, Clarence became solemn.

"Chance is gonna be fine Clarence, you wait and see." "Thanks Sugar Niarchos, you see how Chance let the cotton field's go?" "Yep Pop." "The estate is losing money. I'll harvest them before leaving for New York. He needs to make more money to supplement the hike in his vampire tax. The crops could bring in millions per year. Cotton is in high demand he's letting the fields over grow." "I found them guys." Gabriel handed Clarence eight leather bound books. Gabriel slipped a photo of Zion and Safinah sitting in the Brooklyn house kitchen in the medical book, with a note. "Zion thought you'd like to keep this."

"Who's this little girl Safinah is hugging Clarence?" "Look again Sugar." "Joan? Aww so adorable." I wanna ride with you to drop the books Niarchos." "Take the limo, Niarchos." "Ok pop." Gabriel turned on the news for him. "Return shortly Daddy "Hurry up Sugar." slapping her ass. Gabriel and Niarchos approached the limo, rested on one side with Niarchos sitting across from her.

"You're getting fatter in the ass, Gabriel it's a good thing sexy." Niarchos grinned. "Where's Jupiter?" "He's been running around your estate. I hope he doesn't get ticks Nicky."

"I keep telling you he's not a dog Gabriel." "Yes, he is Nicky. Have you looked up, dingo?" "The dingo is a DOG! It is found in Australia. A medium-sized CANINE! Possesses a lean, hard body adapted for speed, agility, and stamina. Dingos hunt at night, when in a pack they'll target and kill large animal's, such as a kangaroo." "Yes, my Queen."

"Is it true you tossed a girl into the sunlight Nicky?" "Yep, she spat in Pop's face twice. No fucking respect. She was a kid, 15 or so. Mary said rouge vampires turned her." "What's that Nicky?" "They're vampires with no coven. A random vampire bit them and turned em without permission on the streets."

"What happens to them" "Most times a coven linked vampire will get them coven connected. But if I ain't turn you I don't want you ma." She laid her head in his lap. "Why you rockin up under my head Nicky?" "Don't you want the babies honey?"

"Of course." "Four more month's ain't bad Gabriel." "I wanted to explain something, turn on the radio please. I like seeing you cum. Your eyes are so pretty Niarchos. Do you know red is in your eye color when you cum? It's sexy." He kissed her, making sure the cameras in the limo were off. "Sit here ma," moving to the corner. "Why?"

"Blind spot can't be picked up on video." They engaged in a twenty-minute petting session. He touched her through her pants. "Move your hand Nicky before I bite you." popping her teeth. "Those are cute little dice ma." he teased, popping his. "Those are baby teeth Nicky. My husbands are bigger." "Haha."

The limo came to a screeching halt. A barrage of flying bullets hit the bullet proof glass. Niarchos broke the divider glass with his fist, seeing they were surrounded. He pushed four buttons on his phone. Machine guns exited the doors outside the limousine. Headlight guns sprayed a mix of vampire and human bullets.

Gabriel grabbed Niarchos' phone turning the cameras on as Niarchos tossed on his double gun belt.

"Clarence we're under attack! I'm unsure where we are Clarence, hurry please." "Gabriel keep your head down get on the floor." Niarchos shouted. Niarchos drove six miles on the rims to the airport. "They're after the medical journals Gabriel." "How do you know Nicky?" Niarchos looked at the driver he forced into the passenger seat. He was so nervous he pissed his pants. "Here." Niarchos gave Gabriel a gun, "if he tries anything, shoot him." Niarchos cuffed the driver to his arm. "If we die, you die nigga. I should kill ya ass right here." He popped his fangs and so did she. "You ok Nicky?" "Yeah, I'm ok ma."

They arrived at the airport. Niarchos drove on the tarmac directly to their plane. He carried Gabriel while she carried the box, and the driver kept stride locked to his arm as they ran up the plane's steps. Someone in the hanger shot at them. Niarchos rushed Gabriel on the plane, kicking the steps away, locking the door. "Up NOW!" Niarchos commanded. "We're cleared for take-off Elder please be seated." "Gabriel, you have your phone?" "Yes Nicky." "Call pop please." Niarchos uncuffed the driver knocking him out cold with a chin tap.

"Hello? Yes, baby we're alright. No, I'm not hit. We have the box yes Clarence ok hold on," passing her phone to Niarchos. "Yeah Pop? We were 5 minutes away from the airport when 12 men opened fire on us, we were on Tuskegee airmen road. When we got to the plane a man was shooting at us there." "He's vampire Niarchos?" "The driver set this up pop, the shooter is vampire our driver is human. They want mama's medical journals. They don't want us to find a cure for Chance. I'm unsure why." "This plot extends way past his wives Niarchos. Call me when you land in New York." "Ok Pop." "You think Chance cheated someone at cards Nicky?"

"Chance doesn't have to cheat Gabriel. Pop spoke with the vampire treasury, Chance has over $22 billion in cash and assets he's not cash pressed. A company is purposely paying Chance not to harvest the cotton. Something about five-year-old cotton thread count being higher. He's doing well financially Gabriel." "What about the wives Nicky? Did they send the signed marriage agreements from the legal document team?" "Working on it. You're trembling Gabriel." "I'm cold Nicky." "Pilot, please turn the heat on." He closed the partition, dimming the light so they could sleep. "Come." biting the side of his wrist. She fed drifting off.

"My brothers are hungry Gabriel." "Your sisters are hungry." "Them boy's woman so I can turn them into savages like me." "I'm scared someone tried to kill me for the third time." Gabriel put her arms around him, falling asleep on his chest. "Gabriel we're here, in New York." Niarchos gave her a gun with human bullets. He pressed the pilot for his phone, he handed it over. He checked for warnings they may be landing, he saw nothing. Zion met them at the airport with vampire guards. Niarchos tossed the limousine driver from Georgia in the trunk.

Once Niarchos and Gabriel closed the car door Zion raised his hand checking Gabriel's temperature.

"Hello to you too, Dr." "You're warm Gabriel." "We flew with the heat on. Zion I was cold"

"Thank you, Gabriel." passing her a bottle of Clarence's blood. Niarchos gave her a dirty gaze, she drank all of it. "Your blood shows one of the babies is human, Gabriel." "I want them to be vampires, so the human doesn't die Zion." "Let's see how the pregnancy goes." "Don't cry Gabriel. See what you did Zion giving unwelcome news about the babies? "She's tired Niarchos all this action is no good for her or the triplets." "Gabriel? If the child is human, you can make the baby vampire when he becomes of age. You're upsetting yourself for nothing dear."

Twin Oaks......

Clarence dragged the shooter back to Chance's house off the tarmac. Jamaica stripped him naked using a machine he rolled it over his body, and his genitals. "What's that for Jamaica?" "Deactivates anything planted on him like a GPS, to show where he's located Caine." "Pop your fangs." The shooter refused. Jamaica squeezed a gland in his cheeks, they popped. "Niarchos said he was human Jamaica." "The Elders eyes deceived him honest mistake." Jamaica sprayed his fangs with a clear substance. "What's that?"

"Dulls the teeth for 25 days Elder Caine. Biting will be difficult. Let's go!" Jamaica yelled, dragging him to the cells, waking everyone, tossing him in a overcrowded cell with the vampires naked.

The vampresses screamed, and other vampires moved away as pandemonium gave way to chaos.

"Gimme a blanket!" The shooter demanded no one helped him. Mary lay on the cot mattress on the floor as the second wife lay at her feet she had the only blanket which they tore in half to share. Chance's second wife knew the first three wives were innocent. The Spanish one was crazy. She loved Chance, however she couldn't vouch for the last four. "One of you is going to speak up or the Pharaoh is going to starve us." Azaela yelled frantically.

"No, he won't Azaela." "Yes, he will Giselle. You've no idea what he's capable of I grew up a young bride in his house or have you all forgotten?" Mary scoffed. The television came on they watched Clarence's bloody performance at the vampire games on repeat.

"Clarence is an alpha vampire. Did you know he legally adopted Chance? he's Clarence's first turn his first vampire child, and one of you foolish bitches tried to kill his precious son." "Giselle that's enough." "Sorry Mary."

"Hey you? Naked, why you here?" Chance's second wife Giselle inquired. He didn't respond. One of the vampire males slapped him, and the other vampires jumped on him. Jamaica entered banging the bars. "Break shit up, its late!" "Aren't we getting water sir?"

"Who said that?" "Me." one the women said it with an attitude. "Open two!" Jamaica walked up to Chance's fifth wife slapping her to the floor. "Don't hit her!" One vampire yelled in her defense. Jamaica picked her up punching her in the mouth. "Anyone else want to say something? The only fucking thing need to be said is who the fuck in here hurt the Pharaoh's first-born son the Elder Prince of covens! You vampires have no idea who you're fucking with! You thought Niarchos was bad? He's a sweetheart compared to the likes of me. Torture begins six a.m. sharp!" "Susan are you ok?" "He knocked her out Mary."

"They mean business Giselle the Pharaoh is serious if Chance dies, we all die"

At 3 a.m. strobe lights blinked rapidly for one hour. At four a.m. heavy metal music was blasted. At five a.m. preaching from the J-e-s-u-s network. At six a.m. Catholics reciting the rosary on T.V. At 7 a.m. blaring baby cries, by eight a.m. vampires dying horrible deaths.

By 11 a.m. they were worn, thirsty and hungry.

"Good morning how'd you all sleep?" "Mary? The Pharaoh requests your presence." Mary stood wearily fainting in Grip's arms he carried her to where Clarence and Papa Nate waited. "Papa take her upstairs please to your room, give her blood please." "Ok Clarence. I don't like her being a part of all this. Mary's one of us." Papa left upset. "Caine gimme blood from the fridge and Mary's sweater." Caine handed Clarence both. He tossed blood on the kitchen floor popping Mary's pearls, drenching her bright yellow sweater in rich red blood.

"Gimme a knife Caine." Clarence sliced up her sweater "You're mean Clarence Hahaha!" Caine laughed maniacally. "I won't subject her to torture but looks can jar memories" Jamaica entered the kitchen his machete dripping with blood on the kitchen floor. "Next little piggy Jamaica. Don't bring rainbow until I ask, please." "As you wish Great One." Jamaica returned with the young, black, and Chinese vampire. He looked around the kitchen and saw Mary's sweater soaked with her blood. He inhaled, tossing his hands in front of his mouth, shocked to see Clarence spattered in blood with his mouth and chin blood stained.

"Kneel" Caine pushed him to his knees in the bloody mess. "MARY?" He burst into tears at the sight of her blood. "If I killed Mary who I've known for two centuries, what will I do to you?"

"Great One, I swear I know nothing." Clarence nodded at Jamaica.

"Lay your hand on this table." The young vampire trembled. "Who want ta hurt Elder Chance?" Jamaica asked calm with his thick accent, raising the Machete before cutting the tip of his pinky off.

AHHHH no Pharoah mercy please! "We can sew it back on, but you need blood. Who wanted to hurt Elder Chance?" Caine held his hand down, and Jamaica chopped off his middle finger. Elijah opened the basement door; painful screams filled the cells. "Who wanted to hurt Elder Chance?" He raised the machete, "Wait please Pharaoh." He breathed painfully labored.

"I'd question his wives." "Which one's boy? "Three through five, Great One." "Why?" "The first two, were never home. The third one is a little slow...a fortune hunter, I don't think she is smart enough to be involved but you never know. The last four wives heard Elder Chance was leaving for an Indian vampire. They'd be broke if that happened. After that shit got real."

"Language!" Jamaica shouted. "Sorry Great One." He trembled in pain holding his hand which blood soaking his clothes. Give him one pint of blood sew his fingers back on and return him to the cells Jamaica. "Thank you Great One." Clarence turned to Caine.

"BITCHES!"

# Chapter 30

# Hook Line & Sinker

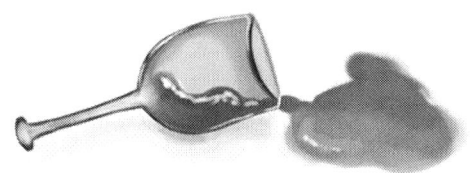

New York Estate....

Gabriel slept three days, Zion reassured Clarence she needed rest. Niarchos stayed at Gabriel's side in the New York house he called Clarence, "What's going on with the investigation Pop?" "We're getting there Niarchos. Did the driver give anything? "I haven't gotten to him Pop waiting for Gabriel to wake up."

"Call when she does, Niarchos." " Yes sir." Zion entered Gabriel's bedroom to listen to the babies. "She's fine, stop worrying and go shower. You want her to wake up to you stinking Niarchos?" Niarchos chuckled at Zion's truth. He showered, drank ten bottles of blood, throwing on a pair of grey sweats and a Black Lives Matter tee.

He slept listening to music. He usually slept by day and was up at night, but this night he dozed lost in the music and by 3:30 a.m. he was deep sleeping. Niarchos was startled out of his sleep to Gabriel on his lap. She bit his neck, drinking, while her other hand rubbed his dick. He placed her back in bed locking the door. He anxiously dropped to his knees before his Queen, parting her pussy, trying to slow himself down. He was going to savor this moment and take time with her pussy, loving on it slow and, easy.

He licked the outside of her left lip, sucking steady, running his tongue up on the inside lip then down the outside lip. He teased her a bit before eagerly making his way to the outside right lip.

Gabriel tasted creamy and ready for him. He teased, moving, licking the pink of her pussy scribbling her name on her inner lips, using the tip of his wicked cream dipped tongue. Gabriel grabbed the edges of the bed, as he drove her into rippling orgasms.

Niarchos grabbed her thighs locking her to his mouth slipping his tongue in and out rapidly. He circled and sucked in relentless combinations bringing her to the edge of sexual release. Her legs trembled under the pressure of his head game. The electric feeling spread through her body as Niarchos controlled the current picking up the pace, ready for her sweet treat.

Using his hand to cover her mouth while popping his fangs, he bit her outside her clit, sucking her pussy while feeding. He was careful not to stain the bed with blood, enjoying every free-flowing drop. All Gabriel's liquid, cream, and blood combination he wanted.... No... needed! Exposing her fat clit, Niarchos treated it like melting ice cream in 90-degree weather.

He licked her sweet through her orgasm. Licking her from the bottom of her split to the top before sucking her lips and plucking her clit. He earned his prize, holding his large hand over her mouth she bit him feeding and shooting cum down his throat.

Latching onto her sugar-sweet clit, holding it hostage, refusing to let go. Gabriel shared sugar-coated pussy tethering the most vicious vampire to live to her soul. Niarchos covered her entire pussy with his mouth he wanted all of her in his mouth. When she was done with him pleasing her, she fell back asleep. He put a towel on the wet spot, leaving an empty water glass next to her on the bed. "Niarchos, I love you." "I love you, Gabriel."

She was every bit as tasty as he imagined. Her snatch smell matching her taste she didn't disappoint.

Zion entered Gabriel's room at 8 a.m. "Did she wake, Niarchos?" "Not sure why?" "The water glass is on the bed." looking at the wet stain on the bed. "She must've sipped some and spilled the rest Zion." "Hopefully, Gabriel's coming out of it Niarchos. Is her purse here? I know it's bad luck to go in a woman's purse." "Is it Zion, why?"

"My mother said you find things not meant for your eyes." as he went into her purse. "Gabriel hasn't been taking her iron pills Niarchos." looking at the full bottle.

"She doesn't like taking them Zion." "It's not up to her Niarchos. Two of the babies are vampires, when they're hungry for blood they're gonna feed from her internally." "She'd better start taking them to keep her iron up and drinking more blood." "How much more Zion?"

"I'm prescribing four bottles per hour." "The 16 oz.?" "Yes." "What if she drinks from the vein?"

"She should drink until she's full." "I'll be sure to tell Clarence. Stay on her and help me Niarchos. It's bad enough, Clarence spoils her. I'm starting a blood drip, I'll return." All Niarchos thought of was her taste. He never bit a woman below. He learned from Chance that women go wild with the sensation of being bitten and cumming at the same time, he wasn't lying. He'd gotten his red wings and ran plenty of red lights when Liza had her menses. In fact, being vampire, he loved it.

Niarchos called the hospital. "This is Elder Niarchos, how is Elder Chance?" "He's sedated Elder the parasite is not multiplying from the powder he's stable."

"If he wakes, call me please nurse." "Of course, Elder."

"Thank you."

"Nicky?" He jumped up, sitting on the side of her bed holding her hand. "Why the drip?"

"You been sleeping Gabriel. "How long this time?" "Three days." "I had a dream it was great." "What was it about, ma?" "You went down." she mouthed.

"Gabriel it wasn't a dream." Gabriel touched his hand. Niarchos winced in pain. "What happened to you?" He opened his palm. "Palm bites heal slower. It'll be gone in a couple hours." "Nicky, how'd it start?" He explained all to her. Gabriel kissed his inner palm.

"I'm sorry Gabriel, I love you and want you. You floated to me, wanting to make love. It won't happen again Great One please forgive me," bowing his head respectfully. Gabriel pushed his chin up. "You're never bad for loving me. I need the love I get from you. I have a confession I woke up during. I knew what was happening and I didn't stop you. Clarence won't understand what we have. I love you both the same, but for varied reasons."

"I won't give you up Gabriel." "You gotta let go Niarchos. I'm begging you," tears rolling. "Shhh none of that. I'm never leaving, you in here," tapping his heart, "It won't let me, Gabriel." "Marry again Nicky. Fall in love stop answering my calls. Allow me to forget us, your Queen is begging." "Never," shaking his head defiantly as the couple love locked in an inseparable embrace when his phone rang. "Pop hey, guess who's up asking to call?" She dialed in. "Sugar!" "Hi Clarence." She sniffed trying to clear her voice of sorrow. "How you doing Sugar?" "Sleepy," showing the blood drip on video. "I'm flying in. I'll be home by 10 p.m. sweetie put Niarchos on please."

"Pop I'll work on him today since Gabriel's awake. How many wives talked pop?"

"Two Niarchos. They were reluctant about working to have Chance killed." "The link is the limo driver downstairs, Niarchos, crack him." "I'm on it Pop, see you when you arrive."

"Clarence?" "What's up Caleb." "I gotta share something important. When Chance made the jump with Gabriel in the valley, she fed from him thinking it was you after Niarchos drained her." "Dammit. Chance's wives poisoned him with parasites Caleb and Gabriel's pregnant."

"I hear they can't survive vein to mouth Clarence." "They can't but what about the babies Caleb?"

"Clarence, the babies will make it. What if there's a cure in Gabriel's blood? If she drank from Chance, then she drank the parasite, but it didn't survive in her." "Inform Zion to check Gabriel's blood samples after the cliff jump and compare them. It may help." "Caleb?" "Yes, Great One?"

"Will Gabriel leave Niarchos alone?" "No Clarence. Give them space. This is a lot on Gabriel. Niarchos makes her feel human. She can say anything, he won't flip out. Niarchos is laid back, you know that. When you argue with her Clarence, she'll seek solace in him. Get used to the south again Vampire King. There is where you'll raise your children and your children's children. Niarchos is in love with your wife, you know this yes?" "I don't like it, Caleb." "You threatened by him Clarence?"

"No title of Pharaoh, nothing I buy can bind her heart to mine. She must want to be bound to me on her own Caleb." "Let Gabriel have her love, let her have something she thinks is hers, something she doesn't have to share Clarence." "The something is Niarchos Caleb?" "Clarence calm down when you blow up you are no good to any of us. Safinah knew you were bark, no bite, Gabriel didn't. Easy old friend this is your counsel and the vision of your seer." "I accept your vision and wise counsel blood is life vampire seer." Caleb nodded his head respectfully.

Niarchos & The Driver....

Niarchos got to the basement pulling his chair to the cell where he held the human Limousine driver.

"Driver you hungry? What were they after?" "Yo man you broke my nose and look at my eye." "You want to see the Dr. human? There's one on staff."

"Call the nigga." Niarchos removed the man's wallet from his sweat jacket hanging outside the cells. "Michael Morgan, 32 Marion Street Brooklyn, I called your house an old woman answered and guess what Mike?

Me and Estelle are eating dinner later tonight. Did you know she was my type when she was younger? I mean Estelle doesn't know I'm technically older than she is to be honest. I explained you had to drive to Florida for an emergency and to let Tina the kids know.

I inquired how they're doing. Your oldest Shamir is graduating from high school. I thought that was impressive. Your daughter Temira? She's a junior in college. College women LOVE me Mike cause' I look their age. I mean I turned in my

20s. I think it's the whole teddy bear beard thing I got going on and these light vampire eyes are icing on the cake. Mike

What were they after Mike?" Niarchos was tired of playing with him.

"Don't hurt my family nigga!" "Your wife Tina, I'm bringing her here to turn her, I'll have the tv on letting you watch while I turn her vampire after she gags on my dick." Niarchos sent a text. "What the fuck are you doing?" "In boxing Temira on IG. dad" Ding!

**Nick: Meet for drinks?**

**Temira: When?**

**Niarchos: Tonight?**

"Look Mike so you know I'm not bluffing. Say what the fuck I need to know. I'm going to strip your daughter, fuck her every which way I please. Then feed from her until her heart slows beneath my naked chest. I'll keep drinking and fucking until I can't hear her pulse.

When I drain her dry you can take comfort in knowing she died happy cause she was fucked good on her way out. What were they after Mike? Who approached you because you been driving for us for a minute, what's up nigga? You a dumb nigga, the Pharaoh is a billionaire and so is Chance. Hell, we all are, they would've paid double." The driver remained silent.

Niarchos shrugged his shoulders leaving the cells. He called Temira to convince her to meet him at club Ambrosia. He left the phone with the security guards. "Charge it up, when you see me calling go downstairs put it on mute and speaker phone so he can hear." "Yes, Elder Niarchos." "Temira, hey, Yeah, I'm free, what you lookin to get into? Club Ambrosia? Yeah, I know It. Brooklyn heights, right? I'll meet you at the bar, of course I'm buying drinks beautiful all on me for you and your friends, in fact get a booth and bottle service. Ok sexy see you soon" "Go down and tell Mike the driver, the conversation you heard, convince him to give up what he knows to stop me." "Yes Elder."

"The Pharaoh returns 10 tonight, make sure all who're awake greet him at the door." "Yes, Elder Niarchos." Niarchos went to see Gabriel. Zion was removing the blood line. "Thank God, I can take a bath before Clarence gets here. I don't want him seeing me this way Zion all pregnant and unkempt." "How do you feel Gabriel?" "Rested Nicky." "Not hungry?" "I think they're asleep. Where are you going?" "To the club with Mike's daughter." "Who's Mike?" "The Limousine driver." "Oh man, SAVAGE! hehe"

"Come see me before you leave. What time you going Nicky?" "Nine thirty ish." Gabriel grabbed his dick. "Your husband will be here." "Hehe." Gabriel felt refreshed. She took a long hot bath adorning herself in perfumed oil. She combed her hair fluffing it to a large afro tying a floral scarf around the middle.

She tossed on sweats and a Black Girl's Rock tee, opening the window for fresh air. The wind carried the smell of Safinah's roses. Niarchos tapped the door before coming in. "Damn Nicky, wow, look at you," wolf whistling. "Cleaner than a Mississippi sheriff, gimme a 360 turn. You cut your hair, and I love the dinner jacket. Don't hurt the girl, Nicky."

"I have to save Chance Gabriel. Sometimes that means hurting someone, it's my job. Will you still love me?" "Always gladiator," pecking his full lips brushing his lapel. *A sweet gentle giant* she thought as he waved goodbye, taking off on his bike. *Sugar I'm there, Niarchos home?* Clarence mind pinged her. *No, he's working. See you soon. Ok Clarence.*

Niarchos arrived before his date. The owner, who was human greeted him. "What's up partner!" "I'm good little bro." "I got you on blood, I keep a stash when vampires come through." "If a girl named Temira comes, bring her to VIP." The ladies entered a few moments later.

"Temira?" flashing a trusting smile. Niarchos hugged her, "Have a seat ladies order what you like on me." They spared him no expense. It's what he wanted. The night was late he led her to the dance floor.

Temira grinded her naked pussy on his thigh. Niarchos knew she wanted to fuck. "You ready to leave Temira?" "Yeah, allow me say bye to my girls." "I'll wait outside." before going to pay at the bar. He came out and got his bike, pulling up front out of camera view. He took her to a hotel. As soon she entered the room she jumped on him, stripping his clothes. He loathed fast women. There were time's he liked his woman taking control, like Gabriel jumping him to feed while grabbing his manhood.

He pretended to like her, but his dick wasn't going up. He thought of eating Gabriel's pussy, rocking up instantly. Niarchos dialed Temira's father Mike.

Security walked the phone downstairs on mute and speaker playing loudly bouncing off the walls of empty cells. "Temira you're a fucking sexy bitch." kissing her neck as she moaned his name. Mike yelled, frustrated. "Are you going to give names?" The vampire security asked. "Why do they want Elder Chance dead?" "Open them legs, lemme meet fat mama."

"Driver, after he fucks your daughter, he's going to kill her, your child! The baby you held at birth? Dead in minutes. Is that what you want? Did you teach her to ride a bike? Nurse her through illness? Saw her in school plays? You're never holding your child again think of that driver."

The moaning continued then the phone disconnected. Security text Niarchos No break Elder. Niarchos set his phone so the room could be seen. He called security on video. The guard turned on the T.V on the wall in the basement outside the cell. Niarchos had the driver's daughter on her knees, deep sucking and gagging on his inches. Niarchos stared at the camera pointing a gun over her skull. She didn't realize a vampire threatened to end her existence she was too engrossed in deep throat.

Mike screamed at the TV, No! Security opened the mic. "Confess! You can end this. She doesn't have to die Mike." Niarchos held her head, "What that mouth do Temira? She sucked faster as he held back her hair in a ponytail. "Nah ma don't make me cum like that." Niarchos held his head back moaning. At her fire head skills.

Security was on speaker, "Again once he nuts driver, he's killing your daughter, your family and he'll kill you violently because you made him kill innocent humans. Who sent you? Who do you work for Mike?" Mike stared nervous and afraid to answer.

Niarchos had his daughter bent over, doggy style banging and pulling her hair. She loved his disrespectful fuck. He pushed her on the bed, holding her down with his foot on her back, pounding with all his weight tossing his back in it. "You need a minute?" "No Daddy, I fucking love it!" She drooled. He grabbed her throat, tonging her down, licking the sweat from her neck and cheeks keeping his grip.

His savage roamed the room. The vampire was eager to drain her. "Take every inch of this dick bitch all of it. Suck it down." Niarchos stopped to sip water and text security.

Niarchos: Did he break? Security: No Elder. Niarchos: Is he watching? Security: Yes Elder. Niarchos: Turn out the light, leave the television on. Security: Yes Elder. Security turned on the video feed from Niarchos' phone linked to the T.V. He opened her legs missionary position, her head hanging off the king-sized bed facing the camera. He dug pussy to balls deep pounding issuing disrespectful sex as he dripped spit in her welcoming mouth drinking all of it like daddy's whore.

Drink it all bitch you better not spill a fucking drop. Fangs popped, he looked directly into the camera biting her jugular vicious hard and painful growling raising her fear index.

Niarchos fed holding her wrist with the opposite hand his thumb on her pulse. She orgasmed several times as he drank, she creamed his dick silky white unaware she was being murdered. Temira didn't understand what was happening. Ecstasy and desire segued to euphoria, terror and fear giving way to chaos ending in the realization she was being killed by a vampire savage. Mike watched and listened to his first-born struggle to free herself from the bogey man she was warned about.

Wiggling, punching, scratching, biting, kicking, nothing freed her from his terrifying grip. He thrust in her ignoring her need of oxygen closing the hand that once gripped her throat in pleasure now clutched it in an unauthorized sexual death pact. "Mmmm....Damn...Shit girl. Whew!"

As life left her eyes Niarchos stared directly into the camera with blood-stained fangs licking her bloody cheek and fingers as chills ran down Mikes spine watching his child cling to life. Her head dropped listless; eyes wide open looking at her dad through the camera. "Damn Mike, I'm unsure what was sweeter her pussy or her blood. Both are sweet as fuck." growling squeezing and shaking her tiny throat theatrically laughing maniacally.

He kicked her dead body off the bed with his foot then stood over her shaking his dripping cum over her face, wiping his dick dry with her hair before cutting the camera. Mike screamed in agony his pain echoed through mansion walls. Every vampire in the house heard through the soundproof walls. "What is that Clarence?" "Niarchos doing his job Sugar." Niarchos made a call. "I need a bus." The vampire cleanup crew showed erasing her, deep cleaning the room of blood and sperm residue, making it spotless. They paid motel staff creating a power outage in the hotel, wiping the video footage clean. They replaced the entire bed and the carpet.

Vampire clean up dropped her to a crematorium Niarchos owned. "Save her ashes, put her in a beautiful urn, and drop it off at the house by morning, please." "Yes, Elder." "Her friends?" "Hypnotized by Elder Elijah to believe she left alone." Niarchos arrived home, beating the sun. He headed to the basement where Mike was on the floor of the cell, screaming and crying in excruciating agony.

"Why man...she was a kid!" "Are you ok, Mike? Sorry for your loss." Niarchos sat in front of the cell as Mike reached to grab and kill him. "It's your fault she's dead Mike, whatever they were offering you meant more to you than your kid. You killed your daughter; you could've stopped it. You could've stopped ME! I gave you several opportunities. It's called don't fuck with me, Mike."

Niarchos tossed something on the floor of his cell, a necklace reading 'Daddy's girl.' "I thought about you. I see Tina tomorrow, Mike." "No! wait I'll speak with the Pharaoh."

"Get some rest Mike. You look like somebody died." Mike clutched his daughter's necklace, crying himself to sleep. Security in the booth laughed. "You a savage, boy." "It's not funny I had to kill an innocent girl tonight." "Sorry, Elder." "The vampire in me loves it, but when the human resurfaces, he brings guilt with him." "I understand, Elder forgive my ignorance." "Did the Pharaoh arrive?" "Yes, Elder." "Goodnight. Thank you."

Niarchos showered, hitting the bed dropping his clothes on the floor. When he woke, Gabriel had his clothes folded. "Good morning, Vampire Queen."

"Good morning, Nicky." "Is the window open?" "Yes bae." "Close the window, Gabriel." "Is fear in the Vampire Gladiator?" "Of course, not woman." "Just because you and Clarence are 100% vampire doesn't mean you can't let the sun in. It can't touch you, Nicky." "It makes us weak, Gabriel, even if we aren't directly in sunlight, UV rays spread like vines." "Are you weak, Nicky?" "Not yet." "When you're weak, I'll close it."

"Stop making excuses, Gabriel. What if you couldn't walk in the sun anymore, would you want to see what you can't have?" "I don't think about depressing things Nicky." "You love sunshine, Gabriel?" "I do. If God sees fit to take it away there must be a good reason. I trust God." "God doesn't love us; we're children of the night, forgotten Honey." Don't say that Niarchos, It's blasphemy. We're a chosen people, uplifted from slavery the mud to show our people the way. We leapfrog through time living an eternity, we help uplift the betterment of melanated people, vampire, or human.

Free healthcare, daycare, afterschool, senior centers, immigration assistance, food pantries, CDL classes, nursing school, and orphanages. How else would these families have made it, Nicky? I'm starting a reading program for those who can't read. That's why we're here: to fix what went wrong, baby. Don't let me hear you say that again. You're blessed and chosen to lead lost people our people understood?"

"Yes, my Queen." He nodded his head in respect of her wisdom. "And about last night the man was crying in agony. He woke me from sleep what did you do Niarchos?" "My job Queen," looking away, ashamed.

"Nicky?" "Nothing, Gabriel." "We lie to each other?" Niarchos looked out the window. There was something about him he didn't want Gabriel to know—his savage side—or ever see; it was his weakness. He wasn't like his father, who allowed her to see all of who he was, scaring her in the end.

"Some things are not meant for a woman to see. This is one Gabriel. I did what I'd do to any human who has something to do with hurting the people I love. Where's your husband?" "I'm looking at him." "You better stop," he grinned. "Clarence is getting coffee. I gotta go before he comes back up." She kissed him, running through the hidden door. "Shhhhhhhh," finger to mouth. He was surprised; he never knew the door was there. Niarchos knocked on his father's bedroom door once he returned.

"Pharaoh, good morning. Mike wants to talk." "I'll see him when we're done," smiling at Gabriel. Clarence loved the north; he wanted to see what the black soldiers he buried in the south died for. What's the hype about New York? Is the negro treated with more respect than in the south? It was true; there was more advancement in the north regarding the negro. Clarence was tired of hiding his love for Safinah. Long after slavery ended, he refused to allow ignorance to enslave him from properly loving his wife; by openly confessing he was negro thus his decision to move North.

"I want to prepare a bath for us, Clarence." "Wait till I return, Sugar. A bath without rose petals? Tsk, shame on you. I'll return, shortly Sugar. Walk with me, Niarchos." They exited. "What happened?" Niarchos told him everything—the girl, how it made him feel during and when he was done.

"All vampires in the house heard it. The news spread on the vampire grapevine, making its way through the covens, to Mara. "You must allow the savage out son, or he'll make his way out. Trust me, and you don't want that. No regrets, ever understand?" "Yes, papa."

"Good stay with Gabriel please." Clarence rolled his hand over Niarchos' head something he did with all his children. "Hold on, Pop," picking up his walkie. "The Pharaoh is on his way. Meet him by the elevator, please."

"I don't need an escort, Niarchos." "I know you don't, Pop. It's a safety precaution. You're an old vampire haha." "Yeah, ok son." Clarence saw Khrista in the foyer. "I hear you made a killing at the games in home and land sales." "I did, Great One. All your rental vacancies have been filled downtown Brooklyn and Georgia. I have a special surprise for you and our Queen."

"Say, you know I love real estate deals Khrista." "I'm working on an estate in Martha's Vineyard, one mile away from

Michelle and Barack Obama, Great One." "Impressive. I have a few houses in the Vineyard already and a 50-acre spread of land. Were you aware, Khrista?"

"No, Pharaoh," her eyes lighting up. "One of the wineries rents lands; they've been attempting to purchase it for decades. The answer is no." "Why may I ask?"

"Why should I sell? I stand to make more money renting it. We are vampires, we never die. The grapes aren't going anywhere. If they decide to leave the land, the grapes remain. I could start a wine line, sell the grapes to supermarkets; there are many business ventures I could pursue. If I sell, do I lose or gain money over a vampire's lifetime?" "Over time, you'll lose it, Great One." "Yes, I will, and time is all we vampires have. Can you and your husband use a weekend alone?" "Yes, Great One, please." "I'll have Joan get you keys Khrista."

"Thank you, Great One. I'll have my lawyers send you the real estate portfolio." "Thank you, Great One." "You're welcome." Clarence stepped on and off the elevator. "Great one," All security kneeled. "What happened...why was the driver screaming? The guard explained all that happened. "In his defense, Elder Niarchos asked eight times about Elder Chance. What is he holding back that cost his child's life, Great One?"

"Elder Niarchos needs no defense nor witness from any vampire. He's a high Elder of the vampire crown a coven leader, head of security and a prince of covens; he owes no one an explanation ever." "Yes, Great Pharaoh, my apologies." Upon exiting the elevator, a vampire security guard drew his gun. "You wanted to see me, driver?"

Clarence looked out of the corner of his eye as the guard cocked his gun before pulling the trigger alerting Clarence who teleported out of harm's way. The bullets he fired lodged in the wall behind where Clarence once stood. Clarence reappeared behind the traitorous vampire security, pushing his head into the wall the bullets were lodged in, restraining himself from killing him. Clarence opened the cell, tossing the betrayer of the crown in.

"Wait! This doesn't have anything to do with me!" The driver yelled. "I want to talk! Please don't hurt my family, please! Great

One, please!" When the elevator opened, guards rushed Clarence upstairs, locking down the estate. The gates were lowered, the doors and windows sealed with steel, time-sensitive digital locks. "Gabriel, don't touch the bars! they're electric."

Niarchos arrived with guns drawn. "Who's with Gabriel, Niarchos?" "Zion and Joan what the hell happened, Pop?" "Chase tried to kill me, get all security front and center now." Niarchos did as told; all were lined up. "ON YOUR KNEES!" Any available vampires in the house were instructed to come to the living room to defend the Pharaoh. The baby vampires were ready to fight; they lived for shit like this.

"You will all, hold up your wrists!" Clarence bit with four fangs, piercing the wrist of each security. He went down the line, gulping mouthfuls of blood, biting the bone. Clarence purposely inflicted pain, reminding them he's King. He'd drink and wait to see if anyone was involved with his assassination attempts.

Clarence grabbed Khrista biting her neck. She never resisted. He drank, rolling rich red blood on his tongue and lips, squeezing her close while she remained under his hypnotic connection. Through her eyes he saw the truth unbeknownst to her.

Before he could run, Niarchos shot him with a tranquilizer bullet. Clarence handed Khrista to Niarchos, who sat her on the couch gingerly. Still entranced Clarence hadn't released her from his telekinetic connection. Clarence continued to bite and drink; no one had anything to do with his attempted murder or Chance's. He locked two of them downstairs in cell three.

Clarence ran up the steps to Gabriel's bedroom, straight to the shower. Gabriel entered the room. "Clarence?" Niarchos stopped her at the bathroom door. "What're you doing? Move, Niarchos. Nicky, move!"

He didn't. Gabriel pushed him; he smiled. She looked around, opening her blouse. When he looked down at her juicy nipples, she ducked under his arm, opening the bathroom door, sliding in on the moist floor. Blood stained her clothes and face. "Baby," she opened the shower door, joining him, checking his body. "You shot?" "No, Sugar," holding him, crying in the shower, thinking he been hurt.

Clarence stared at Niarchos. *How'd you let her get past you? She tricked me, Pop.* "Sugar, can I finish up? You forgot the roses daddy." "Close the door." Gabriel removed her clothes entering the shower, hugging him from behind. "We finish later, Sugar?"

"Yes." He wiped the rain shower drops off her pretty skin. Clarence exited the shower, tossing on clean clothes. "Stay with her, Niarchos. I'll return."

"Nicky? Go next door and get a towel, please." "You used them all Gabriel." He handed her a washcloth.

"Don't tempt me, Nicky" He ignored her. "Ok, you asked for it." Gabriel exited the bathroom, wet, wearing his Gucci tee from the night before. It was see-through; her round, hard nipples pushed through the double G pattern.

"What?" When she went out the door, all he saw and heard was wet fat ass through the back clapping and jiggling like jelly, licking his lips.

"Get the cards, Gabriel, in the nightstand." She got the cards. "You don't want none." "You forgot who my brother is woman?" "Chance is a mathematician; they didn't have a name for it back then, but that's what he's. You know he graduated from Tuskegee? His concentration was math. NASA wanted to hire him; he loves those cards; it's his addiction. Do you know we discovered he's a billionaire? I knew he was rich but not that rich, ma. What about you? Could you care for a wife financially?"

"Yes." "How much you worth Nicky $10?" "You wish, woman. I'm worth enough." "It doesn't matter if all you had was a quarter, I'd still want you. Did you know your father lied to me for two years?" Y'all dated two years?" "Yep, he never slept with me. I thought he was gay. How could he be around all this pound cake and not want a slice, Nicky hehe?" "Weren't you ill, ma?"

"Yeah, and Nicky?" "Pop was concentrating on getting you better." "You knew about me, Nicky?" "Yes, and an no Gabriel. I heard he was creeping, staying days away with no security, doing overnights, not telling where he was. Pop kept the relationship quiet. I understand why; look what happened when he announced his marriage. We were shocked wondering who's the mystery woman?" "I tried hiding my cancer from him; he knew. He'd read until I slept, clean the house, mow the lawn, take out the garbage. Do you know he repaired the roof? Clarence planted roses all around the property; neighbors thought he was a landscaper offering him pay." "Papa, remembered how to do manual labor." "No limos, Nicky. He drove a beat-up red Toyota."

"Haha, you for real Gabriel?" "Yes, cheap clothes, no name we are all we needed in my tiny house in Queens" "You wanna go tomorrow night, Gabriel?" "Sure, I bet it's a mess." "Doubt it. I know Pop, he has someone maintaining it. He's good that way."

The Pharoah & The Limo Drover....

"Clarence went to the basement with three armed guards; he was with the human driver." "What do you want?" "Your son is a savage." "Who sent you?" "I'm unsure vampire."

"Clarence rose. No, wait! A man called the limousine asking if I heard about a cure for Chance. I explained no. They promised if I heard anything, they'd pay three million tax-free dollars." "What did you report human?" "I heard you were pressing his wives in Georgia when we were at the house. Someone said they were going to crack. I mentioned there was a package being sent back to New York, one to help Chance get better."

"They inquired what time we were leaving for the airport. I never knew it was an ambush. They called my cell too. Your son has the phone. The number's on there. I swear it's all I got. Someone high up wants your son dead, Great One. Look at his wives and business transactions. The men threatened to kill my family if I talked, but your son killed my daughter because I didn't. Please, Pharaoh, I didn't know!"

Clarence moved his chair to the security guard's cell." "A vampire attempting to end the Pharoah's life. What punishment does that carry Great One?" "Death, there may be leniency. Who sent you?" "I wish to speak with a vampire attorney." "As you wish." Clarence looked at security; they opened the cell, grabbing his wrist. Clarence drained forty percent of his blood, weakening him. Clarence saw an identical offer presented to him as the driver. He returned to the human. "Stick out your hand." He nicked his hand, drinking blood."

*Same voice on the phone, same offer. Why Chance what's the connection?* "Clarence needed to get to Georgia to examine Chance's paperwork." "Pharaoh, I'm human. Can I please get medical help, a meal...It's been five days?"

"Open cell three." They grabbed Chase Khrista's husband. Clarence bit into his wrist, same man, different offer as the driver the guard received. Clarence saw her husband rifling through his office for paperwork, finding nothing. Khrista, his wife, overheard the call of him reporting findings against the Pharoah. She was about to report him when they were lined up by Niarchos. Clarence instructed security to free Khrista. She got on the elevator, crying and shaken, to her room.

"It's not the money; my wife is in love with you, Great One I want to give her what you have so Khrista will look at me as she does you." "Have I ever returned the feeling toward her Chase? Ever called her to my bed chamber or made a sexual advance?"

"No, Great One." "What is the penalty for vampire treason?" "Death, Great One." "Yo, dude, stop talking. Ask for a vampire attorney." Chase stopped talking. "Feed the human and see to his medical care. The other two, water only, no blood. If they feed from one another, tranquilize them." "Yes, Pharaoh." Clarence exited the basement to the main floor.

"Joan, can you please go outside and get rose petals off the ground?" "Sure, Clarence." She took a Ziploc filling it up. "Tell Zion to come draw my blood please. I fly out tonight, Joan." "Ok." Clarence took the roses to Gabriel, who was losing money. "How much have you lost, Sugar?" "$1000." "You want me to win it back?" "No!" Niarchos laughed at her pouting. Niarchos took his money, putting it in her purse. He loved her; he couldn't take her money.

Clarence lay her down, rubbing her back. They watched the sunrise off the patio. "Remember how we used to lay this way in Queens?" "Yep, I pulled your bed out of the sun. Ms., open the window, it's a new day." "Hehe." He hugged her close, smelling her hair.

"Gabriel, do you love me?" "Why do you keep asking?" "Do you love Niarchos?" "Yes, to both, with all my heart. Any more questions? I love you both differently, I keep telling you." "Will you leave me?" "If you do, I'll die," Gabriel turned to him, staring into blazing brown pools. "Listen to the Pharaoh talk foolishly. I'll never ever leave you. I love you; you saved me." "Is that why you love me, Gabriel?" "It's part of it. I love your hair, smile, the way you look at me adoringly when I'm wrong. How you spoil, kill for me, and protect me. You're smart, funny, kind, and loving--

"Jealous!"

"Yes, jealous. I love you, all of it good, bad, and ugly." Gabriel kissed him, sucking his bottom lip. Clarence readied for their bath, 100% enamored by her. He couldn't blame Niarchos; she was easy to love. What is it about her that's so bewitching? Whatever it was, she him hook, line and sinker.

# Chapter 31
# Strike It Rich

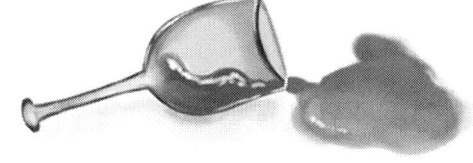

Good morning, Great One;

Please see attached records you requested regarding Elder Chance. The following are included:

Paperwork and marriage certificates for wives and concubines legally claimed, and or any prenuptial written agreements.

Elder Chance's real estate portfolio, including but not limited to all deals he's currently engaged in.

Proof of finances, access to bank accounts in the United States and abroad. These records include deposits and withdrawals for three years.

A list of art and antiquities, including but not limited to jewels, cars, guns, coins, and stamps. Please be advised this sits within vampire vault #05201871. The vault may be accessed by you in the absence of Elder Chance.

If there is any way we may be of further assistance, please don't hesitate to call, Great One."

### -The Vampire Legal Authority-

Clarence sat in Chance's office at Twin Oaks, shifting through piles of paperwork. He searched for anything that might explain why their lives were in danger, finding nothing. Clarence decided to look at Chance's real estate portfolio; for that, he needed Mary.

"Papa Nate, please sneak Mary here. Make sure no vampires are being questioned before bringing her, thank you." Mary entered, closing the door. "Hello, Mary."

"How is Gabriel, Clarence?" "Getting fat and sexier, the way I like." Mary glanced at the paperwork Clarence handed her. "How should we go through it, Clarence?"

"Using deeds we can separate the properties, Mary."

Mary recited the addresses on the deeds, as Clarence made a list; there were five hundred properties. The trio tried figuring out a connection. Papa rested in the corner listening. "Where's Twin Oaks deed?" Clarence and Mary searched again. "Papa Nate, you're correct; it's missing."

"Why would anyone want this plantation, Clarence?" "The historical value, Papa Nate?" "Chance met a woman at the African American Museum in D.C. to declare this land a black landmark, Clarence. Her card is in the desk on the left," Mary pointed. "Her name is Latish I think." "I have it, Mary. Latasha McLarin." Clarence dialed. "Hello, this is Clarence Hollings. May I speak with Ms. Latasha McLarin? I'm sorry to hear. When was she killed? Four days ago? Can you assist? I'm the father of the owner of Twin Oaks, a former plantation and Negro burial ground with original slave quarters. Yes, sir, Chance the gambler." Clarence smiled. "Did the poker tips work? Good. I understand Ms. McLarin assisted in getting the estate declared landmark property. She never filed the paperwork?"

Killed one day before the filing? The filing postponed, till when please? Forty-five days. Yes, please send that. Did Ms. McLarin have a deed copy in her file? Yes, I'll hold. Yes sir, I'm here, no? It is odd, isn't it? Correct me if I'm wrong, Mr.

Warren, would the deed be needed to prove ownership and authenticity of Twin Oaks? I thought so. Yes, we'd like to proceed. The number is 718-556-9990 thank you, Mr. Warren, for your time."

"Why would anyone want this plantation? Why not ask to buy it, Clarence?" "People have over the decades, Papa Nate, but Chance refuses to sell. It was a gift from me." "Chance made sure before he married the others they relinquished claim to this estate, Clarence."

"You too, Mary?" "No sir, if anything happened to him, his ownership reverts back to me." "That's not right, Mary." "What do you mean Clarence?" "I gifted this estate to Chance, I no longer own it, Papa Nate." "What if he never filed the new deed removing you? Chance is superstitious; removing you would mean messing with his luck."

"You both are right, but that doesn't explain why Twin Oaks? I know this plantation like the back of my hand, Papa. At sundown, we ride out have Miguel saddle our horses. Tell Grip I hope he remembers how to ride." "Yes sir." Papa was excited; it reminded him of the old days. "How is Niarchos, Clarence?" "Crazy talking, Papa. How?" "Gabriel's been visiting him; he promised her a buggy ride." "Hehe, how is that big old negro vampire gonna fit in that tiny buggy, Clarence?" "Guess what, Mary? Gabriel's arguing, saying 'we're going on a buggy ride' real fresh."

"Haha, hehe," Mary and Papa laughed at his mocking Gabriel's voice. "I said, 'Gabriel, make sure I'm there cause I wanna see this.'" "He's crazy for her, Clarence. It's something about her." "Is it, Mary?"

"Yes, remember Mother Clarence?" "I do God rest her soul; the church was packed when she died. She purposely requested a sundown service so you could attend the funeral, Mary. She was a good woman, made all my suits. I still have them; I wear them all on all Hallows Eve." "Gabriel reminds me of her, a good-hearted person, a lover of people. These people aren't born often. God placed a light in them, a healing light everyone is drawn to, Clarence." "Thank you, Mary, I hadn't thought of it that way."

Niarchos & The Driver
Cremation....

Niarchos went to the basement, staring into the limo driver Mike's cell sitting in front of it. "I spoke with the Pharaoh; when am I going home?" Niarchos put the urn on the floor. "I purchased you a visitor, Mike."

"I wrapped her all pretty in pink, I said give her the best. I had her name engraved in marble right there. If you make it out here, you can take your child home. At least you'll know where she's, not like some people wondering if she's dead. Not you, Mike. Your answer is here," tapping the urn chuckling. Mike filled with anguish, tears falling. Niarchos sat in front of cell two, glaring in.

"We know about your kids and wife security. Your family buried you and you emerged, vampire," Niarchos bellowed a deep laugh. "Who dug you up, nigga?"

"My wife." "How the hell did she figure it out Dre?" "Said she knew I wasn't dead. She read the autopsy, fang bites. She put it together." Niarchos clapped sarcastically. "Who made you, Dre?" "A rogue vampire Elder, Niarchos. I was taken in by Elder Caine." "That's why I never take in rogue vampire stray dog trash like you, Dre."

You deserve death by sunlight, scum. You ain't shit, vampire." Dre reached to grab Niarchos, the bars burning him. "What's up, nigga, you and me!" Dre was furious. "When?" Niarchos asked calmly. "Don't do it, man." Chase called out. He's an Elder vampire; he's naturally stronger and strength is one of his vampire gifts." "Open cell two," Niarchos called out as he growled invading his personal. space face to face.

"I'm here," Niarchos popped his fangs. "Like I said, pussy ass coward. You ain't shit if you got vampire blood coursing in your veins your business would be handled when I opened the cell, weak ass nigga," pushing Dre to the floor.

Niarchos moved to Chase's cell "Your wife is sexy nigga," Niarchos rubbing his hands. "I'll take care of her after you're executed Chase, make her my new wife. Khrista is afraid to be bitten; that shit, it's a huge turn-on." "You're already making your move on Queen Gabriel; you think we don't know, nigga?"

"Yep, Chase." Mike heckled from the corner cell. "I'm scared. Fuck outta here, clowns. The Pharaoh knows all I fucking do. Good try though. Back to Khrista umm, that ass, lips, and hips, man, I'm gonna tear her up make her an Elders wife. Give her all the shit you're too weak and stupid to get for her fine ass." Chase spat in Niarchos' face. "See, I was being nice. When they judge you who do you think sits on the vampire high court?" "If you say all you know, I may help you both get less time for cooperation with the crown." He removed a tissue. "Since you wanna act like this," wiping his face, "security, no water or blood for cell one three days NBO."

"He's going to die, Elder!" Dre shouted. "Keep talking, I'll add more days to that no blood order. What did you say?" Holding his ear. "I didn't think so."

"Human? You ready for your once slice cheese sandwich?" Niarchos wickedly, walked to the security room, cutting on the mic in the cells.

Mike was speaking to Chase using sign language. Niarchos recorded them calling the vampire legal authority. "Hello? Get me the deaf vampire girl from Elder Vaughn's coven, please This is Elder Niarchos yes, I'll hold. Record them, Jay." "Yes, Elder." "Has anyone called their phones?" "Yes Elder, identical number on all three lines." "Which one gets called the most?" "Chase Elder." Niarchos texted Gabriel.

Honey: Wyd, Niarchos? Nicky: Laying down, you? Honey: Hungry, Niarchos. Nicky: For what, Gabriel? Honey:

Coffee cake. Nicky: I'll get it Gabriel. Honey: Come through the wall between the rooms Niarchos. Nicky: Ok

Niarchos brought her decaf coffee and lemon cake. "Did you take your iron, Gabriel?" "Yes." "I missed you today, Nicky can I ask a favor?" "Yes." "Can you cuddle me to sleep?" "What if I fall asleep too, ma?" "The doors are locked Nicky." "We can't risk it. I'm sleepy too, Gabriel rest. I'll stay up till you're asleep, ma." "Can you rub my back, Nicky?" "Yes, my love." She lay on his lap; his large hands smoldered every curve in her back.

"Did you drink blood today, Queen?" "One." "Gabriel, they'll feed from you. They don't know they are killing you. They are vampires and vampires need blood please ma." Niarchos bit into his wrist; she fed, falling asleep. Niarchos got in his own bed. He tried to turn early morning hours and couldn't because she was nestled behind him. Niarchos opened the adjoining door, putting her back in her bed. Gabriel woke early, dressed, and went downstairs to the jail cells. She got off the elevator, walking past the cells, looking for the human.

Chase and Dre kneeled. "Good morning, Great Queen." "Good morning," stopping at the human's cell offering an orange; he'd been crying, clutching the urn close to him.

"I'm sorry. You've my deepest sympathies. I'll do everything possible to see you home." Security Jay ran to get Niarchos. "Come! The Queen is in the tombs talking to Mike the driver Elder."

Niarchos hyper-sped in pajamas, pulling her back from the cell growling at Mike, fangs in tow. Afraid, Mike cowered to the wall, trembling in fear. The two vampires dared not speak with Gabriel in Niarchos' presence. "Great One, have mercy on me," Chase begged on his hands and knees. "I beg for forgiveness and leniency."

She pushed Niarchos aside. "Don't move Chase or ill snap your neck." "It's ok Elder, he won't harm the Pharaoh's wife, will you Chase?" "No, Queen Gabriel," she put her hand in the cell for Chase; the bars didn't burn her.

He clutched her hand. "Will you confess if we speak alone?" "Yes, Queen." "I'll see what I can arrange with Elder Niarchos." "Thank you, Great One."

She went to Dre's cell. "Tsk did you attempt to kill the Pharaoh Dre?" He didn't answer, holding his head in shame. "Why?" "He's rogue vampire scum Great One no other reason." Gabriel touched Niarchos' arm calming him. "No one is scum, Elder. Were you scum because they forced you into slavery?" "No, Great One." "Were you given a choice to be vampire or was it forced on you, Dre?"

"Someone jumped me, my Queen." "You turned alone with no understanding of vampire law, your Pharaoh, nor his origin?" "Yes, Great One." She shook her head, crying for him. "Were you aware the Pharaoh went through an identical ordeal, attacked and left alone?"

He stared at her, tears in his eyes. "I'm sure if you knew, you wouldn't agree to kill such a magnanimous vampire."

"No, I wouldn't have, great Queen." "I've called you both vampire lawyers; I will pay for your defense from the charitable fund. They'll arrive at 12 p.m." "Thank you great Queen." "Niarchos was livid, controlling himself until they were alone."

Arriving upstairs, they quarreled in front of Joan. "What're you doing out of bed, Gabriel?" "It's visiting day, Joan, haven't you heard?" Niarchos heckled sarcastically. "Gabriel, you went to the tombs alone?" Joan dropped a plate. "Are you crazy, Gabriel? Why would you do that, sweetie? When they don't drink blood, they become ravenous...uncontrollable one could have killed you. If one grabbed, you Clarence would put them to death instantly to make an example of what happens if you touch his Queen. Your action could have gotten a vampire killed sweetie."

"God said to go, so I went Joan" "God said go without security to see the vampire assassins who tried to kill you and, your husband, Gabriel?" "Don't mock me, Niarchos Clarence Hollings, and don't you mock God! I'm not crazy. I hear the voice of God and when I hear him, I obey!" "I'm telling your husband." "Inform him snitch! I don't give a fuck!" Gabriel entered her bedroom, locking her door. "Look what you did, Niarchos."

"Joan, she was in danger." "God does talk to people, Niarchos she may be one." "Let him tell her to take security with her Joan." "Hehe your bad stop fighting with the Pharaoh's wife. Clarence gave her full access to the house. If you're mad, talk to Clarence." Joan walked away. "Don't upset the babies Niarchos you heard Zion make her happy. Fix it!"

He knocked on her door. "Great One? Please allow me to explain." Gabriel ignored him. He went into his room, opening the secret door. "What do you want, how dare you Nicky?"

"You scared me honey," down on one knee, remembering his place. "I told my grandmother sometimes I hear God's voice. When I was diagnosed with cancer, I cried hoping I didn't perish. I didn't know how he was gonna cure me, but he did Nicky not the way I thought. Guess what he said, 'you are not going to die.' I laughed Nicky mocked God I said the doctors said...He cut me off and said 'how dare you! I am your God not the Doctor, I said you shall be healed.' "With that he left me. Weeks later I met Clarence."

"I was six when my uncle touched me. I heard God say, 'I'm sending your grandma to help.' Niarchos, my grandma, worked overnight at the hospital every day except Sunday. Lo and behold, she entered on a Wednesday night catching him red-handed. I wondered, what's she doing home Nicky? I asked her and do you know what she said? God told her to go home Nicky. There's more he shared about you, Niarchos."

"What did he say honey?" "You're not mocking, are you?" "No, honey I swear." "For me to keep drinking your blood because one of the babies is special like you and needs it." "I'm special?" "To God and me, you are." he cried. "God loves me, Gabriel?" "Of course, he does. You and Clarence are special to him. I don't know why yet but he bought you two together for a reason. There is a reason your father was so drawn to you.

That reason is because God made him obsess over you. I knew it when I heard the scroll."

Niarchos leaned in kissing her, she moved away. "No! You can't be my boo today." "Why?" "Because you threatened to snitch me out." She picked up her phone. "Tell him. He won't do anything but yell at you, Nicky." "You wanna bet?" "What do I get if I win Gabriel?" "What do you want, Nicky?" "Kisses for twenty minutes." "If I win?" "Blood anytime you ask, no fighting for two days straight." "Agreed, Nicky. Use your phone since you're dry snitching." "Hello, Pop? Yes, everything's fine. What about you?"

"Discovered what? Wow, you can't be serious. Does Chance know? Did Mary or any of those women know? Is Jamaica questioning them? When are you going to Chance's vault? I want to go. I'll fly out tomorrow. Gabriel can watch herself pop. Pop, ask Grip to stay with her," shaking her head no. "It's not up to Gabriel pop you're Pharaoh. Yes, ok pop. Speaking of which," putting the phone on speaker, "You must speak to Gabriel, pop. She woke when I was sleep visiting the tombs to speak with prisoners with no guard and they're on NBO."

"Why Niarchos?" "God told her to, Pop. Why is her thumbprint added to the elevator keypad for the basement level? She could've been hurt." "If she got hurt, Niarchos, you're to blame." "Why, Pop?" "You're older and wiser. She's a baby vampress hormones all over the place and she is still turning. We have no idea what is going on in her head or her body. Help me care for her like we cared for you when you turned a century ago. How will you explain to your father his wife and unborn vampire triplets are dead by draining Niarchos?" "Pop? I was asleep. She does not sleep through a turn like you or I"

"There is a secret door in the room. I don't want you to tell anyone. At night, lock the doors yours, hers. Then open the joining door Gabriel will show you. You should be able to hear her. You can do that, can't you son?" "Pop, you serious?"

"Yes, Niarchos protect the Queen of vampires and your siblings within her. We need them to strengthen the crown just like I needed you Chance, Grip and Zhou. Should I continue naming the humans I turned and am responsible for making our empire strong? I'm going to call Gabriel and speak with her." "Ok, Pop, why are you hard on me?" "You and your brothers ask the same question of me. When I made you all you were boys, I reared you strong powerful vampire alpha males able to rule this kingdom in my absence including Zhou."

"To answer your question, I love you Niarchos. I trust you with my life and the life of my unborn children and Queen. When I hear you making excuses it irks me because I know that's not the ruthless vampire your mother and I raised, and it sounds like weakness and a copout. I don't raise weak vampire males. Did I answer your question son?" "Yes, pop bye." Niarchos smiled dabbing his eyes. "Hehe! You tried it! He told you off!" Sticking out her tongue teasing him. "Cry baby." Her phone rang. "Your turn wicked witch." Gabriel giggled putting it on the speaker phone.

"Hey daddy." Pretending to be asleep, "Hey Sugar, were you sleep?" "I was earlier I returned to lay down. Must've dozed off reading a new book called Male order bride it a space opera by Blk Qween the vampress author I told you Caleb referred me to." Yes, I've met her, she is a beautiful vampress. How are you, Sugar?" "Better. I wanted to go to the mall?" "Not yet Sugar order offline please. How are our babies?" "Greedy." "Have you thought about the house near the orchard?" "Not yet." "Can I see the estate when I come down?"

"Sugar, I don't think you're traveling away from Zion." "I'm two months pregnant. I'm fine until we get closer to the due date, Clarence." "You went to medical school, Sugar?" "Did Zion say I can't travel Mr. Hollings?" "You should rest as much as possible because your turn isn't complete, Gabriel." "Did he say I can't travel daddy?" "No." "Then it's settled. You take me." "Sugar?" "Yes, bae?" "I'm not ready mentally its triggering." "I understand, Clarence." "I'll buy you another house, whatever one you want, honey." "Clarence, you must expel your demons. A king doesn't run. You've been running for over a century. Aren't you tired?" "Yes, I am, Sugar."

"I'll let the subject go because it upsets you, baby. Mwah," she kissed into the phone, "That's on your neck Clarence." "Gabriel, did you visit the cells this morning?" "Yes, I woke up early. I heard God say, go speak with them, especially the human. Clarence, he's in so much agony. It's tearing him up, I know they're wrong. That doesn't mean we can't show compassion daddy. The man lost his child what if God fixes us for killing someone's child for parental sin?"

"I understand, Sugar, but what if a vampire grabbed you? The cells hold vampire killers. You must trust me, Gabriel. Please obey" "I trust you, Clarence but I'll never trust or obey you more than my God." "Please get Niarchos if you want to see the prisoners, Sugar that's all I ask." "I promise, Clarence." "Thank you. I'd die if something happened to you or our babies. Please don't do that again." "I won't. I'm sorry I scared you, Clarence." "You owe Niarchos an apology; he was petrified." "I will," winking at Niarchos.

The Next Morning New York Estate...

Gabriel entered to find a dozing Niarchos. "What's wrong, Nicky?" "I've been sleepy lately; I'm not sure why Gabriel." "Rest, Nicky." "Gabriel, wake me at 3 p.m." "Alright." Gabriel walked him to the main door. He bent down, hugging and kissing her on the neck. "Stop hehe..go, Nicky. I'll nap too." Niarchos exited the room, zipping his hoodie, feeling cold. He intended to call Zion but dozed off before he was able.

Gabriel knocked on Niarchos' door. He didn't answer; it was 3:15. She went through the joined door to wake him, pulling back the blanket. She was in too much shock to scream. Gabriel face-timed Clarence, who was about to walk into Chance's vault. "Clarence, are you alone?" "Yes, Gabriel." "Like no one around you?" "Grip, papa, and Caine are here." "Go somewhere private, please." "Hold on."

"Sugar, I'm in the bathroom." Clarence smiled at what she shared "Call Zion. I'll be home tonight, Sugar." The baby wolf looked confused. "It's ok, Nicky," hugging his neck, kissing his head, feeding him apple slices from her breakfast tray showing Clarence the large baby wolf on their bed. "It's Nicky Clarence. I'm not letting anyone take him away." "No one's taking Niarchos, honey." "Why is Niarchos a wolf?" "I'm unsure, Sugar. Is the door locked?" "Yes." "Open it only for Zion."

Zion knocked minutes later. "Are you alone?" "Yes, Great One." She opened the door, making sure the secret door was locked. He went to the bed; Niarchos was growling at him. Gabriel laughed. "Nicky, stop. He needs blood."

She held up his paw; he growled low showing sharp baby wolf teeth. Zion handed her a large bottle of warm milk with a nipple used to feed cats. She fed him; as soon as he drank, he slept. "He'll sleep a lot, Gabriel. Don't be alarmed." "Clarence is flying in tomorrow. I told him everything is fine and Niarchos isn't acting wild." "I'll lay some paper down, Gabriel. I'll bring you food and drinks." "Thank you, Zion."

"I love you, Nicky. At least we get to cuddle; no one has anything to say," kissing his paw. She dozed off.

Twin Oaks the Night Before....

Grip had a challenging time mounting his horse. "No one is helping you up, Grip. You should have this I taught you to ride when I turned you." "Pharaoh, it's been years." "It's like stealing a car, Grip; you never forget. Where are your gloves? The reins don't cut your hands?" "In my pocket, Pharaoh." The horse twirled around; he fell off 3 times.

"This is pathetic." Papa Nate dismounted, picking Grip up, placing him in the saddle. "Thanks, Papa Nate." Clarence stared shaking his head. "Do you have horses on your estate in Memphis?" "No, Pharaoh." "I'll adopt a few nags from the humane society. Next time we ride, you will know what you're doing, yes?" "Why can't I get a new horse Pharoah?" "All my sons get an adoptee nag. You'll understand why later in time. Grip, the world will become what it once was; basics will be imperative to vampire survival. I want you to grow something profitable on your land by years end. I don't want you relying only on gun sales as a sole basis for your wealth. Since you're my turn and son the earth must produce for you understand?" "Yes, Pharaoh."

Papa looked at Grip nodding, reassuring him it was going to be ok. "There ain't no profit in herbs Grip." "Says who, Caine? I made three million last year." "Papa Nate, you're a natural farmer; we ain't got green thumbs like you. Them colonizers taught you to get rich Papa they ain't know it." "Haha"

Clarence was hard on bloodline vampires he turned. "See this cotton field Grip? I planted this when I was eight years old. Your brother Chance is reaping profits from something I planted before he was born. This is why you plant; the earth, she will never disappoint." "What do you grow and sell, Pharaoh?" Papa Nate boasted of his accomplishments of how he gained his wealth.

"Roses seventeen types, Grip...baby magnolia trees, apples, cotton, sunflowers and we harvest the seeds, cow milk, goat milk and cheese, eggs, fresh churned ice cream and butter, tobacco, tea leaves, sugar cane, fifteen variations of chopped wood from fallen trees on our acres, wool from the sheep, documented thoroughbred horse breeding, real estate investments, now a salt mine and arabica coffee beans. All organic and hand delivered by his fleet of vintage delivery trucks from the twenties." "Thank you, papa Nate." Papa Nate was proud Clarence built his empire honestly, not from drug money. "Don't forget holiday moonshine and drunken country eggnog." Caine smiled blowing him up. "Yep, and you are my number one customer on blood tox moonshine so shut up." Caine chuckled at Clarence's witty reply.

Clarence hopped off his horse walking in the field, handing his reins to Grip. He wielded a flashlight, trying not to get stuck by the cotton bush thorns. "What the hell? COME!" "Everyone dismounted, except Grip who remained on his horse with guns drawn in case of an ambush.

"You ever seen black greasy cotton?" Caine picked cotton. "This is greasy too y'all." Elijah rode up late, he hopped down looking. "It's oil. Didn't you say these people paid him not to harvest the cotton, Clarence?" "Yes, Elijah. It never made sense. It must be chopped away for new growth. This is millions in loss" Papa removed glass bottles. "What's that, Papa Nate?"

"Oil needs testing to see if it's pure. It must be a certain grade to be worth something Clarence." "It must high grade, Papa, if they want Chance and I dead." "We'll do our own research, Clarence. We don't need outside opinions."

Clarence never argued with Papa Nate. He was much older. Clarence respected his Elders, and Papa was like a second father after Avril passed. He never called him Nathan or Nate, only Papa. Papa took a spoon, collecting several samples of cotton, roots, and soil.

POP! POP! Grip was shooting at trespassing dingos! Vampire Elders ran from cotton fields to their horses. Seeing their swift approach Clarence stripped. Papa, Elijah, and Caine followed suit. "What y'all doing? Grab the guns, Pharoah!" Grip shouted. "Stop shooting Grip."

"What, Pharoah?!" "Do you have a tranquilizer gun?" "Yes, Pharoah." "Use it. No bullets, understand, Grip?" "Yes, sir." They quad vampires shifted to dingo hyper-speeding toward the surrounding woods. Clarence jumped up, landing a dingo. Clarence looked back at Grip, who sat horse high shocked, holding the tranquilizer gun. It went quiet, hair standing on the back of Grip's neck.

Two dingos fought gnashing and growling rang out disturbing the quiet night. Another dingo joined them, two dingos attacking one. Grip didn't know which to shoot. He shot three.

Grip jumped off his horse, rubbing his eyes as they shifted to vampire before his eyes. One was Elijah, and two were unknown. One was missing an ear. He picked Elijah up, tying him to his horse. Clarence, Papa, and Caine arrived in dingo form. Grip knew the big one was Clarence by the way he looked at him.

He glared as the shift into vampires, bones cracked loudly stretching their flesh, the dog's face melting away as paws spread into five fingers of a human hand. "Good job, Grip," Clarence grabbed his clothes. Grip trembled nervously.

Clarence spoke with Grip telepathically. *"It's ok son, I'll explain later."* "Grip, toss 'em in jail. No clothes." "Yes, Pharaoh." "Tomorrow, we visit the vampire vaults." "Papa Nate how many vaults do you own?"

"One. I have the large vault, Clarence, and you?" "Two, because I need a tempered vault. You know oil paintings needs cool airflow." "Caine, how many?" "One, Clarence. They're expensive." "No, they aren't, Caine." "He's always been cheap Clarence ignore him." Clarence remembered when they'd buy slaves.

Clarence laughed loudly. Caine was the one wearing slave attire, after his freedom Clarence shared the memory with them. Caine laughed. "Kept the white man's eyes off me. I didn't draw attention like some folk staring at Papa." "Why Caine cause' I was clean? Bet you still have those old slave clothes." Caine fell silent as Papa stopped his horse. "Say it ain't so Caine." Clarence laughed hard. "I'm calling Lily to ask why in tarnation she ain't burned them?" They arrived at the house. "Have the wives cracked Jamaica?"

"No Pharoah." "No water for three days reward those who talk with water in front of the others Jamaica." "Yes, great one." "Hello, Zion any news?" "Yes, the parasite struggles to stay alive in your blood. I'm going to see if it dies if it does, I may be able to create a vaccine, Clarence." "That's good news, Zion real good news."

New York Estate
Hollings Labs....

"Joan, please hand me the blood sample for Clarence near the microscope." She handed him the sample injecting it into Chance's parasite infected blood. "What?" Joan ran over to look. "Honey!" She saw blood cells eradicating the parasite.

"Joanie, is this Clarence's blood?" She double checked realizing her mistake. "It's Gabriel's blood, Zion." "They're almost all dead Joan, this must be it." "What is it, Zion?" "Pregnant blood with HHG components. The red blood cells are more aggressive when a woman's pregnant, to protect the fetus these are mixed with radiation making them super charged. The cells think these worms will attack Gabriel's Triplets. Currently her antibodies are tripled. Caleb said Gabriel bit Chance if she ingested the parasite her body already built an immunity against the worm darling. You found the cure for Chance Joan." Joan hugged Zion laughing.

She stared at Zion exhaling. "I think Niarchos feeds Gabriel his blood." Zion dropped and broke a Petre dish. "What the fuck is he doing? How do you know, Joan?" "When he's around, she won't drink Clarence's blood. It's a gut feeling. She'll drink when Niarchos is absent." "We can't use that, Joan she's half-human; she may not crave blood." "Alright, Dr., test her blood for traces of Niarchos' blood, better yet check his blood for radiation traces." "I'll check both, but we say nothing to Clarence whatever we find. I never saw him act the way he did on the island when he thought Gabriel was sleeping with Niarchos, Joan." "I agree." "You want the truth, Joanie?" "Always, honey." "It's the sex for Clarence." "Hehe, you think?" "Yes, I do. I'll speak with Niarchos if this is true; there's no harm in blood sharing. Niarchos is an old vampire he's safe with her."

Twin Oaks Estate Georgia....

Grip tossed double dingos into an overcrowded jail cell. "When Elder Chance gets back, he'll be livid at the way we were treated," his fourth wife spewed.

Grip looked. "He's my older brother he ain't gonna be mad about shit. All you bitches are right where you belong." "You are no brother to Chance. I know his brother... Niarchos." "You better ask about me bitch. I was excommunicated. They didn't discuss me, gal." "Yeah, I'll ask," cutting her eyes at Grip.

The limo arrived driving them to the vaults. Clarence needed a vault check to see if he had a copy of the deed. It'd been ten years since he visited his vaults. It would be good to look inside to make certain all he'd sent over the years were present.

They arrived at the vaults located in a closed bank Clarence purchased in the 1950s. The art deco bank had high grey marble ceilings with floors to match. The entry doors were ornate with gold inlay. Clarence passed; original wood desks adorned with green banker's lamps. "Welcome, Great Pharoah. It's a pleasure and an honor you're here." "Thank you, please rise." They rose, keeping their eyes low.

The director of the vaults and scrolls walked him to his private office. Margaret, the Scroll, and vault director was a descendant in his turn line. "How are you, my maker? Congratulations are in order. I hear your new bride is loved by your vampire children. I was excited to proof and read the scrolls from the vampire games."

"Is Steven here?" "Permission to speak freely Great One?" "Of course." "You are causing deep seeded jealousy and unnecessary comradery amongst the senior scroll writers Pharoah." "Why?" "Steven was on vacation in the hotel at the time, so using him is understandable given the emergency hearing." "Yes." "However, once you arrived at the games, you only called Steven to document the sacred scrolls, Pharoah."

"Queen Gabriel summoned Steven my dear, unfortunately I can't dictate whom an Elder chooses to document a scroll, Margaret. In fairness I made them draw names at the games. In the future create a schedule unless an Elder asks for a specific writer, the next name on the schedule shall document the scroll. How is that for a resolve Margaret?" "I agree great one. Thank you for your understanding and wisdom into the matter."

Grant the vice president, who kept the vaults, addressed Clarence. "Great Pharaoh, welcome to the Vaults. I have codes ready for you to access any vault. Great One, while you're here, will Queen Gabriel have access to all vaults?" "Yes Grant." "Will she have her own vault, or share with you?" "Please call and ask her while I'm here. If she wants her vault, we can set it up." "Yes, Great One, right this way."

Clarence's phone rang. "Sugar, I'm on my way to the vaults. Hold on." "Where's the bathroom Grant?" "This way." Papa stood outside the door. "I'm alone Sugar." He saw Niarchos, soft and cuddly. He hated to be away during his first shape shift. "Sugar, stop petting and kissing him; he's not a dog. I'll call tonight."

They arrived at the vault. Clarence laid his finger on a gold pin, then rested it on the scanning pad that spread the blood sample over the blue labyrinth lit scanner. Chance's vault opened. "Can anyone access a vault who's not the owner, Grant?" "Only you possess this power, Pharoah." "May I have a chair, please?" Grant rushed to get a chair. "Thank you."

Clarence saw a shelf with paperwork. Grip picked up a Smith & Wesson Colt. "This is the first model. It's worth millions Pharoah." Grip picked up a blunderbuss gun. "How much is it worth, Grip?" "Twenty million if it works. It's in excellent condition." "It works," the elder trio responded"

A signed copy of Michael Jackson's "Thriller" and "Off the Wall!" Caine took a pic for Lily. "Prince, Rick James, Ray

Charles, Nat King Cole, Etta James, Whitney. He has a thing for songstresses Clarence? "Yes, he does, Papa." "Grip?" "Yes, Pharaoh?" "The deed."

"Oh, yeah. OMG." "What Grip?" "A signed copy of Michael Jordan's rookie card and Shaquille O'Neal." "Put it back, Grip." "I was gonna ask for it when he wakes up, Pharaoh." "Marilyn Monroe!" Papa called out. The vampires turned around. "Ya'll look at this!" Chance messed with her Grip, quiet as it was kept, he met her at a card game when he played DiMaggio." "Elvis Presley's first album, autographed."

"Burn that," Elijah chuckled. "All niggas could do was shine his shoes, fuck him." "Stole our music and wanna discuss us like dogs," Papa added. "I found it." Clarence called out.

"It's the original copy with Alex's name. Look, blood is on it from Chance's beating Papa." Clarence slipped the deed in a file exiting the vault. "Grant, you can lock it." Grant scanned the seal on the dust cover, documenting it leaving the vault, signed out by the Pharaoh's blood.

Upon exiting bells rang, and bars to the vault sealed the doorway. Grip was locked inside the vault. "What happened Clarence?" Clarence glared at Grip. "He has something on him that hasn't been scanned Great One." "GRIP!" Clarence startled him into truth. He held up the Jordan card. Papa laughed. "See what I mean Papa Nate always trying me? Put it back, Grip! A prince of covens is not a fucking thief!" They approached Clarence's Vault. Pricking his finger, they entered. "Watch him," Caine stood behind Grip.

"What're you looking for?" "Something for Gabriel." Clarence unwrapped a diamond crown. "It was Queen Isabella's." Papa unwrapped another. "This has an ankh; it's more her style Clarence." "It belonged to Queen Nefertiti; it has no diamonds. Women love diamonds, Papa."

"She'll love this one." "Clarence, look," Elijah interpreted the deed. "According to the first deed, they knew there was oil under the ground but never pursued it because cotton at the time held more value and digging for oil was risqué. Look, there's a coal mine behind this house. They were going to mine it, but Clara's husband lost the house to Chance in a card game." "Read it in the limousine, Elijah. Let's go."

New York Estate....

Gabriel felt a hand on her. Nicky kissed her. "Why am I in my father's bed naked?" Niarchos shivered uncontrollably. "Alexis, turn up the heat to 71." Gabriel wrapped him in a blanket, laying on top of him to warm him. He wrapped his arms around her. "Is the door locked, Gabriel?" "Yes."

His teeth chattered covering his eyes. "Alexis, lights off." The light hurts your eyes, Nicky? "Yes." Gabriel gave him her sunglasses. "Better?" "Yes, thank you, honey." He saw the picture, looking surprised. "That's you." "No, a wolf how long?"

"One day. Look," handing him a piece of his fur. She put it in her locket. He kissed her, holding her close rolling on top of her, grinding almost slipping inside. Gabriel slid back, breathing heavily. He grabbed her, biting into her neck, feeding. She let him until she felt weak. "Nicky, stop." He stopped.

Kissing between her thighs, licking her pussy, crack, he snatched her breath finding her lost pearl. Her fangs popped Niarchos covered her mouth; she was cumming, salty sweet flowed in his mouth.

He shared her taste with her. Gabriel licked herself off his lips. She massaged his dick graduating to hard jack rabbit jerking. "Gabriel, please ma, you're driving me insane. Gabriel pulled and rubbed twirling her fingertip, rimming his mushroom with the tip of her thumb. Niarchos trembled on his knees before her.

She continued opening her legs wetting her palm with the wetness of her pussy. Rubbing the tip, she put her feet on the floor in front of him opening for visual and smell enticement.

She caressed up his middle shaft, lightly scratching his tip with her nail, as he breathing picked up.

"You're almost there," she whispered in his ear licking his lobe as he stared at the fat of her pussy shaking as she vigorously jerked him off. "You love me, Nicky?" She rimmed her lips with his pre-cum, pulling and rubbing super-fast. "Do you love me?"

"Yes, my Queen, with everything in me," moaning his truth. Gabriel sunk her tiny fangs into his neck feeding "the babies are hungry," replacing what he drained from her. Gabriel covered Niarchos' mouth with her foot as he bit into her toes. She winced, controlling herself from giggling. Her magic fingers worked wonders on his manhood. He fell on all fours, tossing her robe under him; he shot cum load on her robe.

Gabriel opened her cum and blood-mixed hand, licking it clean gazing in his fire burning iris.' She slapped the most feared vampire on the streets, making sure he watched her clean her palm. Seeing this and feeling her dominating slap caused him to bust a double load orgasm, laying his head in her lap, muffling himself, shaking, trembling at her feet. Niarchos showered feeling relieved.

Gabriel looked for the loose brick in the fireplace in her bedroom where Ann showed her to hide Safinah's diaries. She closed the secret door calling Zion. "Niarchos is back; he's in the shower." Zion knocked. "Enter."

He went to his room before I woke. Zion checked on Niarchos. She phoned Clarence. "Yes, sugar?" "Niarchos is back." "That's fast? How long is the vampire gone?"

"Depends on the first turn, a week or so. I'll explain when I come home. You're, ok?" "Yes, honey." "I'll call Niarchos, Sugar." Zion was drawing Niarchos' blood. "Nick, I swear I'll keep it between us. Has Gabriel been feeding from you?"

"No." "Have you been feeding from her?" "Once in the caves, Zion." "I forgot." "Why?" "Your blood has radiation I believe it triggered your wolf shift." "Wouldn't it be out of my bloodstream by now?" "No, Niarchos, radiation has been known to stay in the blood for up to ten years." Niarchos' phone rang. Clarence face-timed him. "How's my, big baby?" "I'm cold pop but good." "We're supposed to be cold; we're vampires." "I'm trembling like a human." "Why the shakes, Niarchos?" "He has light sensitivity," Zion yelled. "It'll pass Niarchos."

"Zion thinks when I drank from Gabriel the radiation triggered my shift Pop." "While you're both on the call, good news I think I found a cure for Chance in Gabriel's blood, Clarence." "How?" Zion explained. . "When are you flying home, Pop?"

"Week or two. The wives aren't cracking. "Toss one of the wives in the light, Pop." "If I do, Nick, they'll say she was the one. All must die if they want to keep secrets. They fear you more than Jamaica; he's been working non-stop, trust me." "You want me on a plane? Come home, Pop, I'll go." "I'd like to try all avenue's before I kill them son."

"Have you learned which wife has paperwork pop?" "Papa, and I are mulling through paperwork over dinner. Elijah and Caine went home for a few days." "What about Grip pop?" "Call him; he saw us shift dingo for the first time Niarchos." "How'd he handle it?" "He did good, I'm proud of him. I'll call after dinner, Niarchos." "Ok pop later."

Zion called. "Niarchos, I prescribed Gabriel iron. Drop the vitamin in her blood twice a day." "Ok, Zion, thanks." "I'm going to rest. I'll check on you both later."

Gabriel called his cell. "How do you feel, Nicky?" "It's been a century since I felt cold." "Is it uncomfortable?" "Humanly so." "Lock the doors so we can cuddle and look at 'Love After Lock-Up'." "Gimme a few Gabriel, lemme call Mara."

"Mara, you alright?" "Yes, Niarchos." "They may've found a cure for Chance." "Oh, God, that's great news." "I'm going on vacation in three weeks, think I'll see you, Niarchos?" "Of course, baby doll, I'd love to." "Call when I'm off?" "I'll be up, Mara, I'm a night owl." He joined Gabriel in her room. "Siree, play power season one."

Zion & Papa Nathan
Dowry Call....

Zion phoned Papa Nathan. "Hey, how are you? I've waited for this call, Zion." "Papa Nathan, I'm calling requesting permission to turn Joan vampress." Papa was quiet. "Joan can't bear children, her daughter is deceased, Isaiah is vampire Nathan Jr.'s bloodline ends Papa. If Joan dies all that's left of her is Isaiah who is vampire. Nathan junior's line will have once descendant residing when there can be two Papa."

"Dr. If I allow you to turn Joan, do you know what type of uproar it'll cause in the bloodlines of Ann and I family? All I've denied prior, adults I let die like Joan's mother...is Joan ill?"

"No, Papa." "Dr., how could we as Elders justify it?" "Please, Papa Nathan, I'm begging you. I'm in love with Joan I can't love then lose her to something so simple as death. I can afford any dowry you set forth...please Elder." "I don't care if you were penniless Zion, as long as you love my granddaughter, that's all I'd care about." "May I call next week to revisit this discussion, Papa Nate?"

"Of course, you love Joan, Zion?" "I have many years Elder Nathan." "I see love in your eyes. The fact you came to me shows the respect you possess for me, your fiancée, and her family. Thank you, Zion. Allow me to think on it?" "Yes, Papa, thank you."

Nicky & Gabriel New York......

"Nicky, I wanna go out." "Where?" "Not sure. Take me where it's quirky." "Quirky? There are underground vampire clubs, vampire sex clubs, human drinking clubs." "What's a human drink club?" "Humans voluntarily allow us to feed from them. You've been before, Nicky?"

"To work the door, not feed. I don't feed off rando's only offerings. I got it Gabriel." "What?" she clapped "It's a surprise. I'm going to make a few calls go dress woman." "How? Dress down, hurry." "Ok." She readied herself. "Hurry, the limousine is coming in twenty minutes, Gabriel" yelling through the wall "Where are we going?!" "It's a surprise woman." He showered and dressed, sexy as usual. "HURRY, ten minutes vampress."

Gabriel scooped her brush, makeup, diamond studs, and the diamond tennis bracelet Clarence gifted her in her purse. She saw the money Niarchos put back and smiled. She checked her bag for gloss, bobby pins, and a rubber band to create a bun.

"Bring your crown!" "What?" "Do it." She opened the safe, removing her headband crown. "What if someone steals it?" Niarchos bellowed a loud laugh making her smile. "Ready!" Her hair was messy. "I'll fix it in the car Nicky."

They rushed down the winding stairs. "Joan, we're going out. If Clarence calls, inform him to FaceTime me." "Text him Gabriel." "I will." They entered the limo, whisking away! "Where are we going?" "Westchester, it's a surprise. Stop asking." She allowed him to brush her hair, as she applied makeup. "You don't need that crap, Gabriel." "That's what all black men say to their women." "We're here honey."

He placed the crown on her head, she pinned it down. "I never knew ladies pin it on ma." "It's gonna fall off if we don't Nicky." Stepping out of the limo, it was dark. There was a huge tri colored tent outside and a red sparkly carpet. Niarchos pushed out his arm, she held it, making sure she didn't trip on the rocky ground under the rug. A loud announcement was made over loudspeakers.

"For the first time under the big top in over a decade, I give you our new Vampire Queen successor to the late and loved Queen Safinah, Wife to our King of vampires, father to us all

Clarence Hollings. We welcome her under the big top Queen of Covens, Gabriel Hollingssssssss."

She walked in, smiling, as led lights danced off her crown. "WELCOME TO THE WORLD'S ONLY VAMPIRE CIRCUSSS!" As soon as vampires saw her, they kneeled. The big tent went completely silent as the ringmaster led her to a podium where a throne adorned in seashells, glitter, and starfish from every place they visited for over fifty years waited for her to sit.

Niarchos sat, next to her, whispering, "They're waiting on your word." "Thank you for such a warm welcome. I'm delighted to be here; please rise, gimme a show!" The tent of vampires whooped, whistled, and clapped. "Let the show begin!" The ringmaster yelled.

Niarchos handed her Clarence's blood to sip during the show. The first act was a woman on horses riding, standing on then and hanging off. She levitated, jumping horse to horse, gliding through the air ballet dancer style to the next effortlessly, landing on her tip toes. There were tightrope acts, contortionists, twins, triplets, clowns, and mimes. There was a vampress who blew up a balloon; her mouth never touched it. She held it back, inflating it.

They brought out small dogs; Gabriel loved them clapping and tapping Niarchos. A poodle jumped on her lap licking her face. They made a joke; the dog wouldn't leave Gabriel. The owner came for the poodle; he refused to get off her lap. The owner got to the exit calling the dog. The poodle ran back jumping on Gabriel's lap; the crowd loved the act as she kissed his nose holding him close.

There were all kinds of vampires, one who could drink 100 bottles of blood non-stop. Vampires bet to see if he could do it. One vampire act mirrored a black mamba; Niarchos stood in front of Gabriel during his act, in case the snake jumped, he could take the bite or catch it.

Then it was intermission. Gabriel checked her phone; Clarence had called 5 times. She Face Timed him.

"Hey, baby." "Hey Sugar, where are you?" She showed him the big tent. He smiled. "Man! How long are they there?" "I'm not sure, you haven't been here in ten years Clarence? They miss you" The owner came over.

"The Great Gideon! How are you, my old friend?" "We're all here, Great One." "Fifty years in the circus business!" "Yes, sir! Don't worry, I know I'm late on the taxes, Pharaoh." "Nobody is thinking about your taxes Gideon; you'll send it when you're able."

"Your wife's pretty yeah?" cleaning her crown playfully. "Thank you!" It made the crew feel good vampire royalty and an Elder came to see them perform; they're totally excited. When Niarchos called, I rushed to tell everyone he and Queen Gabriel was coming." "Thank you for the warm welcome, Gideon!"

"Always, old friend." "You keeping up with your sunflowers?" "Yes, Great One, I have contracts with several sunflower seed companies thanks to you Pharaoh." "Honey, you're missing it!" "I see, are you having fun Sugar?" "Yes, it's elegant, whimsical, intriguing, extravagant, exciting, wrapped in one. Niarchos surprised me." "You're beautiful when you're excited, Gabriel. There's a glimmer in your eyes"

"Thank you, baby! Let me to speak to Niarchos." "Hey, Pop." "Thanks for showing her a good time; she needed to get out." The intermission ended. The acts kept coming, motorcycles, elephants, white tigers, and a monkey gifted her a rose. Vampresses swooned over Niarchos, staring, and pointing.

The ringleader formed a soul train line, picking guests from the crowd. Gabriel and Niarchos came down the soul train line in style; she was prancing, Niarchos was turning her hand, two-stepping behind her everyone loved it. At the end of the show, performers visited her on the red carpet, kissing her hand. Some purchased her flowers and others gave gifts. The motorcycle performers gave a helmet for the Pharaoh and one for Niarchos since they knew he was a rider talking with him about his jump at the games gasping the jump was insane. Gabriel wanted an elephant ride Niarchos said no.

Gideon inquired if the other vampires who wanted to meet her could take a picture, allowing him to charge $5. "Sure." "I don't want anyone touching her. I must frisk them, is that ok, Gideon?" She gave him the eye. "As far as I'm concerned, it adds to the mystery of a royalty title Elder." "The women will enjoy this." "Make sure they kneel before her, Gideon," Niarchos commanded. "As you wish, Elder." Gabriel hit him playfully. "Be nice," pushing her crown back.

Vampresses lined up to meet their Queen. Vampresses were frisked, sparing Niarchos no leeway, moaning, opening their legs, touching his arms and chest, smiling, giggling; he was used to it.

Vampire males were enamored by her, respectfully taking pictures; some couldn't because they would not be seen on film asking, she pose alone. They made the pics funny. She was on Niarchos' back in one; in another, he held her in a chair with one hand overhead. She was given vintage carnival props for a few photos.

Some vampresses wanted to adorn her crown, of course, she let them ask, "Is it real?" They asked her seriously Gabriel replied, "That's what the Pharaoh said. What do you think?" Shrugging her shoulders they laughed at her humor, loving, she wasn't conceited. When they were done, circus performers got free pictures and meet & greets. Some of the women took pictures with Niarchos, him holding them up or him holding them around the waist; it was fun.

Gideon rolled in a wheelchair in it sat an old woman named Gigi. "Hello, Great One. how are you?" She touched her hand, smiling. "With child?" "Yes ma'am." "Pharaoh's child correction Pharaoh's children special they be." Gabriel smiled, holding her hand. "Gigi looked at Niarchos "together again."

"You prayed, begged God, but she belongs to Clarence here," she tapped her head, "here," she tapped her stomach, "and here," she touched her heart.

"But saving one's life is a powerful unbreakable bond a fate Great One. Niarchos, you will never leave Gabriel alone; and Gabriel you will not leave Niarchos." Gigi smiled, shaking her head. "I have not seen a love bind like this in decades." They were alone; Gideon exited as he did for all her readings.

"Niarchos?" "Ma'am?" "She'll never leave your father. She's bound to him first and he is always her maker and the love of her life. The only way is in death, even then they'll find her. Your time has passed, old vampire," grabbing Niarchos' hand squeezing tight whispering. "The life you had is no more vampire warrior, will you stay spiritually bound to a woman who'll never leave another?" Niarchos bowed down eye level with her "Yes Gigi, with everything in me."

Shaking her head, smiling, "Why you make ya life hard? Protect her at all costs. The day will come when you must forfeit your life in exchange for hers be ready, Great One." "Ma'am, I'm not Great One my father is." She smiled, shaking his arm, "We shall see vampire warrior."

"Vampire Queen, you love your husband, and you adore this vampire. You will love Niarchos more than your husband; you will love your husband more than Niarchos. You will have both vampires love locked in eternity," she whispered, giggling. "Gideon! I'm done here. Great Queen, tell Clarence I never got that kiss. He'll know what I mean." "Yes, ma'am." Gideon rolled her out, returning.

"My wife had the biggest crush on Clarence before we wed. It upset Queen Safinah upset; she was the star attraction," he took a picture out, "she looked like Josephine Baker. Clarence promised if she did a reading for Queen Safinah, he'd pay her whatever she wanted. The Pharaoh was thinking money," he chuckled, "however her cost was, *'Pay me with a ardent romantic kiss.'*

"We were not married yet he gave his word promising, *'I'll return alone.'* He never did she never forgot." "She can have it Gideon." "Unselfish and beautiful!" Tipping his hat, "Thank you." He handed her a bouquet of mixed flowers and a circus tote to carry her souvenirs. "We added toys for the children and rompers. Gigi can tell." "Thank you, Gideon."

They approached the limousine. "I had the best time, thank you, Nicky, and Gideon! Will I see you both at the wedding?" "Yes, Great One." "Ms. Gee too, he owes her that kiss later Gideon!" "He shook Niarchos' hand."

Gabriel closed the divider, sitting on his lap. "Kiss me," holding him tight, gazing upon her beautiful crown "How nice of you to let them wear the crown, baby." "Thank you." They didn't kiss; he held her as she laid her head on his shoulder, falling asleep in his arms. When they arrived at the house, Niarchos carried her inside. "Is she ok?" Zion inquired. "Yes, she's fine."

New York Estate
Pharoah's Mansion......

At two thirty-five a.m. a blood-curdling scream cursed the air. Gabriel jumped from bed; Niarchos met her in the kitchen. Joan sliced her wrist from her palm straight up her arm. Blood covered the floor; Gabriel ran over to her.

"Gabriel?" "I'm here, Joan," holding her blood-slick, slippery hand. Joan's blood-soaked body dropped on the kitchen floor.

# Chapter 32
# Control Your Savage

Caleb finished business pertaining to the vampire games. He bought everyone a room; there wasn't an empty bed anywhere on the island. Business transactions were made, millions of dollars exchanged, everyone was happy. His coven members were tired. Lulu had an appointment to meet with Gabriel and Niarchos after the business with Chance settled. Life was good; Caleb was the happiest he'd been in a long time.

He decided to visit Savannah Georgia, hang out at a few vampire lounges, and visit friends. Caleb arrived stores were open late. He loved looking in boutiques and bookstores. After buying Clarence and Gabriel three baby outfits, he took pictures, sending them to Gabriel and Clarence's phones.

Gabriel called. "Uncle Caleb is starting early. I want a baby shower on the island. Clarence wants the wedding shower here." "You have the baby shower where you want; it's not his call Queen." "Try telling him that, Caleb." "Put your foot down with him, Gabriel; he'll try you." "Did Clarence say he graduated from Cooke Bethune?" "No, sir."

"I was thinking about his graduation the other day. You both graduated from historically black colleges." "Not me, I graduated from Medgar Evers in Brooklyn. It's not a historically black college, Caleb." "It should be, they shouldn't limit them to the south." "I met Betty Shabazz, Caleb; she was a strong black woman. She stated no man should yell or hit his woman, said Malcolm X never yelled at her." "He was a good man, Gabriel; I miss him."

"There's a lot about Clarence you don't know. He shares wisdom slowly but steadily. How was the circus? I saw pics on our vampire webpage." "We have our own website, Caleb?" "Chile, yes." "Send the link, Caleb."

"I'll tell them to let you in, Gabriel." "Thank you." "Talk to you later?" "Sure, love you, Caleb." "Love you too." Caleb went to a bookstore he loved because they held author readings from renowned black indie authors. The owner was a lover of Caleb's; he walked to the store seeking an interesting read and found one titled *Crossing Freedom River*. He glanced through the pages, turning them slowly, his anger fueling mixed with outrage brewed with the flip of every page. Caleb held the book so tightly the spine cracked.

Caleb patiently waited for his friend to finish with her packed house. When it was over, she closed the store and went to her apartment in the back with Caleb undressing. "Rosemary, do you know the author of this book?" "Yes, Richard Montclair." "He's a plagiarist, babe." "That's a strong accusation, love." "You know I would not make it unless it were true my love."

"Honey, I've never seen you this way; what is it?" "I authored this book in 1843 through 1860. I lost it the night I escaped slavery with my wife and child." Rosemary saw how unsettling this was for Caleb. She, a renowned author herself, couldn't imagine her work being stolen. "Caleb, what are you going to do? You can't say you authored the book in 1843."

"A white man, Rose! He tossed the book against the wall cracking the plaster. Caleb, please calm down, honey." "Ne me dites pas de me calmer !" (Don't say calm down baby!) "Baby, calm down so we can reach a reasonable solution" "Is this plagiarist coming here to read, if so, when Rose?" "Saturday night, for the live reading series honey." She grabbed her silk kimono off the door, wrapping her toasted almond skin. Caleb phoned Clarence. "Yes, Clarence, the book, a colonizer stole the book! New York Liberty published it and it's a best seller." "Calm down Caleb, we will figure something out, I'm in Georgia already. I'll send the limousine for you, Caleb bring the book." "Ok." "What now, Clarence?"

"Caleb's book resurfaced, Elijah. A puritan stole his work. He wants to confront him." "I'm sure you'll find the underlying cause of it, Pharoah."

New York Estate
Joan, Zion, Gabriel & Niarchos....

"HELLO, Clarence, oh God!" "Gabriel, what?" "Joan took a steak knife slicing her arm, Clarence! She lost a lot of blood; it's all over the kitchen floor; she's going to die!" "Papa Nate!" Clarence called to him inside of Twin Oaks. "Joan tried to kill herself." "Zion put her up to this, Clarence; it's an outrage!" "Papa, they have minutes; Joan's dying." "Do we have a choice, Clarence?"

"No, papa, we don't!" "Let Niarchos turn her, Clarence; he's an Elder vampire." "Zion is as strong Papa." "Niarchos or nothing, Clarence." "Gabriel put Niarchos on. Niarchos, turn Joan. Gabriel put the phone on speaker, allowing Clarence to hear the confusion; Zion was arguing with Niarchos, trying to stop him from doing the turn. "Zion! Niarchos, must do the turn that's final! We have tomust respect Papa Nate's wishes, no more arguing, Zion I've spoken."

"You're Pharoah, Pop, not Papa Nate." "Papa Nate has a treaty, Niarchos; we Elders must respect it." "Fuck!" Niarchos kicked a kitchen stool, breaking it. "Gabriel, FaceTime, please!" She turned on her camera; Joan was non-responsive on the floor, everyone was quiet.

The vampire turn of
Joan Freeman....

Niarchos bent over her body, holding her head in one hand. "Joanie?" faintly she moaned. "Do you understand you're about to die?" "Yes." she slurred "Do you wish to live?" "Yes." "You will no longer be human; you will be vampire, walking amongst the living but will be dead, drinking human and animal blood to survive. You shall never walk in sunlight. Will you die to live Joanie?" "I do Niarchos." Joan coughed up blood.

Zion held her hand Gabriel held the other; Niarchos popped his large fangs, checking her pulse before biting her jugular; Joan's screams echoed through the house. Niarchos held her down as she tried pushing him off, biting his wrist, blood poured his blood into her mouth. Niarchos held her mouth closed pinching her nose, forcing her to drink.

"Of my blood, I make thee," closing his large fist over her mouth. "With my blood, I heal thee," draining his blood into her open wound. "With the blood of our Vampire father, by the power invested in me as a high Elder and a prince of covens and by the King of vampires, Clarence Hollings, in the presence of our reigning Vampire Queen, Gabriel Hollings, who bore witness to this turning and carries the blessed seed of vampires in her womb we baptize you vampress. Blood Is Life." "Blood is life." Zion and Gabriel repeated after him. Niarchos pressed his wrist to her mouth; Joan drank Niarchos' blood until she blacked out.

Niarchos picked her up, carrying her to his bed on the second floor. Gabriel kept the phone on FaceTime. "Let me clean Joan up Clarence. I'll call back, honey." "I'll be here."

Niarchos and Zion exited while Gabriel watched over Joan. "Why, Joan? I didn't think you'd go through with it." Gabriel whispered. Zion tapped on the door, "Is she awake?" "Not yet." "Papa Nathan doesn't want you near her, he thinks you orchestrated it Zion. Clarence texted me." "Thats preposterous and unbecoming of a vampire officiate appointed by the crown

Gabriel." Joan was dressed in a nightgown Gabriel found in her room. "Why did Niarchos bring her to his bed instead of yours?"

"She must sleep in the same space as her maker. The one who made her is the one who explains when she wakes Gabriel." "Why is Nicky upset?" "Niarchos never turned a woman he couldn't make his wife; so, he vowed he'd never make a woman vampress."

Gabriel saw the worry and concern in Zion's eyes. "I'll let Niarchos stay with me tonight; he can sleep on the floor. You sleep with Joan, Zion. I won't tell. I know when she wakes, she'll want to hear what happened from you; you've much to discuss. Call Niarchos when she wakes." "Thank you Great one. How are you doing, Gabriel?"

"Don't worry about me; concentrate on Joan," kissing her head, "Thank you, Gabriel." "You're welcome, Zion." Niarchos was upset. Gabriel sat on the bed, next to him. "Nicky?" In the amber hue of the lamp's light, he looked sad. "You did the turn beautifully; I've never seen something done so lovingly, so welcoming. Who wrote the words for a turn?"

"I did. I thought we should say something welcoming a dying human into vampire life. All vampires memorize and repeat it at vampire induction ceremonies." "What is that?" "When new vampires meet the Pharaoh, he drinks from them; that's why he was able to connect to vampires at the games." "Gosh I said I was gonna call him. Hello, Clarence." "What happened, Gabriel?" She explained. "Did Zion come when he heard the scream Gabriel or was, he already there when you arrived?"

"Yes, baby he came when he heard." "When did we start lying to each other Sugar humm?" She was quiet. Niarchos peered at her, shaking his head yes, as in speak truth. "We had to send for him, Clarence. He was in the lab; he may not have heard the scream. Could you hear it, Gabriel?" "Yes." "If you, a hybrid, heard it, he heard too."

"Clarence, I don't want to get involved." "You're my eyes and ears when I'm not home. You run our home and our people Vampire Queen." "When are you coming home, Clarence?" "I have some things to tie up; Caleb has an issue. Papa Nate wants Zion court-martialed, it's a mess all around. You're tired and I'm tired; sleep Sugar." "The babies have me sleeping a lot; at least when they're born, I won't be alone, Clarence." "Don't do this sugar not now please. I lack the energy for it. Niarchos is there; you're not alone. I love you, goodnight, Sugar." Niarchos peered at her. Gabriel went to the closet to get the blow-up bed.

"Leave it; I can't sleep on it. I'll get my bed roll" Niarchos removed his clothes. He lay on his father's side of the bed. Gabriel turned her back to him; Niarchos held her; he cried like a child. Gabriel turned to him, hugging him close, "Shh, it's alright Nicky," rubbing his back. Niarchos slept in her arms. She understood why they called him the big baby he had a sensitive side.

The next morning, Gabriel closed her bedroom door as quietly as possible, leaving to catch a cab to her house in Queens. When she arrived and opened her front door, she saw the chaise lounge in the living room with a note from Niarchos: My head is three inches from the ceiling woman, which made her smile.

Her house was small compared to the houses her husband owned; however, it was hers and it was cozy. She made hot tea in her kitchen, showered, and lay in her bed with a new mattress set with a note that read, Compliments of the Pharaoh. Turning off her phone, she slept. It was 6:45 p.m. the next evening when she woke up to Niarchos sitting on her bed watching Tubi. She jumped, startled. "How'd you get in, Nicky?" "Why're you here, Great One?" "This is my house; I live here, Nicky." "You live in Brooklyn Gabriel." "Nicky. I live here in Queens. Thats the end of it." Drawing her blanket, turning on her side.

"What's wrong?" "I'm tired, Nicky." "Of?" "I need space; I've been through a lot. I was turned vampire because a wacko vampire who tried to kill me over a nigga that ain't want her ass. I was almost drained by my vampire guard who turned into a wolf by assassins trying yo kill us. I was almost killed at my engagement party; however, I don't remember because my vampire husband wiped my memory clean. I watched my new friend try and kill herself to be vampress because her grandfather, who was supposed to be dead 100 years ago, says no.

I'm pregnant by a vampire king who's way too busy for this relationship and I'm in love with his son I think more than him. I need space, sushi, and quiet Nicky." "You came to Queens to order sushi? From where, ma?" She handed him the menu. "What you want?" "Five orders of number three."

"Hello, can I get five number 3's? Yes, same address as on caller ID thank you." "Pop is going bonkers, Gabriel." "I don't wanna talk." Niarchos moved her hair from her face. "Please Honey?" "No, I need space. I want you to go. Don't crowd me." "We have enemies I can't leave you. He's flying in. We know where you are woman blood share remember we can see you." "It doesn't mean you should follow me stalker much. Don't you need to be with Joan, Nicky?"

Niarchos rubbed her feet. "You like these huge hands on your sexy feet, ma? I'll do this 3x a day if you come with me" "No!" snatching her tiny feet away real nasty. "Pop's gonna come here, Gabriel." "Let him come. I won't open the door and I'm not leaving." "Why're you being difficult?" She pulled the blanket over her head. He put two bloods on her nightstand; she knocked them to the floor. "No nigga damn!" Niarchos' phone kept buzzing. "Hello? I'm here, Pop. She doesn't want to talk. I'm unsure what's wrong. No, she's not crying." "Thirty minutes, Niarchos, see you then."

"See what you did, Gabriel?" "Warn Zion Nicky. He's in Brooklyn in bed with Joan." "I already did, ma."

"I get to sleep with Joan instead of you." "Do you know how that sounds, Nicky?" Gabriel laughed puckering her lips. "No because you keep getting me in trouble with pop slipping away." He shook his head. "You should hear how he reams me out. I ain't finnin to fight wit cho ass fo seven mo months woman. Imma have him put another guard on ya."

Gabriel kept her lips poked; he couldn't resist her. Niarchos pushed his tongue against hers, swirling. "Shh," he broke their embrace, standing behind the door. Gabriel cut the light. The door opened; Niarchos grabbed the person in a chokehold. "It's Papa Niarchos put the gun up Sugar." "Pop, how'd you get in?" "I have keys to the back door." "You gave him keys, Gabriel?" "He was my boyfriend, remember?" "Who else has a key Gabriel?" "I'll give you one too, in case Nicky."

Gabriel shook her head when Clarence wasn't looking. "Stop," she mouthed. "Here, Sugar," handing her the sushi. "He was outside when I arrived. That's a lot; you gonna eat all that?" "Yes, Clarence. Why do you both keep asking? I'm eating for all of us." "They aren't vampires. "Vampires don't eat." They laughed at Clarence. "Yes, they are, at least two, Clarence." "How do you know, Sugar?" "I crave blood mornings and nights. Daytime, the humans want food; it's like they compromise." "One hates chocolate."

"Really?" "Yep, they love ice water like their father. I hate ice water." Clarence touched her stomach, smiling at the story, feeling a baby bump finally. She looked at Niarchos; he was jealous trying to hide it, doing a bad job. "Gabriel, you're royalty. You can't leave, Sugar." "What do you mean, Clarence? Oh? You mean like the oppressors did to you both keeping you on the plantation?" "You know it's not identical, Gabriel." "Isn't it? Just because the prison is pretty doesn't mean it's not jail Clarence."

"Can I take a shower Sugar please?" "Can we watch Lifetime tonight, Clarence? It's the Saturday night movie." "Sure, Sugar. Niarchos, you can go to the mansion we're good." "You don't need me, Pop?" "You need to be with Joan, Niarchos. What if she wakes?" "Zion's there." Clarence darted a dirty look. "Don't start, Niarchos. You know the rules of turning."

"Pop, why me?! Why does she have to live with me for five years?" "Papa Nate called it, Niarchos. He has little trust in Zion. He wanted her turned by an Elder to be a strong vampress...swifter." "He didn't say that when Isaiah was turned, Pop."

"I had to turn Gabriel; there was no time in that situation for me to do both." "I never wanted to turn a woman; you know that pop." "I'm sorry about your vow son, but you have now Niarchos." "Joan isn't going to like leaving New York to live in Georgia, Pop." "She has no choice, Niarchos she must follow her maker. Papa Nate is asking for an inquiry. If he finds foul play, a trial is next."

"The chief vampire Dr. can't be court-martialed. It's in the vampire bi-laws, Pop." "He can if foul play is suspected." "You can't place Zion under arrest, Clarence. We need him to deliver our babies." Clarence tapped her hand assuredly. Niarchos grabbed his helmet. "I'm out." He hugged her and his father. He fixed his fingers to say he was going to text her; she blew a kiss at him.

Clarence watched her. "Stop flirting with my child." "Don't start, Clarence gosh." His eyes ablaze, he stepped into the bathroom to shower. "Gabriel, where's the soap? "In the bottle on the side, Daddy."

When he emerged, she admired her beautiful husband. He smiled at her. "I'm handsome?" "No, you're beautiful inside and out. Let's have a Halloween Masquerade." "You'll put it together, Sugar?" "Yes." "Alright, at Niarchos' house." "Why there? Our house is bigger here in New York." "His house is prettier."

"You do know his was my first house built by the masters, and now for free slaves Sugar haha. That's what Chance says" "The columns out front is beautiful. I love it, Clarence." "They're real marble. I prefer our house." "We had the engagement there; you want me to have our baby shower there when I want it on the Gullah Islands, and I agreed. I want the

Masquerade at Niarchos' house you must compromise Clarence." "If he says yes, Sugar," he agreed reluctantly.

Gabriel grinned. "You're jealous, Clarence." "You know I am, woman no secret there." "Gee says you owe her a kiss. I explained you're gonna make good on your promise, Mister." "Sugar, Gee is 80." "Eighty-eight and you're way older. A promise is a promise, Mr. Hollings."

"What does Gideon say?" "He agrees with me."

"Stop pulling my curls when you play in my hair; look what happens." She rubbed her hand up and down his hard shaft. "You gonna give me some Sugar?" "I might. I know you want it," reaching for her nightstand, grabbing her vibrator wand, removing her tee and panties, sitting on the chair in the corner of her room. Clapping twice, Gabriel's lamp went off. Clarence saw her clear as if the light never went out; she saw his silhouette but not him.

Turning on the wand it lit pink in the dark opening her legs, exposing her pearl, tapping it with the wand until she climaxed, on tippy toes quivering on the edge of the chair. She saw his eyes in the dark; she knew he was watching, wanting, and waiting. Gabriel's hearing was super good; she heard his breathing pick up, sexually aroused.

"Cum for me, let me to see, Sugar." In all his life, he never watched a woman pleasure herself. He wasn't into porn, and women always got straight to sex with him. They never teased him, for fear he'd kill them, he guessed. He was obsessed with her seductive tease. She had him under her spell locked in her sex vice without trying.

He was inches from exploding, watching her weave her web of hot desire. She saw him stroking his long, thick cock in the silhouette. Gabriel turned off the vibrator wand. "Sugar, please don't stop," he begged, his voice shaky. "Don't touch yourself, Daddy." "Yes, my Queen," he inhaled, exhaling his struggled obedience. "Alexis play shake ya ass by Mystical."

Turning the wand on, the glow of the handle flashed revealing his face in the darkness with each pulse of the vibrator. She leaned back in the chair, raising her arched feet and red toes midair as the smell of sweet snatch lit his nostrils. Clarence traced her feet with burning eyes, longing for them to curve as she released, imagining her toes creeping through his hair. That shit was sexy to him. His phone buzzed, he ignored it, trapped in her mesmerizing spell. There was no freeing him; he didn't want it, not from this. Licking his lips, he bit his wrist; he was hot, horny, self-feeding careful not to bite her in passion. "Clarence." "Yes Sugar." "Call for me, Daddy?"

"Gabriel, come ride." She grabbed the seat with both hands. "I'm coming for you, honey, ohhh!"

Her head tossed back as her wild hair flew behind her in the moonlit bedroom. Musical moans tickled his ears as her sexy feet trembled, accompanied by endless shaking. Clarence took one step, dropped to his knees, lapping up cum from the crack of her pussy, ass, thighs, dripping off the chair. Gabriel quickly stood; his dick stood for her his veins throbbed she loved it. Gabriel turned the wand's attention on him, resting it up under his balls on a low setting, twirling her bubble-gum-pink tongue around his sweet pre-cum leaking tip.

"This is sweet icing, Daddy," he moaned, hearing her dirty talk. Gabriel sealed her full lips on the tip, sucking all she could get from the tiny sugar-sweet hole, swabbing inside. Clarence grabbed her hair; she stopped sucking. "Don't touch me."

"Yes, ma'am." His veins pulsed begging for release. "Get this poison up outta me, Sugar." "Not yet." The wand was turned up two notches; he yelled, grabbing the back of her chair cracking the frame. Clarence's knees quivered; he pressed against the wall, disciplining himself not to touch her.

Discipline betrayed him with each suck and lick; his savage side begged him to come out and play. Bending down, Gabriel tea bagged both balls in her mouth, rolling them around like ice cubes while the wand vibrated the fuck out of him. "Damn!" His breathing was rapid; it was time. Placing an ice cube in her mouth, she worked his tip, pressing the vibrator firmly under his balls the setting at its max, sucking steadily locking her mouth snug on his shaft.

She loudly slurped and drooling saliva on him, quickly lapping it up begging for more. "I'm cleaning up my mess; I'm a good slut daddy." Clarence listened to her thoughts. *'Daddy, you taste fucking sweet. I want your sweet nut sliding done my throat. I know you're in my mind.'*

Grabbing the back of her chair, "FUUCKKK!" *'Umm hum, give it to me,'* swallowing every drip-drop, pulling him from her slippery mouth, licking fast, wasting nothing tapping his hardness on her stuck-out tongue. Staring at him, wiping her lips licking her fingertips slow, sexy, and slutty.

Clarence picked her up off the chair putting her on the bed, pushing his tip in, tapping her clit, teasing her, spanking wet pussy with his hardness. With each slap cum splashed his thighs. She pushed his stomach, "no." Popping her fangs, biting his forearm before licking the blood. "No Daddy" pushing him again this time harder yet rubbing his tip saying yes.

She was pushing him off to anger the savage inside of him. She wanted a good fuck. She wanted the kind vampire to go away, the bad vampire to come out and play. Pulling her legs down, he pushed in, but the head wouldn't go in; she was tight. "Let me in, Gabriel," spitting on her split. He worked his way up, pushing slowly and gently. She fed from him; legs spread in the missionary position. "You make me crazy," as he pushed. "It's something about you." "Bang it," pushing, but not too hard, scratching his back. "Got damn," she exclaimed cumming hard, sucking him up into her pussy, her walls grabbing and him relentlessly with every pulsating grip.

"Gabriel, fuck," he exclaimed releasing hard up in her, making her his once again, licking her hard nipples. Gabriel wrapped her legs around him, feeding and cumming. "Love you, Sugar." "I love you too, old man." Clarence didn't distract her from feeding. He felt her tummy on his stomach, his babies close to him. He couldn't wait to meet them. Years of wanting his own children... no money is worth the birth of his miracle vampire triplets. For forty minutes, she fed. His babies needed him, his blood and closeness. Clarence realized his presence was especially important for a spiritual connection to his children during their pregnancy. He never let a vampress feed from him during sex; this was his first experience; he loved the intimacy bridled in passion mixed with love. "Your phone keeps buzzing, Clarence,"

"They can wait, Gabriel." "Check for blood, honey, please." "No, you're jinxing us, Clarence," touching herself. "See nothing ruining the mood." Clarence sighed at her and his relentless phone call. "Hello, Caleb. Yes, brother, I had to leave Georgia Gabriel fled Niarchos I return tomorrow. Meet me at Twin Oaks The book thief's coming for a reading. If I must reveal what we are, I shall. I spoke with the genealogist and our document creation team; they're recreating the book in its original form. I'm having them back-copywrite it legally. You're going to say the book was left in your grandfather's will. The document recreators will send parchment paper for you to draft the book so your handwriting matches the original manuscript. We'll discuss the documents needed with the legal team. We have a conference call tomorrow, Caleb."

"This is in case it comes to a legal battle, which I doubt because no one wants to be an exposed plagiarist. May I spend time with my wife, please, Caleb, I know dad no sex thanks for the reminder." Clarence hung up, irritated. "Damned seers." "What did he say, Clarence? "Are you supposed to be having sex?" "Hehe." "Clarence, are you a wolf?" "No, I'm not, Sugar. Niarchos is the first." "What are you, Daddy?" "I'm the vampire who loves you, and I'm a dingo shifter." "You're serious?" "Yes, Gabriel, old vampires can shift into various creatures." "One day I'll be a dingo?" "Perhaps Sugar."

"The Elders?" "Ann isn't; she turns to mist. "Can you control it let me see?" "Yes, Sugar don't scream. I gotta go down the stairs." Clarence ran, jumping the top stairs. Gabriel tapped the bed for the dingo to sit near her. Clarence's eyes were identical; he licked her thigh. "Stop, fresh." "Clarence?"

He looked, jumping off the bed and down the steps in a leap he shifted vampire. "I want to test something I saw in vampire movie once, Clarence."

"What?" "Can you go in a church?" "No, the ground is consecrated; the dead can't walk on consecrated ground until the original pastor who blessed the ground dies. Never happens with catholic churches because they concentrate every year at Easter. "I can't go to church?" "No, my love. I'll build you a chapel if you wish." "That'd be nice." "Crosses and a bible can you hold them baby?"

"Papa reads his bible daily. Yes, we can wear and hold an unblessed cross. Garlic has no effects, Sugar." "Mirrors and pictures, Clarence?" "Sometimes we show on film and sometimes we don't." "Can we drink blood from the dead?" "Absolutely not Gabriel, it'll kill you once they die; stop drinking." "Who do you love more me or Safinah?"

"I love my queens equally you both have endearing qualities. She was submissive; you're a firecracker. Gabriel, I want you to allow me to lead. You can lead in other areas as the marriage grows. Please, Gabriel, no more running from Niarchos. Promise, Sugar." "I promise, Clarence." "Look, I got you a gift. Close your eyes." He placed it on her lap. "It's heavy, Clarence," pulling it out of the satin bag. "Who's was it, Clarence?" "Queen Nefertiti." "This belongs in a museum, Clarence."

"Donate it; however, I'm sure Queen Nefertiti wanted black Queen adorning it, not stuck in a glass case with the rest of her precious stolen shit." "You sound funny cursing." "It's because I never do it around you." "Don't, Clarence, I love the chivalrous vintage vampire in you." "Ok Sugar." That made her smile.

Zion & Chance
Vampire ICU Vampire Hospital
Brooklyn....

Zion went to administer the vaccine to Chance, checking his vitals. Zion pulled up a chair, crying. "What's wrong, Zion?" Chance asked weakly. "Joan tried to kill herself." Chance struggled to listen, fighting sleep. "I haven't seen you cry since your mother's funeral, Zion." "Life's been good, Chance, there hasn't been a need to cry, Senior Elder."

"What's this Elder mess, brother?" Grabbing Zion's wrist. "Papa Nathan thinks it was staged. I may be court-martialed, Chance." "The chief surgeon of vampires can't be court-martialed; it's vampire law." "I may be excommunicated." Chance scoffed. "Not with Gabriel pregnant. I know our maker; he'd give his life before he saw harm come to that woman."

"Pop will stop anything hindering you. They must prove wrongdoing for you to be arrested. Did you stage it, Zion?" "No, Chance. I told her Papa denied her turn request. She acted fine with it; next I know, she self-harmed." Chance smiled. "Why're you smiling?" "Women, we never know what the fuck they're up to, do we, brother? You turned her, Zion?" "Niarchos." Chance's eyes opened wide, chuckling. "I know, baby brother is vexed. My brother is always trying to keep his head low, not this time, huh? It'll be fine. Pop will make sure. Trust me, you're not going anywhere. Worst case, you won't have Papa's blessing to marry Joan, Zion. Brace yourself."

"Dr., what's wrong with me?" He explained everything and his course of treatment. I detoxed your blood; no tox bloods." "How long have I been out, Zion?" "Thirty-five days." Chance scoffed. "No tox blood?" Zion laughed. "Where's Pop?"

"He returned from Twin Oaks. Currently in New York." Chance looked with huge eyes. "Someone poisoned you; he means to learn who, even if he has to kill everyone to do it."

Zion explained everything he knew, including the executions and jailing of his wives.

"When you were diagnosed, Clarence cried." Chance cried. "Sometimes I think he doesn't love me, Zion." "You're wrong. He left his pregnant bride to go to your house with the Elders, invoking the vacate law." Chance began dozing off, calling Mara and Giselle's name. Chance fell asleep. "Nurse, please add two ccs of sedative; I don't want him waking during the vaccine process." "Yes, Dr. Donovan." "Clarence, it's Zion. Chance woke today." "What did he say?" "Mara and Giselle are all I got. I briefed him. You need to visit. Chance, misses his father." "I will, Zion" "Goodnight, Pharaoh."

Mara & Niarchos....

"Mara, it's Niarchos. What're you up to?" "Showering, about go to bed and you??" "I'm already in bed. How's work, Mara?" "Good, babe." "I sent you money, Mara." "Thank you, bae." "You're welcome; buy yourself something pretty." "You spoil me, Elder." "I'm supposed to." "How's Elder Chance?" "Same." "Tell me if there's a change. Can you visit him, Niarchos?" "Yes, Mara." "Can I come?" "Pharaoh said no." "Please." "I'll see what I can do." "Thank you."

Gabriel & Clarence....

Gabriel got up, showering; Clarence loved waking to her shower concerts. Gabriel sang the black national anthem; he hadn't heard it in years, humming with her. "Good morning, Great Pharaoh," bowing her head in her satin baby doll, handing him warm blood. "Sing a song, Sugar." Gabriel cued the karaoke version of Stephanie Mills' 'I Feel Good' on her phone. "That's how you sing, Sugar," Clarence clapped when she finished. "Thank you, Clarence." He tossed on sweats, no boxers, a black sleeveless tank, and Gucci sunglasses.

Gabriel stared. "I'll take a shower at the house, Sugar." Gabriel snapped a picture of his penis print through his sweats.

"Look." Clarence laughed. "What's funny, baby?" "I was trying to get your attention at the coffee shop. You were reading male order bride by Blk Qween, ignoring me. The women were pointing and giggling. I couldn't figure out why. I sat behind you; your ass was fat, sticking out the back of that chair, my manhood took over. I left so you didn't see. A woman chased me, handing me her number. I now know why." "Yeah, wrap it up, Great One." Gabriel tossed his boxer briefs.

"The limousine is here Clarence." Gabriel opened the front door. A man was there. "What do you want?" I wanna see you, baby. Your neighbor said you were back. You're looking fine Bam-Bam. Are those color contacts? They're pretty." Clarence stepped in front of her. "Nigga, get off the property; my wife doesn't want to see you never come back." "Let her say that big man." "Bam-Bam!" He kept calling. "Donnell! I'm married; this is my husband leave."

"I ain't leaving bae. When you choose a white boy over me?" "When you discovered I was ill, you bailed refusing my calls." "Is it mine?" Looking down at her tummy. "Hell, no we been over fool" Clarence closed the door on Donnell. He banged leaning on the bell, calling her name, begging her to open it. "Clarence, let him go away." Clarence went for the door. "Clarence, Daddy, no." Gabriel tried to hold his arm. "Baby, please? Let's call the police." Clarence opened the door, punching Donnell's jaw, dislocating it, then hyper-sped to the limo with minor burns.

"Lock up let's go, Sugar, please." Clarence's driver jumped out with a gun, waiting for her. Gabriel locked the door, stepping over Donnell. She dared not check on Donnell as she approached the limo; her new husband was livid and jealous. "He's been gone, Clarence. I haven't had any contact with him." "I believe you, Sugar. Men like him burn me up, taking advantage of innocent women, children, and the ill." "Calm down, please." When they arrived to the Brooklyn mansion Clarence hyper-sped upstairs. Truth be told, the ordeal upset her too. How dare he? Seeing him angered her inside, she was glad Clarence broke his jaw. She knocked on Niarchos' bedroom door. "Enter, Queen." Niarchos was reading vampire uprising four. "What happened, Gabriel?" "How do you know something is wrong?"

"Pop's doing push-ups; he does them to calm down." "My ex came by." "Haha, bad idea. What happened?" "Clarence said leave he declined" Niarchos took off his glasses. "What?" "Clarence called him a nigger." Gabriel explained the sordid ordeal. "Haha!"

"Niarchos, it's not funny." "Sorry ma Pop never uses that word." Gabriel's phone chimed. "My Ex is calling Nicky." "Gimme the phone ma," "Yo? Who da fuck is dis?" "You dislocated my fucking jaw, nigga." "If you come around me or my bitch again, I'll fucking dislocate more than dat, nigga." "Where you stay bitch ass nigga?" "You talking slick on da fucking phone nigga." "Pull up, Donnell, 1375 Jackie Robinson Way. I be outside waitin, nigga." Niarchos hung up. Clarence entered. "What did he want, Niarchos?" "He was talking slick, Pop. I told him pull up." "What?" "Come over, Pop I'll handle it he a street nigga; he's gonna find out how street I get. You got enough on ya plate with Chance and his bitch's pop. Sorry Gabriel for cussin."

"Alexis, call Grimy." "Who's that, Clarence?" "A crazy vampire Niarchos turned. A psych patient." "I freed him from those drugs. I liberated him, Gabriel." "He needed those drugs Niarchos. he was diagnosed clinically insane. He suffered extreme child abuse. Niarchos helps keep him under control; he respects Niarchos as his maker." "He belongs to our coven Niarchos?"

"Yep, wears it with pride Gabriel. People need to embrace their crazy and stop using medication to fix it and accept the brain is hardwired that way. I'm not talking about pedophiles or women killers and rapists they need human medications."

As they talked, Joan screamed out. Niarchos held her down. "It's ok, Joanie." Gabriel held her as she returned to sleep. "It's almost over, Joanie hang in there." Clarence kissed Joan's forehead. Niarchos' phone rang. "Grimy, how long till

## Blk Qween

you come through?" "Nah, nigga, six till sundown bring vampires; we got heat." Gabriel went to rest. Niarchos followed her while Clarence called Caleb. "What's wrong?" Gabriel cried. "Why'd he return? He reminded me of how lonely I felt after being diagnosed."

"He tried to place doubt in Clarence's head asking is it his baby?" "That nigga crazy, ma." "What if we weren't vampires, Nicky? He could've caused confusion for a person he left to die with a man who genuinely loves me." "Don't worry, I'll fix him, Gabriel." "Don't kill him. God sits high and looks low; don't get blood on your hands, Nicky if there is no need." Niarchos cut his palm, squeezing his fist over her cup; Gabriel licked his palm. Niarchos entered Clarence's bedroom leaving Gabriel in her room next door. "Why does Gabriel confide in you, Niarchos, and not me?" "Pop, Gabriel is embarrassed that nigga challenged the baby's paternity in front of you. She loves you give it time." "The Queen never has to be embarrassed around me." "You gotta tell her that, Pop."

"Niarchos, Chance woke, he told Zion, Giselle, and Mara." "Where's the marriage paperwork Pop?" "In my office son, get the paperwork; we'll review it." Niarchos returned with the file. "Let's organize wives from concubines." "Chance didn't have any concubines Niarchos." "Do you have self-claims, Pop?" "Yes Niarchos." "Who?"

"Lee." "Will you release her?" "I'm thinking about it." "Do you love her." "I care for her." "I never knew you had an agreement on file pop." "I gotta end it before the wedding; it's part of Gabriel's dowry, Niarchos. I'll honor the agreement with a closing payment." "What did you agree on, Pop?" "Fifty million." "DOLLARS?! Wow, Pop!" "Can we handle this quietly, please Niarchos?" "Yes, Pop." "Thank you."

Twin Oaks....

Grip visited the cells, handing out water and blood. He stopped at the dingo cell. "Lookey here," handing them water.

"Is one of you willing to talk?" "I demand to speak with the Alpha vampire." "You're looking at him, dingo."

The dingo's burst out laughing so loud the women joined them. "You ain't no Alpha vampire, boy. Who you trying to fool?" "The Pharaoh don't wanna talk wit no low-life dingos." "Tell him I got information for him about Chance." "We'll see if he's wanting to hear from, ya, BOY!" Grip moved to the middle cell. "What we got here, anyone got news for Grip? Look what I got," holding up 4 oz. of blood. "Whoever's got something to say can have it." He shook the bottle.

"No response?" Grip cracked the bottle top, tossing it on the cell floor. The wives ravished it like dogs. "Does anyone have something to say? You, Spanish, come here, it's ok, take it, pretty." She took the blood slowly.

"I'll asked my brother for your hand when he wakes. Do you think we can have a private chat tomorrow, mami?" She nodded yes. "Will you share the blood?" Wife 5 inquired of Wife 3. "Why should I? One of you got me into this mess. Don't you get it? The Pharaoh took over Chance's assets! When the Alpha vampire takes over a coven, he gets it all his wives included fool. There ain't shit we can do about it. If Chance doesn't recover, we're screwed." "How old is the Alpha?"

"At the vampire games they revealed he's almost Two hundred Dingo." "How was he turned, vampress?" "The Pharoah said he was bitten during an uprising on a slave plantation." The dingo stood his eyes grew wide. "Hey! Get down here!" A dingo yelled. "I got something to tell!" He tapped the bars with a tin cup.

Grip approached. "Dingo, it's too late for hollerin'. What ya want with the Pharaoh? What happened to your ear, negro damn? The Queen's dingo snatched ya shit off, haha!" "You mean the Vampire Queen Grip?" "Sure, keep that in mind when you're given, ya audience with the Pharaoh?" "Do me a favor, boss. Tell the vampire king two words: Black Lilac."

# Chapter 33
# The Devil Is in the Details

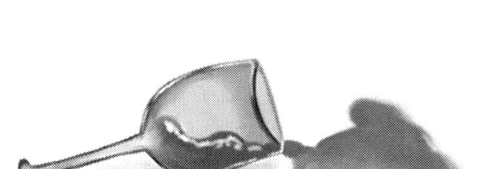

Clarence arrived at Twin Oaks at 10:30 p.m. Grip knocked on Chance's bedroom door where Clarence was sleeping. "What's happening, Grip I'm tired?" "The older dingo is requesting to speak with you," "He mentioned two words: Black Lilac."

Clarence stopped undressing midstream, staring at Grip as if he'd seen a ghost. "I'll be down shortly," changing into a suit. When dealing with vampires in matters of business, he wore suits. Some vampires wore suits because the suit made the vampire, when Clarence adorned one, he made the suit. Clarence walked downstairs. "You look nice, Great One." "Grip, when did you stop calling me Pop? When you feel like it again, you can call me Pop, alright?" "Yes, Great One."

Grip wasn't raised with a father; Clarence was all he knew. Many days, when they were separated, he regretted his decision to live recklessly. Clarence taught him to be a man, to raise and love his children, and never do anything to jeopardize the love of his family, which is exactly what he did. The price he paid was heavy, losing his Vampire family his coven, and the only father he knew.

When they arrived at the last flight of steps, Grip held his father's jacket open; Clarence slipped it on. Grip, walked in front of him, kneeling at the bottom of the steps on one knee with his eyes lowered. Vampires knew the Pharoah was entering; all knelt except the dingos.

Jamaica stood in front of the last cell, kneeling with his semi-automatic chopper pointed inside the cage, held over his left risen knee. Grip brushed the chair before Clarence sat. Staring at the disrespect the standing dingo Clarence glared silently. "You asked to speak with the Alpha vampire, I present Alpha vampire Clarence Hollings, King of covens of all vampires domestic and abroad." The cells were pin drop quiet. Chance's wives were wooed by his smell; Gabriel was lucky, they thought. The dingo, who requested an audience stared in disbelief, pushing his wrist out through the bars carefully and slowly. The dingo invited Clarence to his blood, knowing the king could see a lot with one drop of blood, but a mouthful would share his lifetime. Tears filled the dingos eyes.

Grip drew his rifle, pointing it at the dingo. "This here has UV bullets in the chamber boy. If you try anything—I mean anything—I'll blow your head off and your friend too." The dingo nodded, understanding. "Place your other hand behind your fucking back dingo." He obeyed. Clarence approached the cell, not breaking eye contact with the dingo. "Grip?" "Yes, Pharaoh?" "No hesitation." "With pleasure," cocking the rifle gifted to him by his father when he was turned vampire. The sound commanding unspoken adherence.

Clarence bit the dingos wrist, gulping mouthfuls of blood. The dingo flinched; his bite was strong and gripping. The dingo tried pulling his arm to test how strong Clarence's bite was; he was unable to move his arm.

Grip handed Clarence a handkerchief. Clarence sat, scanning the memories of the dingos life revealed through his bloodletting, allowing him to see the dingos past and present. Clarence rolled the blood on his tongue, allowing it to pool and sit under his tongue, slowly gliding down his throat as he absorbed his memories and lifetime. Clarence opened burning eyes, staring in disbelief. "It's TRUE," the dingo whispered tears of joy streaming down his cheeks nodding yes.

"Let him out, Grip. Bring him to my office. Give him used clothes of Chance's—nothing expensive, you know how your brother is about his dry goods." "Yes, Pharaoh." "Great One, permission to speak before you exit?" the wives requested. "We beg for an audience."

Clarence stopped. "Who requests an audience? Speak." "I do, Great One," we met in Vegas at the inquest held for Chance." "Who's Pia?" "I'm, Great One." Chance's fourth wife responded; eyes lowered. Clarence scrutinized her with elevator eyes, scanning her thoughts; she blocked him. "I'll meet with that one, Grip, after the dingo." "Yes, Great One."

As he left, Chance's third wife asked the fourth, "What does the Pharoah want with you?" "I've no clue." "You're a lying bitch. If I learn you had anything to do with hurting Chance, I'll drain you myself. Mary should've finished your trifling ass off the night you rose against the Pharoah." Grip escorted Dingo One to Clarence's office; where he paced. "What happened, Pop?" Clarence lovingly clutched Grip's arm, thrilled they were reunited, he called him "Pop." "The dingo is my brother, Grip." Grip's mouth dropped. "Blood brother, Pop?"

"Yes, my maker Black Lilac gifted a photo of him which I handed to the scroll writers under a sealed scroll. I need a copy of that photo to be sure the dingo is the same man." He picked up his cell. "Margaret?" "Yes, Great One?" "Please open scroll 73 and send a copy of the photo attached immediately, it's urgent." "Yes, Great One." "Mother had another child. My maker mentioned it before her death, Grip."

Clarence's phone chimed; it was an e-mail from Margaret. Clarence showed Grip the scanned photo. "She identified this vampire as your brother pop?" "Yes, Grip." Jamaica tapped the door; the vampire shifter was shot in the leg, clapped in irons unable to run. "You all may leave." "Pop, no." Clarence shot Grip a disapproving look. "Don't try anything, Dingo. I don't care who you are," popping his fangs. Grip closed the double doors slowly.

"Is my older brother sitting before me? You've no idea how many decades, centuries I've searched for you brother." Tears rolled, the Dingo, wiping with cuff bound wrists. "You tried to kill my Queen...my wife."

"I didn't know who you were; this I swear by God. If I knew you were my older brother, I would've declined the contract." "Contract?" "Brother, there is a bounty on your head, and your firstborn son." "Why?" The dingo reluctantly answered, "Free yourself see us brothers as our birth mother intended." The dingo couldn't help staring at Clarence. "Why do you glare this way? I'm too old to be hypnotized don't try." "You favor our mother. I have an old photo of her; the surviving slaves gifted me. They stated you looked white passing for one during slavery, making it harder to find you. I never knew you passed so well."

"I'm an African American, United States born and raised on a plantation. The blood of our ancestors, who were slaves, is stained on our flag and courses in my veins. I'm a free slave, a survivor of the black American holocaust. Don't let this pale skin fool you as it has our oppressors. A savage killer lurks within ready to introduce himself on sight. This is who I'm and always will be, Dingo make no error. I'll kill you before I allow you to destroy me and all I've built."

"Our mother left letters for you. I have them in a safe; my old masters daughter wrote letters in hope one day you'd get them." "Who sent you, Dingo? I have a number, no name; they put a $5 million dollar contract on each of you, Pharaoh." "Why?" "We don't know we get the contract by phone transmission. Once opened, it's destroyed via virus. "What if you'd succeeded in killing one of us, what proof would they need, Dingo?" "They require us to search for the deed it's all they care for once they have it, we're paid via wire transfer. They never ask for proof of death." "Dingo, you attacked her my wife." emphasizing his gaze on his missing ear.

"I didn't know you nor your Queen; your people call you Pharaoh; the people who hired us assume that's your real name. It wasn't until one of vampires mentioned your name, I figured out you're my elder brother, the reigning vampire king. I know we met under unscrupulous circumstances screw them. I'll explain whatever you need to help us find them. You're my blood; no vampire comes between us."

Clarence picked up the phone. "Call, tell them you have the deed. If they want it, send someone." Dingo dialed, pressed a few buttons, and hung up. Less than five minutes later, the phone rang, "It's for you, Dingo." The Dingo hung up, "They'll call back with a meeting place." Clarence's cell rang. "Yes, sugar, whatever you want, buy it; you never ask, what's mine is yours. Ralph Lauren dress shirts, twenty of them, nothing pink Sugar. I'll call back."

The desk phone rang, "It's for you, Dingo," Clarence not breaking his stare.

*"Ils envoient quelqu'un dans une heure, ils pensent que nous avons tué tout le monde et l'endroit est vide."* (They're sending someone in an hour, We killed everyone, the place is empty. Thank you.)

*"Qu'ont-ils dit, Dingo?"* (What did they say, Dingo?) *"Tu parles français, Clarence?"* (You speak French?) *"Évidemment."* (Obviously.)

"They're sending someone in an hour Pharoah." "The wives Dingo?" "One supplied information for years on your son Chance. I'm not sure which one; we'd find papers in one of the old slave shacks for pickup. The notes she wrote and left for us mentioned you. "Wrote?" "Yes, sir." "If you saw the handwriting again, would you recognize it?" "Of course, there were two kinds of handwritings; we picked up papers a few times in Vegas too."

"Why do you have an English accent, Dingo?" The Dingo was shocked by Clarence's first question, took a moment to think about it. "I mined here a while, made money in gold and silver, moved to London, Paris; all over the UK. Black men were treated fairer in England than the States. I was free so I booked a passage on Queen Elizabeth. I stayed until 10 years ago. I returned to find you; I heard rumors of a black fair skin vampire." "Did you see Josephine Baker perform?" "Perform? I dated her."

Clarence smiled, "She was as beautiful in person as in her photos, Pharaoh." '*Grip,*' Clarence called him telepathically, "Take him to the cells, give him blood before he returns." Grip opened the door, "Let's go, Dingo. "My name is Justice." "Nobody cares what your name is, Dingo" snatching him up rough.

"Grip turned off the lights in the mansion; I want all guards outside surrounding the property. How many do we have?" "I'd say twenty-five, Pop." "That'll work, send ten to the roof and three to the cells, instruct them if anyone cries out, they'll be shot."

Clarence, was gratified meeting his brother, refrained from showing it. Not when he was close to figuring out who was behind this mess. Clarence's phone chimed; he and Caleb texted, "Were you happy?" "About? Meeting your brother for the first time." "Where are you, Caleb?" "Upstairs with Mary." "Come down, bring your rifle."

Clarence tapped the wall behind Chance's desk; the wall opened, revealing an arsenal of various weapons. Putting on his gun belt, he placed two guns in his vintage 1800's holster while carrying a nine glock with U.V. bullets in his right hand. He met Caleb in the hall, opening the front door; they sat in the pitch-black night, waiting, watching, and preying.

New York Estate
Gabriel & Niarchos....

"Darnell never showed, Gabriel, we waited until sunrise. I'll get that nigga, trust. What's wrong, ma?" "I'm cold, Nicky," her voice shaky as she held up her trembling hands. He grabbed a blanket, engulfing her. "Alexis, turn the temp to 75," he locked the door cuddling her close, not that it would help because he lacked body heat. Using a razor, he sliced his forearm open. "No," pushing his arm away. "Please Honey feed. I'll have to call Zion if you don't eat. We can't be alone because Zion's gonna be in and out checking on you all night."

Gabriel grabbed his huge arm, drinking and licking his arm, making his arousal evident. Niarchos timed her, tracing her body with his eyes. He loved her lips they were the perfect hue of rose pink; it looked as though she wore permanent lip gloss. "Nicky, what happened to Rose?"

Rose Isabel Hollings
Origins
Born: 1873 Died:1897...

"Mama wanted a baby, of course, she couldn't have one with a vampire, could she ma? What does a wealthy vampire husband do to make his wife euphoric? Buy her a baby of course."

"Pop purchased a beautiful baby girl, Rose was she—gorgeous, mulatto like Pop, but with sun kissed brown skin like you, and pretty eyes the same color as Pop's when he was human, I'm told by my mother. Hair like yours, thick and soft cotton billows rolling down her back like the river wild. Of course, Rose grew up privileged as she was Hollings blood. She had the best tutors, dresses, perfumes, horses, pets, pianos, and the most expensive riding lessons in DeKalb County. Pop taught her the piano; she mastered French and Spanish.

She had many suitors, but the one she desired loved her too— Dr. Bryan Cartwright. His parents sent him to medical school at Bethune-Cookman Institute which was a grandiose thing for a black person to go to college. They were married after he graduated, a M.D., and started a practice for blacks on the Georgia estate, away from the prying eyes of whites. They were happy and in love.

Pop and I hand built a French Victorian house at the back of our house—five bedrooms, built-in bathroom, state of the art for the time it was built. Rose wanted it to look like a doll house, so her father built her a doll house gifting her 200 acres of Hollings land with it.

It still stands today...like a shrine, everything exactly as she arranged them. She became pregnant, everyone was excited. Rose was the first Hollings to bring new life to our dead existences prior to you.

Then the nightmare began. Rose went into labor; things tumbled down hill; Rose was dying. Mama tried to help her, and so did pop. The baby and Rose were dying. A choice needed making Rose or the baby. As Niarchos told the story, it stormed outside. He stopped, biting his wrist hoping the story was a distraction as she fed, which is what she needed. She was glued to the way he shared Hollings family history. Gabriel sipped comfortably slipping deeper in his arms engrossed in his tale.

Clarence chose Rose, and Rose chose her baby—a boy named after the man who bought her off the auction block. Clarence Niarchos Hollings-Cartwright. It was a dice shoot; the baby was born. Clarence went to turn Rose vampire—she'd lost a lot of blood.

Looking at her vampire father, in French she whispered as if death were listening which he was, *'I don't allow you to turn me vampire papa; if the baby dies, I die with him.'* Remember, pop turns if you agree to being vampire, and if you're conscious to decide. Twenty minutes Pop and Mama Fi begged Rose as they watched the light dim in her beautiful eyes. Rose held her dead baby so tight they struggled to open her arms when she crossed over. Rose died in Bryan's arms.

Mama blamed pop; pop blamed himself for creating the law. It was a mess. For years, my parents didn't speak; they'd be respectful, speak in matters of business but never about themselves or the child they lost.

Pop wrote a scroll about Rose. Mama Fi called the scroll writer commanding him to burn the scroll. This infuriated pop; mama Fi burned the memory of his child. Pop created a law: no scroll is to be destroyed or altered without the blood print signature of the Pharaoh.

Pop moved out of the master bedroom, sleeping in the spare room. Nothing Pop said or did could gain my mother's forgiveness; nothing eased her pain. Isabel spoke with mama Fi, Avril begged her, but nothing moved her Pop was at his whits end. He hired a landscaper to fill the yard with roses in memory of Rose.

He made it the house crest: the blood drop represents the blood he shed and lost. The rose represents their deceased daughter. When mama Fi saw roses of all colors the following spring, how they smothered the house walls and the yard, she broke down crying. Mama Fi ran into pop's arms; they didn't come out of the bedroom for two weeks. No one disturbed them, except for food; my mom forgave him, they never separated again.

When they moved to New York, he did something identical to the garden below this window. Pop clips them in the spring for sales and again before fall. The Hollings rose farm was born. Valentines' day is the biggest sales day of the year with deliveries being made from the New York and Georgia estates Gabriel." "Thats so sad Nicky."

"When you return will you fix the other house for the babies?" "No, I won't." "Why not? It's sitting there, useless." "It's risky leaving the house now Gabriel. You'll remain in the main house where it's secure; don't mess with me, Gabby," scrolling his phone. "Jealous, you better stop, you showed your feelings in Queens. You know Clarence scans thoughts." She was yawning slurring her words. "Get married, Niarchos," Gabriel squeezed his hand with her eyes closed. "I won't marry another vampress; I'm in love with you, Gabriel."

"You don't listen, Nicky." "Do you want to stand witness at the wedding, Gabriel? That's what you'll have to do with

Pop as I marry someone else." "I can give half of me, Niarchos." "I'll take it." Her phone kept buzzing; she turned the screen to Niarchos. "Answer him, ma." "Hello?" "You married to a gangster now, Gabriel?" "Stop calling me; you don't know what you're up against, Donnell." "Yo! Fuck dat nigga, you tryin ta see me or nah, Gabriel?" Niarchos nodded yes. "Where?" "The park, picnic tables. Can you slip away, Gabriel?" "Of course." "Where's ya man?" "Work."

"You're not pregnant, Gabriel?" Niarchos nodded no. "No, Don." "Ok, I'll see you in fifteen minutes." "We're going to the park, Ma." "Only us, Nicky?" "Nope, you, me and Grimy." He's on his way Grimy I sent the location." Niarchos called the limo; they went to the park. Gabriel sat on the swing, her feet in the sand, while Niarchos and Grimy hid in the shadows.

"Hey, Bam-Bam." "What do you want, Don" "I want you back, Gabriel; I miss and love you. We have business to discuss after all It's been years." "Move around Donnell I'm happy again. We don't have business" "That nigga you wit dislocated my jaw; the hospital snapped it back in place." "How does it feel to be hit, Donnell?" "You got mouthy, huh, Gabriel? You trying to provoke me." "You're a low-life woman beater; I hate you and never want to see you again, Donnell." Donnell walked aggressively toward Gabriel. Niarchos hyper-sped, grabbing Donnell's raised fist. "What were you going to do with this fist nigga?" Grimy grabbed Donnell from the back; he couldn't move. Gabriel covered her eyes.

Watching his strength, Niarchos tapped his left eye. "Oh, snap haha!" Grimy yelled, instigating. "One nigga eye to go," Niarchos punched Donnell's right eye.

"Broken eye socket, left or right, Queen?" "Left, Nicky." "You slippin', Grime; hold his ass up." Niarchos hit him feather-light; Gabriel heard his eye socket crack.

"Man!" Grimy laughed wickedly loud. "Busted lip, right, bae?" "Yes, Nicky." "Grime, hold him up damn nigga!"

"Gabriel, I'm sorry," Donnell apologized. Niarchos slapped him open-handed, busting his lip; blood drooled.

"Broken arm, left, or right?" Gabriel didn't answer.

"The faster you answer, Queen, the faster we can leave," Grimy winked at her. "Left," she answered wincing in pain for Donnell. "Upper arm or wrist, bae?" "Forearm, Nicky" Niarchos grabbed Donnell's arm with two fingers pinching applying pressure. "Wait," Niarchos changed his mind wickedly, "I think I'll snap it like a twig."

He wrapped his huge hand around his forearm applying vice grip pressure. CRACK! "Hahaha!" Grimy clapped and laughed maniacally. "What were you hitting my Queen with nigga? Was it the right hand, Grime?"

"Yeah, it was son!" Grimy yelled excitedly. Niarchos squeezed his hand until the bones triple cracked. Grabbing Donnell by the throat, Niarchos popped his fangs. "Will you call again?" Donnell looked at Niarchos smiling over bloody teeth half-conscious laughing maniacally. "Don't kill him, Nicky. Niarchos bit his neck; Grimy bit his shoulder. They stopped feeding three minutes later. "Is he dead, Nicky?" "No, he'll live ma."

Niarchos and Grimy laughed hard. Grimy knelt before Gabriel. "Great Queen, if you need me, please call." "Thank you, Grimy." She hugged him. He hadn't been hugged by a woman in years; he didn't know how to respond. "You're welcome, Ma'am."

Gabriel entered the limousine. "What's your name?" "Richard, ma'am." "May I call you Richie?" "I'd be honored, Queen. Will you come to the Halloween masquerade and our wedding? The Pharaoh is having a bachelor party; you're invited." "Ma'am, I—"

"I won't take no for an answer. I'm your family like you're mine. Say yes." Gabriel looked out the limo; he smiled. "Yes, ma'am." "Good!" "Later, Grimy." He hopped on his motorcycle speeding away. Niarchos entered the limousine staring in her eyes, she stared into his.

Niarchos healed her in a strange way by getting back at Donnell. He fixed something broken inside of her.

Niarchos relieved her of the weight and pain of what Donnell did to abuse her. She hugged him, kissing him while she cried full of gratitude. No words exchanged, only smothering each other with affection wrapped in unspoken love.

Spotted Eagle & Cody
Vampire Colorado
Blackfeet Indian Reservation....

Spotted Eagle threw a huge party for his wife on the reservation. There were five Indians of old, reservation Elders; they knew of Cody and her bloodline. She was an original reservation survivor of the spirit ancestral massacre. Grateful, they welcomed her home with open, loving arms.

The house was beautifully nestled in the private hills of Colorado attached to a large, mirrored image lake where luxury yachts and tiny sail boats floated. It was serene, scenic, and beautiful. The property was gated; as spirit wolves roamed the property for generations and wild colorful birds flew above. Spotted Eagle refused to have relations with Cody. He wanted to re-marry, making her feel special. They had separate bedrooms but didn't need them, falling asleep together, chaste, reconnecting, talking, discussing decades they missed with one another.

The closeness they'd lost returned; the relationship gelled swiftly. The wedding was set for ten days; two months passed since her arrival. Cody wondered how Chance and Clarence were but didn't look back, not while everything was perfect. Eagle knocked on her door. "Enter, honey." "Queen Gabriel sent you a package and letter." Cody opened the box. It was coffee and a letter. She explained the coffee, attaching a coffee maker. "That's nice of her, Hausis." "Yes, it is," Cody agreed. "She has a forgiving spirit, so rare these days."

Cody handed him the masquerade invite. Eagle smiled. "If you want, Hausis." "Cody why do you prefer this name over the one given by your mother? It reminds me of her. My pain is great, Eagle. The Elders call me Hausis. That's fine, they know me from days of old." "So do I, baby." "Please, Eagle, for a little while." "Yes, sweet Cody," kissing her head. "Thank you, Eagle." They watched old Lucy reruns on television. It was good being in his arms. Cody felt like she was home, surrounded by her people who loved her. "Of course, women and vampresses were upset because they wanted her husband."

Sitting on his lap, legs open, she kissed him, stroking his long black hair, seducing him. Cody unbuttoned her shirt, her breasts as he recalled in a sexy push-up bra. "Bite me," he kissed her neck, biting her for the first time, feeding from her as she lay her head on his, smelling his hair. They blood-locked for 30 minutes. "I love you," unbuttoning his jeans.

"Cody, stop, not yet." "Eagle, you're killing me. We're married by vampire and Indian law." "Guess what?" "What?" "We need to rededicate ourselves. It'll be worth the wait, I promise, by our ancestors." Eagle kissed Cody as she grabbed his belt, he ran, laughing.

Cody called Chance's phone; she got Clarence. "How is Colorado, Cody?" "Good. Where's Chance, Pharaoh?" "Chance is in the hospital, Cody," he explained, all. Ask the shamans if they have anything that can help or if they have ever heard of this, Cody." "I sure will." Cody called the Elder Shaman asking to see him. "Of course, Hausis, come. I'm home." Grabbing her mink coat for show, she walked a half mile to his house in the Colorado cold.

New York Estate....

Zion and Isaiah, who recently arrived from school sat by Joan's side. Zion's phone rang. "She woke?" "Not yet, Niarchos." "Coming out of it, Zion?"

"Not yet." "I'm on the way. If she wakes, say a little a scroll must be documented." "Got it Niarchos See you in a few." "Any change, Nicky?" "Not yet, older people turn mad slow Gabriel. I don't believe in turning them, like your time is up, old timer."

"Hehe that's messed up. You're mean for it, Clarence turned, Papa Nate." "It's different, Papa is family, we were the first, the Elders, we needed each other to survive time and circumstances. We're all we had"

We were stronger as a vampire clan than as humans fighting white slavers. We could've been discovered and killed as vampires; whites were cruel worse than vampire slayers. We opted to be vampires to help Pop and Chance if we were attacked, we had strength of one hundred men each.

"Who turned them, Nicky?" "Pop he's, our maker; he can pull rank like he did with Chance when he fell ill. Your maker has the right to supersede any vampire except the Pharaoh. Since all our maker is the Pharoah he has final say concerning all our health concerns" "Is there anything about vampire law, as Queen, I should know, Nicky?" "Anything happens to the Pharaoh, you automatically become his successor." "You know a lot about vampire law." "I studied them when they were being created. It helps to know." "Like what?"

"No, kids are to be made vampires; it's an abomination. "Children can't control their impulses. What happens when they're 40 trapped in a 10-year-old body? I see children vampires, I execute them. There are vampire children, they're 60. They have a house. I leave them be." "Do they know you, Nicky?" "They're afraid of me. I'm the boogeyman." "Leave those children alone, Niarchos Hollings." "They aren't children, Ma." "I wanna see one Nicky." "No, I explained it's a vampire abomination."

"It's not like if I invite them, they're gonna come they fear me." "What about Clarence?" "Pop gave the order to execute them." "They loved our mother, they cried when she died, sent flowers to the house." "They're outcasts for a decision their parents made?" "Yes ma." "Why?" "They're no longer kids, Gabriel." Exhaling agitatedly. "I'll revisit this with Clarence because you're biased, Nicky. I'm having vampire babies."

"It's different--"

"Is it?"

"Yes, they were born this way of two vampires; it's organic, Ma." "Yet, they're vampire children. Will you toss my babies into the light, Vampire?" "Never, Queen."

"The vampire children should be forgiven, welcomed into our covens as family. Place them under Coven One's protection Nicky." "They can stay where they are. I don't want a part of rogue vampire's kids or grown." "You're prejudiced," Gabriel scoffed. You hate rogue vampires. Clarence was a rogue vampire. The definition is one who was turned absent a maker or coven correct?" "Yes, Gabriel." Gabriel's phone rang. "Hey, sugar." "Clarence, were you a rogue vampire?"

Gabriel handed the phone to Niarchos. "She got inquisitive after I accidentally mentioned vampire children pop sorry." Clarence looked blank at him on FaceTime; "Gabriel wants them accepted pop." Clarence inhaled, exhaling aggravated. "Gabriel, the vampire children are taken care of. I made sure of it after Safinah died." "I'm thinking they can be used as one of the most powerful weapons in the Pharaoh's army daddy." "How?"

"Humans speak freely around kids. They don't care what they say, they think kids are slow and won't repeat what they've heard. Humans are loving they adopt children, give them a home and education not knowing they let in a savage. I bet if you put a kid around those wives, they'd speak freely, Clarence." "It's possible what're you proposing, Gabriel? My vampire children despise me for the order I gave, Sugar. They deal with me from a distance." "Do they have respect for you?"

"Of course." "Who's in charge of the children?" "A vampire named Malachi." "What about a female?"

"His wife's name is Savannah. I'll request an audience tomorrow morning Sugar." "I won't be around, Gabriel." "Look at you, Nicky, telling the Queen of Covens what you're not going to do." Clarence laughed loudly. "You two arguing is messy." "There is no argument, Clarence. Niarchos will stay at my side." "Niarchos, Gabriel, I'll call back." "Alright, love you, Clarence." "Come here, Ma." "No, Nicky."

"Don't make me come there." She approached the chair, sitting on his lap, kissing his neck. Niarchos ignored her; his forehead, nose, lips, he couldn't ignore her anymore; he clutched her in his arms "Please, Nicky, be nice? Allow me to talk to them." "Up." She jumped up, running to her bed. Zion tapped the door.

"Come In." "How do you feel, Gabriel? "I feel cold this morning." "Blood?" Niarchos held up four fingers, "Four bloods consumed." "Illness, dizziness, anything?" "No, Zion." "Eating?" "Sometimes, Dr." "Any changes I'm next door. Good night, all." "Good night."

"Your hearing is way better than mine, Nicky." "It gets better with time. Back rub, Ma?" "Sure." She lay on her side; he covered her. In five minutes, she was out like a light. Clarence called back; Niarchos picked up her phone to show she was asleep. "I'll call in the morning Niarchos." "When are you returning, Pop? I gotta go home." "Why do you want to go home son?" "I have business."

"What, is it about vampire kids you hate?" "As an Elder, I'm bringing it to the council for a vote before they're allowed access to us and the covens." "You're going to make Gabriel cross with you, Niarchos?" "They creep me out, Pop." "Niarchos, I'm having vampire children."

"That's different pop." "How?" They'll grow into adults, not remain children." "We can pray, but what if one gets stuck in childhood, Niarchos? Would you hate my child, your sibling? I was outvoted years ago. I didn't want to kill vampire children, but the Elder votes forced my hand. The ones who survived the mass execution deserve to be accepted. They cried the river Jordan when your Ma was called home. Child vampires aren't like us; we're savages, ruthless killers, Niarchos. They're the gentle side of us that died."

"They calm the beast within, because they're this way, they have soft hearts. Can you imagine Gabriel draining a human? She couldn't hurt an animal if she tried. Allow me to handle Gabriel. It's best you're absent when Savannah and Malachi arrive." "Thank you, Papa." "You're welcome." "What's going on at Twin Oaks, Pop?" "One of the dingos is my blood brother." "The one your maker explained about?" "Yes, he matches the photo in the scroll archives. Caleb confirmed it. He's helping us now. However, I'm keeping him locked up until we clear all this against Chance. He may be my brother, but Chance is my child. I'm not willing to stop until I find the underlying cause of this mess." "I hear you, Pop. We took care of Darnell, Pop no more problems If I must get involved, there'll be no talking, Niarchos."

"Yes, sir. I agree." "Stop sleeping with Gabriel and go with Joan, Niarchos." "How'd you know?" "I smell you on my bed linen." "I'm here, Pop, in the next room in case Gabriel or Joan wakes goodnight." "Goodnight, Niarchos." Niarchos sat in the corner chair reading Malcolm X when Mara phoned. Niarchos was turned off since Chance mentioned her but needed to talk to see if she had an angle." "Hey, how are you, Mara?"

"I'm ok and you?" "You've been MIA, Elder." "A lot going on. Sorry." "I understand. When are you coming to see me, Niarchos?" "As soon as we solve the issue with Chance Mara." "Niarchos, are you ok? You sound upset. Why?" "I killed two vampires last week at Chance's house. I tossed them into the sun, Pharaoh's order. Mara, have you met Chance's wives?" "I've met a couple." "Things have gotten serious. No one is exempt, Mara. No one." "I gotta return Niarchos. My break's over." "Do you want a call tonight, Mara?" "Please Niarchos." "Have a good shift."

One day before Darnell was jumped......

"Niarchos, are you reading the marriage agreements?" "Yes, Pop. Let's separate the official wives from the concubines. I have 12 agreements plus Mary's which is super old, Pop. I also have wives two through four. Wife five's papers don't have the vampire signet or your signature, Pop. It's missing along with Chance's blood print."

"Wife five isn't official, Niarchos?" "No, neither are wives six and seven." "To recap son, wives one through four are official?" "Yes, Pop for concubines, there are ten binding on parchment." "Look for Mara, Niarchos." "Got it, Pop. There's a marriage agreement for Mara; you signed it."

"Let me see, Niarchos. It's not my signature son. Check the scroll writers, Niarchos." "Hello Margaret, it's Elder Niarchos Haha, I haven't done anything special that needs documenting. When do you need it? I'm free tomorrow I'll explain what I can. I did make the cliff jump. Did Elder Chance? He did it twice Margaret. I was afraid I'd drop Queen Gabriel but not for myself."

"Margaret, I think you're flirting with me." "What if I am an Elder? I'll have to call later to discuss our options; the Pharaoh's sitting in front of me. Hold on." "Margaret? I need the scroll authenticator to look at the marriage certificate for Mara Thompson. Moving forward, scrolls and marriage certificates are to be personally purchased from our signature authenticator before acceptance and filing. He is to give a certificate of signature authenticity if it's not attached to the marriage certificate it's not valid." "Yes, Pharaoh." "I'll need the authentication report by morning. Please expedite this matter; keep it confidential, Margaret." "Yes, Great One. Good night."

"Falsifying vampire documents, parasites, lies, attempted murder what else, Pop? Your phone's buzzing." "Margaret?" Clarence placed the phone on the speaker. "Steven, I didn't know you were certified to authenticate signatures." "Yes, Great One. I did before turning. My father and his father were in this line of work. Great Pharaoh, these signatures are not yours." "Do you've an idea whose they may be, so I may compare?" "You may check Giselle and Mara's signatures, Steven." "Thank you, Great One." "Good night, Steven."

Niarchos called the gift shop in Las Vegas. "Hello, may I please speak with the store manager?" "May I ask who's calling?" "It is Elder Niarchos." "Oh, Elder, please hold." Immediately the manager answered." "Elder, how may I assist?" "Hey Angela, when Mara came to pick up her bracelet, did she sign for it?" "No, Elder, because you said give it to her. Her friend signed them out." "No worries, Angela. Add the matching earrings. Please have her sign for them. Make up a reason why." "Yes, Elder." "Once she does, please send a copy of the receipt."

"Yes, Elder." "Angela, have Elder Chance's wives signed for anything?" "Possibly. I'll check Elder." "Please send those as well, no matter how old. Inform staff of credit card receipts. It's to be kept confidential, as per the Pharaoh." "Yes, Elder Niarchos. It may take a few days for your second request. Is this, ok?" "Yes, ma'am." "Elder, please stop calling me ma'am. You make me feel old hehe." "How old are you, Angela?" "Twenty-one and eighty years, Elder."

"Guess what? You're technically a ma'am, Angela." "I guess you're correct, Elder. How old are you if you don't mind me asking?" "About twenty-three and one hundred forty." "You were 23 when you were turned, Elder?" "Slaves had no birth records. Dr. Donovan says I was between 23 and 25." "It's been a pleasure speaking with you, Elder." "Oh, Angela?" "Yes, Elder?"

"Did you get new purses in?" "Yes, Elder. What kind Chanel?" "Yes, Elder. Please send one to Queen Gabriel at the Brooklyn estate on my account. A watch for the Pharaoh, something nice not that he needs it." "Someone is always sending him watches. May I suggest cuff links and a matching tie pin, Elder?" "How is my honey bunny Chance?" "Haha, fair to middlin.' Keep him in prayer." "I shall. Inform him Angela's praying for his speedy recovery." "Call when you can. Don't worry about the time, Angela."

Twin Oaks current day....

Clarence and Caleb sat quietly on the porch. Caleb linked to Clarence telepathically. Grip, papa, Jamaica, and Caine, saw a car approaching. Clarence leaned into the dark, wearing all black, covering his face in mud concealing his light skin and brown burning eyes.

Justice stood in the middle of the driveway, waiting for the person's approach. "Who're you?" "I was sent to pick up the paperwork." "Where's my money? I asked for unmarked American dollars." Throwing the duffle at Justice's feet "It's all there as requested." "Since this is over, what's so special about this old-ass plantation, mate?" "It's sitting on an oil field and a lucrative coal mine."

"Why not buy the land instead of stealing it? Justice stalled time counting the money prior to handing over the deed." "They tried over the years the family declined. It's been in Chance's family for generations. He wants to make it a landmark. We couldn't let that happen. If we did, oil and coal couldn't be extracted once declared a negro burial ground, Dingo. We discovered the wives were crooked. He's an old vampire. It won't be easy to kill Chance. One of the wives explained the father was one too when we checked. Two names are on the deed both need to die. We needed vampires to accept the contract. Humans can't compete against vampires."

"Is it all there, Dingo?" "Don't rush me, mate. Ain't no one here. All we have is time. Why'd you all say the father's name was Pharaoh? When I got here, he had an entirely different name?" Justice inquired so Clarence knew he wasn't lying. "Smart." Caleb whispered to Clarence. "No one uses government names. We explained what you needed to know, Dingo." "Which wife? 'Cause Chance has ten." "It's the one who lived here in Georgia and the one in Las Vegas."

*Ask names, Justice.* Clarence requested telepathically. It was a new thing for a vampire to have telepathic connection with him, it was alarming and amazing.

"A few wives weren't here. If they want me to track them, I need names. I'll toss in free of charge to tie off loose ends." "They never gave names Dingo. I saw one once by accident and again when I was in a club in Vegas, man." "What'd she look like?" "She worked; serving the vampire who owns this house. Thick girl, black, about 25. This plantation owner was in a private card game. She's the one who slipped him the worm. We paid her to do it since he took drinks from her when he was gambling. One of the wives gave us paperwork I never saw her face." "It's all here," Justice confirmed, grabbing his wrist knocking him to the ground.

"What's this?" The man inquired, confused. Clarence sat on his black stallion horse, looking down. "I'm the Alpha vampire whom you sought to assassinate. If you say what I want, I'll spare the life of your children and wife." "I'm not married." "Why do you lie, human?"

"Cara, your wife, is pregnant with your third child. Andrew and Kelly are 8 and 11 years of age. You live at 4576 Cedarwood Lane. You took this assignment to pay for college for your children and your mortgage."

"How could you know all of this?" "I am Pharaoh the vampire you seek. I scanned your thoughts and memories over the 10 years, as you spoke with my brother. Yes, Justice is my brother human. Think about the night you were in the bar in Vegas. Access those memories so I may see truth through your eyes." The human closed his eyes nervously, thinking of the day he landed in Vegas.

Las Vegas Forty Days Prior....

Clarence stood in the hallway of the hotel watching him exit the elevator to private gambling games. He was told by one of Chance's wives Chance plays often. He watched Chance gamble for hours. During the break, the human approached Chance's wife. Clarence waited for her to turn around. In the memory, he saw her face. The human handed her a hefty sum of money, passing her a vial containing unhatched parasite eggs. The human explained how it needed to be administered and under what blood conditions for them to hatch and kill properly.

"Human! Why're you blocking the face of the woman?!" Clarence yelled sitting at the bar banging the blackjack table. "Share her face or Andrew will be the first to die as I feast on his virgin blood!" Clarence's Georgia accent was angry and pronounced. The human refused to unlock the memory revealing the second assassin's face. Clarence stepped out the glitzy memory leaving Vegas lights and was atop his horse in Georgia. "Grip! On three, blow his head off." Grip cocked his gun. "1. share, human. 2---"

"Wait!" Clarence closed his eyes reentering his memories. He was transported back to the gambling room of Vegas. He saw the face. Turning to him as they sat at the bar he asked, "Human, are you certain this is the woman who slipped him the parasite?" Staring at the face of his son's attempted killer. "Yes, yes!" He screamed, terrified, slamming his shot glass down on the bar shattering it. "They were lovers!" He continued reluctantly sharing his thoughts. Bang! Clarence looked at the roof behind him. He was transported out the memory abruptly. "Papa Nathan shot Elder Caine from the rooftop of Twin Oaks."

Clarence closed his eyes, concentrating on probing the human's memories, that's when he saw the truth once again solidifying his doubts. He saw Chance kissing her, memories of when the human followed them flooded his mind noticing a camera the human planted in Chance's hotel room.

"Take the human and Justice to the cells, Papa Nate what happened?" "Caine raised a gun at your back, Jamaica saw him." Clarence darted a look at Jamaica. "It's true, Pharaoh." They were in shock. Clarence bent down to check on Caine. "What did you shoot him with, Papa Nate?" Clarence opened Cain's eyes; he was out cold. "A tranquilizer dart. I gave the order not to kill him. We needed answers, Clarence." Tears rolled down Clarence's face. "Lock him up in Niarchos' house. No blood, no water." Papa Nate pat his back reassuringly "It's okay Clarence we'll find the underlying cause of it. Why would Caine try and kill you, Clarence?" Caleb was in shock crying.

Clarence grabbed Chance's motorcycle riding angrily into the fog of night. Caleb and Papa Nate dialed Ann, Blaise, and Vaughn. They would inform Caine's brother Elijah, of his treachery. It was 3 a.m. when Gabriel's phone rang. "Clarence, calm down, slow down." "Wake Niarchos Gabriel" "Niarchos." "Yes, Queen? Your father wants to talk to us," Niarchos walked to the bed. "Pop, what's wrong?" "Caine tried to kill me."

"What?!" "Lily gave him the parasites Niarchos." "Lily?!" "Yes, Niarchos, apparently, she was carrying an affair with Chance. I'm unsure of the details. As I was extracting memories from the human who came for the deed Caine tried to shoot me with UV bullets in the back like a yellow belly coward. Papa Nate sniped him with tranquilizers off the roof."

"Oh God," Gabriel popped up, grabbing her weekend bag. "What're you doing, Gabriel?" "I'm coming, Clarence. I'm coming. We're coming. We gotta before the sun comes up." "Gabriel, no! It's dangerous," she grabbed the phone. "Clarence? I'm not asking. You are visibly shaken. You can't be alone. Me and Nicky are here for you. I'm your wife, not a trophy wife. I love you. I'll arrive in a few hours that's all, Daddy." "Yes, Sugar." "Niarchos?" "Yeah, Pop?"

"You two be careful. This is worse than I thought. The King of covens almost slain by a vampire Elder" "You alright, Papa?" "No, Niarchos. See you in a few ticks." Niarchos alerted Zion of what was happening doubling security at the hospital. "One guard in the room, one at the door, one at the end of the hall, someone must be in Chance's room around the clock. No new medical staff are to administer anything, Zion." "Ok, what happened, Niarchos?" He explained. "What?!" "Yes, I'll call from the plane. The house is under lockdown. No visitors, no one allowed in or out. If they're out, send them to the hotel until further notice staff included." "Yes, Elder." "Zion, if Joan wakes, Facetime, we can explain together what happened, brother." "Thank you, Niarchos." Clarence parked at the mouth of the woods, stripping. He shifted for a run in primal form. Sprinting and jumping, he howled on the bluff's edge in the shadow of the full moon, as high tide saltwater waves crashed on rocks below him.

Gabriel and Niarchos beat the sun, making it to the plane one hour before sunrise. She sat next to Niarchos as usual "What the hell is happening?" Niarchos cut his forearm with his pinky nail. "Hello? This is Elder Niarchos. Send ten Madji to Caine and Lily's house, place Lily under arrest, and lock her up in the Pharaoh's prison in the Brooklyn mansion. If anyone tries to stop you, shoot them in the head. Call as soon as you have her in custody."

"Yes, Elder." "I've never seen you this serious, Nicky." "When an attempt is made on the Pharaoh's life, there are protocols that go into effect." "The Elders must come to Georgia within 24 hours to discuss what happened, per vampire law." "Does Elijah know?"

"Not yet." His phone rang. "Hello, Mya. Gabriel's here," shaking her head. "Where's Elijah? Sure, put him on." "Hey, brother." "Niarchos, what the hell is going on?" He explained what he knew. "Why?" "No one knows, Elijah. Pop hasn't said what he saw. We don't know what Caine was thinking. You need to hire a vampire attorney for your brother, like, yesterday, Elijah. Caine is facing death by sunlight for treason against the crown." "I'm on it, Niarchos." Gabriel was trembling. "You scared?" "Yes, Nicky." "Why?" "What if they killed Clarence? I'm unsure what I'd do." "I'd care for you. You'll never be alone again," kissing his inner hand. "I know, honey. Clarence is the first man who loved me for my flaws. If he dies, I die Nicky."

"He won't die, Gabriel. We're going to see him soon, and trust, those responsible will face my wrath, no more games. As soon as our feet touch the ground, they're going to pay this demon his due and I ain't leaving until I fucking collect in bone blood and ash."

# Chapter 34
# Shit Just Got Real

Clarence ran long; he had no time to shift vampire form sunrise was upon him. He ran to Niarchos' house, scratching the door. Viola opened it, thinking he was Jupiter. Clarence leapt up half the stair landing a naked vampire. Jupiter was asleep in the corner of the bedroom. After showering, he tossed on something comfortable, drinking donated baby blood. The run cleared his head; all he needed was rest on fresh soil. When Clarence woke, Gabriel was snuggled behind him, asleep. Looking at her with doting eyes, he noticed she picked up weight subtly and her baby bump was budding.

Clarence peered under the blanket. "What's in there?" Touching her budging stomach, she woke. Stretching, yawning, pulling up the blanket, Gabriel patted the bed. He rested under the covers, cuddling with his wife. Laying face to face, they gazed through the quiet morning soft light. Stretching his long brown curls, "What happened, baby talk to me?" "It's Lily, Sugar." Gabriel's eyes grew, revealing her shock. "I'm sorry, my love." "Caine knew what I was going to see from the human's memories, thus the assassination attempt." "Since the Elders are flying in, everyone involved should be tried while they're present Clarence."

"I agree, Sugar." "Will you speak with Caine, Clarence?" "It's forbidden, remember, Sugar?" "I'm happy you're not hurt, Clarence." "Whoa, that's a strong hug, Sugar. You alright?" "I don't want you dying; and our children never meeting their father." "When this is done, what do you say we go away, no guards, Sugar?" Gabriel sank into his large arms, tracing his nose feather light with her warm pinky, undressing as Clarence removed his clothes.

No sex, they laid skin to skin, communicating with body language and love enjoying sacred intimacy. "Have the babies moved, Sugar? I can't wait, honey," "Yes, a little Clarence." Gabriel was elated at his excitement. "Where's Niarchos?" "In his room." Gabriel shared what Niarchos explained on the plane. "Jackie's on his way to represent Chase and the vampire security guard. Elijah called Lee for Caine." "Lee?" "Yes, why, Clarence?" "They're trying to avoid execution. Lee handles vampire death cases." "She must be good. Will our lawyer be present?" "Always, Sugar. When it doesn't pertain to us, our attorneys protect us; it's vampire law."

An intrusive knock interrupted their intimate morning. Gabriel grabbed her robe. "Yes, Niarchos?" Clarence called. Niarchos entered. Nick served her hot morning tea. "Where's mine?" his father teased. "What's going on, Niarchos? Gabriel explained most of it. Anything new?"

"Yes, Pop. Elijah and Blaise are sleeping here because Caine is downstairs. Caleb, Ann, and Papa Nate are at Chance's house. Vaughn is at a hotel, Pop." "Tell Vaughn to sleep in one of the covens under our protection, Niarchos, call a 12 o'clock meeting please. Have Margaret and Steven fly in to document the hearings and trials via scrolls. Call the vampire legal team; have them come; we're having speedy trials, Niarchos everyone will need representation." "How many days to prepare, Pop?"

"Ten." "Pop, it's not enough time. Let them argue it in front of the Elders at the presentation hearing." "Pop, permission to speak freely?" "Granted, Elder." "The trials. Must be fair and follow vampire law to the letter. The reason is you're biased,

Pop, because the attempt was made on your life and Chance is hanging on by a thread not to mention Gabriel. I don't want anyone to say your judgment is clouded, casting doubt on the outcome of these trials which may end in mistrials. Please allow your lawyers to speak on your behalf in terms of legalities." "As always, Niarchos, you're wise. Please call Zion, ask him to prepare a medical update for Chance by 12:30 for an Elders debriefing." "Yes, Pharaoh." "Any word on the signatures?"

"I'll follow up with Angela at the boutique; and the deaf vampire from Blaise's Coven. A prisoner in the Brooklyn jail used sign language. I need to know what they were saying. Is Chance awake, Pop?" "No, Niarchos, sedated. Ask Elijah to meet me in the kitchen. Tell no one about the signature receipts, Niarchos." "Yes, Pop." Clarence readied himself, knowing his day would be long and complicated. "Gabriel, please pick out a suit for me." "Do you want a haircut, Clarence?" "Yes, please." He sat, and Gabriel wrapped a towel around him, shortening his hair. "Damn, sugar, you did a good job." "I used to help my uncle in his shop; he was no good with curly hair like yours. I'd scissor-cut; he'd do the shape-up." Gabriel brushed him off, smiling.

"Get dressed Sugar. You're the Queen; you gotta be present; it's vampire law." Gabriel showered and dressed. "You look beautiful, Sugar."

"Thank you." The royal couple entered the dining room, the Elders kneeled before them. "Please rise," Gabriel requested, walking to their chairs. Clarence pulled her chair and sat at the table's head. Gabriel sat on his right, and Niarchos on his left. Niarchos had two guns under the table, one in his hand; none held tranquilizers.

"Thank you for coming. I'd like to start by explaining what's happened thus far. Please understand, this meeting is closed to lawyers and scroll writers. All that's said is between us as family and Elders. Nothing said will be used in any hearing or court case. Instead, what is said may reverse thoughts on decisions I'm pressed to make."

"When we attended the vampire games, Chance fell ill. No one knew why until Zion drew blood. He found a parasite that breeds in the blood of vampires. Once hatched in our blood, they drive us to madness causing us to make irrational decisions and do things out of character. After weeks of infection, the parasite craves sunlight. They mentally harass the host, making him think he'll feel better by stepping in the sun which he would if human. The parasite, when exposed to sunlight, dies, along with the sun-drenched vampire."

"He explained what happened at the games between Chance and Mary, how he detected Chance's illness." "Elder Niarchos and Vaughn, is the description of the incident, correct?" "Yes, Pharaoh." "Zion was testing Chance's blood; Zhou Xie was present; he heard of the worm. Zhou explained someone fed it to Chance through him drinking infected blood."

"Could it be transferred vein to mouth?" "No Blaise, the parasite must be exposed to air to work. First, I thought it was an angry spades player, but our investigations led to his property holdings."

Clarence explained what they discovered at Twin Oaks, about the oil and coal mines and the name issue on the deed. "When I turned Twin Oaks Papa Nate, Elijah, and I discovered my name remained on the deed. Brothers and sisters, the colonizers tried to kill us for our land as history repeats itself. The night we discovered the oil, two dingos attacked we took the into custody."

"I discovered one Dingo Justice is his name is my half-brother we share a mother." "Wow?" The Elders were elated. "I didn't allow it to stop me from getting the truth. I used him as bait luring the men to the estate, wanting the deed in exchange for the bounty Justice was promised if they succeeded with our murders." "Your brother's name is Justice, who named him?" "I'm unsure, Blaise, sorry." "Please continue Clarence."

Clarence explained to the Elders how he probed the mind of the human, extracting the truth about Lily. "That's not all, Lily and Chance are having an affair. I also believe she and Caine may have hired the Indians at the Vampire games I killed in the arena." He shared the warning the Indian gave about the Elders. "In Brooklyn, a vampire security tried to assassinate me; the oil people sent him." He discussed the attempt to steal Safinah's medical journals. This is the fourth attempt orchestrated by the oil people. Niarchos will discuss security measures. Zion is waiting to report Chance's medical progress. Niarchos, please continue."

"Thank you, Pharaoh. Considering the attempt on the Pharaoh's life, I've implemented an immediate lockdown of all covens. Baby Nate is assigned to sit at Chance's bedside 24 hours a day until Zion decides he's discharge ready. Caine, Lily, the two dingos, the human limousine driver, Chase, and all of Chance's wives, except for Mary, are pending further investigation and trial. Information is being collected and shared with all attorneys for the accused, as per Vampire law, statute 91; articles 15 through 35. Are there any questions on security protocol?" Elder's responded no. Clarence took over the meeting. "Thank you, Niarchos...questions?"

"Yes, Blaise?" "Has anyone checked on Caine and Lily, Clarence?" "Lily is being held in Brooklyn while Caine is here in Georgia. I'll allow Elder visits once because of our due process laws. As you're aware, I'm not allowed to visit personally." Papa, asked Elijah, "have you spoken with Caine?" "Yes, Papa, he's standing mute." "He hasn't spoken to his own brother, Elijah?" "No, Papa Nate." Blaise touched Elijah's shoulder. "Will you seek the death penalty, Clarence?" "For all involved with an assassination, yes, Caleb." Shocking gasps filled the air.

"Great One?" Vaughn interjected, "Why not seek jail time instead of death by sunlight?" "Vaughn, when a snake attempts to bite you in the garden, do you allow him to flee, or do you chop his head off ending his return? I have offspring to think of, not only myself. We're vampires; we live forever. Who's to say the same enemies won't rise against my offspring? My life is in direct danger; ALL threats must be eliminated, Vaughn. We kill our enemies; this is how we've survived as long as we have, as free slave vampires."

Vaughn touched Elijah's arm for comfort. "Caine is my brother, my turn by law I can execute him and lily because I turned them, and a maker's decision is final. However, I've decided to share my burden with my Elder vampire family. Do you think this is easy for me to discuss killing vampires I love...vampire I've made?

My heart broke seeing him lying in the dirt unconscious, holding a gun loaded with UV bullets pointed at me after we survived the slave holocaust, and I have no idea know why. This same vampire killed a white vampire who tried to shoot me in the back, the same vampire who kept oppressors at bay by dressing poorly. Lily, I turned vampress, who nursed Safinah back to health single handed after she was brutally raped and assaulted by a viper." Clarence shook his head, wiping tears trembling upset, Gabriel held his arm supportively. "Have I been fair with money, taxes? When we were slaves with nothing, we helped one another; loved one another, we were family." "We still are Clarence," Elijah reassured.

"I've never been selfish." Elders agreed. "What prompted my vampire brothers and sisters, to try and end Chance? A century later, I'm forced to seek death by light for two vampires I love. Please, find evidence so I may withdraw my request of death, converting it to a prison term."

"Brothers and sisters, when white masters had us in chains, raping our wives and daughters, we banded together, rising as one. Here we are today, a living testimony that black people can stick together and grow. Nothing I have, you can't have; nothing you want, I won't give. This has been our way for centuries. Any questions, family?" No one responded, the room was heavy with grief and tears.

"We were slaves with nothing! Blacks today could never survive what we saw nor went through - babies being fed to crocodiles for sport, our women being prostituted and pimped our men raped and broken.

Gang rapes, skin flaying's - our skin used for coats or belts our fat for cooking. We made it through the lash, our children being given away because we showed acts of courage interpreted as defiance. Blaise strung up by white men for sitting at an all-white lunch counter. Vaughn almost beaten to death by white men because he's gay."

"Caleb was shot by Harriet Tubman while running on the underground freedom trail. Papa Nate whipped and left to bleed out on a whipping post for trying to find his children. Niarchos shot the night he heard of freedom from the constables. Chance beaten within inches of his life for helping me avenge the rape of Safinah."

"Zion hung by the clan for sleeping with a white girl at the hospital, trying to secure a maintenance job though his parents struggled to put him through medical school. Caine and Lily gave up their dream of having children to help protect what we built."

Ann allowed me to brutalize her so slavers would see she tried to fight me off when I took Safinah. Where did Lily and Caine lose their way, family?" "God help us" Papa Nate prayed.

Zions Medical Progress Report....

"The vaccine worked; the parasites are dying. I administered the second round of a four injection-vaccine series." "Zion, how soon will Chance wake?" "I'd say during the third vaccine, Papa Nate; this is when most of the worms will die. If the vaccines eradicate the parasites, we'll corner the market on the vampire drug. I'll make sure all covens have the vaccine in case of infection."

"To add Joan accidentally found the cure in Gabriel's blood." Clarence grinned, "How Zion." Zion explained what Joan discovered. "The HHG in her blood is amplified because there are three babies. The HHG attacked Chance's Parasites killing them on contact."

Gabriel texted Niarchos. Honey: Hungry. Niarchos went to the fridge, handing her a bottle of Clarence's blood, tasting his blood mixed in. Honey: You mixed it, :) Nicky? Nicky: Shhh. "Elijah, when is Lee arriving?" "Tomorrow Clarence," she asks if she can lodge at the cabin. "Yes, the attorneys can sleep at the cabin. Give her our bedroom, please." No one thought anything of it, but Niarchos knew what was up with Lee.

"May I speak with you, Elijah?" "Sure, Clarence." "I'm going to rest, Clarence, see you upstairs." Gabriel pecked him, exiting the room. "Caine's standing mute, Clarence." "Is he getting a lawyer, Elijah?" "No, Clarence." "Let's go see him. You wanna wait on Niarchos, Clarence?" "I have you, Elijah."

They approached the cells; Clarence pulled a chair sitting in front of Caine's cell staring blithely. Caine kneeled before him. "Rise, what's going on, brother?" "I stand mute, Great One." "Mute until Lee arrives or mute through the entire process, Caine?" "Mute through the process, Great One," Clarence stared at Elijah. "Do you want to die nigga?!" Elijah yelled. "Yes, Elijah."

"Elijah, add a psychiatrist to Caine's defense. I'm commanding a psychiatric evaluation." "There's no need Great One I will not speak. It's my right as vampire according to our laws to do so, brothers." Elijah tried grabbing Caine through the bars hugging him, but Clarence stopped him. "The bars burn, Elijah."

"Caine, please," Elijah cried, "don't do this!" Caine looked away. "Caine, I love you, I forgive you," Clarence stared in the cell as tears fell exiting visibly jarred, with Elijah following.

**Blk Qween**

Upstairs Niarchos' Mansion Georgia....

Gabriel fainted, Niarchos caught her placing her on the bed. Niarchos handed her a pill. Sucking her teeth she took the pill. "Queen, a gift arrived for you." "Thank you," sitting up while opening it. When Gabriel opened it, there was $10,000 in cash inside the Chanel purse he ordered. "I love it Nicky," she held it on her arm in the mirror. "How does it look, Nicky?" "Not prettier than you," she hugged and pecked him tapping his chest.

Sitting on the bed Indian style, Clarence entered. "What's all this?" "Nicky got me a Chanel bag and money to shop." "How much, Gabriel?" "Why?" "Fifty dollars, Clarence." "My son gave our Queen $50?" "What's wrong if that?" "I know how much, Sugar?" Niarchos, still reading and smiling. "Allow me to see if his raising is still within him, Sugar? $10k is the minimum number."

"Who made that up, Clarence?" "I did," everyone followed. "Why haven't you given me $10,000, Clarence?" He went to the safe, tossing $20k on the bed. "You want more, Sugar?" Tossing her $20k more. "I don't want it, Clarence," tossing the money bricks at his feet. "I'm not a whore, I'm your wife."

She went to the kitchen. "Why're you always the cause of Gabriel's upset, Niarchos?" "You did, that Pop. She's not a money chick, but you knew that, Mr. Construction. We aren't in a competition pop I'm your son not your enemy." Clarence approached the kitchen; sunlight burned his wrist, he hissed frustrated.

Gabriel was alone. "Sugar, please come to me. I'll walk in there Gabriel" Clarence opened the door, scorching his entire arm. Gabriel covered him with her sweater. Niarchos stood in the doorway to the brightly lit room. "What're you doing, Pop?" "My wife won't talk to me son." "Do you want to walk in the light, Pop? Give him six bloods, Gabriel, please." "I'm famished, Clarence." "What do you want to eat, Sugar?" "Fried chicken." She closed the shutters in the kitchen.

"Order whatever she wants, Niarchos." "You do it, Clarence." "Sugar, why does it matter who orders?" "I'm not hungry." Clarence was confused. "Viola?" "Yes, Pharoah?" "What's the name of the seafood chicken spot?" "Keith's Kitchen I'll get a menu," handing it to Clarence who handed it to Gabriel. "I'll take chicken and waffles with fresh strawberries." Niarchos grabbed his phone.

"Not you, Nicky!" "Gimme the menu Sugar, please." Clarence dialed the restaurant. "Hello yes we're at 1975 Old Colonial Way." "Pop, they renamed the street. It's Malcolm X Way." "Sorry, Malcolm X Way dear. Niarchos? No, this is his father--"

"Peaches?" Clarence smiled. "Nice to make your acquaintance young Miss. I'll Inform him, sweetie." Gabriel kissed Clarence. "Thank you, Daddy." Clarence purchased the food, arranging it on a tray with roses and other delicacies in the fridge he ordered, but she didn't know he did. Shortly after, Clarence left. Grip tapped on her bedroom door. "Enter Grip." He gave her a gift Gabriel opened it speedily.

"I love it, Grip!" "I've been meaning to gift it but how do you give a Queen a firearm?" "It's cute; and inscribed 'All Hail the Queen.'" "It was Ginger's idea, Gabriel." "I have to call and thank her. I heard you gained wealth in gun sales, Grip." "It's true." "Do you attend gun shows?" "My kids do, Gabriel." "How many kids do you have Grip?" "Six. Two wanted to be vampires. I turned them. The Pharoah's hard on me because I stole his Rolls Royce. Its's the one he gifted you."

"I have three cars from Vaughn, Clarence, and Niarchos." "You're spoiled, Gabriel." "You spoil Ginger too I saw her jewelry." "The Pharoah's making me grow something in the ground. It's a requirement for his turns, Gabriel, but Pop ain't helping me."

"Parents are hardest on kids; they see greatness it. You and Clarence have been apart a long time; you need to bond again, Grip be patient. Clarence loves you. I got it, weed, Grip!" "No way! You're trying to get me excommunicated again." "Hehe."

Grip paced as the idea swam around dollar signs in his head. "You're crazy, Gabriel!"

"You care about Clarence's feelings instead of doing what he asks? You can have a dispensary Grip. There's plenty of states allowing legal marijuana sales! That's how you pitch it to Clarence. Two birds and one stone. You obey by growing from the earth and make money hand over fist." "Are you offering yourself as my partner, Gabriel?" "Why not? Have you forgotten I'm also a turn? The rules apply to me as well." "We can't tell the Pharaoh until we've researched then we present after our ducks are in a row, agreed, partner?" "Yes, Ma'am." They hugged on it.

Niarchos was pissed he and Clarence left Gabriel but tried not to show it. Every minute he was away from her was torture. *'Stop worrying about her, Niarchos,'* his father telepathically said. *'Why're you in my head, Pop?' 'I saw you were worried.' 'Don't invade my thoughts pop.'*

Niarchos texted Gabriel:

Nicky: You, ok? Honey: You left Nicky. Nicky: Miss me?

Honey: Always I despise when you both leave. What's wrong, Nicky? Nicky: Pop entered my thoughts without permission. My mom would get on him and he stopped. He's starting again. Honey: I'll make him stop. He's probably paranoid. Not making excuses, Nicky, but we can expect he will do it often not knowing who wants him dead or not: Nicky He's being nosey, seeing if I'm thinking of you, Gabriel. Gabriel: Clarence is upset about the bag and money,

Nicky: What makes it hard for Pop is you can't be purchased. Women he dated after my mother's passing gold diggers. Honey: Monetary value means nothing. Nicky Why?

Honey: I was raised to value family by showing love. A man giving his time is how you know he loves you. My grandma said if he buys you the world and never spends a day in bed with you he doesn't love you. That's why I made him get the food; he wanted to run out the door. I wanted him to take time for me.

Nicky: You're special, Gabriel. I love you. Honey: I love you too, Nicky. Nicky: I'm in love with you. Honey: I can't say the words, Niarchos. How can I love two vampires? Nicky: You can Ma. Honey: I'll say it in time Nicky. Nicky: I have nothing but time, ma.

Twin Oaks Plantation....

They arrived at Twin Oaks. "I hate it here." "Why pop?" "How about we stop by your old plantation, Niarchos?" "We can. It's a mall," Clarence grabbed Niarchos' wrist squeezing. "Don't push me, stop eyeballing me now boy." Clarence growled popping his fangs. "Yes, Pharaoh," Clarence released his wrist fracturing it.

"Stop pushing him, Niarchos. He's going through a lot. He has a new pregnant wife he can't enjoy the pregnancy. Four attempts on his life, and Gabriel's, Chance may die, and his other son has eyes for his new bride." "Annie. I--"

"What, Niarchos?" lowering her voice. "We see it in you since the engagement party. Give Clarence space with Gabriel. Let him enjoy their pregnancy. I know you're in love with Gabriel, Niarchos. You look at her identical to how you gazed at Liza."

Niarchos smiled. "Look at that the mere mention of her name lights your heart. You can't love the Pharaoh's Queen, it's that simple. If you do, you must keep it to yourself Niarchos. I'm not Safinah your mother but I'm your auntie. I know you, nephew. If Fi were alive, she'd say, 'leave that woman be,' and you know it. Why do you love Gabriel?"

"She's special, smart, pretty, kind. Not money-hungry, Annie." "All reasons Clarence fell in love with her. Niarchos you're skating on thin ice in July. As soon as Clarence releases you, go home. If Gabriel comes to you, send her home to Clarence." He looked down. "Niarchos, promise please," he looked away. Pulling his chin down lovingly toward her for eye contact. "Promise, Niarchos."

"Promise, Annie." "Good," kissing his hand. "I'm going to freshen up. How's Joanie, Niarchos?" "Turning realextra slow." Ann laughed. "Was it staged, Niarchos?" "No, she acted alone. Joan's impatient she was tired of Papa Nate saying no. Love makes you do crazy things," looking in Ann's eyes. "Not you it doesn't," hitting his arm.

Clarence sat to try once again. "Security brought the wives. They were frail, hungry, and weak as he wanted. They kneeled, tired, worn, emaciated, and best of all, mentally broken." Niarchos stood behind him. "Are you wives hungry?" "Yes, Great One," they said barely above a whisper. "Great One, please," the fifth wife begged blood. Niarchos prowled around them looking down disgusted. "They're skin and bones, Pop. Clarence laughed sinisterly. Jamaica yelled, "You can stop this vampresses eenie, meenie, miny, --" A wife cut Jamaica off.

"Great One, I beg on bended knees and request an audience with our Queen. Per vampire law, article 91, subsections 91a through 91c, it states the following: If the wife of an Elder vampire requests the audience of the reigning vampire Queen before the Pharaoh passes judgment or death, the vampress has the right to her audience request. Als--"

Clarence held up his hand. "I'm aware of the law, wife number two. Are you sure wish an audience with the reigning Queen?" "Yes, Great One I beg your mercy." Niarchos licked the fifth wife's face growling as his savage knocked to be released.

"Inform Queen Gabriel you'll come for her, Elder Niarchos." "Yes, Great One." Niarchos handed the phone to Clarence while Jamaica fanned him as the cool air circulated in the mansion. "Sugar how are you doing...did you nap? Good. How's the food, Sugar?" The wives were shocked that she digested food.

"The strawberries were sweet? Most of them are in Georgia. When I was enslaved, I walked to a strawberry patch in the woods. I wonder if it's still here on Twin Oaks Plantation?" "The strawberries came from the patch behind the kitchen. Isabel planted them decades ago Sugar. Yes, the blueberries too."

"Motorcycle? Niarchos is shaking his head no. Haha, I know, I'm the Pharaoh, he's your guard but he is helping Zion, and your Dr. said no bikes young lady." Niarchos was inhaling wife five's hair, the whiff of her fear teasing the vampire within. "I'll be gentle with you," picking her up, she screamed. "Sugar, hold on please, Niarchos put her down. I'm on the phone, Gabriel can't hear me over the screams. Your brother is going to be cross when he wakes up and finds out you killed his wife without a Queen's audience, Niarchos."

Niarchos dropped her on the cold marble floor, angrily pacing, his savage angry with him for being subdued; the women saw and sensed it in him. "Yes, Sugar sorry, yes, he's on his way. One of Chance's wives wants to speak with you. Why? I didn't ask. Hold on, Sugar. The Queen wants to know what you want?"

"To beg her, to plead with you for mercy." "You heard Sugar? That was wife number two. Gabriel, I know you're tired and its hot welcome to the south, but this is vampire law. Niarchos is coming." Gabriel adorned what she wore earlier. She grabbed the bag Niarchos gave her with the gun Grip gifted her to show Niarchos and Clarence.

"Safety on?" "Yes, Grip. Not you too! I gotta call my girl Ginger, tell ger her you're driving me nutty." "Don't do it, she'll be on me bad Queen." "I spoke with her last night; about the baby. We exchanged sex secrets." "We're in trouble, me and pop." "Yes, y'all are hehe!"

Someone knocked on the bedroom door. "Yes? Come in." "It's Niarchos are you ready, Great One?" "We'll be back, Grip." "Anyone give Nicky?" "Not yet Great One." Gabriel's phone rang. "Hello? Great One?" "Who's this?" There was a child on her line. "It's Savannah. You asked I phone you."

"May I call when I'm alone?" "Of course, Great One." "Tonight?" "Yes, ma'am." "Ma'am? No way, you're older than me," Savannah laughed. "Call me Gabriel." "Ok, Gabriel." They arrived at Twin Oaks. "It's beautiful this house is huge, Nicky!" "This is your husbands childhood home ma." Niarchos opened the doors for her. When she entered, everyone knelt. Clarence hugged her. "This is where you grew up daddy? It's beautiful, Clarence. Especially this large twin oak trees at the front."

"A beautiful prison, isn't it, Sugar? I didn't grow up in this house; I grew up in the barn with the horses," Clarence pointed out the west window. "So did Jesus born amongst animals in a manger. They were kinder than your oppressor, no?" Clarence kissed her, smiling. "You always see good in evil deeds, Sugar such an endearing quality in my Queen." "Honey, why am I here?" Niarchos handed her ice water.

"One of the wives quoted vampire law before an execution. They have rights to speak with the Queen of vampires." "Which one, Clarence?" He pointed. "Permission to speak Great Queen." "Granted." "Great One, you may remember me from the hearing in Las Vegas." "I do. How are you?" "I've been better, Great One." "How may I help?"

"The Pharaoh, in his infinite wisdom, wishes to put one of the wives of Senior Elder Chance Hollings to death. He may execute the wrong vampress. Great Queen, the culprit, isn't going to reveal herself. I personally don't wish to die because someone is lying, I beseech your intersession into this matter. I beg you to assist me in swaying your husband's decision regarding a mass execution." Gabriel sat on Clarence's lap fighting sleep.

"In all fairness, my husband attended this matter for a month. He's given ample time for any vampire or vampress to share information. "Have you wives cooperated?" "No one has, Great One." "Vampresses, you leave my husband optionless. It's difficult to know who the culprit is and who is innocent. Elder Chance will be upset; however, in lieu of what's transpiring, my husband's wisdom surpasses ours we must trust the process vampress."

Gabriel looked at Clarence; he mentally connected to her. *'Nothing on the scans, Clarence?' 'No, they're blocking me, Sugar.'* "Help the Vampire King. Why protect the person who tried to assassinate the vampire you love and who loved you through all your woes? Unless anyone has anything to add?" The room was pin-drop quiet. "Elder Niarchos, please continue I'm sorry vampresses."

"He didn't want Gabriel seeing him kill a woman," she slightly nodded yes. Gabriel watched as vampires whimpered, hissed, and cried out as tension and fear gripped the room. Gabriel's sexual excitement grew; she'd never seen Niarchos kill, licking her lips the vampress inside anticipated the kill. Niarchos smelled her sexual arousal rolling on the semi-warm air. Gabriel stared into his eyes although she couldn't see his eyes through his sunglasses. Niarchos knew her eyes rested on her, which aroused him severely.

"Which one, Queen? Please do the honors." "That one pointing at wife five as Clarence grabbed the paper fan from Jamaica removing his jacket ignoring his son and wife as he tried to cool down. Niarchos grabbed her, removed his serrated knife, cutting her hair.

Niarchos tossed stringy hair on the remaining wives like confetti after all his party was about to begin. "Pardon Great One pardon please!" Wife five screamed and trembled. Niarchos grabbed her, holding her waist from behind tethering her to him. His huge arms made it impossible for her to move. Niarchos pushed her head left, his long strong fangs slipped slowly from his gums. His growls echoed as he bit hard; the pop of her skin was loud and pronounced. Blood oozed down her shoulder, crossing her arm sliding on golden-brown skin. It trickled off her fingers, resting on cold marble beneath her dangling feet.

"One of the wives, crawled to the blood, lapping it savagely off the floor." "Why is she doing that, Clarence?" "She's hungry. When vampires are denied blood, they feed off one another or resort to drastic measures like this Sugar. Jamaica." Jamaica kicked her away from the blood as the remaining wives popped fangs hissing at the smell of her blood.

Niarchos' eyes never left Gabriel. He continued to feed, his hard dick pressing on wife fives back hidden. Wife five squirmed, trying to free herself. Niarchos was too strong. Gabriel was in heat, watching him drain her. In her mind he drank and fucked at the same time. Niarchos saw Gabriel's nipples harden through her dress. The smell of sweet blood swirled in the air wrapped in the aura of her arousal. Round red blood drops hitting the floor were thunderous in her ears, tapping the marble like a leaky faucet."

"Niarchos growled, locking his prey tighter, slowing his drain making her death last in the memories of her sister-wives. Instilling the realization, they could be next unless they confessed. Licking the blood from her neck, slurping her shoulders. He raised her slender fingers, placing them on his tongue, licking them clean one by bloody one as he escorted her to deaths door. Resting her hand behind his neck. Niarchos stared at Clarence's wife vertically as she breathed fast, imagining her fingers rolling on warm tongue.

"Clarence, where's the bathroom?" "Down the hall Sugar." Gabriel was excited she couldn't take it. Her fangs were exposed, and her dress was stuck to her body. Gabriel ripped her panties off, sitting on the sink, rubbing her clit feverishly as she watched herself in the mirror. She had to cum, or she was going to explode. Gabriel watched herself inhaling seeing her clit the largest it had ever been as her wet pussy lips glistened under florescent vanity lights. Gabriel moaned as low as possible, trying to rush her climatic release."

"Clarence knocked hearing pleasuring herself from the foyer. He was hard, listening to her sexy moans across the mansion and through the door. Clarence put his nose to the door, smelling her dampness. "Gabriel unlocked the door." Gabriel turned the lock but didn't open the door. Clarence rushed in as Gabriel clawed his back ripping his shirt off in shreds, kissing him savagely.

Clarence placed her on the sink, snatching his belt off she unzipped him anxiously. Gabriel held her torn damp panties in her hand, sliding them under his nose as he closed his eyes inhaling deep getting high off horny. Clarence entered her sweetness, as they exhaled sigh of relief, they were one. He drilled her hot box, pulling out white gooey goodness. Gabriel opened her legs more inviting him to stand up in it. She cut the cold water on splashing it in his hair and chest cooling him while she fucked him.

"Slow down, Sugar," his southern drawl drove her wild, she bit his neck gulping mouthfuls of his blood his cologne making her wetter. Hopping off the sink, Gabriel faced the mirror holding the edge. Clarence pushed inside her. "Look, Daddy." Clarence's reflection made a cameo appearance adding to the growing sexual tension between them. Clarence smiled. Twelve years passed since he'd seen his reflection. He stared watching himself fuck—a first for him, causing a dick leak inside her. Gabriel was on her toes. "What's gotten into you?" She didn't answer because she didn't know.

Clarence pulled pins from her bun, releasing her wild, crown of hair. He buried his face in her scalp, intoxicating himself with her touch and scent and sexual cat calls. Staring at their sexual engagement in the mirror he released hot sweets inside her panting as stress left him. Gabriel stared at his image counting how my pumps she felt during his release bumping against her tight walls. He was fine as fuck to her—tall, strong, and sexy with wild half kinky brown and blond curls. She loved every bit of him and was eager to see which child was born in his likeness. Clarence's eyes were glued to the mirror, staring at her. He dick taped her clit nodding until she orgasmed loudly. Pulling her dress down, he exposed large breasts, spilling out of her bra, nipples, begging for tongue attention.

Clarence cupped chilly water, massaging her sweet nipples. Gabriel's walls pumped and pulled, sucking him deeper. She held her head down as she came, he pushed up her chin forcing her to watch herself tremble at his touch in the mirror. *'See what I see when you tremble beneath me.'*

Clarence spilled his love in his wife, then sat her on the vanity, holding her heavy breasts in his hands, licking water drops from them as she struggled to get breath. She tried to calm down, breathing heavily. "What happened, Sugar?" "The smell of blood,...I wanted you."

"Watching Niarchos kill turned you on. You never saw one of us kill to feed; you liked it?" "Yes, Clarence." "When I killed, it scared you." "It looked sexy, the way he was holding the vampress. It's like she had no idea she was dying. Her life slipped away. It was sexy less violent"

"She didn't know Sugar. When a person is being drained, they fall into a state of euphoria an unpainful death. When a vampire discovers what's happening, it's too late." Clarence bent down, kissing her tummy secretly, checking if he smelled blood. "Sugar, get my spare suit while I clean up, please. You shredded this one to ribbons." "Hehe."

Gabriel exited the bathroom, baby hair stuck to her temples with free-flowing hair wreaking of Clarence. Walking past Niarchos he smelled her cum, catching the strong scent on the cool air tennis eyeballing her as she slipped past. Vampires smelled Clarence's sex on her, smiling. His smell was intoxicating to the female vampires. Bisexual wives were horny by the scent of her freshly fucked cum filled cunt wishing they were her cuckhold. "I'll return shortly," she ran to the car, the smell dragging on the breeze behind her out the door.

When she dropped the suit, she cleaned herself up. "I have no discipline when it comes to you. I'm not used to losing control, Sugar." "How does it make you feel, Clarence?" "Free but bad." "Don't feel bad about loving me." She left Clarence in the bathroom. The dead wife on the floor was at Niarchos' feet. She looked like a sleeping doll. "Ladies, please tell them what they want to know. I implore you," Niarchos texted her.

Nicky: Were you fucking? Honey: yeah why? Nicky: I smell it, hear it. Your scent makes me horny. Honey: You turned me on; I couldn't control it. I went to masturbate. Clarence entered. You stared at me like you wanted me. I had to cum, or I was going to pop my clit throbbed so bad that never happened to me. You make me horny to the point of craziness Niarchos.

Clarence returned; she tucked her phone away, deleting the texts. "Nice suit, Pop," Niarchos whispered. "You whisper now vampire?" Niarchos grinned.

*"Honey, I think you should waltz with one of the wives,"* telepathically speaking. *"If you waltz, it relaxes the mind, hypnotizing her. You can see the thoughts. Cue the music on your phone, Sugar. How long, Clarence? Five minutes, minimum.*

"Niarchos?" "Yes, Pharaoh?" "Giselle" Niarchos snatched her off the floor, she smelled rank. "Pia, have you waltzed with Chance?" "No, Great One." "Niarchos, do you waltz?" "Yes, Great Queen," she smiled. "Niarchos is better than me, Sugar." "No one is better than you, Great Pharaoh." "Thank you, Elder Niarchos," Clarence held Giselle in waltz position. "Great One, I'm unsure what I'm doing." "That's the beauty of the waltz, vampresses. You need no knowledge on how to waltz if you allow your partner to lead."

Gabriel cued the music. Clarence twirled Giselle, who stared into Clarence's eyes. Clarence lifted her off the floor, suspended five feet in the air. Vampresses gasped in awe looking up. Giselle breathed heavily, sexually aroused, as Clarence bit her neck, extracting thoughts from her mind through his fangs. He saw the day she met Chance in the 1980s. Clarence watched her life and all Chance's good and bad deeds.

Giselle eavesdropped at the door while Chance spoke to Cody about leaving his wives. Clarence saw Giselle on a midnight run when a man who offered her twenty million dollars to find the deed to the house and keep Chance away from a doctor if he fell ill. Giselle declined the offer, when she heard Chance plotting to leave with Cody, she phoned the adversary, making the deal bringing wives five, six, and seven in.

Clarence saw them toasting when they heard Chance was dying. Clarence kept drinking the blood falling from above their heads, wives licking the floor. Clarence drained her for plotting against her husband and his son. Her blood revealed her truth to Clarence and her scheme to cover the tracks of her failed diabolical plot. She made a call to Vegas, trying to gain access to the hospital to finish Chance off, which was recent.

Giselle called Lily and didn't get an answer. Then she made another call. Clarence slowed the memory as Giselle spoke coherently. *'Hello, Mara?'* She discussed the money and how it'd been used. Mara explained she was dating Niarchos and wanted out. Giselle stated she couldn't get out; gears were in motion it was too late. chastising Mara, *'You gave Chance his second dose of larvae because the first set didn't work so because you're falling in love with Niarchos, screw us?'*

The memories were fading fast as Giselle was dying. She whispered, "Pharaoh, tell Chancie I love him. I do. I'm sorry." Clarence stopped drinking, gently laying her next to the dead wife five.

"I have half of what we need Niarchos. House arrest wives three and four; the rest stay in jail. I need to speak with you, Jamaica," who entered the foyer from the basement. "Gabriel, please wait for us in the limousine," Gabriel exited. "Ok, honey."

"Call Vegas, have the head of security place vampress Mara under arrest son I'm sorry, Niarchos. She gave Chance his second dose of parasite when she fixed his drink. For the record, she tried to get out of it when she fell in love with you Niarchos." "I'm not in love with her, Pop. I cared for her." "Hello, this is Elder Niarchos. As per vampire King Clarence

Hollings arrest Mara. No visitors unless it's her lawyer thank you. Arrange transfer for her to Twin Oaks." "What did you see, Pop?" He told Niarchos and Jamaica everything.

Niarchos shook his head. "I'll get Gabriel home and inquire when Zion will wake Chance pop." "Call the driver, Niarchos he must've gone around back." Niarchos called Gabriel's phone with no answer. The limousine crashed into a tree. Clarence and Niarchos hyper-sped, "Gabriel! Gabriel!" The limo driver was dead, two shots to the back of his head. There was a syringe stuck in her hand with God knows what in it.

"She got the fucker, Pop look!" "Sugar my baby! call the vampire hospital, tell them we're on our way Niarchos." Clarence swept up a limp Gabriel in his arms. "Pop don't touch the needle. What if it's the parasite Pop?" "Niarchos removed it from her hand pulling the driver onto the ground, rushing to the hospital.

"This is Elder Niarchos phone Dr. Donovan, explain we're coming with the Queen and Pharaoh." Clarence's phone rang. "Zion, hi." "Hey, Clarence, I called Dr. Richardson; she's in charge at the Georgia hospital she's vampress, and waiting for you." Clarence rushed an unconscious Gabriel inside the hospital as blood fell from an open head wound. Hospital staff panicked, kneeling when he entered. "Rise, help the Queen. Help my wife please!" Clarence was torn to tatters.

"I'm Dr. Richardson. This way. Clarence laid her on a gurney rush rolling Gabriel to a private room. Niarchos handed the Dr. the syringe; she passed it to the lab tech. "Take this to the lab; we need to know what's in it." "Dr. she's pregnant, Dr." "I'm aware, Dr. Donovan briefed me. Great One." Niarchos Facetimed Zion, allowing him to see what was happening.

"Dr. Richardson began a Vaginal exam. "Elder Niarchos, please leave the room." Niarchos left his phone for Zion; Clarence stayed, of course. The lab tech returned with report. "She's fine Great One; it's a sedative. They tried to put her to sleep for a few days. I checked for parasites; there weren't any in the cavity of the syringe." "Great One, there is no subtle way to ask, did you engage sexually your wife prior to the accident?"

Exhaling, "Yes, Dr., an hour ago." "Thank God, I thought he took liberties." "She should wake in an hour or so. I want to do a sonogram if it's ok Great one." "Yes please." The Dr. undressed Gabriel, placing a hospital gown on her. She put the machine on her stomach. Clarence smiled it was the first time he saw his babies. "One is larger, Dr." "Yes, my king, the big one is more developed than the rest, Great on you will be blessed with our vampire prince. Can't tell with the others yet."

"They're fine, Dr.?" "Yes, Great One, they're sleeping0 It's an honor to see your miraculous children and our future crown leaders." "Thank you." "You're welcome doctor how much bigger is he?" "By one whole pound Pharoah." She said Jovial. "Look at his fat tummy," Clarence smiled, glued to the screen squeezing Gabriel's sleeping hand. She printed pictures for him and Gabriel. Clarence waited for her to wake. Gabriel woke screaming and fighting. "Shhhh I'm here baby." Niarchos burst into the room. She popped up, hugging Clarence. "What happened, Sugar?"

"I entered the limo; he tried to drive away I couldn't stop him. I opened the partition to see out the front; he started leaving Twin Oaks. The driver pushed me back hard, telling me to 'shut the fuck up and sit back,' pushing the syringe into my hand only getting some of it in me. I grabbed the gun Grip gifted me, shooting him in the head. The car careened out of control." Gabriel cried hysterically.

"Clarence, tea please," he exited to get it and speak with the doctor. Niarchos hugged and kissed her lips. "Shhhh, Nicky," wiping his face. "It's hard for me to hide my emotion. I'd die if something happened to you Gabriel." Clarence entered the room. "What're you doing, sugar?" "I'm going home. I want to sleep in our bed."

"Yes, my love. Grab her file and purse, Niarchos." "Yes, Pop." Clarence carried her to the limo. "Tell the Dr., I'll have her come to the house tomorrow," as he walked by the nurses' desk. "Yes, Great One," no one said a word about him discharging her prematurely. Clarence entered Niarchos' house. He grabbed Grip, hugging him tight. "You saved my wife and our babies, Grip."

"How, Pop?" He shared the sordid ordeal. "The years you were gone, I missed you, son. There were times I cried." Grip was crying. "Don't ever disappear on me again, understand?" "Yes, Pop." "We're going to war, son. We must wake Chance. This shit is bigger than us. They're trying to kill us for our land. I need strong vampires on deck, ruthless savages. Get Grimy on board, Niarchos." "That's what the fuck I'm talking about, Pop. Shit just got real!"

# Chapter 35
# Liza Hollings

Savannah Georgia

Rosemary's Book Store....

Caleb was ready to face the Charlatan who stole his book. Clarence had paperwork recreated by the document division. They looked authentic down to the calligraphy handwriting on aged parchment paper. "The motherfucker had the nerve to steal the book verbatim," Caleb spewed angrily.

As Caleb rewrote the book, he cried several times, thinking of his wife and daughter, allowing memories of them to fade far from thought over the decades. His book was an anchor, bearing his soul. No one was profiting off his emotions and loss.

Caleb and Clarence entered the cozy bookstore. It was packed with readers who loved Caleb's book. The book thief read a passage from the book, speaking about love and people taking it for granted. Caleb recalled writing this piece because he saw his wife in town; she was owned by another oppressor, he wasn't allowed to speak with her, fearing Massa's wrath, thinking they were plotting an uprising.

Fans of the book and Clarence clapped. The visitors inquired about the book's origins; lies were shared by the plagiarist to cover his thievery. "Why were you clapping, Clarence?" "It was beautiful Caleb. I clapped for you." The thief signed books, with each signature, Caleb's temper grew. Clarence advised Caleb not to speak unless he gave permission because of his temperament. The reading room cleared, the four of them remained.

Rosemary knelt in front of Clarence; she was human, it wasn't needed. Caleb explained that Clarence was vampire royalty, she showed as much respect humanly possible. "Please rise; have a seat, dear."

The thief was confused. "Hello." Clarence greeted him calmly. "Hello. Are you a fan of my work, sir?" Clarence smirked passing his fedora to Caleb. "Your work?" "Yes, my work, sir." "You're certain you authored this manuscript?" "I'm the author."

Clarence handed him the recreated documents, including the backdated copyright certificate. Clarence paid one million dollars to the clerk who did the honors. The book thief went over the documents, his hands shook as the reality of his truth set in, snatching his glasses off nervously. "What do you want?"

"An apology, to begin with. You stole the works of Caleb's great-great-grandfather. How dare you, a white man stealing the book of a common slave." "I'd think as another white man you'd understand my short comings," the thief retorted. "If I were white but, I'm a black man." Rosemary and the book thief were shocked. "Here's what you're going to do: you'll send me copies of the contracts you signed with your publisher as well as any movie, television rights, or endorsements and proof of monies received in connection with the book thus far."

Clarence turned to Caleb, "Eighty percent of proceeds?" The thief's jaw dropped. "No. 95% Mr. Hollings." "You'll wire 95% of all funds ascertained in connection to this book. You will continue scheduled book tours and fulfill your contract."

"I don't have the funds." Clarence removed a manila envelope containing the thief's financial portfolio and net worth. "I did my homework, Deveraux. You've quite the inheritance and real estate holdings, fifty million from trust?"

"It has nothing to do with the book, Mr. Hollings."

"Mr. Deveraux, I don't care where you get the money, just pay it. This book was written by my uncle who went after the book, subsequently losing his wife and child in the process. For you, a white man, to steal the work of an accomplished writer, pawning it as your own, is despicable, Deveraux. If you don't have the money by one p.m. tomorrow, this is the letter I'll send to the New York & Chicago Book Sun Times, exposing you as the plagiarist, liar, and charlatan you are,"

"Be careful of the words that escape your tongue, Deveraux or I may be forced to rip it from your head. This can be a quiet or very sordid public affair. You won't write any sequels. If a movie is made, all monies will be donated to this charity," Clarence handed him the name of their nonprofit, owned by Blaise and Caleb. "What say you, Deveraux?" "You have me at a disadvantage, Mr. Hollings." "I have a question," Caleb interjected. "Where'd you find the original manuscript Deveraux?"

"Georgia, I was digging the grounds on the property creating a koi fishpond. The book and everything with it were deep underground, covered in bricks and mud. It was wrapped in burlap, which preserved the book in the leather binding."

"Grandfather mentioned photos in the book. Do you have them, Deveraux?" "I do, Caleb they're in the car along with the original manuscript. Would you like me to fetch them, sir?" "Please," Rosemary unlocked the door, walking Deveraux to his car, returning with pictures in an envelope and other items.

Caleb opened his beat-up leather satchel, putting them inside his satchel without looking at them. "May I have those back, Mr. Hollings?" "They don't belong to Deveraux; they're family heirlooms. It's scttled, Deveraux. If you fail to keep your agreement, you know what follows. I'll visit your wife and children. I won't be civil are we on identical pages, Deveraux?"

"Threats aren't necessary, Mr. Hollings," Clarence turned to Caleb shocked. "Did you hear a threat, Caleb?" "I didn't, Mr. Hollings," "Mr. Deveraux," Clarence extended his hand, but Deveraux ignored it. "Goodnight, Rosemary." Deveraux rushed to the door embarrassed his lie was outed. Caleb kissed Rosemary as she wiped his tears of joy mixed with the relief of personal closure. "I'll call, baby."

The old vampires entered the limousine. Clarence didn't ask to see the photos, though he was excited too. They arrived at Niarchos' house. Caleb was crying, hugging Clarence. "This is why I love my maker. I couldn't ask anyone to handle it better. Thank you, old friend." "It's fine, brother. I'm sorry this happened. However, I'm glad the book is in our possession and a part of our history as vampires." "Clarence, be careful with this land business. These people are wicked. They are serious about Twin Oaks. Don't underestimate them."

"What have you seen, Caleb?" "I saw Gabriel giving birth without you, Clarence." "Why, Caleb?" "I'm unsure. I'm seeking answers. A bit of news for you, not sure Niarchos is gonna like it. You wanna know?" "Yes, Caleb." "Gabriel found her a nanny, Clarence. It's Savannah." "I see, Vannah's good with babies, and she's family." "How are things with Niarchos?" "I feel like I'm competing with him for Gabriel." "It's in your head, Gabriel has enough love for all of us, Clarence."

"Niarchos admitted he's in love with her Caleb. Am I supposed to ignore it, brother?" "Let things happen the way they're meant to. Stop trying to control everything, Clarence. Some things aren't meant to be controlled. Moment of truth?" "Of course, Caleb." "Clarence you're a good husband trust the process Great One. Why do you hate Twin Oaks Clarence, it's about growing up there enslaved isn't it?

"I was fucking the slave owner's wife at 14 It's one reason why I despise Twin Oaks Caleb." "You never said where in the mansion?" "In Chance's bedroom when Alex was away. Avril instructed me on what not to do." Caleb laughed. "It's not funny Caleb." "Yes, it is Clarence. Old Avril giving sex tips." "He taught me to pull out you think I'm proud of that? Having to fuck a bony, white, pedophile bitch. She saw the size of my dick and became obsessed."

"You need Niarchos like you need Chance and Grip Clarence. When Niarchos was ill you were ill with worry. I saw you crying over Niarchos and Chance. With Niarchos you watched him way before you turned him." Clarence snatched a shocked look. "How'd you know that Caleb no one knows that?" "I saw it. You removed a lot of bad memories from his mind. Why not remove all of it Clarence?"

"No child should've gone through that. "Clarence Niarchos is a demigod. When men laid with angels, they created extra-large humans, giants. Today, there are people like Shaq and Niarchos—big humans, half man, half angel." "You believe that, Caleb?"

"Wholeheartedly." "Niarchos is gentle with Gabriel. There's a side she loves and it's, something I'm missing. It's driving me mad Caleb because I'm unsure of what it is and I can't buy it." "Haha listen to the rich man. It's Niarchos himself. He was the same with Fi. You despised her doting on Niarchos. You hate sharing your women and she was the boy's mother Clarence. Ann spoke with Niarchos. Give it time."

Clarence arrived at Niarchos' house after dropping Caleb. He opened the door to find Gabriel and Niarchos in a dice game in the foyer. "What is this, Niarchos? I don't allow dice in my house." "Baby, this is Nicky's house," Clarence scoffed. "He knows better, Gabriel." Clarence went upstairs. Niarchos and Gabriel chuckled. Gabriel joined Clarence. She was lying in bed and jumped on him, kissing all over his face, tickling him. "Clarence, mad over dice? Shame on you, daddy." "I've seen vampires killed over dice so has Niarchos Sugar"

"Lighten up, Pharaoh. It's a friendly game between vampires there are no strangers playing." "Gabriel?" "Yes, honey?" "I know you see me as a strong leader. However, I'm a victim in your hands. I'm a vampire who loves you. I'd give my life for you. There's something about you I'm enamored by your deep love. In your arms, I'm a fourteen-year-old slave wanting the love of a good woman but never admitting it for fear she'd be sold like my mother, Gabriel." "They ain't gonna sell or take me away, Clarence. I'm never leaving. If I do, I'm ill. Come get me." Clarence snuggled her neck, crying. "Baby, what's wrong?" "You make me complete, Gabriel. You and our babies. You're giving me something I've wanted and could never have—natural children. I love our adopted children as my own, but this is different. When Safinah died, a part of me went with her. I didn't think I'd ever love again until we met. I knew when I saw you, Sugar, you'd be my bride."

"Mr. Hollings?" "Yes, ma'am." "What if I said no, sir?" "I wouldn't stop trying." Gabriel smiled. "Clarence, what did I do to deserve you?" "I'm unsure, woman, but I'm here." Clarence kissed her. "I'll return in a few, ok, Gabriel?" "Yes, baby."

Gabriel sat on the bed and sent Niarchos a song, 'I'm Ready for Love' by India Arie." Seeing this Niarchos sent her Isaac Hayes' "I Stand Accused."

Honey: This is how I feel about us. I may not be able to say the words 'I love you,' Nicky, let this song serve in its place until I'm able. Let me know if you like it.

Nicky: Love you more, ma. Niarchos listened to the song, texting Grip, Grip: Wyd?"

Grip: Nothing, Nick. torturing these women in the cells.

Nick: Leave them vampresses be, they're about to light walk. Let them make peace within themselves. You flying out before trials start? Grip: Yeah, gotta check on Ginger. Give her some dick. What do you want, negro? Spit it out. Nick: Gabriel sent me a song, Grip. Grip: Which one?" Nick: India Arie's 'I'm Ready for Love.' You know it? Grip: Hell yeah, I know it. Ginger loves it. What're you doing? If Pop finds out, you both are dead, Nick. Nick: We ain't doing nothing, Grip. Grip: Yet.

Have you lost your mind? Leave the vampress be, Nick! Nick: Can't do that, baby bro. Grip: You don't want to be excommunicated Nick. It's bad, Niarchos. As the years drag by, you'll miss your vampire family. She's not worth it. Nick: Yes, she is, Grip.

Grip: Nick, you hear yourself? Snap out of it, bro! She's your father's wife! The Alpha vampires Queen. SMFH, you're treading in dangerous waters, Niarchos. What's up with Pop's bachelor party?" Nick: You know Pop ain't down for bitches on his lap, Grip. Grip: Don't matter what Pop wants. We're gonna show the fuck out for him, Nick. Vampire strippers on deck. I'll come see your ass before I fly out. Leave the woman alone, Niarchos. Nothing good can come from it. Nick: Later, Grip. Hit me when you're back in Georgia. Tell Ginger hey.

Clarence returned with a cup of tea and roses. "Gosh, they smell wonderful, baby. Thank you. I like it here, Clarence. It's better than New York."

"I don't want to raise our children in the south. City people have a different mindset than southerners. They're swifter with thinking. More business oriented." "That's shocking coming from you, Clarence." "What do you mean, Sugar?" "You're a country boy, though you hate admitting it. Born and raised in the south."

"Did Safinah want to migrate North, Clarence?" "No, Sugar but when she saw the difference in the way blacks were treated, she liked it. We could walk down a damn street holding hands without judgment or fear. People made comments; however, they didn't try to hang me for it. Won't you miss our cozy hideaway in Queens Gabriel?"

"I'm married. I know what comes with it. I heard you make all your 'turns' grow something in the ground. Does that rule apply to me Clarence? I have something to grow marijuana."

"Grip." "Hehe, why do you say that, Clarence?" "Woman, I know my children." "It's my idea. I suggested marijuana plants. Before you give a fast 'no,' I'd like you to consider a slow 'yes' Clarence." "When it comes to matters of business, you're not my wife. I'll be hard on you Gabriel treating you like my turn no favors." "I understand." She giggled at his attempt to speak sternly.

"The babies make me sleepy Clarence." She yawned, pulling closer to him. "Let me show you something, Sugar," grabbing her medical file. "The Dr. took these when you were asleep. Niarchos has the rest."

"They're getting big. Look at this one, the babies are huge. He weighs four pounds. He's our boy, Sugar." Gabriel smiled. "What about the rest?"

"They have their legs closed. Gabriel knew the baby would be big because of Niarchos' blood. She was overjoyed to see what his blood was doing. She was going to have a huge boy like Niarchos.

The Next Morning Georgia Estate....

Niarchos checked on Caine, who was asleep before he left for the airport. He transported all prisoners to Chance's house. Vampire lawyers were arriving later that day. Clarence had a mandatory meeting scheduled with them at the cabin where he had to be present. The limo arrived at 4:30 a.m., the truck for prisoner transport arrived at the estate the night before to transport those from the New York Estate to Georgia.

"Chase, Lily, Mara, and Mike the human driver, were in chains. Mara couldn't keep her eyes off Niarchos. They were put in the back of the truck, with no windows. Lily rode in the limousine with him in chains.

The driver headed to Chance's house; the jail was crowded. Niarchos wanted them to be uncomfortable while in custody. "What happened, Lily?" "I stand mute, Niarchos." "You both can't stand mute, Lily. One of you Must speak, or you both will die. This is a plot, Lily. Guess why? The land has oil and coal on it. The white man is trying to kill Chance and Clarence for the land. Sound familiar, Lily? Rosewood? People don't know Rosewood sat on oil, Lily. They tried to kidnap Gabriel yesterday in exchange for the transfer of deed we figure. You and Caine? Pawns. But why take their dirty money Lil?"

"Lily, you were there to remember when pop purchased my mother's plantation after she was raped? Who cared for her, Lily? Who cared for me when I slept for a month after my turn? Who sat with Chance after those white men tried to hang him, icing neck burns so they wouldn't stay as a reminder when he completed his turn, Lily? Who sewed bullet holes closed so they wouldn't be a constant reminder to him?"

Lily, cried. "Why were you sleeping with Chance, Lily?" She smiled seductively. "It's not funny Lil Don't you see what you and Caine have done? You've divided us the Elders our little family, Lil." Lily reached for Niarchos' hand; he snatched it back wiping his face. "No, Lily, fix this. You and Caine are family. We love you. Don't stand mute. Don't make us pass a death judgment on those we escaped chains with. Don't allow me to watch you walk in the light. Don't force me to carry out a vampire execution."

Lily, cried staring out the window, they arrived at sunrise. Niarchos placed Lily in the cell next to Caine's in his house. They held hands, careful not to touch the bars, kissing the bars scorching their faces. "Your lawyers are here. Elijah hired Lee for you both."

Twin Oaks Plantation Holding Cells......

Niarchos went where the accused were added to the already crowded cells. When Niarchos entered the basement, it got quiet. He made an announcement, "You all are vampire fugitives awaiting vampire trial. You all have been charged by the crown for egregious crimes to be heard before the Vampire Elders of the high court. You can compare notes, talk to the people who hired you before trial. Human, you don't get a trial, but you get a vampire attorney Compliments of Queen Gabriel. You're being charged as well." "With what, vampire?" "Conspiring to commit murder." "I'm not vampire."

"Doesn't matter. You answer to breaking vampire law. We'll turn you lose once your time is served. Dingos, you get attorneys. Compliments of the Pharaoh." "What about me?" "Oh, the human who delivered the money to Justice." Niarchos snapped his fingers. Security rushed in the cell strapping his to a vintage chair they used in psych wards in the 1940's. "Bolt it to the floor and leave humans in this cell only." Niarchos pushed an IV in his arm draining his blood. "Two bags a day for the rest of your life should due." The white man screamed as Niarchos slipped him a sedative.

"You're Justice?" "Yes." "You have your own attorney." "Thank you, nephew." "I'm not your nephew; it's Elder Niarchos." Nick approached wives 6, 7, 8, and Mara, sharing a cell. "Tsk tsk, conspiracy to kill a vampire Elder, attempted murder, poisoning an Elder, conspiring against the crown with humans, and conspiring to kill the king of covens and forgery the list goes on. You all have attorneys. Good news, they're fresh out of vampire law school."

"Niarchos?" He looked back at Mara. "Elder Niarchos, what's up?" "Nothing." "By the way, good try with the document forge, Mara." She held her head down. "If a vampire doesn't want you, get someone to create paperwork, huh Mara?" "Water will be given you're all on a no-blood no feed order. If caught feeding from one another you will add ten years per feed to your sentences. Have a good day," Niarchos exited the cells.

"We're going to die, I sense it," Chase said to the driver. "If you die, go with honor. You messed up. Pray and ask whatever god is listening to allow you into heaven. Go with peace, not fear," Justice advised.

"You weren't there, Justice, when Niarchos drained two wives." "A draining is a better death than sunlight. It's not painful, wife Six." "How would you know, Justice? I'm an old vampire. When you're drained, you black out. It's euphoric pray for this type of death trust me."

## Blk Qween

Niarchos arrived at the airport to get the lawyers. Two scroll writers, a signature authenticator, a stenographer, a clerk and one paralegal. "Lee!" she hugged Niarchos. "Look at you, all grown." "Where's that old man of yours?" "He's coming after I drop you all at the cabin." "Do I meet my clients today Niarchos?" "Of course." The other lawyers followed her lead.

Gabriel called and texted Niarchos soon as she woke. Niarchos purposely ignored her; he promised Grip and Ann he'd pull away from her. It felt like crack withdrawal or so he'd heard and seen during the crack wars; she was relentless with the calls and texts. Every time she called, he paced the floor, begging the phone to stop ringing.

"Gabriel, please come pick out my suit." Gabriel picked Clarence's suit for the day. "Gabriel?" "Yes, honey?" "Please cut my hair." Clarence sat; she cut it. "Thank you. What's wrong you're agitated, Sugar?" "I'm not, Daddy. Babies kept me up last night. You can rest if you like. Grip can come with me to the meeting, and Niarchos can stay here." "Do you need me there?"

"No, it's a pre-hearing attorney meeting. I must brief the attorneys, state what charges the crown is pressing for each prisoner. In a few days, we will have a meeting; all Elders will be present. You must be present for that one." "Of course. When trials begin, guess what, Sugar? We wear crowns." "Are you serious, Clarence?"

"It's vampire law." "Do we have matching crowns?" "No, however I can have them forged." "I've never seen you in a crown, Clarence. I'm excited. Reality will set in when I see you in a crown daddy." "Elders wear robes, roped, and a sash representing their covens. It's marked with the year they were turned with their coven crest."

"This is serious, huh Clarence?" "Yes, honey. Vampires may be put to death. This is as serious as a human capital murder trial. It can turn ugly. Brace yourself, Sugar." "Niarchos will arrive shortly, Sugar." Gabriel walked Clarence to the limo. When she returned, Viola had a cup of coffee and lemon cookies.

Gabriel got to her bedroom smelling Niarchos' cologne; he was near. Gabriel dozed off; the cologne smell was stronger. She opened her eyes; Niarchos was in the chair, staring.

Gabriel approached Niarchos, open handed slapping him. Niarchos sat emotionless staring. Gabriel slapped him again. He tried to forget about her; she knew it, tearing up. He approached the door, locking it then opening the secret bedroom closet. Gabriel entered; Niarchos closed the door behind them. Gabriel raised her hand to inflict the pain of loneliness he inflicted on her all day.

Grabbing her wrist, Niarchos kissed her inner palm as she struggled to free herself from his loving stronghold, his tears dropped on her fingers. "How do you expect me to move on if you won't allow me, Gabriel?" He whispered, looking away in shame.

Niarchos rubbed her hand on the spot where she slapped him. Closing her eyes as she rubbed, getting lost in his chemistry. "You don't get to do that, Nicky. You can't up and go, while I'm pregnant. I want to show you something," Gabriel went in her sweater pocket showing him sonogram photos. Niarchos grinned. "You see the big one? Why do you think he's huge, Nicky?"

"You're drinking my blood, Gabriel." "God said for me to drink it now we see why." Niarchos kissed the Picture and her tummy; a boy Honey." Niarchos picked her up, kissing and holding her. "I'm sorry, Gabriel. I want you. Don't you want me?"

"Yes, Nicky. There's something with you. It's more than lust. It's deeper." "That's why it's dangerous woman. We're connected in some odd way. When I attended the engagement party, and you saw me what did you feel in your heart?" "Like I knew you from somewhere, puddin." "What did you call me honey?"

"Puddin I've called you that in my head from when I saw you." Niarchos sat as if he'd seen a ghost. "Nicky, what's wrong?" Niarchos was visibly shaken and upset. He picked up his phone. "Do me a favor, Gabriel repeat to Caleb exactly what you said to me." "Why, Nicky?"

"He's my spiritual advisor please, honey humor me baby." "Alright, Nicky." He passed Gabriel his cell phone. "Caleb?" "Hey, boo." "Hey, Nicky and I were speaking and--"

"Tell the truth, please, Gabby." "Alright, Nicky calm down please." She rubbed his back. Caleb felt the love between them; it was amazing. "Caleb, Nicky, and I were speaking. I got upset because he ignored my calls. When I commanded him to call, he refused. When I woke, he was here. I got a little rough with him Caleb." Caleb saw her slap him; he smiled. "When I saw him at the engagement party, he asked what I said in my heart? I replied, Like I knew you from somewhere, puddin"

Caleb dropped the phone. "Hello? I'm here, Gabriel." Nicky inquired, "Why did I call him puddin'?"

"I've called him that since I laid eyes on him, before I knew his name, Caleb." "Is Niarchos ok, Gabriel?" "He's upset did I trigger him in a bad way Caleb?" "Honey, have Niarchos leave the room." "Nicky, Caleb said to go to another room. He wants to speak with you." Niarchos opened the door. "I'll return, Gabriel." "Ok," Gabriel sat eating a cookie, confused. Niarchos went to his old bedroom. "You ok, Niarchos?"

"Whose wife is she, Caleb? I'm asking, is she, my wife?" Caleb knew the answer; he saw it the night he met Gabriel. "She's Clarence's wife, Niarchos." "You didn't answer the question, Caleb." "If I answer, promise you won't act on it." "Can't do that boss." "Yes, it's Liza. She doesn't know she's Liza boy." Niarchos burst out laughing maniacally. "What's funny Nick?"

"The pearls. She carries them in her purse every day, Caleb. I placed those on her when she died, remember? The undertaker returned them. I was so upset I it was too late.

They'd already covered her with earth." "I remember she carried or wore them every day. Why those pearls, Niarchos?"

"I gave Gabriel Liza's Rolls. She went to the glove compartment. I asked Gabriel, 'what're you looking for?' She said MY scarf. It was her first time in the car, why would she look for her scarf? Gabriel can't sleep unless something near her smells like me. She told me that, Caleb."

"The way Gabriel touches my head, like Liza. The tea Liza loved her tea, Caleb; two shots of honey, like Gabriel. Do you know Gabriel gifted me a beautiful red lamp? A RED lamp, Caleb." Caleb smiled. "Liza had them throughout the house, remember? Thats why I told Gabriel no to the lamp at the games it wasn't a money issue it was a memory issue" "She's Clarence's wife now Nick; he found her in THIS lifetime. She belongs to him. Clarence loves Gabriel as much as you. He's bewitched by Gabriel, she's the jewel in his crown. He's lost in her. Clarence lets himself go in her arms. You had your life with your time with Liza, Niarchos, it was a good life, but this is Gabriel. Liza returned as your father's wife, Niarchos."

"I don't want to hear it, Caleb." "The truth hurts, and often we don't want to hear nor accept it, Niarchos." "I tried today not to answer Gabriel's calls. She slapped me."

"I saw, haha!" "It's not funny Caleb. I'm chained to her. I'm getting a second chance, Caleb. If pop catches me, he's excommunicating me or death." "Is it worth it, Niarchos?"

"Yes, she's my Liza Caleb and vampire just as she promised." "Niarchos, you can have any vampress you want in our kingdom. Let this one go to your father he deserves happiness after so many years of grief." "No, Caleb." "It's worse than I thought, Niarchos. You must listen please. Clarence knows how you feel. I'm afraid for Gabriel. Clarence is extremely jealous, Niarchos. You heard what he did at the cabin?" "Yes, pop scared her terribly, Caleb."

"This is true Niarchos. I say this to bring it to your attention: have you seen him like this with Safinah or any other woman?" "No, Caleb." "If he thinks Gabriel is cheating, he's going to go bonkers. There isn't anything you're going to do if he kills her because Clarence can prove her infidelity before the Elders." "I beg you, Niarchos proceed with caution." "I'll call back, Caleb."

"Gabriel, I need a favor." "Sure, Nicky." He walked her to another room in his house on the second floor. When we had people in the house where did we hide jewelry?" "Nicky, this is your room."

"No Honey. I know it sounds crazy but please concentrate. I'll explain, real soon Gabriel." Niarchos held her hands. "Close your eyes and concentrate ma." "Open the window, Nicky, its warm in here I don't understand what I'm doing." "It's nothing special, Gabriel. concentrate, please, honey."

Gabriel sat quietly for fifteen minutes, she sat for fifteen minutes more. She felt something tugging in her mind. She rose, opening the bedroom door, leaving she went into his old bedroom, moving a boot box on the floor in the far corner. Gabriel got on her knees, popping a floorboard with her fist. She put her hand in the hole, there was a velvet bag. In it were Liza's wedding band, engagement ring, and Niarchos' wedding band.

"This was your master bedroom when you married. Your wife liked it because it was smaller cozier, Nicky." "Why do you like those pearls you carry all the time, Gabriel?" "Because you gave them to me, Niarchos."

"When, honey?" "At the party, silly." "Gabriel, when did I give you those pearls?" "On our second date." "Close, it was the third." "It wasn't, Niarchos, it was the second." "Yes, it was, Gabriel. How do you know?"

"I--I was there Nicky." He leaned into her, kissing her neck with tears in his eyes. "It's me, Gabriel." He whispered holding her close. "What is, Nicky?"

"It's me Liza...look in my eyes my love. You and I were married in your last life, Gabriel remember me...remember us sweetheart. Your name was Mrs. Liza Hollings." "You were mine."

To Be Continued........

# Follow Me

### TIKTOK

### FACEBOOK

### AMAZON

### INSTAGRAM

### VAMPIRE UPRISING TEA TALK

VAMPIREUPRISINGS.COM

Made in the USA
Middletown, DE
19 March 2025